"….Freedom is a very important attribute for a human being. When a man is free, he can express his thoughts to others in an open and fearless way. If a man is not free, his thoughts – howsoever great or useful for others – will be buried under the sands of time."

'Gulamgiri'

MAHATMA

JYOTIRAO PHULE

Dr. RAVINDRA THAKUR

Translated by

RESHMA KULKARNI-PATHARE

Mehta Publishing House

✆ +91 020-24476924 / 24460313 / Mob. No. 9545000513
Email : production@mehtapublishinghouse.com
Website : www.mehtapublishinghouse.com

MAHATMA JYOTIRAO PHULE by Dr. RAVINDRA THAKUR

Email : author@mehtapublishinghouse.com

Translated from Marathi to English by Reshma Kulkarni-Pathare

Publisher : Mehta Publishing House
1941, Sadashiv Peth, Madiwale Colony, Pune 411030. INDIA

Printer : Parksons Graphics

Cover Design : Mehta Publishing House

Price : ₹ 795.00

Publishing Date : March 2020

P Book ISBN 9789353174415
E Book ISBN 9789353174040
E Books available on : amazonkindle Apple Books Google Play Books

Dedicated to the memory of the eminent biographer,
Late Shri. Dhananjay Keer, whose biography
'Mahatma Phule' was the source of inspiration for
me to write this book

PROLOGUE

This book is a sincere effort to present before discerning readers, the thoughts, personal facets and the story of a lifetime devoted to serving humanity by the great Mahatma Jyotirao Phule. I do not know how successful I have been in capturing all these elements in one book – I leave that decision to my dear readers. The success of this book will really depend on how many readers get truly and deeply affected by the personality and the yeoman service that the great man toiled to give the society, all his life. For, the magnitude of Jyotirao Phule's work and his thoughts, is so humungous, deep and multi-faceted, that it would be foolish to even claim to be able to fit it into one book.

It goes without saying that the present-day society has been keenly influenced and moulded by the Mahatma's thoughts. Not just in India but even abroad, there is a huge demand for his literature; which is why, his literature is being made available in several languages apart from Marathi. However, I doubt, how many Maharashtrians realize what a gem they have given to the world?! In that sense, our condition is that of a musk deer, who does not realize that it carries a much-coveted treasure in its own belly. The truth remains that, the roots of many a progressive ideologies present in today's society, can be traced to the thoughts expressed by Mahatma Phule. He had written extensively about need of new technologies in agriculture, entrepreneurial education, technological education, environmental concerns, reservation policies, abolition of untouchability, abolition of the Devdasi system, need to eradicate superstitious beliefs, need for gender equality and so on. He had also toiled incessantly to bring about societal change in all these spheres. A lot of thinkers and researchers have tried to study and dissect the thoughts and work of Mahatma Phule. However, the common man almost never gets access to (or, is not interested in reading) such academic journals that carry these theses. Hence, I decided to put forth the thoughts and work of this great man, in form of a book. This is not a work of fiction; but, since it is written in a format that should be appealing to a large demographic of readers, it would be helpful to not view the book with conventional parameters of critical analysis. My book is more of a character narrative of Mahatma Phule. Although it is traditionally believed that books are not academic journals and thus might contain exaggerated information, it would not be farther from truth in the case of this book.

I find it pertinent to describe, what made me turn to writing about Mahatma Phule's work; especially when, there already have been reams written about him in the past. I have read a few of those writings (not all). However, even though those books gave a decent representation of the Mahatma, as a reader, I was left wanting for more. When I started expressing this feeling of dissatisfaction in front of my friends, a couple of them suggested, "Then, why don't you write a book that will fill in those gaps?" That's when I realized that their suggestion held promise. It is easy to criticize and find fault in someone else's work. The real litmus test is in writing something that will cover up those gaps. Many more discussions and self-introspection sessions later, I decided to write a book in the form of a character narrative. Thus it was that I took up the challenge of writing my version of Mahatma Jyotirao Phule's life and service.

As I started writing the book, the topic engulfed me in its embrace! I could think of nothing more than Mahatma Phule. Someone suggested that I write a play based on his life-story; but, the scope of the Mahatma's work is so huge, that I was not sure it would fit into a theatrical play of mere two hours. Around the same time, someone else had come up with a play about the Mahatma; and, the dismal treatment that it gave to this great man's work, left me even more skeptical of going towards that route.

Of course, that is not to say that no one can ever write a play on the Mahatma. In fact, I really hope that some day a very wise, evolved and mature playwright and director will come along, who can do justice to Mahatma Phule's work in a theatrical representation. But, writing a book and writing a play are two totally different things. It does not mean that a play is less potent in its effect. Rather, to the contrary, sometimes a book may not achieve that kind of a ripple effect to bring about societal change, that a small play may. However, speaking for myself, with the kind of writing style that I have, my mind kept gravitating towards expressing my thoughts through a book, rather than any other medium.

Thus, once my decision was made, I started reading and researching extensively on the Mahatma. Reading, noting, re-reading, re-noting, self-critiquing...this cycle continued for many months. When I felt a bit confident about some authentic matter being collected, I started writing parts of what later became this book. Of course, there were many deterrents and interruptions that came in the way; but, my indefatigable willpower finally led me to success.

Writing this book was a revelation to me about what exactly happens when a person gets besotted by something!! I feel that I have spent the last 5-6 years living with the Mahatma himself!

Today, when I have finished writing this book, I can look back with detachment and realise the value of all those years.

There is a mixture of emotions in my heart – sadness at the fact that I can no longer savor the literary closeness of the Mahamanav (great man), and joy at the fact that finally, I'm being able to devote this book to my dear readers.

Looking back, I feel that, even I was a part of those famine-affected people who went to Phule's house. Even I had savored the small piece of bhaakri that kaku kept on everyone's hand. I was amongst those who basked in kaku's motherly gaze. I was also amongst those who heard the cries of new-born babies in Phule's house. While writing this book, I would also laugh and cry at certain junctures. It just goes to show how overwhelming the experience must have been for me.

The book represents Mahatma Phule's ideologies and thoughts at a lot of junctures. It would have been incorrect to obliterate those parts of Phule's personality, just because this is a piece of literature. Rather, it would have made Phule's life-story seem incomplete; because, his evolved, liberated thoughts are what made him great in the first place. Thus, in the book, I have tried to describe Jyotirao's thought-processes in as much an interesting way as I could. Of course, Mahatma Phule's life was 'embellished' with enough dramatic events whose description in itself would have made my book creatively interesting. But, that was not the aim of my writing. I wanted the context behind the Mahatma's thoughts, as well as, his thoughts to come forth my readers, in order to give a complete personality sketch. Also, I felt it pertinent to tell the readers about the churning of ideologies that had begun in the 19th century and the important role played by Mahatma Phule in bringing about an ideological and societal revolution on that backdrop.

Trying to weave creativity with research requires a lot of help. I was fortunate to receive such help via the writings of Pandharinath Patil, N. V. Joshi, Dhananjay Keer, Hari Narke, Sitaram Raykar, Y. D. Phadke, S.G. Malshe, N. R. Phatak, V. B. Govande, P. B. Kulkarni, and P. B. Salunkhe. Specially, the book written by Dhananjay Keer, proved to be a guiding light while writing my book. Thus, I have dedicated by literary effort to Keer, with sincere gratitude. I have taken a bit of creative liberty where I could not find facts; but, due care has been taken to see that that liberty is also rooted in the soil of reality. Readers will realize this as they read the book.

For instance, we can see that a few of Mahatma's trusted accomplices, left him alone in his later life. The reasons for this could have been personal selfish gains, or incompatibility of thoughts – we do not know for sure. Nevertheless, the Mahatma kept doing his work in spite of growing illnesses. The Kranti Jagar movement that the Mahatma started, later spread into many other sectors. The service provided by Lokhande, Bhalekar and Mukundrao Patil are proof enough for this fact.

However, there are some places in the book where readers may feel a lack of semblance or continuity. That is because, where I could not get credible proofs for certain events, I have preferred to not write anything, instead of writing something untrue. In the interest of readers' faith, I preferred to not let the book be marred by fictitious things under the pretext of creative liberty.

I have tried my best to write about almost all events and facets of the Mahatma's life. But, that does not mean that I have compulsively covered every tiny detail.

Certain important things also transpired after Jyotirao's demise. A few friends of mine felt that I had to include a bit about those happenings too. For instance, when Jyotirao was on deathbed, Mama Parmanand tried valiantly to get some help from Maharaja Sayajirao Gaekwad. He also wrote a letter to the king after Jyotirao's demise. Jyotirao's family did get financial help due to Mama's efforts. But, since my book ends closer to Jyotirao's demise, I did not find it pertinent to include this development in the same. Interested readers may find out about such other developments from other sources.

I gave a lot of thought to the title of this book. Two titles stood out more prominently than the rest: 'Mahamanav' and 'Mahatma'. Since Jyotirao was not in favour of the concept of a soul, I had earlier decided to go with the name 'Mahamanav'. But then I thought, how could I ignore the status of a 'Mahatma' (great soul) attributed to Jyotirao by the people themselves? Thus it was, that in reverence to popular vote, I named my book 'Mahatma'. I hope my readers will agree with this rationale. After all, the emotions behind a word matter more than the word itself.

After I began working on penning this boo, I realized that encapsulating Mahatma Jyotirao Phule's work and life in a few pages, was a gargantuan task! The effort tired me out many a times; yet, I kept going on with self-perseverance, but more so, due to the support and constant encouragement of a some very invaluable people I would like to thank here.

Revered Guru Dr. Nagnath Kottapalle stood as my biggest pillar of strength. He read my writing and gave immensely valuable suggestions to help improve it. Along with that, discussions with certain learned and wise individuals proved to be highly encouraging and value-adding from time to time. These include, Dr. A. H. Salunkhe, Nilu Phule, Dr. L.R. Nasirabadkar, Dr. Vasant Joshi, Dr. S. S. Bhosale, Dr. Sitaram Raykar, Dr. Pandit Taapre, Dr. Rajan Gavas, Dr. Avinash Kamble, Hari Narke, Dr. Vasudeo Mulate, Dr. Krishna Ingole, Professor Dr. Harish Bhalerao, Dr. G. R. More, and Dr. G. P. Mali.

Had my student-colleague Professor Madhav Patil not kept egging me on with his constant encouragement and reminders, probably this book would not have seen the light of the day. Many of the chapters in the book have been written following extensive discussions with him; but, he would not like a formal word of thanks. So, I'm refraining from the same. Another student-colleague, Dr. Mahendra Kadam, helped me a lot during writing the final draft of the book.

I would like to thank my daughter Ms. Sharmishtha, for helping me write a substantial number of pages of the final draft.

A heartfelt word of thanks is due to my wife, Mrs. Nalini Thakur, but I do not know whether thanking her would show enough gratitude for the silent support she gave me all these years that I was writing the book. From noting small nuggets of information for me to peruse over, to maintaining a conducive atmosphere at home for allowing me to write in peace, to not letting any problems reach me so that I could concentrate on my task... her help has been immeasurable and invaluable. I can never forget or repay (her) for the same.

My book has also received direct and indirect support from many other important people. I would like to sincerely thank my publisher, Shri. Anilbhai Mehta, for taking time out to read and re-read the drafts, suggesting changes to make the final book as flawless as possible.

The sharp editorial acumen of Shri. Mohan Velhaal has lent a unique sheen to what I wrote. I was pleased to realize that he was just as emotionally involved in the book's narrative, as I was. Every discussion with him, added a lot of value to the book.

In spite of all this, whatever flaws remain, are entirely my responsibility. For, literature regarding Mahatma Phule is being constantly written by someone or the other. Thus, I cannot claim my book to be the last word on this great personality.

This book is an effort to resurrect the legendary persona and work of Mahatma Jyotirao Phule as it was learnt and understood by me. Once again, I make no claim that this is the best representation of the luminary's life. My book is a humble effort to portray the greatness of Jyotirao Phule before my readers. I hope, readers recognize the sincere basis behind this endeavor.

Penning a biography of Mahatma Jyotirao Phule is perhaps akin to measuring the height of the Himalayas with a ruler!

But, even though the task is mammoth, it does not mean no one does it, isn't it?

Our country, our society owes a lot to this great man. This book is a small attempt to repay that debt. I'm sure, my large-hearted readers will accept this gift with love.

What more do I say now; words fall short
I prostrate at your feet; humbly so

– Dr. Ravindra Thakur

LIST OF CHARACTERS

Moro Vitthal Walvekar Sadashiv Ballal Govande Sakharam Yashwant Paranjape Vasudeo Babaji Navrange Usman Sheikh	:	Friends of Jyotirao
Thomas Penn	:	Author of books like 'The Rights Of Man' and 'The Age Of Reason'. His writings had a great influence on Jyotirao's ideologies
Saguna Aau	:	The daughter of Jyotirao's maternal aunt i.e. his cousin sister. She was like a foster mother to Jyotirao and raised him with great love and care.
Fatima Sheikh	:	A friend of Savitribai's, who also became her co-teacher at school

Chimna Aai	: Jyotirao's step-mother Chimna was also the name of Jyotirao's real mother who expired early on. In those days, it was a convention to accord the second wife the name of the first one.
Rajarambhau	: Jyotirao's elder brother
Sadubhau	: Savitribai's brother. Tukaram was his son
Gyanoba Krishnaji Sasane	: The son of Jyotirao's cousin brother Krishnaji. His daughter Radha was given in marriage to Yeshwant. After marriage, Radha's named was changed to Lakshmi.
Krishnaji Phule, Ranoji Phule	: Jyotirao's paternal uncles
Babaji Phule	: Ranoji's son; Jyotirao's paternal cousin
Mahadba and Sadba Phule	: Sons of Babaji; Jyotirao's nephews
Ganpati	: Rajarambhau's son; Jyotirao's nephew
Gajanan	: Ganpati's son

Sahadu Waghole	:	Husband of Thakubai, the niece of Jyotirao. Their son was Mahadu Waghole
Devrao Thosar	:	Jyotirao's neighbor and friend
Tukaram Hanumant Pinjan	:	Son-in-law of Devrao Thosar. He was present during the foundation of Satyashodhak Samaj
Ustad Lahujibuva Salve	:	The expert who mentored Jyotirao and Vasudeo Balwant Phadke in military studies
Dr. Murray Mitchell	:	A Christian Missionary who was a teacher at Jyotirao's school
Rev. James Mitchell	:	A Christian Missionary and the Director of the Missionary school
Tatyasaheb Bhide Sadashivrao Hate Jagannath Sadashivji Annasaheb Chiplunkar Bapusaheb Mande	:	Jyotirao's colleagues who helped set up the girls' school at Budhwar Peth
Prof. Kero Lakshman Chhatre Raghoba Pandurang Tarkhadkar Annasaheb Sahastrabuddhe	:	Well-wishers and supporters of Jyotirao's school. Helped him from time to time.

Tatyasaheb Bhide	: Gave space in his own house to start the girls' school; also extended financial help for the same
Annasaheb Chiplunkar	: A wealthy money-lender in Pune. He provided proactive support for the girls' school, and also gave space in his house at Budhwar Peth for the same.
Mrs. Farrar	: Wife of Rev. C.P. Farrar; started a girls' school at Nagar
Mukta	: Jyotirao's student belonging to the Scheduled Caste. Her essay outlining the rejection and plight of people from Mahar and Maang (scheduled caste) communities was published in the magazine called 'Dynanoday' in 1855
Keso Trimbak Dhuraji Appaji Chambhar Ganu Shivaji Maang	: Teachers in the school started for children of Mahars and Maangs
Jagannath Sadashivji	: Son of Sadashiv Govind Hate. Responsible for acquiring space for the girls'

	school. Secretary of the executive committee of the school. A clerk in the government's PWD department. Probably, must have helped Jyotirao when the latter was trying to get government contracts.
Justice John Warden	: Judicial Commissioner, Chairman of the Board of Education
E. C. Jones	: Collector of Pune; a patron of the girls' school
Mrs. E. C. Jones	: A valuable and generous patron of the girls' school
H. W. Reeves	: Revenue Commissioner. Gave generous patronage to Jyotirao's schools. Would personally come to check on the progress of students enrolled in the school for Ati-Shoodras
Keshavrao Bhawalkar (Joshi)	: Government school teacher. Taught Savitribai. Proliferated the work of Paramhans Sabha in Pune
Major Kandy	: Principal of a school in Pune

Justice Erskin Perry	: Judge; Chairman of the Board of Education for a few years; a hearty supporter of Jyotirao's schools
Viscount Falkland	: Governor of Bombay
Dadoba Pandurang Tarkhadkar	: School Inspector; Founder of Paramhans Sabha
Dr. Ram Balkrishna Jaykar	: Chairman of the Paramhans Sabha. A great social reformer. Jyotirao has dedicated his powada on Shivaji Maharaj to Dr. Jaykar
Raosaheb	: Justice Mahadev Govind Ranade
Raobahadur	: Lokahitawadi Gopal Hari Deshmukh
Thorale Shastribuva	: Krishnashastri Chiplunkar
Dhaakte Shastribuva	: Vishnushastri Chiplunkar; Writer and editor of Nibandhamala
Pandita Ramabai	: Founder of Arya Mahila Samaj; was bestowed the title of Pandita (lady scholar) for her intellectual genius. Lived in Pune for few years

Maharshi Dayanand Saraswati :	Founder of Arya Samaj; stayed in Pune for few years
Ramchandra Dhamanaskar Bhau Kondaji Patil Narobabaji Mahaghat Patil Balaji Kusaji Patil Ramaiyya Venkaiah Ayyavaru : Jaya Yalappa Lingu Jaya Karadi Lingu Ramshet Urawane Dr. Santuji Ramji Lad Ramji Santuji Aawate Dr. Vishram Ramji Ghole	Well-wishers and colleagues of Jyotirao at Satyashodhak Samaj
Tukaramtatya Padwal :	An eminent social worker from Mumbai; author of 'Jaatibhed Vivek Saar'
Mama Parmanand :	A great respected political mentor and reformist. Also known as an accomplished writer, editor and journalist
Narayan Meghaji Lokhande :	A labor-leader from Mumbai. Editor of 'Deenbandhu'. The government had bestowed him with the title of 'Justice of Peace'.
Krishnarao Bhalekar :	Editor of 'Deenbandhu'. Founder of the Deenbandhu Sarvajanik Sabha. Orator,

		writer, editor. Author of the novel 'Baliba Patil'
Ganpat Sakharam Patil	:	Nephew of Krishnarao Bhalekar; expired at a young age
Sitaram Raghunath Tarkunde	:	Student of Gyanoba Sasane; helped make copies of 'Shetkaryacha Aasud'
Dr. Shivappa Rajanna	:	Family physician of Maharaja Sayajirao Gaekwad. A Satyashodhak colleague of Jyotirao. Gave a lot of help for the Victoria Balashram at Dhanakawadi
Bhau Mansaram Naik	:	A well-known contractor from Pune. Gave his new house in Vetaal Peth for the weekly meetings of Satyashodhak Samaj
Bapuji Hari Shinde	:	A Satyashodhak volunteer from Buldhana
Tarabai Shinde	:	Daughter of Bapuji Hari Shinde; author of 'Stree-Purush Tulna'
Dynaangiribaba	:	A seer and follower of Sant Kabir. Presented a critical appreciation of 'Bijak', a compilation by Sant Kabir

Madhavrao Rokade	: Worked to proliferate the importance of education, in Mumbai
Krishnaji Arjun Keluskar	: Student of Madhavrao Rokade
Gopalbuva Valangkar	: A student and colleague of Jyotirao. Author of 'Vitaal Vidhvansak'. Served in the army for some time
Sitaram Jabaji Alhaat	: A neighbor and domestic help at Jyotirao's house. His was the first wedding to be conducted according to the Satyashodhak Samaj rites
Govind Ganpat Kale	: A clerk at Satyashodhak Samaj
Kashibai	: Yeshwant's mother
Kashibai	: A widow who was sentenced to life imprisonment for committing the crime of feticide. She used to work as a domestic help in the house of Sadashiv Ballal Govande
Baba Padmanji	: A well-wisher of Jyotirao Author of Yamunaparyatan'. Editor of 'Satyadeepika'

Gangadharshastri Phadke : Acquaintance of Jyotirao. Well-wisher of the Samaj. An officer in the Department of Education

Raje Umaji Naik : A self-declared king who challenged the British government

Vasudeo Balwant Phadke : A brave freedom fighter who challenged the British government

Tatyasaheb Rode : Son of Dhondiba Rode

Dhondiba Bin Lahuji Salve : Son of Lahujibuva Ustad

Gangamai and Rangubai : Widows working as domestic help in the Phule household

Nana : Son of Sheth Raju Babaji. Student at Jyotirao's hostel

Venkaiah, Yalappa, Bapu : Sons of Jaya Karadi Lingu. Students at Jyotirao's hostel

Linganna : Nephew of Jaya Karadi. Student at Jyotirao's hostel

Shantaram, Lakshmi, Shiva, Babu etc, : Orphans reared by Jyotirao at his home-grown orphanage. After the first girl named Lakshmi died,

	the next girl born was named as Lakshmi again
Hari Raoji Chiplunkar	: A well-wisher of Satyashodhak Samaj
Gangarambhau Mhaske	: An eminent advocate from Pune
Narayan Kashiba Karhekar Nhaavi	: A Satyashodhak volunteer from Talegaon-Dhamdhere
G. B. Shivubai Vithoba Bhujbal	: A lady Satyashodhak volunteer from Talegaon-Dhamdhere
Vithoba Bhujbal	: A mendicant from Talegaon-Dhamdhere
Nanasaheb Peshwe	: The adopted son of Bajirao Peshwa II. Leader of the mutiny of 1857. He took cover in the forests of Nepal after facing defeat in this rebellion and died an anonymous death there itself
Tatya Tope	: Nanasaheb Peshwa's General in the 1857 mutiny. Arrested and hanged to death

Sarvajanik Kaka	: Ganesh Vasudeo Joshi. Founder of Sarvajanik Sabha. Famous by his nickname 'Sarvajanik Kaka'
Lord Litton	: Viceroy of India. Enforced the Press Act and banned the publishing rights of Hindi publications
Lord Rippon	: Viceroy of India. Reinstated the publishing rights taken away by Litton
Lord Dufferin	: Viceroy of India. Jyotirao sent the handwritten manuscript of 'Shetkaryacha Aasud' to him
Sir William Wilson Hunter	: The government had incorporated a committee under the chairmanship of Sir Hunter, to study the challenged related to education in India. Jyotirao's insights proved invaluable for the Hunter Committee
Behramji Malbari	: Editor of 'Indian Spectator'. A gutsy social reformer who fought for the rights of women
Frederick Maxmuller	: A professor of modern

European languages, at Oxford University. A scholar of Oriental learning. Translated the Rigveda into English. In India, he came to be called 'Mokshmuller'

Dynanoday : A journal started to proliferate Christianity in India. Some of Jyotirao's writings were also published in Dynanoday

Satyadeepika : A magazine started by Baba Padmanji. Few of Jyotirao's powadas were published first in Satyadeepika

Dnyanprakash, Pune Vaibhav, Dnyanchakshu : Newspapers published in Pune

Vividh Dnyanvistar : A magazine edited by Ramchandra Bhikaji Gunjikar

PART 1

1

The watchman rang the bell to announce that school was over for the day. Jyoti walked out of his classroom. The road was deserted. Students from the Free Church Mission had not yet been left from their classes. Today, Jyoti's attention was not diverted by the tower of St. Mary Church. Neither did he pay attention to the missionary dwellings or places of worship of the way. He was rushing to reach home and start reading through the writings of Thomas Penn. He knew that a visit to the akhaada and Parvati were non-negotiable, but yet, he could not think of anything more than Thomas Penn and his views. Till date, he had never read such evolved and uplifting thoughts on human rights, human dignity, freedom of expression and abolition of slavery. Penn's expressions were buzzing in the young Jyoti's head. He kept ruminating on what

Penn said: "The world is my country, my religion is to do good" and "My own mind is my own church".

The cycle of thoughts churning in his mind, Jyoti didn't even realize when he crossed Nagzari towards Ganj Peth and reached his house. He hung his satchel to a knob and rushed out to Janaai's farm where the akhaada was located. On reaching the doorway to the akhaada, Jyoti cautiously looked around and softly knocked on the door.

The akhaada was tucked away in a discreet corner of Janaai's farm. Very few people had access to this place which was not just a training ground for wrestlers, but also a place for revolutionaries to brainstorm about their radical ideas. Radicalist youngsters would learn to wield weapons with deft in this akhaada, under the able guidance of Lahujibuva.

Someone opened the door, took Jyoti inside and slammed the door back again. All in a few seconds.

Jyoti stood rooted to the spot, observing some youngsters wield the sword; others swinging a gauntlet-sword with ease, as Lahujibuva kept an eagle eye on their maneuvers. Lahuji was a hands-on teacher. He would keep going around the akhaada, guiding his students via demonstrations rather than theory.

In the beginning, Jyoti would only stand in one corner and observe the others as they wielded their weapons. Yet, the sheer energy of the akhaada was so infectious, that Jyoti could not wait for the time school would end and he could rush to the akhaada. Slowly, he too started handling the weapons. He became proficient in all types of weapons, but his true skill lay in wielding the gauntlet-sword, more commonly known as a dandpatta. The smoothness, with which Jyoti would play the dandpatta, would leave others watching him agape!

Jyoti would lose sense of time when he would be in the akhaada.

Revolutionaries had again started getting active in the akhaada. Sometimes, at night, when the cannon signifying prohibition would be blown, revolutionaries like Bapu Bhangre and Bhau Khare would come to the akhaada. They would be joined by valiant youngsters like Raghu Bhangre, Nana Darbare and Chimnaji Jadhav. These people would sit with Lahuji through the entire night, planning and plotting their next move. Their ploy to upturn the British regime and hand over the reins of the kingdom to the Peshwas had become unsuccessful; but, that did not deter these brave-hearts from their goal. Ramoshi of Purandar, Koli from the Sahyadris and Umaji Naik's son were all keen to join them in the next mutiny, whenever that happened.

The young Jyoti would get excited and incensed at the same time, hearing the talks of his seniors. He also wanted to be a part of the mutiny. He wanted to become a martyr for his motherland.

However, today, something was amiss. Jyoti was not reacting with his usual fervor at the akhaada. The sight of other youngsters wielding their weapons was not arousing him like it usually would.

Just then, Lahuji came ahead and handed over a sword to Jyoti saying,

"Jyoti, come on. Spar with me."

"Yes, Ustad "replied Jyoti.

He bowed low before his teacher and started sparring with him. In spite of his advanced age, Lahuji remained a nimble warrior. Jyoti was trying his best to defeat his teacher, but something was seriously amiss. Lahuji picked up on Jyoti's lack of concentration and said to him,

"Your mind is wandering somewhere else today, son."

Jyoti was embarrassed to have been caught out. He hung his head low and stuttered,

"No...umm... no, Ustad... I...I..."

Lahuji smiled and replied,

"I know, you wish to fight with those hat-wearing enemies, isn't it? But to be able to do that, your training has to be flawless."

"Yes,Ustad. I understand."

"It won't suffice to just wield the dandpatta. You should also be an expert in using the sword" said Lahuji, walking away to oversee other students.

Jyoti stood standing there, his face ashen. Ustad would always praise him for his skills in dandpatta; but today, when he himself came for a swordfight, Jyoti had fared badly. It was not done. Jyoti thought of practicing his dandpatta, but his mind was too preoccupied for that. Then, he wore a loincloth and started exercising, but soon stopped that too. Today was simply not his day. Finally, Jyoti gave up. He took a quick bath, changed his clothes and started walking towards Parvati.

Sadashiv came running behind him, calling out,

"Hey, Jyoti...what happened? Why are you leaving early today? Did something happen? Did Ustad say something to you?"

"No, nothing..." Jyoti mumbled.

Then, they both started walking towards Parvati. Soon, they reached the hillock and climbed up towards the Goddess' temple. They sat at their favorite spot, observing the sky turn pinkish orange as dusk started settling. The bells in the temple were tinkling. Devotees were lining up to visit the Gods. Brahmins dressed in nothing but a white dhoti were climbing up and down the stone pathway of the hillock. Other people were cautiously moving to the side-lines on seeing the Brahmins approach, taking care to see that their own 'polluted' air did not touch the 'pure' Brahmins. In case some hapless non-Brahmin were to come closer, the Brahmins were yelling and cursing at them, sprinkling water from their tumblers to purify themselves and their surroundings.

Jyoti was utterly enraged on seeing this scene.

'How can one human being behave so disgustingly with another? And why? What permits one person to curse another for polluting him by his shadow? How ridiculous is that?! And that too, in the name of God and religion? No! This has to stop. This is going to have terrible repercussions. Colonization of religion has shifted from Europe-America to India. Our original Hindu religion may be having some truly elevated ideas; but these new-fangled concepts will lead our society to nothing but divisive ruin. Our society requires someone like Penn to educate them. It is necessary for someone to deliver Penn's thoughts to our masses….'

Sometime later, they saw Moro and Sakharam walking towards them. Looking at Moro, Sadashiv asked sarcastically,

"So, Moru? Did you go to pay your respects at the temple?"

"You are well aware of my inclination, Sadashiv? What joy do you get in needling me in spite of that?" Moro asked.

Turning to Sadashiv, Sakharam chimed in saying,

"Sadashiv, to be honest, we can never be sure of you. On one side you may curse the Brahmins and the Hindu religion, but then you may even turn up at some temple some day!"

Sadashiv got alert of hearing this comment. He did not take the matter laughingly. Instead, with a grave stance, he replied,

"It is true that the values ingrained since childhoods are not going to be erased from my mind very easily; but, I'm trying. Sincerely so. Yes, it becomes very difficult to stop doing the Ekadashi rituals and Bhagwat paath that I have been doing for so many years. It is not easy denouncing the faith that I have held so dear all my life. I do realize that these rituals are more of a show-off but old habits die hard."

Moro added,

"Indeed, there will not be any other religion in the world that might be shackling its followers through an incessant spate of mindless ritual practices. That is why I was saying, that if we have to free ourselves from these rituals, we should all become Christians!"

"But how will that conversion help in erasing the values that we have held dear to our heart, all these years? Can anybody guarantee that?" asked Sakharam.

"Well, maybe not; but at least, those people in Pune who take pride in being called religious fanatics, may come to their senses...." ventured Sakharam.

Jyoti, who was quiet all through this conversation, now piped up saying,

"Don't think about them, Sakha. Those people will never come out of their slumber. For, they have chosen to remain in that state. Even when they are wide awake, they pretend to be sleeping, shutting their eyes tight against the light of knowledge and progression. Three Brahmins in Pune have undergone Baptism. But, do you see any difference in their mannerisms and attitudes? The embers of the Shripat Sheshadri matter have yet not calmed down. In fact, now they are talking about making him atone his so-called sins. No, this is not the right time to convert our religion. We need to think of some other way."

No one said anything. The answer to this riddle was not an easy one. Then, Jyoti said,

"I think, the views expressed by Thomas Penn will prove to be a good guiding light in this sticky situation."

"What does this Penn say?" asked Sadashiv.

"We shall talk about this after two days" replied Jyoti.

"Alright."

These four friends would thus discuss and debate on many such topics. They would lose all sense of time, when their discussions would ensue. However, today Jyoti was not very keen on prolonging the discussion. Thus it was that the four friends bade goodbye, and Jyoti rushed home to read the writings of Penn.

The progressive and educated Brahmins in Pune would advocate that in order for Indians to reach up to the level of French, Americans and Russians; we first need to drive the British away from our country. They would try to substantiate their views using Thomas Penn's ideologies. However, in reality, Penn's ideas were very different. He would never let blind patriotism and selfish religious views mix with each other, in his writings.

Jyoti was thankful to Vasudeo for sending him these invaluable books from Mumbai. Had he not gotten access to these books, he would have remained deprived of such a treasure of knowledge. Jyoti thought that his friends would also benefit from reading these books. They could then discuss on Penn's views together.

After a quick dinner, Jyoti pulled the small oil lamp closer, and started reading through one of Penn's book. Each sentence seemed to have started getting carved on the young Jyoti's mind.

'God is one; there is only one God, and what matters is how deeply do you abide by Him, in your heart. You do not require any sacred texts or mediator for a communion with the Almighty. All human beings belong to only one religion – the religion of humanity. Sincere faith in the Almighty and true practice of morality are the two most important pillars of humankind. Who decides to follow which religious faith, is a personal matter which should not be interfered into by others. Nor should it be governed by others. Even though sacred texts are considered holy, they have not been directly ordained by the Almighty. These texts have been written by human beings like you and me. These are written expressions about human understanding of the concepts of religion and are thus subjective in nature. However, certain conniving people take undue advantage of popular faith and twisting the concepts to suit their evil purposes. We should remember that the creator of this universe, is One. Thus, his message should reach everyone in only one form, as it was intended for the collective progress of humanity. Dissent and discords arise because selfish human beings distort this message in the name of religion. Thus it is that man-made religious sects are responsible for driving wedges among human beings; God can never do that work because for Him, all his children are the same.....'

Jyoti was hungrily devouring the new concepts that he was getting to learn about. Penn had made strong criticism on the untoward practices of Christianity, even as he advocated the need for human rights and freedom of religion.

Jyoti was overwhelmed on reading about Penn's ideas regarding governance and religious structures; his affinity towards the farmer and labour class; his role in the American freedom struggle; and his courage in taking on any oppressive force in the world. Jyoti was deeply affected by Penn's determination in the face of repeated insults, criticism, harassment and imprisonment. So loyal was Penn to his thoughts that, he even had to fight with his own friends to defend his views. Penn was one of the greatest thinker-reformer of the 18th century, who even suffered imprisonment in defense of his ideas about freedom of expression and freedom of thoughts. This man, who had not been able to complete his formal education owing to lack of money, turned out to shake the very core of European society. He was an unbiased thinker, who was not afraid to point out the faults of the very people he was fighting for. Critiquing the American capitalists who had pushed thousands of blacks into slavery, Penn had said,

"Till the time you continue to employ slaves, you have no right to protest against the concept of slavery."

At one point, Jyoti kept the book down and started thinking...

The state of our Indian society is far more terrible than that described by Penn as oppressive societies. Our kings and leaders themselves are slaves to various religious sects. Even though the governance may have changed a bit, people are still shackled to the conventional concepts of religious differences and continue giving exaggerated importance to empty rituals. What's worse is that, they find happiness in doing so! How terrible is that! The physical slavery of blacks may even end some day, but this emotional and psychological slavery is going to be extremely difficult to cast off. Half of our society is denied the basic right to be able to live like a human being. They do not understand the basic concepts of what religion means. We are constantly abused on the name of fangled rituals and rules. In other religions, everyone has access to religious scriptures. Then, why do our Brahmins claim monopoly over our texts, hiding them from non-Brahmins? Probably because, those texts may hold the key to our subjugation? If that is so, then this religion is not ours. We do not need such a religion. We do not need those scriptures that subjugate, instead of elevating us. This seems to be some connivance of the Brahmins. We need to pierce through it. Till that happens, those people who are not Brahmins, will never be able to lead a happy and dignified life in the Indian milieu. These differences of caste and creed have not been created by God. They are man-made. We need to become unified to eradicate the roots of humiliation and mental slavery heaped upon us, in order to lead a better life...

"Son, get up. Time has come for your real test to begin. But, don't be afraid. I'm with you..." A faceless voice seemed to murmur in Jyoti's ears.

Jyoti snapped out of his trance with a start! A storm of thoughts was brewing in his mind.

What is a better option? To spread terror in the name of revolt, or, to wage a war for restoring the human rights of thousands of underprivileged?

The flame of the lamp started flickering, but Jyoti was not paying attention to it. His thoughts refuse to ebb.

'The revolutionaries are talking about ousting the Company Sarkar; but, it would be aimless, and even thoughtless, to start a political revolution without paying attention to the social oppressions happening around us', mused Jyoti, even as he started feeling that the feverish discussion about a revolt, going on at the akhaada, was pointless. What's the use of a revolt if it is again going to set in a divisive Peshwai regime?! We do not want such a revolt that will again lead to Brahmin oppressors sitting on our heads.

The flame of the lamp was now dying out. Darkness was engulfing it from all around. Jyoti lay tossing and turning on his bed, even as the watch-tower signified the arrival of dawn.

Jyoti had not been able to sleep the entire night. As the bells in a nearby temple began to tinkle, he woke up with a start, rubbing the sleep off his eyes.

Someone had covered him up in a blanket. Jyoti was amazed to think that he had been so lost in his reverie, that he didn't even realize who had come to cover him up!

Sitting up in bed, Jyoti's head calmed down a bit. The fervor for patriotism in his heart had been replaced by the urgent need for employing human rights. He started looking beyond the borders of one's own region, state, country, language and lineage towards the global citizen. He was ready to pounce on any oppressive force who dared to trample on the human rights of people, anywhere in the world.

'The road ahead for you is fraught with many battles. But, don't be afraid; I'm there to hold your hand'... Lord Christ was saying with his arms outstretched.

2

After finishing his daily discourse, Father James Mitchell was hurrying towards the prayer-house in the military cantonment. He had been late in leaving from the discourse. Glancing at his pocket watch once again, Father Mitchell picked up pace.

Just then, some youngsters who had been waiting for Father Mitchell in the adjoining lane, jumped in front of him and started teasing him.

Father Mitchell did not react. It had become a regular spectacle by now – The Father walking ahead with his book of Psalms and the youngsters following him, teasing and hooting.

The sight had become a sort of twisted entertainment for onlookers, some of who would also join in the 'fun' by encouraging the children or even adding an insult or two of their own.

Harassing Christian missionaries had become a permanent time-pass for idle youngsters in Pune. The missionaries had started schools, dispensaries and hostels in the cantonment. Some poor children used to study there; physically disabled people would receive love and care in those sanctuaries. But, the fear remained that the Christians would convert them forcibly; thus, people would usually shun these places. It was the same case with their discourses. No one would turn up for the discourses, even when they were free of cost. Some idle youngsters would go for the session to get free books but would then keep heckling the priest giving the discourse.

Father Mitchell was a very simple man. He would talk lovingly and earnestly with everybody, even giving away free books for them to read. There must not have been a single person in Pune who did not wrangle free books from the simpleton Father Mitchell.

The Father continued walking down, not heeding the children. Suddenly, out of nowhere, a stone came hurling at hit Father Mitchell on his head. The whack left Father Mitchell reeling in pain. Till then, Father Mitchell had been the recipient of many insults, barbs, heckling and even being targeted with cow dung. However, he had never been stoned till now. Nevertheless, he had expected it to happen some day.

Blood started gushing from the wound on Father Mitchell's forehead. As he saw his starch white robe getting drenched with blood, the Father held the crucifix dangling from his neck and looking skywards he whispered,

"Amen!"

A man from a neighboring house came ahead and asked Father to come into his courtyard. Father refused politely. Then, a few more people congregated to show false sympathy and ruminate about who must have thrown the stone. Father was not interested in knowing that.

Just then, Moro came running and held Father's hand to steady him. Seeing a Brahmin boy holding the Christian man's hand, many of the onlookers turned away their faces in disgust. One of the remaining onlookers asked Father,

"How do you keep bearing all this?"

"Tolerance and patience are two of Lord Christ's biggest teachings, Shastribuva" Father replied politely. "Fire never extinguishes fire. Thus, a discord can never end with another discord. Why should I hate the boy? The Lord will forgive him. The Lord is the most compassionate."

In spite of being Christian, Father Mitchell's accent was devoid of Western nuances. He would speak as effortlessly as any Brahmin. Somehow, this effortlessness was enough to anger Shastribuva. He retorted agitatedly,

"Hmm! Compassionate, is it? Very good! Our children will stone the head of that compassionate Lord of yours…what will you and he do then?!"

Everyone started laughing. Someone called out,

"Be wise and leave Pune before you suffer more."

Moro got uneasy on hearing these comments. He turned to Shastribuva and said,

"Buva, it does not befit you to talk like this."

"Oh, shut up you hypocrite!" Shastribuva said to Moro with disgust. "You are a Brahmin, but yet you go to study in the schools of these impostors and then speak against your own people?!"

"Buva, he is going to be converted very soon…" someone from the crowd piped up.

"God knows what has happened to these Brahmin kids of Pune. They have lost all sense of propriety" said someone else.

Moro realized that it was futile to debate with these people.

Father Mitchell knew that it was not appropriate to go to the prayer house in this state. He raised his hands upwards and begged for forgiveness from the Lord. Father was unhappy at having missed the prayer; he knew that people must be waiting for him over there, but he was helpless. The physical wound did not hurt him as much as this fact that he faltered in the service of the Lord.

Father Mitchell was remembering the words of Lord Christ.

'When you devote your life to spreading my word, people will torture you to no end. They will hurt you, insult you, spread malicious gossip about you. But, whatever happens, you should stay calm. The prophets and followers before you had also been through the same pain. But, your devotion will receive just rewards in the kingdom of God.'

Moro was walking alongside Father Mitchell. Seeing his questioning eyes, Father said to Moro,

"The work of spreading the Lord's message among people is bound to be fraught with difficulties. I need to keep going on in the face of all adversities."

They both kept walking for a while, after which Moro asked Father Mitchell,

"May I leave you up to the Mission?"

"No, my son. Thank you, but that won't be necessary. I will manage" replied the Father.

Moro left Father Mitchell and started walking towards Parvati, the cycle of thoughts whirring in his mind.

....Father James Mitchell was the friend of his teacher, Dr. Murray Mitchell. It was with Dr. Murray's help that Father James had started an English medium school in the Scottish Mission. It had been a great help for children who were keen to gain education. Both, Dr. Murray and Father James would give religious discourses at the Scottish Mission. The Mission not just imparted knowledge about reading and writing, but also taught attendees about religion, morality, manners and values. The Mission was where Moro had found like-minded friends like Jyoti, Sadashiv and Sakha.

It pained Moro to see Father Mitchell being repeatedly

humiliated by the people of his own clan. Their behavior seemed nothing less than barbaric to him.

As Moro kept walking along, he heard Jyoti calling out.

"Moro..."

Moro turned to Jyoti and asked,

"Oh! How come you are here just now? Did you not go to the akhaada today?"

"No. I have decided to stop going to the akhaada from now on" replied Jyoti.

"What?! Why so? And, why did you not come yesterday? We were waiting for you."

"I will tell you everything. First, let us go to our regular place and sit peacefully. By the way, why haven't you been coming to the akhaada?"

"It is such a pain to skirt everyone's watchful eyes and come to the akhaada. That exercise delays me and then I don't feel like coming at all" replied Moro.

Moro and Jyoti climbed up the Parvati hill. Moro narrated the recently happened episode to Jyoti. Jyoti was immensely despaired to hear about what had happened.

"That's their last weapon!" he commented with a deep sigh.

Moro too shared Jyoti's despair. He said,

"Father Stevenson also receives such barbaric treatment. I do not like it at all. Actually, I feel, their way of spreading awareness about their religion is quite exemplary. They do not coerce anyone. They only try to to convert a person's heart by teaching and talking."

Jyoti agreed with Moro's views. He had experienced it personally too. As a child, he would accompany Suguna Aau to Father's John's house. Father John and his wife Mary would shower immense love on little Jyoti. They treated him like their own son. It was at Father John's home that Jyoti had been blessed with a friend like James. The association with Father John's family had led him to getting acquainted with Father James Mitchell and Dr. Father Murray Mitchell. Jyoti received a lot of knowledge regarding Christianity from Dr. Mitchell and Madam Mitchell. It was due to them that Jyoti could read wonderful books written by scholars like John Wilson and many others. The family was always hopeful that their discussions and advice would some day lead Jyoti to convert to Christianity, but they had never once forced him to do so, in any way.

Sadashiv and Sakharam joined Moro and Jyoti. On reaching them, Sadashiv asked,

"Jyoti, what's up with you? Why have you stopped coming to the akhaada?"

"I have decided to stop coming to the akhaada at all" replied Jyoti.

"But why?" asked Moro. "You very well know how many bullets we have had to dodge to start coming to the akhaada. And, now you are talking like this? Why so?"

"No need for you to dodge bullets from now on…" Jyoti replied cryptically.

"What are you saying?!" Moro asked exasperatedly.

"Moro, our aim cannot be replacing the British regime with Peshwai. I have given it much thought, and I find it utterly foolish. There will be no societal upliftment by doing so."

"What's this now?" Sadashiv piped in with surprise. "Till yesterday, you were talking about toppling the Company Sarkar's regime, and now what's this new thing you are talking about? Have you forgotten, that we all had decided upon this aim after reading the biographies of Chhatrapati Shivaji Maharaj and George Washington? The winds of rebellion are blowing strongly in Pune. All preparations are being made. Secret meetings are happening daily. So many youngsters have pledged to devote themselves to this cause… and now you are saying…"

"What I am saying is that, we need to critically re-evaluate our aim in the current situation, Sadashiv. The revolutionaries want to upturn the Company's regime and reinstate Peshwai. But just think, what will be achieved by that? Have you forgotten what all happened when the Peshwas were in power? As it is, they have long trampled upon the concept of Swarajya laid down by Chhatrapati Shivaji Maharaj. Shivaji Maharaj's regime was one that practised social justice. His concept of Swarajya embraced every citizen, irrespective of their caste and lineage. In his Swarajya, everyone received due justice, sans any bias. Peshwai broke down this very social justice. Shivaji Raje never gave undue importance to Brahmins, but divisive casteism grew manifold during the Peshwai. In fact, Peshwai was nothing but the regime of Brahmins. The fruits of that oppressive and divisive regime are being suffered by us till date. There is a great difference between the social conditions of America during Washington's times and those in our society right now. It will not suffice for us to keep political independence as our sole goal. We may even be successful in driving out the Company Sarkar, but then, who will we replace them with? The Peshwas? Those very rulers who trampled the shoodras mercilessly, stripping them of all their human rights? Of what use is such independence to us?!"

Jyoti was speaking passionately. He continued,

"Our progressive scholars have not thought deeply regarding the writings of Penn. Our society has been divided into fragments due to ignorance about the correct tenets of religion, which have led to formation of castes and sub-castes. This fragmentation has allowed the aggressors to worm their way into our society to divide it even further. What happened in the past with the Muslims, is happening now with the British. It is not justified to lure innocent and ignorant people towards incorrect notions of patriotism in the name of selfish religion-based concepts. That cannot be true patriotism."

His friends were listening carefully, even as Jyoti continued,

"Unless we all are unified beyond the divisions of castes and religion, we can never succeed in driving out the British. If we wish for a country that belongs only to Indians, then we first need to become one as a society. Until that happens, ironically, it is in our benefit to have a British regime. That's because, unless we become unified as a society, even if we drive out the British, we will only be replacing them by our own orthodox fundamentalists who will do nothing but create even bigger chasms amongst us all. Ultimately, we all will prove guilty of helping create our own but a very divisive and hierarchical country. Please think carefully about the oppressions that happened during the Peshwa's regime. Being Brahmins themselves, they thought of no other clan than their own. They misused their power in the name of being from the so-called uppermost caste. Such an unjust regime was bound to topple some day; because, it was never in the interest of the whole society. No wonder, the farmers and ladies breathed a sigh of relief and the idle, lazy Brahmins shed tears when the Peshwai ended. Those lazy Brahmins have become so used to being saluted for nothing, that they still behave as if the Peshwai is continuing. They do not want to work. They are happy livings on the offerings they receive, thinking of it as their birth-right. However, apart from the Brahmins, other people were indeed relieved when the Peshwai ended. They have suffered immensely during that phase. If we pick up weapons right now, it will be an indirect help to those people.... People's regime can become the real sovereign power in our country; but, now is not the right time for that to happen. First, the boundaries of caste and religion need to be erase from amidst us. We need to be united beyond those divisions. Only when that happens, will the rule of people be established in India. Albeit, the Company Sarkar will not be present here to witness that; because, by then we would have ousted them."

Jyoti was saying all this, but what Sadashiv had earlier said was also not untrue. Till yesterday, Jyoti was also planning to be a part of the big rebellion brewing. The thoughts of a rebellion had got even more firmly rooted in his mind after reading the biography of the King of Dongar, Umaji Naik. Raje Umaji Naik's progressive views, the way he functioned keeping Chhatrapati Shivaji Maharaj as an idol, the respect he held for women, the lack of any addictions, and the big sacrifice he had to give…all these were stories that till now, Jyoti would never tire of telling his friends about.

A boy, who, till yesterday, was speaking about being a part of the rebellion, was singing an entirely different tune today. His friends could not fathom as to what had happened to change his mind so drastically, overnight?!

"But, what about the fact that Umaji Naik's son and his followers are also going to join the rebellion?" asked Sadashiv.

"They are not understanding the deviousness of these cunning so-called patriots. When Raje Umaji had cried out for everyone to set aside the differences of caste and religion to unify against the British, where were these patriots? Were they asleep? No; they were pretending to be asleep because they did not want to heed a king from the Ramoshi clan. Raje Umaji's caste was enough to erase all his great qualities. In fact, he was the best ideal of how a king should be. He never squandered away his time and energy in wasted pursuits. He did not loot his subjects on the pretext of unfair taxes or fines. He was the most just ruler who looked out for the benefit of all his subjects. Did any of our so-called rulers ever behave like that? Their rule meant nothing more than looting and harassing us. We do not need such a regime again."

"What Jyoti says is right" said Moro.

"But, do we not need to have any self-respect for our own country?" asked Sakharam.

"We do hold that self-respect; but, our definition of that aspect is different from the usual. The people who consume the urine of cows, considering it holy; but, treat fellow human beings worse than animals, considering them impure just because they are from another caste… we do not subscribe to their selfish and narrow-minded definition of patriotism and self-respect as Indians. Only that person who toils for the upliftment of every fellow countryman, can be truly called patriotic and as one having self-respect as an Indian. Please remove the narrow-minded definitions of patriotism perpetrated by the Brahmins, from your head. They will not lead us anywhere" replied Jyoti.

"So, do we change our decision?" asked Sadashiv.

"Yes, that's what I have decided. Our aims are not going to be fulfilled with a rebellion or revolution. Thousands of poor and downtrodden people have been suffering from the tyranny of the Brahmins. These Brahmins have also crawled into the administrative offices and are torturing others through the power of their pens. Our first duty remains, releasing the downtrodden people from the oppressive clutches of the Brahmins; and, the time for doing that, is right now. It is not easy to rebel against the Company Sarkar yet. As it is, in a way, the Company Sarkar has done us a good service by defeating the Peshwas. We need to worry about the fact that our Ramoshi and Koli brethren are going down the suicidal route by joining hands with the revolutionaries and rebels."

"But then, won't we be called out for being biased towards, or, in favour of the British? We will be labeled traitors, in a way" Sadashiv asked in a frightened voice.

"That is bound to happen, irrespective of what you do, Sadashiv! Company Sarkar is not going to be in India forever. They are bound to leave some day. But till they are here, why not use that time to liberate the persecuted people from the draconian clutches of these lazy, idle Brahmins?" relied Jyoti.

Jyoti's firm stance rendered Sadashiv speechless. A few minutes passed in silence, as everyone kept ruminating about what Jyoti had said. Then, Sadashiv said,

"I can see that Thomas Penn's writings have had a profound effect on you, Jyoti... Do lend those books to me also."

"Absolutely! Please take them from me today itself. Your thoughts will also change overnight, as mine did. You will be surprised to see how those writings have been misused to fill our heads with utterly wrong notions of patriotism."

Moro asked,

"What are Penn's views about religion?"

Hearing this, Jyoti replied with a laugh,

"Moro, the termites of region and conversion refuse to stop gnawing your brain!"

Everyone laughed at this comment. The tension in the atmosphere was broken a little. Then, Jyoti said,

"Thomas Penn opines that true belief in God and remaining faithful to one's morality and values, is the real meaning of being religious. What is moral and what is immoral, is defined by each person's own internal compass. There is no need to take the crutches of sacred texts/scriptures or follow certain rituals to become religious. Even though scriptures are considered holy, they have not been created by the Almighty; they are man-made. Conniving religious leaders have placed undue importance on sacred texts, just to forward their selfish gains. But, Penn believes that this universe created by the Almighty is the biggest scripture in itself. Anyone can read it without requiring any kind of mediator. The religion of all people in this world is one and the same; it is the religion of humanity. It is due to the absence of such a formally-established religious sect, that today people have got segregated into multiple religions. Having said that, no one has a right to interfere or dictate someone else's choice of religion. If anyone tries to create obstruction's in someone's religious choices, it should be the government's responsibility to protect the victim. Every person should have the liberty to savor his/her natural, social and religious rights without any prejudices and threat. It is the government's duty to ensure the creation of such a society where people won't face prejudices or threats for following their religion of choice. For, the government is but created by the people themselves. A government is a social contract between people and administrators. The day this contract is violated, the administrators lose their power to be in office. A government cannot be run on the lines of heredity. It cannot be a dynastic rule. Not just that, every generation has a right to create a governance that best suits their needs and demands….."

The three friends were listening to Jyoti spellbound. This was a completely new and refreshing line of thought that they were hearing. Sadashiv mused,

"Humanity is the only religion and religion is a personal choice. So, by that logic, conversion achieves nothing substantial."

Jyoti said,

"No religion enjoys an exclusive privilege or status in today's times; because, every religion has become contaminated by some imperfection. Like in the Hindu religion, Christianity also requires some things to be accepted solely on the basis of faith. Since the roots of all religions is in our conscience, behaving morally remains the best way to become truly religious. Baba Sane has said the same thing. Since no religion has remained in its original form, unaffected by other influences, religious conversion makes no sense. I think we took a wise decision by not converting to Christian religion on the basis of half-baked information."

Jyoti looked at Moro with the expectation that he say something. Moro had also accepted Baba Sane's advice, but Jyoti's views had raised many questions in his mind. Until he got satisfactory answers to those questions, Moro was not going to be able to agree with Jyoti entirely.

"All in all, it's best that we because wise in time" said Sadashiv.

"No. We need to analyze Thomas Penn's views in more depth" spoke up Moro.

"Please do. And then, reanalyze your thoughts about religion accordingly" replied Jyoti.

Moro did not retaliate to Jyoti's sharp comment. But, he did feel bad that Jyoti should comment like this when everything thus far had been done with everyone's consent. Moro was well-acquainted with this trait of Jyoti. He would not force his views on anyone, but would also strongly oppose the person who would defy his views. Jyoti would keep poking that person with sarcastic barbs till he acquiesced.

Unable to keep quiet, Moro finally huffed,

"Did you forget that we had been drawn towards the idea of conversion by mutual consensus, Jyoti?!"

"But, of course! What's surprising in that? The tenets of that religion are itself such that anyone would be drawn to them. It advocates winning over our enemies with love. Who would not like such a religion? But, do not forget, that has not absolved the religion of the tyranny of its leaders. That is why, I have long left the thought of conversion behind me."

"Oh! So you mean to say that I haven't, isn't it?!" Moro asked, gnashing his teeth.

"Well, I can only say, if the cap fits, wear it. And better still, extricate yourself from that cesspool soon" Jyoti replied cryptically.

Sadashiv added to this, saying,

"You do know about the torture being heaped on Shripat Sheshadri in Mumbai, don't you, Moro? Every Hindu temple is being 'purified' with lamps of pure ghee. The pandits of Kashi have decreed that Shripat should not be allowed back into the religion. The people of Pune are vying to ostracize Baba Biwalkar, who tried to support Shripat."

Hearing this, Moro yelled in frustration,

"This all is a ploy of the Brahmins to loot money! Shripat Sheshadri never became a Christian at all; so, where does the question of ostracizing him or taking him back , arise? But the attitude has now become that of, what we decide is the religion and what we do is the karma. How does it make sense to allege that just because Shripat stayed with a brother who became a converted Christian, he too became one? The missionaries feel that just because Shripat's brother converted, Shripat should too; and that's exactly what these orthodox Hindus don't want. This whole conspiracy is being cooked in order to scare people off conversion. The Brahmins of Kashi don't know anything about this. They just take their dakshina and mend the religious rules to suit the querent's purpose. Tomorrow if someone gives them more dakshina and tells them to say that it is alright for both these brothers to convert, they will parrot just that! Their religious rules change to the tune of the dakshina offered."

Shripat Sheshadri's case was a sore point for Moro. He would get tremendously incensed at the injustice being meted out to Shripat.

Progressive thinkers such as Balshastri Jambhekar, Gangadharshastri Phadke and Nana Shankarshet had made efforts to re-include Shripat in the religion after making him do due penance. But the Brahmins in Mumbai were singing only one tune. Their opinion was that Shripat's crime was so heinous that no amount of penance would suffice to forgive him for it.

Babaji Biwalkar had come back to Pune but no one was ready to listen to him. Rather, no one was even willing to give him an audience! The Brahmins of Pune held a big meeting at the temple of Lord Muralidhar and decreed that before Shripat Sheshadri, first Baba Biwalkar must do thorough penance for even daring to ask forgiveness for a sinner like Shripat! They all wanted Baba to rub his nose at their feet, as the ultimate act of begging for forgiveness. They opined that if sinners like Shripat and Baba were forgiven easily, then it would not take much time for the purity of the religion to get vilified. Thus, they wanted corruptors like Baba and Shripat to be expelled from the fold, to set an example in front of others thinking of carrying out such monkey tricks against the religion.

Sadashiv said,

"There are fundamentalists in every religion around the world; but, I doubt if any of those are more cruel and unbending as the Hindus! Rather than following the tenets of our religion, we are taking pride in following and coercing empty rituals, without wanting to understand the meaning behind them. It is these mindless ritual that are turning believers like me into non-believers. It is this coercion in the name of religion that forced my young sister to go Sati ! It is just terrible!" said Sadashiv, getting visibly disturbed at the thought of his sister. With a deep sigh, he continued,

"It is indeed a very confounding paradox that, on one hand it is said that our religion does not allow the practice of Sati, and then on the other hand, we are given the examples of history to show how Sati is honourable! Religious scriptures have multiple connotations and views about the inhuman ritual of Sati. So, irrespective of how many scriptures one reads, it is impossible to make one strong belief about the same. Originally, this practice was never present; but no one knows how and when it begun and got perpetrated in the people's mindset. The only thing that is true, is that, we have become slaves to this practice, Moro!" Sadashiv said with anguish, continuing, "What Jyoti says, is right. This is not the true path of religion; but conversion also will be of no use really."

Sakharam said,

"Either we stay in our own religion and try to improve it; or then, we try to proliferate the views of Thomas Penn. Until that happens, neither will such inhuman and baseless practices end, nor will the perpetration of wrong notions stop. Friends, words will fall short when we talk on these topics. Come on, let's get going. It is getting late."

Sakharam was right. It had become quite late at night. The sentries had started making their rounds to shoo away the stray people who were still loitering on the hill. Not much time was left for the cannon to blow off signaling the closure of Pune's entry gates and borders for the day. As the four friends started climbing downhill, the cannon went off.

3

The atmosphere had become very pleasant, due to the strains of the musical instruments being played. The marriage procession, which had started from the temple of Lord Maruti, had now reached the marriage venue. Dusk was fast settling in and the procession was hurrying up in order to start the rituals before sunset. The musicians were heading the procession, followed by the bridegroom on the ceremonial horse, Brahmins wearing the choicest of clothes and pugrees, and lastly, the other invitees. Since it was the wedding ceremony of two Brahmin families, non-Brahmins were taking due care to not vitiate the proceedings in any way. They were standing carefully at the edge of the road, to let the procession pass through without a hitch.

Jyoti, Sadashiv and Moro were walking with the procession, chatting happily with each other. It was the wedding of Sakharam's brother, so he was busy with the preparations. Adorned in a nice outfit, Sakharam was running along to see that all preparations were in place.

Sadashiv and Moro had also worn their special pugrees. Amid the sea of red and yellow pugrees, Jyoti's plume-embellished red turban was standing out prominently. The three friends were walking along with the other Brahmins. Suddenly, a few guests started frowning at the three of them. Someone else's attention was caught on, and he wrinkled his nose. A few guests turned around to see what the murmur was about and the veins on their forehead began pulsating in anger. Soon, the murmurs began getting stronger and people started moving away in disgust from the trio of friends. A lowly Kunbi's son was walking among the high-caste Brahmins! This was scandalous!

"This is simply unacceptable! Sinners! You all are sinners!" someone spat out in disgust.

One of the pugree-bearers came rushing ahead and

screamed,

"Hey! You lowly Shoodra! You deplorable Kunbi! How dare you walk along with us Brahmins? You think yourself to be equal to us? You have zero concern for the rules of caste and rituals don't you? You think our ancestors were fools to lay down those regulations? Get out from here! Right now!" scowled the Shastribuva, trembling in rage.

Another man screamed out,

"Have you gone blind? Don't you see other non-Brahmins walking behind us?"

"Shiva! Shiva! This over-smart lowly boy has corrupted this pious occasion!"

"Shastribuva, looks like the Brahmin caste has been polluted to no end today!" said another man in a frustrated voice. He was behaving as if the sky had fallen on his head!

Those poisonous barbs hurt Jyoti's heart and mind to no end!

'What was my fault? Just that, I participated in the procession with my friends? Does such a simple, harmless act warrant such a heinous treatment?!' Jyoti kept thinking, his head buzzing with the atrocities heaped upon him in those few minutes. Suddenly, unable to bear the pounding of his head, Jyoti darted out of the procession.

Seeing him go, someone proclaimed in a victorious voice,

"Nowadays these people have started behaving in quite a wanton manner!"

"That is what happens when foreigners start establishing their power over us. They have no sense of our customs and rules. Would anyone have dared to do this kind of a shameless act during the Peshwai?" said another.

"That Shoodra's son is one senseless fellow, but have the sons of Govande and Walvekar also lost their to bring him along with us here?!"

"Idiots all!"

"Whose son was he, by the way? The shameless one?"

"Govind, the gardener's..." replied a man, with a distasteful expression on his face.

Over there, Jyoti went back to his house, dizzy with anger! What he had heard about happening with others, had now happened with him.

Jyoti was bursting like a volcano when he entered his home. Dada was bewildered to see the usually tranquil Jyoti having become so incensed. He recognized that something seriously unfavorable had happened.

Dada was immensely proud of this son of his, who was taking education in English medium. At the behest of Munshi Janab, Dada had re-started Jyoti's schooling that had been stopped in the interim. Jyoti would always be seen with some or the other English book in his hand; and, that would make Dada's heart swell with pride. When Munshi Janab would praise Jyoti for his excellence in studies, Dada would beam with joy. Saguna Aau would say,

"My Jyoti will become a learned and respected man like Father John Sir. He will teach and uplift the uneducated. He will serve the poor and downtrodden."

In the recent times, Dada and Aau were keeping a keen eye out on their young lad. He was growing up. They trusted his to be wise, but sometimes, his thoughts would also worry them.

As Jyoti sat down on the bed, Dada came up to him and asked softly,

"What happened, Jyoti?"

His father's loving question made Jyoti burst into tears!

"Insult...They insulted me terribly! Why? Just because I walked along with them in the procession" Jyoti burst out, struggling to keep the volcano of emotions bubbling within his heart from exploding! His face had become red and he was breathing fast in a mixture of anger and anguish.

'So...Jyoti had polluted the procession! Oh my God! ...' Dada was gob-smacked thinking about the repercussions of what had transpired. He did not appreciate the way Jyoti had behaved and was afraid of the consequences which were soon to come. 'Perhaps the Brahmins may make their displeasure on the Mali community known....Perhaps, fearing the wrath of the Brahmins, other Mali families may ostracize us... Oh God...what are we to do?!'

Dada was tremendously angry with Jyoti, but he bit his tongue to stop himself from creating a scene. He realized that this was not the time to berate Jyoti. He needed to be explained tactically. But how?....

Dada kept thinking, wiping his forehead with his scarf, even as Jyoti kept barreling on.

"Their religion does not get polluted by the presence of the horse, an animal...but we human beings? We pollute them with our mere presence, is it?! This is what their religious texts teach them? This is their behavior?"

"Jyoti, my son...this is just how it is. Brahmins enjoy a privileged position. They do feel polluted by us. Why go to become an equal with them? Let us live in peace instead of stirring up unwanted storms. You are lucky that they only insulted you. Had the Peshwas been in power, you would have been punished by being trampled upon by an elephant! Our entire family would have been ruined" said Dada, trying to pacify Jyoti.

"Yes, sure! They would have trampled me...hmmph!" Jyoti thundered. "Their and my religion is one. I'm as much a Hindu as they are. Then, how come I become inferior to them? I am also a human being. Then, on what basis do they think me as lowly? Why should I take this nonsense?"

Jyoti's utterances made Dada even more anguished. He said,

"I agree that the list of their cruelties is very long, my son. But, truth remains that their caste is higher than ours. Even today, they hold the power to ruin us. They can get us ostracized. They can do anything! Who will stop them?"

"Me!!" thundered Jyoti! "I will stop them. I will bring out

their atrocities in the open. I will see to it that these atrocities and injustice stops!"

Jyoti's words were creating a huge wave of terror in Dada's heart. He did not know how to stop his son. In a helpless voice, Dada reasoned,

"Jyoti!! Please accept that we belong to a lower caste. Our job is to serve the higher caste people. That has been ordained by God Himself."

Jyoti was beyond listening. Dada could see that, but the father in him refused to sit quiet without extricating these rebellious ideas from his young son's mind. He continued,

"Still, we are better off today than we were during Peshwai. Those times were nothing less than the Dark Ages for the low caste people. During the Peshwai, even the smallest and most innocent attempt to level ourselves with the Brahmins would lead to terrible punishments. There were strict rules about how to drape the dhoti, how to draw the vermillion mark on one's forehead.... Only the Brahmins had a right to drape the dhoti horizontally, and draw the vermillion mark horizontally. Have you heard what happened to Shenu sutaar ? For his 'crime' of wearing a dhoti horizontally, the Peshwas ordered for his butt cheeks to be sliced off!! When the Sonars started drawing the vermillion horizontally, their foreheads were seared with hot iron! Nhaavis and Telis could not step out of their houses in the morning time. If they did, the Brahmins would beat them black & blue. The condition of Mahars and Maangs was the most deplorable. They would be fed oil and vermillion and buried alive in the foundation of new constructions, without any compunction. They were not permitted to enter the city limits till noon. And, if they did, they were forced to hang a tumbler around the neck to spit into and wear a tell-tale cloth around their waists. What do I tell you, son? As young boys, when we would go to the Peshwa's mansions, we have seen such atrocities, that those memories still make me quake with fear. Once, a low caste woman took water from a pond meant for Brahmins. She was made to sit at the Shaniwarwada for three days, after which she was brutally raped and then let off, after being seared on her private parts. The good-looking wives of the poor and downtrodden would be surreptitiously taken away to the Shaniwarwada for unspeakable decadent pleasures of the high caste people…"

"But Dada, the Peshwai no longer exists today. I will not tolerate such heinous treatment and shall also not allow others to be treated like this" Jyoti said in vehemence.

"My son, why do we need the Peshwai for the atrocities to continue? These people feel polluted by our mere shadow. They have been known to torture such 'pollutants' to death at the Gultekadi grounds. I'm warning you, Jyoti. Don't try to become a hero and mess with them. You are lucky they allowed you to come home in one piece" said Dada.

But, instead of containing him, Dada's sermon served to only instigate Jyoti further. He thundered,

"Who the hell gave them the right to do all these atrocities in the first place?! They torture us, treat us contemptuously, and still, we need to look up to them? We need to treat them as royals because they claim to be direct descendants of God?! What kind of a religion is this? What kind of justice is this? What religion advocates treating fellow human beings in such a dirty manner? No, this is not religion. No religion advocates meting out such inhuman behavior to a fellow human being. All this is a farce, a sham! They have created these rifts for their own selfish gains and have conveniently placed the blame on God's shoulders to torture us under his name. We all are the children of one God, isn't it? Then, is God really so cruel as to be so biased against some of his children? Who decides the reason for why we pollute them? And, who decides, what is it about us that is so impure?! I'm as much a human as they are. Their and my religion is the same. So, how do I become inferior, and they become superior?"

Saguna Aau and Savitribai were listening to Jyoti's incensed talk from the doorway of the kitchen. Saguna Aau's somber face was lined with worry. Savitribai's serene lovely face too contained traces of worry, but it was laced with interest. This facet of Jyoti was new for her. She knew Jyoti as the studious young man who would keep studying way past midnight; who would read out interesting extracts from books to her and Aau. But, today's Jyoti was a newly dynamic man who was speaking so earnestly, that Savitribai felt like carving every word of his onto her heart.

Jyoti turned Aau and said,

"Aau, give me some clothes. I will not feel peaceful till I take a bath and wash off the hypocrisy of those empty-headed fundamentalists, from my body!"

Saying thus, Jyoti paced away to the well and kept pouring pails of water on his head, for a long time.

Dusk fell. Savitri lit lamps all over the house. Jyoti was still fretting over the incident. He did not even have his dinner. Rajaram took his dinner and went to the farm. Dada ate a few morsels on Aau's insistence and lay on his bed.

Jyoti's mind was still abuzz with thoughts.

'This has to stop. We need to come out of this cesspool. All these ideas of racial supremacy owing to birth, heaven-hell, the hierarchies of castes and sub-castes, the hollow rituals, the concept of thirty-three crore Gods overlooking our every action...all this is a farce! This is nothing but the connivance of those shrewd Brahmins to ensure their supremacy over others. They are the ones who have created these casteist segregations and pitted one human being against another.

The society has also fallen prey to this connivance, owing to fear. People are willing to sit in their cubby-holes of complacence instead of daring to challenge these stupid notions. Not just that, they have accepted their inferior status with pride! How absurd is that?! I doubt if such a ghastly situation might be found anywhere else in the world? What torment must those people going through who face the agony of being treated as untouchables every day? How must they be feeling to parade around with a tumbler dangling from their necks to hold their spittle and the branches of a tree tied to their waists, to sweep the ground they walk on? Must their hearts not be bleeding from the daily humiliation? How many of their generations must have suffered thus? Who must be pacifying them at such times? Today, one incident has wounded me so much; what must those people be suffering from, who live with the unfortunate tag of an untouchable all their life?!'

Jyoti felt ashamed of himself on realizing that today was the first time he understood the pain of the untouchables. He was ashamed to have been so ignorant about it earlier.

'If the Brahmins think Shoodras are untouchables, then how do the Shoodras think of those even lower than them to be untouchables? What gives them the right to consider themselves superior to their own kin? For the Brahmins, everyone lower than tem are untouchables. But then, shouldn't the Shoodras treat their lower-caste brethren with compassion and equality, instead of letting deplorable thoughts of hierarchy create rifts amidst them? Who spoiled their minds to think like this? So, what we are following, is it really the Hindu religion, or would it be more apt to call it Brahmani religion? Why don't people unite and fight the Brahmins? Or, have years of mental slavery deadened their minds to such a possibility?'

Jyoti's mind was churning out one question after the other. On one hand, spiritual laws tell us that God lives in the soul of every being. I am the Universe and the Universe is me. But then, when it comes to ground reality, these laws are conveniently kicked off to torment people in the name of religion. Not stopping at that, these Brahmins deny access to education to the lower caste people so that they do not get capable enough to unravel the former's evil misdoings. It is very easy to string along someone who is not educated; whose vistas are not broadened. It behoves the Brahmins well to keep the low caste people uneducated for achieving their selfish gains.

The only reason that low caste people are suffering for generations, is the lack of education! The only way to upturn the unjust dominance of Brahmins, is to educate the lower castes. Make them aware of their rights and show them how their rights have been trampled upon. We need to provide education for women and low caste people. The root of this problem is ignorance. We need to train the axe on this root itself. Unless the darkness of ignorance is dispelled, this injustice will never end. Education....yes, education is the only answer! We need to start right at the bottom, with the lowest of the Shoodras. In that too, we need to start with the ladies of that bracket. When a woman gets educated, the whole family gets educated; and that leads to the whole society getting enlightened. We need to start with educating the women of the lowest castes...'

"Jyoti..." Aau called out.

It was quite late in the night. Aau and Savitri were waiting for him. Aau had yet not had her dinner, in spite of being tired from the days' work. Savitri too would toil in the farm with her elder sister-in-law, but she would not even have water until Jyoti had his dinner.

Jyoti realized that these two ladies would not eat till he had eaten. Thus, he got up and said,

"Aau, please give me my dinner."

The two ladies started serving. Jyoti washed his hands and sat to have his meal.

The next day, Jyoti sat reading from morning to evening. He did not even go to school. He would read and then keep thinking to himself for couple of minutes. In this way, apart from Penn, Jyoti started poring compulsively through the works of Gautam Buddha, Mahatma Baseshwar and Tirthankar. Among the Marathi saints, the verses of Sant Tukaram, tugged the strings of Jyoti's heart. Soon, he learnt many of those verses by-heart. The critical analyses of Hindu religion, as put forth by Prof. Wilson and Sir William Jones, appealed to Jyoti tremendously. Martin Luther's biography made him see a compelling need for brushing away the conventional notions of religion.

That evening, Sadashiv, Sakharam and Moro came to meet Jyoti. They couldn't muster enough words to pacify their dear friend.

Moro said,

"I asked my father, why do you see Jyoti as inferior even when he is more educated than so many Brahmins? My father replied, that mere educational degrees do not suffice to make a Brahmin of a Shoodra."

Sakharam was feeling extremely sad that the unfortunate incident took place during his family's ceremony. Jyoti did not react when Sakharam expressed his grief. Instead, he himself pacified and consoled his friends.

After his friends left, Jyoti again got engrossed in his books.

At night, father and son sat down together for their dinner. Savitri was serving them. No one spoke anything. Dada finished his dinner and got up. Jyoti was merely pecking at his food. Aau was observing him silently. His fair-toned face seemed to have acquired a different glow altogether. Despite herself, Aau smiled to herself with a sense of satisfaction.

Seeing that, Jyoti asked her,

"What happened, Aau? Why are you smiling?"

"Just like that."

"No, you never smile just like that. Tell me, what is it?" coaxed Jyoti.

"Well, I was smiling thinking that here, you took a bath to wash off the hypocrisy of the Brahmins; and there, the Brahmins must have taken a bath to wash of the 'impurities' you polluted them with. So, in the end, while the body got cleansed, the thought of impurities remained as they were, in both your minds."

"Aau, leave that topic now. I spoke in anger" replied Jyoti, even as he kept thinking that Aau's comment indeed made a lot of sense. He began thinking about why did he need to react like that?

Jyoti glanced at Savitri, who was looking at him, tongue-in-cheek. Savitri's face was a gentle, smiling one. Thus, at times like this, when she would smile intently, she would look even prettier. Aau was also like that only. She would speak only when necessary, but her comments would be witty and exact.

Jyoti said,

"Aau, you are right. I need to cleanse my mind off the feelings of revenge. But, it is not easy when something so humiliating happens. And, they behave like this with everybody..."

"Jyoti, I will only tell you one thing. Let them do what they want. You do not hold anger for anyone in your mind. Anger does nothing more than corrupt a good intellect. Even Lord Jesus has preached loving one's enemy...." replied Aau.

That night, Jyoti kept thinking about Aau's advice for a long time.

'These people, who dare to label fellow human beings as impure...are they our enemies or friends? We belong to the same country, the same religion. What, then, warrants these segregations amidst us? Or, do the roots of this segregation go beyond what it seems on the surface?'

Jyoti was confused.

Aau's words were prickling his mind.

Father Murray Mitchell's words were coming to haunt him. He would keep telling Jyoti:

"Son, try accepting Christianity as your religion. Until then, you will never be able to see religion in its most pure form. Lord Christ was a prince. He was the son of God Himself. Yet, he never considered himself above other fellow human beings. He would give equal respect to a fisherman, a miner and even a prostitute. He would spread the word of God to make everyone think in the right direction. The Jews would consider him to be the son of a carpenter; they would mock his teachings. Yet, Lord Christ did not waver from his aim. He exposed the hypocrisy of the fundamentalist Jew leaders. Lord Christ's teachings are so simple! He simply says, do not lie; love your enemy; and, do not make a circus of your religious beliefs. Rather than conducting an hour-long prayer in the midst of a busy road, one minute of prayer done in peace and with complete faith reaches God better. That is what the Christ preached... But, Jesus Christ was framed for being rebellious, owing to these views that he propounded. The fundamentalist Jews made him stand trial before the Governor Pilate of Rome. What an irony! Jesus, the King of Jews, was labeled a criminal by the Roman court of justice. He was crucified brutally... nails were battered into his hands and feet...he was made to wear a crown of thorns and paraded bleeding all over the town, to be crucified to death."

Father Mitchell's words kept ringing in Jyoti's ears.

"Son, try accepting Christianity as your religion. Until then, you will never be able to see religion in its most pure form..."

Jyoti had asked him,

"Father, is it mandatory to become a Christian in order to ingrain the principles propounded by Lord Christ? Plus, if Lord Christ was also simply a messenger of God, a mediator between man and God; then, of what benefit will it be to follow his lead?"

However, in response to all his questions, Father Mitchell would only keep repeating,

"Jesus is the son of God. He has come with a message of human upliftment. He is the only one who can wash away our sins."

Sleep kept eluding Jyoti. He came into the courtyard.

The sky was twinkling with stars. Jyoti was awestruck thinking about the enormous expanse of the sky. He kept looking into the dome-shaped expanse. Unbeknownst to him, his heart was getting filled with the glow of awareness.

The darkness was being dispelled to show a new path.

4

Jyoti left the mission school. After that, he would mostly remain at home. At most, he would go to the farm sometime. He tried engaging in work, but nothing seemed to excite him. He did not feel like meeting anyone. In spite of trying sincerely, Jyoti had not been able to forget that humiliating episode which had happened so many days back.

However, after a few more weeks, the dark clouds crowding in Jyoti's mind, began to dissipate. He began squinting towards a new direction, which was yet not becoming clear; but, was there. The cobweb of questions was yet not becoming resolved. One question would lead to another. In between, Aau's advice would pop up in mind:

"You do not hold rage over anyone. Lord Christ also gave the message of loving one's enemies."

What Aau says, is true. The Brahmins have sowed the seeds of malice and hatred; we should work to remove them, instead of adding to it. The core of our work should be humans and humanity. There also are some rational and progressive people among the Brahmins; we can enlist their help in this task. The Missionaries too might be able to help us. As it is, they are ready to teach the children of Mahars and Maangs, but our people are the ones who hesitate to go to them.

The web of questions kept spinning round and round...

'....The oppressive Peshwai has ended, Company Sarkar has established its regime. Our physical slavery has ended, but the psychological slavery continues. A major chunk of our society is stuck in the slavery of the tenets of religious scriptures. They simply refuse to let go of the fallacy that Brahmins are the messengers of God. The society simply does not realize that it is still a slave! It does not realize who it is serving as a slave! Enlightenment about these truths will not come unless they receive due education. Only education will make them think in the right direction, make them realize that they are being oppressed, and then make them stand unified in rebellion against this injustice.

This government is also quite a cunning one. It took away the affairs from the farmers' hands and encouraged the Brahmins to keep getting educated. The school in Vishrambaug, now also teaches English, apart from Sanskrit. The Brahmin children are happily receiving good education over there, with all their ritualistic purities kept intact. On festive occasions, those schools also have arrangements for cleansing rituals and good food, for the children. The Shastri, pundits and students partake of tasty savories while learning newer things. A hefty portion of the school's budget is kept aside for these festivities.

The biggest irony is that, the head of this school, Major Candy, is treated like an untouchable! He is not allowed to enter the Vishrambaug wada . His office is located in a room towards the roadside, at one end of the mansion. The arrangement is such that he should come and go from outside itself; not pollute the students with his presence! Once when he had stepped into the mansion by mistake, the Brahmins had performed an elaborate cleansing ritual to wash away the pollution! Till date, when Major Candy starts walking, one person follows him, sprinkling water to purify the path he walks on. Candy Sir takes all of this in his stride. His Missionary tolerance serves him well!'

Finally, the tides turned in Major Candy's favor. The Brahmins tired of the daily cleansing ritual. They made a convenient exception saying, kings are the reincarnation of Lord Vishnu, and Major Candy is the messenger of the king. So, there may not be any real reason to say that he is impure! That's just how their rule bend. Conveniently.

Tired of these hypocrite rules, Sadashiv enrolled himself in the army' Missionary school. But, that was before an English medium school began in Budhwar Peth. Sadashiv's main aim was to learn English and since, that time there was no other school teaching English, Sadashiv and Jyoti both went to the army's school. That's where they became good friends. Sadashiv entered the gang of Jyoti, Moro and Sakharam and soon, they became inseparable. They would go together everywhere – to the akhaada, to Parvati… there wouldn't be a single day wherein they did not meet and discuss something.

Then, after the school in Budhwar Peth began, Sadashiv enrolled himself there. Over there, he found progressive and brilliant friends like Gopal Hari Deshmukh. Some time later, Sakharam and Moro also quit schooling altogether. Only, Jyoti remained.

After a brief hiatus in his schooling, when Jyoti rejoined school, he had turned 15 years old. Till then, Sadashiv had finished his education and worked for a brief period as a teacher in the same school. After that, he got a job as a clerk in the Company Sarkar's department of roads and ponds. Moro and Sakharam were also searching for jobs. Only Jyoti remained a student.

All these children had been long married. At the age of 14, Jyoti was married off to an 8-year old girl. In spite of being married, he continued his education, realizing that only a good education can give him and his family a life of value and dignity.

Jyoti would see a lot of children his age in his neighborhood. He realized that if they were to lead a good life, it was essential that someone – probably, Jyoti himself – should teach them, make them educated. But for those children, school and education were very alien concepts. Nevertheless, Jyoti was getting firmer about the fact that someday, he would teach them. He would enlighten them.

Times were changing; Jyoti was trying hard to anticipate the coming changes well in time.

The intelligent Brahmins of Pune had already recognized the winds of change from much before. They had begun realizing that it was not prudent to keep hawking the old concepts of purity and impurity.

By then, it had so happened that even those Brahmins who would live off alms, had started realizing the importance of learning English. It was a given that, they would continue to receive alms irrespective of what they were learning. Just that, probably some orthodox person would wrinkle his nose, once in a while! Thus it happened that, the Brahmins in Pune began learning English, even as they kept cursing the British on the sides. Again that famous convenience came into play. They would wrap up their traditional garbs while going to school; and then, on returning home, they would simply take a bath to cleanse themselves of the pollution caused by touching English books! Those books, that would be written using ink made from cow's fat, would be kept outside the boundary of the house, lest the animal fat not pollute the pure atmosphere in their home.

Jyoti would keep thinking…

'Giving the excuse of duty, the Company Sarkar has started encouraging more and more people to get educated in English medium. The Sarkar knows that it requires thousands of clerks for their increasing work, and there is no better than the industrious Brahmins to do this job. Thus, they have started teaching English even in the hardcore Sanskrit medium schools. News is that, that school is soon going to be converted into the Poona College. Funny thing is, the Brahmins still do not allow children of any other caste to learn in that school. They still follow their regulations about purity and impurity in that way. The Company Sarkar also does not object to this hypocrisy. It is happy to keep entertaining the Brahmins, who they need. The Company Sarkar does not take any solid steps to educate low caste people. How will they? They know that that is not going bring any money into their coffers. Instead, they will end up hurting the Brahmins, whose help they need to run the country. Even the Governor Elphinstone who took many steps for improving education in India, did little to benefit the low caste people.

Worst part is, our people have no clue about all these things happening. They are sitting complacently, wrapped in their dreams of some magic wand being waved and the Peshwai coming back on throne. So many of them are still living off the earnings they get from the land parcels given to them by Bajirao. Their only work is to sit eating the whole day and keep praising the non-existent Peshwai. Their equally dumb followers keep listening and nodding in acquiescence to these idle talks. Bajirao went off, giving away the last of land parcels to even cooks and water bearers. But he paid no heed to what will happened after he is gone. The ones who got the land parcels have been indiscriminately looting the others in the name of unaccounted for taxes. Else, they plunder away people's homes and estates. Not to mention the enmity that keeps brewing amid those land holders themselves. Utter chaos has reigned! No one knows when one land owner may just charge upon another to loot his estate. Law has gone to the dogs. During Bajirao's times, there were generals who sent their wives to pleasure the ruler and got favors in return. They are known as Paithani Sardars. Now that nothing remains to show off their valor, they keep flaunting their erstwhile pride by throwing lavish parties, where courtesans dance till the wee hours. Rumor has it that these courtesans are paid huge sums of money for their services. Of course, who can blame the Sardars? They copied their master, who himself was a 'connoisseur of beauty' to put it mildly. The Sardars have followed in his footsteps as sons may follow their father.

Don't even mention the exploitation being carried out in the name of religion. Pune is the capital of Brahmin caste; so, the Brahmins of Pune behave as if the sole responsibility of protecting the purity of religious hierarchy (whatever that means), rests only on their bloated heads. But, how many people are aware of the fact that these so-called pure Brahmins, who keep sprinkling water everywhere to get rid of impurities, are ardent spectators of the lascivious dance shows that go on at night?! How many people know that, come nightfall, these very Brahmins slink into the disgraced alleys of prostitutes, and set out to ask for alms from there itself in the morning? How many are aware are many of these Brahmins, who keep preaching from their high-horses about morality, themselves have chattels on the side? And, many of them even conduct unaccounted business of providing loans at exorbitant interest rates?

The malpractices that have perpetrated in the city of Pune, will make even the most hardened player blush in shame. Alcohol, non-vegetarian consumption and illicit relationships are eating away the moral fabric of Pune like termites. Peshwas gave status to alcohol consumption; the British gave fillip to this status. So many Brahmins shamelessly consume alcohol, labeling it as Somras , and then fall by the roadside in an alcoholic haze. They feel that there is no knowledge beyond the Vedas and no world beyond Pune. They have no doubt in thinking that, there's a faraway island by the name of Calcutta, from where the monkey-faced British came to Pune. These Brahmins boast that Pune also had airplanes during the times of Ramayana-Mahabharata, but then their fortunes turned and the airplanes vanished. The British stole our knowledge and came to dance on our heads. How else would these monkeys have any sense? The Brahmins believe that it is all a game of fortune. Once again, the wheel of fortune shall turn in their favor, and the British will run off with their tail in their legs.'

When a globe was installed in the school at Budhwar Peth, so many people came to look at it in curiosity. But, these Brahmins refused to believe the geographical theories propounded by British teachers. They kept harping that, those learning English are the king of fools. According to them, English education brought nothing but atheism and maladies.

They strongly encouraged stopping education in English.

They kept cursing the city of Mumbai for having sent the tenets of religion to the dogs. Many people were rumored to have turned Christians there. One person had apparently violated all good sense and went across the seven seas to England. 'My God! That's blasphemous!!' they said. 'Why just that? Some people also eat biscuits and ice! Some drink a weird concoction called tea! Thank goodness, Pune has not fallen prey to such blasphemy. But, who knows about tomorrow? Just see, as it is, some people are now being swayed by those foolish British and are saying that the earth is suspended in the universe. Now, who can stop such idiotic blabbermouths? And, who are you trying to convince about the high knowledge of these fair-faced ones? Can there be any knowledge higher than the Vedas?! Why do we need some foreigners to come and teach us that the earth stands balanced on the head of Lord Sheshnag? If we try to prove ourselves wiser than the scriptures, one day this earth is going to be submerged under water! Anyways, why would the Company Sarkar be keen to educate us, unless they wanted to convert us? All this is simply their ploy....nothing more!'

Sometimes, these Brahmins also extol the teachings of the ancient scriptures. How much ghee would be required for arranging a wholesome lunch for hundred Brahmins? How many kilos of stuffing is required for a puranpoli in summers, and how much in winters? Such 'brilliant' topics are up for discussion amongst them. Sometimes, they also discuss truly serious topics. For instance, they may start pondering about, how does rainfall occur? In response, one is treated to some stunningly brilliant answers by these scholars! One scholar might say – Lord Indra is the God of Rain. The clouds are his elephants. He commands the elephants to start moving, and rain starts falling! Or sometimes, they may even deliberate over the benefits of women going Sati. They opine that, 'instead of bald-headed widows going around the city, polluting others; it is best that they go Sati behind their husbands! The British abolished Sati for their selfish gains. They want to convert us all by polluting us through these widows. How will these ignorant foreigners understand that by going Sati, the poor woman gets to live in heaven for as many number of years as there were hair on her husband's body – 350 crore, to be precise! These self-serving louts are going to burn in hell for trying to pollute our religion. They will die childless. We pity those idiotic so-called progressive thinkers who cry their heart out for the pain of the widows. What bloody pain? Their entire time goes in washing utensils and clothes. Many of them become widows during childhood itself. They don't even remember their husband's face. What pain are you talking about?'...

When such discussions go into a frenzy, these scholars get drunk even without alcohol.

There is a spot near Bhaangya Maruti, where idle Brahmins, cooks and water-bearers congregate to gossip. Their talks are so useless and filthy that they are seen as akin to the gutter-water running from a drain near that spot. Nevertheless, it is a popular spot for those looking for free entertainment.

One day, one person at that gossip spot said,

"Did you all hear? The women in Mumbai have started roaming around on streets...alone! Blasphemy at its best, I tell you! Oh Lord, have mercy... If you don't believe me, read the newsprint... it's all there in black & white!"

This man's enthusiasm got him in trouble, as someone asked him,

"What are you saying? And, anyways, when did you start reading the newspaper?"

The first man fumbled as he replied,

"Ahemm... Where will I go to read the newspaper? I heard this from that man...you know, that nosey fellow, who reads newspapers...he told me... I do not read the papers, please! I do not want to corrupt my religious morals, do I?"

In response, another idle fellow piped up,

"I would say, better to be corrupt than go mad!"

Everyone giggled like schoolgirls on this silly joke.

This is the usual pattern. Someone says something stupid, others laugh, or then languish in remembering the lost glory of the Peshwai, saying,

"Oh, such beautiful days were those, when the Peshwai was thriving. Brahmins were given their due respect. There would be no dearth of luxuries for them. Now, all that has gone. The Peshwas themselves have lost their power; so, who will ask us any more?"

As night falls, most of these people start visiting the tamasha camps. There commotion goes on till the wee hours of night. One can see so many patrons of the tamasha, roaming around the empty streets of Pune around midnight.

If at all no tamasha troupe is on town, then these so-called pious people do deem going to some bhajan-kirtan m arranged at Tulshibaug or Belbaug. They feel, those rare visits might quell them off their sins. But over there too, they are surrounded by their sycophantic admirers and prostitutes.

Such is their hypocrisy and need for fake appreciation, that they still try to observe the 18 rules of being a gentleman, laid down by Bajiraosaheb. Some of these include, wearing a fitting tunic, maintaining a big moustache, eating all tasty delicacies and having a beautiful wife. When these brainless idiots start going around town wearing a pugree and a shawl draped on their shoulder, it seems as if they are some big scholars, out for an important discourse; but, in reality, they are simply off to beg for alms…

Such fools get invited to big feasts, simply because they are Brahmins. But a poor, hungry Shoodra will not be given even a drop of water on mercy. Save for those staying in a few select alleys of Pune, the rest of the citizens are finding it difficult to even have two square meals a day; but no one seems to care. Yes, the British regime has brought in peace, but it led to the farmers and tillers to lose their employment in the army. Now, they have to rely only on their ancestral occupation of farming, which hasn't remained so easy. Incessant taxation and oppression by landowners has made life difficult for this group of people. Ignorance and lack of education spawning generations, along with constant subjugation by the Brahmins, has brought the farmers and other such people to the brink of troubles.

Ganj Peth, Meethganj, Bhavani Peth, Nana Peth, Ghorpade Peth, Vetaal Peth holds the clusters of these sub-castes itself. The languages and lifestyles in these Peths (localities) differs according to which sub-caste of people stay there. Jyoti stays in Ganj Peth, which beholds varied communities such as gardeners, oil pressers, Ramoshis, Mahars, Maangs etc. There are also some Gir Gosavis and followers of Sant Kabir staying along side. Apart from the holy month of Shravan, no Brahmin rituals can be seen being carried out in this locality. Rather, one can here the dohas of Saint Kabeer being sung by believers such as Dyangiribaba, who stays in Nana Peth. Dyangirbaba knows the Brij dialect very well and can often be seen holding discourses that would annotate the meaning of the dohas.

These people are well aware of how cunning the Brahmins are; yet, when the Brahmin mendicants come to see horoscopes or tell about auspicious days etc, they go away with sack-loads of grain from these 'low caste' people. They keep spinning these people in a web of rituals and house-purification pujas, in a bid to keep getting things from them. Alms and donations are not the only way in which the low-caste communities are harassed by the Brahmins. Some Joshi may come in the morning as a mendicant to ask for alms; and will again turn up in the afternoon as a moneylender to ask for his installment! Jyoti had never seen such a system where moneylenders would take money from people, give it back to them as loans, and again charge a hefty interest on it!

As much as Jyoti gets agitated at the Brahmins, he feels equally confounded at the behavior of the low-caste people, who keep venerating the Brahmins in spite of knowing all their connivance. He does not understand, why do they keep feeding the Brahmins, even taking loans for it at times? They address the Brahmins with respect on their face, but then curse them behind their backs. Then, why don't they dare to confront a Brahmin headlong? A common imprecation these people heap on each other is, 'May a Brahmin fall into your matters'. It is said that this utterance began due to the bad experiences that people had by shovelfuls at the hands of Vaijnath Bhat, a Brahmin during the Peshwai. His recommendations to the Peshwas led to such exploitation of the poor and downtrodden, that from then on, the latter would take Vaijnath Bhat's name in the most vicious way possible.

Today, almost every farmer is submerged under the burden of massive loans. So many of them have written away not just their farms but even their wives and children in mortgage deeds to the moneylenders and squires. Owing to this, the men toil in the farms of these lenders and squires, whereas the women toil at their mansions; many a times, also forced to trade their bodies in lieu of lessening the loan. Truth remains, whatsoever they do, the loan only keeps getting piled up. The state of widows living in the hallowed houses of the Brahmins, is even more pitiable and heart-rendering. Each day is a living hell for those widows, many of whom are widowed in mere childhood. They keep living for decades, counting each passing day, waiting for when death comes to claim them.

Mahars and Maangs live in Meethganj Peth. Ever since the Company Sarkar's regime has begun, they have become free to walk on the roads at all hours, but the social ostracism continues as ever. These very people, who were the foot soldiers for protecting the wealth of Maharashtra, have been reduced to living in utterly deplorable and inhuman conditions.

Jyoti was feeling a tremendously strong tug to do something constructive for all such oppressed and subjugated people. He kept thinking about what a thorn-laden path would be in store for him, once he decided to follow his heart.

One evening, Devrao Thosar came home. Father Mitchell had once gifted Thosar a copy of the Bible, as a reward for writing an excellent essay in English. Remembering that episode, Jyoti remarked,

"See, Devrao? Those foreigners have no compunction in rewarding the students from the Shoodra communities; but our own people, the Brahmins, can never even think of such a thing."

Devrao replied,

"What can we expect from those people who do not even allow us to enter their schools?!"

Jyoti said,

"Brahmins will never take the lead the educate us. They find it below their dignity to teach low caste people. But, the question is not of our education. The question is, who will educate the lower castes? The Shoodras and Ati-Shoodras? I doubt if even the British will be able to achieve that..."

Devrao started thinking about what Jyoti had said. He knew that the Brahmins would never educate the lower castes, but he had never thought about whether the British would do it, or not.

Breaking his train of thoughts, Jyoti said,

"Devrao, the Company Sarkar has made all arrangements to educate Brahmins, because they see their own benefit in it. At most, they may agree to educate us, but I'm sure, they will take no interest in educating the Ati-Shoodras. Isn't it proof enough, that they refuse to give admission to the children of Mahars and Maangs, in their schools? The Company Sarkar has to keep the Brahmins happy in order to rule here properly. They are smart enough to know that, without the co-operation of the Brahmins, they will not be able to have a seamless administration. Brahmins too see their own gain in this arrangement. Don't you see what is happening in the villages? The Brahmins have issued threats to the Company Sarkar, that if they admit the children of Mahars and Maangs, they will withdraw their own children from the schools. Who can the children of Mahars and Maangs turn to then? In reality, the rules of governance say that, it is every government's duty to provide free and compulsory education to its subjects, irrespective of any biases. But, the government is turning a convenient blind eye to this fact. That is why, this responsibility rests upon us. We need to take the reins of educating the Ati-Shoodras, in our hands!"

Devrao kept staring at Jyoti's face, uncomprehendingly. Jyoti kept talking,

"If we want our society to progress, we need to educate the ladies and our Ati-Shoodra brethren. They form a substantial part of our society and yet they are kept devoid of education. Equipping them with the right education can actually lead them to become strong pillars of our society. Devrao, I am going to take up this challenge. You tell me, how will you help me in this work? Also, remember another thing. The Missionaries have realized that Brahmins will never agree to teaching the Shoodras. That is why they started missionary schools. For that, I shall remain eternally grateful to the Missionaries. Even if I make shoes out of my own skin and make them wear it on their feet, it won't be enough to repay them for the education they have bestowed me with. But, it won't help to hand over the responsibility of educating the Ati-Shoodras to the Missionaries. The onus of this task lies on us. If the Missionaries can educate us, in spite of coming from a foreign land, why can't we do it for our own people?"

"I'm ready to help you in any way I can" said Devrao, inspired by Jyoti's commitment.

Nevertheless, Devrao was also a bit confused by Jyoti's talk. He agreed with the thoughts that Jyoti had expressed and was also indeed willing to help him; but, he could not fathom how Jyoti intended to carry out his mission.

After Devrao went away, Jyoti again sat by himself, immersed in his thoughts.

Someone's soft footsteps were tapping behind the door. Savitri was coming. She was on the brink of turning into a young lady and thus, looking prettier by the day in her nine-yard sari, with a horizontal vermillion mark on her forehead. She kept standing at the doorway, looking at Jyoti expectantly. He understood that she wished to say something. He prodded her with his eyes to speak up.

"Did you not agree with what Aaubai said?" she asked.

Jyoti laughed and replied,

"Oh that? I long forgot about that topic..."

"Is that so? Then, what do you keep thinking about all day? You haven't even gone out for last few days..."

"Hmm...I have been thinking about what can I do to wipe off the dark blemish seared onto our foreheads? How can I help make our society live with pride?"

Savitri did not reply. She had come to see if she could pacify Jyoti in some way. But this is what would happen every time. She would come to talk about something simple and Jyoti would steer the conversation on some high-brow topic, making efforts to get Savitri to agree to his point of view. Savitri would not understand many of the things that Jyoti would say, but his earnestness and commitment would make her feel ever so proud of her husband. Then, even she would start thinking. However, the woman in her would keep seeing the difficulties that lay on the way. Was it so easy to chart an entirely new path? Poor Savitri's condition would become that of a person caught between the devil and the deep sea.

"Come here, Savitri. Come and stand before me" said Jyoti.

Savitri became very conscious. She looked around cautiously and slowly, came in front of Jyoti.

"There's only one way to make this change happen. Education. And, it will not be enough to educate only the men. Even women need to get educated. Education and progress of women are the two strong pillars of social and societal reform. This work needs to start with the women of

Ati-Shoodra communities." Jyoti halted in his tracks... A few moments later, he looked up at Savitri and asked her,

"Savitri, will you learn to read and write?"

"What will I do, learning to read and write?" Savitri asked with a giggle.

"Do not giggle, Savitri, This is a serious topic. We cannot achieve social reform by merely talking about it. Talks need to be accompanied by serious and proactive actions for change to happen. If you get educated, people will start taking our thoughts seriously. Change must begin at home..."

Savitri was dumbfounded! She didn't know what to say.

"Do you agree with what I feel, Savitri?"

"Umm...yes...I do...but..."

Jyoti bore his eyes into Savitri's and asked,

"But...you are afraid about what Dada will say, Sadubhau will say...isn't it?"

Savitri kept staring mesmerized into Jyoti's grey eyes. Jyoti lowered his voice and continued,

"There is no sin in getting educated, Savitri. Aau and Dada only got me educated, isn't it? Then, why do you fear them? Or, are you afraid that people will react unfavorably? That is to be expected; because, they themselves are uneducated. But, one day, they will also realize the importance of women's education. Instead of thinking about what people will feel, think about what you feel about all this in your heart. That is more important."

Savitri was seeing substance in what Jyoti was saying; but, she was also realizing that this was going to be a huge step in the future. It was too big a challenge to fathom. She was wondering about what reply to give. But soon enough, Savitri's trust on Jyoti won and she replied,

"Yes, I will learn to read and write."

Honestly, Savitri herself could never tell whether she had said this on her own conviction or had just blurted it out with some divine intervention's push!

But whatever it was, Jyoti was thrilled to hear Savitri's decision. His eyes reflected immense pride and love for his wife. He said,

"That's great, Savitri. We shall begin from tomorrow itself. Take Aau with you and go to Lady Mitchell's school in the Mission. I shall tell them to admit you and Aau both."

Savitri was taken aback to hear about being admitted to the Mission school. She had not anticipated this. She had thought that Jyoti would teach her at home itself.

Jyoti could see the fear reflected on Savitri's earnest face. He said to her,

"Don't worry. No one converts you to Christianity just because you attend their schools."

"But, how will I be able to attend school daily?". Savitri ventured, the responsibilities of domestic life standing before her.

"That's okay. When you won't be able to go to school, I shall teach you at home. Aau can read; she can also teach you" Jyoti said enthusiastically, and then again became introverted. After some time, he looked at Savitri and said,

"The work that I intend to take up.... I may require a lot of your help in it, Savitri..."

"How's that?" Savitri asked in a confused voice.

Just then, somebody called from outside,

"Jyoti, are you at home?"

It was Sadashiv.

Seeing him approaching, Savitri quickly went inside. The topic remained incomplete.

Sadashiv came into the living room. Jyoti asked him,

"How come you haven't come here in so many days?"

Sadashiv replied,

"You are asking this to me? We keep waiting for you over there....but you don't come... What face do we have to come here, you tell me?"

"Don't worry about that, Sadashiv. In a way, it is good that incident happened. We got a learn a lot from it."

"Means?" Sadashiv asked.

"It showed us what we need to do..."

"What do you have in mind, Jyoti?"

"We need to start a school. We need to educate those people who are living like animals...we need to get them back into the human fold. To begin with, we need to start a school for ladies. The biggest victim of exploitation by the Brahmins, is a woman. We need to first start with educating the women; because, once they get learned, they can teach their children. They can teach the entire family. Thus, the ball of education will start gaining momentum and then it won't take much time for the social conditions to change. I am going to start a school for the Maharas and Maangs. I hope you will support me...?"

Sadashiv had been listening so intently to Jyoti, that the question surprised him. He replied,

"Yes, of course, Jyoti! What is there to ask in it? I'm with you always. Sakharam and Moru also have a desire to dedicate their life to teaching. They will also help you. I will do as much as I can from Nagar."

Now it was Jyoti's turn to be surprised.

"Nagar? What do you mean?!"

"I have been transferred. Received the orders yesterday only" replied Sadashiv, adding, "By the way, Jyoti, have you thought of the challenges you will face in this mission?"

"Yes, I have, my friend. But, it won't do to scamper back fearing those challenges. Remember what Thomas Penn has said? The more challenges you face, the more victorious you shall emerge. Nothing is impossible if we take due efforts. Now, look at this...your Vahini has agreed to learn reading and writing."

"What are you saying?! That's great" exclaimed Sadashiv, adding, "Please tell her to encourage the lady at our place too."

Bangles tinkled from somewhere inside. Savitri, who was intently listening to their talks, ran to the kitchen, her face aflame.

Both the friends burst out laughing. Then, Sadashiv became serious and said,

"But, Jyoti, do think seriously about the problems you will face. It is not going to be an easy trek. Even though your intentions are good, the Mahar Maangs will not be ready to send their girls to school. I would rather propose that we first start a school for Brahmin girls, and then, maybe emulating them, the Mahars and Maangs will be ready to send their daughters to school. In today's scenario, even that will be a lot of social service. Also, think like this... if we start a school for Brahmin girls, we can also get the support of the reformist Brahmins of Pune. Tatyasaheb Bhide, Sadashivrao Hate will readily support us."

After much deliberation, Jyoti agreed with Sadashiv's viewpoint. Bhide and Hate had already expressed readiness to help any cause that would forward the education of girls. Thinking about the present scenario, the limitations faced by reformers and Sadashiv's transfer, Jyoti agreed that what he was saying, made sense.

If Tatyasaheb Bhide would give floor space for starting a girl's school, Jyoti's problems were going to be reduced by half. The history of opening girl's schools in Pune, was not a very happy one. Before this too, the Christians and Missionaries had tried opening up such schools, but in spite of running them in utmost secrecy, the schools shut down in barely a few months. One Mrs. Wilson had a god experience of running girl's schools in Calcutta and Mumbai; she tried making the same effort in Pune. But, the tremendously orthodox societal attitudes of Pune, made it impossible for her to continue. It was going to be a big challenge for Jyoti to start his school, on the backdrop of these events.

Their discussion then moved onto, who else can chip in, in what way, if at all Tatyasaheb gave them a place. Most importantly, they both agreed upon not letting anyone know of their plan till the school actually began.

Sadashiv said,

"The Missionary school at Nagar is very famous. In fact, it is run by a lady. You accompany me to Nagar. Let us visit the school and see what curriculum do they have, what methods of teaching do they use etc."

Jyoti liked Sadashiv's idea. Nothing like personal experience to make a new start!

The friends kept talking till dusk. Soon, night started falling, but their talks still continued. Finally, they both decided to meet Tatyasaheb and Sadashivrao the next day itself, and then immediately proceed to Nagar.

Jyoti returned from Nagar with a renewed zeal and vision altogether! Madam Farrar was very pleased to show him around her school. She had a long discussion with him about what teaching methods can be best employed for the children. She also expressed immense satisfaction at the fact that youngsters like Jyoti and Sadashiv were stepping up to do something constructive for the empowerment of women, whose conditions were pitiable to say the least.

After returning, Jyoti waste no time in meeting Tatyasaheb. He, along with Sadashiv and Moro, had a meeting with Tatyasaheb, which turned out to be very productive. Tatyasaheb Bhide was indeed a very progressive thinker. He immediately agreed to give them the space. Not just that, he also gave them a big donation of Rs. 101 to start off the preliminary preparations, and also promised to give Rs. 5 per month for monthly expenses. Sadashiv promised to send blackboards and books from Nagar. Jyoti was going to do the teaching himself.

The logistical problems were getting resolved one by one; but the real problem that lay in front of Jyoti, was of getting students into the school. At that time, Sadashivrao Hate came forward to hold Jyoti's hand. He personally met his friends and requested them to let their daughters accompany his own daughter to Jyoti's school. Slowly, around 8 girls got registered in the school.

The day of the school's inauguration came closer. Jyoti told Aau and Savitri about what was going to happen the next day, and again went outside to the Bhide's mansion. He swept the room that was given t him for the school, put up the blackboard on the wall, and filled an earthen pot with water. The school was ready for getting inaugurated tomorrow.

That night, Jyoti went to Gaffar chacha . He was very pleased to know about Jyoti's endeavour. He said,

"Your intent is wonderful, my son. I always knew that you would do something different in life. Just one advice: do not step back now, come what may!"

He also met Usman, his childhood friend. Even though Jyoti and Usman were very close, everything had happened with such speed that, till now, Jyoti had found no time to tell Usman about what was happening. Jyoti and Usman had become dear friends after Jyoti had started attending classes with Janab Gaffar chacha. Later, in spite of facing opposition from his community members, Usman had started learning English. He had a sister. He had decided to educate her too.

At this meeting, Jyoti conveyed to Usman about his plans. They both sat reminiscing about their childhood days. It was in Usman's presence that Jyoti had been witness to the lowly attitudes of the Brahmins. Now, Usman also pledged to help him, which served to boost Jyoti's confidence even more. It was quite late in the night by the time Jyoti returned from Gaffar chacha's house.

The next morning, the first day of the girl's school began in Budhwar Peth, and in the next few hours, Pune was boiling with fury!! Someone had seen 7-8 girls enter the Bhide mansion and on getting to know the purpose behind it, had started spreading the word.

Every alley of Pune was abuzz with angry remarks and curses of the Brahmins.

"Educating girls? Is that man crazy? This is nothing but

the beginning of anarchy! Education does not agree with women. They will be widowed if their heads get bloated with knowledge. They will lose their morality and become characterless. They will start insulting the elders. What is the need for women and girls to get education? Do they need to go out to work, like we men? As long as they know how to cook, clean and serve their husband, they are good. So many centuries have gone by without such blasphemy occurring...what have the women been left wanting for? Instead, they get looked after very well by their able husbands. And, tell me one thing, if women start attending school, then will men have to start cooking? Manusmriti has rightly said '*Na stree swatantrya arhati*' – Women do not deserve freedom. Was that great man a fool to write those tenets?! If women get educated and start dancing on their husband's heads, who is to blame? Nonsense! Those so-called progressive teachers will not get a place in hell too, I'm telling you! They are committing the vilest of sins possible."

Even as the first day of school was going on at Budhwar Peth, the Brahmins congregated their own class at Belbaug. They heaped the vilest of curses on Jyoti and his friends. They lambasted him in derogatory terms and pledged to stop this sacrilegious act immediately.

"We can still understand about that Jyoti...but what about his Brahmin friends? Have they mortgaged their brains somewhere? It is a matter of profound shame that in spite of being born in the purest of Brahmin clans, they have been corrupted to such an extent that they are actually supporting this farce! What hope can we have for our clan if our next generation is going to behave so treacherously!? No, no, all this must stop... we have to stop things from going so bad...."

5

Things were heating up by the day. Ram Dikshit, Apte, Bandu Nana were hearing all sorts of things; but, Jyoti was composed. He would go to school teach the girls, meet people after school, come home and get engrossed in studies. His own schooling had stopped in the midst of all this activity. Whenever he would get time, he would teach Savitri. Sometimes, Aau would also join in this unique class.

Savitri also took her classes very seriously. She would regularly attend Madam Mitchell's school, along with Aau. To give company to Savitri, Aau also took up the slate and pencil again. Seeing their progress, Madam Mitchell fast-tracked them to Grade 3. Just one more year of learning like this, and Savitri's education would be completed.

Everything was happening seamlessly. They had even formed a committee to ensure a smooth running of the school in Bhide mansion. The committee would deliberate on various issues and take decisions as per consensus. There was no quarrel or disagreement. Yet, Jyoti was restless. He was sleeping with satisfaction. He would lie awake till the wee hours of night, thinking and planning. His goal was to open a school for the daughters of Mahars and Maangs. That had not materialized yet.

The main problem was that of space. Once they got a place, they could start preparing to establish a school. Sudamji Alhaat from Vetaal Peth would always praise Jyoti and his friends for their service. He had space in his mansion. Jyoti thought, why not ask him?

The next day, Jyoti went to Alhaat to request him for some space for the proposed school. Sudamji immediately agreed. An exhilarated Jyoti did not waste a single second after that. He spoke to Savitri about his plans. He held elaborate discussions with his friends. He did not want to delay his plans by even a day more.

Then one day, Jyoti woke up with renewed vigour and conviction. Today, he was going to Meethganj Peth to talk with the Mahar Maang families staying there. First of all, he was reminded of Raanba, the loving watchman. Jyoti would often meet him on his way to the farm; but, he had never been to Raanba's house. Nevertheless, Jyoti was sure that Raanba would at least give him a patient hearing.

Jyoti reached Meethganj, and asking around for Raanba's address, finally reached his house. Raanba was sitting outside his modest dwellings, eating his breakfast. Seeing Jyoti, he immediately got up, washed his hands and asked him,

"Come, come Jyotiba. What a pleasant surprise! How come you are here today?"

"I have come to meet you, Raanba."

Hearing this, Raanba's face swelled with happiness. he laid down a mat for Jyoti and sat at a distance from him. Two of his small kids were peeking out from the door of the house, with curiosity.

"Yes, tell me Jyotiba… What brings you here?"

"Raanba, I'm starting a school for our children. Send your children to my school from day after tomorrow."

Raanba was perplexed. He could not fathom what Jyoti was trying to tell him. He asked,

"Umm… school? Means, the type of place where you would go? Where you read, write.. that one?"

"Yes."

"What? No, no, Jyotiba….What are you saying? Mahars and Maangs to learn reading and writing? That's unheard of! When has that ever happened?"

"It may have never happened till now, Raanba; but, now on, it will happen. It is the need of the hour that Mahars and Maangs get educated, if we wish to break free from the shackles of slavery. Let us make that start" Jyoti explained in an even tone.

By then, the entire neighborhood had gathered around

Raanba's house, intently listening to their conversation.

Raanba was still confused. He asked Jyoti,

"You are asking our children to write. But, how will they ever understand such difficult things?"

"There's nothing difficult in that, Raanba. We will be teaching them easy subjects like reading and basic calculations. They will understand about morals and values while they read. They will learn about manners and hygiene in the same way. Most importantly, they will understand that they are also human beings, and have every right to live like one. That is such an important thing to know, don't you agree?"

Someone piped in,

"Jyotiba, all that is okay…but people will spit on our faces! What you are proposing is blasphemous!"

"There's nothing blasphemous is getting educated" Jyoti replied calmly. "As for those who you fear will spit on your face, they will shut up very soon. You have been bearing so much oppression for so many generations. Bear a bit more and get free from the bondage of slavery, for ever!"

Someone else said,

"If our children learn to read and write, they will turn into Christians!"

"Don't be silly. I myself have studied in a Missionary school. Have I become Christian? Please listen to me. Unless we are equipped with education, we will not be ale to live like human beings. And, till that happens, the stigma of being untouchables, will also be never wiped off from our foreheads. All this nonsense about untouchability and impurity is nothing but the Brahmins' craftiness to maintain segregations in the society, for their selfish gains. If we get educated, we will be able to see through their scams, and thus be able to topple their subjugation. Time has come for us to start getting learned now. Don't let this opportunity go wasted."

"But…sending girls to school means…" ventured Raanba.

Jyoti stopped him in his tracks saying,

"Raanba, it is utmost important to teach girls. If girls get educated, the whole community, the next generation gets educated. And why just girls? Send both your boys and girls to school. Let brothers and sisters study together."

"Yes…but…"

"Raanba, now there's no time for your ifs' and buts'" Jyoti said persuasively. "Times are changing rapidly. In the Company Sarkar's regime, no one can stop our children from attending school. The Sarkar itself may not open schools for our children, but unlike in the earlier regime, the Sarkar will also not stop us if we decide to educate our children. And I'm also sure, that ultimately, the Sarkar will also open the doors of its schools for us!"

For a long time after that, Jyoti kept reiterating the importance of education; of, sending girls to school. He also told them that they wont have to spend a dime. All the books, stationary, tiffin-food and uniforms would be provided by the school itself.

A few people agreed with Jyoti's perspective; few, did not. But, even those who did agree, were not getting ready to send their girls to his school. They simply could not fathom how they could send their daughters to school at a mansion where they would not be able to even set foot inside the doorway. One query kept leading to another, and chaos reigned supreme.

Then, at one point, Raanba said,

"Jyotiba, this is not going to work. We all shall discuss about your proposal at night and convey our decision to you tomorrow. Your views are correct, but it is best that the decision happens with everyone's consent."

Jyoti had no option but to wait till the next day. He returned home.

That night, Jyoti could not sleep a wink. Early the next morning, he dressed hurriedly and went to meet Raanba. Seeing Jyoti, Raanba exclaimed,

"Why did you take the trouble, Jyotiba? I was going to

come to you…"

"Leave all that. Tell me what have you all decided?" Jyoti asked pensively.

"Ahh yes! Oh, what a meeting we had last night! Utter chaos! No one was ready to listen to each other. Much yelling and shouting ensued. Finally, I said, I don't care what you all do; I am going to send my children. Lahujibuva was also there. I told them, I know Jyotiba very well. If he has taken up this work, it will definitely reap something good for us. Listen to me, and you all also send your children to his school. Finally, after much deliberation, everyone has agreed!"

Jyoti's joy knew no bounds! He could have leapt with joy, had he been alone. A very difficult obstacle had been successfully surmounted.

Soon, the other people from the neighborhood began congregating around Jyoti. They started asking all sorts of questions. But, Jyoti did not have much time to answer them all. He started taking down the names of the children who would attend school from the next day. There was much to be done.

Lastly, Jyoti requested the people to leave their children at the school tomorrow morning. But then, he realized his folly. So, he said,

"No worries. I shall come to take your children."

But, Raanba interjected saying,

"Don't worry about that, Jyotiba. Leave that duty to me."

Seeing strong people like Lahuji and Raanba standing in his support, Jyoti was indeed overwhelmed. He knew that if his idea would not have appealed to them, all his efforts would have gone down the drain. He thanked God and said to Raanba in a gruff voice,

"You have helped me beyond my imagination, Raanba!"

Jyoti took everyone's leave and started walking back home. On the way, he saw several malnourished, poorly clothed children wandering around listlessly. Jyoti felt a severe tug at his heart on seeing those children. He kept thinking about, which of these children would he see at school tomorrow. He wondered about, when these dark pockets of population, who did not even know the meaning of the word education, would ever become enlightened? When would these people come out of the pitiable conditions they lived in?

The Company Sarkar had started a few schools, but people were not ready to send their children to those schools. The only remedy to that problem was starting home-grown schools. But, it was hopeless to expect the established educationists to do something in that direction. The British were not helping matters by propounding gems like the 'filter down theory', which believed that if the upper castes were educated, the lower castes would follow suit via a trickle down effect. They seemed to think that this was as easy as water trickling from one pot into another! Some Brahmins were holding p this theory too, but Jyoti was not convinced – more so about the Brahmins, than about the theory! Those who had kept the lower castes in ignorance for generations on end to satisfy their personal greed, could not be trusted to turn a new leaf over, anytime soon.

Jyoti was sure that even though his effort was small in size, its effects would be far-reaching and its direction was correct. If every village turned up supporters like Raanba, his mission would soon be accomplished. Shoodras and Ati-Shoodras would start understanding the importance of education, and they will start living with dignity. Times will change.

Smiling away in anticipation of that golden period, Jyoti picked up pace. The next day was a very important one for him. But soon, the thought of tomorrow cast a web of worry on Jyoti's mind.

Tomorrow, when the children come to school, where did he have the books and stationary to give them? He barely had a few slates and boards that Sadashiv had sent. Jyoti had never thought that the problem of convincing parents to send their children, would get resolved so soon. He had been prepared for a long wait to begin his school. But, now that the children were coming from tomorrow, he had nothing much to give them.

Again, Jyoti started off on another mission. He want home, gathered whatever slates and books he had, and kept them in the room at Alhaat's mansion.

The next day, when the first day of Jyoti's new school began with the boys and girls of Mahars and Maangs, Pune seemed to shake with tremors of the highest seismic scale. The orthodox Brahmins banged their heads in frustration, crying out loud for the blasphemy of Goddess Saraswati being sent to the houses of the lowliest of creatures. They cursed that the sinners rot in hell.

Now, Jyoti was finally feeling better. Sakharam and Moro started handling the school at Bhide mansion. Jyoti would be at one school in the morning and the other one in the afternoon.

Finally, Jyoti had found the purpose of his life. The road ahead was yet sheathed in mystery, but Jyoti was sure that the future was bright! Jyoti's immense willpower had finally given him the direction and success he was restless for. Now that the journey had begun, the possibilities were endless. Jyoti knew for sure, that he was on the brink of something really huge.

6

Both the schools were running nicely, but Jyoti was sad about one thing. He had not had a proper conversation with Dada for so many weeks. Earlier, Jyoti would look after the accounts and other affairs of the farm, but after he had started these schools, Dada had stopped talking with Jyoti. When Jyoti went to look into the farm's account books, Dada had spurned him off. Actually, Dada had been enraged from the time Jyoti had started teaching Savitri. It was simply unheard of! There was no other house where daughters and daughters-in-law would sit with a book in hand…and more so, be taught by their husband.

Jyoti knew that Dada was opposed to his ideologies and work, but he knew he had to go on nevertheless.

One day, Jyoti finished his work in the farm and returned home. Evening had set in. Aau was working in the kitchen. Jyoti called out to Savitri. She came and sat in front of him with her slate and pencil in hand. She could read and write quite nicely now. So now, Jyoti had started teaching her Maths. That day, Jyoti started her off with a simple calculation. But somehow, Savitri was just not being able to crack it. Jyoti could see that Savitri was distracted. He asked her,

"What happened, Savitri?"

"Nothing…Nothing at all" Savitri replied, wiping her nose.

Jyoti did not say anything for some time. Savitri was also quiet. Her gaze was fixated to a faraway place. Jyoti asked her again,

"Savitri, speak to me frankly. What is wrong?"

"Till when will this continue? This standoff between you and Dada? Dada is not eating properly. Aau remains constantly sad. Nobody talks properly to each other. This school of yours and my education have created so many problems! Our happy home has turned into a silent, sad house."

"What do I do, Savitri? Even I do not like this situation, but I am at a loss to understand how can I resolve it?" asked Jyoti.

"Do something, please! Open a dialogue at least. Hear them out…" Savitri requested earnestly.

"Alright. I shall speak to Dada tomorrow evening" Jyoti promised her.

Dada would usually be home before dusk-fall; but after this standoff with Jyoti, he would prefer remaining out in the farm till dinnertime. He would do so to avoid talking to the people he would unfailingly meet on the way. He was not interested in answering all sorts of questions that would come up about the 'weird' behavior of his son and daughter-in-law. He had started becoming petrified of the thought that people were laughing at him behind his back. Thus, Dada would come home quite late at night.

That evening also, the same thing happened. Dada appeared in the courtyard much late in the night. Savitri offered him some water, which Dada accepted wordlessly. As Dada washed his hands and feet and went to rest on his cot, Jyoti came and sat besides him. Seeing Jyoti, Dada turned away his face in anger. Still, Jyoti ventured,

"Dada, I know that you are angry, but..."

"Just shut up! Shut up right now!" Dada exploded! Jyoti was stunned to see the normally peaceful Dada erupt like this. He kept staring at Dada's face, as Dada continued barreling,

"Why did I educate you so much? I had thought that you would take up a good job and have a life better than we had. But no! What did you do with that education? You are using it to teach those Mahars and Maangs?! Are you beyond stupid? What are you trying to prove by mingling with those low caste people?! What are you trying to do by teaching them to read and write?!" Dada roared, his white moustache quivering with rage.

"I am not doing anything wrong in this, Dada..." Jyoti persisted.

"It is against the laws of religion to educate womenfolk. You have dared to go beyond the religion too?!"

Jyoti realized that it was difficult to explain everything to Dada. In a helpless voice, he said,

"Dada, no true religion prevents any person from getting educated; and if it does, it is not a true religion."

"Wow! How learned you have become, Jyoti?!" Dada commented sarcastically. "You fool! It is my mistake that I allowed you to learn English. Those Christians have spoiled your mind. I should have anticipated this, but I was blinded by my love and faith in you...I'm so regretting my decision."

"Why, Dada? You did nothing wrong by sending me to the Missionary school."

"Yes…but you do everything that is wrong…okay?! Go against God and religion…you have become very smart, isn't it?"

Dada would have said more, but Aau interjected,

"Dada, Jyoti is not saying anything wrong. It is always a meritorious thing to give and receive education. Jyoti saw through the deceit of the Brahmins, well in time. We should also start seeing things with a clear and unbiased view. You had stopped Jyoti's school listening to that Krishnaji clerk. But even you realized later that it was his deceit to make you do so, isn't it? Krishnaji knew that he would have no scope to fudge the accounts and steal money if Jyoti got educated. That is why he was telling you all sorts of religious tenets to stop Jyoti…isn't it?"

"Yes, but isn't it enough that he got educated and became a wise man? Why does he need to teach this girl to read and write? He wants to make her an English madam, is it?!" Dada bellowed.

Nevertheless, Aau continued pacifying him saying,

"Dada, don't get agitated. Jyoti is doing nothing wrong…"

Dada kept muttering for a long time after that. Jyoti could hear a few snippets.

"How will such a behavior ever be tolerated by the society? We have to stay within the society. We are normal people, not heroes or kings that we can do what we please. How many people shall I face? What can I keep telling them?...." he kept muttering.

Finally, Aau requested him to eat his dinner saying,

"Come on now, Dada. How many days are you going to keep being angry like this? Come on, let us all eat together."

Reluctantly, Dada sat to have his dinner. Jyoti also quickly went and sat besides him. They ate in silence.

After dinner, Jyoti went to lie down on his cot, but the

thoughts in his head refused to abate. He tried reading in order to keep them at bay, but it was useless. He could understand Dada's agitation, but he also realized that he would have to keep cruising ahead, without giving into Dada's insistence that Jyoti leave this 'nonsense'.

Jyoti kept waiting for Savitri to join him. He had many things to talk to her about. Finally, Savitri closed the kitchen and came in with a tumbler of water for the night. As she sat besides Jyoti, he said to her,

"Dada is right in his own way, Savitri. I understand that at this age and stage, he cannot wipe of the notions that have been fixed in his head. He comes from a generation that has been led to believe that the Brahmins are correct in assuming that we are ineligible for education due to the castes we come from. We have no right in even asking to become educated. We are not even completely human to demand human rights! The condition of Ati-Shoodras is much more terrible. Probably, stray cats and dogs must be getting a better treatment than they do. But, all this is unacceptable to my brain, Savitri. I cannot close my eyes to such blatant injustice going on in the name of religion. It disturbs me tremendously..."

Savitri could see agony writ large on Jyoti's face. She could sense the fervency with which he was speaking.

Looking at Savitri, Jyoti said,

"Savitri, don't think about Dada or anyone else. Loo into your own heart and tell me honestly – do you think I'm doing something wrong?"

Savitri did not require even a moment's thought to reply,

"No. You are doing the right thing. The service you are rendering is priceless."

"Are you sure? Are you saying this from your heart?!" an overjoyed Jyoti asked with a smile on his face, adding, "Now, we have to see that the school does not close down for any reason. Yes, I do need to earn for a living too, but I will take up some work which will not interfere in my duties towards the schools. All the other elements of nature, be it animals, birds, rivers etc., all toil for the benefit of others. Human beings are the only ones who toil only for oneself. This has to change. I will begin that change from myself. Friends are coming forward to help me, but for now, I will have to do all the teaching myself. There will be many challenges on the way..."

Jyoti went into a trance as he kept speaking. Suddenly, he snapped out and asked his wife,

"Savitri, if you trust that what I am doing is not wrong, then will you keep listening to me in the future too?"

"Yes, absolutely; but, why are you asking this?"

Jyoti had no answer for this question. Her answer had reassured him many times over, and also boosted his confidence. He could never forget that Savitri had always listened to him and had kept her word. When he decided to start the schools, Savitri had said:

"You start off...I shall help you as I can. If needed, I will also come to the school. You teach the girls; I shall discipline them..."

How easily had she extended her support...how selflessly!

Even now, Savitri rebuked Jyoti saying,

"I'm telling once and for all. Never again ask me such a question, as if you do not trust me. I will always be standing by you, come what may."

Jyoti replied,

"Don't be angry, Savitri. But, this task is onerous. The path ahead is frught with challenges...so..."

"Whatever it is, I am with you!" Savitri said with determination.

Jyoti's eyes were filled with tears, even as his heart swelled with pride.

"Then, I don't need anything else. Now, no one can stop us. Oh, by the way, I forgot to tell you...Vahini has invited you to Nagar."

"Oh, you tell me the most important thing after so much

time, is it?" Savitri asked with a laugh.

Sorry, sorry, it just slipped my mind."

Saraswatibai and Savitri were very close friends. Saraswatibai had also taken a unique decision by joining her husband at Nagar. It was simply unheard of for women to follow their husbands like this. But, Saraswatibai had left quite unexpectedly and in a hurry.

"She is quite worried right now..." said Jyoti.

"Why so?"

The family members think that Sadashiv will get converted to Christianity if he stays alone over there, surrounded by Missionaries. That's why, Vahini has gone to Nagar."

Now, Savitri understood why her friend had left without any notice. She asked Jyoti,

"But, I thought, you had left that thought behind...?"

"Yes, we have; but Sadashiv's family members refuse to believe it."

You don't worry; I shall speak to Vahini. How are her studies coming along?" asked Savitri.

"Sadashiv said, her studies are coming along well. By the way, Savitri, when you go to Nagar, do visit Madam Farrar's school and tell me what you think about it..."

That night, Savitri slept enveloped in the joy of meeting her friend soon.

The two had kept talking quite late into the night. At some point, Savitri had slept off, but sleep eluded Jyoti. His mind was whirring with thoughts and dreams...

Somehow, his tired brain gave itself up to sleep during the break of dawn. But soon enough, the bells ringing at the nearby temple woke Jyoti up for a new day.

7

Community members had congregated in the meeting room of Jyoti's house. Ranoji, his son Babaji, Satwaji, Khanduji and many more men had come together. Voices were rising, disagreements were being expressed vocally. Dada was listening to them without a word.

"Our community is deeply ashamed of what Jyoti has done. Just tell us, if he is going to stop all this or not?" asked Ranoji.

".... And also tell us whether you want to stay in the community or step out of it?" said another.

"Your son's antics have made us all bow our heads in shame!"

"Yesterday, a few Brahmins happened to meet us...." an elderly man said, shaking his head in regret, even as another person added,

"One Shastribuva has warned us directly. He said, rein in Jyoti or the consequences will be very bad."

"They said, everyone will have to bear the punishment for Jyoti's sins..." another man piped in.

"They told us, better we ostracize your family. For once, we agree with those Brahmins. But that is not going to solve this problem. We can ostracize you any time, but finally, even we will face the same fate."

"And what about the wrath of Gods? Have you or Jyoti thought about that? Who is to blame if some misfortune befalls us all because of Jyoti's stupidity?"

"We do not feel happy troubling you like this; but, if Jyoti does not mend his ways, we will have no other option but to ostracize your family."

Finally, Dada spoke up with helpless agitation:

"What can I do, my friends?! I'm as helpless as you are. I have tried everything possible to make Jyoti see sense, but he is behaving like an obstinate bull. He has even started teaching his wife! I am at my wits' end due to this boy! You only try driving some sense into his head now..."

This news did not surprise anyone. By then, the news of Jyoti teaching Savitri had spread like wildfire. But, no one wanted to take up the responsibility of speaking to Jyoti. They told Dada,

"Do not pass the buck on us. You need to rein in your boy. That's not our job."

"Yes, that's right. Try to resolve this matter within the house. Tomorrow, if this reaches to the Gram Panchayat , things will get really messy."

"You just tell us one thing..."

"How does it look, huh? No woman in our community had sat reading books till now..."

"Kaka, I'm telling you, keeping the regard for your age in mind. Stop that girl's education, and also tell Jyoti to stop this nonsense of schools..."

"Nonsense? It is much more than that. It is blasphemy!"

"That's what. Tell him to stop it, Dada...else, the results will be very bad, I am telling you..."

Utter chaos had ensued. Some people were shouting, some were threatening Dada...no one was willing to listen, and poor Dada had no choice but sit listening to all of them. He was seething about the fact that he had to bear such humiliation from his own people, owing to Jyoti. He had no answers or explanations to give these squawkers.

Just then, a few people parted away, and began whispering in hushed tones. A few of them became so stunned that they just shut their mouths up! Many of them tried to escape from the scene, as if they were not yelling a mere few seconds back.

Jyoti knew why they had all come here. He wanted to explain his thoughts to the community members, but he knew that now was not the right time. Jyoti cast a fearless glance at the crowd, and went inside his house. Savitri and Aau were seeing all this from the doorway, their faces filled with fear.

When Jyoti came outside after freshening up, the courtyard was empty. Dada was sitting on his place with a sad face. Today, his courtyard contained no friends!

Jyoti still had a long day ahead of him. They were thinking of providing uniforms to the girls. For that, they required money; thus, Jyoti was planning to meet some generous people in the village, to request them for donations. He pulled ahead his writing pad to write letters requesting donation. He had to write a letter to the Government as well. He kept writing till late at night.

He ate dinner much later, and again sat to work. Soon, Savitri came inside. Seeing the worry on her face, Jyoti said to her,

"Why are you worried about those people, Savitri? These people will shout and scream for a few days, and then keep quiet. It won't do to cow down to them at this stage."

"No....you are right...But, I really could not bear the way they spoke to Dada. They threatened him, insulted him..."

"That's because, Dada listens quietly. Why didn't he tell them to talk to me directly? Why did those people slink away after I came home? There can be only one reason – they had not come on their own accord; they were sent by somebody. For all you know, those people also knew that we are doing nothing wrong by giving education."

"But, did you here what vile threats they were giving?!"

Jyoti laughed in scorn and said,

"Oh? All those threats about ostracising us, isn't it? Who cares? Neither do they want to extricate themselves from the cesspool of casteism and ignorance, and nor do they want the others to do so. These habits are tough to break, and to add to it, the selfish Brahmins pour oil in the fire. They are the ones who have sowed the deceptive seeds of pride about one's caste, into these people's heads. Who do we blame?" Jyoti cried out in frustration, adding, "What I feel most bad about is that, our people have put a blindfold on their eyes and are following these beliefs blindly. Brahmins treat us so shabbily, yet our people feel happy following the rules they have propounded for their selfish gains. Anyways, leave all this. I wanted to talk to you about something important today."

Savitri looked at Jyoti expectantly.

"The time has come for you to fulfill your promise to me,

Savitri. From tomorrow, you will come to teach at the school. I do not fear being shamed by people. In fact, sometimes people shaming helps us see a new direction. Brahmins have stooped to an all-time low. So now, it is upto us to step up our standards. The Brahmins have perpetrated this myth that if women get educated, they will behave promiscuously. We will upturn this myth on its head!"

Savitri started seeing the innocent faces of the little girls in Jyoti's school, in the eye of her mind. She felt very sorry for those girls who barely had enough food or clothing to survive; and she couldn't help but feel disgust about the evil minds that thought so lowly of them.

"Has the number of girls coming to school, been dropping?" Savitri asked.

"Not yet, but who knows how long their parents will hold out before they succumb to the brainwashing being carried out? Those vile people use the lowliest of means possible to forward their gains."

"Is that why you are asking me to teach?"

"That is one reason, yes. But otherwise too, I need an able partner to help me in this growing endeavour. Not to mention that, once these girls start growing up, they may feel awkward to learn from a male teacher. That is why, I want you to take up this responsibility from now itself. Of course, you will need more education yourself too, but I hope you are prepared to start from now?"

"Yes, I am."

"Oh really, Savitri?!" Jyoti exclaimed with joy. "I cannot begin to tell you how relieved I am to hear this. Gradually, you will only be handling that school. Once that school is firm on its feet, I wish to take this mission to another level."

"…. And, where will you get female teachers for those schools, from?" asked Savitri.

"You are going to make teachers like yourself very soon, Savitri. Why should I worry about that?"

Hearing this, Savitri's face broke into a sweet smile.

Jyoti moved ahead and clasped Savitri's hand in his own. Soon, she melted into his loving embrace. As Jyoti patted her back lovingly, Savitri felt like the strength of a hundred elephants was charging through her. Soon, Jyoti said to her,

"Savitri, you go off to sleep now. I will finish my work and join you. Tomorrow morning, I shall reach you to school and then go to meet Uravane Sethji ."

"You don't worry…I shall go to school alone" replied Savitri.

"Alone?!" Jyoti asked, marveling at his wife's courage.

"Yes…"

Jyoti was stunned by the strength displayed by his young wife.

8

Jyoti had a hurried breakfast and set off for the town. He was going to go to school directly from there. Dada was getting ready to go to the farm. Savitri was running around busily. She had yet to send Rajarambhau's breakfast….prepare lunch… Aau was helping her as she could.

This would be the routine every morning. Jyoti would rush out early. He would always have someone or the other to meet. Savitri's mornings would be terribly rushed as well. She would push the envelope to ensure that Jyoti had a good breakfast, because once he set out, lunch would be a forgotten or half-baked affair. Most of the times, Jyoti would not come back home for lunch; he would go to the school directly.

Dada got even more saddened after Savitri started teaching at school. Thus, her responsibilities had increased manifold. Savitri would do her best to ensure that Dada would not get angry for any other reason. She would see to it that she did not falter in any of her household duties in favor of her teaching job. Savitri would also try to find out what was on Dada's mind, but he would barely say anything. Lately, he had even started ridiculing Aau, putting her down for supporting Jyoti. Then Aau would also sit in one corner, dejectedly. With everyone withdrawing into their own shells, Savitri's little heart would flutter like a caged bird.

Chimna Aai would not participate in any of this. She would be completely detached from it all, content with working on the farm all day.

Savitri finished all her work in the kitchen and ate a little bit. Then, she kept aside a few bhaakris and chutney for Jyoti, knowing that he would not have eaten anything during the day.

In the morning, Savitri started off for the school. Actually, the Bhide mansion was not too far from Savitri's house; but somehow, the road seemed too long to her every day. She would almost run from the house to the mansion, waiting for the moment when the safe embrace of the mansion would take her inside the school.

Every morning, people would stand at the doorstep of Jyoti's house, jeering a Savitri as she made her way outside. They would insult her, make rude comments, and keep sniggering shamelessly. Not just men, even women would participate in this 'fun'. Sometimes, Savitri would be attacked with cowdung and slush for her daredevilry.

Savitri would steadfastly ignore all this and keep walking towards the school.

Sometimes, Jyoti would accompany her, but that time, people would behave even more savage. They would find it funny to sneer at the procession of husband and wife, walking to the school. Savitri would find this more insulting.

That day, as Savitri set out, someone whistled and commented,

"Ohho, the Madam has set out for school...!"

Soon, the same insult reverberated from an adjoining lane.

Savitri started walking faster, but the insults refused to stop.

At one point, she felt like a crowd was following her. Her

heartbeats fastened, but she did not dare to look behind. Just then, somebody said,

"Stop her, somebody stop her right now! Where will you wash these sins, you vile woman?!"

"Stone her!!"

Three youngsters were crossing the lane in front of Savitri. As they heard the last words, one of them picked up a stone and flung it at Savitri.

The stone hit her near the ear. Soon, a stream of blood began oozing from the wound. Savitri felt faint. Her view blackened for a few seconds. But then, she held one end of her sari to the wound and resumed walking.

Realising the gravity of what he had done, the youngster slunk into the lane, wordlessly. His friends followed suit.

But, the men standing behind Savitri could not contain their laughter. They said to her with scorn,

"You low-caste woman! You need to be taught a lesson like this only!"

"Step back, else you will die here itself."

"Leave aside religion for a minute…but, are you not ashamed of flouting the norms meant for women, so easily?"

A gaggle ensued. Savitri was feeling increasingly pained by not her wound, but these comments flying thick and fast. Unable to bear it any longer, Savitri composed herself and turned around.

The crowd was startled to see her turn and look at them with a steady gaze. They kept quiet. Savitri addressed them and said,

"Brothers, I'm doing a sacred work of teaching my younger sisters. Today, the attitude you have demonstrated has only strengthened my resolve that my sisters indeed do need education at the earliest. Brothers, I shall continue with my service with a pure heart. If you stone me for it, I shall bear those stones like flowers. May God keep you all happy."

The Brahmins shivered from head to toe, seeing Savitri's

composed fearlessness. Nevertheless, trying to gain a one-upmanship over her, they yelled,

"How dare you speak like this in front of us Brahmins, who are embodiment of God on earth?!"

"Give this useless lecture of yours to the children in Mahar localities…not here…"

Savitri kept walking. However, she felt very drained out.

When she reached Bhide mansion, she found Jyoti waiting for her on the steps. Seeing Savitri with her sari clutched to her head, Jyoti rushed ahead and took her bag from her hand. As she came inside, all the children congregated around Savitri. Jyoti rebuked her saying,

"This is the reason why I said we will go together!"

"It's okay. I'm not hurt that badly."

"Are you joking, Savitri? Just look at this wound…" Jyoti exclaimed worriedly.

Soon, a wad of cotton and some turmeric was brought in for Savitri. Jyoti dressed up her wound, and the blood stopped oozing out. A girl got some water for Savitri.

"Savitri, I shall teach today. You take rest…" said Jyoti.

But, Savitri refused, saying,

"No, don't worry; I'm okay now. I shall teach. I have got some bhaakris for you. Please eat them."

Saying this, Savitri stood in front of the girls, as if nothing had happened. Today she was teaching them a lesson from an extract written by Balshastri Jambhekar regarding morals and values.

"Children, not all rich people are egoistic; many a times, even poor people behave egoistically. Thus, if we presume that material possessions bring about ego, then all rich people should be egoistical, shouldn't they? But, that is not the case. Thus, it is wrong to presume so, too. Ego stems from one's mind. Anyone who thinks that I am someone great or special, is egoistical. Just as water does not flow to the peak of a mountain, similarly, ego does not flow to the head of a wise, learned person.

Thus, one who wishes to be learned, should first shed his/her ego. He/she should stop thinking that they are great. Just as the branches of a tree laden with fruit bend downwards, similarly, a person whose head is filled with education should always be humble. That is where his/her true greatness lies. Only growing in age does not make anyone great. Greatness is in how much education one has; how learned one is. Thus, leave your ego aside and concentrate on becoming as well-educated as possible, so as to lead a fulfilling life."

9

All efforts had gone down the drain. Jyoti had not shut down his schools. The community members ostracized Govind gardener's house. They even exhorted Sadubhau to come from Naigaon and fill some sense in his sister's head. Sadubhau came and tried talking to Savitri, going as far as to tell her,

"If you are being compelled to do this vile work of teaching, come back home."

Savitri resolved his misconceptions and warned him never to bring anything like this in his mind again.

Meetings were being held almost every day at Belbaug. Incensed Brahmins were pledging to look into this matter personally. The common theme of all meetings was that Jyoti was wreaking revenge on the Brahmins, just because he could reconcile to their natural superiority. Schools and education were meant to be domains of only the Brahmins. Now, thanks to Jyoti Phule, even those low-caste people were being able to replicate the upper caste Brahmins. The Government is foreign; they will never understand the havoc that will happen if the pure Goddess Saraswati is sent to the filthy houses of low caste people. The Government may be oblivious, but didn't this so-called educated Shoodra realize what was good for him?! A lowly gardener's son had no business and absolutely no right to interfere in something as holy as education. Jyoti and his wife are sinners of the highest order. They will not get a place in hell as well! Women will get widowed if they learn. Racist upheavals will ensue in this sacred land of the Peshwas! Oh, how horrible!

All the meetings were halting at only point: Let us meet Govind gardener and tell him to put a stop to his son's antics.

Then one day, a group of seven-eight Brahmins stood in front of Govind's home. Jyoti and Savitri had left for their work. Dada was sitting in his living room, musing with sadness over what was happening. Just then, he heard a typically tell-tale nasal voice calling out,

"Govinda, are you home?"

Dada felt a lump of fear settling in the pit of his stomach. He peeked out to see a congregation of Brahmins, standing outside his door.

"Please, come in, Maharaj ..." Dada pleaded.

"No! We are not going to enter your house. You come outside" one of them ordered in a shrill tone.

As Dada came outside and stood before the group with his head hung low, they all started squawking.

"Govinda, if you can't control your son, then at least try reigning in your daughter-in-law! How can you allow such monkey tricks in your house?"

"Your son has put a big black blot on the tenets of religion. Tomorrow, if the children of those Mahars and Maangs get educated and become officers, are we supposed to salute them?!"

"Tell him, this is not Calcutta or Mumbai. This is Pune – a Punya Nagari. A holy place. Such sacrilegious antics are not tolerated easily in Pune."

"Haven't you seen how angry the Brahmins are?"

"Govinda, put a stop to this nonsense, else you will suffer from the wrath of all Brahmins."

"Your lineage will not continue..."

"Forty-two generations of your will rot in hell!"

"You will suffer a lifetime of insults..."

Dada was feeling weighted down with every curse being thrown his way. He tried to say…

"Maharaj…please…"

However, the Brahmins stopped him in his tracks, saying,

"Don't you dare speak a word! This nonsense has to stop immediately. This is our command to you. If you cannot stop them, then throw them out of the house."

Dada stood like a stone! He did not know what to say.

"Come on, let's leave. He has no other option but to listen to us" said the Brahmins, as they walked away in a huff.

Dada collapsed in a heap! He had never felt so humiliated and helpless before.

Till now, even though Dada was rebuking Jyoti, he was also realizing that Jyoti is not doing something entirely wrong. Albeit, he was not understanding the meaning of what Jyoti was doing, but he was trusting Aau and was hoping that some day, he would come to his senses and stop this 'little project' of his. But now, Dada's patience had dried up. It was time to take a firm decision.

Today, even Aau's requests went unheeded. Dada was furious!

Jyoti got to know what had happened. He was tremendously enraged that the Brahmins had sought out Dada alone and terrorised him. Jyoti rushed back home.

Seeing him, Dada bellowed,

"You husband and wife have blackened my face!!! I cannot step out of this house without being subjected to torment!"

Aau tried pacifying him, but Dada was relentless. Jyoti, however, stuck to his guns as he said,

"Dada, we have not done anything that you should be ashamed of."

Dada was in no mood to listen. He asked Jyoti,

"Tell me your final decision. We have already been ostracized by our own people. The Brahmins have come to pick on us like vultures. Just tell me, are you going to stop your stupidity, or not?!"

Jyoti looked towards the door. He saw Savitri coming home from school. She had packed the children off and come home behind Jyoti.

"No. I won't" Jyoti replied firmly!

"What?!! You won't?!" Dada yelled.

"No, Dada. I shall not leave this work till the end of my life" Jyoti persisted.

"In that case, you and your wife will not stay in this house. Get out!" Dada said, delivering an ultimatum.

Jyoti had been mentally prepared for things to take such a turn some day. Yet, hearing those words from Dada's mouth struck a chord of deep hurt in Jyoti's heart. Nevertheless, he composed himself and said,

"Okay Dada, we shall leave this house. Do not worry any more. If people come to hound you, tell them that Jyoti does not stay here any more."

Dada had been muttering to himself all this while. When he heard what Jyoti said, unknowingly his eyes started watering up. He looked at Jyoti and pleaded,

"My son, why are you behaving this way? Did I raise you, educate you, so that one day you might leave us?!"

"Dada, please do not think that I am leaving you. Our relation is too strong to be broken by anything."

"Isn't it?" groveled Dada. "Jyoti, I do understand your views. I also understand that what you and Savitri are doing requires immense courage. But, I am not as strong as you are. I do not have the strength to fight all these people."

"How will you have the strength, Dada? For generations on end, we have been taught to keep our head low and bear all insults without retaliation."

"That's what I am trying to tell you, Jyoti.... you do not try to break from the mold. It is a very difficult path ahead if you do not toe the line" Dada tried explaining once again.

But, Jyoti's mind was set. he replied,

"No, Dada. That is not possible. I have chosen my path. There won't be any going back on it now."

Saying this, Jyoti looked at Savitri expectantly. She replied in the positive with her eyes. Aau picked up on the meaning of this mute conversation and burst into tears!

Jyoti and Savitri went inside to pack their belongings. They put all the stationary and books in a big sack, bowed low to pay their respects to Dada and Aau, picked up little Ganpati to give him a kiss and then, Jyoti went to stand outside the door. Savitri hugged Aau once more and followed behind Jyoti.

Jyoti and Savitri started walking. They did not know where they were going. They kept walking – Jyoti in front and Savitri trailing him like a shadow. Ultimately, they decided to go to Janab Chacha's house.

10

When Usman got to know that Jyoti had arrived along with Savitri, he rushed to welcome them inside. He gave them space to stay at his house; gave them some utensils to cook. Sometimes, Aau would come to visit them, bringing some food or grains.

Ever since she had started teaching at the school, Savitri's own education at the Missionary school had halted in its tracks. Jyoti was working hard to make Savitri finish that course from home. Sometimes, Sadashiv would also give her a few lessons.

While staying in Usman's house, Savitri got another dear friend in the from of Fatima. They would often study together.

However, back at school, the number of students had started declining rapidly. Funds were falling short, so they had not been able to give food to the children for last many days. They could barely afford giving them books and slates. Savitri started stitching blankets in order to supplement the income. Both, Jyoti and Savitri started doing backbreaking labor to keep the funding afloat.

However, even as they were striving to keep the school running, the opposing parties were getting a stronger hand on them by spreading vile rumors. One of the strongest rumors that caused many girls to drop out, was that Jyoti and Savitri's school was a façade to convert innocent children. Sudamji too received a threat of getting ostracized from the community; following which, he withdrew all this support. Finally, the day came when Savitri's school was shut down. The only respite was that the school in Budhwar Peth was still running.

In this period, Savitri and Saraswatibai Govande started the Mahila Seva Mandal. They organized a haldi-kunku program on the eve of Sankranti , wherein Mrs Jones, the wife of Collector Jones was invited as the Chief Guest. The invitation card to this unique event, clearly specified that all women will be made to sit together on the same carpet, sans any casteist segregation. The program went on as planned. Many women visited and were given their offerings of haldi-kunku and a til laddoo without any segregation.

11

Savitri was tending to a bag of leftover cloth pieces, segregating the good ones from the unusable ones. Then, she arranged all the good pieces in a square in front of her and gestured to Jyoti who was sitting before her with a needle and thread. He started threading the pieces together to make a blanket, according to Savitri's guidance.

Just then, they saw Sadashiv and Keshavrao Bhavalkar coming to their house. Quickly, Savitri wrapped up the blanket-in-making and went inside.

Keshavrao was very fond of Jyoti's vision and work. He had even come to visit the school a few times. Jyoti too held Keshavrao in high esteem. Keshavrao was the one who had started the Paramhans Sabha in Pune. It was in his circle that Jyoti could get acquainted with the thoughts and works of great people like Ram Balkrishnaji Jaikar. Ram Balkrishnaji and Dadoba Pandurang had entrusted Keshavrao the responsibility of taking the work of Paramhans Sabha ahead. Moropant Walvekar was ready to proffer him any help as was required.

Keshavrao and Sadashiv took a seat. Sadashiv asked Jyoti,

"Any change in Sudamji's stance?"

"No" answered Jyoti, adding, "Our community people have threatened to ostracize him. He feels compelled to make us shift our school."

"Alright. I have decided one thing. We shall start the school in my house. Ideally, Baba won't object too much."

"But, what about the money? Unless we pay the children at least a small sum, they will not be willing to come to school."

"I shall think about that too. Today, Keshavrao has come to talk to you about something" said Sadashiv, looking at Keshavrao.

Keshavrao began,

"Yes, today I have come here with a special purpose. If we want to speed up the process of educating women, we need to have trained lady teachers to teach them. I am planning to start such a teacher's training class; and I wish that Savitribai attends that class."

Jyoti had been confident that once Savitri finishes her own education, she would capably handle one school on her own. Savitri had also been confident about it. But, after having returned seeing Madam Farrar's school, Savitri had realized the lacunae in her own education. She had been toiling day & night to cover up the portion. She would take the guidance of able teachers like Aau, Jyoti, Madam Mitchell and Sadashivrao. She was trying to soak up as much knowledge as possible.

Jyoti was thinking about all of this, even as Keshavrao said,

"If it will be difficult for her to come to the training center, I can come here and train her. As it is, I'm yet to set up a proper facility. Till then, I can easily come her and train

Savitribai. In that way, your school also will not get hindered."

Jyoti was happy to hear Keshavrao's proposal. Of course, first they would have to re-start the school that they had been forced to shut down. But obviously, Keshavrao was not going to be able to help them with that aspect. The help he was proffering was invaluable in its own way.

Jyoti said,

"We really need such training centers. Our ladies find it difficult to go to Madam Mitchell's school. Savitri definitely needs more education. We are certainly going to re-start our school soon. Till then, if you take up the responsibility of training her, she will be better equipped to teach when we re-open our school, and will also be able to devote the time of her studies in teaching at the school."

Again, the topic of funds came up. Jyot said,

"We require donations."

Sadashiv said,

"I will let you know about the place, tomorrow itself. I will also send more slates and books on going back to Nagar, and will keep sending Rs. 2 per month for distributing food to the children. Whatever happens, our school should start again at the earliest."

The next day, they received place at the Govande house (Sadashiv's house) . Jyoti was elated. He started working with renewed enthusiasm. He did the rounds of Meethganj, Bhavani Peth, Nana Peth etc. and talked extensively with the people staying there. He resolved all their doubts patiently and requested them to start sending the children to the new school. Savitri continued to go to the school at Bhide mansion, tolerating the stone and cow-dung pelting that was still going on. Now, she started coming to the new school as well.

The description of Jyoti and Savitri's efforts reached to the Principal of Poona College, Major Candy. He sent a stack of books as contribution from his side.

Now, the children attending school started to get food,

but the problem of water was yet to be resolved. They had to walk for miles to get to a well where they would be allowed to drink water. Being the children of Mahars and Maangs, they would not be allowed to drink water from the nearby easily available sources. Jyoti and Savitri could not bear this torture. S, they started purchasing water for the children. The funds were as it is falling short to buy enough food; to add to it, now they had to purchase water too! Whatever funds they were getting were falling short to run the school on a sustained basis.

Once again, Jyoti was immersed in worry. He saw no other way than to meet Lahuji Ustad.

Much had happened in these interim years after Jyoti had left the akhaada. Colonel Macintosh had cracked down on the rebellion led by the Bhangares. Bapu Bhangare had been imprisoned. Raghoji Bhangare had somehow escaped and was in hiding. The government had announced an award of Rs. 5000 for anybody delivering Raghoji to them.

The ploy of gaining control over the kingdom in the name of Peshwas, had fallen right on its face! After the arrest of Umaji Naik's son, the crusades in Purandar and Satara had died down in a day!

But, Lahuji was still obsessed with driving the British out. He came from a lineage of warriors and had grown up hearing their tales of valor. Lahuji's recounting of the stories of brave-hearts who got martyred while protecting the motherland from enemies, had been responsible in enabling so many young men, including Jyoti. Jyoti's ancestors had also laid their life down for the Marathi motherland. Ranoji Gore had been a chevalier in Shivaji Maharaj's cavalry. He was martyred while fighting alongside the Chhatrapati during the battle of Bijapur. Jyoti's grandfather Chaphaji, had died while protecting Narayanrao Peshwe. Jyoti had also inherited that hot, courageous blood from his ancestors, but the ill-treatment being meted out by the Brahmins had left him disillusioned.

The Marathi kingdom had been razed to the ground. The

king had vanished; the subjects were left to their own devices, without any help. People had been forced to beg and steal for one square meal. Yet, the desire for independence remained as strong as ever. One of the early crusaders for this cause, Umaji Naik, was sent to the gallows, but till his last breath, he refused to bow down to the British. Umaji's children also followed suit. Lahuji too was carrying on the same path.

But, Jyoti had one question burning bright in his mind; the answer to which, no one was ready to give. Will we ever get back that Swarajya, which Chhatrapati Shivaji Maharaj had laid the foundation of?

Ustad would say,

"The day the Marathi flag went down from the Shaniwarwada, we pledged to upturn the caricaturish government formed by these red-faced monkeys ! My father died fighting against these red-faced monkeys. I shall not stop till I avenge my father's death; even if I have to lay down my life for that!"

When Jyoti reached Janaai's farm early next morning, Ustad had just finished his morning exercises and was taking a small break.

Seeing Jyoti, Ustad broke into a broad smile and said,

"Come, come Jyotirao. What brings you here today? I should address you as Tatya now...you have become a teacher, isn't it?"

Jyoti bowed humbly before his Ustad and sitting besides him, replied,

"Ustad, you must be knowing about the school we have started."

"Yes, of course. It is a very good work" encouraged Lahuji, the pride for his student reflecting transparently on his face. However, he added, "Albeit, I used to feel you would make some use of all the training you received in the akhaada..."

Jyoti understood the subtext of what Ustad was saying. he replied,

"The British are going to leave some day, Ustad. But what is required for the long term progress of our society, is that education reaches to the masses, across all barriers."

"That is true. Jyotirao, you are learned. What you are saying is absolutely right. But, how can mere education suffice to achieve our aim?" asked Lahuji.

"It will, Ustad. It will. Even though the British have established their rule over us, our physical slavery is over. But what about the mental slavery that the Brahmins have locked us into? Don't we need to start thinking about how and why are we Shoodras, Ati-Shoodras? As much as the British are our arch-enemies, so are our home-grown Brahmins, who have locked us into mental and physical slavery of different sorts over all these decades. They enchanted our valiant ancestors and made them believe that these casteist segregations were beneficial for them. But, that is not true. They have very cleverly ensured that they close the doors of education for us, so that we may never come out from under the shadows of ignorance and see the truth. This manipulation is the main reason for all the traumas that our communities are facing till date. Ustad, the Company Sarkar is bound to leave some day. They have not come to stay here permanently. Our true and deadly enemy is the rank of lazy, idle Brahmins who hegemonize all others in the name of the self-proclaimed racial superiority."

Ustad agreed that what Jyoti was saying, was true; but, his heart would not allow him to carelessly disregard the British so easily.

Ustad said to Jyoti,

"What you are saying, is true. But, how can we forget how the British are ill-treating the Mahars and Ramoshis too? Umaji was sent to the gallows. Raghoji is being forced to be in hiding. You have selected a different track altogether. I have no qualms about that; but, this is not our Government. These are not our people. I won't rest in peace till they are driven out of here."

Jyoti replied,

"On one side, the Maangs and Ramoshis are dying fighting against the British, and on the other side, the Jahagirdars appointed by the Peshwas are having their fun, attending dance programs where they make the poor womenfolk of low-caste dance while they leer at them! How unjust is all this! How will any rebellion be successful in such a scenario, Ustad?"

"I'm not banking on that at all! I will fight till my last breath. Even if I die fighting, I will feel my life has lived its purpose" said Lahuji.

Lahuji was firm on his view; however, he did agree that education for the masses, was the need of the hour.

Finally, Lahuji said,

"Let it be, Jyotirao. Let's agree that we disagree on this topic. But, it is a good thing that you started the school. I know what you have gone through. Always remember, people will never forget this service of yours. Not for generations on end! I hope the school is doing well? If you require any help from me, let me know."

"Thank you, Ustad. I know you realize the worth of my work. Hence, I have come here today with a request..." Jyoti ventured.

"Sure, sure...Tell me frankly..."

"Students are dropping out of school very fast. Will you please have a talk with the community elders and tell them to send their children to school?"

"Oh. is that it?! Don't worry. I promise you...by tomorrow, you will see double the number of students in your class. That's my word."

"No, no, Ustad... we do not have the space to accommodate newer students for now. I would be happy to have the present ones back for now."

"Why do you worry for that? Start another school in the Mahar locality! I shall give you place for that" said Lahuji.

"Yes, we shall think of that too. But, for now, please tell the parents to start sending the children back again" said Jyoti, as he prostrated before his teacher and took his leave.

The next day, the entire locality of Mahars erupted in a huge chaos. Ustad Lahujibuva and Raanba ploughed their way into each house and made every family agree to send their children to school. Sometimes they spoke sweetly, sometimes they yelled... some children were literally carried and brought to the school! Jyoti and Savitri spent most of that day wiping the children's tears.

After a few more days of this unique admission process, the number of students attending school regularly, began to swell like a river in monsoon. So much so, that the place started falling short for accommodating so many children. Yet, news of the school started spreading like wildfire and parents from neighboring villages started bringing their children in, carrying them on their backs if needed!

12

One evening, Jyoti sat in the house doing the accounts, while Savitri sat in the courtyard, preparing for the evening's meal. Just then, she heard someone call out,

"How are you, teacher Madam? Is Pantoji tatya at home?"

It was Moro. Savitri smiled at him and said,

"True that. Your tatya had a definite reason for making me educated."

"Ohh, so Jyoti, that means Vahini finally saw through your plan" laughed Moro as he entered the living room and sat besides Jyoti.

The school children would address Jyoti as tatya and Savitri as kaku. The names had so stuck, that by now almost everyone called them tatya and kaku itself.

Hearing Moro's comment, Jyoti looked at Savitri with a glint in his eye. Savitri stole a glance at Jyoti, who was trying hard to suppress a smile.

Moro had come with some good news. He turned to Jyoti

and said,

"Jyoti, we no longer have to worry about having a good teacher. I asked Vishnupant Thatte and he had immediately consented to teaching at our school."

Jyoti did not react. He sat thinking.

Seeing this, Moro asked,

"What happened, Jyoti? Are you surprised?"

"Well, it is a surprise, isn't it?" remarked Jyoti with a hint of a smile.

"It is a sign that the society is finally realizing the value of our work" said Moro.

"The society has started realizing it long back; but, what I'm surprised about is that people like Thatte have reconciled to it so soon!"

Jyoti's sarcasm did not escape Moro's attention. He replied,

"You are misunderstanding, Jyoti. Thatte has high regards for you and Vahini. He said, 'just because the Brahmins ridicule Jyotirao's work, that does not lessen the value of the contribution he is making towards the society'. Thatte has invited you to meet him. Agreed, he is somewhat of a traditionalist; but, if we are getting his help, and that too, snubbing the orthodox members of the community, what more do we want?!"

But, Jyoti was unmoved by Moro's enthusiasm. He remarked,

"I don't believe it. He will come for two days, and then leave it in the name of repentance."

Savitri could not help giggling at this pointed comment, which made Moro even more abashed. Yet, he pressed on saying,

"We shall see that later. But for now, at least I do not see anything wrong in taking his help."

Finally, Jyoti relented to his dear friend's insistence, and they both started off to meet Vishnupant Thatte at his house.

Vishnupant was truly pleased to see Jyoti come to his house. He greeted Jyoti and Moro warmly, and said,

"I have deep appreciation for the work that you all are doing. Actually, this step should have been taken long back by those like us who claim to be the educated class; but, we failed to do so. It is very regrettable that people from our community torture you in heinous ways. I cannot stop them all, but I can definitely contribute to this noble cause. With this thought in mind, I am prepared to assist you in whatever way I can. Moropant has briefed me about everything that has happened so far. In the past, Christian Missionaries had tried setting up similar schools for the womenfolk of the Shoodra communities; but, they could not run those schools for long. On that backdrop, it is specially commendable that you have taken such a bold step. More than Christian Missionaries, when our own youth takes on the onus of empowering the society, their efforts should be encouraged in all possible ways."

What Vishnupant had said, was true. In fact, the failure of Christian Missionaries had led to the orthodox Brahmins becoming even more brazen!

Vishnupant started coming to the school, from the next day itself. It was another shcok for the conservative society of Pune.

The number of students in the school were constantly increasing; but, due to that, they were facing a serious paucity of space.

When Janab chacha saw this condition, he said to Jyoti,

"Jyotiba, there's place nearby that belongs to a Muslim man. The children can also get ample water there. Only… you will have to pay some rent."

Jyoti checked out the place. It was quite a big one. Paying the rent was going to be a difficult proposition, but at that time, Jyoti had no other option.

The school shifted from Govande's mansion to the new place in Ganj Peth. Everyone started toiling for the school. Suddenly, one day, Vishnupant stopped coming to school. Things happened just as Jyoti had anticipated.

Jyoti had no time to cajole Vishnupant. By now, the scope of his work had broadened beyond the Peth. Jyoti was getting invited by many neighboring villages to start similar schools over there. However, that was not resolving matters of Jyoti's monthly income. He required a steady flow of money to run the house. For that, Jyoti started a tailoring shop. He kept a servant to man the shop, but still, he had to look into it personally too. Whatever time he would get from the teaching duties, Jyoti would spend visiting the shop, or then, visiting people for donations. Apart from that, Jyoti was also travelling to the villages that were requesting him to start schools. Thus it was that, Jyoti's schools started at far-flung places like Hadapsar, Otur, Saswad, Kasba Pune, Talegaon Dhamdhere, Shirur, Shirval, Anjeerwadi, Karanje and Bhingar.

In all this, Jyoti had not forgotten his conversation with Lahuji, wherein the Ustad had requested him to start a school in the Mahar locality. Finally, one day, a school was established for the children of Mahar and Maangs, at Meethganj. Saguna Aau took up the teaching responsibilities of that school.

13

Pune was abuzz with various activities and disagreements, all the same. A group of conservatives were talking about staging an open rebellion against the few progressives in the city.

The names of Annasaheb Chiplunkar, Keshavrao Bhavalkar, Bapusaheb Mande were much in discussion. Some application had been sent to the government, requesting it to change its stance on the donation-funds that had been given to the Brahmins for long by then. The applicants had requested that half of those funds be diverted for forming a pool of prize money to be awarded to Marathi novels and books.

Lokhitawadi Gopal Hari Deshmukh was the forerunner of this demand. He had been toiling for this change to happen, for the last three years.

Something funny happened in regard to this application. Bapusaheb Mande wrote the application. Annasaheb took it to the school at Vishrambaug wada, for getting the signatories to sign on it. Some teachers had barely signed the application, when suddenly, the principal of the school, Balaram Kirad, hollered accusatorily that the application was a weapon against the Hindu religion! A fight ensued. Amidst that chaos, Annasaheb tore up the page that had the signatures, and grabbing the original application, dashed out of the school. A few students chased him and also blocked his way, demanding for the application to be demolished. But, Annasaheb was adamant. The application was sent to the government without signatures and that led to the matter escalating into a bigger problem.

Actually, now the question of donation-funds was not limited to the Brahmins. Everyone was feeing that the government needed to rectify its stance about the funds. The library in Budhwar Wada would always be abuzz about discussions regarding this issue. Jyoti had also participated in these discussions; but, the Brahmins, who had gotten used to the free flow of money coming their way, painted the whole issue in such a light that the whole perspective shifted. They tried every trick in the book to get the application withdrawn. Once, when Gopal Hari Deshmukh had gone to Tulshi Baug, around 5000 Brahmins surrounded him and threatened him to sign another application. Recognizing the delicate situation, Deshmukh signed the application over there, but then, he immediately went home, and sent a letter to the government, requesting them to consider his original application as the real one.

It was understood that a few members from the Paramhans Sabha had also signed the application. Keshavrao was a prominent member of the Sabha. The orthodox Brahmins found another scapegoat. The issue was going in multiple directions, with no real solution in sight.

Jyoti was surprised to see that the usually diplomatic progressives had taken such a firm stand on this issue. Keshavrao was unusually staunch on it. Of course, this pointless Peshwai custom of donating free funds to idle Brahmins, irrespective of what they were doing for the society, should have ended with the end of the Peshwai itself. However, the British had played safe by not abolishing these funds, because it was in their benefit to keep the Brahmins happy.

The Brahmins of Pune were being obstinate on only one point. They felt that the useless progressives were wasting good money over educating Brahmins. Brahmins were supposed to be educated by the virtue of their caste. What was the need to allocate special funds for educating the already-learned Brahmins again?! Were the Peshwas fools to keep giving such large funds to us? Was that Elphinstone gentleman a lunatic to have kept the custom thriving, and even allocating excessive funds for it? If these evil progressives have their way, tomorrow the Brahmins will be reduced to doing menial labor to fill their tummies. Oh, what pomp we Brahmins used to live in?! After finishing our ablutions in the morning, someone or the other would come requesting our services for some holy puja or ritual. The Peshwai was a golden period for us! Shaniwarwada would host thousands of Brahmins every day…oh, those delightful motichoor laddoos, those wispy soft puranpolis , that heavenly basundi-puri …. Times have indeed turned worse for us Brahmins.. Oh, how we miss that golden era…

That evening when Jyoti returned home, he was constantly talking on that one topic itself. Often, he would keep glancing at the door.

Savitri was cooking while talking to him. She asked Jyoti,

"Who are you waiting for, so eagerly?"

"Keshavrao is going to come. He had sent a message saying so."

Savitri was surprised. It was unlikely of Keshavrao to keep a message like that. When she said as much to Jyoti, he replied,

"Yes, that's true; but he wishes to keep this meeting a secret."

"These progressive people are very afraid of everything...." Savitri remarked.

Jyoti laughed and said,

"Well, who can blame them? Even though they are progressive, they still have to remain within their community. They wish to be progressive within the confines of their community."

Dusk was giving away to the night, but Keshavrao was yet to arrive. After some time, they heard someone knocking the door.

It was Keshavrao. He was cautiously entering Jyoti's house, looking here and there to confirm that no one was keeping an eye on him.

"Why are you so afraid, Keshavrao?" Jyoti asked him.

"No one should get a whiff of this meeting. If they do, it will be a big problem. I have come here to ask your help for a very important task, Jyotirao..."

"Yes, I realized that on getting your message. Do tell me; I shall help in whatever ways possible."

Keshavrao sat on a settee with a sigh and said,

"The problems are snowballing beyond control. The Peshwas made the Brahmins idle by lavishing them with money and gifts. Those habits will die hard. On the other hand, we have been asking for Marathi novelists to get due appreciation. We wish that they should be given some awards from the donation-funds. But this topic has become a huge bone of contention amidst our community members. You must be aware of how Gopalrao Deshmukh was besieged. To tell you the truth, we had never dreamt that this topic will acquire such epic proportions. I have never seen such attitudes in Mumbai. The Brahmins in Pune are really too much! I made a mistake. We had got enough signatures on the application. I sent the letter to Vishrambaug wada to get more signatorial support. I had also gone with Annasaheb that day, but I had waited outside. We both literally ran for our lives; else, we would have definitely been injured badly. Now those people have sent written notices to seven of us. We have been asked to stand before a committee in Tulshibaug tomorrow and ask for forgiveness...else, we are going to be ostracized!"

Jyoti heard Keshavrao out silently and then replied,

"Tatyasaheb, are you sure that what you have done, is appropriate?"

"Yes..." replied Keshavrao.

"Then what are you so afraid of? Why are you so afraid of being ostracized?" asked Jyoti.

Wiping the sweat off his forehead, Keshavrao replied,

"I'm not afraid about that thing for myself. Mainly, I have no desire to beg for anyone's forgiveness. I have already made it clear, that I am willing to take all responsibility on my own shoulders. I am only afraid of one thing: in spite of all the reassurances, if even one of us backs down at the last moment, the whole thing will turn topsy-turvy against us and we will not be able to raise our head ever again!"

Jyoti was listening to all this, silently. He could not understand Keshavrao's fear.

Keshavrao asked Jyoti,

"Do you agree that what we have done, is appropriate?"

Jyoti replied,

"Yes, of course. Please do not have any doubts about that. The government has no right to blow up people's hard-earned money on these lazy Brahmins. It is utterly wrong on the part of the government to keep continuing this foolish practice started during the Peshwai. A simple inauguration of a bridge is also taken as an occasion to distribute funds from the exchequer, to the Brahmins. How is this justifiable? I'm completely supportive of your views on this topic."

"Then, there is only one way to resolve this dispute" said Keshavrao.

"And, what's that?" Jyoti asked.

"To tell that, you have written the application."

Jyoti kept silent. He could not fathom the rationale behind what Keshavrao was proposing. He asked,

"That will resolve this issue?"

"Yes, it will; and along side, the progressives will also gain some strength and courage" Keshavrao replied with conviction.

"Have you discussed this amongst yourselves...?" asked Jyoti.

".....Yes, and I have taken up the responsibility of getting your consent" replied Keshavrao.

"Oka. If that's the case, then do tell my name" said Jyoti, without pausing for a second.

Hearing Jyoti's reply, Keshavrao breathed a huge sigh of relief, and said,

"Jyotirao, you have unburdened me of such a big worry! I cannot thank you enough... Now, I have only one more request... If you could please come along with us...."

"Okay. If such a need arises, I shall come and say it myself."

"Thank you, Jyotirao! I need to go and convey this news to the others...." said Keshavrao, getting up to leave. The flush of happiness on his face was instantly replaced by worry, as he said, " Also, let me see what has transpired in all this time..."

Jyoti reassured him saying,

"Don't worry, Tatyasaheb. You are doing the right thing. Hence, I find it my moral duty to help you. You go ahead and prepare yourself for facing the Brahmins. I shall see to it that no one touches even a strand of your hair!"

Keshavrao darted out of Jyoti's house and soon disappeared into a narrow alley.

The next day, Pune started heating up with news and rumors. Someone started spreading the news that last night, something was cooking at Jyotiba Phule's house in Meethganj Peth, although no one could confirm what had really transpired. Nevertheless, this much information was enough to know that now, Jyotiba Phule had become involved in this matter. The city was abuzz with speculation. Bandunana Ranade's house was being frequented by pot-bellied Brahmins. Many of them started feeling that Jyotiba was the real instigator behind this matter. In order to teach him a lesson, the seven of them had to be brought to book. They were even ready for fisticuffs, if the occasion arose.

Early that morning, Jyotiba had been to Janaai's farm. Lahujibuva's messages were hand-delivered to all concerned people. Around fifty wrestlers were going to be present at a designated place, at a decided time, without fail.

That afternoon, Tulshibaug was crowded as if there was some carnival going on! A judge's chair had been placed high up on an altar. Bandunana Ranade himself was going to chair the proceedings. Keshavrao and others had already congregated at Gopal Hari Deshmukh's house in Shukrawar Peth. Somebody came to summon them. That time, they realized that it was already 12 O' clock. The sun was burning overhead.

The seven of tem started walking the short distance from Shukrawar Peth to Tulshibaug. People had thronged on both sides of the road to see this procession of the 'shameless progressives' as they had been dubbed. Seeing them walking down, the crowds started cursing, "Hypocrites! Traitors! Atheists! Wicked! Evil!" The seven of them kept walking wordlessly.

Jyotiba was standing near the mansion of Baramatikar, with fifty-sixty wrestlers in tow. Seeing them, Keshavrao gained strength. The wrestlers surrounded the progressives and started walking with them. Now, they had no reason for fear.

However, this scene served to incense the onlookers even more. They started cursing even more furiously at the Brahmin progressives, for having taken the help of the impure Shoodras and Ati-Shoodras.

The procession reached near Budhwar wada. The British officer Turqwand, who was serving on Nana's roster, was standing at the door of the mansion. He had been reading the newspaper in the courtyard, when he heard this commotion; and thus, came outside to see what the matter was.

"What's the matter, Mr. Mande?" asked the officer.

When Bapusaheb told him what was transpiring, the officer flew into rage. He called out,

"Sepoy! Go immediately, and call the police Sub-inspector here."

The sepoy rushed to the police station. Soon, sub-inspectors Sheikh Hassan Fareed and Abhyankar came there with a batch of twenty-five policemen. Seeing them, the truant Brahmins who had been jeering so far dispersed like rats during a flood!!

Officer Turqwand ordered Abhyankar to make sure that the procession reached Tulshibaug safely. Abhyankar belonged to the orthodox group, but he was not in a position to disobey the Officer.

Soon, the group reached to Tulshibaug. The rest of them stopped a few feet away from Tulshibaug's entrance, to allow Keshavrao to move ahead. The meeting room was packed to the gills. One could see a huge group of students from Vishrambaug wada school. The teachers from that school, physicians, Shastris and other Brahmins sat reclined on bolsters.

Bandunana sat on the judge's chair, flanked by Moroba Shastri, Baba Sathe, Narayanshastri Thatte, Krishnambhatt Gokhale, Vishnubhat Jatapathi and few more esteemed Brahmins. Bandunana was visibly furious!

Keshavrao came forth; the others followed suit. They all came and stood before the jury.

Bandunana looked at Bapusaheb pointedly, and asked,

"Why have you brought all these people with you?!"

Bapusaheb glanced around pensively. The audience strained its ears to hear what Bapusaheb would answer. But, Bapusaheb was silent.

Seeing him unresponsive, Bandunana asked in an emphatic tone,

"I'm asking you, why have all these people come here?

What's their role in the meeting of our community?"

There was no real need to answer this question.

The crowd started murmuring among itself. Soon, somebody piped up,

"This should not be tolerated....!"

"This is a meeting meant to resolve an important issue concerning only Brahmins."

Soon, Bandunana raised his hand and roared,

"Okay, enough now. Keep silent, everybody."

The crowd fell silent as if gagged!

The wrestlers standing outside had scared many Brahmins out of their wits! The remaining ones were shaking in fury at the audacity of it all!

Bandunana looked at the jury. He was even more furious by now. The jury too were disgusted. One of them simply threw a deplorable glance at the accused, to signify, "Ask ahead…"

Bandunana cast his sharp glance at the six of them and asked,

"Where is the application?"

No one said a word. In reality, there was no point in asking this question, since the application had already reached the government. But, who would dare tell that to Bandunana?

Seeing everyone silent, Nana again roared,

"I'm asking, where is the application?"

"Annasaheb gave the application to… to this man…" stuttered a student, pointing towards Keshavrao.

"Who is this man?" asked Nana.

"I'm Keshavrao Bhavalkar."

"Ohh… and where are you from?"

"I am from Junnar. I was staying at Mumbai before coming to teach at a school in Pune."

"Did Annasaheb give that application to you?"

"Yes."

"Give it to me."

Sorry, but the application is not with me anymore."

"Then, where is it?"

"It was sent by post, on that day itself, to the Honorable Governor Bahadur."

"Okay. Do you have a copy of the application?"

"No."

"No? Okay...who amongst you had written that application?" Bandunana asked, gauging Keshavrao's face.

Keshavrao kept silent. Seeing him like that, Bandunana became even more irate. He bellowed,

"What am I asking you? Can't you answer?!"

The onlookers were excited beyond belief. They couldn't wait to hear that traitor's name, who had written the application.

Keshavrao realized that this was the right time to give the rehearsed answer. he replied,

"Jyotirao Phule!"

The crowd turned quiet on hearing Jyotiba's name. This was an unexpected twist in the plot. Another round of murmurs started going around. Then, somebody said,

"You are lying. We know that the application was written by Sonyabapu... not by Jyotirao."

"Well, Jyotirao has come here with us. You may ask him."

"No need! That won't be necessary!" Nana snapped with a wince of a scorpion whose sting got broken.

He did not dare to question Jyotiba Phule in a community meeting. Neither did the jury.

Seeing Bandunana silent, the jury racked down hollering,

"But, that does not mean that you are not guilty!"

"Why did you sign the application?" screeched another jury member.

Keshavrao chose to remain quiet. Bandunana tried putting all his legal skills to use by asking in a different way:

"When you could plainly see that the application was going against the learned, pure and God-gifted Brahmins, how could you sign it, in spite of being a Brahmin yourself?!"

"He is lying...the application was written by Sonyabapu."

"These people are out to drown all religious ethics..."
"Hypocrites!"
"Evil men!"
"This is all a ploy of that Shoodra fellow, Jyoti..."

Utter chaos ensued. The jury did not know how to handle the matter. There was no strength left in any argument. The environment had become unnaturally tense. Keshavrao realized that there would be no better time than now, to make an exit. he said,

"Nana, we are leaving..." and started walking away without even waiting for Nana's answer.

"Wait! You cannot leave without the jury's permission..." screeched an old jury member.

But Keshavrao did not stop. Somebody called out,

"What are we waiting for? Stop them!"

"Stone these traitors!"

The crowd started yelling and screaming. Anticipating something terrible to happen, people started running helter-skelter. But, no one dared to raise their hand. Keshavrao and their friends escaped from Tulshibaug and soon vanished amidst the security of the wrestlers.

14

Jyoti was planning to open a school at Mundhwa. He had gone that morning to scout the place. When he returned in the evening, Keshavrao was tutoring Savitribai and Fatima. Seeing Jyoti, Savitri got up to make preparations for his bath and then came back for her studies. Keshavrao gave them both a sum to solve, and then turning to Jyotirao, he said,

"I happened to have a detailed discussion with Annasaheb Chiplunkar, about what we spoke day before yesterday. He agrees with our view that even upper caste ladies need to get educated. At the end of our discussion, Annasaheb proposed that if you are willing to take the initiative, he would like another school for the Brahmin ladies to be started. He is ready to give us place in his mansion, for this work. Annasaheb is very impressed with the way you took a courageous stance during the donation-funds issue."

Jyotirao was pleased with Annasaheb's proposal. He had been thinking of starting such a school, for a long time now. Finally, his discussions with Keshavrao on this topic, had reached fruition.

Nevertheless, Jyoti was also being skeptical about the proposal. It was not intentional; but, the experiences that he had got so far, had made Jyoti cautious enough, to not take everything at face-value. Also, so far, Annasaheb has just been all-talk-no-work. He would only spout progressive views, but had not matched them with actions, so far. Jyoti had not yet forgotten his cowardly stance during the donation-funds issue. Jyoti said to Keshavrao,

"Tatyasaheb, I have not yet forgotten the way Vishnupant backed out. I'm thus wary of any such proposal coming our way."

Keshavrao smiled in response and said,

"But, I don't think Annasaheb will buckle under the pressure of the orthodox Brahmins."

"Really, Tatyasaheb? When it comes to these vocal progressives, I don't believe that they ever get totally rid of the pressure from the orthodox segment. Do you really think, Annasaheb won't buckle?" Jyoti asked, looking at Keshavrao in the eye.

"Well, Jyotirao, social reforms happen at a snail's pace only."

"I do not believe in thinking like this and sitting complacent. Instead of sending this proposal to us, why doesn't Annasaheb start the school himself? We are certainly in favor of emancipating all women. But, that does not mean that we take on the onus of educating Brahmin women as well, and these so-called progressives sit on the fence and get applause for doing nothing."

"It is obvious that Annasaheb does not have the courage to do so" replied Keshavrao.

"That is why I said that he is not totally free of the fear of the orthodox. He can be generous enough to give us place for the school; but, he cannot dare to do the 'impure' work of teaching. I do not like this hypocrisy. we can see the pitiable conditions of their women, and they cannot see it, is it? If they call themselves progressives, then should also act to justify that title. It is easy to praise others and sit tight."

"So then...what do we do about that proposal?" asked Keshavrao.

"See, it is good that Brahmins too are thinking positively about women's education. We shall think about his proposal. It's a good thing that we are getting the place."

They kept talking for some more time and then, Keshavrao left soon after.

Jyoti and his friends had a meeting, wherein they accepted Annasaheb's proposal. Accordingly, another school for Brahmin girls started at Budhwar Peth in the mansion of Annasaheb Chiplunkar.

The school started off with only eight girls on the roster. Then, the founders started toiling to increase the class strength. They would go from door to door to request Brahmins to send their daughters to school. But more often than not, people would slam the doors on their faces. They would curse them, and threaten them with dire consequences.

Annasaheb said,

"Jyotirao, probably it will be easy to convince illiterate people; but, convincing these over-smart Brahmins is something that even God will not be able to do!"

However, there were a few progressive Brahmins like Raghoba Pandurang, Krishnashastri Chiplunkar, Lokhitawadi Hari Deshmukh and Bapusaheb Mande aka Sonyabapu, who recognized the worth of this task and contributed generously in all ways. Funds started getting raised via monthly contributions and donations. Apart from slates, books and food, the girls had to be given uniforms too. In spite of the donations and contributions, the funds were falling short to address all these needs. People were not coming forward to donate generously, owing to a generic apathy towards female education, coupled with negative propaganda by the orthodox Brahmins. However, Jyotirao's willpower was too strong to be broken by these problems. When Justice Thomas Erskin Perry from Mumbai, got to know about this appreciable endeavor started in Pune, he sent a generous donation of Rs. 50 as help from his side. Not just that, he promised to send this donation every month. Even though Vishnupant Thatte had taken a backseat, newer progressives like Vamanrao Kharadkar were coming forth to join hands with Jyotirao.

Soon, Savitribai was transferred from the school in Ganj Peth to that in Budhwar Peth. She was made the headmistress of the new school.

The conservatives were even more agitated than before. Savitribai was still being tortured; to the extent that, the committee deputed Balwantrao Kolhe to accompany Savitribai to & fro the school, to maintain her safety. Plus, the committee was also responsible for maintaining the safety of the girls coming to school. Balwantrao would also have to ferry the girls to & fro school.

With Fatimabai's help, Savitribai started another class for young, married women. This class had to be taken in utmost secrecy.

Days were melding into nights, but Jyotirao's efforts showed no signs of abating. He had forsaken food, water and rest to keep up with the growing demands, problems and responsibilities. Everyday, he would spend a few hours in the school at Ganj Peth and then come to the school at Budhwar Peth.

The executive committee of the schools, included eminent people like Annasaheb Sahastrabuddhe, Bapusaheb Mande,

Prof. Vishnu Moreshwar Bhide, Prof. Krishnashastri Chiplunkar, and Vishnushastri Pandit. Jagannath Sadashiv was made the Secretary of the committee.

The workload was burgeoning by the day.

Jyotirao had recently embedded another feather in his cap, by starting a girl's school at Raasta Peth.

A few days later, word came from Mumbai that Justice Perry and judicial secretary Lumsden were coming to Pune to see Jyotirao's schools. Even though Justice Perry was a generous donator to the schools, this news brought its share of tension for Jyotirao. He did not want the presence of a British man to hurt the sentiments of the parents who were sending their daughters to schools. The daughters were being sent on the strict promise that they would not be seen by any strange man, much less a foreigner. The condition was even more stringent for married women. In such a situation, a visit by Justice Perry was going to be a tightrope walk.

Just a few days earlier, Justice John Warden of Pune had come to visit the school at Budhwar Peth. He was keen to see the training center being run for married women. But, Savitribai had been compelled to politely refuse his wish, not wanting to risk the wrath of the families of those women. Thus, Justice Warden had to leave after seeing only the school attended by the small girls. Jyotirao did not want an encore of that incident.

15

One evening, Jyotirao sat checking the mail. A letter from the Superintendent, Government Vernacular School, caught his eye. He opened the letter and saw that it was signed by supervisor of vernacular schools, Dadoba Pandurang Tarkhadkar. Jyotirao found this letter important on the backdrop of visits from Justice Perry and judicial secretary Lumsden. He was convinced that the government was now taking notice of his work.

Justice Perry and Sir Lumsden's visit proved very fruitful. The girls in school and the ladies in the training centers gave very satisfactory answers to both of them. However, Jyoti had to take immense efforts to convince their parents for this visit. Nevertheless, Jyoti was happy that now his schools were taking root in the societal psyche.

Educated progressives like Bapusaheb Mande had now started taking increased interest in this work. In fact, Dadoba's brother Raghoba Pandurang was one of the forerunners in the committee's work. Thus, Jyoti started thinking about opening more schools. He wanted to open the next school for boys and girls of the Mahar, Maang and Kunbi communities, in Vetaal Peth. If possible, he wanted to make separate classes for boys and girls.

The next morning, Jyotirao conveyed the good news to the other committee members. He went to Raghoba Pandurang's house to tell him the news in person. It was indeed a matter of great pride, that an eminent scholar like Dadoba was going to visit their schools. Annasaheb was thrilled with the development. Jyotirao was piqued to meet Dadoba. He had heard a lot about the Paramhans Sabha that Dadoba had established; and, also knew about the work that Dadoba had done for the Manav Dharma Sabha. Jyotirao could identify with the tenets of Paramhans Sabha. He could see Thomas Penn's ideas resonating in the concepts of one God and humanity beyond religion, as propounded by the Paramhans Sabha.

Annasaheb made all preparations to give a befitting welcome to Dadoba. Keshavrao was at the forefront of all preparations. The orthodox Brahmins were ruffled about all the importance being given to a Shoodra. According to them, the fact that a Shoodra like Dadoba should learn the Vedas and preach on religion, was the biggest blasphemy ever. They were sure that such audacity would have met with severe punishment during the Peshwai. That gave them even more reason to lament the absence of Peshwai.

Finally, the day arrived when Dadoba Pandurang came to inspect the schools. The principal of Pune College, Major Candy, was also present on the occasion. Dadoba congratulated the committee for setting up such wonderful schools in such less time.

The occasion gave Jyoti a chance to interact with Dadoba on a personal level. He was quite impressed with Dadoba's views about using the best tenets of all religions to improve social and religious conditions for all. The government was putting obstacles in Dadoba's way, but unmindful of those, he continued doing his work. However, one thing about Dadoba's views that bothered Jyoti, was that, even though Dadoba agreed that no religious text is above humanity (since it has not been created by God, but by man); he also did not out-rightly reject the greatness of the Vedas. Rather, he often used the Vedas to elucidate his views.

Nevertheless, Jyotirao found a resonance with Dadoba's views on humanity. Both of them were striving to elevate the conditions of poor and exploited people. Both of them advocated the importance of education for this elevation to occur. Until the exploited person knew that he/she was being put down, he/she would not rebel against that injustice; and for that, educating them was the only way. Education would give them the understanding of their inner human being that needed to be honored. Till the time they were ignorant and illiterate, they would not understand heavy concepts like one God and religion of humanity.

No religious or social reform was possible without education. For that, starting a few schools was not going to suffice. Such schools needed to be opened in every alley of every town and village.

Jyotirao started making arrangements to start a school at Vetaal Peth. But, the main problem was about, who would teach there? Jyotirao started looking out for a capable teacher.

Around this time, the committee decided to hold the first formal examination at the school in Budhwar Peth.

A big program was arranged on the occasion. Since the place at Annasaheb's mansion would have proved insufficient to seat all guests, the program was held at Phadke mansion. All committee members, including Keshavrao, Sadashivrao, Moropant and Bapusaheb got engrossed in preparing for the big day. The Phadke mansion wore a festive look, as family members of the students trooped in with curiosity to see what the girls had learnt. Justice Brown was invited to preside over the function.

In his speech, Justice Brown elaborated on the benefits of women's education and said,

"I'm glad to see that at least a few people in this country have started thinking in the right direction and have started taking proactive steps to reform the country. May God give them success."

Justice Brown also announced a big donation for the school.

Jyotirao was happy to see the girls giving correct answers to the questions that were posed to them. More so, he was happier that the importance of women's education was percolating in the fabric of the society.

16

It was evening time. Jyotirao was sitting at home, writing down the accounts for the school of Mahar Maang children.

C.S. Harrison: Donation Rs. 10 per month, Gopalrao Hari Deshmukh: Donation Re. 1 per month, Dadoba Pandurang: Donation Rs. 5....

The balance sheet expenses getting heavier than the income. Funds were falling short for payment of salaries to the teachers. They were, as it is, facing problems in getting teachers; and the ones they would get, would soon leave due to lack of a good salary. Financial troubles plagued Jyoti. The application sent to the government was yet to be decided upon. So far, Jyoti had only got a letter saying that his application had been set forth before the Dakshina Prize committee.

Nevertheless, generous people were springing up with unexpected help. Once, a stranger named Balacharya, contributed - Rs. 12 - his salary of one month, to Jyotirao's school.

The school in Vetaal Peth was going along fine. But, young girls started feeling hesitant to sit with boys. Thus it became imperative to start a separate classroom for them. Jyotirao established a separate committee to oversee the working of this school. Sadashivrao, Moropant and Sakharam became the main members of this committee; Jyotirao was content taking on a general membership. Nevertheless, he would still have to look into many matters personally. Earlier, Devrao Thosar would help Jyotirao in managing the correspondence; but, after he accepted a job in the police force, Jyotirao and Moropant had to take on the added responsibility of sifting through the post. Annasaheb was handling the Budhwar Peth school, but Jyotirao was worried about handling the matters of the Vetaal Peth school. He again together his three best friends for the task.

Somebody came to meet Jyotirao.

"Come in..."

It was Jagannath Sadashiv. He looked elated!

"Jyotirao....the Dakshina Prize committee has sent a reply to our application. They have agreed to give us Rs. 75 per month!" announced Jagannathrao.

"What?? Is that correct?" exclaimed an equally thrilled Jyotirao.

He took the letter from Jagannathrao's hand, and after hurriedly reading the contents, shouted out to Savitri saying,

"Savitri, come here...fast!"

Savitribai came running. Handing over the letter to her, Jyotirao exclaimed,

"Read this! The Dakshina Prize Committee is going to fund

our schools!...Usmanbhai, did you see this? he said to Usman who had just come in.

They had been trying to get these funds for many months now. The education department had eminent people like Nana Shankarshet and Bhau Daji. Major Candy had seen Jyotirao's work from close quarters. For the sake of this letter, Major Candy had been requested to go through the committee's accounts and pen the perfetc application for the Dakshina Prize Committee.

Jyotirao sent a message for everyone to come to his home next morning. The letter was read aloud in front of everybody. A lot of discussion ensued. They were all thrilled about the development. It was another tight slap on the faces of the orthodox Brahmins, especially in the light of the recent failure they had faced.

Moropant Walvekar said,

"Now, we will be able to regularize our pay to the teachers. I think, even Vahini and Jyoti should accept a monthly salary."

"No!" Jyotirao stated emphatically. "Me and Savitri will not take a penny from these funds. Let all this money go only for the upkeep of the school. Our service and our livelihood are two distinct things."

Moropant was sad to see that his suggestion was taken in another light. He explained,

"Jyoti, please understand what I'm trying to say. We all are chipping in for the school, keeping our jobs intact. But you and Vahini have wholeheartedly devoted yourself to this cause. You also need a livelihood, don't you?"

"Yes, we do; but that will not come from these funds. The income from my shop is good enough for both of us" said Jyoti.

Thus, the topic ended there itself. The conversation moved to other topics, such as, starting separate classrooms for girls. Jyoti also wished to start a library for the school. They decided to work towards the same, and the meeting ended on that note.

By that evening, the news of Jyoti getting a generous donation from Dakshina Prize Committee, spread like wildfire! The Brahmins beat their breasts over how the world was getting closer to its end, now that the funds that were supposed to be kept for holy Brahmins, were being squandered on unholy and useless pursuits. They declared that the government had lost its marbles for having agreed to cheap pursuits like literary prizes and donations to women's schools. The government, Jyotirao Phule, the progressive Brahmins contributing to this sin by teaching and donating money.... all were the target of the unutterable curses spewed by the Brahmins for many hours afterwards.

17

"Tatya has come...Tatya has come..."

The girls started chirruping like sparrows. Someone got a pencil. Someone got a slate. Someone who wanted a storybook was consoled saying she will get it tomorrow...

"Tatya, you had asked me to write an essay, isn't it? See, I have written one..." said Mukta, one of Jyotirao's favorite students.

Mukta was a very studious and sincere student. She would pay rapt attention to everything that Jyotirao would teach. She would finish her homework in time... would keep writing something or the other...would participate in elocutions...

Jyotirao started reading Mukta's essay.

The depth with which she had written the essay, brought a broad smile to Jyotirao's face.

"Very good, my child!" Jyotirao praised Mukta. She smiled broadly and went to sit on her place.

However, Jyotirao was so impressed by what Mukta had written, that he felt like reading out the essay to all the children. He told them to be seated, and told Mukta to read her essay aloud:

'The Brahmins say that the Vedas are their domain only. We are chosen to absorb and propagate knowledge about the Vedashastras. By alternation, that means, we people of the other castes, should have nothing to do with religious texts. Well, if the Vedas are meant for Brahmins alone, then they should also behave according to what the Vedas teach them. And, if we are to be away from religious texts, then what religion should we follow? Please tell us, God...So that, we can behave according to the tenets of that path.

During Bajirao's reign, our caste people used to be treated akin to donkeys. They had no compunctions about stuffing the throats of our ancestors with oil and vermilion, and burying them alive in the foundations of new constructions! During that time, if any Mahar or Maang would dare to go across the taalimkhaana , he would be ruthlessly beheaded at Gultekadi.....'

Further, Mukta had written about how the condition of Mahars and Maangs became better after the British regime came in. While ending the essay, Mukta had written:

'Oh, poor and exploited Mahars and Maangs... If you feel sick, please give your brain the tonic of education. Education is the only magic wand that will make the cobwebs of ignorance disappear from your mind, and make you see the light of sense, knowledge, morality and rights......'

Jyotirao's chest swelled with pride! After so many years of toil, his aim was seeing the light of the day. A small child from the Ati-Shoodra caste, had become emancipated enough to think independently. She had become enabled enough to be able to pen those thoughts in a logical and clear way. A picture of a bright future started getting formed in front of Jyotirao's eyes:

Children like Mukta and Raaynak are getting their due rights. They are the baton-wielders of social reform. They will be the youngsters who stand up against injustice. They will enlighten the others of their community to stand up for their rights. So much so, that the ones who think of meting out injustice to them and their brethren, will themselves feel ashamed of their thoughts. Everyone will live together in harmony, reaching across the boundaries of caste and religion. The society will be one happy family...

All the children loved Mukta's essay.

Jyotirao folded the paper on which Mukta had written the essay and kept it in his pocket to store in his locker. He then gave a speech on the evils of casteist segregations. He told the children about the uselessness of the ignorant notions being propagated in the name of Hindu religion. He taught them that Ved meant Bhed (differences). Jyotirao was very keen to see his students grow up into conscientious, thinking individuals; not just bookworms. To achieve that, he would constantly keep talking to them about what concepts were right and what were wrong.

That evening, Savitribai also read the essay.

Jyotirao said,

"It is important that the children are getting aware. Anybody can study and get a job. But, true education is that which molds a human being in all ways. These children are intelligent; they require higher education to build a better future. But, sadly, we cannot help them in that. Even if they go to the Missionary school, the Brahmins will drive them away from there. That is the reason why Raaynak could not continue learning English... Mukta's education too will be thwarted in the same way...so will that of Vetaala...the cobbler's son...such a bright child, but I doubt if he will be able to study further..."

Coming face-to-face with his limitations, made Jyotirao feel suddenly very helpless.

A few minutes went in quietude. Then, Savitribai said,

"Aau had come. Dada's health is not very good."

Dada's deteriorating health was a matter of immense worry for Jyotirao. Dada would keep falling ill from time to time.

Jyotirao found himself guilty for having become the major reason for Dada's condition.

Defying Dada's express wishes, Aau had also started looking after the Meethganj school. She would get extremely tired looking after her domestic duties, the farm and the school. Add to that, Dada would pour out all his anger on poor Aau. On the days that Dada's anger would become unbearable for Aau, she would come to visit Jyoti and Savitri. She was bearing it out for these two.

"Has Dada sent any message?" Jyotirao asked Savitri.

"No."

Jyoti would keep hoping that some day, Dada would call him home, ask him to bring Savitri along. So far, this dream had not manifested. But Jyotirao did not lose hope. He knew that some day, Dada would find the courage to do so.

Jyotirao cast a glance at his wife... exhausted, hungry and strained due to circumstances...

He felt sorry for having broken her from her in-laws, as well as from her parents... Since the last three years, no one had come from Naigaon, nor had they sent a message. Aau would come intermittently, and they could get to know about Dada only from her. Else, there was no relation left. Savitri would never complain about the situation, but Jyotirao could see that she was very sad about the way things had unraveled.

Jyotirao felt a strong pull to go and visit Dada.

After dinner, Jyotirao set out for a stroll.

18

Jyotirao had got a message that Major Candy was coming home to meet him that evening. Thus, Jyotirao came home earlier than usual. The Major was known to be a stickler for time. He had come to the schools a couple of times, and had always been present at the time conveyed.

Jyotirao was surprised to know that Major Candy wished

to see him at home. Thus, he sent a message to his friends and committee members to join in the meeting too. Accordingly, Bapusaheb Mande, Jagannath Sadashiv, Annasaheb Chiplunkar, Sadashivrao Govande, and Moropant Walvekar also came home that evening.

At the given time, a horse carriage stopped in front of Jyotirao's house. Jyotirao stood in the porch with his friends, to welcome Major Candy. The Major wore an ankle-length coat and carried a walking stick. He wore gold-rimmed spectacles on his eyes, which made his face look even more serious than it was. A white beard flowed to his chest.

Jyotirao and the Major exchanged pleasantries and they all went inside the house.

Jyotirao's house was lit up in the soft lights of diyas. Requesting Major Candy to sit on a chair kept specially for him, Jyotirao sat near his desk. The others also claimed their places.

Some small talk later, Major Candy said,

"Jyotirao, today I have come to meet you for a special reason. The government has decided to felicitate you for your yeoman service in the field of women's education. I have come to get your consent for this honor."

Looking at his friends with a broad smile, Jyotirao replied,

"Major Candy, I'm honored knowing the government's intent. But, this work is not my own alone. It would not have been possible without the help and support that I received from these friends of mine. So, truly, they deserve this honor more than I do."

"I understand your sentiments, Jyotirao. But, I request you to accept this honour on behalf of all these gentlemen" requested Major Candy.

Understanding Major Candy's well-wishes and looking at the immense help he had given them thus far, it was not possible for Jyotirao to decline his request.

Jyotirao smiled and conveyed his acceptance. Major Candy

got up, took Jyotirao's hands in his own and congratulated him formally.

Major Candy was deeply impressed with Jyotirao's humbleness. He narrated the details of the meeting to the government. Details about Jyotirao's work had reached right up to London.

The Major said,

"The work that you have done is more valuable and substantial in comparison to public schools. Specially the fact that you are educating people from lower castes, is extremely impressive. Tell me, has the problem of teachers in the Vetaal Peth school, been resolved?"

The Major had special fondness for the Vetaal Peth school. In the last meeting, he had promised Jyotirao that he would appeal for Rs. 25 to be given every month from the Dakshina Prize Committee specially for this school. The appeal had been granted and the money had also started coming.

"No, Sir. That problem is a persistent one. The Brahmins teachers are not ready to teach those children, and we do not get able teachers from the lower castes. That's why, we teach them as it gets possible for us. One Brahmin youngster had dared to join the school, but the Brahmin community drove him away. I have heard that your school is also facing a similar problem, is it?" asked Jyotirao.

"Yes. The Brahmin teachers have refused to teach children from other castes. Thus, I have to take their classes myself."

An idea was being propagated that the Sanskrit schools in Pune should be thrown open to children of all castes; but, the Brahmins were vehemently opposed to the idea. Some of them were so fierce in their opposition that they threatened to resign if the change was made.

Jyotirao was aware about the troubles that Major Candy faced from teachers and students. He was sure that the government's decision would add fuel to the fire.

"Actually, they are afraid of being ostracized. In Mumbai,

many Brahmins have started teaching Sanskrit to people of other castes, as well as, to the British. In fact, in many other places, people from castes other than Brahmin, have started getting admission in schools. Pune is very orthodox in comparison to these places. I happened to meet Reverend Mitchell. Had you sent a lower caste student to his school?" asked Major Candy.

"Yes. I did. He was very keen to learn English."

"Reverend Mitchell was telling me about that student. He felt very sad that he could not help the child in any way."

"That is okay. Mitchell Sir need not feel sad about it. It was the other students who refused to accommodate the child amidst them. They threatened to stop coming to school if that boy was given admission. Obviously, Reverend Mitchell must have become helpless. I feel very sad about the fact that not one teacher came forth to talk in favor of the boy. The ill-treatment that he received from the children, has made him bereft of education for all his life. Many students are facing the same fate" stated Jyotirao.

"I don't understand these people. They are okay with being touched by us, but they cannot tolerate their own countrymen just because they are from some other caste..." mused Major Candy.

"Oh, it's convenient thinking at its best! Their religious texts and tenets are also based on nothing but convenience. You are the government... that is, rulers or kings. And according to them, kings are the reincarnation of Lord Vishnu. Thus, they outwardly tolerate your touch, and then take a bath the moment they go home!"

The Major laughed and said,

"Well, that's true. I'm taking this experience on a daily basis."

Just then, Savitribai came in bringing some snacks.

Major Candy said to her,

"Bai, I also congratulate you for your work. Please accept

our honour."

Savitribai did not reply. She felt awkward receiving such profuse compliments. She glanced at her husband and went inside.

"Jyotirao, Bai has contributed immensely to this work, as well."

"Absolutely!" Jyotirao replied heartily.

They all kept talking for some more time. Soon after, Major Candy took Jyotirao's leave.

Jyotirao accompanied the Major to the porch. The horse carriage was waiting for him. Bidding goodbye to all, Major Candy went away.

19

Finally, the day of 16 November, 1852 arose. In the week prior, the 'Poona Observer' had printed the news of Jyotirao being felicitated by the British government. From then on, the Brahmins of Pune weren't tiring of cursing and uttering profanities in the name of the government who, according to them, was foolish enough to bestow an honour meant only for learned Brahmins, onto a lowly Shoodra! They had never seen such shameless blasphemy before.

The Vishrambaug wada was being decorated for the occasion. Bapusaheb was personally overseeing all preparations. The road in front of the wada was decorated with festoons and buntings. Towards the right hand side of the dais, special seats with pillows and bolsters were arranged for the officials. On the platform behind that, carpets had been laid out for the ladies. Chairs and sofas had been arranged for the foreign dignitaries. Jyotirao's students were happily helping in the preparations. The government had also sent a servant to lend a helping hand.

Late in the afternoon, people started thronging to the Vishrambaug wada. The excitement of the last six months was finally reaching culmination today.

The time came closer for the program to begin. A few girls came and shyly sat in the open space near the dais. They were going to undergo a small exam, on the eve of the program. The girls were casting quick glances at the crowd and shyly covering their faces with their palms.

Soon, the generals and officers started arriving. The fragrance of frankincense filled the entire assembly hall, which was filled to the brim.

Saraswatibai Govande brought Savitribai into the hall. Saguna Aau and Fatimabai followed them.

As Major Candy's horse carriage came to a halt near the doorway, everyone started straining their neck in excitement. Bapusaheb rushed to welcome him inside. Annasaheb Chiplunkar, Moropant and Sadashivrao had already been waiting at the doorway for the welcome ritual.

The horse carriage halted. Major Candy and Jyotirao alighted from it. A satisfied smile played on Major Candy's lips, as he saw the number of people who had assembled.

Graciously accepting the welcome given by the hosts, the Major and Jyotirao started walking towards the dais. Jyotirao wore a red turban, white dhoti and reddish coat. He lead from the front, eyes shining bright with pride and confidence. His glowing, resolute face reflected the fearlessness in his mind. The small beard of his mid-20s, lent him a uniquely male handsomeness. Jyotirao's friends walking alongside him, were also beaming with pride.

As they all entered the hall, the audience broke into a spontaneous applause, that stopped only after the guests of honor took their places on the dais. The servant who had come with Major Candy, brought a salver with shawls and other gifts and placed it on the table.

The program had been meticulously planned. The Major ran his eyes on the program details printed on the card and smiled with satisfaction. After Bapusaheb made the introductory speech, Major Candy rose to talk:

"Dear brothers and sisters, today we have assembled here to honor our dear friend, Shri. Jyotirao Phule. I find myself fortunate to have been chosen by the government to bestow this honor on Jyotirao, for his yeoman service. The work that Jyotirao has been doing for women's education and empowerment, is an in valuable and unforgettable one. It was certainly not an easy task, considering that social scenario of Maharashtra. But, Jyotirao cruised through all those problems and challenges on the strength of his indefatigable willpower. I must specially thank his wife Smt. Savitribai Phule, and his friends, for supporting Jyotirao at every step. Today, we will also be felicitating Smt. Savitribai Phule for her equal contribution to Jyotirao's work. I hope that she will accept this honor too."

Saying this, the Major took one shawl from the salver and held it open for Jyotirao saying,

"I would first like to congratulate Jyotirao and offer him a small token of our respect..."

Major Candy draped the shawl on Jyotirao's shoulders, offered him a bouquet of flowers; after which, Jyotirao humbly bowed to the audience and sat on his seat.

Then, Savitribai was honored with a sari and blouse; and bouquets were presented to Annasaheb, Moropant, Sadashivrao and Sakharampant.

The programme went on with speeches on some scholars like Moreshwarshastri, who spoke about the importance of women's education. Finally, Jyotirao stood up to speak:

"My dear brothers and sisters... first and foremost, I'd like to thank the education department of the government for considering me worthy of such an honor. This honor is not mine alone. It belongs as much to my friends, Savitribai, Raanba, Lahuji, my students and to all of you who believe that women need to be educated. I cannot forget the support given by Sadashivrao and Annasaheb, who gave place for the schools.

A lot of generous donors have helped us all along by providing much-needed financial help. A lot of well-wishers and friends supported us in myriad ways. Major Candy Sir has been a staunch supported all along, sending us books, stationary, funds and even getting us financial help from the Dakshina Prize Committee. Thus, I feel specially happy to have received this honor from him...."

"....Friends, the condition of Ati-Shoodras is really bad in our country. They are steeped in ignorance, and that is the root cause of their misery. God showed me the direction that while education is important for all, it is specially important to educate the women of those castes, because once a woman is educated, they can teach the next generation. Mothers are the ones who sow the seeds of education in a small child."

"After seeing the Missionary school at Ahmadnagar,

I realized that foreigners are striving to uplift our society, but our own educated class is taking no interest in spreading the light of knowledge amidst those deprived. That

thought pained me to no end; and hence, I decided to do something proactive about it. My work received a lot of

support form like-minded people, all of whom I'm immensely thankful to."

"The government has definitely helped us a lot so far; but, its responsibility does not end here. We will require the government's help further, to open up newer schools for Shoodras and Ati-Shoodras in various villages and towns."

"Friends, I was guided by my conscience into towards taking up this cause. Frankly, I have simply done the duty that God ordained for me. I take no credit for doing something huge... I would instead be really pleased if my educated brethren join hands and uplift their ignorant countrymen, to enable a bright future for us all...."

An overwhelmed Jyotirao could say no more. He bowed before the audience and took his seat.

The audience had been equally overwhelmed with Jyotirao's

speech. No one spoke anything for the next few minutes. They sat absorbing the gravity of Jyotirao's words, in their hearts and minds.

The final part of the program was also a very important one. People were equally keen to see how the girls would perform. Savitribai and Fatimabai came forward. They questioned the girls in mathematics, simple reading etc. People were impressed to see the girls answering with confidence.

It was almost evening by the time the event ended. The guests started meeting Jyotirao to congratulate him personally and to take his leave.

At one point, Jyotirao saw Janab chacha standing in the crowd. Jyotirao weaved his way through the crowd to reach Janab chacha and bowed low to touch his head to chacha's feet.

"Oh, please get up, get, Jyoti..." said a visibly proud and moved Janab chacha. He held Jyotirao close to his heart, his eyes soaked in tears.

"Inshallah ! You have done a lot of good work, my son... you deserve every ounce of the respect you are getting..."

Jyoti was smiling outwardly, but his eyes reflected a deep inner turmoil. He kept thinking,

"Dada should have been her today...!"

That night, the entire Ganjpeth had gathered at Jyotirao's house. Today, all those years of Jyotirao's and Savitribai's toil had reached due fruition. Saguna Aau had come to meet them on the happy occasion. But, in spite of all the cheer, Jyotirao was in turmoil. One part of his heart was raring to soar higher, but the other part was still stuck in the grief of the past. He was remembering the sacrifices made for him by Saguna Aau. In reality, she was his elder cousin sister, but she had become a mother for him. Saguna Aau had supported Jyoti all through his education and work.

Jyotirao kept thinking, what would have happened to him if Saguna Aau had not stepped in to take care of the infant

Jyoti... But God had been kind... He had taken away Jyoti's real mother but had given him Saguna Aau in her place. What justice was this?

Jyotirao kept looking at Saguna Aau and kept thinking....

'Aau, you are the one who raised me... fed me... taught me the difference between right and wrong. You were the one who spoke to Janab chacha and convinced Dada to re-start my education. You were the one who took me by the hand and led me to Father Mitchell's school. You chose Savitri as my bride. You were so right in your choice. All what I have achieved today is a fruition of your hard work. If you had not put me into school then, how would I have ever realized the importance of education? You are really great, Aau! You made me realize the true meaning of humanity. You gifted me the treasure-trove of education. You taught me to love all human beings equally, without any segregations. I lost my home...my parents... but you have always been there for me...with me... like a shadow...I shall never forget your sacrifices, Aau... I'll remain forever indebted to you!'

20

A wave of excitement was coursing through Jyotirao's school. The President of the Board of Education, Honorable Sir John Warden, was coming to visit the school. After Jyotirao's felicitation last year, this was another important event which was taking place.

Everyone started preparing for Sir Warden's visit. The good results of the latest exams had given immense confidence to the girls. Scholars such as Narayanshastri, Ganesh Ramchandra and Balshastri Thakaar were not teaching at Jyotirao's schools.

The small sapling planted two years ago, had started growing into a huge banyan tree. There were almost 275 girls on the combined rosters of both schools. A new school had been started at Raasta Peth; the committee was thinking of starting another school at Vetaal Peth too.

The exams of the schools at Budhwar Peth, turned out to be a memorable affair. No event in Pune had seen such a crowd before. A big event of the examination was held at the Vishrambaug wada in Poona College Chowk, on 12 February 1853. A special canopy was erected for the occasion. Brigadier and Mrs. Trydell, Collector E. C. Jones, Mrs. E. C. Jones - a generous donor to the Female Education Society, Reverent James Mitchell, Mrs. Mitchell, Principal Major Candy,

Prof. Frazer were the foreign dignitaries attending the event. Along side, eminent countrymen such as Mehendale,

Sardar Dajiba Pendse, Sardar Balasaheb Patwardhan, Sardar Raosaheb Khasgiwale, Sardar Krishnarao Tulshibaugwale, Prof. Kero Lakshman Chhatre, Prof. Vishnushastri Chiplunkar were also present. So many people had thronged to be a part of the program that the Poona College Chowk started falling short to accommodate everybody. People clambered onto adjacent balconies and roofs to see the program.

The event turned out to be a huge success. Bapusaheb Mande presented the committee's report. He emphasized on the fact that child marriage was one of the biggest roadblocks to education.

In his speech, Annasaheb Chiplunkar cracked down heavily on the selfishness of the Hindus. Expressing deep disappointment about the fact that Hindus find women's education to be blasphemous, he elucidated on the benefits of educating women. Giving the examples of foreign donors to the schools, he said,

"...While we are deeply indebted to the foreign donors who have supported us thus far, it is also a matter of shame for us that while we are receiving help from foreigners, our own educated people do not feel empathy for this cause. Truly, they will have no place in the court of God. Time has come for all of us to think about our future generations. If we want to make them capable, we need to start educating women from today itself."

The crowd was speechless on hearing Annasaheb's candid views.

After that, the girls' examination began. The girls were found to be specially proficient in English. Some of them calculated difficult mathematical sums in English. Nanashastri Aapte's younger daughter Durga, was found to be so intelligent that she translated an entire lesson of Marathi into English. The crowd was taken aback with her feat!

The thanksgiving speech also turned out to be a lesson of sorts of the onlookers. Major Candy requested Prof. Frazer to issue a vote of thanks to the committee. Frazer said,

"Gentlemen, a society that takes pride in subjugating women and considers them inferior, can never make real progress. Until women are empowered, mankind will continue to remain weak. Women's education is the need of the hour."

The program ended at 6 pm.

A funny thing happened during the program. Mrs. E. C. Jones was distributing saris and books to the award-winning girls. When her turn came, Sumati Mokashi said to Madam Jones,

"Madam, we do not need awards. We need a library. Can you please give us one?"

Everyone was proud to see the girl's confidence. Sumati was a very brilliant and quick-witted girl. She would study till midnight. At a tender age of 6 years, she could read and speak English fluently.

In her innocent way, Sumati had brought forth an important lacuna in the school; but, she also gave inspiration for a new direction. A decision was taken to open a library in each of the schools!

The examination ceremony of the Vetaal Peth school, also saw a similar crowd of people. On that occasion too, eminent guests like Mr. & Mrs. Trydell, Captain Gilmore, Major Candy, Rev. James Mitchell, Prof. Frazer, Prof. Nilkanthshastri, Prof.

Chhatre, Annasaheb Sahastrabuddhe, and Wamanrao Paranjpe were present. Jyotirao had thanked Lahujibuva and Raanba in his speech given on that occasion.

All these events served to bring more and more girls to school. Noted people like Sardar Vinchurkar, who were earlier sceptical about the concept of women's education, now started their daughters to school on their own volition. The schools would often get well-wishing guests like the Trydell couple and Major Candy. The newly appointed Commissioner Reeves started paying special attention to the Vetaal Peth school. He had sanctioned a donation of Rs. 10 per month and would come personally to enquire about the children's progress. He would encourage the girls to study harder. Sadly so, one of the schools' earliest patrons, Justice Perry, had returned to his motherland.

Jyotirao's schools set new precedents in the field of education in Pune. Teachers would give personal attention to each child's progress. Classes had been segregated into divisions and each class had a separate teacher.

As opposed to this, the Brahmin schools would seem like a cattle-shed. Children of varying age groups would be herded into one cramped room, and one teacher would teach them all. Someone would be rattling off multiplication tables, while some smaller child would be singing a poem. For most times, the teacher would have no time or interest in listening to what the children were doing; busy as he would be in cursing and hitting some or the other student! It would indeed make for a very 'pleasant' sight of what a school should be like!

Jyotirao stopped the practice of verbal memorization and put in place a system of teaching with chalk and boards. He also did not advocate hitting any child, and instead asked the teachers to explain with patience and love.

Before Jyotirao's schools began, it was a common occurrence in Pune that those Brahmins who failed at even begging, would take up teaching. One can imagine what a sorry state of affairs it must be to have such incapable people become teachers to young, impressionable minds. Some of these teachers were so bad that they would beg for alms in the morning, teach the children in the afternoon and spend the night at a brothel! Quite a few times, these teachers would get late in reporting to school. At such times, they had to be sought out at the brothels and dragged to school where the children would be waiting for them, wide-eyed. Apart from the schools at Budhwar Peth and the Missionary school, there were a few more English schools in Pune; but, till Jyotirao's schools came in, the condition of all those schools was similarly pathetic.

One day, Major Candy sent a message that he was going to visit the Vetaal Peth school.

On the D-day, Jyotirao and the committee members of both schools, made due preparations to welcome the Major. They reached at school earlier than usual and saw to it that there would be nothing lacking in his welcome. Water, snacks for the children, the library etc. was all kept ready.

Major Candy's horse carriage stood in front of the school at 8 am sharp. John Warden went ahead to help Major Candy alight. After all, the Major was in his 50s by now. But, years of military discipline had kept him agile even at that age.

Major Candy was genuinely happy to see all the people who were waiting for him. Warden Sir went around inspecting the school, even as Major Candy spoke to a few students and gave a detailed report of the school's progress to Mr. Warden. The school had children of various age groups. The children from the Ganj Peth school had now been shifted to this school. Lahuji's son Dhondiba showed excellent progress in his studies. Since Dhondiba was also an ace sportsman, Jyotirao had tasked him with looking after the physical fitness of the other students.

Warden sir was overwhelmed to see the devotion of the students, who, in spite of their poor economical conditions were so eager and sincere about learning. He was equally touched by the devotion of the teachers and committee members and the overall conducive atmosphere that they had created for learning, even amidst all the problems they had encountered. Congratulating Jyotirao, he said,

"You have done a fantastic job here. Our public schools are lacking on many counts, in comparison to your schools."

"Yes, that's true..." averred Major Candy.

Then, the group moved onto the school at Budhwar Peth. There, Savitribai, Saguna Aau, Annasaheb and a few more people were waiting to welcome them all. Jyotirao requested Warden sir, if he would like to visit the training center for married women, since he had not been able to do so earlier.

Warden immediately agreed, saying,

"Oh sure! I know what you mean to say. Times have changed for the better now. You don't mind it any more. I can understand, Jyotirao. You have faced immense challenges while doing this work. Even in European countries, people like you who had taken up the cause of education, had to face similar challenges. I know that success for such difficult work is not possible without perseverance and conviction in face of constant adversities. As for me, I love my work, and this is also part of my work."

Saying thus, the Warden laughed heartily and Jyotirao was amazed to see that he had not been displeased with the last episode. Instead, he had looked at it without prejudice. Jyotirao felt that it was silly on his part to have kept that matter in mind for so long.

They all walked to the Jogeshwari alley, where the training center was running at Annasaheb's house. Jyotirao couldn't help but remember of the times, two years back. They had to run this center in utmost secrecy, behind closed doors. Whatever few married women were being sent there, were coming on the strict condition that no stranger would be able to see them. That is why, Warden sir had to be refused the visit to this center, two years back. But now, the center opened its arms wide for Sir Warden.

21

John Warden was very pleased with the progress of the schools. He promised continued co-operation to the venture. The meeting held after Sir Warden's visit, brought up newer issues. A new building was required for the school of the Mahar Maang children. It was decided to approach the government for financial help to build this school. The committee secretary Moropant Walvekar, wrote an application for the same. Addressed to Hon. Lord Falkland, the application highlighted the plight of Mahar Maang children, as well as the committee's constraints. He wrote:

"The people of other communities have ostracized the Mahars and Maangs, and lack of education is continually adding to their plight. The Lord Sir is renowned for the immense care he has for the people of this country and the work that he keeps doing for their happiness and upliftment. I'm daring to take the liberty of sending five copies of the results of the examinations held at Jyotirao Phule's schools, on 21 March 1853. I request Lord Sir to kindly accept and peruse through these results.

Our school does not have sufficient funds to take care of the burgeoning costs of teachers' salaries, salaries to the students, watchmen salaries, books, maps, stationary, rent etc. It has been a year & a half since we started this school. The children are also studying properly. Thus, we are feeling the need to have a qualified and sincere teacher who can guide the children better. Finding a teacher may be easy, but retaining him is a very difficult part. No teacher gets ready to teach the children from ostracized, low-caste communities, unless they are promised a hefty pay-packet.

We need to keep replenishing the stationary in school. In order to keep the children from leaving school in between, we need to keep paying them to come to school. The older students need to be promised with a monthly salary for them to keep attending school. The place where we run the school presently, is in very bad shape. We do not have sufficient funds to build a new school or take some place on rent. If we get help to build a new school building, we will be able to accommodate more students, and will also help them stay healthy.

We are writing in to request you to please recommend to the Collector of Pune, to help us build a school building that will accommodate 150 boys and 100 girls. We wish and hope that Lord Sir will take positive action on our application."

Yours sincerely,

Pune – Moro Vitthal Walvekar,

Secretary of the committee looking after schools that educate Mahar and Maang children

16 December 1853

The next day, the application was sent to Mumbai via post, after getting everyone's consent on its content.

22

A strong gust of wind was blowing through the window. The monsoon clouds lent a dreamy feel to the atmosphere. Jyotirao was sitting in his house, the light of the lamp highlighting his rugged silhouette. He was engrossed in reading something, and was marking on the pages with a pencil.

Midnight arrived, but Jyotirao still continued reading. He had only halted to pour some oil into the wicker lamp. His day had went extremely busy as usual, but yet, there were no signs of tiredness on his face. That was how Jyotirao was. Howsoever busy his day might have gone, he would never forsake reading at night. Especially, if he came across a new, good book, then he would even sit reading till dawn!

Savitribai was awake too. The thoughts in her mind refused to cease. Lately, Jyotirao's name was being tossed around in another whirlwind. The government had allotted place near Trimbakji Dengale's ordnance factory, for the school building for Mahar-Maang children. It had also ordered the collector's office to give them Rs. 5000 as donation. The city of Pune was mired in speculation and discussions of all sorts. Jyotirao was quiet through all of it; because, Lord Falkland, through whose efforts this order had been passed, had returned to England just a few days back, and Jyotirao was sure that in his absence, the Brahmin clerks would see to it that the order would never be executed.

Add to that, today itself, a group of Brahmins had openly cursed Jyotirao. Jyotirao had committed a grave sin, according to those Brahmins.

It so happened that, in the after-wake of heavy rains, garbage had been openly rotting in the by-lanes of Pune, causing the spread of various infectious diseases. People were falling very ill with dysentery and vomiting. Pune would suffer from this problem every year. Either the contaminated water, or the infections that devotees would bring back from their annual pilgrimage to Pandharpur, would cause deadly epidemics in Pune. There would be a spate of deaths in Pune after the annual pilgrimage.

That morning, Jyotirao had decided to do something constructive about this problem, and thus, taking along a few friends from the akhaada, he had started collecting the garbage lying on the streets. He had sprayed disinfectant in the open wells. Wherever possible, he had also taken the help of police. This work went on from morning to evening. Apparently, this act had angered the Brahmins, who alleged that Jyotirao had 'polluted' the waters!

Jyotirao's reading habit had rubbed onto Savitribai as well. They both would sit reading till late into the night and would often discuss on the contents of the books. Sometimes, Jyotirao would read out something interesting to his wife. At times, Savitribai would be so tired from the day's work, that she would fall asleep the moment she would take a book in hand. Nevertheless, she could not sleep till Jyotirao also went to bed.

In recent times, Savitribai had started writing educational sayings and phrases for the girls. When Jyotirao would start reading, she would sit and start penning newer thoughts to share with the girls the next day.

One day, as Savitribai sat penning her verses, Jyotirao sat engrossed in some letter.

"What are you reading so intently?" Savitribai asked, seeing her husband thinking deeply over the contents of the letter.

"It's a dispatch sent by Sir Wood. He has made a very important suggestion to the government. He opines that no one should be refused admission to a public school, on the basis of caste" replied Jyotirao.

"Oh! If the government accepts this suggestion, it will be such a wonderful thing for the children. They will be able to learn at any school, without needing to travel for miles..." exclaimed Savitribai.

"Exactly! I'm thinking the same thing. How can our two-four schools suffice for everyone? The government needs to take this issue up on a large scale. Providing education to all, is the government's responsibility. However, I fear that the Company Sarkar's selfish intentions may present an obstacle. The government finds it profitable to spend money on educating the Brahmins, instead of the Mahars and Maangs. After all, they want to keep churning out clerks to fill their coffers. It is a good thing that there are good people like Sir Wood to make such nice suggestions,; but, I doubt how long it will be before the government starts acting on those?!"

"The government should make a law to that effect!" said Savitribai.

"Well, laws are for those who abide by them. What about those people who treat law like a rag? Even if a law is made, who is to say that the Brahmin teachers will indeed behave unbiased and give good education to the children of lower castes? What is the condition of public schools right now? The Brahmin teachers refuse to let go of their ideas of purity and impurity. Not just that, they keep drilling biases into those tender minds, confusing them to no end. In reality, they do not want the children of Shoodras and Ati Shoodras to learn. The government is adding to this chaos by appointing Brahmin teachers to public schools. Teachers who do not have an innate interest in igniting young minds, and also have no knowledge of how to do so, can never create a good learned generation. These people are ones who become teachers just because they do not want to become beggars. What lofty expectations can we have from them? If the government indeed wants the lower caste children to become educated, then they should make education compulsory for those castes; and, appoint teachers from the Shoodra and Ati-Shoodra communities to teach these children. That is only when chane will occur" Jyotirao stated emphatically.

"What else does Sir Wood say?" Savitribai asked.

Jyotirao told her all the salient points of the letter and then said,

"Apart from this, another important development is that, the Scotland Mission has decided to start a school for girls; and, they want our help for the same."

"And what about our schools?" Savitribai asked.

"I have thought about that too. I will go to the Mission school every morning for four hours."

"Will it be possible for you?" asked Savitiribai, Jyotirao's already packed routine swimming before her eyes.

"Well, I will have to make it possible. Where there's a will, there's a way. It would be an honor to teach at a school of the Mission that made me learned. It is a good thing that they are starting a school for girls" replied Jyotirao.

Savitribai did not say anything further. She kept looking at her husband...his eyes heavy with sleep but sparkling from the dreams to be achieved yet... his broad chest that would take on any challenge that came their way.... his weather-beaten body... Jyotirao's efforts refused to cease. From the crack of dawn, he would get busy in getting ready to teach at the schools, look after the shop, meet people to secure donations and more.... There would be no time for having one decent meal or a full glass of water. Now, he was planning to take on more work... His body had not yet started complaining about the various burdens that Jyotirao was heaping on it, and even if it did, Jyotirao had no time to pander to those demands. Savitribai was worried for her husband, but she knew that he would not listen...

Jyotirao had many new ideas brimming in mind; the latest being, starting a night school for farmers. Presently, he was engaged in convincing people about the idea. He was also planning to develop a street play to promote the idea, but was not getting the time to write the script for it.

"From when will you be going?" Savitribai asked.

"From tomorrow...everyday..."

They talked for a bit more, till Jyotirao drifted off to sleep. Savitribai had lost her sleep, though. She kept sobbing wordlessly, in the dark!

The next morning, as Jyotirao was getting ready to go to the school, someone called out from the courtyard:

"Tatyasaab.. are you home?"

It was Shidba, who worked as a watchman in the school at Bhokarwadi. That school had become quite big by then. Shidba was also tasked with taking children to & fro school.

"Come, Shidba... Good you came...I was myself planning to visit the Bhokarwadi school. If you listen to me, please leave that thought..." said Jyotirao.

"What to do, Sir? I'm back-broken with this poverty..." replied Shidba, adding a litany of his complaints.

Jyotirao heard him out, and then said,

"What will you get on converting to Christianity? Have you thought about that?"

"Maybe...a job in the Mission...?" Shidba ventured.

"Shidba, it will be unwise to convert your religion for the

sake of a job. Have you studied the tenets of that religion?"

"No...I haven't...that's why I have come to meet you..." said Shidba.

"No, Shidba. I will definitely not advise this. Especially not, in the hope of getting a job..." Jyotirao said, handing over a letter to Shidba.

"Take this to Jagannath Sadashivji. He will increase your salary. I will also talk to him personally about it. But till then, this letter will suffice."

Shidba thanked Jyotirao profusely, and went his way. Jyotirao started off for the Mission school.

23

It was way past midnight. Jyotirao kept writing...he had to finish the first part of the play today, at any cost. Kondiba Patil had been asking about it daily. Finally today, Jyotirao had promised him that by tomorrow, the first part of the play would be ready for reading. Savitribai was also excited that, this work which had been pending for so many weeks, was finally reaching fruition.

The children of the farmers and tillers were becoming sane, but their parents were still falling prey to the deceit of the Brahmins. Jyotirao was writing this play to show them the reality in a way that they would understand easily.

The rampancy of superstition in the society, would make Tatya very uneasy. The hold of superstitious beliefs on ignorant minds was so strong, that be it the arrival of a child or a death in family, they would bring in a Brahmin to conduct rituals and pay him large sums of money, sometimes at the cost of taking loans, or even staying hungry for the same!

Farmers from neighboring villages would start bringing their children to Jyotirao's schools, carrying them on their hips and walking barefoot for many miles. But, come new moon or full moon, and the number of children of start drying up like water during the summers! The school would almost empty on those days. Sometimes, a child would just stop coming to school. When Jyotirao would go to enquire, the child's parents would tell that the child was hale & hearty; it started falling ill only after coming to school; so, they had found it prudent to stop its education. Some farmer would suddenly stop his intelligent daughter from coming to school; when Jyotirao would ask the reason, he would say, 'if the girl becomes too learned, then she will become a widow!' There were so many superstitions around, that Jyotirao would sometimes be at his wits end as to how was he going to weed out these false notions. Some people believe that holding a book in one's hands was a surefire way of becoming a lunatic!

While it was very taxing for Jyotirao to keep talking to the people and make them leave these superstitions behind, his perseverant streak refused to let him leave that task unfinished. He would convince the farmers to get them to start sending the children back to school again.

However, the farmers would simply not understand why it was so important for the children to be educated. Jyotirao would explain to them:

"If the children do not study, they will become wastrels. They will go down the wrong path and become thieves or criminals. That will only add to your and our misery. Plus, the government will have to spend more to erect courts to punish such errant children. Will it be happy about that? No. Plus, tomorrow, when your children are paraded down the streets as criminals, with their faces blackened, will that be a very happy day for you? Think about it..."

Frightened by such possibilities, the parents would again send the children to school.

Jyotirao realized that for letting the children learn in peace, it was necessary to educate their parents and remove the superstitious ideas crowding their heads. For that, he spent that entire summer in the effort to start a night-school for farmers. After prolonging the matter with excuses such as, 'now is the time for cultivation', 'now is the time for harvest', 'we don't have time to come to school just now', finally the school had started. Instead of going to some spiritual discourse and get bored listening to the same mythological stories, the farmer men and women started finding it interesting to listen to Tatya and Savitribai's practical talks. They would walk for miles together to come to the night-school.

Jyotirao knew that simply teaching them alphabets or numbers was not going to be enough. That is why he had scripted the play, to make them realize the atrocities being heaped on them by the cruel Brahmins. Jyotirao's play was aimed to remove their rose-tinted glasses, as well as, make them realize the importance of education.

As Jyotirao finished writing the last sentence, he heaved an audible sigh of relief. Savitribai understood that the play had finally been written. She asked Jyotirao,

"Can I read it?"

"No...I will read it out to you" Jyotirao said with a smile.

He pulled the wicker lamp closer and started reading. Savitribai had read the earlier part of the play, but she was keen to know how Jyotirao had scripted the ending.

Jyotirao had ended the play with a scene that, recognising the importance of education, the farmer couple starts walking towards Jyotirao and Savitribai's night school. Savitribai felt shy about having being made a part of the play. She blushed and asked her husband,

"What's this? Why did you end the play like this?"

"Oh, why? Because I included your name? But, what's wrong in that? You are also working at the night-school. So, obviously, you will be mentioned in the play, isn't it?" replied Jyotirao.

Savitribai could not argue with him, but nevertheless she continued remaining embarrassed about being mentioned in the play.

Jyotirao looked at her and asked,

"Now, tell me…what title should we give to our play?"

Savitribai playfully bit her lip and said with a smile,

"You must have already thought of that too! Why are you asking me then?"

Jyotirao smiled and said,

"Knowledge is a human being's third eye. Since our play talks about the importance of education, I have decided to name it, 'Trutiya Netra' (The Third Eye)".

"If you ask me, I would prefer the name 'Trutiya Ratna' (The Third Gem). Do you remember telling me about the axiom that says, water, food and knowledge are the only real three gems found on earth; but, foolish are those people who take stones to be gems and value them. Since our play is about education…"

"Absolutely, Savitri! What a great idea!" exclaimed Jyotirao, as he dipped his pen into the inkpot and wrote on the cover page: 'Trutiya Ratna'.

"Tatyasaab, today I will not leave without hearing the script!" Kondiba announced, the moment he came to Jyotirao's house. Some more people had also gathered there.

When Jyotirao announced that the script was ready, the people sat up with interest. As Jyotirao started reading through the script, the audience started reacting – slowly at first, and then guffawing loudly! They were piqued to see their own lives reflected in the play, in such a funny way.

The character of Joshi in the play, was a very sly one. He tells one woman that the birth of her son is destined to bring misfortune to her husband; and, to escape that fate, she must feed some good Brahmins. The woman succumbs to the ploy, but then a Christian Father comes by and he exposes Joshi's fraud. Jyotirao had also included the character of a clown, who would keep making funny but critical comments such as, 'If Brahmins can eliminate the miseries of others, why can't they do so for themselves?' The audience was in splits. Savitribai was specially tickled by the last scene.

At one point, the clown says something that makes everyone introspect. He says,

"God sent the British to our country to compel the Brahmins to stop monopolizing education, and let everyone have access to learning. But tomorrow, if the British start torturing our countrymen, then, the educated Shoodras and Ati Shoodras will establish their own rule (like Raja Shivchhatrapati did) and will govern their own selves, like the Americans did. Come what may, the evil and inappropriate Peshwai will never return to our land again!"

After finishing the reading, Jyotirao said to the people,

"Brothers, think of the British rule as an end to our slavery. What was impossible during the Peshwai, is easily possible now. Teach your children. Make them wise. The British government is not going to stay here for ever. Make you progress till they are here. If we do not utilize this time and the privileges they are according us, it will be a misfortune for us and our future generations."

The audience started introspecting. They realized that Jyotirao was talking sense.

"Tatyasaab, we agree with what you are saying..." said Kondiba.

"Our children have been telling us that Kakusaab has also written a book of verses, that teach us important truths. If Kakusaab can...." said another person.

"Yes, yes, we would love to hear from her too..." said Kondiba.

Savitribai had not expected such a request. She felt shy at first. But then, unable to deny their collective request, Savitribai relented and started reading out:

"Wake up, dear brethren, dear Ati-Shoodras,
Wake up to break off from the chains of slavery,
Wake up to learn, get enlightened!"

The program went on till late that night.

24

After travelling to Nagar and Mumbai for his job, Sadshivrao settled in Pune in a job at the Inam Commission Office. Two years into the job, Sadashivrao started finding more time to devote to the schools. He again began getting involved in the work of the schools. But, this time, he kept feeling something is amiss. He was not liking the way some things were happening. Hence, his enthusiasm started diminishing. Superficially, things were going on as usual. Sadashivrao had to present a statement of accounts in an upcoming meeting. For that, he had to meet Jyotirao beforehand.

One afternoon, he reached the school at Vetaal Peth along with Moropant. Jyotirao was busy in teaching the children. Jyotirao asked his friends to wait; he had to finish this lesson today, come what may.

Today's lesson was about the futility of the concept of various forms of God. The children were chortling, even as Jyotirao's friends were hearing them, sitting on a bench outside. Jyotirao was saying,

"Children, from a young age, you must be listening to stories about battles between the Gods and the devils, and how the devils are always defeated at the end. However, in reality, these stories are about the battles that ensued between Aryas and Anaryas. The Aryas who came from Iran, waged battles with the Kshatriyas living in our country. The Aryas defeated the Anaryas and pushed them into slavery. Those continue to be called as the Shoodra and Ati-Shoodra classes today. Parshuram waged 21 battles with the Kshatriyas. He did not spare even their women and children. The Aryas forced their Gods and rituals upon our society. In reality, we must feel the highest hatred for Parshuram, who heaped so much injustice on the Kshatriyas. But, look at the twist of fate! The vile person who killed the just and able king Baliraja, is revered as God. The Brahmins claim the Parshuram lives on even today; but, truth be told, no human being is immortal. These claims are nothing but ploys to keep us all under their thumb. If Parshuram was indeed alive, why doesn't he ever come before us? I challenge him today…'O! Parshuram… If you are present, come before us…' Let's see if he does…"

The children laughed aloud!

Outside, Sadashivrao turned to Moropant and asked him "Moro, what do you think of the way Jyoti teaches?"

Moropant was listening to Jyotirao intently. He turned to Sadashivrao and asked,

"Are you meaning to ask about his method, or, about the content he is teaching?"

Sadashivrao was a bit taken aback at Moropant's direct question. But today, he wanted to speak his mind out, without hesitation. He replied,

"What had we decided when we started these schools?"

"Come to the point, Sadashiv! What do you want to say?" Moropant asked directly, as was his nature.

Sadashivrao answered candidly,

"The main, or rather sole, aim was to make the children of Ati Shoodras worldly-wise. Isn't it?"

Moropant realized what Sadashivrao was trying to say. He said,

"Well, it seems that your and Jyotirao's thoughts were running on different lines then… Honestly, that time, I had not given so much thought to this issue."

"That means, you are doing it now, isn't it?" Sadashivrao asked, cleverly trapping Moropant in a corner.

Moropant tried salvaging his side saying,

"Why are you saying all this today, Sadashiv? The main premise of these schools was that, certain facets of the Hindu religion are responsible for the subjugation of the lower classes. So obviously, the schools were meant to eradicate those lacunae…"

"The question is, what exactly are we teaching the children? If this propaganda against Brahmins continues, it won't be long before our community faces mass rebellions!"

Moropant became thoughtful. He said,

"We had turned to Christianity because we had become tired of the false notions perpetrated in the Hindu religion, and then when we decided to not go ahead with the conversion, we decided to educate the masses, isn't it? Have you forgotten all that?"

"No, I have not forgotten anything. I have not forgotten how Jyoti saved us from going down the wrong path that time. I also understand that even though he may use harsh language, his thoughts do not stem from personal hatred about the Brahmins. But, think on a larger scale; what is all this going to culminate into? We have always believed that, in any religion, one has to accept certain things with faith, and leave aside those that do not appeal to one. Then, why not think about the Hindu religion in a similar way? I'm saying this from a political angle. I have been thinking a great deal about it , lately…. we cannot turn a blind eye to the need for political independence."

"Do you mean to say that Jyoti does not want political independence?" asked Moropant.

Sadashivrao replied,

"Jyoti's idea of independence is very different. But, if we wish to attain freedom from the British in the recent future, then it won't do for the lower castes to lose their respect about the Brahmins. If that happens, they will support the British against the Brahmins. They will stop trusting the Brahmins in every aspect, and if that happens, then our political aims will go for a toss. In reality, we Brahmins are caught in a weird position. At one level, we have to go against our own people, and on the other hand, we have to pretend being friends with the British. This is resulting in us getting even more unpopular with the masses."

Moropant became thoughtful. He could see sense in what Sadashivrao was saying. It was difficult to predict how and when the orthodox groups may revolt. Already, there was talk about Jyoti's life being in danger. What if something terrible really transpired? Moropant could not even bear the thought! But, he also could not ignore the purity with which Jyoti was carrying out his mission.

Moropant stood thoroughly confounded!

Sadashivrao was saying,

"We definitely require our political freedom and rights. Simply harking about social empowerment is not going to help much."

Moropant could see prudence in what his friend was saying. He replied,

"But Sadashiv, if these intrinsic differences amidst us come to the fore, won't it prove detrimental to the continuity of our mission? That will only serve to strengthen the orthodox group further..."

It was a tangle of questions and problems, with no easy way out, in sight.

Soon they saw people congregating into the courtyard and thus, wrapped up their discussion.

Moropant said to Sadashivrao,

"Take up this topic in the meeting, day after."

Soon, school was over and the children rushed out like bees from a hive! The parents took their children and went away, leaving the three friends to chat.

25

The committee meeting was being held at Moropant's house. All the members were present. Sadashivrao Govande was chairing the meeting. Being the Secretary, Moropant gave a small welcome speech and the meeting commenced.

The topic of the government dillydallying in giving the sanctioned place and funds for the new school, came to fore. It was decided that Babaji Manaji Dengale would pursue the matter.

The officers in the Collector's office would keep delaying the process with silly excuses. Sometimes they would say that the tenders had not come; or, they would crib about the price of raw materials having increased sky-high, owing to the new public constructions going on.

This kept going on, until one day, a letter signed by Collector Davidson, stating that they had suspended the plans for erecting the building, was sent to the government. It was hoped that now at least, the government would give them the long-sanctioned Rs. 5000; but, that was not to be.

Caught between the 'brilliantly practical' government, who wondered what benefit will it accrue for itself if they educate the lower castes; and, the overt enemies of the lower castes aka the Brahmin clerks, the organization had almost zero hope of getting any help. Thus, it was decided to focus on other, more practicable issues.

Jyotirao suggested that they should talk about what changes and improvements could be brought about in the curriculum of the Vetaal Peth school. Sensing the commencement of an unpleasant topic, Sadashivrao's face turned bitter. He said,

"Rather, I feel, we need to talk about what improvements should be made in the teaching style that is being adopted in that school... The other members are free to provide their inputs too."

Jyotirao was a bit taken aback by his friend's comment. This was unexpected. Sadashivrao continued,

"Along with that, we also need to focus on avoiding talking to the children about Hindu religion and their religious texts, as we pointedly avoid talking about politics in front of them."

Saying thus, Sadashivrao kept silent.

Moropant added,

"I agree with Sadashiv on these aspects."

Jyotirao was even more taken aback by this silent protest commenced by two of his dearest friends. Finally, after some deliberation, Jyotirao said,

"We have set up this committee so that the school is run on consensus. Thus, everyone is free to air their views frankly. I feel that our teaching policies cannot be the same in the schools for Brahmin children and Shoodra, Ati-Shoodra children. For the latter set, our aim cannot be limited to teaching them to read and write, but rather, it has to go beyond that, to teach them to live like human beings. We need to equip them with the confidence to live with dignity; and, while doing that, we need to tell them to challenge any person or ideology who seeks to become an obstacle in letting them live with pride. Unless we do that, these children will never become aware of their basic rights and thus will never fight to retain them."

"But, this attitude will also contribute to the two sects developing enmity and hatred amidst themselves!"

"Which two sects? Against who will the hatred develop? Against those Brahmins who consider themselves as agents of God and trample upon others because they think they have the license to do so? Well, the Brahmins who still live with the Manusmruti in their brains, should definitely be hated! And remember one thing... this ignorance will not stay forever. If we do not educate the lower castes, somebody else will...but, one day, the curtain is bound to be removed from before their eyes, and that day, they are bound to understand the ploys that were plotted against them in the name of religion."

"But, I still feel, we should not fall into this. It will lead to a lot of dissatisfaction" said Sadashivrao, refusing to let go of his viewpoint.

However, Jyotirao too was adamant. He refused to cow down to Sadashivrao's persistent explanations. Jyotirao said,

"Strife is the foundation of the Hindu hierarchical set-up. The entire society has been based on that foundation; so, why has this fear of political freedom come up today only? Our basic aim was (and remains) to educate the masses. Have you forgotten that? So many social evils are rampant around us... the widows are living a life in hell, farmers are being exploited to no end.... It is amply clear that the main reason behind all these evils are the mindless rituals and ideas prescribed in Hindu religious texts. In that scenario, do we do something proactive to remove those evils, or, do we turn a convenient blind eye to them? I have no interest in digging up graves. But, I certainly wish to make people see the truth. If you do not subscribe to my views, I will gladly resign from this committee. You are free to run the schools according to your ideas. But, kindly do not keep your Shoodra and Ati-Shoodra brethren bereft of education. It is my humble request to you all" Jyotirao said with folded hands.

Seeing the usually firebrand Jyoti in such a humble position, Moropant softened his stance. He could not think of the school sans Jyoti. Thus, Moropant said,

"Jyoti, please do not misunderstand. This school cannot run without either of you. Please do not let our disagreements morph into unresolvable quarrels."

Jyoti could not refuse his dear friend's request. He replied,

"Alright. I shall continue teaching at the school. But, henceforth, let the committee look after the working of the school, and let us start finding able teachers who can take on the teaching work."

No one said anything on this. There was nothing left to say.

As usual, Jyotirao said a prayer and took everyone's leave.

26

That night, Jyotirao could simply not sleep. There was a storm of thoughts brewing in his mind. The city was abuzz with rumors that Jyoti and Savitri had been converted. Jyotirao was not bothered about that. He was more concerned about his friends who had been caught up in the notions of caste hierarchies.... about the youngsters caught up in the snarls of Macaulay...

Macaulay's policies were creating clerks and officers who were brown-skinned but would talk the language of the fair-skinned. These people would scale the heights of administrative hierarchies and oppress their own countrymen. The overall condition was that British were the kings, but these brown-skinned officers were the rulers. The Shoodras and Ati-Shoodras were getting even more subjugated in this unusual regime. The new bracket of clerks and officers were finding it proud to dress and behave like the gora sahibs . They started feeling ashamed of their own vernacular brethren.

On the other hand, the orthodox group had resurrected the ghost of Manu. The scarecrow of Missionary preaching was also standing alongside. Resultantly, the society was getting increasingly ritualistic. What the British said was being held as the law, and, what the Brahmins said was being held as religion. The lower castes were getting wrung in between.

The school in Vetaal Peth was like Jyotirao's own soul. He was dismayed that disagreements should arise around that school. Jyotirao was becoming aware of the fissures getting prominent on the surface. He knew that disagreements were morphing into a bigger problem.

Jyotirao was agonized to see that his childhood friends, with who he had dreamt, brainstormed and worked so far, were now getting farther. Their ideas seemed to have delineated from Jyotirao's. The only loved one who remained close, was Savitri. Jyotirao was specially surprised about

Sadashiv's attitude. He could not fathom as to what had happened to that Sadashiv who would send money and stationary from Nagar for the school? Who would send Rs. 2 as a monthly donation so that the school may keep running? Who had travelled high and low to get a place for the school? Who had convinced his father to give place in his own house for the school for Mahar Maang children? How and why had Sadashiv changed so much?!

It was easy to dismiss the British as foreigners... But, if the British regime was not there today, would the Brahmins had allowed us to become educated? Would they have let us become learned? Would we have been able to achieve all this without the financial and moral support of the British? The answers to all these questions were coming in the negative. Jyotirao was sure that, had it not been for the British regime, the Shoodras and Ati-Shoodras would have still been languishing in the Dark Ages.

The thoughts in his head kept growing and growing....

It was 2 a.m. Jyotirao had fallen asleep, tired out by the whirlwind of thoughts in his head. Something rustled outside. The alert Jyotirao woke up with a start. Rubbing the sleep from his eyes, Jyotirao squinted in the dark to see shadows near the window on the opposite side. In an instant, he focused on the dandpatta hanging on the wall.

Savitribai was sleeping at some distance, on the floor. A wicker lamp was casting its weak light on the wall, from where Jyotirao could make out the shadows coming nearer....they were now in the house...

At one point, Jyotirao leapt for the dandpatta and shouted, "Who is it?!"

Hearing Jyotirao's voice, Savitribai woke up and clung to him. Jyotirao could make out the sharp blade of an axe shining in the frail light. Once again, Jyotirao asked,

"Who is it? What do you want?"

This time, a man spoke up:

"We want your life!"

Jyotirao squinted in the dark and saw a couple of men, wielding axes, with their faces blackened with soot, standing in their house. He held Savitri closer and asked,

"What for? What have I done?"

The men did not answer. Seeing this, Jyotirao gripped the dandpatta and raised his voice to ask,

"Tell me...what is my offence?"

"We don't know all that. We have been tasked to kill you. We have taken up the job..."

"For what?" asked Jyotirao.

"For money."

"For money? That means, you are not dacoits, are you?" Jyotirao asked, his heart beating fast but his grip on the dandpatta loosening, as he asked them,

"How much money are you going to get by killing me, my friends?"

"Rs. 1000 each."

"Alright. If you are going to benefit by my death, please kill me. Till date, I spent my life for your betterment. If my death is going to be of any use to you, please kill me. I will be happy to die for you. Go on, do your job. But, first just tell me one thing... do your children go to school?"

The hit-men did not answer. Then, Jyotirao said to them,

"Then, please agree to one last request of mine. Send your children to school. That will ensure that at least they will not need to resort to such means in the future."

Jyotirao's words melted the hearts of those hit-men. It was the first time that they were seeing a man who was so fearless in the wake of a raised axe. Unbeknownst to them, the axes fell down from their hands, and they both prostrated at Jyotirao's feet pleading,

"Forgive us, tatyasaab...please forgive us..."

"Our life is truly worth spitting upon, tatyasaab! We agreed to the hellish work of murdering the Godlike man who educates our children to make their lives better!"

"Get up, friends...get up..." said Jyotirao, even as the men kept weeping,

"You are God in human form, tatyasaab! Our sins will take us to hell!"

Jyotirao was overwhelmed to see their change of heart. He looked at Savitribai, who was also weeping tears of happiness and relief.

The innocent men started talking candidly. Jyotirao asked them about their identities. They were Dhondiba Rode and Dhondiram Kumbhar.

Savitribai poured oil into the wicker lamp and requested the men to wipe the soot off their faces. Jyotirao recognized one of them. He said,

"Oh, you are Dhondiram Shaahir ! I have heard your compositions."

Dhondiram was embarrassed to hear Jyotirao praising him in the light of what had transpired.

"Tatyasaab, till date, we had not met a man like you, who spoke to us with such affection. You have indeed shown us the right path. Henceforth, we will do whatever you say" said Dhondiram.

Dhondiba added to this saying,

"Tatyasaab, please allow us to do one thing. We wish to eliminate the person who tasked us with this evil work.

"No, Dhondiba. Don't even think of it" cautioned Jyotirao. "Just because he made one mistake, you do not commit another. This cycle has to stop somewhere; so, why not stop it here itself? Forgiving that person will be his biggest punishment. Our ignorance is the root cause of why all this happened. So, let us strive to remove this ignorance. Revenge, murder and such other negative things have never achieved any good. We all are the children of one God. So, by that relation, we all are brethren. How can we ever think ill for our own brothers? One day, that person is bound to feel regret for what he was doing. That will be his real punishment."

"But, Tatyasaab… your life is in danger…" said Dhondiba.

"Is that going to go away by killing one person? I do not fear death. We are all mortals. Death is waiting for all of us somewhere or the other. If I die while doing something good for somebody, it will be the happiest moment for me. And, why should I worry about all these things when I'm surrounded by good people like you who can discern between good and bad? Now, just do one thing: do not tell anybody about whatever has transpired here."

Both of them nodded their heads in acceptance, but then Dhondiba said,

"But, Tatyasaab, listen to me. If you need to go anywhere, do take me along."

"Yes, tatyasaab… what Dhondiba says is correct. You need to be careful" added Dhondiram.

Jyotirao could not refuse these two gentle souls. He agreed, and then turning to Dhondiram, said,

"You also have to agree to one thing… Henceforth, utilize your gift of poetry to educate the masses."

"Oh, Tatyasaab… I'm hardly a poet! I can barely put a few words together to entertain people, that's it" Dhondiram said shyly.

"Dhondiram, mere entertainment is of no use for our people. Rather, if you do not change the content of your poetry, they will continue to remain ignorant. Please use your poetry to elucidate the benefits of education. Education is the only thing that can uplift our people now."

"Yes, tatyasaab…I shall try my best…"

By then, it was almost dawn. The two men wiped their faces once again, and fell at Jyotirao's feet, saying,

"Allow us to take your leave now, tatyasaab. Aaisaab, please forgive us. Henceforth, we will never let our faces be blackened – literally, and figuratively too!"

27

Savitribai had come to her parents' house for Diwali, after almost seven-eight years. Seeing her mother after all these years, Savitribai could not resist weeping in her loving embrace! Lakshmibai was over the moon to see her daughter again. The next two days went by in talking late into the night. After all, they had a lot to catch up about.

However, two days later, Savitribai's health took a downward turn. She became bedridden. Lakshmibai's heart was aflutter to see her dear daughter fall so ill. She and Sadubhau kept tending to their daughter, day & night. It took almost a fortnight for Savitribai to get better.

Savitribai was amazed to see her brother look after her so tenderly, after having refused to see her face for the last decade!

Savitribai was getting well, but she was still too weak to go home. Her medicines were also continuing. Savitribai was constantly worried about the school. Finally, one day, she said to her mother,

"Aai , I must go! I cannot stay here any longer."

Lakshmibai was taken aback. She asked,

"What? In this tender condition?!"

"I'm feeling better now…" said Savitribai.

"No ways. We are not letting you go till you become perfectly alright" stated Sadubhau.

Savitri knew that talking about the school would anger her brother; hence, she said,

"They must be waiting for me, back home…"

But Sadubhau could see through his sister. He bellowed,

"Don't talk nonsense. I know, you want to go back for that wretched school! Please, at least now stop that evil work! What good is such a mission that has led you to get ostracized and has created so many problems for us? Now at least, behave according to the wish of Gods and the Brahmins. Your life came under danger, yet you both refuse to listen to any sane word of advice. Tatya has become too big for his boots after he started reading those English books. You, as his wife, should have filled some sense into his head.... but, no! You also decided to help him in this vile work" Sadubhau spat out his restrained anger held within for all these years.

Savitribai did not mind her elder brother venting his anger, but it pained her to see him saying mean things about her husband. She was especially sad to see that Jyotirao's work was receiving recognition from strangers – even, foreigners – but his own family refused to see the merit in the same. Lakshmibai could see the dejection on her daughter's guileless face. She rebuked her son, saying,

"Don't speak like this, Sadu. Such language does not befit a maalkari like you."

Savitribai added to this, saying,

"Brother, you are a maalkari and a warkari ; but, your intellect has been blunted by the false teachings of the Brahmins. You love to touch and feed cattle; you have no compunctions serving milk to a snake on the eve of Nagpanchami ; but, you find Mahars and Maangs to be untouchable and impure, in spite of the fact that they are human beings just like you? These Brahmins, whose propaganda you stand by, consider you to be untouchable, in spite of being a maalkari. So, in a way, they also look at you as a Mahar! Have you ever thought of that?"

Sadubhau was shocked to hear this fact. The truth stood in front of him, but his ego refused to admit that his sister was right. Sadubhau said,

"But, what is the need to educate Mahars and Maangs? The people of Pune curse you, torture you... we get to know everything, and we cannot tolerate it! Not just that, even in this village people keep talking dirty things about you, as well as us. How long can we tolerate all this?"

"Brother, there is no difference between an animal and an uneducated person. Education is the only thing that elevates a human being. We teach Mahars and Maangs so that they can live like human beings. What is wrong in that? Brahmins spread vile rumors about us because our work presents a threat to their existence. People like you also fall easy prey to their propaganda. But, I tell you, my swami is God is human form. No one can match up to him. You just keep muttering the name of God, but he is actually doing God's work on earth. I feel gratified to be able to help him in this work. I get to see so many different forms of humanity."

Sadu and Lakshmibai kept listening intently to Savitri. Lakshmibai had tears in her eyes as she said,

"My daughter, how unique have you become?! You are blessed by Goddess Saraswati herself. You speak so wisely!"

Sadubhau too had a change of heart on hearing what Savitri had to say. He said,

"I'm sorry, Savitri. I said a lot of wrong things to you. My mind was prejudiced. But now, I realize the worth of your work."

Sadubhau felt specially distressed by the fact that all this should have happened when Savitri had come home after so many years, and was also not keeping well.

On her part, Savitribai decided to postpone returning to Pune, in the light of what had just transpired. Some time later, she sat down to write a letter to her husband. A lot of thoughts were swirling in her head. Finally, after a long time, she started writing in her beautiful handwriting:

"To,

Satyaroop Jyotiba Swami,

Sincere respects from Savitri.

I'm writing this letter to inform you that, I fell very ill during this trip to Naigaon. However, my dear brother Sadubhau, nursed me back to health. He has done a lot for me during my stay here. I'm feeling much better now, and the credit goes entirely to Sadubhau. Please do not worry about me. Fatima must be having trouble covering up for me there, but I know, she will not complain...."

Further, Savitribai wrote about the incident which had happened. Finishing off the description, she said,

"... So, you must have realized that, just like in Pune, here too there are a lot of clowns who are spreading bad things about us. Why should we be afraid of such people? We will not cow down to them. We shall continue doing our work. Success is bound to be ours in the near future."

PART 2

28

It had been five years since the revolt in North India had died down; but, even now, there were many people who were daydreaming about expelling the British from the country.

Gossipmongers would keep talking about the hearsay tales from the revolt, and rue the fact that the British were almost ready to pack their bags, but fate smiled on them at the last moment.

Soothsayers and conmen were having a field day by giving irrelevant and useless advice to the kings and others. For instance, once, some astrologer told some king that, 'it had been a hundred years since the British had come to India. Hundred was a magic number that would change their fates for the worse. The British were sure to leave the country this year.'

This 'prophecy' spread like wildfire around the country. Kings and princes from all over, started buzzing in the joy of their imminent return to true power. It had indeed been a century since the British had begun conquering India by winning the Battle of Plassey. After fawning over the foreigners for many years, most of the rulers had started cursing them for the various oppressions they wreaked on the rulers. The British had started conquering their territories, abolished their privy purses, and were basically creating havoc all around. The rulers were united in the thought that it was time to drive out the foreigners on an immediate basis.

Nanasaheb of Bithoor, the utterly dissatisfied and disillusioned adopted son of Bajirao Peshwe, and, Kunwarsingh, the aged ruler of Bihar, were ready to charge on the British at any moment. Rani Lakshmibai of Jhansi, and, Begum Hazrat Mahal of Ayodhya were also ready for a revolt. Almost all the rulers had some bone to pick with the Company Sarkar.

Nanasaheb wanted the annual maintenance of Rs. 8 lakh that was being paid to Bajirao, to be continued even after his death. But, the Company Sarkar brutally rejected the request. Rani Lakshmibai was locked in a bitter battle with the government, regarding a boy's adoption. Begum Hazrat Mahal was also fighting tooth & nail with the government, with her younger son in tow. Dissatisfaction with the British rule was bubbling over the cauldron. Nana Peshwe took the lead. Messages were sent across many states and regions. A major revolt was planned; even the date was fixed. 31st May 1857. As the day came nearer, secret meetings and last minute onceovers gathered steam.

However, the row over cartridges, led to an uprising happening before the planned date! The soldiers deployed in British army would be given cartridges layered with animal fat. They had to break open the seals of the cartridges with their teeth. When the Hindi soldiers came to know of this fact, they were shaken to core! They had unwittingly conducted blasphemy!

This knowledge led to a soldier in Meerut cantonment, named Mangal Pandey, to get tremendously instigated against the British. One day, he started firing indiscriminately at any British soldier or officer in sight. He also gave a call for revolt to his Hindi soldier brethren. However, the British army proved heavier than Mangal Pandey. He was arrested and hung to death in the next eight days. The other soldiers who were suspected to have supported him, were sent to the dungeon.

But, Mangal Pandey's sacrifice did not go waste. He had sparked an agitation, that kept gathering steam. The soldiers become very disturbed by the death of Mangal Pandey. They started killing the British indiscriminately. The dungeon was attacked; they helped the imprisoned soldiers to escape and proceeded to Delhi. A huge uprising took place in Delhi, that led to Delhi being snatched out of the hands of British. Bahadurshah Zaffar, the dethroned emperor of Delhi, was again made king with a lot of pomp and pageantry. Bahadurshah took on the responsibility of the revolt upon himself.

What started off as one man's agitation, soon snowballed into a countrywide movement. Hindi soldiers went far & wide, carrying the message of revolt against the oppressive British. If a man was seen entering a village with a bundle of chapattis in his hand, it was a signal for the people that the revolt had come to their village. They would take those chapattis from the man, give him fresh ones, and would join the revolt under the oath of food.

Nanasaheb Peshwe had no time left to wait for the pre-planned day. He slayed almost every British person seen in Kanpur and established his firm control over the region. However, the British were not to let this attack go unheeded. They launched a counter-attack and expelled Nanasaheb from Kanpur. Seeing their ruler retreating, general Tatya Tope rushed to the Peshwa's help. He fought valiantly, and re-established

Peshwa's control over Kanpur. However, subsequently, Tatya Tope was defeated in the battle with General Havlock.

After escaping from Kanpur, Tatya again put together his army. Many soldiers from the British army too came to join Tatya Tope. They won over the fort of Kalpi. Tatya and Nanasaheb Peshwe decided to help the Rani of Jhansi.

Over there, once the Rani of Jhansi entered into the revolt, Sir Hugh Rose launched an attack on Jhansi. Rani Lakshmibai fought valiantly; but, she fell prey to deception by traitors. She broke through the siege laid by British soldiers, to reach Kalpi. The soldiers were in hot pursuit behind her. With her adopted son Damodar tied to her back, Rani Lakshmibai was nearing Kalpi. She was hopeful that if Nanasaheb reached in time, she would benefit by his help. But alas, that was not to be. The valiant queen was martyred in this battle.

On the other hand, Tatya Tope was riding on the wind, with the British in hot pursuit. Tatya extorted money from almost all major princes and kings in North India and came to Maharashtra. From there, he went to Gujarat and then proceeded towards the jungles of Rajputana.

Richard Meade was perseveringly behind Tatya, but Tatya was outsmarting him at all junctures. Sadly, again treachery became the brave Tatya's death-knell. One of his most trusted men backstabbed Tatya and handed him over to the British. His arrest signified the end of the daring revolt that Tatya was planning so painstakingly. The soldiers, who Tatya had gathered with so much trouble, scattered away in an instant.

Bahadurshah was trying his best to retain Delhi. Bakhtkhan Rohilla of Bareilly had come to his aid. Bahadurshah made Bakhtkhan his sepoy-general. Under Bakhtkhan's guidance, Delhi waged a war against the British.

John Nicholson got prepared to tackle the agitators with long-range cannons. He did not need to work too hard to conquer Delhi. Internal rivalries and a spate of treacheries had already driven holes in the revolt. The Badshah refused to listen to guidance given by Bakthkhan who was a Rohilla. One of Badshah's relatives turned treacherous to the extent of letting the British army enter Delhi like a cakewalk! There was no limit left to the bloodshed and torture that ensued thereafter. Delhi was defeated and Bahadurshah Zaffar was imprisoned.

The British meted out very humiliating treatment to this last of India's emperors. His general and relatives were paraded through the city on donkey-back, after which they were publicly shot dead. The emperor's sons were mercilessly beheaded, and their cut heads were presented to the emperor on a salver.

The countrywide revolt started crumbling in the face of this defeat. The British tortured and massacred thousands of soldiers. To serve a lesson to others planning to rebel, they hung many of the soldiers' dead bodies on trees in public places. Many brave-hearts had to live in disguise to save their lives. Nanasaheb Peshwa took on a mendicant's garb and disappeared into some dense forest. His soldiers also vanished with him.

Rana Jungbahadur of Nepal joined hands with the British. Out of fear for his life, he handed over thousands of Hindi soldiers, who had taken refuge in Nepal, to the British.

Revolts that had stirred up in Patna (Bihar) and Maharashtra, were crushed before they could even stand on their feet. Chimasaheb, the brother of the Chhatrapati of Kolhapur, was arrested by the British. Traitors unveiled the plan of revolt made by Rango Bapuji in Satara. The British started a witch-hunt for those involved in planning that rebellion. Rango Bapuji managed to escape, but many of his accomplices were not that lucky; they were caught and hung to death.

The revolt spread like wildfire, in one pocket after another; but that itself turned to prove the biggest weakness of our people. The absence of unity and strength of the masses, made the revolt incapable of upturning the massive Company Sarkar. It became very easy for the British to snuff out small rebellions as they kept erupting from place to place. The neutral stance taken by princes such as Shindes and Holkars, served to benefit the British. Had the princes not taken a short-sighted view of how they could (not) benefit from the revolts, and had seen the larger picture, probably the British would have tasted defeat.

In Pune, the very vocal patriots, who would be ever ready to give lectures on patriotism, sat hidden in their homes during the revolts. However, they did not leave any occasion to smear Jyotirao's name. After Ganpat Mali and Maulavi Nur-ul Huda were arrested, similar rumors started wafting about Jyotirao. The people remembered Jyotirao's old connections with the rebels. Ganpat Mali was flogged in public, near Budhwar Peth, and was then imprisoned. Nur-ul bhai was charged with having joined hands with the rebels of Karnataka.

As was wont to be, the rumors regarding Jyotirao started having an adverse effect on his good relations with the British. The British gentlemen who would hitherto have a smile on their faces on seeing Jyotirao, started frowning on seeing him. Having experienced this with a couple of English people, Jyotirao stopped interacting with them.

Many other people reeled under the after-effects of the revolt. Many soldiers lost their money and household and were forced to live in extreme poverty. Many soldiers died a brutal death, while many others were forced to live (and die) in compelled expulsion. The leaders of the revolt found themselves mired in endless legal proceedings brought over them by the Company Sarkar.

Tatya Tope was charged with treason; he wore that charge proudly while going to the gallows. Bahadurshah was expelled from his own land and imprisoned in Rangoon (Burma), for rebelling against the government. The last big emperor of India died a pitiful death, languishing in a fort of Rangoon. No one knows what happened to Nanasaheb Peshwe. Some say that he continued living like a mendicant, while some believe that he died in a jungle of Nepal.

Queen Victoria of England got t know about this

tremendous dishevelment that had happened in India. She ordered for the Company Sarkar to wind up their operations in India and handed over the governance of India to the British Parliament. Effectively, now India came under the direct rule of the Queen of England.

The Queen issued a special declaration for the people of India. She promised them that henceforth their rights would not be abused, and no one would interfere in their religious matters. A traumatised population started becoming calmer after these assurances.

However, those imprudent people who were still living in the haze of the Peshwai, had no joy or sorrow about the changing situations. They were still busy in plotting the ostracization of the Nhaavi community. Apparently, some Brahmin had uttered the pure shlokas from the Vedashastras at the house-warming ceremony of a nhaavi (barber) family. As a result, the orthodox group had not just tortured the Brahmin in question, but also decided to ostracize and un-communicate all nhaavi families in the city. The troubled nhaavis went to Jyotirao to take his advice. The quarrel went on for many days, but ultimately, the Brahmins had to eat a humble pie before the nhaavis.

The barber community won this battle but it resulted in even more troubles for Jyotirao. He was cursed for interfering in every matter – be it the proposed ostracization of Gopal Hair Deshmukh (in the past), or this latest issue.

On his part, Jyotirao was facing opposition from all sides. Earlier, at least, he had the British on his side. But now, the British and Missionary well-wishers had withdrawn their hand of friendship, and, there was nothing much to be expected from his own countrymen too.

The only silver lining to this dark cloud was, the consistent progress being shown in school by the children of Mahars, Maangs, Chaambhars and Kunbis. New dashing teachers such as Ganu Shivji Maang and Dhuraji Appaji Chaambhar had risen to teach the new generation of students. They started working with zest along side people like Ramchandra Moreshwar, Ragho Sakharam, and Keso Trimbak. Under their able guidance, students like Lakha, Nama, Tukaram, Ibrahim, Parvata, Ganu, Vithu, Sadhu, and Dhondi started making great progress in studies.

The committee held the examination program of the Mahar Maang students, at Babaji Dengale's warehouse. Many local and foreign guests came for this function. Educational Inspector Lester sent a list of the excellent students to the government and wished them success in the future.

The committee was still working to keep the schools running, but somewhere, the initial enthusiasm had worn off. The proposal to build a new school building had remained on paper only. The amount sanctioned by the government for this work, still remained in the government coffers itself. Internal disagreements were taking a vicious turn. Jyotirao was faced with an unusual deadlock. Those who were earlier not interested in education, were turning towards it; and when the time had come near to build more schools for them, they were being forced to cut down on the existing schools.

But, Jyotirao's life was too fluid to get entangled in one matter only.

In the interim, Jyotirao shifted to a new house in Meethganj Peth. All his friends came for the house-warming. Jyotirao had been able to buy this place due to Saguna Aau and Sadashivrao's help.

Around the same time, family quarrels rose their ugly head. Jyotirao was not interested in getting involved in disputes regarding ancestral property. He even went for his niece Thakubai's wedding with a lot of affection. But even at that time, the bitterness brought about by the disputes, rose its head. His own relatives refused to speak with Jyotirao. A big quarrel ensued during the festivities itself. Jyotirao tried to intervene by telling everyone to resolve this matter with rationality and patience; but, no one was in a state to listen to him.

Even as his personal troubles were growing, Jyotirao's mind was also getting disturbed by the increasing distress being faced by widows all around. Those innocent women were so traumatized that, while on one hand they would be staring at a vacuous and unsure future; on the other hand, they could not even voice their grief with abandon! If a widow was found crying, she would be severely rebuked for being shameless enough to cry because she had no man in her life! The physical and emotional abuse suffered by the widows while they waited pitifully for death to claim their unfortunate loves, clawed at Jyotirao's heart day & night. The mute ululations of those widows were pointing towards a new mission for Jyotirao to pursue. He was anguished to see doll-like 8-9 year old girls being widowed at an age when they had not even had a chance of a marital life. He could see young widows living in the perpetual shadow of fear and slavery as they buried all their dreams, toiled like oxen, and fell prey to the lust of unscrupulous men who saw them as nothing more than playthings. It was not uncommon to hear of suicides and feticides committed by these women who found themselves stigmatized for no fault of theirs. Many a times, someone would find an abandoned fetus washed away on the riverbank or floating in the water of a well. At times, one could also see the corpse of that fetus' mother floating alongside. Those widows who did not have that much courage to commit suicide, would either abscond out of public eye or would be pushed into prostitution. There were many such women who had run out of their marital homes and become prostitutes, in the hope of getting a wee better life than they could envision at their homes.

Widows would be looked upon with extreme derision. They would be seen as a walking-talking misfortune; a calamity, whose shadow could pollute the purest of things. Once a woman became a widow, her own parents, siblings, in-laws all would become her enemies. No one would feel like reassuring or even consoling her for her loss. Instead, they would fear that if they showed affection to a widow and not torture her, they would face the wrath of God! A widow's life was living hell, but no one thought that they were making a travesty of humanity of meting out such inhuman treatment to these women. This attitude was yet another terrible gift given by the Peshwai to the society.

Baba Padmanji, a friend of Jyotirao's, had described the pitiable state of widows through his book titled 'Yamuna Paryatan'; but such efforts, although very commendable, were falling short to reform the societal attitude. Even the judiciary was not being able to curb this evil practice. Even the so-called progressives had turned a convenient blind eye to this aspect of the society. Jyotirao had respect for Baba's anguish for the widows, but he did not agree with Baba's view that converting to Christianity was the only answer to relieve the widows of their sorrow. As it is, the cunning Brahmins had laid down a maze of rules that prevented a widow from being given away as someone's wife more than once. Their theory was that, a girl can be given away only once in her life. Who would give away a widow?! even if she is alive and her husband is dead, a widow belongs only to her husband. No other man can claim right over her, lawfully. Either a widow should go Sati, or then, if she stays alive, she has to live like an ascetic, with her head shorn, body devoid of any adornment whatsoever, and starving herself to look as unattractive as possible. After all, how would God give her an entry into heaven if she adorned herself like a hussy?! According to these 'learned' men, there was no reason for the society to grieve over the condition of these vile women. As it is, how many such women were there? And why should centuries old religious laws be changed for them?! It did not make sense to them.

During a brief stay at Nagar, Jyotirao happened to hear the tyranny spread by a man called Shankaracharya. This man had been travelling all over with a blade, forcibly shearing the heads of any long haired widow he would come across! Such was his fear that if news came around of Shankacharya coming to their village/town, long-haired widows would flee from their location and go into hiding. The unfortunate amongst them who would get caught, would be forcibly shorn off! The same thing happened at Nagar. One child widow was caught doing something that she should not have done. Her father had to pay a heavy price for his daughter's immorality. He had to wash Shankaracharya's feet and drink up that water to purify himself and his lineage of the blemish that his daughter had stained them with. As for regaining the girl's own purity, Shankaracharya suggested a very 'unique' way indeed. He told the father to create a hollow in the stem of a mango tree and make the girl sit inside. Then, fill the hollow with dried leaves, and set the stem on fire! After enough fumes are generated, the girl should be brought out and tonsured, and then the father should feed one thousand Brahmins, as penance!

But apparently, a few brave widows had also threatened to call the police if this Shankaracharya forcibly tonsured them. On those occasions, this 'great man' had no option but eat a humble pie.

However, such women were far and few. Most widows were helpless before the generations old customs and their merciless family members.

Jyotirao used to feel extreme anger about the fact that when even the Shoodra and Ati-Shoodra communities had accepted the idea of widow remarriage, then why couldn't these so-called progenitors of knowledge still not wind their heads around it?! It would make him furious that old men on the way to imminent death would have no compunction in marrying girls as young as 10 years! He had no respect for such religious tenets that held no concern for human beings, just because they were female.

Another event happened around this time, that contributed to Jyotirao's resolve to do something concrete to alleviate the pains of the widows. In fact, the gruesome incident happened in Sadashivrao's house itself. A maid named Kashibai, who used to work at Sadashivrao's house, had slit her newborn child's throat and thrown the corpse in a well behind the house! Someone saw the corpse floating in the well and raised a hue & cry. The police were called; Kashibai admitted to her offence; and, she was taken into police custody.

Jyotirao was specially restless on experiencing such a thing so close to home. He could not forget the bloated body of that tiny child, floating on water. A Shastribuva staying near the Govande's house had taken advantage of the beautiful, genteel child widow that Kashibai was.

Kashibai was charged with infanticide. A helpless widow who had fallen prey to mindless customs and societal prejudice, had to stand in court to defend the death of her own child.

That was when Jyotirao knew that something definitely had to be done to help these widows; and, no one, except for Savitribai could help him in this endeavor.

29

The sessions court had sentenced Kashibai to life imprisonment. The verdict had shaken entire Pune to the core! Such a punishment was unheard of for a woman.

Jyotirao read about the verdict in a newspaper and decided that, this should not happen again. Such an incident, which put a big blot on the face of humanity, had to be kept from repeating itself. He decided that, widow remarriage was the best way to save the lives of many such widows and small or unborn children.

Savitribai came outside and saw Jyotirao immersed in deep thought. She asked him,

"What are you thinking about?"

Jyotirao looked at her and replied,

"Savitribai, you are seeing the worsening condition of

widows, aren't you?..."

Jyotirao's rhetorical question was enough for Savitribai to realize what he was thinking about. Jyotirao continued,

"Savitribai, women are such an integral part of society, but they are being constantly subjected to injustice, pain and trauma. In spite of being superior to men in so many ways, women are being harangued by the evils of a male dominated society. Read this news..." said Jyotirao, handing over the newspaper to his wife.

An incident had happened in the Maadha village of Solapur. A Brahmin man's widowed sister had died due to one part of the house collapsing on her. But, since she was not tonsured in spite of being a widow, Brahmins refused the let her brother conduct her last rites. Ultimately, she had to be cremated at the hands of a Shoodra.

"This is terrible! The ritual of Sati sounds bearable in comparison to such injustices. It is better to die once and for all, instead of dying crumb by crumb every single day of one's life" Savitribai said with a deep sigh.

Jyotirao said,

"Centuries of slavery also makes a person habituated to it. They start finding it a way of life. Then how can we even expect someone to oppose a practice that they have been accustomed to? The same thing has happened with women. After living a tortured life for many years, they find Sati to be a welcome embrace for ending their pain. Till recently, women were going Sati in Pune too. The Brahmins have kept themselves on the apex of societal hierarchy for many years now; but, they never behaved befitting that status. The Muslims and then the Company Sarkar thought of banning the ritual of Sati, but these evil Brahmins curse the Company Sarkar for abolishing Sati, instead of praising them for it. They have the audacity to still approach the government with tenets of religion that 'prove' that Sati was a good practice. How absurd it is to claim that Sati was a good practice in any way?! If they feel that sitting on a burning pyre expedites a woman to heaven, then why don't these learned people use the method for themselves?!

Listening to Jyotirao, Savitri was remembering the many stories about widows that Saguna Aau had told her about. A widow named Radhabai was made to go Sati. Unable to bear the pain, she had leapt out of the burning pyre and started running towards the village, her body aflame. The Brahmins raised a hue & cry about the widow polluting everyone with her presence, instead of trying to help her. She was screaming her heart out, but no one had the heart to take her in their house. Finally, some British soldiers took pity on her and tried to recuperate her. But, the unfortunate woman died of serious burns, three days later.

Another such woman who had leapt out of the burning pyre and run towards the river to save her life, was forcibly back by the Brahmins, who pushed her back into the pyre, threw more logs of wood onto her to keep her from escaping and watched her die a horrible death as she flipped in the fire!

Savitribai got tears in her eyes on remembering that episode, as Saguna Aau had narrated to her.

"We only write the scriptures and we only validate our actions in their shadow!" Savitribai said with a smirk.

"If women had written the scriptures, its contents would definitely have been been more compassionate" said Jyotirao, adding, "Nature has made women more stronger than men. But, men took undue advantage of her physical frailty and pushed her to slavery. These hypocrite men who want their women to be so loyal to them that she goes Sati after they die...have they ever thought of whether they will climb the pyre if the woman were to die first?! Hypocrites who shamelessly bring another woman into the house in the presence of their wife...will they accept it, if their wife brings a man into their house, in their presence?! Widows are not allowed to remarry, but widowers can! Why so? Who granted them this liberty? Do the cunning Brahmins have any proof in their scriptures to validate how and why has this distinction been made? In whose favor has it been made? What good can come out of it? Truth be told, Brahmin men have particularly seen to it that they create biased and irrational tenets, so that they can rule over women. They forget that, such evil actions only lead to subjugation of women, who can otherwise be very able partners to them. They forget that they were born to a woman. I feel ashamed to see that this is the way these evil men are obliging the wombs they came into this world from! Savitribai, exploitation of women will take this country nowhere but downwards. If we wish to see progress in our country, we need to do something to stop this exploitation!"

"Tell me what you are thinking to achieve this..." said Savitribai.

"I feel, we should start an orphanage for widows, to save them from committing crimes like infanticide."

Savitribai started thinking. A few Missionaries were taking care of such children, but their aim would be different. Many women would kill their children thinking that, it is better for them to die than live as a Christian. That would start off a chain of other problems for the already traumatized women.

"Tell me what do you think of this, Savitribai? I feel that no woman should suffer the fate that Kashibai did..." said Jyotirao, looking at his wife expectantly.

"Let us do it" said Savitribai. "By taking on this responsibility, we may need to live even more frugally; but at least, we will be able to stop innocent children from dying for no fault of theirs."

"Thank you, Savitribai! I knew you would not refuse..." Jyotirao exulted with tears in his eyes.

"You know , I will never refuse you. But, have you thought of any place for the orphanage? Where shall we keep all those children?" Savitribai asked.

"Let us start from our home itself. We do not require anybody's help. Those men who could not snatch the razor from the hands of the barber who came to tonsure their widowed sisters, what help can we expect from them?! We will need to do this work ourselves, without expecting any type of help from anybody. As for the schools... Sadashiv is handling the Vetaal Peth school. We shall task some other teacher with your school. Annasaheb will not refuse...." Jyotirao clarified.

Savitribai could see Jyotirao's determination and eagerness to help, through his hurried words. She knew that the work he was planning to do was an invaluable service to humanity; she was equally eager to play her role in it.

"Let us start this work at the earliest!" said Savitribai.

Savitribai's encouragement served to strengthen Jyotirao's resolve even more. The direction of his life had changed yet again.

Today, Jyotirao was remembering Saguna Aau a lot. She was no longer alive to give them her staunch support. She had long passed ahead of the mortal world, leaving yet another vacuum in Savitri and Jyotirao's hearts.

Jyotirao did not know his birth mother; she had died soon after giving birth to him. Saguna Aau was the only woman he knew as his mother... the one who had shaped his mind, body and soul. Saguna Aau had gone to Fursungi for some work, and fell ill over there itself. Savitri and Jyotirao rushed to bring her back, as soon as they got the message; but, it was too late.

During Aau's funeral, Jyotirao kept reminiscing about the journey of her life, as he knew it.

Jyotirao's mother Chimna Aai and Saguna Aau's mother Dhondabai, were real sisters. The daughters of Zagdewadi Patil.

One daughter was married to a family in Ganj Peth of Pune, while the other at Hadapsar. Chimna Aai gave birth to two children and died around nine months after Jyotirao's birth. After Dhondabai's death, Saguna Aau soon became a widow at a very young age.

Saguna Aau had seen her aunt die and leave a hungry, crying baby Jyoti behind. Aau could not bear the plight of that baby.

She left Hadapsar and came to Chimna Aai's house to tend to Jyoti. Dada remarried a few years later; the new wife was also named Chimna Aai in memory of his first wife. But, Jyotirao never got his Chimna Aai back. He grew up with Saguna Aau only.

Aau used to work as a nanny at the house of a Christian Missionary called John. Over there, she got a dear friend by the name of Mary. It was due to Mary that Saguna Aau started taking interest in education, and further went on to give the same gift to Jyotirao.

Saguna Aau passed away, but not without giving another big gift to Jyotirao – that, of loving other's children selflessly. Jyotirao decided to open an orphanage in his house – a house that they had built with Saguna Aau's help. That was going to be the best homage he could pay to his Aau.

30

As dawn broke, the city of Pune started stirring to life after a fitful sleep. A priest, Ram Dikshit was hurrying to the nearby temple, with his salver in hand. He could see something written on a wall across the road. Curiosity got the better of Dikshit, as he crossed over to read the small notice. As he began scanning the words of the notice, Dikshit's eyes got as large as saucers, and his mouth fell open in awe!

Save yourself and your child from disgrace

- Dear widowed sisters, if you have unknowingly fallen prey to the lust of conniving men and have become pregnant through it, then please come to Jyotirao Govindrao Phule's house to deliver your baby safely. The name of the woman will be kept under utmost secrecy. You may take the child along with you, or if you cannot do so, we will be happy to rear it. The choice remains yours.

The cool morning breeze did little to stop Dikshit from sweating! He cast furtive glances around. Seeing that no one was around, he kept down his salver, pounced on the notice stuck on the wall, and tore it into tiny pieces, cursing Jyotirao all the time. Just then, he saw another priest coming towards him, muttering curses for Jyotirao under his breath.

As people began gathering in the temple for the morning's hymns, there was only one topic being discussed – that of the content on the notices stuck all over town. Many of the people had read and even torn off the notices that they had seen. Dikshit finished the hymns half-heartedly and then turning to the crowd, he bellowed,

"Go, people, go! Tear off those filthy notices from wherever you see them, and be sure to sprinkle gomutra (cow urine) on the walls from where you tear those notices."

The people started rushing to do the deed; but, there were too many notices stuck all around for a handful of people to remove them all. The city of Pune started quaking as if some earthquake had hit it. The cannonball fired by Jyotirao Phule had shaken up the orthodox Brahmins from their idle sleep.

Little did they know that such earthquakes were round the corner for Pandharpur, Nashik, Wai and Kashi as well!

Tongues began waging indiscriminately about Jytoirao Phule's latest blasphemous act. If his earlier deeds were sinful, the latest one took the cake and the bakery, according to those orthodox men who simply could not stop cursing the sinner. "First, he polluted a pure thing like education; and now, he is trying to give a life of dignity to wanton widows?! Not just that, even his wife is supporting this latest craze of the man?! Has she gone mad? Oh Lord, have mercy on us! God is not giving an offspring to the couple, that is why they have become so desperate that they are ready to take care of the illegitimate children of spoiled widows?! These are sinners of the highest order. They will not get a place even at the bottom of hell! Such nonsense practices will only serve to embolden those wanton, filthy women! You idiots, did God put some good practices into place, only for people like you to trample over them? The practice of Sati was good for this reason only. Such blatant blasphemy would have never dared occurred then."

Humans who had forgotten the basics of humanity were openly cursing humans who were trying to perpetrate humanity in the society. But, Jyotirao was determined to not let any opposition stand in their way.

Two days later, past midnight, somebody knocked on Jyotirao's door. He opened the door to find a heavily pregnant widow standing outside, her face a mixture of fear and hope; her tonsured head casting a pitiable look on her young face; and a prominent burn mark on her forehead. As the door opened, the widow stepped back like a scalded cat, almost as if she was not expecting anybody to answer the door. She went and stood in the dark. Savitribai came forward and affectionately took her inside. Once inside, the widow sprawled on the floor and started crying loudly.

"Who are you, sister?" Savitribai asked, patting the crying woman on her back.

"Please don't ask me that… I won't be able to tell… please don't…" cried the woman, hiding her face with her red widow's garb.

"Alright…it's okay. I will not insist. Don't worry; you are completely safe here. Your name will remain a secret" Savitribai assured her.

"Really?" the widow asked, her eyes filled with tears.

Suddenly, she got up and started running to the door shouting,

"I don't want to kill my child… I don't want to kill it…"

"Savitribai went behind her and said,

"That is what this orphanage is for. Don't worry. You can come here whenever you wish. We will wait for you."

The woman wanted to say a lot more, but she was shaking with fear at the thought of someone seeing her at the Phule household.

"I shall come, Bai. But, you will take care of my baby, won't you? Please?!" she pleaded with Savitribai.

"Yes, sister. I shall look after it like my own child" Savitribai assured her yet again.

Soon, the woman rushed off in the dark. Looking at her retreating figure, Savitribai sighed,

"Poor lady! She will take hardly one more day to deliver."

The next night, the woman knocked on Jyotirao's door again. This time, she was moaning in pain. Her contractions had started. Savitribai took her inside and lovingly patted her back to comfort her.

A few hours later, the woman delivered a son. Savitribai heated up some water to clean her up and then skilfully cut the umbilical cord. Soon, the house reverberated with the cries of that little boy.

Savitribai cleaned up the baby and offered it to his mother. Seeing that, the woman got startled like a deer and began to get up. Seeing her getting up from the bed, Savitribai said,

"Don't get up, please! You are not in that condition...."

But, the woman was adamant. She said,

"No, I'm sorry! I won't be able to stay for a minute more. They will kill me! Just once...please show me my baby just once..."

Savitribai held up the baby towards his mother. She looked at him with tearful eyes and rushed out of the door, into the darkness. A few minutes later, Jyotirao came inside.

"Did you see that woman rushing out?" Savitribai asked him.

"Yes, I did. What a sad condition these poor women live in?! This poor woman mustn't have seen the sunlight for the last so many months. And today, when she has finally delivered her child, she cannot even hold him in her arms. The only silver lining to this dark cloud is that today, we were able to save two lives. Else, this woman would have surely committed suicide. The government abolished Sati for its own gains; but, unless the practice of widow remarriage perpetrates in the society, these problems will not abate" said Jyotirao.

The new-born baby was wailing in hunger for its mother's milk. Jyotirao's heart skipped a beat on seeing him thus. He said to Savitribai,

"Give the child to me."

But Savitribai refused saying,

"I'm yet to give it a bath."

The child was born very weak, owing to the ill-effects of multiple abortive medicines that his mother had taken. Jyotirao's eyes welled up with tears on seeing its condition.

Soon, Savitribai got some warm water to bathe the baby. Together, they both gave him his first bath.

This scenario started repeating itself every few days apart. A few babies would die stillborn, while others would be too weak to survive more than a few hours after birth. Nevertheless, there were also enough babies being born to fill the orphanage up faster than the couple had imagined. They both had turned parents to the many children that were being secretly delivered at their house. The entire day would fall short in caring for so many infants. Thankfully, Shaahir Dhondiram and Dhondiba Rode came forward to help them.

One day, someone knocked on their door late at night. Jyotirao opened the door to see that first widow who had delivered there, standing in their courtyard.

"Come in, please…" said Savitribai.

"My baby….Where is my baby?" the woman asked.

From the five-six infants wrapped up and kept on a blanket, Savitribai expertly lifted up the widow's son and said,

"Here. This is your Shantaram."

"Shantaram? You gave him this name? Oh, what a nice name!" the woman exclaimed, even as she eagerly held her son to her bosom and kissed him all over, tears streaming down her eyes.

Savitribai and Jyotirao kept admiring the beautiful scene from afar. Then, Savitribai asked her,

"You met your baby... heard his name.... but, you still haven't told us your name, sister...?"

The woman again got startled.

"Don't worry; if you are afraid, do not tell us."

"Godi... I'm called Godi..." the woman replied with a stutter.

"Godi? That means, Godavari, is it? Such a beautiful name you have! Why do you address yourself as Godi?" Savitribai asked in mock anger.

Probably, it was many years later that someone was talking so lovingly with Godavari. She burst into tears, and then composing herself after a while, she turned to Savitribai and said,

"When I was a child, my mother used to lovingly call me Godu or Goda. After I got married and then became a widow, I have been spitefully addressed as Godi or Gode!"

Godavari sat staring into space, reminiscing about her difficult life. Suddenly, she said,

"I just wanted to see my baby once. Thanks to you, that wish of mine is fulfilled. I shall never return here again...."

Savitribai asked her,

"Why do you say so, Godabai?"

"What else do I say, Savitribai?" Godavari asked, sobbing aloud. "Why should I live this wretched life?"

"No, Godabai. Please don't think like that. Please stay here with us. We will take care of you too" said Jyotirao, echoing his wife's thoughts.

"Godabai, please think about Shantaram at least...." Savitribai exhorted Godavari.

"This Company Sarkar shall rot in hell!!" Godabai cried out in anguish. "If the practice of Sati had been allowed now, I would have happily jumped into the pyre, instead of being forced to live this cursed, humiliating life. How long do I bear all this? Even cats and dogs must be having more courage than I do. But, I cannot take this anymore. Who is there to support me? How do I live this long life alone? Please....Please do not shackle me in the chains of love, Savitribai. You came into my life as a form of God. You have already done a lot for me. Please, now just become a mother to my Shantaram. That's all that I will request you. How I wish, I had got a mother like you! But of course, I'm hardly that fortunate... " Godabai kept sobbing for a long time. Probably, she had got a chance to free her suppressed emotions and tears after a very long time.

"Godabai, please do not worry about Shantaram. He is ours now. But, do you really wish to leave your dear son and go? See, there are so many children like your Shantaram, over here. They are all starved of a mother's love. Why don't you become a mother for them too, Godabai? Please stay here..." Savitribai said, trying to reason with Godavari.

Savitribai's loving request melted Godavari's heart. It had been ages since somebody had spoken so lovingly with her. Finally, her resolve broke down and she decided to stay over.

Godavari kept talking to Savitribai for a long time after that. She was pouring out her heart before the kind lady. Savitribai could not help but keep looking at the prominent burn mark on Godavari's forehead. Finally, unable to control herself, she asked Godavari,

"Godabai, what is that mark on your forehead?"

In reply, Godavari slapped a hand on her forehead and exhaled,

"Hmmph! This mark?.... I was a child that time... My husband had died, but I simply could not remember that I was not a widow and was not supposed to wear the vermillion powder on my head, as married women do. Finally, a very 'gentle' relative, made sure that I would remember the rules, by branding my forehead!"

Savitribai was shaken to the core on hearing this take of cruelty. She could not imagine, how many such widows were languishing in their dark rooms, getting subjected to cruelty every day of their life?

Godavari was looking at all the children lying on the blanket. One of the babies started twitching its small limbs, crying out for milk. Instinctively, Godavari held it to her chest, and fed the hungry baby.

"Thank God, at least I was not subjected to getting my eyes ruptured or my ears or nose cut off, as a punishment for my husband's death" Godavari said sardonically.

The next day brought a fresh start for Godavari's life. She was no longer going to live as an impure, evil soul. She was going to live as a mother of the children kept in the orphanage. She was going to live as a soul sister to other women, who like her, were subjected to irrational abuse for being widowed.

Tatya was feeling immensely proud of his wife. Without being worried about what the society would say, Savitribai had shown the courage to house Godavaribai. He was so overwhelmed that he felt like asking Savitribai as to where did the reservoir of her immense strength, stem from? But he did not do so; he was too awed by the strength of her character.

However, after all this, Godavari's resolve crumbled mere days later. She could not bear living with the thought of societal criticism. The third day, Godavari left home, never to return. Savitribai and Jyotirao kept waiting for her, but she had vanished in the unknown!

31

News about the stellar work being done in the orphanage, reached up to Mumbai. As a result, many well-wishers such as Tukaram Tatya Padwal, Raobahadur Madan Shrikrishna, and, Mama Parmanand wrote to Jyotirao with letters of encouragement and promises of financial help. In Pune, progressives such as Lokahitawadi and Vishnushastri Pandit came forward with proactive support. Jyotirao again got immersed in the task of keeping accounts of the donations that started flowing in.

Everything was going well; yet, Jyotirao was still not feeling that inner satisfaction. One day, he said to Savitribai,

"Until and unless, widow remarriage gains societal acceptance, this problem will not end in totality. Legal recourse is not the only solution. People need to start accepting the remarriage of widows."

Glancing at the darkness spread outside, Jyotirao proclaimed,

"That day will soon come...just you see, Savitri! Widow remarriage will gain social acceptance, and then, we will no longer need the sort of orphanages that we are running now. These are nothing but a symbol of our society's failure to think progressively."

Savitribai cast a glance at the small children who had been kept in their shelter by their helpless and often, anonymous mothers. Saved from their lives being snuffed out, those small beings were trying their best to lead a life of a human being. She looked at Jyotirao and asked,

"You were going to orchestrate one remarriage, isn't it? What happened about that?"

"Preparations are going on. The progressives have taken a lead..."

"....and, they are waiting for your help, isn't it?! Hmmph! These people call themselves progressives, and what do they do? Very cleverly, they only talk more and do little. They do not do anything that will spoil their image or peace of mind" roared Savitribai.

Jyotirao was amused to see his usually diminutive wife, take such a fierce stance. He said,

"Oh, Savitribai...So now, even you have started berating the progressives, is it? See, I agree with what you are saying; but, for now, whatever little they are doing, is also more than enough to forward these difficult causes. It is indeed helpful to have people like Vishnushastri Pandit doing so much to support the cause. Anyways...Savitribai. I have one more plan for after this remarriage ceremony happens. We should meet with the barber community and dissuade them from taking up tonsuring of widows."

"Vishnushastri won't come along for that work...I hope you realize that.." replied Savitribai.

"I don't even expect his help for that work!" replied Jyotirao, as he looked at his wife and smiled saying, "This work will have to be done travelling, not just across Pune, but even in neighboring towns and villages. And, for that, I will require, not Vishnushastri's, but Savitribai Phule's help."

"I'm always with you...." replied Savitribai, as she drifted off to sleep.

In the morning, Jyotirao and Dhondiram Shaahir were sitting in the verandah. Savitribai was busy in tending to the children. Jyotirao was poring over the account books. The servants had to be paid; grocery had to be purchased for the house. Just then, Dhondiram called out,

"Tatyasaab, Sakharampant has come."

"Oh, come , come Sakharam...Good to see you after a long time" said Jyotirao, looking up from the account books to welcome his friend.

As Sakharampant climbed up the stairs to Jyotirao's house, his face was clouded over with the guilt of not having met his old friend for so many weeks.

"I heard about your latest work. So, I thought of coming and meeting you" said Sakharampant.

Jyotirao was well aware of Sakharampant's nature. He would talk straight and to-the-point. Jyotirao appreciated this quality in Sakharampant, as well as, Moropant. Both these friends would not hesitate to air their views with candour, but, without letting any disagreements affect their relationship. However, Sadashivrao was exactly the opposite. He would let his thoughts fester in mind for long and then one day, would vent it out so acerbically, that the relationship would get marred. Himself a frank person when it came to airing his views, Jyotirao could communicate better with Sakharampant and Moropant.

Breaking his train of thoughts, Jyotirao glanced at his dear friend, who was standing in front of him like a stranger for now.

"Truly, Jyoti... You have done, what no Brahmin progressive dared to do" said Sakharampant.

"One important news, Sakharam... Soon, there will be a widow remarriage taking place. If required, we will need to go there" said Jyotirao.

"I have been hearing snippets about this remarriage. But, were exactly will it be happening?"

"The venue and time is yet to be decided; and everything is going to be kept under utmost secrecy. Very soon, a 'Punarvivaahuttejak Samiti' is going to be formed. This remarriage will be happening under their aegis itself.

"I hope, this is not like that Raghoba Janardan's episode..." Sakharampant commented sarcastically.

Jyotirao's face became serious as he looked at his friend pointedly, and replied,

"No. If it was anything like that, I would have never come ahead to support this remarriage; nor would have told you to help us. It is an extremely shameful thing that an educated member of the society felt no compunction in marrying another woman, on the pretext that she was a widow, in spite of having a wife at home. Anyways, there was another thing that I wanted to discuss with you. A lake is being built at Khadakwasla. I'm trying to get the contract for the stones that will be required for the construction. If you become a partner with me..."

"Yes, sure. Why not? I'm also in search of some good work" replied Sakharampant, taking on the responsibility of chipping in with some funds and also helping to complete the paperwork.

Sakharampant had come to visit Jyotirao with a vexed mind; but, he returned with a new ray of hope.

Savitribai was talking to someone from within the house. Excusing himself from Sakharam's company, Jyotirao went within to see what the matter was.

A message had come from Jyotirao's home; Dada's health had deteriorated badly. He had called Jyotirao and Savitribai to meet him. Sadubhau had also come down with his family, from Naigaon.

An old lady was helping out Savitribai. From her attire, she seemed to be a widow.

"Who is this lady?" Jyotirao asked Savitribai.

"She is Gangamai. She is alone. She does have relatives, but no one is ready to look after her. She is also not getting any work as a domestic servant to support herself. Thus, I have told her to stay here with us henceforth."

Jyotirao was happy with Savitribai's decision. He asked after Gangamai's health etc, and agreed to pay her 2 aanas more than what she would have got at some other house. Gangamai was very happy with this pronouncement, and started working with more vigor.

Dada's health had taken a turn for the worse, a long time back. But now that Jyoti had taken on the onus of helping widows, he had become even more ill than usual. Jyoti would go to meet Dada once in a while – sometimes on his own, and sometimes when Dada would send a message for him.

For quite some time now, Dada had only one relentless demand from Jyoti: he wanted a grandchild at the earliest! He wanted to say something different in that regard, but so far, he had not been able to say it openly. Dada's nature was such that, he would take some time to accept newer ideas, but then even after accepting them, he would finally bow down before convention.

The last few days had been very busy for Jyotirao; hence, he had not been able to meet Dada. Dada had also not sent any message for him. Hence, when Jyotirao got the message that Dada had called to meet him and even Sadubhau had been summoned, he could not help but feel that this meeting was going to take on a different hue.

Savitribai and Jyotirao reached home in the evening. The little Tukaram was playing in the courtyard. Savitribai lovingly lifted him up, even as Jyotirao held up some candy before him. After playing with Tukaram for some time, they both went inside.

Everyone was waiting for them. Sadubhau was sitting near Dada's cot. Jyotirao folded his hands before everyone, even as Savitribai bowed down in respect before Dada and Sadubau and went inside.

So many turbulences in the interim period had fortunately not affected the blood ties between these people.

Dada's gaunt face was looking even more weak due to the spikes of beard that had grown on it. A strange tension was being seen on everyone's faces.

Tukaram came toddling inside. Jyotirao took him close and started talking to everyone. He noticed that Rajarambhau was giving curt answers. At one point, Sadubhau made a pointed comment:

"Tatyasaheb, a hungry stomach demands bread. That time, it isn't enough to tie a piece of bread to one's stomach and convince oneself to be full."

Jyotirao's face creased into a frown on hearing this comment.

"Sadubhau, do you feel, we do this work only because we do not have children of our own?" Jyotirao asked.

"No, not entirely like that....but, do think of Dada's wishes too, won't you?" Sadubhau ventured.

"Oh, so you also feel the same way, is it?"

"Tatyasaheb, everyone feels the need to have someone to carry his lineage forward. What is wrong in that? It is not at all a good thing to die childless! Thus, if you decide to remarry in accordance with Dada's wishes, then we will not have any objection... that's all I want to say..." averred Sadubhau.

"Well, you may not have any objection, but I do!" replied Jyotirao.

"How's that?" asked a befuddled Sadubhau.

The topic that Jyotirao had desisted from addressing so far, had now come onto an open forum. He decided to tackle it once and for all.

"Sadubhau, if a couple is not bearing children, then how come the fault always lies with the woman? Why should we always blame the woman? Isn't that unjust? Can we not ponder on the fact that sometimes, the fault might be lying in her husband?"

Everyone was stunned to hear what Jyotirao had said. They could not fathom how a man could be sterile. Jyotirao continued,

"...And, as for a remarriage.... if the wife of a sterile man proclaims that she wishes to marry another man to become a mother, how will that man feel? Will he be too happy about it? Obviously not. Then, should a man not think of his wife's feelings while deciding to remarry?"

"A woman thinking of remarriage when her husband is alive?! What nonsense! How is that even possible?" exclaimed Sadubhau.

Jyotirao replied calmly,

"Why not? The same reason that gives a man to remarry while his wife is alive, should be reason enough for the wife to remarry when her husband is alive, isn't it?"

Sadubhau was very irked with the way Jyotirao was behaving. He had come all the way from Naigaon, only at Dada's behest, so that they could convince Jyoti to take on another wife for procreation. But, Jyotirao was playing another tune altogether. Nevertheless, Sadubhau realized that this topic was a very delicate one; it would not do to have a war of words. He ventured,

"Tatyasaheb, we are proposing this only in view of Dada's deteriorating health. Savitri is my sister. Do you think I will feel happy if she gets a co-wife?"

"Sadubhau, you are placing the blame for our childlessness

squarely on Savitri's shoulders. But I feel that, remarrying simply because your wife cannot give you children, is a very inhuman and disgusting practice. No thought is given to a woman's emotions. As for me, I cannot even think of remarrying" Jyotirao declared, cutting the topic once and for all.

There was nothing more left to say. Sadubhau kept quiet, smarting from Jyotirao's harsh words.

Everyone had a quiet dinner, following which, Jyotirao took leave with a silent Savitribai in tow.

32

The sun was shining bright. Sweat was dripping down the body. Work was going on in earnest. Carts were coming from the mining site to the construction site, emptying their contents, and immediately returning for bringing in more stuff. Jyotirao was personally supervising the work, even lending a helping hand wherever necessary. There was still time for the construction of the dam to begin. Preparations were underswing. Many more stones were required before the work could begin.

The last five-six days had been specially hectic. Gyaanoba Sasane had stationed himself in Pune. He would come to the mine early in the morning. As soon as the bullock carts would arrive, the work of bringing in material would start off. Jyotirao would join in soon after.

Sometimes, the British officers would come by to supervise the work.

One day, as a couple of bullock carts were going up and down the hillock, Jyotirao could see a man come running towards him. He squinted against the sun to see that it was Sitaram.

As he came near, Jyotirao wiped his face with a hand towel and asked,

"What happened, Sitaram?"

"Tukaramtatya has come from Mumbai…" Sitaram replied.

"Tukaramtatya? When?"

"In the morning… after you came here…"

Tukaramtatya was the father of 'Jaatibhed Vivek Saar' and a generous patron of the orphanage.

The remarriage of Nana Bhide had not taken long to spread to Mumbai. While the ceremony was originally planned to take place in Pune, the venue was shifted to Mumbai at the last minute, knowing that the orthodox group would create a ruckus if they got a whiff of what was happening. Nana Bhide had gotten remarried to the widowed sister of his dead wife. Vishnushastri Pandit had done the kanyadaan . Tatya was aware of the efforts taken by Jyotirao, Vishnushastri and Balwantrao Gopardikar for this widow remarriage. Tatya had written to Jyotirao about wanting to meet him personally on the backdrop of this courageous act.

Jyotirao sent a message for Gyaanoba to replace him for some time, as he went to meet Tatya. As Gyaanoba arrived, Jyotirao said to him,

"Gyaanoba, Tukaramtatya Padwal has come from Mumbai. I need to go to meet him. Will you stay here for some time, please?"

"Yes, tatyasaab…Don't worry, Sakharampant will also be arriving soon."

Jyotirao tied his turban and started walking. Gyaanoba called out to him….

"Tatyasaab…"

Yes, what is it Gyaanoba?"

"Take the bullock cart along…"

"No, no…I shall walk. You will need the cart for work."

"Then at least, have some food and leave…" Gyaanoba persisted.

"No, we shall eat at home now" Jyotirao smiled as he gestured to Sitaram to walk along.

Jyotirao reached home to find Tukaramtatya waiting for him eagerly. The details of Jyotirao's thoughts, work and courage had long reached him. Hence, he was eager to meet the man in person.

An important fixture of Mumbai's social scene, Tatya was also one of the foremost members of the Paramhans Sabha. In recent times, the Paramhans Sabha was dissolving to give way to a new Prarthana Samaj. Tatya was involved in the formation of this new organization as well. Additionally, he also ran a clinic in Mumbai.

From afar, Tatya could see a smart young man walking towards him, dressed in a dhoti, jacket and red turban. His fair-complexioned face bore the maturity that comes with immense reading.

The seriousness and resolve on the young man's face was enough to tell Tatya that this was the famed Jyotirao. He required no other introduction.

The two gentlemen met like long-lost friends. Jyotirao asked after Vasudeo Babaji. A great misfortune had befallen Babaji. His business had become bankrupt, but he was not going to return from abroad unless he paid all his creditors. It was Vasudeo Babaji who had published Tukaramtatya's book. The two men were discussing various matters, but Jyotirao's attention was diverted by some commotion from inside the house. The little girl Lakshmi, was crying incessantly.

"Are there any copies of your book that still remain?" Jyotirao asked Tatya.

"No, I'm sorry. I need to go for a reprint."

"Please do so; and, do send some copies to us... please excuse me for a moment" said Jyotirao, unable to halt any longer. The topic was cut down there itself.

Jyotirao went inside to find Savitribai taking care of all the babies. Lakshmi was lying on her lap, crying loudly. This newest addition to their family had stolen Jyotirao's heart. Two months back, as Jyotirao had come into the courtyard in the morning, he had found this infant lying their in a makeshift crib that the couple had set up near their door. The fair-skinned cute baby was named Lakshmi, in remembrance of Savitribai's mother. The couple had gotten specially fond of this baby girl, but Jyotirao was always afraid that Lakshmi would soon leave them and go away, because she would be constantly ill due to the ill-effects of the abortive medicines that her mother had taken during pregnancy.

Most of the children who would come to Jyotirao's orphanage, would be in more or less the same condition. The couple had to really strive to make them live.

Gangamai was making preparations for lunch. Gangamai would do all other housework, but for some unknown reason, she would desist from touching any of the children.

Jyotirao carried the crying Lakshmi outside, where Tatya was waiting for him. As Jyotirao cradled her, Lakshmi stopped crying and started looking around with her button-eyes.

Tukaramtatya asked Jyotirao,

"Have you established a committee or formal organization for this orphanage that you are running?"

"No" replied Jyotirao, adding, "and I don't plan to do so in the future too. I do not want an encore of what happened in the committees established for running our schools. People who cannot see the grief that their sisters, who became child-widows, are going through, will be of no help to this cause. The world is changing rapidly. In the States, Abraham Lincoln has abolished slavery and laid the foundation of a country that will run on the platform of equality. But over here, we are still stuck in the Dark Ages. The so-called patriotic Brahmins are still grieving over the end of Peshwai, which was nothing but a legitimate form of slavery. Not just that, they are still dreaming about bringing back the Peshwai! Who needs such an unjust and cruel governance?!"

"Do you feel the same about the revolt in the North?" asked Tukaramtatya.

"Tatyasaheb, if Nana Peshwe's revolt had become successful, it would have again brought back the same unjust Peshwai to the fore. The seeds of hope that have been sown for the progress of Shoodras and Ati-Shoodras in the British regime, would have been crushed to death. The British are not going to be here permanently. The main question is, when will our social slavery end? My friends got agitated when I poked fun at Nana Peshwa's revolt. But, you tell me…a revolt that begins on the excuse of a few cartridges, can it really be called an uprising?! The neighboring princes supported that revolt for their own selfish gains; not for the country. What do they want? Privy purses worth lakhs of rupees, legitimacy for adopted children, and what not… And what do they want all this for? To oppress the subjects yet again! I care two hoots for this farce. I don't care who says what about me, but I refuse to kowtow to this drama. I feel very sad about the fact that our society cannot see trough this farce."

Jyotirao was speaking as if some volcano had erupted from his heart! All the thoughts that had gathered in his mind over the years, were coming out like hot molten lava…

"….. Those people who treat us worse than animals and then have no compunction in licking the shoes of the British, how can they be our brethren?! If they and their ancestors knew what self-respect and true patriotism was all about, they would have been the first to oppose the subjugation that perpetrated in our society on the name of religion. Those hypocrites find it great to drink the urine of an animal, but get polluted on drinking clean water at the hands of a Shoodra. Manipulation flows in their veins along with blood; they can go to any extent to fulfil their gains. They go to lick the boots of the British, and when we go to them to ask for justice and education, they call us traitors! A mere few years of political bondage has become heavy for them to take; then, why can't they think about the centuries of social bondage that have been heaped upon us? Do they think, what pain must we have gone through all these years? Who gave the Maratha empire in the hands of British? This, Raghobharari! They were the ones who got the British to Talegaon. They played all sorts of games to make beggars out of the Mali and Kunbi community members. And now, when the British have started getting big for their boots, now these deceitful people are advocating the power of unity, is it?! Now they want our help… they want us to become cannon fodder against the British. That is why, they are advocating the benefits of patriotism and unity. But, who can trust them any more? These are utterly selfish people. Once their work is done, they will not even turn to glance once at us. If they really believe in the shenanigans of unity that they are blowing right now, they should give up the evil Brahmin religion; abolish all social and communal segregations; and behave equally with everyone. That will lead to real equality, which will lead to the progress of the nation. It is only when we all forget the hierarchical segregations amidst us, that we will be able to get rid of the problems plaguing us. But these people are two-faced; they say one thing, and do another."

Lakshmi had gone off to sleep. Jyotirao placed her in the crib and came back. Tukaramtatya said to him,

"You are right. The root cause of all our social evils and pain, is casteism. Actually, the wise seers and mendicants have never advocated casteist segregations. So, the Brahmins claim that these differences stem from religious teachings, is untrue to say the least."

Jyotirao replied,

"I do not trust those religious tenets propounded by the Brahmins, even one bit! All their thoughts, words and actions have been in keeping their importance as Brahmins at the core. But sadly, people have been too much brainwashed to realize the folly of the Brahmins. They need to realize that casteism is evil; it does nothing but regress the society bit by bit. That is why, we require more books like 'Jaatibhed Vivek Saar' to be written. If the earlier copies have been sold out, more copies need to be printed. The saints in the Warkari panth may have done a lot of social good; saints like Tukaram also did a lot to educate ignorant people through his simplistic writings. However, almost none of these saints did anything to free the lower castes from the bondages of social slavery. Instead, many of these saints actually saw merit in the caste system. Thus, I have no belief in the tenets of the Warkari panth. Tatyasaheb, the British regime may have freed us from the physical slavery of the Brahmins, but we are still not mentally free from those chains. The only way to achieve this freedom, is education and awakening. Times are changing rapidly; and, a society's laws must change in accordance with time. It is high time we threw away the biased scriptures like Manusmriti and draft new laws based on present social conditions."

Tukaramtatya was not too happy to hear Jyotirao's views on the Warkari panth; he was a believer of the same. However, he did agree to the other rational and fearlessly expressed views of the young man. Thinking over Jyotirao's words, tatya said,

"I need to get more copies of my book printed; but, I do not know when Vasudeo Babaji will return. Hence, if possible, you only print more copies of the book. No one else, apart from you, shall dare to do this work."

Jyotirao gave an instant assent to Tukaramtatya's suggestion, and took on the entire responsibility of publishing more copies of his book. Looking at the immense work that Tukaramtatya had done for the upliftment of the followers of Hindu religion, no one would have imagines that long in the past, tatya had been besotted with the ideas of Christianity!

The next day, Tukaramtatya left for Mumbai, and soon after, Jyotirao started making arrangements to get his book printed.

Published under the title of 'Ek Hindu', the book reached every house in Pune, simply because it was published by Jyotirao. The book held Brahmins responsible for the casteism that had become rampant in the society. It alleged that taking undue advantage of their education, the Brahmins had tampered with the original religious scriptures and inserted tenets that would maintain their status at the apex of society. The author had substantiated his argument with many references from the original Sanskrit scriptures, that he claimed were tampered with by the Brahmins. The sole aim of the book was to let the common man know, why and how were they being bound in social slavery and thus free themselves from the same. Even if one reader would take the book's message in the spirit that it was intended with, it was going to be a huge victory for the author. The name of the author was kept in secrecy; he/she was going to announce one's name if he/she felt that the name would contribute to the success of the book. The epilogue of the book stated that:

'The religious and casteist difference being practiced in the society, have no firm affirmation in the scriptures. These segregations show no overt benefit to the society; instead, it only leads to material and spiritual loss for the society as a whole. Wise saints and philosophers have also always condemned such differentiations among human beings. They have always said that such divisive practices deteriorate the societal fabric. Why then, must we human beings remain ignorant and slavish to such vile practices propagated falsely in the name of religion?'

Looking at the content of the book, it was conveniently assumed that it had been written by Jyotirao only. Yet again, the winds of scandal enveloped Jyotirao in its midst. Temples and the homes of religious men saw aggressive meetings happening for many days to come. Demands were made that, the author of this scathing critique on the great Hindu religion, be declared a religious traitor!

In reality, Jyotirao had not at all liked the fact that Tukaramtatya refused to disclose his name as the author of the book. The work of Paramhans Sabha would also be carried out in such secrecy itself. The Paramhans Sabha worked on the principles of 'one God', and, fraternization. It worked towards progressive goals such as abolishment of casteist differences, widow remarriage, abolition of child marriage and so on. However, when the names of the members of that organisation came into the open, much running and hiding had ensued! Seeing stalwarts like Dadoba Pandurang, Ram Balkrishna Jaykar and his friends like Moropant and Keshavrao adopt this secretive stance, had put Jyotirao off the organization.

He was of the firm view that casteism required to be tackled headlong; not in secrecy or covertly.

Nevertheless, it was not a small thing that tatya's book was going to expose the cunning of the Brahmins. That is the prime reason why Jyotirao had agreed to publish the book.

Newspapers were spilling over with aggressive reviews about the book. But, the dart had hit its target. Brahmins were hopping mad about the contents of the book. Jyotirao was in for more trouble.

33

Jyotirao was supervising the working at the dam. 300-400 workers were toiling in the sun. The dam was now being built. 100-150 workers were toiling at the actual site as well. Everything was going on as per typical government attitude. The supervising British officers were busy in parties and hunts. Contractors were adulterating the cement. Clerks were rigging the signatures to show more attendance than there was, to pocket extra money.

Jyotirao was working equally hard along with the workers. As the stones were being ferried around, a few stones would slip and hurtle away. Jyotirao kept running around, gathering those errant stones and taking them upwards.

For a long time, a young man was observing Jyotirao from a distance. Jyotirao called out to him and asked his whereabouts.

"I'm Piraji, from Bhamburde. I was working at the lake till

yesterday...but, the contractor gave me the boot..."

"Oh! Why so?" Jyotirao asked him.

"I attended the lecture that you were giving all the workers in the afternoon. The clerk did not like that...he told the contractor..."

"Ohh, that means my lecture cost you your job..." said Jyotirao expressing sadness at what had happened. "No problem, come join our work.."

"Okay Tatyasaab!" exclaimed Piraji, as he started working with Jyotirao. Then, as an afterthought he added, "But, Tatyasaab, I have not got any food with me today. I had only come to meet you."

"Don't worry about that. We have brought enough food. You will not go hungry."

Piraji was embarrassed on hearing Jyotirao's reply. He started working. As Jyotirao started talking to him, it turned out that Piraji was Pandurang tatya's neighbor. Jyotirao asked about tatya's health. Piraji replied,

"He has growing old now. His health is also not that good."

Pandurang tatya of Bhamburde was a distant relative of Jyotirao's. Jyotirao remembered seeing tatya at his home in Bhamburde. A devour Warkari, tatya would never miss the annual pilgrimage to Pandharpur. He would give wonderful discourses, and was specially skilled in interpreting the Dynaneshwari . He had also prepared a dictionary explaining the difficult terms of the Dynaneshwari. Jyotirao was attracted to Saint Tukaram's teachings due to Pandurang tatya itself. Tatya was working as a worker on the government's payroll, in Bhamburde.

Dr. Mitchell was also a great proponent of Saint Tukaram's teachings. He found Saint Tukaram more relatable than the others because he would speak to the people in a language they would understand. Dr. Mitchell had also translated a few abhangs of Saint Tukaram into English. However, Jyotirao and Dr. Mitchell disagreed on the topic of saints and their work because according to Jyotirao, the saints had not done much to abolish the social slavery of the Shoodras and Ati Shoodras.

Every time Jyotirao would read Saint Tukaram's works, he would get reminded of his discussion with Tukaramtatya. Even though Jyotirao had published tatya's book, he was not totally convinced with the latter's stance. Apart from a few saints like Tukaram, none of the others had done much to erase the caste differences in the society. Rather, saints like Ramdas had actually accorded merit to the caste system. He had not given a single thought to the betterment of Shoodras; rather, he advocated denying them education and equal status.

That afternoon, everyone sat together for lunch. Jyotirao introduced Piraji and asked him to share their lunch. He also told Piraji to convey his regards to Pandurang tatya.

The contract work had considerably eased out Jyotirao's financial worries. A new bridge was going to be built at Yerawada. Jyotirao was thinking of bidding for the contract of supplying limestone for this work.

Even though Jyotirao would be physically present at the constructions sites for most of the day, his heart would be engaged at home, thinking of Savitri. Lately, Savitribai had been alone at home, since Gangamai had gone to her village at the behest of some relative. Sitaram was there, but Savitribai had to do everything for the children on her own.

That evening as Jyotirao reached home, he first went to check on the children. He took Lakshmi in his arms and glanced lovingly at Shantaram who was sleeping soundly on his bed. He called out to Savitribai. As she came outside, Jyotirao asked her,

"Has Gangamai not returned? It has been fifteen days since she went..."

"She won't be coming back. That man had come to take her, so that she would not work here..." Savitribai said.

Jyotirao had this niggling doubt ever since Gangamai had

left abruptly. No wonder, that relative had suddenly developed concern for Gangamai and come all the way to take her. The Brahmin women in the city would taunt Gangamai constantly; the men would curse her. That is why, she would rarely dare to venture out of the house. She was left wanting for nothing in Jyotirao and Savitribai's house. They both would treat her like a mother. She would also get paid 2 aanas more than the market rate. Hence, Jyotirao was understandably agitated at Gangamai's abrupt departure.

"This is definitely the doing of those useless, idle Brahmins roaming around here! They could not see the dignity of labor; they could only see that a Brahmin woman was washing utensils and clothes at a Shoodras house. These evil people will not let a widow live in peace!!" he bellowed.

"It's okay, let it be..." Savitribai tried pacifying Jyotirao.

Jyotirao kept quiet, but the incident did not get erased from his mind so easily. He vented his angst through a starkly risqué and critical powada . Jyotirao would often write such powadas, that Dhondiram Shaahir would then sing in his robust voice. The powadas were specially popular among the workers at the construction site, who would understand how Brahmins were misleading them under the name of religion. The sarcastic and humorous way in which Jyotirao would elucidate about how Kulkarni appa was pandering to the Brahmin officials and cheating the farmers; or, how religion was used as a weapon to subjugate ignorant low caste people, had become so popular with the masses, that they wanted Jyotirao to publish a book of his powadas. Finally, Jyotirao relented and the book was published.

After Gangamai's exit, Savitribai had to shoulder the entire responsibility of the orphanage.

One day, Pune was grasped by a deadly epidemic. The children started falling violently ill, and Tatya and Kaku had a tough time caring for so many sick children together. Sadly enough, not many of them survived the epidemic. Born weak, they succumbed one by one to the life-wrangling fever that they contracted. Tatya and Kaku were heartbroken to see their children leave tem one by one. Their dear Shantaram was also among them!

34

The clock announced the arrival of dawn. Jyotirao woke up, finished his ablutions, fed his horse and set off for his daily walk. This was the only exercise regime that Jyotirao could now follow, after having left the akhaada all those years back. The last few years had been so hectic that his morning walk had also been discontinued. But now, after he bought horse to travel to & fro the construction sites, he had revived the morning walk, to ensure at least some exercise for the body.

The streets were empty. Jyotirao was walking, his stick tapping on the road in tune with his feet. Jyotirao came to the temple of Lord Devdeveshwar and sat on the steps. Dawn was yet to break properly. Tatya liked sitting on these steps and see the sun rising on the horizon, washing away the darkness of the night as it came up. The gold-plated pinnacle of the temple would start shining as the first rays of the sun would fall on it. Then, the entire atmosphere would get bathed in light, making the surrounding houses and the St. Mary Church Tower properly visible.

The sunrays would also bring into visibility, the surrounding pieces of farms and the small roads leading to the neighboring villages like Khadki, Wanowrie, Yeravade and Bhamburde. Bhamburde was a small village hidden in the forests beyond the river...

That day, as Tatya sat on the steps as usual, he could sense some movement in the bushes near the temple. He squinted in the dark to see some person standing near the bushes. Tatya knew that many people from neighboring villages, wanting to try their luck in Pune, would come and rest their worn off bodies in the temple premises. Tatya called out to the person, asking,

"Who is it?"

"It's me... Hari Raoji Shinde..." came the voice of a barely 16-year old young boy.

Tatya was surprised to see such a young boy waiting outside the temple. He went closer and found that the boy was shivering in his tattered clothes. His physique was proof enough that the boy was accustomed to physical labor and had bore a lot of toil from a very young age.

"From where have you come, son?" Tatya asked affectionately.

"From Konkan...Chiplun..." the boy stammered.

"Chiplun? That far? Why so? What brings you here?" Tatya asked.

But Hari did not answer. His silence told Tatya that there was more to Hari's story than he was willing to tell. Tatya prodded him saying,

"Tell me, son. What brings you so far?"

Jyotirao's loving demeanor boosted the boy's confidence and he told him about his journey.

Hari hailed from Chiplun. His father's name was Raoji. He had been orphaned at a very tender age. From then on, he had been constantly travelling in search of work and food. He had been educated barely enough to read and write the basics. Till recently, he was at Thane and from there, he had come to Pune a day or two back.

Jyotirao said to Hari,

"Hari, today you come along with me to my house. If you wish to study further, do that. If you want employment, I will try to help you for that too."

Just then, the bells of the temple began chiming. The sun had risen; darkness had given way to light!

Jyotirao and Hari started climbing down the steps of Parvati. Jyotirao kept thinking about where he could seek employment for the boy. Bholageer Maharaj was looking for some helped for his shop. Probably, Hari would be good for the job...

Tatya reached home with Hari in tow. Savitribai welcomed Hari affectionately. They both had their baths and then sat down to a frugal breakfast of milk and stale bhaakri. Tatya would love eating stale bhaakri with milk; Savitribai would always make two extra bhaakris the previous night, for Tatya to have it in the morning.

Tatya crumbled the bhaakri and pored milk over it. Hari emulated him. Both began eating. Realizing that the boy must not have had food the previous night, Tatya quietly placed one quarter of his bhaakri in Hari's plate. Hari got awkward, but he took the bhaakri wordlessly and kept eating.

Today, Jyotirao had to go to Bhamburde for Pandurang tatya's funeral. Piraji had conveyed the sad news yesterday itself. Jyotirao felt bad that he could not see tatya for one last time before his demise.

After breakfast, Jyotirao set off on his horse and reached Bhamburde in no time. People started gathering as word spread that Jyotirao had come. Jyotirao paid his condolences to the family members, including tatya's old father Bhausaheb. Everyone insisted Jyotirao to speak a few words about tatya. Jyotirao spoke about how Pandurang tatya was the epitome of goodness in a human being.

On reaching home, Jyotirao went and met Bholageer Maharaj to put in a word for Hari. Bholageer was very happy to get a decent young man like Hari to work in his shop. He immediately employed Hari. From now on, Hari was going to be known not as Hari Raoji Shinde, but as Hari Raoji Chiplunkar.

35

Yet again, the orthodox group was up in arms. The reason was Jyotirao's friend Vishnushastri Pandit. Vishnushastri had taken up the cause of widows very seriously, and was doing everything in his capacity to accord them a better life. He had even resigned from his government job and had established the 'Punarvivaahuttejak Mandali' in Mumbai with Mama Parmanand's help. Vishnushastri would also edit a journal called 'Induprakash'; the journal started expressing candid thoughts on the need for widow remarriage. The organization was doing proactive work to forward its cause. Vishnushastri had gotten a Brahmin widower named Pandurang Vinayak Karmarkar, married to a widow named Venubai. Vishnushastri himself had given Venubai away as a daughter. The earlier remarriage of Nana Bhide had been done covertly; but, Karmarkar's remarriage was deliberately done openly and with much fervor, to prove that the Mandali had nothing to be ashamed of. Renowned guests like Dr. Bhau Daji Lad and Prof. Ramkrishna Bhandarkar attended Karmarkar's wedding. The invitation card to this courageous remarriage was signed by seven eminent progressives including, Justice Ranade, Raobahadur Gopal Hari, Vishnushastri Pandit and Shrikrishnashastri Talekar. Interestingly, the invitation card also came with a questionnaire attached. Jyotirao had been thrilled to see the card.

The marriage ceremony took place in Mumbai in the bungalow of Justice Moroba Kanhoba. But, barely had the ceremony finished when, the orthodox group turned aggressively up in arms.

A huge chaos ensued as curses were openly flung on the blasphemous people who had dared to take such a blasphemous step so openly! Religious scriptures were brought out to prove what a grave sin had been committed! This blatant attack on the purity of religion was not going to be tolerated easily, they warned! Once again, the verbal-happy progressives were caught in a bind. It was a testing time for them. Time would tell who buckled under the pressure and who stood to match their actions to their words...

At this time, Jyotirao was busy with the orphanage. The epidemic had passed and only five children had survived. Tatya resumed his work with renewed vigor. Moropant had suggested that they build a separate structure for the orphanage. Jyotirao had been able to save some money. He felt, it would be best used for this noble work.

One evening as Tatya came back from work, he found Sitaram waiting on the steps for him. The children were playing in the courtyard.

"Tatyasaab, kaku has gone home. Bhau had come to call her..." Sitaram conveyed the message.

Tatya immediately set out for his house. The last one month had seen Dada's health deteriorating very badly. The illness had eaten up his insides. Jyotirao would go every other day to meet Dada...feed him medicines... Dada had still not given up hope. He would keep conveying his thoughts through his eyes, but Jyotirao could not agree to his wishes.

As Jyotirao reached home, he saw Vahini preparing some medicine. Everyone else had gathered around Dada's cot.

Dada looked at Jyotirao with hopeful eyes and then again shut them. Jyotirao came and sat besides Dada.

Dada was muttering something. Jyotirao strained to hear:

"Rajaram... The British government honored my son for his work, and I did not even have the grace to attend the occasion. Had I been witness to that event, I would have been able to die a content death. Oh God, what was the big fear that kept me away from my son all these years?!" said Dada, tears streaming down his gaunt cheeks.

"Shhh... Dada..." Jyotirao said, trying to stop him. But Dada was determined to speak his heart out today.

"Tatya... At least now do not stay far from us all. Come home... Both of you brothers..." Dada started wheezing and coughing with the effort of talking even these few words. His words got swallowed in the bout of violent coughing.

Jyotirao looked at Savitribai. His face was glowing with contentment at Dada's words. Even Dada seemed at peace after having unburdened himself of what he wanted to say all these years.

Dada kept shedding silent tears; he had forgiven his Jyoti for everything.

Jyotirao also could not help crying at the memory of all the toil that Dada had done, all the torture he had bore for Jyoti's sake. Dada had been an innocent man who would easily trust anything that anyone said to him. Even Krishnakaka's nature was the same. The elder brother Ranoji had snatched away all the land that they had inherited from Zagde grandfather and what had been received from the Peshwas as a gift. That time too, these brothers had been left wringing their hands, because they came to know of the fraud only after the land was taken away from under their noses. A lot of arguments, fights and litigations had followed; but they got nothing. From then on, the family got divided. The two warring parties refused to see each others faces. They would not visit each other even on festive occasions or during a death in the family. In such a scenario, Dada hoped that at least they two brothers should stay together till the end.

Two days passed, and then one night, Dada left the mortal world.

Jyotirao sidestepped all the typical Brahmin rituals while conducting Dada's last rites. He burned away archaic rites along with lighting his father's pyre. The huge amount of food that would otherwise go to idle Brahmins, was distributed among the orphans and physically disabled. The money that would otherwise have been spent on mindless rituals, was used to purchase stationary and books for the schools.

Both the brothers got an equal share in Dada's property. Jyotirao got the house that Dada stayed in, whereas

Rajarambhau got the neighboring one-storied house. Dada had kept Rs. 5000 and two houses in Shukrawar Peth and Kasba Peth for Chimna Aai. Both the sons were not ready to let their mother stay alone; but, they could not do much against Dada's wishes. Jyotirao was pained to realize that Dada did not trust both his sons to take care of their mother after his death. Chimna Aai went to stay in the house at Kasba Peth.

It was almost after 17 years that Jyotirao came back to live at his original house. Both the brothers started living together in harmony. Jyotirao loved this house of his with its big living room, verandah, inner quarters, kitchen and a well. The house was large enough to hold the orphanage. The kitchen was a big one, with a large courtyard in front of it. Jyotirao decided to build the orphanage there itself. The back-door of the house was close to that part, and the walls of the well were high enough to ensure no one feel into the water. Thus, the location was ideal from all points.

The north-facing house held a banyan and peepul tree in its courtyard. There was also a small temple devoted to Lord Markandeshwar. The children would get ample place and shade to play around.

Jyotirao converted one of the inner rooms into a small library for him and Savitribai. He had an impressive collection of books of various topics. His friends and family members had open access to the library at all times.

Tatya also arranged a desk for himself in the same space. The temple in that room, along with its idols, were sent to Rajarambhau's house. Tatya only kept one impression of Lord Jotiba of Ratnagiri with himself. Lord Jotiba… the Kshatriya king… the God of Shoodras and Ati-Shoodras…

While shifting from his house in Meethganj Peth, Tatya met all the people with whom they had formed such fond realtions. Lahuji Buva, Raanba, Dhondiba Rode and many more… Even though Tatya was shifting house, these relations were never going to end. Nevertheless, Tatya felt sad that he would not be meeting these people every day.

Tatya was earning nicely through the contracting business. From there, he branched into a business of selling raw materials required for construction. After the contractual work ended, Tatya gave a feats to all laborers. When Gyaanoba sat down to account for the expenses incurred in the feast, Tatya stopped him saying,

"Gyaanoba, the sin we would have taken on our head by feeding one Brahmin, is erased by feeding these hard-working laborers. That's the only accounting that matters."

The feast was scrumptious – tempered daal, rice, onion and bhaakri. It was after a long time that the Phule Wada was seeing such a celebration.

To augment his income further, Tatya took on an agency of moldings. Vasudeo Babaji had cleared all his debts and returned to Pune. He had brought along the sole agency of moldings. That time, one could not get good quality mouldings in Pune. Tatya wrote to Babaji to request the Pune agency for the moldings in exchange for a hefty commission. Babaji agreed to his request. The contractor Jyotirao had now turned merchant. His workload increased so much that Tatya had to employ a servant to help him.

The shop eased out a lot of Tatya's worries. He did not need to run around any more, and could devote time to his studies. Sitaram was manning the sales part, whereas Rama was handling the daily affairs of the shop.

This shop, which was located at Vetaal Peth, became an important meeting point in Pune. The shop had a loft, where Jyotirao would usually station himself. When someone would come to meet him, Rama would call out the visitor's name and send him upstairs after getting Jyotirao's approval. Ramshet Uravane, Vinayakrao Dengale, Advocate Lingu, Ramchandrarao Shinde, Advocate Gangarambhau Mhaske, Rambhau Mansaram, contractor Shinde, Raobahadur Gopal Hari Deshmukh, Dyangiri Baba and many such important local people would come to meet Jyotirao in that loft. People from beyond Pune, such as, Narayanrao Kadlak, Narayanrao Nagarkar and Devrao Thosar would also pay visits once in a while. Jyotirao had got new friends like Dr. Vishram Ramji Ghole, an assistant surgeon with an affinity for reading. He and Jyotirao would have intense discussions about whatever they would read. Eminent people like Justice Raosaheb Ranade would also drop in some times. In that sense, the congregation that would happen on Sunday afternoons, would be an important one. People would stay on till late at night on Sundays, discussing, debating and brainstorming with each other.

36

Leaving Rama to man the shop, Tatya headed home for his lunch. Lately, lunch had become a task to complete due to the busy schedule in the shop. He knew that Savitribai would be waiting for him. Tatya intended to finish his lunch quickly and return to the shop to complete the day's work and also catch up on his reading and writing.

Lately, Tatya had fervently resumed his reading and writing. After his powadas critiquing the Brahmin community had become popular, Tatya was keen to write more on those lines.

One day, he penned a powada about Brahmin teachers working in public schools. In a funny manner, the powada described how these teachers would slack in their job while teaching the children of Shoodras and Ati-Shoodras; would teach the children hateful things about the government while taking hefty salaries from that government itself; would spend the daytime cursing the lower castes and then go to read scriptures at the houses of Malis and Kunbis at night, thinking nothing impure about taking food and money from them at that time.

Shaahir Dhondiram singing this particular powada in his

robust voice, had made it immensely popular among the masses. In fact, Baba Padmanji liked the powada so much, that he got it published in his journal 'Satyadeepika'.

Apart from creating powadas, Tatya also started reading about the history of various countries. He was surprised to see that not many countries had the inhuman tendency of human beings treating each other worse than animals owing to caste differences. He wondered why would that be so. He began researching intensely about the Brahmins and the reasons behind their inhuman treatment to the lower castes. After much deliberation, Tatya came to the conclusion that the Brahmins were originally not from India. They came here from foreign lands and conquered the erstwhile Kshatriyas via incessant attacks, making them their slaves. The offspring of those Kshatriya ancestors were the Shoodras and Ati Shoodras today. The rules that were established by the Brahmin king (Brahmaraja) to keep the slaves under their perennial captivity, were called 'Bhed'. Later on, the word got corrupted and turned into 'Ved'. After the main Brahmin king died, the remaining Kshatriyas waged 21 wars with Parashuram. That is how they got to be 'Maha Ari' aka the Great Enemy. The term must have got colloquially converted to Mahari and then Mahar. Mahasubha aka Mhasoba, Khandoba was a great Kshatriya warrior who got martyred. Our country must have been originally called Balisthaan. Bali was the king of this country. Vaman seized the kingdom away from Bali, by deceit, and pushed Bali into hell. This history is what probably prompts women today to pray that may all evils burn away and may the kingdom of Baliraja come again.

Later on, cunning, selfish and evil kings like Manu wrote scriptures that multiplied the importance of Brahmins many times over than was warranted. To top it, he claimed that those scriptures were written by God Himself; so as to crush any opposing voice that may get raised against them. These scriptures advocated nonsense such as, Shoodras emanated from the feet of Lord Brahma whereas Brahmins emanated from his mouth. In order to ensure that the Shoodras and Ati Shoodras remained their slaves for ever, the Brahmins spread the poison of casteist hierarchy. Just so that no one could understand about these tricks they played, the Brahmins wrote these scriptures in the Sanskrit language, that no else except for them, knew. They also made arrangements to see that Shoodras and Ati Shoodras did not get access to education. In short, they proclaimed themselves as God, reducing even the real God to a position beneath themselves!

Tatya's head was whirring with myriad thoughts…

At a well on the opposite side, some Brahmins were having their afternoon bath. They were also giving lavish baths to their children. At a well beyond this one, people from other castes were taking a bath and washing utensils etc. Women from the Mahar Maang communities were sitting at a distance from these two groups, pleading them for some water. Their small children were also sitting alongside with small earthen pots in hand, looking at the children of their age having happy baths. The Mahar Maang children had not had a bath for several days. They were gathering the water that flowed from the cleansed bodies of the other people and sprinkling a few drops on their body. Their elders were scolding them not to do so. People were past them were yelling and cursing them to stay away, lest their shadows pollute them. The reservoirs in Sadashiv Peth, Narayan Peth, Budhwar Peth etc would be overflowing with water at all times; but, for people staying in Meethganj Peth, Ganj Peth etc, water would be a luxury. The nearest reservoir for them would be Naagzari. While the Naagzari reservoir would fill up during monsoons, it would fall dry in the other seasons; causing these poor people to rush helter-skelter for water.

Today was an especially hot day and the Mahar Maang people were thirsting for a glassful of clean water. They were pleading with the others to show them some compassion but their pleas were falling on deaf ears.

This was a regular scenario. Tatya would be distressed to see that while Brahmins were behaving as they had always behaved, even the Shoodras were finding it proper to put down their Ati Shoodra brethren. In spite of many requests, the Municipality of Pune had done little to improve the basic living conditions of these hapless communities.

Suddenly, somebody started screaming,

"Oh, you bastards! Has that well in your Maharwada dried up?! Why are you coming here to pollute us all?!"

"Sorry sir, sorry…it has indeed dried up to the core…that is why we came here… please…" someone replied.

"Sir, madam…brother…sister… please show some compassion…please let us have some water…" some other person pleaded.

Tatya was seeing all this. At one point, his agitation got the better of him and he went near the Mahars and Maangs. Seeing Tatya coming towards them, the crowd started chanting his name and began pleading,

"Tatyasaab, please help us with some water… please help us tatyasaab…"

Tatya saw that the crowd comprised of a lot of children and also some old men and women. His heart went out to them all. Looking closely, he saw Raanba Naik's father among the group.

Tatya came closer… the crowd again chanting calls for help, holding out their bowls before him. But, instead of going towards the well to draw water for them, Jyotirao took Naik's earthen pot in his hand and said to him,

"Naik, come along with me."

No one could fathom what was going on. Silence pervaded for the next few moments till Jyotirao again looked behind and said to the crowd,

"Come along. All of you…come with me…"

The onlookers were horrified with the thought that Jyotirao

intended to pollute the wells by getting the Mahars and Maangs near them. They stood rooted to their spot.

The Mahar and Maangs also demurred coming along with Jyotirao. Naik pleaded,

"No, no, Tatyasaab.... please give us water here itself..."

Jyotirao turned to him and said,

"Naik, I'm inviting you all over to my house, to draw water from my well. Now will you please come?"

The crowd whooped with joy on hearing this pronouncement. Soon, a procession of Mahars and Maangs followed Jyotirao to his house. Onlookers were bewildered to see that unusual sight. No one knew what to make of it. By then, neighbors had started peeking from the windows to see what the commotion was all about.

Tatya came to the backdoor of his house and handing over Naik's earthen pot to him he said,

"Come Naik, go ahead and take your fill."

Naik hesitated.

"No, no, Tatyasaab, how can we touch your well?"

Seeing Naik backing down, everyone else too started going back. They could not fathom what Jyotirao was thinking. It was incomprehensible for the group that Tatya would invite them to touch his well, instead of drawing water from it and giving it to them from a distance.

Seeing Naik's hesitation, Jyotirao surged ahead, took the pot from Naik's hand and let it down into the well. The crowd started staring at Jyotirao agape! They had never seen something like this. How did Jyotirao have the courage to touch their pots? They were untouchables, weren't they?!

Jyotirao drew out on pot of water, placed it before Naik and said,

"Now you won't have any problem of untouchability, will you? Please listen, all of you... you may come here whenever you need water. You can touch this well, you can draw water from it yourself... There is no need to beg anyone for water henceforth. And if this water falls short, then go straight to the Phadke reservoir and start drawing water from there. Till that happens, the municipality is not going to rouse form its slumber."

Naik's eyes were filled with tears as he said to Jyotirao,

"Tatyasaab, you are God for us! How much do you do for us!? How can we ever repay you?!"

But Jyotirao did not wait to hear this praise. He went into his house, leaving the crowd free to draw as much water as they wanted, knowing that they would still be hesitant in his presence.

At Naik's behest, the people swarmed to the well. Children, women, old people all clamoured to draw water to have a bath or wash utensils. Soon, the news of Jyotirao having opened up his well for Mahars and Maangs, spread like wildfire and people started making a beeline for the well.

After having his lunch, Jyotirao went back to his work. People kept coming and asking Savitribai to give them water. She kept telling them to draw the water themselves, without any fear. She also kept telling them that they need not ask for anyone's permission henceforth.

On one Sunday, Jyotirao was sitting in his shop, trying to finish his work before the regular members came for the evening's meet-up. Gyaanoba Sasane came from Hadapsar with a new work. A tunnel was to be built at Katraj; Gyaanoba was hoping that Tatya would sign up for a sub-contract of the same. Just then, Rama came upstairs and told Jyotirao,

"A student has come to meet you."

Jyotirao asked him to be sent upstairs. Soon, a young, lanky boy came up. He folded his hands and stood humbly before Jyotirao, who was observing him with his piercing eyes.

"Come, sit here. What's you name?" asked Jyotirao.

"Tukaram Hanumant Pinjan."

"Where do you stay?"

"At Devrao Thosar's house…"

"Oh, Devrao is a good friend of mine. Are you related to him in any way?"

"Yes. He is my father-in-law."

"Oh, good, good... That means, you are our son-in-law" said Tatya with a smile. "Did you have any work with me?"

Tukaram faltered. He did not know how to talk his heart out before Jyotirao. Tukaram would often go by the shop, and see eminent people sitting and discussing about a variety of matters there. He would be very curious to know what those people would be discussing. That is why he had come to meet Jyotirao today; but, having come face-to-face with him, Tukaram would not dare to broach the topic directly. Thus, he said,

"Nothing special, Tatya. I just wanted to meet you personally."

"Good... Glad to hear that. Study well. If you face any problem, let me know" replied Tatya with an encouraging smile.

They talked a bit more about sundry matters, and then Tukaram took Jyotirao's leave. Jyotirao invited him to come over whenever he felt like. The invitation made Tukaram float on air! He had got what he wanted. He would now be able to drop by to hear the important people talk.

37

Tatya took up reading the Shivcharitra again. The interpretation of those words was very different from when he had first read it as a student. Twenty years back, Chhatrapati Shivaji Maharaj's valor had invoked an aggressive patriotism in Jyotirao. He had been ready to upturn the British empire on its head.

Jyotirao sourced out the biographies written by historians like Grant Duff and Murrey. Noe, a very different image of the Chhatrapati started shaping up in Tatya's mind. He could see Shivaji as a king of farmers and tillers, who created his own kingdom (Swarajya) with the help of Shoodras and Ati Shoodras. Swarajya was not created by the Brahmins of Peshwai! No, Sir! Instead, they gobbled the beautiful Swarajya created by the Chhatrapati and made a big hue & cry of religious rituals. The Peshwai took Maharashtra to the lowest of rungs. Sovereignty drooped its head before religious torment. The tenets of Manusmriti replaced the law of the land. Rituals perpetrated by the Brahmins became the new rulebooks to be lived by. Casteism made life impossible for the lower castes. Women started getting sold as if they were cattle. It was a lament that all this was happening in the land where Shiv Chhatrapati gave every woman the status of a mother.

The oppressive Peshwai regime saw farmers being made to stand on hot frying pans, if they were not able to pay their taxes on time. They would be made to sleep on a pan laden with chilies, with its smoke going into their eyes and nostrils! The acts were barbaric to say the least.

Shivaji Maharaj was helped by Deshastha Brahmins. They were also the original people of this land. However, the cunning Chitpavan Brahmins took them to their side by giving them the titles of Kulkarni and the like. They were the ones to raise this rumor during Shivaji Maharaj's coronation, that Shivaji was not a Kshatriya at all! They also elevated Saint Ramdas, the staunch proponent of Vedas, to being Shivaji Maharaj's guru, and gave the title of 'Gobrahmanpratipalak' aka 'the protector of cows and Brahmins', to Shivaji Maharaj!

Tatya was fascinated to read about the attitude, ideas and exploits of Chhatrapati Shivaji Maharaj who had brought the biggest Mughal emperor to his knees! He kept thinking about how would be the thought process of this valiant king who brought Hindus, Muslims, Brahmans and Shoodras, Ati Shoodras on one plane? How did he manage to bring about such equality among such a myriad group? How did he have so much compassion for every person, sans any segregation?

Jyotirao started feeling an intense urge to visit the fort and pay homage to the shrine of this great man. Finally, one day, Jyotirao set off for Raigad. He travelled for two days to reach Mahad, and from there, he went to Raigad.

Jyotirao felt awestruck on seeing the seat of power nestled in the formidable lap of the Sahyadri mountain ranges. The majestic fort of Raigad looked to have risen directly out of the Kaal river that flowed at its feet. Surrounded by cloud-touching mountain peaks, the fort looked like a diamond paved in a fine setting by an ace jeweler. The slopes of the Sahyadri mountains were pitch black, gleaming like black diamonds, without the sign of any vegetation on them.

Witnessing the symbol of Shivaji Maharaj's farsightedness and prudence, filled Jyotirao's heart with happiness and pride.

Tatya climbed up the entire fort. Many of the things on the fort had turned derelict, but they still stood testimony to the greatness that once was. Tatya was keen to see the Chhatrapati's shrine. He kept asking every passer-by about the shrine's whereabouts. But, no one could give him proper directions to the same. Tatya was determined to not leave without seeing the shrine. He climbed down and met the village head, a Joshi. However, he also was dismissive about the topic. Tatya again climbed up the fort and started asking the laborers working there about where the shrine stood. A few of them told Tatya that there was a foundation stone that remained somewhere around, but it was almost impossible to reach that place. The place was surrounded by thick shrubbery and tress, and it was dangerous for anyone to attempt going there. However, no amount of persuasion was going to dissuade Jyotirao. He was adamant about not leaving from the fort till he paid homage at the shrine.

Jyotirao took an axe from one of the laborers and went on the route leading to the shrine. He started cutting down the errant bushes that were coming in his way. This task continued for three days. His stock of bhaakris had finished long back. The laborers started getting bhaakris for Jyotirao. He would keep cutting the shrubbery for the entire day, eat some bhaakri at night, and go to sleep after a round of talks with the laborers.

On the third day, Jyotirao finally reached the foundation stone of the shrine, hidden in the clutch of bushes and vines. With tear-filled eyes, Jyotirao folded his hands to the Chhatrapati. His heart wrenched seeing the pitiful condition of the shrine of the great man. The weather-beaten shrine had sturdy, errant plants coming out from the foundation stone at many places, causing immense cracks in the same. Jyotirao again lifted his axe and cut down the grass and bushes that were growing wildly around the shrine.

Then, Jyotirao went to a gardener's house and requested him for a pail of water. He brought four pails of water in all, and washed the shrine till it gleamed. Then, he plucked a few wild flowers and paid a sincere homage to Shiv Chhatrapati.

Jyotirao was wandering in his own universe…oblivious to anything happening around, he was reminiscing about all the tales of valor that he had heard about Shiv Chhatrapati, from childhood.

He was snapped out of his reverie by someone's footsteps approaching the shrine. It was the head of the village – a Brahmin. He was spitting fire! He simply could not accept that some low caste outsider should come out of nowhere and dare to clean up the shrine! He was even more enraged on seeing the flowers on the shrine. Furious, he screeched,

"What in hell is going on here?! How dare you pay so much respect to this low caste king of yore? And, that too, without thinking of paying respects to me, Joshi, the head of this village? A Brahmin?!"

In that fury, Joshi stomped ahead and kicked the flowers off the shrine! Then, he again turned to Jyotirao and started screeching,

"Oh, you Shoodra! You lowly tiller! Do you think your Shivaji was some God, that you are paying so much respect to him, placing these flowers on his grave?! Shivaji was nothing more than a rogue leader of low caste people. He had not even been given the ritualistic ordinations that are so important to raise a good boy. What worth was he of?!"

Jyotirao's head started spinning! Joshi's evil words spewed a bucketful of venom and rage in Jyotirao's mind. He was so furious that he could have torn off Joshi's tongue, on the spot! But, Jyotirao composed himself thinking at the futility of this raving lunatic standing in front of him. In reality, this Joshi was supposed to be responsible for taking due care of the shrine. Instead of doing that, he was spewing nonsense about the king who had enraptured even the British with his way of governance.

Jyotirao kept wondering as to, what bestowed such hollow pride about their caste on these Brahmins?! How did they conveniently forget that this so-called Brahmani regime of the Peshwas was given to the Peshwas by the very Shivaji Maharaj, from whose shrine this audacious Joshi had just now kicked off the flowers from! How utterly, despicably ungrateful could these people be?

'The Chhatrapati's title of Gobrahmanpratipalak was a fake one. It was given to him by you mean Brahmins, for your own personal gains. Shivaji was the king of the masses. The true leader of the lower castes. How could people like Ramdas Swami and Dadoji, who never understood his idea of an equal society, ever be his gurus? It was just impossible! It was all your ploy. How dare you people make slaves out of the original people of this land? How dare you kick off the flowers from their king's shrine?!'... Jyotirao's head kept spinning with furious thoughts.

The village head finally stopped talking and left in a huff! Tatya plucked a few more flowers, placed them on the shrine, folded his hands in reverence, thanked the people who had helped him and set off from the fort, the sea of turbulent emotions kept locked up in his heart.

Slowly, the wave of anger receded from Jyotirao's mind, and he started thinking calmly. The fault also lay with the Kunbi community. They had forgotten their valiant king. They had forgotten his acts of bravery. It was time to remind them about it all. He realized that it was time to draft new powadas, reminding listeners about Shivaji's tales of valor.

On the way back home, Jyotirao could see the various historical events related to Shivaji Maharaj, dancing in front of his eyes. On their own, his lips started murmuring verses that he would put in the powada.

"I'm singing the powada of Bhosale, the king of Kunbis;
Of Chhatrapati Shivaji;
The protector of Kunbis, the tormentor of Muslims;
He treats everyone equally…."

Jyotirao kept writing:

"Jyotirao Phule is singing the praises of the king,
who was the patron of Shoodras,
and also of the Peshwas!"

The powada ended with a hymn directed at the Queen of England, in which he wrote:

"You are ruling our country, oh, Queen;
But the countrymen are ignorant;
Brahmins have rubbed the inks of their pens;
On their eyes;
Brahmins rule the universe here;
There's no voice for the Kunbis;
Jyoti exhorts you…. come fast;
Save us from these tyrants!"

Shaahir Dhondiram was very happy with the new powada. He went around the entire city, singing it in his mountainous voice!

Jyotirao had drafted the powada using simple words, that would be easy for his ignorant, illiterate brethren to understand. He took Baba Padmanji and Gangadharshastri Phadke's counsel for adding editorial finesse to the powada; wrote a small prologue for his book of powadas, explaining the rationale behind the new verse; and promised the readers that if they liked his new attempt, he would write more verses on heroes like Mahasubha too. Jyotirao dedicated the new powada with affection and reverence to the Late Ram Balkrishna Jaikar. Baba Padmanji took a copy of the powada to publish it in his 'Satyadeepika'.

Importantly so, in spite of his earlier experience with the Dakshina Prize Committee, Jyotirao sent the powada to it, on the behest of Dhondiram Shaahir.

As expected, the progressive and wise people like the powada a lot. Jyotirao too fulfilled his promise and wrote a scathing powada on the cunning of Brahmins, titled 'Brahmananche Kasab' (The 'skills' of Brahmins). The first part of the powada described the terrible battle that had happened between Parshuram and Mahasubha & Khandoba. It also talked about the ghastly atrocities inflicted by Parshuram. The words in the powada were kept simple, so that people could easily by-heart them.

"Oh, of what use is your futile life, O, Brahmins?!,
You first eat fresh food and then think of work!"

said Jyotirao, adding elsewhere,

"Understand the cunning of Brahmins,
They thug you with their brains, not brawn"

The aim of this powada was to make the government understand how the Brahmins were cheating lower caste people, and why it was thus necessary to equip them with education. The powada served its purpose, causing funny ripples in the society.

38

Tukaram was in a happy state of mind ever since he had seen the play, previous night. Funnily titled as 'Adnyaanrao Bhole Deshmukh', the play also spoke of the same views that Tatya would keep expressing through his talks and writing. Tukaram had been hearing of this play causing a stir in

Bhamburde, and had been waiting to go for it. Finally, last night, Tukaram had been able to go to Bhamburde with a couple of friends and seen the play.

That evening, he could not resist coming to Tatya's shop. He was too eager to tell Tatya about the play. He was sure that if Tatya were to see the play, he would also be full of praises for the ensemble that had put it together. Tukaram went upstairs to meet Tatya, who was busy writing something, with heavy tomes laid open in front of him for reference.

Seeing Tukaram, Tatya smiled and said,

"Come, Tukaram…Sit here…"

"Tatyasaheb, I had been to Bhamburde last night…to see a play…" Tukaram gushed.

"Oh, is it? Which play was it?"

"Adnyaanrao Bhole Deshmukh!"

"That's the name of a play?!" Tatya asked in surprise. "Who has presented it?"

"A student called Krishnarao. He has written the play and also acts in it."

Earlier, Tatya had heard of some student from Bhamburde having written a farcical play about the Satyanarayan puja ritual. He could not help wondering if the latest play was also the same student's presentation…?

Tukaram said to Jyotirao,

"Tatyasaheb, you should definitely see this play. You will really like it. I'm sure you will praise the students for their efforts. They have put up a fantastic play."

Jyotirao smiled seeing Tukaram's enthusiasm. Tukaram continued,

"….Tatyasaheb, the farce is a clever critique on the ignorant Deshmukh and the havoc that Brahmin priests and clerks wreak on the hapless man, taking undue advantage of his ignorance."

Tukaram described many comical instances and observations from the play. It piqued Jyotirao's curiosity. He felt like seeing the play and meeting the writers and cast members to congratulate them personally. He said to Tukaram,

"Inform me when the play is showing next. I would like to go and see it...talk to the cast members and specially, the writer..."

Tukaram was exhilarated to see that Tatya had taken his suggestion so seriously. He said,

Really, Tatyasaheb?! That will be great! Your praise will prove a great encouragement for those students."

"Alright, I shall go to Bhamburde tomorrow itself then..." said Jyotirao.

"Thank you, Tatyasaheb!"

Dhondiram Shaahir had come to see Jyotirao at his shop. Lately, Dhondiram had been nettled with the Dakshina Prize Committee's biased attitude. Ganeshshastri Lele's poem had received the first prize. Mahadev Moreshwar Kunte's mediocre and uncouth piece on Chhatrapati Shivaj Maharaj had received the second prize. Actually, this situation was expected, but Dhondiram could not reconcile with the unfairness of it all. He was incensed that such mediocre pieces should get governmental recognition, instead of the popular and most deserving powadas written by Jyotirao.

That day, as soon as he came into the meeting, Dhondiram asked Jyotirao,

"Tatyasaheb, you have so many good contacts in the government...yet, how come your powada did not receive any award? Marathi literature started getting recognition due to your efforts, and your works are being blatantly ignored! This is not fair."

Jyotirao tried to calm him down saying,

"It's okay, Dhondiram. It is not a compulsion for them to give us an award for that reason. The people who publish the powada are themselves afraid of backlash...so much so, that they even felt the need to publish an explanation...what do we expect from others then?"

Jyotirao's wan smile did not escape Dhondiram's eye. He also knew the reason behind the same.

A new storm had arisen after the powada had been published in 'Satyadeepika'. Another journal called 'Vividh Dynaanvistaar' had published a sharp critique on the historical facts in the powada being misleading. Immediately, Baba Padmanji had printed a retraction in 'Dynanoday' saying that he had only seen the words of the powada while taking the decision to publish it in his journal; he had no concern or connection with its content or the views expressed therein.

Jyotirao was used to well-wishers pulling out of a tricky situation, abruptly. Rather, he was happy that Baba had shown the presence of mind to issue an immediate retraction, before the issue blew out of proportion. However, the content of the retraction did leave an unpleasant taste in Jyotirao's mouth.

Jyotirao tried explaining to Dhondiram that, Chhatrapati Shivaji's merit was not going to become reduced due to not getting an award; but Dhondiram refused to listen.

"Nothing doing. Now, let us dig out feet in to promote 'Brahmananche Kasab'. We will not just be satisfied with an award; let that powada reach each and every school in the city" he exhorted.

"Dhondiram, even if the British feel like giving an award to our work, the Brahmins should let them do it, shouldn't they? They keep poisoning the ears of British committee members against us. Did you forget, why the draft of 'Trutiya Ratna' came back? I cannot keep singing praises of the government so that they can give me some silly award. Let us be practical; the present political situation will not allow the British to award a book or any work that goes against the Brahmins. The Brahmins will definitely not like to award us themselves. So, let us make peace with the fact that those awards are not meant for us. The committee has never supported Shoodra writers; and, where a powada about Chhatrapati Shivaji does not get an award, what hope do we have for a clear-cut anti-Brahmin powada like Kasab? It will be foolish on our part to expect that kasab will be incorporated in school curricula. And Dhondiram, please realize one thing.... never use wrong means to get a good work done. Else, the purity of that work gets blotted. So what if they rejected one draft of mine? God has been very kind; He has not left me wanting for anything."

Shaahir did not know what to say on this! He kept quiet. Then, Jyotirao changed the topic saying,

"Let that be... See what this Tukaram is saying.... There's a nice play happening at Bhamburde..."

- The next day, Jyotirao really set out for Bhamburde. He took Hari Raoji along. They knew nothing much about the play, except for that it was written by a student named Krishnarao, and that it would be staged in an open space outside the temple of Lord Vitthal. Jyotirao and Hari Raoji crossed the Mutha river and came near the temple. They caught hold of a passer-by and asked him,

"Day before yesterday, some play was staged here. Do you know where the playwright, Krishnarao, stays?"

"Oh, you wish to meet Krishna, is it? Please wait here, I shall get him..." said the man, hurrying away on his way.

Jyotirao noticed that the man seemed quite proud of Krishnarao. They kept waiting for Krishnarao to come. Jyotirao started observing the temple precincts. He noticed a cupboard full of books and newspapers standing in one corner of the temple. Going closer, he saw a few issues of 'Dynaanchakshu' and 'Lokakalyanecchu' lying there.

Soon after, a young lad of 18-19 years of age, clad in a white attire, came and stood in front of Jyotirao.

"Are you Krishnarao?" Jyotirao asked him.

"Yes, Tatyasaheb. How come you..." Krishnarao could not fathom what brought a great man like Jyotirao, all the way from Pune to him at Bhamburde.

Jyotirao realized his perplexity and said,

"I have heard a lot of hood things about your play. So, I felt like coming personally and meeting all of you."

Krishnarao was stunned! It was beyond his wildest imagination that a great man like Jyotirao would hear about their small play and come all the way to encourage them. He simply could not hide his delight at the occurrence.

Krishnarao said to Jyotirao,

"Tatyasaheb, please wait here. I shall get the entire team along here itself."

Krishnarao rushed off to the village. In a little while, he returned with his cast members such as Narayan Kanade and Narayan Pandhare. A crowd of villagers had also followed them along, since word had soon spread that Jyotirao was in their village. Krishnarao introduced his team members to Jyotirao; then, they together showed Jyotirao their small library, and narrated how they were inspired by Joshi kaka to start the library.

Jyotirao was immensely happy on meeting this inspired youngsters. The villagers began requesting Jyotirao to give a speech. He could not deny their affectionate request. Krishnarao asked everyone to get seated, and then Jyotirao began to speak. More than a formal speech, it turned out to be a session of informal talks between Tatya and his young friends. Jyotirao praised Krishnarao and his cast members saying,

"My brothers, I find it a good development that you have started recognizing the evil lurking behind the cunning of Brahmins. Youngsters like you have the resources to take this movement ahead and free your Shoodra, Ati Shoodra brethren from the shackles of Brahmin bondages. That was my main reason to come and meet you today."

At the end of his speech, Jyotirao said,

"It would probably be a lesser loss for you if some dacoit looted your house, than being bamboozled by the snake-like Brahmins."

A hearty laughter erupted on this comment.

After Tatyarao's speech, the audience requested Krishnarao to say a few words. Tatya was not aware that Krishnarao was also a good orator. He started talking in his dynamic style and unknowingly, began taking logical cognizance of the pointers that Jyotirao had mentioned in his speech. Tatya found his fearless and courageous style of talking to be praiseworthy. Krishnarao's oratory was a bit aggressive due to his young age, but his thoughts were well organized and lucid. He exhorted that, apart from the Brahmins, the land-owning barons were to be equally blamed for the pitiable condition of the Shoodras and Ati Shoodras. He had elucidated this idea in his farce too, and had heavily criticised the Brahmin clerks who poisoned the ears of the barons.

As Krishnarao finished his session, Jyotirao said to him,

"The reasons behind the barons of Shoodra community behaving erratically against their own brethren, is the Brahmins itself, isn't it?"

But Krishnarao was firm on his views. He argued,

"Brahmin clerks may tell them anything; but have they mortgaged their brains that they cannot think for themselves? It is the idleness of these barons that makes it easier for the Brahmins to fleece them. These Shoodra community barons will have no compunction in paying hundreds of rupees to the Brahmins for mindless rituals, but they will not cast a glance at a Shoodra brother who dies in poverty."

In spite of marginal differences in their views, Jyotirao agreed that what Krishnarao said, was true. Changing the topic in a bid to not extend the argument ahead, Jyotirao asked,

"Krishnarao, what's your father's name?"

"Pandurang Ranoji Bhalekar."

Jyotirao was surprised to hear the name. He exclaimed,

"Pandurangdada? Oh! What a coincidence! We knew each other for a long time. I used to come to your house often."

"Yes, you had also come during Dada's demise" said Krishnarao.

Jyotirao was happy to see that Dada's son had grown up to be such a talented and intelligent young man. He asked after everyone in Krishnarao's family. Krishnarao was presently studying in the Mission school in Ravivar Peth.

Soon, Jyotirao began to leave. Krishnarao requested him to come home for a meal.

"Not today, son. I cannot stay more today. Now that I know you study in Pune, come by the shop. We have a shop in Vetaal Peth."

Saying thus, Jyotirao set out. Krishnarao and his friends accompanied him to the village border.

39

A joyous occasion arose in the Phule household. Ganapati got a son. Rajarambhau became a grandfather, and, so had Jyotirao. Jyotirao was happy that he would finally have one child from his own family to play at the orphanage.

However, Jyotirao's happiness over this expectation turned out to be short-lived. His relatives refused to enter Jyotirao's house! Speculation was rife that Jyotiba Phule had converted to Christianity; else, there was no way he could have allowed Mahars and Maangs to fill water at his well. Only the Christians would not look at those people as untouchables. Thus, it was obvious that Tatya had also become a Christian.

People of their community had started threatening to ostracize Jyotiba. He tried explaining the facts to them, but no one was in any mood to listen. Rajarambhau was also siding with the community people, against Jyotirao.

On his part, Jyotirao kept calm amidst all the chaos going around him. He kept reading extensively. From those readings, his principles started getting firmer. He was planning to write a book, expressing his newly-found thoughts. He was especially studying the period of slavery in America. After slavery was abolished in America, the slaves had also become mentally and emotionally free from slavery; but in India, the Hindu religious scriptures had created such a deep impression on the followers minds, that the Shoodras and Ati Shoodras simply refused to come out of their mental bondages.

After the Paramhans Sabha got dissolved, Dr. Bhandarkar and some other people came together to form the Prarthana Samaj in Mumbai. Last year, a branch of the Samaj had been established in Pune, with the initiative of Justice Raosaheb Ranade. However, sadly enough, this Maharashtrian offshoot of the Brahmo Samaj did little than hide the shambles of the Hindu religion. The Brahmins had played one more ploy to hide the misdoings of their ancestors.

The curtain had finally fallen on the remarriage initiated by Vishnushastri Pandit; but, a lot of things had come into the open. The orthodox group had exerted so much pressure, that the progressives fell slack in between. They could not hold onto their own under that pressure. Even Raobahadur Gopalrao Hari was amongst those who backed down. In fact, Raobahadur did not even attend the wedding. His daughter's mother-in-law sent a dire warning from Baroda, that if Raobahadur went to the wedding, she would send his daughter back home for ever! Else, better still, she would push her into a river…! But, she would not be taken back into the house for any reason.

It was indeed unfortunate that, Raobahadur, who had himself sent so many invitation cards with a personal note requesting the invitees to attend along with their families to show unity and support, had himself left town on the eve of the occasion.

Jyotirao was specially pained to see such a fearless crusader being reduced to a heap of nothingness. There was no other person than Raobahadur who could wield his pen so fearlessly and could also turn so many Brahmins in their favor. He was the first one in Maharashtra to have publicly spoken about the immorality and evil in the Brahmin-perpetrated philosophies.

Vishnushastri, however, stood firm on his ground. While

on one hand Vithoba Anna Daptardar was crusading zealously against widow remarriage, at the same time, Vishnushastri was propagating the merits of widow remarriage. Pune was in immense turmoil.

A big meeting was held at Tulshibaug, wherein it was decided to ostracize all the seven progressives involved in the widow remarriage. The progressives surrendered, but the orthodox group was in no mood to forgive. They wanted to eradicate the progressives from the root, once and for all!

Coincidentally, at the same time, Jagadguru Shrimant Shankaracharya had come to Pune. The orthodox group decided to let the Guru serve due justice in this matter, according to the rules of the religious scriptures.

Eminent Brahmins were invited to come aboard the panel for discussing whether widow remarriage was moral or immoral according to the scriptures. Gopalacharya Karhadkar from Gwalior was made the chief jury from the side of the orthodox group. Prof. Krishnashastri Chiplunkar became the main jury from the side of the progressives. However, the orthodox group took objection on Chiplunkar's deputation, because he had committed the sin of eating fruit and ice along with the Europeans! They insisted that in order to wash away that sin and become eligible to sit on the panel, Chiplunkar would first have to pay a fine of Rs. 500. The progressives had also suggested that Prof. Ramkrishnapant Bhandarkar be made the main jury from their side. But, his candidature was also rejected on the premise that he was a Saraswat Brahmin, and it would be a huge sin to let a Saraswat Brahmin participate in a holy matter like this.

The arguments went on for nine days in the presence of Jagadguru Shankaracharya. People would sit all day long, listening to both the parties. The city of Pune would be abuzz with discussions about the proceedings of the day. Both parties were given amusing names: The 'religiously upright' orthodox group was named Shuklapaksha , whereas the 'sinning' progressive group was named Krishnapaksha !

To advocate their stance on widow remarriage, the progressives took the reference of a shloka in Parasharsmruti that prescribed remarriage for a woman whose husband was dead; had renounced the material world; was a lunatic; or had committed apostasy. But apparently, the Shankaracharya said to Raobahadur that, his son had committed apostasy by crossing over the seven seas. Thus, taking the aforementioned shloka as the base, she should also be allowed to remarry. Raobahadur could say nothing on this argument. His logic had backfired badly on him!

Then, Krishnashastri Chiplunkar brought forth a reference that said that, if a girl becomes a widow before reaching puberty i.e. she is a virgin, then the scriptures do not disallow her remarriage in any way, even though they do not specifically mention that such a marriage is allowed. However, this argument was also blown off on the pretext that scriptures only tell us what to do. They do not specify anything about what not to do. Thus, this point comes under a grey area, and since the scriptures do not openly advocate widow remarriage, any form of widow remarriage is not acceptable in their book.

Utter chaos ensued as both warring parties kept coming up with numerous references from numerous scriptures. Most of the scriptures being written in Sanskrit language, each word could be interpreted in myriad ways. Who was to decide which meaning was the perfect one?!

The progressives kept fighting with all their might. Prof. Bhandarkar burnt the night oil trying to find references that would strengthen their argument. However, the orthodox group kept giving them a tough fight and finally, they decreed that any interpretation of the scriptures that prove the progressives' point, does not hold credence in the Kaliyug !! That put a full-stop to all arguments, rendering the progressives mouth-shut!

Another reason why the progressives suffered a massive blow was that people from their side started playing hypocrite.

Krishnashastri Chiplunkar turned his back and started talking things in favor of the orthodox group. Seeing that the progressives were fighting a losing battle, Krishnashastri and Kerunana came ahead to surrender and do atonement.

After all this chaos, the decision was finally taken through a vote. It was a sorry situation that a grave question such as the fate of so many widows, was decided through voting. The nine-day ordeal turned out nothing but a farce. The progressives were asked to do atonement. The orthodox group proclaimed themselves a winner and shot off a wire to the 'Times Of India' declaring their victory.

Amusingly, even though the bickering continued for nine days, no one actually saw the Shankaracharya speaking! Whether the Shankaracharya did not understand the arguments, or, he did not wish to talk… that remained a secret. But, it was always the orthodox group members who kept talking on his behalf.

Finally, all the progressives had to do atonement by rubbing their noses to the ground. Vishnushastri Pandit, Vishnu Parshuram Ranade and Raosaheb Ranade had to face ostracism.

While Pune was embroiled in this drama of arguments and ostracism, another widow remarriage took place in Mumbai. Justice Kanhoba Vijaykar married a widow called Sumitrabai, at his bungalow near Gavlyacha Talao. The ceremony happened with pomp and gaiety. His first marriage had also taken place in the same bungalow.

The orthodox group were severely pinched by this snub. Alleging that it was especially shameful for a judge to behave in this way, they started making life hellish for Vijaykar and his wife.

As time passed, certain things started coming out of the woodwork. Apparently, the orthodox group had terrorized a progressive called Venkatshastri Mate and got him on their side. Irrespective of what the Shankaracharya thought, it was already decided that the ruling would be in favor of the orthodox group. Lokahitawadi undertook the atonement, but later he wrote a letter to the panel of jury that he would still continue doing his work.

The principles of the endeavor of 'public meetings' started by Joshi kaka, were good; but the working did not involve Shoodras and Ati Shoodras in any way. In a way, it was nothing more than a public congregation of the Brahmins. Sadashivrao Govande handed over the working of the school for Mahar Maang children, to the government's education department, and became the secretary for the public meetings.

Sadashivrao's name would stir up many memories for Jyotirao. He was pained to hear that nowadays, Sadashivrao had been enraptured by some soothsayer. Jyotirao could not fathom how and when had their ways become so different?! At one time, the four friends were determined to follow one single goal; but all that had been left in the past now. Everyone had gone their own way. Moropant and Sakharampant had gone to Mumbai. Moropant had become a member of the Prarthana Samaj. He had also taken on the editorial responsibility of 'Subodh Patrika', and was going to be permanently stationed in Mumbai for that work. Sakharampant too had decided to stay on in Mumbai for his work.

Where were all those work, with whose help Jyotirao had started his crusade? After being promoted as Assistant Supervisor for schools in the Thane and Colaba district, Keshavrao Bhavalkar did not return to Pune at all. From Mumbai, he went directly to central India as a Tehsildar. Fatimabai had also not met them after her marriage, which had happened many years back. Usman had met Jyotirao in recent times, but after a gap of many years. Dr. Mitchell, Rev. James Mitchell had long left for their motherland. Major Candy had shifted to Mahabaleshwar.

Lately, Raosaheb Ranade had been transferred to Pune. So, the work of Prarthana Samaj and the public meetings was being done under his able guidance.

Even though Raosaheb could not personally participate in Jyotirao's work, he had immense respect for the same. Raosaheb had been hearing about Jyotirao's courageous crusades for a long time. Hence, he had come to visit Jyotirao to congratulate him personally. Jyotirao also understood Raosaheb's limitations, but he could not help being touched by Raosaheb's intelligence, curiosity and sincerity towards work.

Raosaheb and Jyotirao kept meeting often, exchanging thoughts and discussing important matters for hours on end.

When Raosaheb's sister, Durgabai, got widowed, Jyotirao went to meet her. That time, Raosaheb was not at home; but, when he got the message that Jyotirao had come to meet his sister, he was overwhelmed and sent a message that he would come to meet Jyotirao that evening.

That day at precisely 6 pm, a horse carriage came to the door of Phule mansion. Dressed in a starch white kurta (tunic), with a satin scarf wrapped around his shoulder, Raosaheb alighted from the carriage. He was short in stature, but the glow of intelligence on his face was unmistakable. His impressive personality became even more prominent due to the pink pugree he wore on the head. He wore no accoutrements as such, but, his calm visage shone with the glow of wisdom. Raosaheb was such an avid reader that one of his eyes had become weak, and would keep shutting down, due to his habit of constant reading!

Seeing the orphanage in Jyotirao's house, Raosaheb said to him,

"I wish to open such an orphanage at Pandharpur. I have taken the liberty to invite Lalshankar Umiyashankar to see your orphanage, for that purpose."

Jyotirao was happy to hear that. He said,

"You are right. Such an orphanage is required at places having religious shrines, because there, the society is even more bound by religious norms. That is why, I had advertised my orphanage at Wai, Pandharpur, Nashik and Kashi too. A few women from there also came to our orphanage. Widows hailing from religious centers often commit suicide, unable to withstand the societal pressures. Thus, orphanages such as mine, are required even more in those places. It will be possible to save the women and their children; not to mention, probably, educate the orthodox people there about the futility of troubling those hapless women."

"The orthodox people will never get enlightened! It's useless to expect that their stony hearts will ever spurt compassion. Didn't you see what happened with us?" Raosaheb said with a wan smile.

Both the men kept talking for a long time after that. It was evident that Raosaheb was still unhappy about the agony they had to face while helping the remarriage. Add to that, his own sister had been widowed. Times were testing for Raosaheb.

"It is easy to talk; but, bringing in proactive change is a very difficult task. Raobahadur, who opines that the Shastras also need to be changed as per time, is himself not open to change. How can such an attitude work?" said Jyotirao.

"But, Tatyasaheb, in spite of that, he has provided support for the group promoting widow remarriage, hasn't he?" said Raosaheb.

"If words are not supplemented with actions, then of what use are hollow words, Raosaheb? Simply writing articles and giving speeches is not going to help in such a sensitive matter. For that, one needs to be in the thick of things; one needs to share the torment of those affected. Till that happens, one's thoughts – howsoever good – keep rusting like a sword kept in its sabre" averred Jyotirao.

Everyone, including Jyotirao, was aware of Raobahadur's familial problems. He also had deep compassion about the same. But still, Jyotirao would be pained to see a dynamic man like Raobahadur becoming a slave of mindless conventions for the sake of familial pressure.

Raosaheb said,

"Even I was under pressure… But I stuck out my head nevertheless."

Jyotirao added to this saying,

"Irrespective of all the commotion created by the orthodox group, tell me how does widow remarriage prove to be a sin in any way, Raosaheb?! Widow remarriage has been going on in the Shoodra and Ati Shoodra castes for so many generations now. People like you bow your head before the scriptures presented by the orthodox group; that is why they get empowered. When progressives like you decide to remove the bondage of these scriptures from your mind and heart, these orthodox people will vanish in thin air along with their foolish, baseless ideas!"

"Hmm…the scriptures…" sighed Raosaheb.

"Which scripture says that widow remarriage is a sin? Tell me, Raosaheb…?" Jyotirao persisted.

"Well, no scripture says that widow remarriage is not allowed. But, since no scripture also openly says that it is allowed, thus the matter remains in a limbo. That is exactly what happened in the nine-day argument, isn't it? This proved to be the undoing for the progressives. Apparently, whatever progressive tenets were supposedly found in the religious texts, are not applicable in Kaliyug, they said." said Raosaheb.

"Well, if the progressive tenets are not applicable in Kaliyug, then how come the regressive tenets can still be considered applicable? That means, time has come to change the scriptures altogether, isn't it?" argued Jyotirao.

Raosaheb kept quiet. He kept thinking for some time and then said,

"Convention. That is the only law. What did not happen till now, will never happen in the future too. Our home too was singed in the same fire. Anways, Tatyasaeb…we have our own limitations. Best is to accept them…" said Raosaheb, wiping his tear-filled eyes with his scarf.

Jyotirao could understand his pain. Both kept quiet for

some time. Then, Jyotirao said,

"Whatever happened was indeed very unfortunate. It should not have happened. But Raosaheb, the lady who has been widowed is the sister of a progressive."

Hearing this, Raosaheb promptly sat up. He was understanding the subtext of Jyotirao's comment. Jyotirao said to him,

"Raosaheb, please don't let your sister live the cursed life of a widow."

"But...Tatyasaheb..." Raosaheb stammered.

"Raosaheb, you have been a forerunner in insisting that the society should change. Then, why don't you let this change start from your house itself? You are getting a chance to bring your thoughts into reality. Please don't leave this chance. Please take the lead and get Durgabai remarried" Jyotirao averred, adding, "The main aim of any religion is to bring about progress of mankind. And, service of humanity is the service of God... That's what you have always told the society, isn't it, Raosaheb?"

After long last, Raosaheb said,

"Tatyasaheb, such decisions definitely become epoch-making in the road to progress. But, the person making those decisions has to face immense opposition and turmoil. You know what happened with Moroba Kanhoba... How much torment did he have to go through...! My family is still bearing immense trouble from the society, just because I spoke in favor of widow remarriage. My wife is not invited to any social function. If she is invited, then it is only for taunting her openly. Servants also refuse to work in our house, fearing ostracism from their communities. Today, our situation is so dire that, if there happens to be a death in the family, we are not sure if we will get people for the funeral! To even think of my widowed sister's remarriage in such a situation, means..."

"No good work has ever happened without a fight, Raosaheb! Societal change is not going to happen on its own. It has to be made; and for that, it needs to be started off by somebody. If you truly believe that widows are entitled to a better life, then have the courage to get your own sister remarried. It is only when our words are supplemented with actions that people realize the importance of what we have been saying" urged Jyotirao.

"But, Tatyasaheb...don't we also need to consider the emotional status of those who se lives we are planning to change?" asked Raosaheb.

"Thoughts and emotions are never going to change unless we bring about progression. Constant counseling helps in changing even the most rigid mind-sets" said Jyotirao.

Slowly, Raosaheb's doubts were melting in front of Jyotirao's resolve. Finally, Raosaheb said,

"Jyotirao, I think you are right. Durgabai is hardly 20-21 years old. She has a long life ahead of her, and there's no reason she should spend it in misery of being a widow. But, I shall need to think of my father. He will be tremendously unhappy with my decision to get Durgabai remarried. Not to mention, the Brahmins will ostracize our family for ever, and probably my father will not be able to bear that."

"Well then, stop your hypocrisy of branding yourself a progressive!!" Jyotirao retorted sharply!

Raosaheb was stunned by this unexpected comment. He shied his eyes away from Jyotirao and mumbled,

"Tatyasaheb, a progressive also has to think of the society some times... after all, he stays in the same society, doesn't he?"

"Thinking of the society, and, reneging on one's views at the last minute are two different things, Raosaheb! People like you, who profess the need for bringing about a change in society, should follow up their words with due actions when the need arises. Else, there words are nothing but bubbles. Societal attitude will change slowly, but surely. Why worry about that so much?!" said Jyotirao.

Raosaheb kept quiet. Night had fallen. Raosaheb soon took

Jyotirao's leave and went his way.

Kaku was deeply disturbed with the way Tatya had spoken with Raosaheb. He would never speak like this with any guest who would come to their house. Rather, he would talk more humbly with the Brahmin scholars who would visit them, because he did not want anyone to think that Jyotirao was an enemy of the Brahmins. Usually, Tatya would be so soft-spoken that it would be difficult to believe that he was the same Jyotirao who would crack a whip on the behavior and policies of Brahmins through his speeches and powadas.

After Raosaheb left, Kaku berated Tatya in unsparing words. Tatya was sheepish, but anger about Raosaheb's attitude was still simmering in his mind. He said to Savitribai,

"They want progress; but they want other people to do it. Those people who cannot bring about change among their own family, what change will they be able to bring about in society?! If he cannot hear his own widowed sister's tragic pleas, how can he ever wipe the tears of hundreds of widows who are crying out for help? These people are just paper tigers. They can only talk about change; but are ineffectual in doing anything to bring in change."

Savitribai did not wish to stretch the argument any further. As it is, work was beckoning her from the kitchen. As she left for the kitchen, Jyotirao went to play with the children. After some time, Savtribai peeked out of the kitchen and saw Jyotirao immersed in playing childish games with the children. Suppressing a smile, she wondered if it was the same Jyotirao who was so incensed a few minutes back!

40

Jyotirao got the contract for providing stones for the construction of the Katraj tunnel. Gyaanoba was handling the daily affairs related to that work. Jyotirao was handling the shop and was suing whatever little free time he got, to write

'Gulamgiri'. The book was a seminal dissection of the tenets of Hindu religion.

A few days back, Jyotirao had written and publicized a letter aimed to educate his ignorant brethren. The title of the letter was:

'How can the Shoodras free themselves from the slavery of demoniacal Brahmins?'

The letter had Jyotirao declaring that he had been able to free himself of the aforementioned slavish bonds due to the early learning of writings by American and European thinkers. Further, he exhorted his Shoodra brethren to do the same, and also promised that if he came across any Shoodra who had freed himself from this bondage and was making efforts to build a morally upright, clean life; then, Jyotirao would treat him like a family member and proffer any help he possibly could.

Jyotirao sent copies of this letter to many newspapers, but the Brahmin editors of all of those newspapers refused to publish it. 'Lokkalyanecchu' went so far as to writing that, Jyotirao had used nefarious means to send them this letter but they were taking a morally upright stand by not publishing anything that was so viciously anti-Brahmins.

Only the Christian magazine 'Shubhavartaman Darshak', which was published in Kolhapur, published the letter with a remark that, many more such men were needed to progress the nation.

One evening, Jyotirao came home to find Savitribai dressed up and the little Yamu pestering her to take her along.

"Where are you off to?" Jyotirao asked Savitribai.

"We have been invited for a wedding. Saraswatibai is also coming along" replied Savitribai.

Jyotirao had a lot of respect for Saraswatibai. Under the guidance of Sarvajanik Kaka and Justice Ranade, he and Saraswatibai Joshi had recently started the 'Stree Vicharvati Sabha'. They were keen that Savitribai also participate in the work of this organization. Both the families were coming together on his pretext. Tatya was happy that Savitribai and Saraswatibai were going together for the wedding.

"Please go..." said Jyotirao, lifting Yamu up on his shoulders. Just then, Gajanan also came crawling and caught Jyotirao's leg. The little boy had just about began crawling now.

After Savitribai left, Jyotirao played with the children for some time, and then after handing them over to Sitaram, he sat to write. He became so immersed in writing that he lost track of time. After long last, when he looked up, it was completely dark outside.

Jyotirao came out of his room and went to the children. Sitaram was giving them dinner. Savitribai had not yet returned.

Jyotirao saw that Yamu was refusing to eat. When he asked Sitaram about it, he said,

"I told her many times...but she simply refuses to eat."

Jyotirao came to her and said in a soft voice,

"Yamu, come on...have your dinner..."

Puffing her cheeks even more, Yamu resolutely nodded in the negative. Jyotirao picked her up. He and Savitribai were specially fond of this sprightly little girl. Ditto for Shivaji. He would remind them both of Shantaram. Lakshmi and Babu had grown bigger now. It was time to enroll them in school.

Jyotirao said to Yamu,

"Will you eat with me?"

"Yes."

"But I will be eating late...After Kaku comes...will you wait till then?"

"Yes."

"But you will get very hungry by then..."

"No, I wont."

For a long time after that, Jyotirao kept waiting for Savitribai with Yamu on his shoulders. Finally, as Savitribai arrived, Jyotirao rebuked her saying,

"What is this? Did you see how late it is? Do you not care

about the children?"

Ignoring his anger, Savitribai said to Sitaram,

"Go and bring a lamp..."

"Lamp? What for? Has anyone come along with you?" asked Jyotirao, his voice going low by several octaves.

"Yes. Saraswatibai has come along" replied Savitribai.

"Ohh! Is it? Then why haven't you invited her inside? This Yamu has been crying for you, so I... wait, I shall get the lamp..." Jyotirao said in a sheepish tone.

Jyotirao got the lamp and asked Sitaram to reach Saraswatibai to her house. Savitribai took Yamu inside, and soon they all sat for dinner; Yamu ensconced on Jyotirao's lap.

41

'Gulamgiri' was published in June 1873. It was a logical dissection of how the Brahmin-written texts are full of baseless concepts; how their tenets are hollow and hypocrite; how the Brahmins came down from Iran; how they were originally meat-eaters; how Baliraja, Jotiba, Khandoba, Mahasubha, Bhairoba were the original rulers of this land; what were the customs during their reign; how Vaman sent Baliraja to hell; what hoaxes did Naarad and Shankaracharya come up with to enslave the Shoodras, and so on. The vivid description of the tyranny wreaked by Parshuram was capable of bringing tears to the eyes of the most hardened reader. Along side, Jyotirao had also critiqued the idle princes, the Kulkarnis, landlords, Brahmin clerks working for the government, the education department, Municipality, the Dakshina Prize Committee and Brahmin editors.

The prologue of the book compared the slavery being bore by Shoodras and Ati Shoodras to that which had perpetrated in America. Jyotirao showed how the slavery in our country was much more horrifying in comparison to that in the West. He explained that the lower caste people in our country had become so effectively brainwashed by the Brahmins, that they would go against the very people who were trying to uplift them. The Brahmins had systematically inserted the venom of caste hierarchies in their minds, so as to keep their superiority and income, intact. He strongly alleged that the Brahmins were responsible for the pitiable and slavish state of the lower castes today. He also appealed to the government to take firm steps to spread education among these classes, so that they could break out of the bonds enforced on them owing to their ignorance.

In a special message, he exhorted the Shoodras to realize that the British are not going to stay on in India for ever. Thus, it would be prudent for them to free themselves of the slavery by taking due advantage of the resources they are getting, before the British leave for their motherland.

Even though the book was priced at 12 aanas, Jyotirao announced a 50% discount for the Shoodra and Ati Shoodra readers.

Jyotirao had dedicated his book to those people in America who had strived to abolish slavery and had expressed a wish that our countrymen would also follow their example soon. Along side, Jyotirao had also expressed gratitude towards the progressive Brahmins, who had broken away from their ancestors' unjust thoughts and were contributing towards building an equal society.

However, the Brahmin community was up in arms against the book! They were breathing fire over Jyotirao's claims that Brahmins had come from Iran; that, they were originally meat eaters; and over the impure ideas that he had expressed about giving education to Shoodras. A letter written by Jyotirao addressed to Parshuram, had instigated the Brahmin community beyond belief. In that letter, Jyotirao had challenged Parshuram that if he was indeed as immortal and omnipresent as the Brahmin scriptures said, then he should make his presence felt within the next six months of this book being published.

If he did not do so, then the Mahars and Maangs would be free to call out the Brahmins hiding cowardly behind their Mhasoba and give them their due 'rewards'.

Pune was abuzz with rumors and murmurs. Allegations were flying thick and fast that Jyotirao Phule was betraying his own kin. Some said that, it was a big ploy of the British and Jyotirao was not thinking about the fact that he was being used as a pawn in the big game.

These mischief-mongers had pushed Justice Moroba Kanhoba and his wife to commit suicide. They had been responsible for making Raobahadur Gopalrao Hari do atonement by rubbing his nose on the ground. They had also driven a good progressive like Raosaheb Ranade up the wall with their wicked thoughts and antics. However, Jyotirao was proving too strong for them.

While so much of agitation was going around him, Jyotirao was calm as ever. One evening, he was sitting in his shop, going over the accounts with Gyaanoba. That evening, Dynaangiribaba was going to give a discourse. Jyotirao was keen to attend it.

As dusk fell, avid listeners like Ramshet, Vithoba Guthaal, Kushaba Mali, Dhondiba Kumbhar, Gyaanoba Zagde, Krishnarao Bhalekar, Tukaram Hanumant Pinjan started gathering at the pre-decided location.

Dynaangiribaba started his discourse with a verse by Sant Kabeer, that said,

"Cows may be different in color; but the color of milk remains the same;

Then, how are we different even if you may be Brahmins, and we may be merchants?"

Dyaangiribaba's flowery oratory soon captivated the audience by explaining them what was written in Braj dialect. The audience found resonance in what was written by the Braj saints and what they were going through.

42

It was pitch dark all around. The steps seemed unending....spiraling downwards as if into eternity. The well was surrounded by huge trees with vines as thick as ropes growing on them. It was difficult to determine if it was day or night; for, the trees made it impossible for any light to pass through. Descending down the steps into a well-like structure, it was getting difficult to breathe. Every effort being made to come up from the stifling well, was being met by failure. Cold-blooded, slimy reptiles seemed to be licking at the ankles while trying to stumble around the pit of the dry well....

Jyotirao woke up with a start!! His throat was parched. Lately, he had not been sleeping too well. His thoughts were disallowing him from sleeping soundly. He recognised that the well that he saw in his dream was not a well, but a prison. A prison without bars, but more stifling and suffocating than it otherwise would be. A prison of the religion-based society built by the Brahmins.

Jyotirao was deeply disturbed. Myriad thoughts about religion and its various interpretations and forms, were running through his mind. It was getting imperative to show the Shoodras and Ati Shoodras, the real meaning of religion; to make them live a life like human beings. For that, they had to freed from the oppressive and subjugative hold of the Brahmins. For that, they had to be explained the real meaning of religious tenets in a language and format that they would easily understand and be able to follow.

Again, a storm of thoughts began raging in Jyotirao's mind. He kept thinking of what Dynaangiribaba had said in his discourse. Saint Kabeer's views on morality and basic human values had appealed to Jyotirao tremendously.

His sleep had been broken; he realized that now it would be futile to attempt sleeping. Thus, Jyotirao came into the courtyard. Gusts of wind were blowing, causing Jyotirao to shiver. He kept looking at the play of the moon and clouds that was going on in the sky. The vastness of the universe kept beckoning him as he kept looking at the clouds playing hide n' seek with the moon.

.... This vast, immeasurable universe...the elements that seem suspended in it... the natural cycle that has been going on for eons... everything is run by some invisible but tremendously powerful force. That force means God. God is the one that has created us all; He is the one who has provided us all the means to survive. Everything happens according to His wishes alone.

As these thoughts kept coursing in his mind, unknowingly Jyotirao folded his hands at the vast universal space in front of him. At that moment, he was reminded of Saint Tukaram's verses, that said:

"You are the savior; we can tell our troubles to you and you, alone;

Who else do we go to with our lament, Oh, creator of ours?!"

Thoughts kept whirling around in his mind, refusing to abate.

....The creator has given birth to everything, including human beings. He created plants, animals, humans everything... So, in a way, human beings are not different from any of the other creations of God. However, what differentiates human beings from the rest, is intellect. God made human beings stand on two feet instead of four; but compensated him with a much superior brain. What must be the reason behind giving human beings a superior intellect? Surely, God must have wanted that humans use this intellect to accord an enriched life to the human race, the animal kingdom and the botanical world. But alas, humans have not lived up to this expectation. Rather, he has demeaned this gift in the most vile ways possible. Man has misused his intellect to push a certain section of human beings into slavery. He played on the strengths and weaknesses to show one's section superiority over another. Some humans are smarter than others. They used that smartness to their advantage and left the other bereft of their basic human rights. Going ahead, they created a scarecrow of tenets meant for a good life, by converting them into religious ideas and using them to terrorize the masses into psychological slavery. They wrote down the so-called 'word of God' into scriptures and made people follow them like lambs.

This is exactly what happened in the kingdom of Bali. The evil Brahmins captivated the masses with their religious ideas and sovereignty went to the grave. Racism and social hierarchy became the norm, creating horrific segregations in the once-unified society. Racism and hierarchy based on religious tenets is anathema for any society, because it differentiates people not on the basis of merit or achievements but on the sole basis of his birth. According to the theories propounded by Brahmins, a person's birth is determined by his/her actions in his/her previous birth. Thus, the lineage of his/her birth determines his/her behavior, attitude, and actions in the present life. Supplementary to this theory, the Brahmins believe that only it is only the Brahmin caste which gets born with Sattva Guna and vice versa. The ones born in lower castes are born thus, because they have been attributed by the Raajsik Guna owing to their sins in the last birth. People with Rajasik Guna are essentially immoral, and thus, when they try to come up to the level of Saatva Guna-endowed Brahmins, they are only adding to their list of sins. The system of segregation used by Brahmins goes thus: Gunas determine actions; actions determine caste. Thus, caste came to be the premier point of social differentiation.

.... Jyotirao did not see any sense to this segregation, and the ideas of superiority and inferiority that had become entrenched fro the same. If fools were found amongst the Shoodras, so were they found amongst the Brahmins too. Then, how come Brahmins are considered superior and Shoodras, inferior? If Brahmins gush about them being the paragons of patience and forgiveness, then how come they start giving the choicest of expletives when a shadow of a Shoodra falls on them? Do they not lose their 'Brahmin-ness' with this behavior of theirs?

Brahmins have held sway over the lower caste people with their oft-repeated statements that propound the Brahmins' words to be the words of God. However, the only truth is what is seen in the creations of God. The flowers, fruit, water, sun, moon, food...all the essentials created by that supreme power to help living beings live a good life, is the only truth. As much as thirst is real, so is the cool water created by God real. However, Brahmins have mind-numbed the others into believing that only they (the Brahmins) are entitled to savoring the bounties of the creator, whereas the 'dharma' (duty) of the lower castes is to give up attachment to all those things, and 'donate' it to the Brahmins to 'erase their own sins'.

Has any Brahmin seen Lord Brahma in reality? If they have, let them describe to us how He looks? We would also like to hear!

Truth remains that Brahmins have used their intellect to mesmerize the guileless people by feeding them on hollow, false claims for generations on end.

They have misused the name of God to perpetrate philosophies that keep them entitled to all luxuries, while making the others shamelessly bereft of the same. These hypocrites have had no compunction guzzling alcohol, calling it 'Somras' . They have no qualms in killing innocent animals in the name of religious sacrifice. They are utterly shameless in prescribing rituals like the Anang Vrat Daan to the women of Shoodras and Ati Shoodras and taking undue advantage of them on that pretext. They call us lowly, but I doubt if there will be anyone more lowly than the Brahmins who have had no misgivings in twisting natural rules and subjugating others to the point of torture, for their own selfish gains. Animals might be more forgiving than these Brahmins who do not have the humanity to treat a fellow human being like a human. The myth that they have perpetrated of Brahmins being the most reverence-worthy of all, needs to be broken down immediately.

The cobwebs of ignorance need to be brushed off. A new social order based on the tenets of morality and true ideas of religion, needs to be established.

This universe is God's creation. When He created everybody similar, who are the Brahmins to dare create segregations and differentiations among us all? God has never attempted to create segregations on any basis, in any of our minds. All the things in this universe have been created for equal use by every person that God puts on this earth. How does it happen then that, certain people claim sole rights over certain things?

A human being's real religion is to behave with each other with equality and truth. When God has created every person, how can there be different religions and castes for different people? The thought seems illogical in every way. Humanity is the only religion accorded by God to all human beings. Some people have shamelessly kicked off this basic truth and created rules of their own. Not just that, they are shameless enough to claim that those rules are what God ordained in the first place! These people are outrageous enough to dethrone God and propagate themselves to be the ultimate superiors! What have they done this for? To create walls between people! To pit one man against another! To make them fear humans more than God!

God is a very kind entity. He is our father. He would have never thought of making his children fear him. This fear of religion and higher power has been perpetrated by the priests and so-called guardians of the seat of religious powers, to keep their hold over the unwitting masses intact.

True religious tenets aim to spread the message of morality and duty. However, all those ideas have long gone into oblivion owing to selfish motives.

The need of the hour is to bring back those ideas and help them take root in the minds of all people, crossing over the boundaries of caste and race. People should either be empowered to not follow any religion at all, or they should be equipped to follow the right kind of religion. One that teaches them to follow the path of morality and humanity.

Self-embalmed religious gurus have put the obstacles of biased scriptures and stone idols in the way of people and the Highest power. It is not just in Hindu religion; this hara-kiri can be seen in Christianity as well, where the papal system has been subjugating masses in its own way. Islam too has its own good side, but it does not have the largesse of heart to incorporate women in its folds.

Jyotirao was being reminded of people like Shidba, who were successful dissuaded from going in for religious conversion; but, there were many more people who were blindly following that path in the hope of freedom. Were they ever going to get bathed in the light of the true meaning of religion? Some educated people were veering towards the Prarthana Samaj, but be it Prarthana Samaj or Arya Samaj, these were simply eyewashes to cover up previous mistakes. The Shoodras and Ati Shoodras who were joining these organizations, were being heavily mislead. If this dangerous trend was to be halted in its tracks, then they had to be shown the true meaning and tenets of religion very soon. Every religion beholds the same truths; but some of the selfish religious leaders of each religion have hushed up those truths to keep their personal superiority and hold over the followers intact. Some tenets in Christianity, Islam, and Buddhism are really good. A new religious path can be etched by taking the good of what these religions have to offer. That will lead to the ideas of 'religious freedom' and 'freedom from religion' getting perpetrated among the masses. There won't remain any compulsion on people to follow only a certain religious path, irrespective of whether they like it or not. They will be free to choose whatever religion they want, and pray to the Almighty in whatever form they want to…

….The night had given way to dawn. It was time for Jyotirao to go on his morning walk. He called out to Savitribai, woke Sitaram up and taking his walking stick, set out for his round. The clickety-click of his chappals (footwear) was reverberating with the thoughts that were still whirring in his mind. A very important decision was being shaped up…

43

Once again, Jyotirao turned to Thomas Penn for inspiration. Penn had always considered belief in the Almighty, and, a life of morality to be the real way of leading a religious life. He did not feel the need for any mediating factor (like, some scripture, or, idol) to show or prove his religious leanings. He firmly dismissed the idea that scriptures were ordained by God. Instead, he believed that God meant for differences to be present in terms of religious ideas; because, if there were no differences, how would there ever be any discussion, debate or exchange of ideas vis-à-vis religion? Penn believed that religious choices were a very personal matter; the government or other people had no business interfering in any person's choice in this matter.

Jyotirao found inspiration in entities like Saint Kabeer who washed away the cobwebs gathered over religious ideas, and, Thomas Penn who strived to release the masses from the torment of religious leaders. Jyotirao endeavored to create a new religious discipline for the people of his community, but he knew that it was going to be a very challenging task to make tem accept the new ideas, conditioned as they were by the deep-rooted, ancient ideas and rituals. He was not finding the way to break through the shackles of the old systems.

The orthodox group had started a strong movement against the Christian missionaries and their work of spreading knowledge about Christianity. In Mumbai, public debates were ensuing amid the Christian Missionaries and Hindu orthodox members. Their repercussions were being seen on Pune as well. Scholars like Morbhat Dandekar, Krishnashastri Chiplunkar and Vishnubuva Brahmachari had gotten sucked into these debates.

After some scholarly Missionaries like Dr. Murray Mitchell, Rev. James Mitchell and Rev. H. H. Wilson had begun lifting the lid off the hypocrisy perpetrated by the Brahmins, Hindu fundamentalists had started scrambling to save face and make half-hearted amends, by establishing organizations like the Brahmo Samaj and Prarthana Samaj. However, these were clearly half-baked attempts at salvaging their wounded pride and showcasing a farce of being progressive. It was clear that these acts were short-lived, and were also not going to serve any concrete purpose in hiding the earlier misdoings. It was an old habit of the propagators of these organizations to advocate the theory of 'one God, one religion', confute casteism, and then do a U-turn to go back to the old scriptures. They had no wish to reach right down to the Shoodras and Ati Shoodras. It was foolish to believe that those people, who were 'invisible' to them till now, would suddenly start getting visibility on their mental landscape.

Baba Padmanji, a staunch supporter of the Free Church Mission, was an old friend of Jyotirao's. After having converted to Christianity, Baba had settled in Pune itself. Earlier, while he was in Mumbai, Baba had established the Satyashodhak Sabha. Comparative analysis about different religions was one of Baba's favorite topics of discussion. Thus, that was the basal idea of the organisation he had established, as well. Each meeting with Baba would give Jyotirao more fodder for thought. Idolatry, sanctity of scriptures and such other topics would often come up for discussion amidst them. Many of their discussions had led to both of them realising that no scriptures were ordained by God; but strangely, Baba refused to let go of the thought that the Bible was directly ordained by God. Jyotirao found this attitude strange. Even though he found the tenets of Christianity to be more reformist than many others, Jyotirao refused to believe that they were the sole way towards achieving social progress.

Jyotirao's mind was flipping like a fish out of water. He was feeling a dire need to raise a totally new and different religious sect that would become a guiding light for the entire society.

On one Sunday's meeting, Jyotirao elucidated his thoughts before his audience.

"Brothers, you are aware about how the Brahmins have enslaved the other caste people by brainwashing them through scriptures that they claim to have been ordained by God Himself. There is an urgent need to entrench the thoughts of Saint Kabeer within the masses. Unless they get free from the slavery of religious scriptures, they will never realize what their human rights are, and will never be able to follow religion in its real, intended sense. There is no merit in claiming that maintaining a beard or serving Brahmins leads one to 'real' and 'fulfilling' religious paths. We need to form an organization for making people see the light of truth."

The audience heartily approved with Jyotirao's idea. There was no doubt in anyone's mind about the cunning practices of the Brahmins. Everyone started chipping in with their suggestions regarding the philosophy and aims of the proposed organization. The discussion turned so frenetic, that it went on for the next two weeks! Finally, an organization was established by the name of 'Satyashodhak Samaj' – Satya, meaning truth; shodhak, meaning finders; and samaj, meaning a group of people on a mission to find the truth. Jyotirao was declared the founder and chief of Satyashodhak Samaj.

The base of this organization was going to be very different. The organization was not going to propagate or promote any one religion as good or perfect. It was going to put forth its free views about religion as a concept, and rather than simply halt at discussing about religion amongst its members, it was going to strive to reach the thoughts among the masses. The main aim of the organization was to reach newer, liberating thoughts about the concept of religion among the society and give them an opportunity to change their life in a holistic manner.

The members of Satyashodhak Samaj decided to have a big meeting on 24th September 1873. It was decided to invite people from Mumbai, Nagar etc. Jyotirao, Krishnarao Bhalekar, Shaahir Dhondiram all started toiling towards making the meeting a success. Invitations were being sent out, drafts of the program were being made and remade... Tatya did not know at that time, but soon enough, a new generation of farmers, labourers and the educated class would become very keenly involved in the Satyashodhak Samaj.

44

Soon, the D-day arrived. The Phule mansion was abuzz with excitement since morning. Many people had come from out of town. Govindrao Bapuji had come from Bhillar, Narayanrao Shinde had come from Parvati. Gyaanoba and Sitaram were immersed in overlooking the last minute preparations. Narayanrao Nagarkar, who had arrived last evening itself, was deep in discussion with Jyotirao. Narayanrao Kadlak, Krishnarao Bhalekar, and Shaahir Dhondiram were busy writing the declarations.

The meeting began at noon, with around 60 people in attendance. Jyotirao was requested to start the meeting with a speech, in which he said:

"Brothers, religion forms an important aspect in the foundation of any society. But sadly, today our society's attitude towards the concept of religion has become like that of the blind person in the fable of the blind man and the elephant.

Each one is interpreting religion in their own way, but without any independent thought. In fact, their capacity of thinking independently has been dimmed to such an extent that they have been rendered incapable of asking questions and raising doubts regarding any thing concerned with religion. Thus, they have been shackled in the slavery of scriptures. The Brahmins find themselves great by parroting the verses of holy scriptures, and the Shoodras find it gratifying to drink the water off the feet of such Brahmins who they consider to be the agents of God. However, this is not true religion; rather, it is the travesty of religion as it was meant to originally be. It is the insult of the Almighty who has created us all."

"The Hindu religion as it stands today, is nothing but a distorted, contorted version of the real religion, done by sly, selfish Brahmins. They have made a business of religion by steadfastly entrenching casteism and the principles of birth being decided by past karmas. They claim to live according to the Vedas, which they claim to be the ultimate truth. However, they themselves do not live according to the principles of Vedas. This hypocrisy is also an insult of the Creator. Sadly, this openly conducted deception escapes the eyes of majority in the society. We have been reduced to such a blind, deaf and dumb mass that 'the Brahmins talk and we listen'. We have stopped questioning, doubting, and arguing about anything that the Brahmins tell us. This needs to stop. We need to stop thinking that the Brahmins are the ultimate knowledge-bearers. Here, I would like to thank Dynaangiribaba for showing us the right direction in this regard. It is not in the capacity of one person to fight against this cunning of the Brahmins. We all need to join hands to fight this evil. That is why we have established our Satyashodhak Samaj."

"Brothers, there is religious basis to parroting from the scriptures and offering food-water to stone idols. This is a ploy perpetrated to keep the kitchen fires burning in the houses of a select few. In order to keep this practice running, the concepts of caste differences and rituals have been firmly entrenched in the social mind-sets. So many Shoodras, who are born with immense intellect, keep thinking of themselves as unworthy, simply because they have been born into a Shoodra household. Such negative thoughts lead to immense loss for the country, because the country loses precious resources owing to such debilitating ideas. If we want our country to progress, we need to uproot the evil ideas of casteism and untouchability. We all need to strive to educate each and every person in the society. That is the best way to justify our birth as a human being."

"A person becomes superior through his/her merit. Not through his/her caste or the family he/she is born into. How is it justifiable that a decent Mahar is considered inferior, even as a vile Brahmin is considered superior, just because of their castes? W also need to introspect about this factor. Do not find it great to wash a Brahmin's feet and drink that water! Instead, try to improve your own social and educational conditions."

"The concept of religion has been horribly distorted to suit selfish purposes. Our Shoodra brethren have blindly accepted those distorted versions. Understand: rearing sheep is a shepherd's job, not his religion. Making furniture is a carpenter's job, not his religion. Similarly, cheating the Shoodras of their human rights is not the Brahmins' religion; it is their attitude. Let some Brahmin answer me this: if they justify taking donations of food and money from the Shoodras to expedite their dead ancestors to heaven, then who do the Brahmins pay donations to, for expediting their own ancestors in the same way?! These mindless rituals are nothing but clever ideas of the Brahmins to keep their kitchen fires burning without doing any exerting labor."

The audience started chortling. Jyotirao continued,

"If three brothers from the same family have three different occupations, then does that mean that they follow three different religions?! No. Thus, it is important to weed out absurd ideas and work towards a new concept of religion that accepts that God is one; He is the ultimate truth. He has created every living being; thus, there can be no differentiation amongst them on any basis. Every person has equal right on whatever is present in the universe. The Creator has ordained that every person should enjoy every thing without any differences. He is not going to be appeased by offering the same flowers that He only created. True appeasement to God can only come by each of us helping our fellow human beings grow and prosper, in whatever ways we can. Each of us behaving fraternally and morally, will be the best form of service to God."

"It will bode better for human beings to not keep searching for how does God look like, and where does he reside? It is beyond human comprehension and capability to find answers to such questions. God is all-pervading. God is the ultimate power. We do not require any intermediate link to offer our prayers to Him. We all are the children of one God. Just as a child does not require its father's permission to talk to its mother, so also we do not require anybody's permission or recommendation to communicate with God. He is our mother and our father too. We do not require these priests to talk to our own parents. Stop being so dependent on them."

"No scripture can provide you with one ultimate truth. That's because, in every religion, the cunning and selfish people of that religion, have manipulated the texts to serve their own purposes. Thus, no one scripture can be said to be entirely beneficial for man. Yes, every scripture will have some tenets that are worth following; but often, those tenets have been hidden or distorted by the manipulative elements. It is our duty to find and follow those good tenets."

"Fundamentalism and casteism are evils that erect walls amidst people of one God. We all are one. We have equal right to enjoy the universe's offerings. But sadly, we face many challenges in letting that happen."

".... There are so many rivers on this earth. All rivers go

and join some sea or ocean. How then, can it be justified to say that, only one river is the purest of them all? Thus, when we all human beings have been endowed with the same physical features and brains, how can a handful of them prove superior simply because of the family they have been born into? Brothers, time has come to think and introspect. Look within. See what we are doing wrong Stop gambling. Stop getting addicted to alcohol or tobacco. Get your children educated. Become industrious. Don't keep blaming the stars for your misfortune. Industriousness can be the key to vanquish any misfortune you may be suffering from."

"Brothers, true religiousness is in realizing the truth about religion and then following that path only. Truth is morality. Truth is action. Truth is the true religion. Follow the path of truth to achieve eternal happiness. Remaining happy is the best service you can offer to the Creator. This thought is the foundation of our Satyashodhak Samaj."

"Brothers, religion is not the ownership of a handful few. No one can claim monopoly over it. Everyone is free to follow a religion. Sadly, the Hindu religion expels women and lower caste people from its folds. Christianity, Islam and Buddhism can be practiced by anybody; but not so with Hindu religion. Another factor about the Hindu religion is that, once you are born into it, you are compelled to follow it for life; irrespective of whether you agree with its teachings or not. I'm not saying that other religions are completely error-free, or that you should convert to those religions. No; those religions too have their problems. Thus, there is a need to start a totally new religious sect that will be of benefit to everyone, irrespective of their background and status. We believe that all human beings are one; truth is the only religion; and thus we are putting forth before you a religious sect called 'Satyadharma' aka religion of truth. We will not coerce anybody to follow our sect. Our religion will not interfere with the present religion you may be following. Instead, we only pray to God that may such a day come soon, where we shall see many Satyadharma followers co-habiting in the society harmoniously. Our religion will have no rituals and no priests. Our religion only exhorts its voluntary followers to try to find the truth in everything, and follow on its path tenaciously. Today, the people of our community are suffering very badly. They are being looted by unscrupulous Brahmin priests in the name of mindless donations. We need to extricate our ignorant brethren from these scams and the subjugation that comes along with them. I request you all to put forth your suggestions on whatever I have said so far."

Pin drop silence ensued for the next few minutes. Tatya's speech had pulled at the heart strings of each person present there.

Then, slowly the murmurs started, and soon escalated into an outpour of suggestions. People started expressing their thoughts freely.

Krishnarao said,

"Tatyasaheb, will our brethren become free from the psychological slavery of Hindu religion, if they start walking on the path of Satyadharma?"

"Undoubtedly!" said Jyotirao. "The Brahmin-enforced Hindu religion is founded on a bed of lies. Following the tenets of Satyadharma will definitely help exorcise the ghosts of the untrue Brahmin Hindu religion. The Hindu religion had come to be monopolized by Brahmins. It has no place left for Shoodras and Ati Shoodras. But, our Satyadharma will be all-encompassing. We will not promote idolatry or mindless rituals in any way. The aim of Satyadharma is not just religious reform. Rather, we wish to educate people that they are free to follow any religion that enhances their life. They are not bound to meekly follow what the Brahmins, or any other religious guru, tells them. Satyadharma will endeavor to first remove the basic idea of religious slavery from the hearts and minds of those who have been oppressed for generations on end. Thomas Penn, who gave a great critical analysis of Christianity, did not establish a new religion by himself. But, he gave us the direction to do so. Thus, Satyadharma wants to remove the slavish notions and establish the idea of free thought and freedom of religious choice among the society."

Then, the discussion shifted to what should be the basic tenets of the Satyadharma religion. A few of the points that were highlighted, included:

1. There is only one God and He is reflected in truth. He is the creator of all living beings on earth.

2. Just as a child does not require its father's permission to talk to its mother, so also we do not require anybody's permission or recommendation to communicate with God.

3. A person does not become superior or inferior by his caste. That is decided solely on his attributes and behavior.

Any person who agrees with these ideas can become a member of the Satyashodhak Samaj.

The ideas expressed as the foundation of this organization, were deliberately kept very simple, so as to enable everyone to understand them easily.

After Jyotirao, Narayanrao Nagarkar, Narayanrao Kadlak, Krisnarao Bhalekar, and Dhondiram Shaahir too spoke about the need for entrenching Satyashodhak samaj in society.

Then, Jyotirao elaborated on what would be the initiation ritual for becoming a member of the organization. Before that, he asked the audience if they wholeheartedly agreed with the ideas that the Satyashodhak Samaj would be based on.

Narayanrao Nagarkar asked Gyaanoba,

"Gyaanoba, do you agree? Do you feel that these ideas hold merit?"

"Absolutely, Sir. I agree with what Tatya has been saying" replied Gyaanoba.

The others also expressed their acceptance of the ideas. Then, Jyotirao started the simple ritual of initiation with a prayer addressed to Lord Khandoba and Bali Raja, and a promise from all present that they will strive to uphold the ideas of the Satyashodhak Samaj.

Then followed the public reading of the oath that exhorted the members that they would henceforth believe wholeheartedly in the concept of one God; they would not depend on any intermediary for communicating with God; they would educate their sons and daughters; and they would always behave in keeping with morality.

Then, Jyotirao was declared as the Chairman and Treasurer of the organization, and Narayanrao Kadlak was named the Secretary. Then, everyone started enrolling their names as members.

It was the dawn of a new era. A surge of renewed confidence was coursing through the people present there. They were not going to be enslaved anymore. They were going to follow a new path that would lead them to becoming much better and emancipated people.

45

Evening had set in. Jyotirao finished the day's work at his shop and started for home. He was in immense hurry. That night, Shaahir Dhondiram was due to give a speech near the Shaniwarwada. Jyotirao had promised to write some notes down for the speech, but he had been so burdened with work that till now, the notes had not been readied.

The work of Satyashodhak Samaj was going on in earnest. The members had celebrated the small festival of Tulshicha Lagna without calling any Brahmin priests to conduct the ritual. As this news spread far and wide, places like Bhillar, Bhamburde, Hadapsar and Parvati started scrambling to open branches of the Satyashodhak Samaj. Meetings and speeches stared happening at multiple venues. News of Jyotirao Phule expected to come for a meeting would lead to people traveling for 10-20 miles to attend the same. After excellent orators like

Dhondiram Shaahir, Krishnarao Bhalekar and Bhimrao Mahamuni started traveling to give speeches, the crowds began intensifying beyond belief! Farmers and tillers who would otherwise find entertainment in dance programs, started abandoning them to make a beeline for meetings of the Satyashodhak Samaj. A powada written by Krishnarao, about Raghu Gaadiwan, started getting specially popular. The society of Pune started buzzing with electrifying energy. Soon, the vibes spread to other parts of Maharashtra as well.

Places as far as Thane, Mumbai, Buldhana and Satara started being positively affected by the Satyashodhak movement. Youngsters like Krishnarao Bhalekar, Pandharinath Abaji Chavan, and Raoji Shirole began participating enthusiastically in the movement. They started conveying the messages of Satyashodha Samaj to the masses via writing, poetry and speeches. Krishnarao came up with a great idea of having daily speeches in the Peths of Pune – for instance, a speech in Budhwar Peth on Wednesday (Wednesday is called Budhwar in Marathi), in Guruvar Peth on Thursday (Thursday is called Guruvar in Marathi) and so on. Such was the effect of these meetings that, the Brahmins started quaking in their boots with every new meeting being organized. Except for Raobahadur Gopal Hari, no Brahmin dared to come even nearby the venue of the meetings. Raobahadur, however, was invited for presiding over quite a few of these.

Dr. Santuji Lad of Thane, Ramchandrarao Dhamanaskar of Satara, Bapuji Hari of Buldhana and Ramaiyya Venkaiah Ayyavaru of Mumbai, became the prime flag-bearers of the Satyshodhak Samaj in those locations. Many eminent people of Pune, such as Ramshet Uravane and Vitthalrao Guthaal, came together for supporting this cause. The committee members were meeting every Sunday. Every alternate Saturday would see a public speech being given on varied, socially-relevant topics such as idolatry, mindless rituals, importance of education, need to forego addictions and so on.

Donations were pouring in from several quarters. People were coming forward to help in various ways. People started coming from beyond Pune, to attend the Sunday meetings. Soon, the number became so high that the shop started falling short in accommodating so many people. So, the venue for Sunday meetings had to be shifted to Dr. Sadoba's Gaawde's bungalow. Now, the Sunday meetings had morphed into Satyashodhak Samaj meetings.

Jyotirao's poetic mind started getting more fodder for thought in this scenario. He started getting inspired to write many powadas and couplets, some of which he would use during his speeches, much to the audience's liking. Dhondiram Shaahir would also exhort him to keep writing. Dhondiram would also request Jyotirao to keep writing texts for his speeches, which he would then make copies of, and distribute among the followers of Satyashodhak Samaj.

Surprisingly, the gossip rags of Pune had not yet got a wind of the formation and activities of Satyashodhak Samaj. A magazine called 'Vividh Dynaan Vistaar' had written a disparaging article regarding 'Gulamgiri', calling it a loony piece of work by a madman called Jyotirao Phule. The article also went on to make derogatory comments about 'Jaatibhed Vivek Saar', calling it the idiotic base for Phule's literary 'rag' that had foolish and false thoughts expressed about history, logic. language and religion. The reporter had gone onto say that 'Jaatibhed Vivek Saar' was clearly written by a person who had converted to Christianity and soured by his experiences there, had become a jealous, frustrated, vengeful man who gave Phule a platform to air his biased thoughts from.

Few days later, Jyotirao had to take time out of his busy schedule to attend a funeral at Raosaeb Ranade's home. This was the second time in two years that there had been a funeral in the Ranade household. Raosaheb's wife Rama had been ill with tuberculosis since the last two years. Finally, one day, she gave up her fight with the disease and succumbed to death.

After his sister's sudden widowhood, Raosaheb now had to battle with the grief of his wife's untimely death. His progressive friends started badgering Raosaheb to get remarried to some widow; but Raosaheb was not making any comment on this suggestion.

It was quite late in the evening by the time Jyotirao returned home. The frontage of his house bore the phrase 'Satyamev Jayate' (Truth Always Wins), and a red flag fluttered on the roof. He returned to an empty courtyard. Tired of waiting for him, the younger children had gone off to play at the neighboring houses. Usually, they would wait till their Tatya came home and then, they would all play and chat for a long time. It was one of Jyotirao's favorite pastimes to engage with the children. But today, there was no one.

He called out for Savitribai, but there was no answer from her too. Flummoxed, Jyotirao sought out Sitaram and asked him about Savitribai's whereabouts. He replied,

"Kaku has gone somewhere with the lady from Govande house."

Jyotirao went inside the house. The older children were doing their homework. He gave them some treats that he had got along; gave some instructions to Sitaram; and then sat to at his desk to write. Just then, Shaahir Dhondiram came inside. Seeing him, Jyotirao exclaimed,

"You have come at any opportune moment, Shaahir! Listen to what I have just written...."

"Wah, wah... absolutely, Tatyasaheb" the Shaahir said heartily.

Jyotirao started narrating the verses he had written:

"We are created by one God; Revere him, all ye' men;

Enjoy the things he has created; but with equality, sans differences;

Cast aside the segregations of caste and religion; follow the path of righteousness, always;

Let each and everyone be happy; prays Jyoti, to his Creator!"

"Oh! That is really great, Tatyasaheb!" Shaahir exulted.

Jyotirao replied tongue-in-cheek,

"I hope you didn't feel surprised that I did not write anything critical about the Brahmins?" adding, "Shaahir, we all need to remember that no individual belonging to the Brahmin caste is our enemy on an individual basis. Our enemy is the divisive attitude harnessed by the Brahmins as a community. Our aim is to release our ignorant brethren from the psychology slavery, that, blindly following religious rules has forced them into. Satyadharma can be adopted by anyone and everyone. It is all-inclusive. It is as much for women and lower caste people as it is the Brahmins. There cannot be separate religions for humankind. That's because, we all have ben created by only one God. The humankind is one entity; so, it is bound to have only one religion. However, sadly, we do not have any such religion at present, that unites every person under one canopy. That is why, the concept of 'freedom of religion' is missing from the lexicon of society. However, Satyadharma abides by 'freedom of religion'. When people of different religions start co-existing harmoniously, the society will become a very happy place. Listen to this verse..." said Jyotirao, as he started narrating various verses to Dhondiram.

Just then, Sitaram announced,

"Tatyasaheb, two people have come to meet you."

"Send them inside."

Seeing the two middle-aged men who came in, Jyotirao realized that they had been present at last Sunday's meeting. The men introduced themselves and said,

"Tatyasaab, we wanted to ask you something..."

"Yes, tell me?"

"You say that even if we pray in our Marathi language, those prayers reach to God properly. But, how is that possible? God only converses in Sanskrit language, isn't it?" said one of them.

The other man added, saying,

"We were going to ask this question at the meeting, but we didn't..."

"Then why didn't you?" asked Jyotirao.

"How could we, Tatyasaab? People would have laughed at our ignorance."

"What is there to laugh in that? And anyways, why did such a question come in your mind?"

"There's a priest who comes to our home for conducting rituals. He says that prayers reach God only if they are said in Sanskrit, because that is God's language. That is why, all scriptures, hymns and prayers are written in Sanskrit, and only the Brahmins have a right to learn and use that language."

"He also said that it is a sin to conduct prayers or rituals in Marathi language."

Jyotirao smiled at them and said,

"Brothers, you sing the hymns written by saints like Tukaram, Chokha Mela, Savta Mali and Gora Kumbhar. What language are they written in? Marathi, isn't it? Then, do you mean to say that they committed a sin by writing hymns in Marathi?"

The two men looked at each other in bewilderment and replied,

"No."

"So, you do agree that their prayers and service did reach God?"

"Yes, absolutely" they replied.

"Then, remove this doubt from your mind. No other country follows Sanskrit language. They all speak and pray to God in their own language. Their prayers do reach God, don't they? God is omnipresent and the ultimate power. How will he not understand your prayers? Tell me one thing... if sinners say lies or do some other sin in some language other than Sanskrit, then would you say that God will not understand what they are doing?"

"No, not at all. How can that be? God is sure to understand" the men replied.

"Correct. That's why I said, do not worry about whether God understand our language or not. Just keep praying to Him with a sincere heart. Truth is the only way of life. Truth is the only religion. People who are telling you lies in the name of God, are undermining His capability. If the Vedas are meant to uplift all of humankind, then why are they written in a language that only a handful can understand? If the Vedas were truly written by God, who has created us all, then they would have been written in a language that would have been understood by all, isn't it?" said Jyotirao, as he continued,

"See, there are many languages in this world. The list of languages and dialects will keep growing as the population keeps increasing. Can God really be so selfish and narrow-minded to convey his message in a way that will be understood only by a small section of this ever-increasing population? Don't pay attention to such false claims. These are simply clever ways to hide one's flaws. The Quran and Bible are open to al. Then, why aren't the Vedas? That's because, they don't want their falsities to come out in the open. Even though these scriptures are supposed to be about religion, they are not really so. These are manipulations on paper, nothing more. Do not fear Sanskrit; do not fear God. Go on, learn English…learn Hindi… Become knowledgeable. Everyone should know English, Hindi and Marathi. That is the best way to our progress. Do not fall prey to foolish claims made by these selfish people. They want religion to be concentrated only in their hands, so that they can lead an idle life. We need to realize this ploy. Brahmins are only concerned about looting the ignorant Shoodras, taking undue advantage of their ignorance. These people leave absolutely no occasion or festival to beg for alms from Shoodras on the name of dakshina. From Diwali, to Ganesh Utsav, to even the sun and moon eclipse… they will leave no occasion to cull money!"

The two men started laughing heartily. Jyotirao continued,

"Be it the pilgrimage to Pandharpur, or to Alandi…these people will be present with their hands outstretched! If we were to write a list of all the ways in which they are looting the Shoodras, it will become one big book in itself! This loot has been going on for years on end. So many past generations of ours have fallen prey to these atrocities. Sadly, the tormented have become complacent about the torment, and that has served to make the tormentors more shameless than ever. I'd say, dacoits are more preferable than these slick-talking thugs. At least, dacoits make their intentions clear."

The two men seemed relieved. They turned to Jyotirao and said with a smile,

"Now we shall not get lured by their claims, Tatyasaab. Please make us a member of the Satyashodhak Samaj."

"This Sunday, few people are coming to get their membership. You may also come that time. This is going to be one of the main aspects of our movement henceforth. We are not going to tolerate the hypocrisy of these Brahmins. They treat us lowly but have no qualms taking money and food from us in the name of dakshina. They are playing the devil's advocate by creating divisions of superiority and inferiority even amongst the Shoodras and Ati Shoodras. Please, always remember: God requires no mediator. These people, who claim to have seen God and have spoken to God, are nothing but fraudsters. Seeing God in His eternal form, is beyond the capacity of the human brain. We humans are too small to even claim to have seen that omnipresent power. We can only do service to it by behaving properly and righteously. Since these devil's advocates claim that they have seen God, let them tell us how He looks? Can they do that? Let them show this God to us also… we will also ask Him, why has He made these differences of caste and religion, if at all it is ordained by Him as these people claim...! Brothers, keeping fasts, following ornate rituals, idolatry, or singing bhajans are not the real ways to offer service to God. Real service to God lies in following a righteous, moral life that will make your and others life happier."

"But Tatyasaab, what do we call this God that you are talking about? What is His name?" asked one of the men.

"Do not bind Him in the box of names. Call him a Creator or Ishwar; but realize that, He is one; He is the ultimate power; He has created us all. He does not reside in any stone idol or in any temple. God is only one entity. This hoax of there being 33 crore Gods, is just that – a hoax! If you keep praying to each one of those Gods every day of your life, your entire life will go only in praying! You will not be able to do even a single work."

The two men got sheepish on hearing what Jyotirao was saying. He had pointed out exactly what they had been doing so far. All the same, they also realized why Jyotirao was labeled an iconoclast by the society.

Jyotirao said,

"Brothers, those people who build huge temples and loot the devotees in the name of the idol they install there, are nothing but thugs and sinners. Look at David Sassoon. He started a charitable dispensary for the benefit of the poor; but the rich people in our country can never think like that. The Shinde Sarkar gave a feast to one lakh Brahmins in Pune. Had they used that money for doing something good for the society, they would have got so many blessings. But of course, why will the idle Brahmins advise them to do that?!"

"Tatyasaab, people call you a heretic and an apostate. They say, you are out to blacken the face of religion…" one man ventured to say fearfully.

Jyotirao laughed and replied,

"People who shamelessly use the name of God to loot others, are the true sinners. They, who have no qualms manipulating religion or the government for their own selfish gains. Every time someone has raised a thumb to snub their selfishness, they have retaliated in exactly the same way. They are the real heretics, not me! They have been blinded by the smoke coming out of the sacrificial offerings they keep doing time and again! They, who do not see the tons of grain and ghee being wasted in the name of oblations, can never claim to see or know true God and religion. This lament is not new; rather, it has been there from time immemorial. In the past too, Lord Buddha, Charvaak, and Bruhaspati made stern criticisms on these wasteful aspects of Hindu religion; but, these Brahmins are so thick-skinned, that no criticism penetrates their brain to make self-reforms. When they cannot silence their critics by labeling them as heretic, these Brahmins then gang up to bring the opponents into their realm. What happened with Buddhism and Jainism? These religions were among the first to refute God in the form of idols. But then these astute Brahmins labeled Lord Buddha himself as the ninth form of God! They have befuddled the whole society by writing scriptures with texts that directly contradict each other. Our Shoodra and Ati Shoodra brethren have yet not understood this confusion created in the name of religion. It will still take them time to make sense out of all this. These cunning people used their knowledge and scriptures to torture the ignorant; and, then they had the gall to term the scriptures as 'true knowledge' and thus kept the lower castes away from reading them. In reality, harming the society became the religion of the Brahmins, and, taking on their torment complacently became the religion of the other castes."

"But Tatyasaab, then you only guide us...What do we ignorant people do in such a scenario?" asked the men.

"Do only one thing: Test anything that is told to you, against the meter of your intelligence and personal views. Don't even believe me entirely, just because I am saying it. That would also be blind following. Think about what appeals to your mind, and follow only that much. Behave with others as you desire them to behave with you. Do not fear anybody except for God. While doing anything, think if it will be liked by God or not. Once everyone starts behaving in accordance with that moral compass, then the society will soon become a happy and healthy place for all. Truth is God; God is truth. Behave truthfully in whatever you do. That is the true meaning of being a Satyashodhak. Do not sit chanting God's name emptily. Instead, behave with truth and God will be pleased with you. Do not think of any person different or inferior than yourself. Any scripture that advocates creating segregations between human beings, consider it to be a fraudulent text created by selfish people. The Sanskrit language has been used to make a monkey out of us. They kept telling us that it is God's language and thus meant to be followed only by a select, privileged few. In order to keep the Shoodras and Ati Shoodras away from knowing the truth, they wrote the scriptures in Sanskrit and then very cleverly, prevented the lower castes from acquiring knowledge. It was nothing but a ploy to keep their evil deeds a secret. But, this situation is now going to change. Anybody who decides to see the scriptures through the lens of rationality, is condemned for being a non-believer by these Brahmins. But tell me, is there a shred of logic in the scriptures that they have written? Creating Gods out of thin air and then declaring themselves higher than those Gods, is nothing but a sham. God has created this entire universe – and these people claim to have created God! Can there be a better example of atheism and malarkey than this?!"

Jyotirao continued further, saying,

"Without testing these scriptures against the parameter of rationality, if we keep trusting the tenets of casteism and rituals, it will be the biggest foolishness on our part. If we keep believing that the reason for our problems in this life is hidden in our actions in the past life; or that, we are unhappy because being unhappy is the destiny written for us by God, then all that is pure nonsense. It is a very clever way to cripple the society so that we all become putty in the hands of the Brahmins. If a Shoodra kills a Brahmin, he is sentenced to death. But, if a Brahmin kills a Shoodra, he is let off with some meager punishment, or simply atonement. What kind of justice is that? A religion that attributes such a meager value to a Shoodra's life cannot be embraced as our religion! Please stop thinking of Brahmins as agents of God. Stop worshipping them. Stop fearing them. Our ancestors have suffered long due to the biased laws of the Brahmins. Today we are happier because the British government does not follow those laws."

The two men were entirely satisfied with Jyotirao's explanations. They took his leave and left.

Here, Jyotirao started thinking. The movement was now getting powered up. Turmoil was around the corner. The Brahmins were going to become savage, once they realized that their livelihoods were in danger.

It was quite late in the night. Savitribai had yet not returned. Jyotirao became worried. But soon, he heard the back door open. Kaku was entering with a newly born infant in hand. Jyotirao rushed ahead and took the child from her. He had slept after wailing for a long time. The bloodied umbilical cord was still hanging from his belly.

Tatya asked Kaku,

"Who was the poor woman, Savitribai?"

"There's a widow named Kashibai who stays in the house of Kesopant Sindi. She is from Kalyan. Her elder brother is a Collector. Apparently, he left her here. Actually, she hails from the Natu family in our town. But, no one is willing to support her. The poor woman has been reduced to working as a domestic help. She was going to commit suicide, but thankfully I could stop her in time. She was not ready to give the boy. Only after I promised her that I would look after him like my own child, did she relent. Poor woman, she was so reluctant to hand over her son...." sighed Kaku, looking at the little baby lovingly.

"Why didn't you tell me all this, Savitri?" Jyotirao asked, taking the baby in his arms.

Kaku looked at him with a wan smile and said,

"Where do you have the time to listen to these things?"

Jyotirao became sheepish. Savitribai was right. With his work increasing manifold, Savitribai was looking after the orphanage singlehandedly.

"I know, Savitri. But, it is due to your support that I am unworried about the orphanage..." said Jyotirao.

"That's also true..." said Savitribai, taking the baby from him.

They both went into the kitchen. Arrangements had to be made for the new guest.

"Savitribai, what should we name this baby?" asked Jyotirao.

"You suggest...?"

"No, you tell me..."

"No, I would like you to suggest some name..."

"Yeshu....Yeshwant...? Did you like it?"

Kaku smiled and gave her affirmation. Tatya asked her,

"Well, that's good. But, you didn't ask me, why I chose this name only?"

"I understood. You chose it because it is the colloquial name for Lord Jesus, isn't it?"

"That's right" said Jyotirao with a smile. "It is the name of the great man who gave the message of 'love thy enemy' to make humans out of every man. Every time the name Yeshu is uttered, people will be reminded of that divine soul!"

46

It was imperative to start a branch of the Satyashodhak Samaj in Mumbai, imminently. Jyotirao was in constant communication with Swami Aiyyavaru regarding the same. Swami Aiyyavaru was staying at Kamathipura. Many Telugu families of the Phoolmali caste were settled in that area. Many generations back they had left for Telangana, but had now returned to Mumbai. They would undertake contracts of building houses and roads. Swami Aiyyavaru was a rich and learned personality from that community. He too had a business of undertaking contracts. Last year, he had come to Pune for some business and had specially gone to meet Jyotirao that time. He had expressed a desire to participate in the Satyashodhak movement. He himself had already started a school and library at Kamathipura. Even though Vasudeo Babaji and Tukaram Tatya had become members of the Prarthana Samaj, they were definitely going to help the Satyashodhak Samaj too. Dr. Santuji Lad had also written a letter of support to Jyotirao and had invited him to come to Thane as soon as he could.

Jyotirao was wanting to take a tour of Mumbai and Thane, but his work in Pune had burgeoned to such an extent that, he was simply finding no time to draft any travel plans. Add to that, opposition was growing stiffer against the Satyashodhak Samaj. Naysayers were up to nuisance tricks such as suspending the members from their jobs, poisoning the minds of British officers, ostracizing and cursing people who became members, throwing stones on their houses and so on. The moment they would hear that some person was planning to become a member of the Satyashodhak Samaj, the Brahmins would go and waylay him at his house itself! Gyaanba Malhar Mistri had been successful in making members of fifty people; but, he had to suffer immensely at the hands of the Brahmins for this act of his. His boss, a Brahmin, troubled him so much that finally Gyaanba was forced to leave his job. Narayanrao Kadlak was transferred to Mahabaleshwar. Vitthalrao Guthaal advised Mahadevrao Suryawanshi to conduct his housewarming pooja without Brahmins. Both of them were immensely troubled by the Brahmins for this daring act. The Brahmins poisoned the ears of Vitthalwao's business partners, and Vitthalrao had to suffer a big loss to his business.

In spite of all this, the Satyashodhaks were not faltering or stepping back. Membership was growing. The organization was primarily undertaking the work of education. Membership fees and donations were being used for giving scholarships to promising children. Many schools were opened along side opening of new branches. Jyotirao was happy but his mind was still restless. He now wanted to entrench the concept of social and festive events happening according to progressive norms instead of the conventional ones. He was going to lead by example in this aspect.

Jyotirao's helper Sitaram Alhaat was leading the life of a widower. He hardly remembered his marriage, which had happened when Sitaram was a mere toddler. Jyotirao had been thinking of getting Sitaram remarried and resettled. Radha, the daughter of Gyaanoba Nimbankar, who stayed in Jyotirao's locality, was perfect for Sitaram. Her mother, Bajubai Nimbankar, would often come to their house, and was friendly with Savitribai.

Jyotirao decided to broach the topic with Sitaram that evening.

When Jyotirao came home that evening, he saw Babaji sitting with his sons Mahadba and Sadba, in the living room. Savitribai was talking with them. Property matters had caused a rift among the brothers.

Jyotirao folded his hands to Babaji. Then, Mahadba and Sadba too got up and touched their younger uncle's feet. Jyotirao blessed them wholeheartedly, and asked after everybody's health.

Casual talk went on for some time more. Jyotirao could not understand the purpose of this surprise visit. Seeing that Babaji had come, Rajarambhau also came and sat in the living room.

Finally, Jyotirao asked Babaji,

"So, what brings you here today, Dadasaheb?"

"Well...I thought...how long will all this continue? We all are the branches of the same tree. Why not live together and happily then?" replied Babaji.

Jyotirao was pleased to hear what Babaji said. The dispute

had been started by their respective fathers, but had spilled over to the next generation for no reason at all. Jyotirao was going to be happy if these useless arguments went to grave.

However, Rajarambhau could not control himself. He spat out,

"Yes sure, why not?! Now that there is nothing left to give or receive, that is when you have come ahead with an olive branch, isn't it? What do you have to lose by doing so?!"

"I agree, Rajaram" Babaji said in a soothing voice. "But, see, these quarrels were started by our fathers. Now, they both are no more. So, how prudent is it that we keep fighting just because they had fought?! I could see my father's mistake even at that time, but how was I going to be able to intervene, you tell me?"

Seeing Rajarambhau still trembling with rage, Jyotirao intervened saying,

"Bhau, let us not extend this dispute any more..."

Using that opportunity, Babaji said,

"Tatya, we are really happy to see the work you have been doing for the lower castes. We too would like to become members of the Satyashodhak Samaj."

Jyotirao was indeed happy to see that the long standing problems were getting resolved and the brothers were finally coming closer. However, Rajarambhau was not convinced. After Babaji left, he said,

"Tatya, I smell a rat in all this. I don't believe that these people simply came after all these years and extended a hand of peace. I find something fishy in all this..."

Jyotirao was understanding what Bhau was trying to say, but today his attention was focussed on the topic of Sitaram's marriage.

As he broached the topic with Sitaram, the latter's face came alive with joy. He trusted Tatya to do only good for him. After getting Sitaram's approval, Jyotirao spoke to Savitribai. She liked the idea, and agreed to talk to Bajubai, who would then be tasked to speak to Gyaanoba.

Soon, dinner was done and Jyotirao retired to his room to read.

Just then, the door creaked. Immediately, Savitribai got up to see who had come. Seeing her rush, Jyotirao understood that Savitribai was already expecting someone. Jyotirao could hear some woman speaking to Savitribai in hushed tones and crying for a long time. Then, the door creaked again.

As Savitribai came inside, Jyotirao asked her,

"Who was it?"

Savitribai replied,

"Yeshwant's mother."

Jyotirao was deeply perturbed. It was beyond comprehension that a mother had been reduced to sneaking like a thief for seeing her own child! Jyotirao had yet not seen Yeshwant's mother. He said to Savitribai,

"Why didn't you call me? I too wish to meet Yeshwant's mother."

"Kashibai will not come in front of you, Shetji . She feels, she has committed a grave sin. She is losing her mental balance due to that thought. It gets very difficult to calm her down."

"Savitri, whatever happened was bad. But, it can never be a sin to save a baby's life, can it? And, if that is a sin, then what about those evil men who shamelessly took undue advantage of a helpless woman's condition?..."

Just then, Dhondiba came calling out for Jyotirao…

"Tatyasaheb…Tatyasaheb…."

"Yes, Dhondiba, what is it?" Jyotirao asked, coming out of the room.

"Tatyasaheb, Dhondiram has been arrested. He has been taken to the police station. Please come soon."

"Arrested? For what? He was scheduled to give a speech today, isn't it?"

"Yes…that speech was going on near Shaniwarwada. A policeman from the station opposite the fort, had come for the speech. He objected saying that Dhondiram was smearing the Brahmins and their religious thoughts and took him to the police station. The Brahmins have created a chaos out there."

"Come on, lets see..." said Jyotirao, stepping out in an instant.

Soon, they both reached the police station. The police officer was perturbed to see Jyotirao having arrived. Jyotirao asked him,

"Sir, why has this man been arrested and brought here?"

"I caught him singing songs that were objectionable and defamatory to the Hindu religion" the officer stammered, trying to build a defense for himself.

"The people in the audience were also Hindu. When they did not find anything derogatory in those songs, then how did you?" Jyotirao asked.

"He openly curses the Brahmins. Stokes public fury against them..." said the police officer.

"Sir, please get your facts right" said Jyotirao. "Dhondiram does not curse anybody; he simply speaks with a lot of agitation, and that agitation is nothing but the suppressed lava of fury about being mistreated for generations, coming out through his speeches and poetry. You do not know anything about his inner turmoil; because, you have never felt it necessary to know about it. If you do not know his identity, let me tell you. Dhondiram is a Shaahir, and a studious one at that. Whatever he says via his poetry, is said only after due research and fact-checking. I can assure you of that. If you prove even one statement of his to be untrue, you may arrest him. And why just him? You may arrest me too; because, quite a few of those poetries have been written by me as well."

The officer was stumped by Jyotirao's open challenge. He had no proof against Dhondiram. He had taken the brash step only to curry favor with his fraternity. Yet, he was finding it difficult to accept his mistake directly.

Seeing the officer dillydallying, Jyotirao said,

"Alright, officer; in that case, I think I will have to meet your superior then."

That's when the officer's mask of carelessness fell apart. He started grovelling for mercy saying,

"Tatyasaheb, please forgive me, Tatyasaheb... I'm sorry. I made a mistake. I shall leave him immediately. Please do not let my boss know about all this."

As Jyotirao stepped out of the police station with Dhondiram in tow, the onlookers who had gathered to see Jyotirao being humiliated, ran away like mice chased by a cat.

By the time Jyotirao left Dhondiram to his house and returned home, it was past midnight.

Jyotirao himself would often face such situations too. During a speech, someone would stand up and randomly ask a clearly biased question. Jyotirao would try to answer such questions with immense calm. At times, some onlooker would launch into an argument, but Jyotirao would cut the topic off before it could escalate any further. Shaahir Dhondiram and Krishnarao were also adept at slamming down such mischief mongers. Some people would make it a point to attend the speeches, simply to create trouble – be it through posing random questions, or jeering the speakers. Such people would not just belong to the Brahmin community; in fact, there were many ignorant people from the lower castes who would also participate in this tomfoolery. Jyotirao would be pained to see that the people for who he was fighting, would get swayed by mere sweet talks being spoken by the others.

Even more painful was the fact that, sometimes people from Jyotirao's own community would go to any lengths to demean him.

At one such meeting, one person from Jyotirao's community came ahead and put a garland made of flowers and a dead snake, in his neck. The audience was engrossed in the speech to notice the snake immediately; but then, one man from the audience started screaming 'snake...snake...!'. Jyotirao retained his composure and said to the audience members,

"Brothers, do not worry. The snake won't do anything to me. And, he too has a soul like us all. If I do not hurt his soul, he will not hurt mine."

Sometimes, people would invite Jyotirao home on the pretext of wanting to host him, and would then try to make a fool out of him. But, Jyotirao never fell into their traps. At times, these experiences gave him friends for life too!

Jyotirao would deal with such mischievous people using the weapon of logic and rationality. One such episode was quite funny:

After the Samaj was formally established, one day, two Maalkaris came to visit Jyotirao at his home. Since Jyotirao was not feeling too well that day, he had not gone to the shop. Balwantrao Kolhe and a few more people had come to visit him too.

One of the Maalkaris asked Jyotirao with a straight face,

"Tatyasaheb, you have set out on the path of truth and become a Satyashodhak. So then, please look into the mirror of your heart and tell us, what do we have in this closed fist of ours?"

Jyotirao understood the real intentions of these two people; but, under no circumstances would he offend a person who had come to his house as a guest. He thought a bit. Ever since the men had arrived, there had been a lingering smell of Tulsi leaves all around. Jyotirao said,

"Look brothers.... I'm a Satyashodhak, not a magician. But, I will be able to tell you this, that you are holding Tulsi leaves in your hand."

Hearing this answer, the two men begged for forgiveness from Jyotirao and immediately left the house, shame-faced.

The people siting around were stunned to see Tatya's wit and rationality.

Tackling many such experiences and people, the journey of Satyashodhak Samaj kept going ahead.

47

Sitarama's wedding took place in a simple ceremony. Many people tried to not let the wedding happen. They went as far as to poison Gyaanoba Nimbankar's ears. But, Bajubai remained firm in her resolve. She did not let any naysayers mar the marriage from happening.

The bride and bridegroom garlanded each other and recited wedding vows written by Jyotirao for the occasion. Members of the Samaj were the main attendees for the ceremony. Bajubai, Savitribai and a few more women donated money for the couple to bring items of daily usage to begin their married life with. The ceremony ended there.

Members of the Phule family, such as Babaji Ranoji, Maruti Satwaji, and Tukaram Khanduji had come for the ceremony with their family in tow. Many people from the Mali community were also in attendance. After the ceremony, Babaji Ranoji, Maruti Satwaji, and Tukaram Khanduji took the membership of the Satyashodhak Samaj. Jyotirao was very happy to see that the estranged brothers had finally come together, and had also become members of his movement.

During the same time, Raosaheb Ranade also got remarried. But, Jyotirao was not at all happy with the fact that, the 32-year old Raosaheb, who would talk fervently in favor of widow remarriage, should marry a mere child of 11 years! It had not even been a month since his wife's demise that Raosaheb had brought in a new child bride. His excuse was that he could not defy his father's wishes. But Jyotirao was convinced that Raosaheb's progressive stance was hollow from within.

One day, Zaverilal Umashankar Yagnik came to meet Jyotirao along with a few of his friends. They were planning to open orphanages at Pandharpur and Mumbai. They spoke to Jyotirao at length about the process and problems that they would encounter in this work. Jyotirao was also happy to see their earnest involvement in the work. He made them stay at his house for the night. The next day, while leaving, Yagnik gifted a sari and some clothes for Savitribai and the children, respectively.

The Samaj was very happy due to having successfully conducted the first widow remarriage on their own steam. But, Bajubai was facing immense problems due to the same. Her husband, as well as, people in the society had started torturing her in myriad ways for taking the bold step that she did. Nevertheless, Bajubai took everything in her stride confidently.

Many such incidents were coming to light in the meetings of the Samaj. Vitthalrao Guthaal had suffered tremendous loss to his business. So much so, that he was not left with any money to even continue his children's education! Getting to know of this dire situation, Advocate Gangarambhau Mhaske started a scholarship of Rs. 3 per month for Guthaal's children. Gyaanba Zagde Mistri had also had to leave his job, and was facing a tough time managing his home. But in spite of that, he continued working for the Samaj tirelessly. He also facilitated a remarriage at Ghorpadi. Seeing his dedication to the work of the Samaj, the members started helping him out financially. The occasion proved to be a showcase for the humaneness of the Samaj members and the generosity of its donors. Hari Raoji Chiplunkar started giving Rs. 5 per month as scholarship to a promising student named Ghanashyam Kiraad. In an effort to promote education of girls, Bhikobadada Chavan donated uniforms for many of the school-going girls.

Baba Padmanji's 'Satyadeepika', Moropant Walvekar-edited 'Subodh Patrika', and other journals like 'Pramodsindhu' and 'Induprakash' started giving due publicity to the work of the Samaj.

A meeting of the Samaj was going on. Members and well-wishers were present in a large number. Everyone was narrating their own experiences. Naysayers had been tormenting the Samaj members by pelting stones at the houses, hurling abuses at them in public, and defaming them to all and sundry. There had been other inventive methods being used as well. Vitthalrao said,

"Tatyasaheb, the Brahmins are trying every trick in the book to make our community members ostracize us. They have been going around saying that any wedding ceremony that is taking place without the consent and presence of Brahmins, is illegal, and, the offspring being born from such marriages will be considered illegitimate! Such rumors are causing people to develop cold feet."

"That is why we need to strengthen our movement even more now" said Jyotirao. "Only when the entire Shoodra and Ati Shoodra community comes under the umbrella of the Satyashodhak Samaj, will these naysayers fall by the side. Maybe that time, having been left in solitude, they themselves will need to join us!"

Jyotirao's words gave immense encouragement to the members. They said,

"We shall not back off now...come what may!"

After the meeting ended and Jyotirao set out for home, one sentence uttered by Krishnarao kept whirring in his head. He had said,

"Tatyasaheb, now the wedding season is fast approaching. We need to travel to villages in the vicinity and start a spate of widow remarriages. Until that happens, these opponents will not cow down."

Presently, Jyotirao had been thinking about Gyaanoba's marriage. Gyaanoba had also come to a marriageable age by then. But, Jyotirao was not getting time from his work to do the whole process.

Gyaanoba was a very close relative of Jyotirao's. He was the son of Krishnaji, the son of Jyotirao's maternal aunt. This aunt, Raahibai, had taken care of Jyotirao immediately after his own mother had expired. She was the one who handed him over to Saguna Aau at their house in Hadapsar. Saguna Aau would keep narrating those incidents to Jyotirao when he was a boy.

Gyaanoba had grown up in abject poverty. Thus, Tatya and Kaku had special affection for him. Gyaanoba had left home at a very young age to go with a bunch of mendicants. He returned home at the age of 16. He came in contact with Jyotirao while working for some contractor in Hadapsar. Very soon, he developed a close bond with Tatya and Kaku. They treated him like a son. Gyaanoba knew a bit of English. Jyotirao would be happy to see him writing the few alphabets that he remembered. Gyaanoba was proving a big asset for Jyotirao in his contracting business.

Savitribai was also keen to see Gyaanoba married. She would keep telling Jyotirao,

"You got Sitaram married; now you need to look out for Gyaanoba."

In reply, Jyotirao would tease her saying,

"Don't force him into marriage, alright? What if he again runs away to become a mendicant!?"

"Why would he do so? Marriage makes a man happy…" Savitribai would say, looking pointedly at Gyaanoba, who would soon find an excuse to slip away.

One evening, Jyotirao broached the topic during dinnertime. It was decided that Narayanrao Shinde would be requested for an alliance with his daughter Lakshmi. Looking at their age and attributes, the couple seemed to make a perfect fit.

After dinner, Jyotirao and Savitribai both sat reading their respective books. Too many thoughts were going on in Jyotirao's mind – the trouble being created by the Brahmins; the staunch support of members in the face of immense opposition; the many invitations flooding in from beyond Pune; Gyaanoba's marriage… and so on. The mystery of his brothers coming ahead to become members of the Samaj, had also been resolved now. Maruti Satwaji and Tukaram Khanduji had proposed that Tatya take their children under his wings, in his orphanage. However, Jyotirao had steadfastly ignored their proposal. Babaji also had similar plans in mind; he was going to broach the topic to Jyotirao, at an opportune moment.

He did not realize when sleep captured him while reading; but after some time, Jyotirao heard the door creak. He woke up to find Savitribai missing from her place. Sitaram was sleeping in the living room. The children too were fast asleep. Jyotirao craned his neck and saw Savitribai speaking to some woman. Some more time went by, and the woman left after pleading something to Savitribai.

As she returned, Tatya asked Kaku,

"Who was it, Savitri?"

"Yeshwant's mother, Kashibai. She had come to see him."

"Why don't you wake me up at such times? It is not safe to open the door alone at such late hours of the night" Tatya chided her.

"I know what time she comes..." replied Kaku.

"Well, that's alright; but...."

"Shetji, only a woman can understand another woman's pain" Kaku said with a sigh. "She is not eating anything. She has contracted tuberculosis. Her son is the only thing that is keeping her alive."

Jyotirao felt a searing pain for the poor woman's state. He exclaimed,

"That means she will not...."

"Yes, she may not live long. Her brother will not accept her, and the people around us are making it difficult for her to live here."

"Please request her to stay with us. We will look after her. Yeshwant will also get his mother's love for some time at least."

"Not possible, Shetji. The woman is so scared that she does not even venture out of her house in daytime. There is no chance, she will agree to stay with us."

Tatya was flummoxed as to what to do to help the woman. Finally, they both decided to try speaking to Kashibai.

After eight-ten days, Kaku's persistence paid off. Kashibai

came to stay at the Phule house. But, her health kept deteriorating instead of improving. Kaku was taking due care of her, but Kashibai's health refused to improve. Tuberculosis, coupled with lack of nutrition, and constant stress, made a skeleton out of her once beautiful body. It was as if she had given away all her beauty to Yeshwant, and had been reduced to nothingness.

Yeshwant looked ditto like his mother. He was growing into a beautiful baby. Tatya would be mesmerized by his little antics.

Kashibai was happy to see that her son was in safe hands. But nevertheless, she would keep worrying incessantly about Yeshwant's future. How would he grow up? Would he be educated? Would he get married? Would he have a happy married life? Would people trouble him for being a widow's son? Many such thoughts would keep going on like a carousel in her already weakened mind. The stress would become so unbearable that Kashibai could not even step out of her room for days on end. Dr. Ghole would come regularly to check on her; but his medication was proving futile in the face of the stress that Kashibai was taking. Her tuberculosis kept strengthening beyond control.

One day, Jyotirao saw Kashibai sobbing incessantly. He could bear it no longer. He went near her and said,

"Kashibai, do we not understand your sorrow? We do…."

Kashibai looked at Jyotirao expectantly. He continued,

"Please do not worry about Yeshwant. Now, he is our son. We shall never let go of him. We will take care of him in the same way in which we would have taken care of our own son, if we had one. I do not know what else to say, so that your worries may cease."

"Kashibai, haven't I told you the exact thing, so many times before?" Savitribai asked earnestly.

"Better still, we shall legally adopt him. Will that make you happy, Kashibai?" proposed Jyotirao.

Hearing this, Kashibai began sobbing. Savitribai held her close and consoled her.

Jyotirao kept thinking...he had given his word to Kashibai in a moment of emotion; but, would they be able to live up to it They had made the similar promise to Godabai, the mother of Shantaram. But, Shantaram had died soon after his mother's demise. Jyotirao had not been able to keep his word. He did not want the same thing to happen again.

There had been so many children like Shantaram, who had grown up with Jyotirao and Savitribai. They had not been able to see or even know the names of the mothers of many of those children. Somebody would come and lay a mewling infant at their doorstep. Tatya and Kaku would then tae them inside and try to give them a good life. But, many of those children would die in mere weeks or months. It would be an ordeal for Tatya and Kaku to erase the memories of those tiny lives that would have played, eaten and slept in their home for so many days. Quite a few children would be born with handicaps or other anomalies, owing to the abortion-inducing pills that their mothers would have taken during pregnancy. Those children would also be fighting a constant battle with death. No one could tell when and how the battle would end. It was a very difficult journey indeed. Babu and Lakshmi had grown to 7-8 years of age. They now were school-going children; but, they would constantly remain ill due to some reason or other. Shiva and Yamu also suffered from delicate health. No one knew what the future would bring for these little ones. In such a scenario, Jyotirao had given a very big promise to Kashibai. He just prayed that God would give them both, the strength to see it through the end.

48

Finally, Gyaanoba's wedding took place without any untoward incident marring the ceremony. Now it was imperative to concentrate on going to Mumbai. Monsoons were fast approaching; it would not do to delay the visit any further. However, some or the other problem was cropping up. Shivaji and Yamu had fallen ill. Kashibai's health had also become a cause for worry. Nevertheless, unable to delay the visit any more, one day Jyotirao set off for Mumbai, leaving Savitribai to deal with the problems at home.

As the train snaked its way across the Sahyadri mountains from Pune to Mumbai, a chain of thoughts started forming in Jyotirao's mind, about the events of the past few weeks....

.....Gyaanoba's wedding had proved to be a major challenge for the Samaj. The opponents had done everything in their capacity to see that the wedding did not happen. Narayanrao Shinde from Parvati had agreed for his daughter's alliance with Gyaanoba, at Jyotirao's request. He also convinced Krishnabhau for the alliance. However, the community members who had graced Sitaram's wedding, went against the Samaj at the last moment. They fell prey to the rumor that Satyadharma was a covert way of converting people to Christianity. However, truth be told, they had lost interest in the movement after learning that Jyotirao was going to legally adopt a widow's child. Once again it had become clear as to what had really prompted the sudden decision of his brothers to become members of the Samaj. However, Babaji Ranoji had assured Jyotirao of giving full support to Gyaanoba's wedding, and he had also stayed true to his word. On his part, Jyotirao would also help him out in times of need, financially or otherwise. Babaji was the only one among the brothers who had remained close to Jyotirao now.

Gyaanoba's wedding was to take place at Hadapsar. Tension started mounting as the date of the wedding came closer. Some people from Pune poisoned the minds of people from the Mali and Kulambi communities in Hadapsar. Gyaanoba was threatened to not going ahead with the marriage. He was threatened that, "We will cut the water supply to your house if you go ahead with the marriage with the support of the Samaj".

Gyaanoba got frightened with these threats. He came running from Hadapsar to meet Jyotirao and begged,

"Tatyasaheb… I shall stay unmarried all my life, but I shall not be able to take this torment any more. Please excuse me from this alliance!"

Jyotirao understood Gyaanoba's dilemma. He tried to explain him saying,

"Gyaanoba, this is not the Peshwai any more. We are living in the British rule, where they cannot carry out any of the threats they are issuing. Do not cow down now."

But, Gyaanoba was not to be convinced. He replied,

"Even though the regime might be British, their clerks and officers are Brahmin! They will torture me badly, Tatyasaheb. I will not be able to do anything!"

Jyotirao tried hard to explain to Gyaanoba that not all Brahmin officers were bad. British officers were also quite helpful. At long last, Gyaanoba got a bit convinced, but the problems were far from over. There were many more battles to be fought.

Finally, as a precautionary measure, Jyotirao decided to conduct the marriage ceremony at his house itself. The bride and groom were quietly brought into the Phule house, on the night prior to the ceremony. This obliterated the possibility of someone abducting the bride or groom; but, another problem cropped up due to Jyotirao's brothers, Maruti Satwaji and Tukaram Khandoji. At the last minute, they decided that they also wanted to get their children married on the same day as Gyaanoba's wedding was slated to happen. Incidentally, their children were mere 2-3 years of age! The ploy was to dissuade as many community people as they could, from attending Gyaanoba's wedding.

Not stopping at that, they also arranged for goons to beat up the Samaj members on the day of the wedding.

But Jyotirao was not going to cow down for any reason

whatsoever. Babaji Ranoji and Vitthal Guthaal started the preparations in earnest. Jyotirao met his advocate friend Polsani Rajanna Lingu, who got him in touch with Advocate Gangamarambhau Mhaske. Advocate Mhaske helped Jyotirao connect with Police Inspector Mr. Train, who agreed to provide police protection during the event. Friends and well-wishers from Meethganj also came for the wedding. The presence of police and wrestler friends from the akhaada ensured that the ceremony would go without a hitch.

The ceremony did indeed go without a hitch, but Jyotirao was very sad in his heart. He had expected opponents to crop up, but had never imagined that his own brothers would go to such a low and behave the way they did.

As Jyotirao reached Mumbai, he found Swami Aiyyavaru ready to receive him at the station, along with a few other people. Meetings of the Samaj had already been started at Kamathipura. Swami had roped in moneyed and influential people like Vyanku Baloji Kalewar, Raju Babaji Vanjari, Jaya Yalappa Lingu, Jaya Karadi Lingu and Narsingrao Saaybu Wadnala.

Swami got Jyotirao to his house in Kamathipura. Jaya Karadi and Narsingrao stayed in the same neighborhood as Swami. Each of them had their own business. Vyanku Baloji, Swami Aiyyavaru and Jaya Yalappa were big contractors. Many big buildings in Mumbai were being built by them. Swami Aiyyavaru and Jaya Yalappa had started a school and library for the Telugu community. Jaya Karadi, the younger brother of Jaya Yalappa, was a big grain merchant. Both the brothers were taking keen interest in the social work that had been started by their father.

Jyotirao met all these people. After giving a couple of speeches at various locations, the Mumbai chapter of Satyashodhak Samaj was announced to be formally established at the hands of Jyotirao. Many of the attendees pledged to behave as per the norms of the Samaj, and also promised to spread the same amongst the society at large. For instance, till now, during every Ganesh festival, Vyanku Baloji would offer a feast and donations to a thousand Brahmins. He pledged to now use that money for the benefit of the poor and handicapped. Yalappa too pledged to stop the donations to Brahmins and use that money for giving scholarships to promising students and a gold medal to one student who would come first in the matriculation examination.

Many feasts were arranged in Jyotirao's honour. Soon, time came for Jyotirao to go back to Pune. Narsingrao Wadnala honored Jyotirao with a dhoti and shawl. Vyanku Baloji and Swami Aiyyavaru promised to send a printing machine for the Samaj's Pune office, so as to help the printing and propagation of the Samaj's literature.

Jyotirao also got a few young friends during his stay in Mumbai. Jaya Karadi's son Vyanku and Swami Aiyyavaru's son Keshavswami, became very good friends of his. The children would always remember their memorable meeting with the great reformer. Swami's wife Ratnamma, was also a very scholarly lady. Jyotirao found himself quite enlightened with his discussions with Ratnamma.

During his stay of eight-ten days in Mumbai, Jyotirao was happy to make some very precious and lasting connections with some very loving and welcoming people –a rarity for him! He also got to meet Mama Parmanand, Rajaramshastri Bhagwat, Vasudeo Babaji, Tukaram Tatya and Moropant Walvekar.

His heart overflowing with the affection received in Mumbai, Jyotirao travelled to Thane.

While in the train to Thane, Jyotirao saw a poor man sitting in front of him. His clothes had become threadbare. Overcome with compassion for the man, Jyotirao gave him the dhoti and shawl he had received from Vyanku Baloji.

It had been a long time since Dr. Santuji Lad had been urging Jyotirao to come to Thane. Finally, his wish came true when Jyotirao landed at Thane station. Dr. Lad and all the members of the Samaj had come to receive him at the station.

Jyotirao had the same experience in Thane as he did in Mumbai. People were very keen to hear his thoughts about Satyadharma and showed readiness to follow the norms too.

All in all, Jyotirao's tour to Mumbai and Thane, turned out to be a very successful one. He found those societies to be quite less orthodox in comparison to Pune. Thus, he found the social atmosphere very conducive to spread the word and work of the Samaj. In Pune, most of Jyotirao's energies would be expended in warding off the negative forces who would keep trying to disrupt the activities of the Samaj.

Finally, after a long stay, Jyotirao took leave of all the affectionate people he met in Thane. His heart was now looking forward to meet the children. The worry about Kashibai's health was also a Damocles sword on his head.

As soon as he reached home, Jyotirao asked about his little girl, Yamu. However, he was compelled to hear the most grievous news from Savitribai, that, his little doll Yamu had expired while her Tatya was away in Mumbai. Savitribai wept as she narrated to him about how Yamu constantly kept chanting 'Tatya, Tatya' even while burning with fever.

Yamu's death left a deep wound on Tatya's heart. Clasping the remaining children to his heart, Tatya wept like a child himself! Savitribai had never seen her indomitable husband sob so helplessly before!

49

Jyotirao had been very busy since morning. The work was piling up as the hours went by. Reluctantly, he made his way home for lunch, knowing that a mountain of work stood in front of him after he returned.

After finishing the work of Katraj tunnel, Jyotirao had taken up the contract for another work. After the Khadakwasla dam had been built, tenders had opened for building canals near the same. In partnership with Ramchandra Hari Shinde, Jyotirao established the 'Poona Commercial and Contracting Company' and won the contract for supplying stones for building the canals. They also included Krishnaji in their company. Krishnaji was a young, promising lad who was working as a clerk in the court. He had left that job and was working as a clerk with a contractor named Ramchandra Mahadev. The society, as well as, the company required enthusiastic youngsters like Krishnaji.

Jyotirao's relationship with Advocate Polsani Rajanna Lingu became stronger after Gyaanoba's marriage. Advocate Lingu also become a member of the Samaj. Dr. Ghole and Ilaija Shaleman (who was in a government job) also soon became members of the Samaj. Well-wishers like Advocate Gangarambhau Mhaske were helping the Samaj in different ways. Ramchandrarao Dhamanaskar had come from Satara to meet Jyotirao; he had established a branch of the Samaj at Satara. Having risen from poverty to become a Head Clerk, Ramchandrarao found it his duty to help poor but promising students. Jyotirao was convinced that people like Shaleman and Ramchandrarao who had themselves risen from poverty to become success stories, would be an invaluable help in acquiring justice for the Shoodra communities.

Many illustrious people had come ahead to support the Satyashodhak Samaj. But, there were equal number of opponents who were getting aggressive with their tactics to shut down the same. One gang had taken it upon themselves to pelt stones at the houses of the Samaj members. However, the cowards that they were, they would run away the moment somebody would shout at them. Finally, with Advocate Lingu and Advocate Ghole's help, the police caught these stone-pelters and scared the wits out of them. That's when the pelting ceased to happen.

Jyotirao also went to Hadapsar. Gyaanoba's house had been

ostracized. The lives of his family members were in threat. Yet, they all were standing up courageously in the face of all such adversities.

Those people who had extended a hand of help at one time, also started raising their selfish agendas. Babaji Phule extended a proposal of adoption before Jyotirao. He had never thought that Jyotirao would really adopt the widow's child, over his son. He tried influencing Jyotirao in various ways, but after all pleas fell on deaf ears, Babaji broke off from his brother. Rajarambhau had predicted long back that such a thing would happen. He had warned Jyotirao that his selfish brothers would forget everything that he had done for them and would break off, the moment Jyotirao would refuse to accept one request of theirs. Jyotirao was seeing a very unpleasant side of his own relatives; the experiences he was getting were so strange, that any simple person would stop believing in the goodness in humankind.

As Jyotirao turned into the alley that led to his house, he saw an old man sitting outside Abaji Alhaat's house, picking up grains that had scattered all over the ground in front of him. The old man's bag was so torn, that the grains that he was putting inside, were again falling down. Jyotirao felt deep empathy for the man. He rushed ahead and removing the scarf from his shoulders, he held it towards the beggar saying,

"Take this, baba. You bag is torn. You won't be ale to hold any grains in it."

Without glancing at the person who had offered him the scarf, the beggar took the scarf gratefully and mumbled,

"Thank you... you too see like a kind man...just like Jyotiba's wife.... she is a universal mother...may God bless her and Jyotiba..."

He finished picking up the grains and looked up at Jyotirao with gratitude. However, he did not recognize him to be Jyotirao.

As Jyotirao came home, he saw Savitribai engrossed in

reading her favorite magazine, 'Gruhini'. Moropant was the editor of this magazine, which would be published from Mumbai. Savitribai would wait eagerly every month, for her copy to come in. At Moropant's behest, Savitribai would also write articles and poetry for the magazine, but on the condition that her name would be kept under wraps.

Seeing Tatya, Kaku kept the magazine down and got up to receive him. Tatya felt something amiss; the children had not come running to him as usual. He asked Kaku,

"Where are all the children?"

"Sitaram has taken them out to play" she replied.

"Have they eaten?"

"Yes."

"Has Kashibai taken her medicines?"

"Yes, Shetji..." Kaku replied with a smile, adding, "Where's your scarf?"

Tatya answered,

"You gave alms to that beggar, but it must have slipped your eye that his bag was torn. The poor man was sitting in front of Alhaat's house, picking up grains from the floor. So, I gave my scarf to him."

Kaku smiled at her husband's generosity, and went inside.

After his meal, Tatya sat in the living room, going through his correspondence. By then, he had become used to letters written in uncouth, abusive language. Today also, there was one such letter. The anonymous (and thus, cowardly) writer had ended the letter by threatening to kill Jyotirao, unless he closed down the Satyshodhak Samaj immediately.

Before this, two such letters had been delivered to the shop's address. But when Jyotirao refused to cow down to them, the writer(s) had taken to sending the letters to his home address.

Putting the letter down calmly, Jyotirao remarked,

"This writer needs to be conveyed that his letter has reached me. But, I have no way of doing that."

"Why so?" Savitribai asked innocently.

"It seems, the writer has forgotten to mention his name and address" Jyotirao smirked, as he tore the letter and threw the pieces in the dustbin.

"Why did you tear the letter?" Savitribai asked him.

"It was a well-wisher's letter.. he had heaped praises upon the Samaj and its work..."

Savtribai was well-versed with her husband's type of sarcasm. She asked him,

"But then, was it so bad that you could not even show it to me?"

"Well, you can say that, Savitribai. Would I have torn it otherwise? But, don't worry. He had given very regular, random threats. 'You will face trouble...Your house will be pelted...' and all that."

Jyotirao laughed aloud, and taking another scarf, left for the shop again. However, Savitribai was not feeling so casual about the whole thing. She knew that even though her husband was trying to make light of the happening, these threats were growing by the day, and it would be foolish to ignore them as random.

That night, Tatya kept reading late into the night. Sleep was eluding him somehow. Today, he was remembering Yamu a lot. Yamu would often sleep besides him. After her demise, Shivaji too had gone into a shell. Lakshmi and Babu were quite older than him. Shivaji had lost his companion of play, and had become a recluse. Tatya was worried about him.

Kaku gave medicines to Kashibai and came to sleep on the carpet. She took the little Yeshwant in her arms, and made Shivaji sleep alongside. However, she also was not being able to sleep. The letter which had come that afternoon, had spoiled her peace of mind.

Kashibai was coughing as usual. However, soon, her cough seemed to intensify. Tatya and Kaku could hear her wheezing and racking with cough. Tatya asked Savitribai to have a look. Savitribai went inside and came out running, saying,

"Shetji, please call the doctor. The situation seems serious." Saying thus, she rushed to Kashibai's side.

Jyotirao sent Sitaram to call Dr. Ghole and went to Kashibai's room.

The medicine bottle had been flung to the ground; its contents were lying on the floor, making the whole room reek of the putrid smell. Kashibai was flipping in agony, like a fish out of water. In that helpless situation too, she was frantically waving her hands as if saying, 'No...No...'.

Tatya looked at Kaku questioningly. She explained that Kashibai was requesting them to not call the doctor.

Tatya went near Kashibai's bedside and said to her,

"Kashibai, please don't stress yourself. Please don't talk.... Try to rest..."

But, clearly the situation was out of control. Kashibai now had eyes for only one person. She kept muttering,

"Yeshwant... My baby... Yeshwant..."

The couple saw that there was no time to lose. The writing on the wall had become clear. Tatya brought baby Yeshwant inside and handed him over to his frail mother. With great effort, Kashibai sat up, put her baby on the lap, and started caressing him with her weak, bony hands.

A few minutes later, Kashibai started seeing her son's face blurredly....soon after, she could not see it at all...her breath started coming in spasms...she turned breathless....and then, at one moment, the world turned black!

- Kashibai left her son an orphan!

50

Kashibai could not live to see her son's official adoption by the Phules; but Jyotirao stood true to his word. He hosted a ceremony to adopt Yeshwant officially, in front of the society. His decision turned his relations sour with a few of his family members, but Jyotirao did not go back on his word.

The first anniversary of the Satyashodhak Samaj was round the corner. The members decided to carry out a procession of the organization's flag, all around the city. Everyone started preparing for the event enthusiastically. Bhau Kondaji Patil of Otur also consented to grace the occasion. Patil was successfully running a branch of the Samaj at Otur. Similar stellar work was being done by Bapuji Hari Shinde at Buldhana. Being a government servant, he was being tormented in various ways for lending support to the Samaj. But Bapuji persevered; and in fact, exposed the Brahmin officers who were troubling him. From then, his opponents started laving Bapuji alone. The Samaj was getting strengthened by such positive developments.

In Pune too, the problems faced by the Samaj members, started decreasing slowly. Vitthalrao Guthaal restarted his business. Gyaanba Mestri got another job.

The Satyashodhaks were going out of their way to help each other. Guthaal wrote a heartfelt letter to Gangarambhau, for all the help he offered.

Soon enough, the anniversary celebrations stood merely two days away. Jyotirao and Narayanrao were sitting at the shop, preparing the agenda. Many other people like Vinayak Bapuji Bhandarkar, Dhondiba Rode, his son Tatyasaheb, and Gyaanoba Sasane were also present. Work was going on in an atmosphere of cheer and bonhomie. Tatyasaheb Rode, who at one time would openly criticize Jyotirao, had now turned a member of the Samaj. Jyotirao would often go to Dhondiba's house. During one such visit, he had said,

"Dhondiba, your son Tatyasaheb has become quite a courageous lad. He openly argued with me at the meeting last evening; but honestly, I am happy that he had the wits and bravery to speak up. The society requires more youngsters like him, instead of the dumb fools that we see around. His views today are the product of teachings by Brahmin teachers; but just you see – one day, he will be at the forefront of our movement."

Jyotirao's prediction had come true faster than he had expected. During one meeting, Jyotirao had quelled all of Tatyasaheb's doubts, and from then on, Tatyasaheb had developed immense respect for Jyotirao's work.

As they all sat chatting in the shop, word came in that some gentleman had come to see Jyotirao. Soon after, a smart-looking elderly man, flaunting a thick moustache on his wheatish face, and wearing a dhoti and jacket, climbed up the stairs. On reaching upstairs, he folded his hands before Jyotirao and said,

"Namaskar, I am Bhau Kondaji Patil."

"Ohh... Namaskar...Namaskar. Welcome please...." Jyotirao effused as he got up to welcome his esteemed guest. Taking Patil by the hand, Jyotirao led him to a settee. Soon, avid talks began in the room.

Bhau Patil was a very eminent and established man. After having been the Patil of Otur for many years, Bhau had accepted a job at Gwalior. In his decade-long stay at Gwalior, Bhau rose to the post of a Mamledar . Then, he returned to Otur and spearheaded the work of the Samaj in the areas of Otur and Junnar.

Patil briefed Jyotirao about his work in these regions and said,

"Tatyasaheb, the farmers in our region are being badly exploited by landowners and money-lenders. We are thinking of hosting a big meeting, and would be obliged if you come for it."

Jyotirao accepted the invitation happily.

Many people came for the anniversary celebrations, from beyond Pune. The procession started at 9 a.m. and ended at Sadoba Gawde's house in Somwar Peth, at around 3 p.m. Jyotirao Phule, Bhau Kondaji and Krishnarao Bhalekar spoke on the occasion. Narayanrao Kadlak presented a synopsis of the work done by the Samaj in the last one year. In his speech, he thanked well-wishers like Vinayak Bapuji Bhandarkar and

Sitaram Sakharam Datar for their support to the organization. He also thanked well-wishers like Gangarambhau for helping the Samaj members during troubled times.

Some posts and positions were shifted – while Jyotirao remained the Chairman and Treasurer, the secretarial assistant's post was given to Narayanrao Nagarkar. A youngster called Krishnarao Bhalekar was inducted into the managing committee.

The anniversary celebrations turned out to be a roaring success. Sadoba Gawde's big house fell short for containing all the people present. The speeches created a deep impact on the minds of the audience.

Soon, Dr. Gawde's house started falling insufficient to accommodate the growing members of the Samaj. However, that problem was resolved soon after contractor Rambhau Mansaram Naik attended one meeting, and agreed to give them space at his new residencd that was being built in Vetaal Peth.

Another good incident followed soon after. Vinayak Bapuji, a friend of Jyotirao's and a well-wisher of the Samaj, got his widowed daughter remarried. Best part was that, Bapuji did not blow any trumpets of being a progressive, and also did not conduct this remarriage in secrecy. The ceremony was conducted in full view of society, with many Satyashodhaks in attendance.

Among the progressives, only Vishnushastri Pandit stood the test of his word. Without kowtowing to any opposition, he got married to a widow. People had not yet forgotten the suicide of Moroba Kanhoba, which he did with his wife. On that background, Vishnushastri had indeed taken a big step forward. He could do so with the strong support of stalwarts like Phule and Mama Parmanand.

Moroba Kanhoba's suicide was a heart-wrenching incident. The bodies of both, husband and wife, were seen floating in the well behind their house, tied to each other! No one knew if they had tied themselves to each other and committed suicide, or they had been tied up and pushed into the well! Either ways, the people who had seen that gruesome sight, could not get it out of their heads for months on end.

Moroba Kanhoba was actually a very courageous man. Without fearing the staunch opposition by the orthodox group in Mumbai, he had got his widowed daughter remarried. However, the poor girl was not at strong-minded as her father. One day, she jumped into a well and ended her life. After such a heart-breaking incident too, Moroba kept championing the cause of widow remarriage. He arranged for many widow remarriage ceremonies to take place in his bungalow. Not just that; he himself got remarried to a widow. But alas, finally the man met a tragic end.

However, even though people like Moroba perished, their work kept being an inspiration for the younger generations.

51

Whenever he would get time, Jyotirao would love to explore neighboring villages along with his friends. That day's stroll saw Bhau Kondaji being included in the group too. Jyotirao, Bhau, Bhimajirao Birmal, Marutrao Navle, and Dhondiba Rode, all went to Hadapsar.

However, that day's visit did not turn out to be as fruitful as expected. The weather was hot, and many people had gone to Alandi for the annual pilgrimage; so, they could not meet a lot of them. That particular summer had been relentless in its heat; farmers were waiting for a torrent of rain, to see a bumper crop.

That night, a lot of Satyashodhaks gathered at Jyotirao's house for informal chatting. Shaahir Dhondiram had gone to a discourse by Swami Dayanand.

Presently, Swami Dayanand was staying at Pune. His arrival had caused quite a stir in the city. Swamiji had come directly from Lahore to Pune at the behest of Raosaheb Ranade,

Raobahadur Gopal Hari, and Mahadev Moreshwar Kunte. Last summer, he had established the Arya Samaj at Mumbai. Plans were afoot to start a branch of Arya Samaj at Pune now.

Swamiji was giving daily discourses every evening at Bhide's bungalow in Budhwar Peth. People would throng to the discourses in spite of torrential rains. Raobahadur Gopal Hari and Raosaheb Ranade were daily attendees. They, along with advocate Gangarambhau Mhaske, would take due care of Swamiji's routine and needs. Raobahadur and a few other people had taken membership of the Arya Samaj.

Jyotirao also went for Swamiji's discourses for a few days; but soon, he was disillusioned due to the ideological two-sidedness in Swamiji's teachings. On one hand, Swamiji would tell people that casteism was wrong, and untouchability had to be abolished; but then, on the other hand, he would give references of the Vedas. Add to that, Jyotirao found nothing new in his exhortation to shun idolatry.

Swami Dayanand's eloquent oratory won him many admirers in Pune; but, Jyotirao was not one of them. He found Swamiji's talks to be nothing but empty talks about progression, spoken from behind the veil of the Vedas.

That day, when Shaahir Dhondiram returned late at night from the discourse, the Phule house was still reverberating with talks and laughter.

Seeing him approaching, Jyotirao asked,

"Come, Shaahir. So, how was today's discourse?"

"As usual, Tatyasaheb. Swamiji was saying, do not follow idolatry... do not believe in casteism... but then, was given references of the Vedas. Frankly, I don't understand this fuss."

Jyotirao smiled and replied,

"That's precisely the aim of all these people, Shaahir....That we should not understand the fuss ever. They intersperse their speeches with smatterings of Sanskrit – making the listener feel, 'Oh, I'm hearing some scholar's speech'. But, if one were to think properly about the content of their speeches, they crate more confusion than resolving the existing ones. These people feel that they can hide their forefathers' sins by speaking in Sanskrit... but that is an unreal assumption."

Bhau Patil said,

"But, Swamiji's oratory is really beautiful. He speaks as if the Creator has placed sugar on his tongue."

"Well, that's true" said Jyotirao, adding, "That is one trait of his worth emulating. Our Krishnarao must have been present at today's discourse, was he?"

"Yes, he was. Some people from Bhamburde were also present. They want to invite Swamiji to their village."

"Oh well..."

Thus, these talks continued for a long time after. At one point, Shaahir Dhondiram said,

"Tatyasaheb, the pilgrimage of Alandi is beginning tomorrow. It will be nice to have a few of your speeches there, to raise awareness about the Samaj."

Jyotirao had been fond of pilgrimages since childhood. He would go to the Alalndi pilgrimage every year with Dada. Similarly, when Tukaram tatya or Vasudeo Babaji would come from Mumbai, he would accompany them to the pilgrimage at Dehu. Narayan Sadanand of Dehu had become close friends with Jyotirao, due to this long time association. Lately, Jyotirao had become too busy with the work of the Samaj to be able to go to Dehu.

However, he found it pertinent to speak to the masses about the work of Satyashodhak Samaj. on the backdrop of an occasion honoring Sant Tukaram, who always spoke up against following any faith blindly. In fact, impressed with the philosophy and teachings of the Satyashodhak Samaj, many people from the Warkari sect had become members of the same.

Jyotirao heartily accepted Dhondiram's suggestion. He too found the pilgrimage to be a great platform to reach to the ignorant brethren. Immediately, it was decided that the group would leave for Alandi in the morning itself. Jyotirao and Bhau would give speeches, whereas, Dhondiram would sing powadas.

The next morning, Shaahir arrived at the crack of dawn at Jyotirao's house, bringing along his tambourine and a small packet of lunch. Soon, Dhondiba, his son Tatyasaheb, and Marutrao also arrived. It was imperative to start early if they wanted to return that night itself. Everyone took their lunch packets along.

Nevertheless, they got a bit late in starting off. Hence, they all started walking fast towards their destination. On the way, a couple of warkaris (who were known to Jyotirao) also joined them.

One of the warkari winked at his friend and asked Jyotirao,

"Tatyasaheb, you Satyashodhaks are not known to be devotees of Sant Dyaneshwar. What, then, takes you to the pilgrimage?"

His question was a reflection of the misconceptions that had taken root in society, regarding the Satyashodhak Samaj and its ideologies. Many people felt that the Satyashodhaks were a band of atheists; some also felt that they were secretly Christian in their beliefs.

Jyotirao understood the sarcasm in the man's question. He replied,

"Brother, when truth is deliberately kept hidden under the darkness of ignorance, it becomes necessary to carry a lamp and search for that truth. That is what this Samaj endeavors to do. Our God is truth; and, morality is our religion. Our Creator – God – is One. He is all-pervading and omnipresent. We are going to Alandi to spread only this message."

That man was silenced by Jyotirao's answer, but not his friends. They kept asking weird questions. Jyotirao said to them,

"Brothers, if you think that Satyadharma is heretic or irreligious, then, you are wrong. We Satyashodhaks strongly believe that God is an omnipresent power, which is not confined to some idol or a person. Satyadharma has no place for idolatry or blind faith. These are the things that led to the spread of idle Brahmins becoming princely. But, we believe that the true religion of any human-being is morality and truthfulness."

Soon, the group had reached Dighi. Finding it futile to waste time talking to people like those three men, Jyotirao decided to fasten his pace and reach Alandi in time.

The weather was very sultry. Trees and shrubs adjoining the road, seemed to be looking up at the sky in the hope of a few drops of rain to fall on them. The road beneath their feet was also burning hot.

Just then, a group of pilgrims crossed Jyotirao's group from the other side of the road. Jyotirao's eye fell on a very old man, who was walking very slowly behind the others. He was very weak, and the searing sun was making it even more difficult for him to walk straight. Even as Jyotirao was looking at him, the man suddenly collapsed on the road.

Seeing that, Jyotirao ran ahead to see if the man was hurt. Most of the people from his group had walked far ahead. They were not even aware of the old man's plight. Three youngsters who had remained behind - chatting idyllically as they walked - smirked and said,

"Hey, old man, what made you do this over-smartness of going on a pilgrimage at this age? Do you realize that this may well be the beginning of your last & final pilgrimage?"

They started cackling at their own joke, but the old man could not hear what they were saying. He had fainted owing to the heat and exertion.

Jyotirao carefully took the old man's head on his lap and started fanning him with his scarf. Calling out to Marutrao, he said,

"Please see if you can find some water nearby."

Dhondiram's son Tatyasaheb, and Marutrao, scanned the surroundings. They saw a well standing on a farm nearby. Immediately, went running to draw water from the well. However, there was no pail or rope to draw water. Tatyasaheb took off his scarf and let it into the water. Then, he quickly drew up the wet scarf and they both came running towards where Jyotirao, Bhimajirao and Shaahir had brought the old man under the shade of a tree.

As Jyotirao wiped the man's face with the cool scarf and dripped a few drops of water from it into his mouth, the man came to his senses.

Seeing him awake, Jyotirao took out a bhaakri from his lunch pack, and offered it to the man, saying,

"Baba, please eat some bhaakri. You will feel better."

The old man's eyes filled with tears of gratitude at Jyotirao's kindness. He looked at Jyotirao and said,

"My son, I had gone to Alandi to see Sant Dyaneshwar. I did not get to see him there, but I saw him in you right now!"

Saying thus, he held Jyotirao's feet and kept sobbing.

Jyotirao instantly held him in an embrace and said,

"No, Baba. Please do not touch my feet. It is every person's social and moral duty to take care of our seniors. I did not do anything special; it was my duty. In a way, you can also say, I behaved selfishly. After all, some day, even I am going to get old, am I not?"

The old man was stunned to hear Jyotirao's words. He remarked,

"Praise be to the mother and father who raised such a wonderful son like you!"

The man slowly finished his bhaakri. He started feeling better. Heaping blessings on Jyotirao, he then set out on his way.

Jyotirao's group too resumed walking. They now had even lesser time to reach Alandi.

The men, who had earlier been arguing with Jyotirao, now said to him,

"Please forgive us, Tatyasaheb. We were sparring with you for no reason."

Jyotirao smiled, and resumed walking.

Soon, they could see the golden apex of Sant Dynaneshwar's

temple in front of them....

52

One night, two men came to Jyotirao's house with a message from Raosaheb. As soon as they left, Jyotirao sent an urgent message for Lahujibuva's son Dhondiba, and Tatyasaheb Rode, to come to his house.

"What happened, Tatyasaab? Why have you called us at this hour?" Dhondiba asked as he arrived at Jyotirao's house.

"Dhondiba, tomorrow evening, an elephant-back procession of Swami Dayanand procession is going to be carried out through the town. The Brahmins have decided to create a ruckus in that procession. They are going to bring a donkey in that procession...."

"Understood. How many men will you require?" asked Dhondiba.

"I think, 15-20 would be enough for those cowardly Brahmins" Jyotirao replied.

However, Tatyasaheb was not convinced about offering help for the occasion. Somehow, Jyotirao managed to convince him that unless they stood behind the progressives, the back of the orthodox group would not be broken.

At long last, Tatyasaheb got convinced; then, they both went to their homes.

Jyotirao kept thinking about Swami Dayanand's Pune sojourn. The last two months had seen Swamiji giving a lot of discourses in and around Pune. Gangarambhau had arranged for discourses in various Peths in Pune and also in the surrounding villages. Krisnarao had arranged for discourses in Bhamburde. Jyotirao was not in favour of all this. He simply could not wrap his head around the fact that, the Vedas – which were the root of all segregations – were being used as reference material while speaking to the low caste farmers.

The orthodox group of Pune had become wild after

Swamiji's arrival. Already fuming over the activities of the Satyashodhak Samaj, the orthodox group now had to contend with Swami Dayanand's preaching as well. Dayanand had been speaking out against casteism. He had been telling people that women's education and widow remarriage were accepted by the scriptures. Obviously, the orthodox group was up in arms against him!

Swamiji was soon to leave Pune. The procession was planned as an ornate farewell to the eminent guest. But, as soon as the orthodox group learnt about the procession of 'that heretic man', their leader, Ramdikshit Apte, called for planning a ruckus at the event.

The atmosphere was tense; but, the procession was going to be carried out as planned. Police protection was probably not going to be enough to control the commotion. It was little wonder than, that during such a Catch-22 situation, Raosaheb Ranade felt it prudent to rope in Jyotirao. Their friendship was intact in spite of all their differences, and Jyotirao too found it wise to offer his help, in order to crush the orthodox group.

The procession was planned for evening; but, the foolish orthodox group became so impatient that, they began carrying out their own procession with a donkey, right from 6 a.m. The people of Pune were treated to a comical procession, which saw a donkey being walked around the city to the tunes of trumpets and drums.

While this drama was going on in the city, people were preparing for Swamiji's farewell speech at the Bhide bungalow. At around 4 p.m., Jyotirao set out for Bhide's bungalow, accompanied by Gyaanoba Sasane, Tatyasaheb Rode, and Dhondiba Lahuji. They were followed by 15-20 wrestlers armed with thick sticks. The wrestlers had been duly briefed about what their role would be.

The living room of Bhide's bungalow was packed with people. Swami Dayanand sat on the dais, a bright yellow shawl tied to his head like a turban.

Swamiji's personality and oratory, both were extremely charismatic. His shining intellect coupled with an elephantine memory would lend immense profoundness to his enchanting speech.

Around 4.30 p.m., Swamiji got up to speak. Today, there was no particular agenda to his speech. He wholeheartedly thanked the people of Pune for coming to his discourses religiously, and also expressed a hope that the teachings of Arya Samaj would soon proliferate among the citizens.

Some light snacks were served, after which, the people came out of the bungalow for the procession. A beautifully decorated elephant was standing in the open ground outside Belbaug. The wrestlers stood guard around the elephant; some with flambeaus in hand. 8-10 policemen were also standing guard at a distance.

Raosaheb Ranade, Jyotirao Phule, Lokahitawadi, Gangarambhau Mhaske and a few other people escorted Swami Dayanand to the elephant. Raosaheb requested Swamiji to sit atop the elephant. Cymbals and drums started playing to signal the mahout to lower the elephant for Swamiji. Soon, Swamiji climbed onto the houdah to the tunes of clarinets.

Just as the procession was about to begin, the donkey's procession started from an alley right opposite Belbaug.

The youngsters holding onto the donkey started shouting,

"Swami Gardhabhanand ki Jay!

Swami Gardhabhanand ki Jay!"

The donkey was decorated to resemble Swamiji. A yellow shawl was tied to its head; a blanket with Swamiji's photo painted on it was put on the donkey's back; and, a garland of flowers with a board of Swamiji's name tagged to it, was hung in the donkey's neck. The poor animal was followed by around 100 Brahmin youngsters, their bodies smeared in mud and muck. A few children from the Mali and Kunbi communities too could be seen among the crowd.

In a matter of moments, the donkey's procession came and

merged into the elephant's one....and....utter chaos ensued! People started screaming slogans...they began pushing each other... Scared by the sudden chaos, the donkey started kicking around, causing the youngsters holding onto him to get a few kicks on their legs!

Nevertheless, Swamiji's procession started surging ahead as planned. People who were on Swamiji's side, began ignoring the donkey's procession and moved ahead behind the elephant. This served to anger the youngsters even more. They started swearing at the people moving ahead. But, they could not do anything more than that, because the police and the wrestlers were protecting the procession fiercely.

The youngsters were frustrated to see their plans going bust. They did not know what to do. Just then, someone saw some muck on the ground, and their devious minds began ticking again...

As Swamiji's procession kept moving ahead, suddenly, balls of muck started raining on the backs of the people walking along side! Some mischief-mongers standing along the roadside, started cackling to encourage the Brahmin youngsters. But nothing was going to dissuade Swamiji's followers. They kept walking.

The British police officer accompanying the procession, was waiting for Raosaheb to give him the signal. But, Raosaheb wanted to handle the issue as peacefully as possible. The procession moved from Raviwar Chowk to Daruwala Bridge. Seeing that the opposite party was not showing any dissent, the Brahmins felt more empowered. They started pelting stones at the procession. Three-four people got hurt. That's when the procession was halted.

By now, the British officer was furious! He was enraged to see that a handful of mischief-mongers could create so much ruckus. His police force was waiting for his orders; they were ready to make a lathi-charge on the miscreants. But, even the officer could not do anything without Raosaheb's express permission.

Nevertheless, seeing the British officer looking at them in fury, the miscreants started quaking in their boots. They started running helter-skelter. In a few minutes, the street got emptied of the mischief-mongers.

The procession was cut short abruptly; they all returned to Bhide's house, where the farewell speeches began in earnest. Moments later, they could again hear the calls of 'Swami Gardhabhanand ki Jay!' coming from the alley outside Bhide mansion. Soon, this was followed by pelting of muck on the attendees, from the windows and doors of the mansion. Even after the windows and doors were closed, the chaos refused to subside. Instead, the rogues now started insulting people by taking individual names. Finally, the speeches had to be stopped.

By now, the attendees to the event had become tremendously enraged. They filtered out of the Bhide mansion, and began hurling blows on any person coming in their midst! In that tumult, someone ended up hitting the donkey. As a result, the donkey got wild and started kicking out unbidden. A few Brahmins tried to hold onto its reins, but the donkey had become so frantic, that it started running with the Brahmins hanging onto its reins! It would have made for a very funny sight, had the occasion not been such a serious one.

Just then, news came in that a big fight had erupted in Budhwar Peth. The Magistrate himself rushed there to intervene. Swami Dayanand was safely escorted to his place of residence.

At long last, the chaos abated. Jyotirao took Raosaheb's leave and returned home.

However, the Brahmins had not yet had their fill. They again found out their donkey – the scared animal had gone into hiding – and kept shouting slogans till late that night.

Jyotirao was very displeased with the way events had unfolded. He was specially pained to see that some youngsters from the Mali and Kunbi communities had also been brainwashed enough by the Brahmins to join in the hooliganism. For a long time, he kept thinking uneasily about what the future would bring for these misguided youngsters?!

53

Maharashtra was crying out loud for a few drops of rains, but over there, Gujarat was crying out for the lashing of torrential rains and flood-storms to stop! Just after Swamiji left Pune, news started pouring in about people in Ahmedabad becoming homeless due to floods. Lots of people and animals had lost their lives already. The Satyashodhaks came together and decided that, instead of spending money on elaborate 2nd anniversary celebrations of the Samaj (which was round the corner), they should contribute that amount for flood relief.

Jyotirao was keen to hand over the Chairmanship of the Samaj to some mature and intelligent person. He could not think of a better man than Dr. Vishram Ramji Ghole, for this task. He was sure that the independent-minded Dr. Ghole would do complete justice to the post.

Till then, no Chairman had been formally elected to the Samaj. Jyotirao had been declared both, the Chairman and the Treasurer, by the founding members. Jyotirao invited Dr. Ghole for a meeting and soon after, his name was formally declared as the new Chairman during the board meeting of the Samaj's 2nd anniversary. Bapuji Hari Shinde's brother Lakshmanrao Hari was made Deputy Chairman. Ramshet Uravane was made the new Treasurer. Advocate Lingu was made President of the managing committee. These arrangements were made to ensure that the working of the Samaj be carried out in a democratic way, without one person or caste having a monopoly over the proceedings. The Samaj did not follow any segregations of caste or religion. When Ilaija Shaleman showed interest in becoming a member of the Samaj, he was immediately taken on the managing committee without any second thoughts. Jyotirao decided to remain a simple member instead of taking on any post.

On the day of his induction, Dr. Ghole passed the resolution to help the victims of the Gujarat flood. After getting his wholehearted support, the members began working enthusiastically to collect funds for donation. They travelled within and outside Pune to collect funds. Members in Mumbai also began their efforts. Soon, a good amount of money got collected. The funds collected at Mumbai were going to be sent directly from there itself.

When the Prince of Wales came to Pune for a visit during Diwali, the Samaj hosted a program to felicitate him, because loyalty to one's rulers was one of the regulations that the Samaj abided by. The members arranged for a prayer meeting; Shaahir Dhondiram Kumbhar and Krishnarao Bhalekar sung paeans to the Prince; Krishnarao also read out an essay elucidating about the work being done by the Prince.

During this time, talks also ensued about starting their own newspaper. The printing machine given by the Mumbai members, was lying idle. Krishnarao was excited to take on that responsibility. However, the question of the ownership of the printing press was still in a limbo. No response had come to the correspondence made with Mumbai in this regard. The Pune members were not ready to take the topic ahead till they got clarity about the ownership. Thus, the matter kept pending.

While some matters were unresolved, others were getting resolved quickly. Lately, the orthodox group had started announcing that the marriages conducted by the Satyashodhak Samaj were illegal, and, the progeny born out of such alliances were misbegotten. The Samaj members decided to take legal advice regarding this matter from the Mumbai High Court translator Raghavendrarao. A letter requesting his help, was dispatched without further delay.

The Samaj was constantly working towards counseling

people about the importance of education and helping poor but promising students to get higher education. Niloba Ramji Karade was a poor man staying near the Phule house in Ganj Peth. He was a labourer and his two elder sons worked as tillers. Niloba wanted his younger son, Govinda, to get educated. He decided to seek Jyotirao's help for the same.

Govinda had completed his education in the Marathi medium; but, putting him in an English medium school for further studies, was beyond Niloba's financial means. Jyotirao promised to help Govinda. Jyotirao would help such promising students from his own funds, as well as, from the funds of the Samaj. The Samaj members would meet wealthy people and request them for donations and scholarships to help such students. Patrons like Hari Raoji Chiplunkar and Gangarambhau Mhaske would always donate generously for this cause. Hari Raoji would donate Rs. 60 annually. Jaya Karadi would send Rs. 25 every year from Mumbai. Tukaram Tatya would help as per his means. Jaya Yalappa Lingu had declared a gold medal for the child standing first in Matriculation exam every year; he had also sent the requisite amount for it to the Samaj. Annasaheb Sanglikar gave a one time donation of Rs. 35.

Apart from financial help, the children would also require assistance for getting admission in the English medium schools. Many promising children would drop out of school due to lack of funds. Jyotirao had been in touch with patron Sir Chattfield for allowing at least 5% of the students in every school to be admitted for free, from the Shoodra community. Jyotirao was keen that the children of shudra communities become not just literate and bookish, but instead grow up to become engineers of the future. He was seeing the future of Maharashtra becoming industrial in nature. Cloth mills had started in Mumbai. The industrial revolution was fast spreading to other parts of Maharashtra as well. It would not do for the Shoodra community to lag behind. But, till date, no Shoodra had acquired admission in an engineering college. Jyotirao decided to meet the Principal Sir Cook in this regard.

In that week's meeting, Jyotirao broached the topic of financial aid for Govinda. The committee sanctioned Re. 1 per month for Govinda, but on the condition that he would have to submit a monthly progress report of his studies as well as behavior.

Another topic came up for discussion in that meeting. Sakharam Satwaji Bhongle, an active member of the Samaj, had recently expired, all of a sudden. Thus, his family was facing immense problems. His wife as partially blind. It was impossible for her to teach her children. The committee decided to sanction those children Rs. 2 per month, on the same condition that they put forth for Govinda.

This condition had been out after reports that, many children from poor households, would skip school and while away their time in useless pursuits. The Samaj members decided that it was essential to keep the children away from foolish distractions. Thus, they decided to appoint a guard, who would accompany the children to & fro school. It was also decided to donate Rs. 5 per month from the Samaj fund for people who could not afford paying the children's fees.

Every meeting would see many such issues crop up and be resolved by mutual consent. During one meeting, Treasurer Ramshet Uravane declared an award for Shoodra writers writing literature pertaining to developments in the agrarian sector.

After many requests by Jyotirao, Sir Chattfield agreed to let 5% students of every school be included from the Shoodra community and be taught free of cost. Principal Sir Cook also agreed to admit students from the Shoodra community into their engineering college. 2-3 such students were also given immediate admission.

During a meeting to draft formal letters of thanks to these generous patrons, Jyotirao said,

"If we want more & more students from the rural belt and

poor households to gain education, we need to think beyond classes and stationery. We have to provide them with hostels where they can live and eat free of cost, or at least, at very minimal costs. That will accord them the peace of mind required for taking education."

The proposal was accepted by all the members. Instantly, a committee was formed to start work on such a hostel. Gamgarambhau Mhaske, Jyotirao Phule, Advocate Lingu, Lakshmanrao Hari Shinde and Vinayakrao Bhandarkar were appointed on that committee. They immediately started sending letters full of heartfelt requests to patrons, requesting them to think about the benefit of future generations and donate generously for the hostel.

As decided in another meeting, Phule, Vinayakrao Dengale, Vitthalrao Hirave, and Balaji Aadhav paid visits to the schools of Shoodra and Ati Shoodra students in Pune. They took the students' examination; gave them treats and prizes.

Krishnarao Bhalekar was running a library at Bhamburde. Alongside, he also started a night-school for farmers.

During another such meeting, one of the members read out a letter sent by Raghavendrarao from Mumbai. He had written that, marriages carried out by the Samaj were completely legal. This news served to boost everyone's enthusiasm to carry out the marriage ceremonies which had been kept on hold till clarity was got on the issue.

In the same meeting, Jyotirao proposed developing good orators, who would serve to dispel the ignorance amongst Shoodra, Ati Shoodra brethren through their speeches. In view of developing such orators, it was decided to hold elocution competitions. Dr. Ghole and Krishnarao Bhalekar accepted the responsibility of conducting these competitions. Topics such as 'Pros and cons of casteism', 'Pros and cons of Idolatry' and such others were decided upon for the contestants. It was decided to host the first elocution competition in the upcoming summers. The winners were to be given handsome prizes.

By now, the membership of the Samaj had swelled beyond 300. People from various socio-economic strata were coming forward to become members. Jyotirao was immensely happy to see such a diverse populace congregate under the banner of the Satyashodhak Samaj. It was a sign of the society having accepted and endorsed the values and ideas of the Samaj.

54

Jyotirao was looking forward to the much-pending trip to Otur. Preparations were under-swing for the four-day trip, when the devastating news of Yalappa Lingu's demise filtered in from Mumbai. A generous patron and supporter of the Samaj had gone too soon!

The Samaj members called for an urgent meeting. A condolence letter was drafted and sent on behalf of the Samaj to Jaya Yalappa's younger brother, Jaya Karadi. However, Jyotirao could not think of not going to Mumbai personally; thus, off he went.

In the travel from Pune to Mumbai, Jyotirao kept reminiscing about Jaya Yalappa's yeoman service to the society, especially in the education sector. He was the founder of education for the Telugu community in Mumbai. He himself would teach at the Telugu-Marathi school at Kamathipura. Jaya Yalappa's life was a saga of immense hard work and sacrifice. It was necessary to do something to preserve his memories for the future generations. Jyotirao kept thinking about what kind of commemoration could be done for this selfless soul.

Jyotirao met a lot of people during the condolence meeting.

After returning to Pune, he put forth a proposal that, the members should collect funds and declare an award in the name of Jaya Yalapppa, to the student standing first in the annual elocution competition. Everyone agreed to the suggestion.

The first elocution competition was held in the newly built bungalow of Ramchandra Mansaram Naik, in Vetaal Peth. The students had come well prepared. Dwarkanath Sonar, Damodar Shimpi and Anandrao Ranchhodji were declared as winners. They received awards from the Samaj funds, as well as, from the personal funds of Dr. Ghole and Ramshet Uravane, who declared prizes on their own accord to encourage the winners. Gopal, the son of Dr. Ghole, also gave a speech in the competition. Jyotirao gave him a special award for speaking so eloquently and fearlessly, in spite of his young age.

Dr. Ghole's appointment as Chairman, had eased out quite a few bottlenecks in the working, due to his go-getter attitude. Since space was falling short at Sadoba Gawde's house, the meetings of the Samaj were now being taken at Naik's bungalow. Many Marwari merchants of Vetaal Peth were wanting to rent space in Naik's huge bungalow. They were willing to pay whatever rent Naik quoted. If such a deal got struck, the Samaj would again be left wanting for place. Anticipating this problem in due time, Dr. Ghole went to meet Naik. In a pleasant turn of events, Naik agreed to give his entire bungalow to the Samaj for a small rent of Rs. 10 per month. Additionally, he also gave a generous donation to the Samaj.

Jyotirao's proposed trip to Junnar got prolonged yet again. Even though the farmers' agitation had become a bit subdued, dissatisfaction still bubbled over in their minds. It was difficult to say when and how the dissent would erupt again.

That year was particularly bad for the farmers. Rain had played truant; it was almost a draught-like situation. Indapur, Miraj, Tasgaon had not received even a few drops of rain. At many houses, it had become impossible to get one square meal a day. People had become impoverished overnight. It was difficult to predict what problem would arise next.

During this time, Jyotirao was shouldered with yet another responsibility. Taking into cognizance his yeoman service towards social empowerment, the Pune Municipal Corporation made Jyotirao a Member. The ambit of his work expanded yet again.

55

Krishnarao would never forget the meeting that took place in Raobahadur Veerjangamaiyya's living room. He was ready to take on the entire responsibility of the newspaper. He took a formal oath for the same. When the question of ownership of the printing press came forth, Krishnarao also showed readiness to pay its rent from his own pocket. However, Jyotirao did not agree to anything that Krishnarao said. After a lot of arguments, it was decided to send the press back to Mumbai.

Krishnarao had been slogging for the last two years to have the Samaj's own newspaper. He was very sure that, a newspaper would be the perfect vehicle to reach the views of the Samaj to the masses, as also to, convey the people's problems to the Government in an effective, democratic way.

Till then, majority of the newspapers in Pune were controlled by Brahmins. They would almost never be ready to publish articles written by the members of the Samaj, or those that would propagate the views upheld by the Samaj. Rather, most articles in those newspapers would berate and insult the Samaj and its members. Krishnarao was raring to give a befitting answer to all those naysayers through the Samaj's own newspaper. He was confident about running the newspaper independently.

However, from the beginning itself, Jyotirao was not keen on starting their own newspaper. Seeing Jyotirao's unenthusiastic response, Krishnarao got some influential people to talk to him and make him change his mind. However, Jyotirao's response remained unchanged. He kept saying,

"For people who do not even know what a newspaper is, there's no point in starting one. We need to first spread education among our community, before taking up such initiatives."

Krishnarao did not agree with this opinion of Jyotirao's. He was sure that a newspaper would help in myriad ways. In fact, Jyotirao and a few other members had made a bigger issue out of the ownership of the press, than it warranted. Actually, the people in Mumbai too were not very rigid about it. A lot of members in Pune also wanted the press to be handed over to Krishnrao, so that he could start a newspaper. But, Jyotirao was unbending.

Krishnarao decided to give it yet another try before the press was sent to Mumbai. Seeing Jyotirao's curt behavior in the last few days, Krishnarao knew that it would be fighting a losing battle; but, yet he was going to try.

One morning, when Krishnarao's horse-carriage halted in front of Jyotirao's shop, Jyotirao was getting ready to go to a site. A lot of canals were being built at Hadapsar and Maanjri. Plus, bridges were also being built on the canals. 'Poona Commercial and Contracting Company' had got the contract for supplying stones for this construction.

Usually, Krishnarao's carriage would arrive at the pre-decided site before Jyotirao arrived. Seeing Krishnarao at the shop that day, Jyotirao was a bit surprised.

"Come in, Krishnarao. What brings you here today?" Jyotirao asked, beckoning Krishnarao inside.

"I came to meet you, Tatya. I strongly feel we should rethink about sending the press back to Mumbai" sad Krishnarao, without mincing words.

"That's not necessary" replied Jyotirao.

"Why so, Tatya? A newspaper is very necessary to proliferate the views of the Samaj…" Krishnarao insisted.

Jyotirao responded in a firm voice,

"Krishnarao, the people for who you wish to start this newspaper for….do they even know the meaning of that word?! The letters in the newspaper would be nothing more than blobs of ink for those ignorant and illiterate brethren. To run a newspaper consistently, we require renowned and scholarly people to contribute articles on a regular basis. How many such writers can we find in the Shoodra community? And the readers will be these people of Pune...who will read anything only if they get it for free! They won't spend a penny to read a newspaper... they will simply walk off, turning up their noses saying, what's so great in it to read?! What newspaper will you run in such a scenario? Today's time demand the proliferation of education; it is not a conducive time to run a paper. When a big chunk of our society becomes educated, that is when we shall start a newspaper and run it according to the Samaj's principles."

Krishnarao was taken aback by Jyotirao's stern talk, but he also knew where the sarcasm was stemming from. Krishnarao had arranged Swami Dayanand's discourse at Bhamburde; during which, Swamiji had expressed some views about farmers, which had not gone down well with Jyotirao. That time, he had even expressed his dissent openly, saying,

"The farmers, for who you are claiming to have so much empathy for.... what has Dayanand done for them? This scholar, who roams around citing passages from the Vedas... does he even know what pathetic conditions are the farmers living in? Before conveniently ignoring the atrocities being committed by Brahmin money-lenders, and, making brash statements like 'farmers are debt-ridden because they cannot control their spending', he should have visited a farmer's house and seen the truth for himself. He can raise a finger on the defenseless farmers, but not dare to criticize the atrocious money-lenders, is it?! How convenient!"

Jyotirao had yet not softened his stance on this issue. Albeit, Krishnarao knew, that was not the sole reason for Jyotirao's displeasure. He was equally displeased with Krishnarao for the harsh treatment he gave his wife. Jyotirao had not expected such behavior from an educated youth and a Satyashodhak like Krishnarao. Even though Krishnrao felt that Jyotirao was being a bit too stringent, the latter was firm on his opinions. Even though he had never expressly voiced his displeasure about Krishnaroa's behavior, Jyotirao would try to shun Krishnarao's participation in the activities of the Samaj, as much as possible.

Realising that Krishnarao had understood what he wanted to convey, Jyotirao said,

"The people for who you want to start this newspaper, cannot read; and those who can read, will not want to hold your newspaper in their hands. People who find it better to invest in a new blade when the barber raises his fees by 2 aanas, are never going to spend their precious money buying your newspaper. And, the government, whose eyes you wish to open through the paper... does it have the time or inclination to read even one page of that paper?"

Seeing Krishnarao in a thoughtful mode, Jyotirao softened his stance a bit and continued,

"Krishnarao, Maharashtra is suffering from acute water shortage. A draught is not too far away. People have far bigger worries to think about rather than reading a newspaper and changing their views. We need to think about how to help people get the basic requirements of life, instead of thinking of starting a paper. If we do not think of people emphatically, how are we different from those Brahmins who stay enveloped in their own bubble and view the world through their rose-tinted glasses? Newspapers and magazines are subjects okay to be discussed by those for whom reading and writing is the only work in life. But, we represent a larger mass of people, who are not only ignorant, but presently are finding it difficult to have even two square meals a day. Would they be in a frame of mind to receive a newspaper in such a scenario? Think about it."

In spite of all this explanation, Krishnarao was still not ready to listen. He persisted,

"Tatyasaheb, I do not agree with you. If you do not wish to hand over the press to me, that's fine. But, I will stick t my resolve of starting a newspaper! My decision will not change. But please be rest assured that I shall carry on the work on the paper in keeping with the principles of the Samaj. I am a true

Satyashodhak at heart."

Jyotirao could understand Krishnrao's anger and obstinacy, but without caring a tuppence for it, he replied,

"Krishnarao, every member of the Satyashodhak Samaj is tied to the Samaj through the thread of humanity. We place humanity and humaneness on the apex of all the principles we stand for. It is not in my place to comment on your domestic matters, but, I would only say... behave in keeping with humanity in your home, and then call yourself a Satyshodhak."

Jyotirao's words were a stinging slap on Krishnarao's face! He stood stunned and speechless! Jyotirao had put a finger on his weakest – albeit, yet hidden – point.

No one said anything for some time. Then, Jyotirao said,

"Come on, let's leave. We are getting late."

Krishnarao mutely followed Jyotirao in his carriage, and soon, off they went to Hadapsar.

All the way to Hadapsar, Jyotirao kept trying to convince Krishnarao, but he was in no mood to listen.

56

When Jyotirao's carriage reached the site, he saw the supervisor yelling at the laborers to do their work faster. The laborers were rushing as fast as they could, lugging heavy stones on their head.

After that day's visit, Krishnarao hardly ever came to the site. He was preparing to launch a newspaper on his own. Jyotirao was hearing several things, but he had decided not to confront Krishnarao about them at all.

Jyotirao tucked his dhoti at the waist, and started helping the labourers in carrying the stones. Soon, rivulets of sweat started flowing down his body, but he did not stop. At one point, as Jyotirao lifted a stone, it suddenly cracked; and one big chunk of the stone landed on his foot! Jyotirao screamed in agony! For some moments, his brain went numb with the pain. Slowly, he removed his sandal, and saw that three fingers and the toe had been badly crushed. Blood was flowing profusely from the wound. Jyotirao took some mud and applied it to the wound. The blood stopped flowing.

The laborers dropped their work and came running to see what had happened to their dear Tatya. They were immensely worried to see the wound. Mukunda said,

"Tatyasaab, this mud may have stopped the bleeding for now; but you need to visit a doctor immediately."

Jyotirao replied,

"Mukunda, I am a farmer at heart; and, a farmer's mother, father, doctor…everything is this earth…this mud. As it is, who is going to ask us at the doctor's clinic? My earth-mother is the best medicine for my wound. At most, when I reach home, I shall apply some turmeric or herbs. See, the bleeding has already stopped. Come on everybody….let's get on with our work."

The laborers returned to work, but Mukunda was still worried. He said,

"Tatyasaab, my house is close by. Please come there. I shall apply some ointment. You also need to rest awhile."

Jyotirao could not refuse Mukunda's affectionate insistence. He accompanied Mukunda to his house, which was a small hut in a wasteland nearby. The wasteland was actually a farm, but the draught-like situation had rendered it into a wasteland. Two bullocks, thinned to the bones due to lack of food and water, were sitting nearby wistfully. A hen and her scraggly chicks were clucking around.

Jyotirao asked him casually,

"So, Mukunda…Is all okay?"

Mukunda replied,

"Well, I would say so, Tatyasaab… what else can I say? This draught is out to kill us. The land is bare. One does not get two decent buckets of water a day. If this work of the canal hadn't come up, we would probably have perished in this draught."

Mukunda brought some ointment for Jyotirao. As he was applying it, two-three hollow-stomached kids came running from the adjacent hut and ran back inside. Jyotirao was immensely pained to see those half clothed, hungry looking children.

Just then, Jyotirao heard someone talking inside. He asked,

"Who is inside, Mukunda?"

"It's my mother. She is running a high temperature for several days. Add to that, ever since the moneylender snatched our small piece of land from us, it has affected her mind badly, and she keeps shouting and crying."

Inside, Mukunda's mother was crying aloud:

"Oh God! Please have mercy on us, God! All my life, I spent whatever little money we had, on feeding these idle Brahmins. They kept telling us one ritual after the other, and we did it all to please you. But you still do not seem pleased by us. Why, oh why, have you reduced us to such a pitiful stage?!"

Just then, a middle-aged man came out from the hut and asked,

"Who is it, Mukunda?"

"Tatyasaab contractor has come to our house."

"Oh?! Tatyasaab contractor? Greetings, Sir..." said the man, who was Mukunda's elder brother.

After a few casual talks, Mukunda's brother said,

"What do I tell you of our troubles, Tatyasaab?! Those evil Brahmins levied double the tax on us. When I said that I would like to go by the books, they said, I would have to bribe them to readjust the accounts. From where would I get that kind of money? Finally, I had to mortgage my small land to pay the enormous tax..... and...and... that moneylender, who was hand-in-glove with the Brahmin clerks...he gobbled up our land, Tatyasaab!! We have lost everything sir...every little thing we had..." he said, sobbing like a child!

Jyotirao was immensely pained to hear all this. He asked,

"Why don't you lodge a complaint against the moneylender?"

"With whom?" Mukunda's brother asked in a defeated tone. "The money lender's wife's brother is a government officer. His uncle works in the Collector's office. His elder sister's husband is a sepoy. His wife's father is a police officer at the district level. Plus, apart from that, wherever we may go, he has employed Brahmin clerks who dance to his tune. So, where do we go hoping for justice, tell us? The irony is, we have lost everything, and yet, we keep getting charged on some or the other crime that we can never even dream of committing! We cant even think of hiring a lawyer; he will bleed us dry. What can be more agonizing for a father than having to sell of his married daughter's jewelry to wipe off his troubles? But, Tatyasaab, I am such a sinner who has been compelled to do just that! It is because of me that my innocent daughter has been kicked out from her marital home. It is a vicious cycle, Tatyasaab! Very vicious!"

Jyotirao was listening intently to the poor man's heart-wrenching narration. He was talking his heart out, saying,

"My children are dressed in tatters. They go asleep on an empty stomach. What kind of a life is this? Sometimes, I feel like ending this wretched life of mine. But then, I think, who will look after my wife, my children....what about my old mother? You tell us to lodge a complaint.... But, Tatyasaab...this British empire is not going to be here forever. Once they go, these people are not going to let us live in peace. They will take revenge for the next seven generations of mine!"

Saying thus, the man started bawling out! Jyotirao was stunned. Somehow, he pacified the man and said,

"What you are saying is correct. The British are not going to be here for ever; most of the Brahmins are out to wipe you all off. But don't worry. I know a few good Brahmins who will surely help you. I shall talk to them."

Hearing this, both the brothers began groveling at Jyotirao's feet.

"No, please don't do that" said Jyotirao. "Mukunda, tomorrow come along with me to the city. I will do everything I can to help you. This evil age of Brahmin domination needs to end somewhere. Do not live under the threat of what the Brahmins will do after the British leave. Tomorrow's regime is going to be that of educated, enlightened farmers. The children of farmers are soon going to be educated and empowered and they are the ones who will drive the British away from our country. Please do not live under the fear that the cruel Peshwai regime will return. It won't."

Mukunda's brother then requested Jyotirao to help them. Jyotirao also met and pacified Mukunda's mother, promising her to help them all.

Soon, he took Mukunda along and left for the site. On the way, he kept thinking...

'Due to lack of education, these farmers do not even know what they are made to sign on. The British legal system has broken their backs even more. It is such an irony that, the ones who feed the society, are themselves dying out of hunger. We need stringent laws to prevent this exploitation of the farmers and save their lands from getting snatched by unscrupulous people. The revolution that had recently happened at Junnar-Ahmednagar, was required to happen here as well. The entire country needs to be up in arms against the Brahmins...'

That evening, Jyotirao came home with his head buzzing with horror stories about exploitation of many farmers like Mukunda and his brother. He kept thinking about who all he should meet tomorrow to resolve Mukunda's plight.

As he came home, Jyotirao saw a new newspaper lying on the table. Curiously, he picked it up and saw the name of the newspaper and its editor as:

'Deenbandhu,

Editor: Krishnarao Bhalekar'.

So finally, Krishnarao had had his way. Jyotirao was not

ignorant about what had transpired in the interim. Krishnrao had sold his wife's jewelry and mortgaged his house to start this paper. He was in the process of getting a typesetting machine from Mumbai and was ready to even mortgage his land for the same. Krishnarao's brother Ramchandrarao was helping him realize his dream.

While on one hand Jyotirao was impressed by Krishnarao's courage and perseverance, one the other hand, he still thought that it was a kneejerk decision. It seemed, Krishnarao had not thought of many factors like the draught situation, the need for consistent circulation of the paper, subscribers and so on.

Jyotirao began reading the first edition of Deenbandhu. Krishnarao had minced no words in conveying that, Deenbandhu would highlight the problems being faced by the ignorant, low caste members of society.

57

Finally, everyone's fears came true, as Pune got enveloped by a terrible draught. Villagers began crying out in anguish. Debt-ridden farmers were pushed further into a black hole as money-lenders began tormenting them for money. Even when they could plainly see that in absence of a crop, the farmers had no way of repaying their debts, the hard-hearted money-lenders started putting legal charges on the hapless farmers. It became a common sight to see some poor farmer being dragged off to the police station for 'cheating' the money lenders.

This was a commonly used ploy by money-lenders at other times too. In the draught, they became even more evil. Many of the farmers were already repaying debts left for them by their forefathers. For that, they had mortgaged their own small lands, homes, cattle, and even their wives and children to the lenders. For so many years, they would take their entire harvest to the money-lender's house, keeping not a single sack for themselves. But, decades of sleeping on empty stomachs had still not been enough to free them from the vicious cycle of debt. Instead, the debts kept mounting. Their future generations were already harnessed to taking up their share of the debts as soon as they grew to a certain age.

The farmers understood the money-lenders' ploy, but they were too afraid to speak up in protest. That's because, they were afraid that after the British government went away, the money-lenders and the Brahmin officials would not let them live in peace. They knew that even know the British had brought some legal sanity into the country, the lenders and the Brahmins would not let farmers take recourse to that law. Farmers were the most exploited lot. Sadly so, even if they took loans from the rich people of lower castes, they too would find nothing wrong in exploiting the farmers.

It would be impossible for the farmers to pay taxes after keeping every possession of theirs mortgaged. Again they would be reduced to groveling before the lender itself. Usually the lenders would give them more credit, but this year, seeing that the farmers would find it impossible to ever repay them, the lenders tightened their purse-strings more than ever before.

The farmers got caught between the devil and the deep sea. There seemed no end to their troubles. No on was willing to show them any empathy. Money was non-existent; debts had mounted beyond sanity; and the money-lenders refused to abate their harassment.

Finally, as was bound to happen, decades of dissent got unleashed like a volcano! The farmers stood up united in one of the most fierce revolutions known to India.

The first ember of this revolution was lit in a village called Karde, in the region of Shirur. Babasaheb Deshmukh, a retired official from the Shinde regime, faced forfeiture by a Marwari money-lender. Once a well-respected officer, Babasaheb too had sunken into the cesspool of debts.

Babasaheb had pleaded a lot with the money-lender. He had even mortgaged the jewelry that adorned the idol of Lord

Vitthal in his ancestral temple. But, in spite of all that, he had not been able to repay the loan in the given duration. Using that as an excuse, the money-lender had snatched away the God's jewelry! That served to be the breaking point for Babasaheb, as well as, the beginning of a severe agitation against the years of torment by unscrupulous lenders.

Babasaheb appealed to the farmers in his village to stand along with him. The distressed farmers immediately sprung into action! They boycotted all the lenders in the village. After decades of traumatizing the poor, it was now the lenders' turn to face the heat. Not a single shopkeeper in the village would agree to sell them a grain of salt! Nobody would rush to help them in case of some problem. People started flinging dog carcasses inside their houses. It became impossible for the lenders to step out of their homes. Matters reached to such an end that the lenders had to request police protection against the agitated village-folk. But, that served to escalate the tension even more.

The revolt in Karde served to be the first ember of the fire that was soon to spread over many regions. In a matter of days, the entire region of Shirur blew up in agitation. Just as the police and government officials managed to bring some peace to Shirur, a similar revolt started in Supe. A gang of farmers started viciously attacking the homes of money-lenders. One Marwari lender's house was set on fire. Many of their houses were ransacked. People would simply charge inside, pluck out whatever documents they could, and make a bonfire of them on the road!

Soon this revolt, which started getting recognized as 'Khat Phaadiche Band' , spread to Indapur and Pandharpur. Just as those areas came under control, violent rebellion restarted in Shirur. A Marwari lender was killed by an aggrieved mob in Naavrya. This led to merciless murders of many lenders all around. The farmers had decided that enough was enough. They had crossed their limits of patience. Farmers started forming systematic gangs. Armed with weapons, they would barge into a lender's house, threaten him and his family, and ask for documents. If the lender refused to give the documents, the gang would simply set the whole house on fire! At times, the lender would be locked up in a room and be made to suffocate to death with the fumes that would light up his house. Often, the lenders would invite death into their fold by locking themselves up in a room, to save themselves from the merciless anger of the crowd. But that would serve to irk them even more, and they would light up the house. At Nimbhaat, the farmers sliced off some Marwari money-lenders' noses. At Karhaati, a money-lender's granary was looted to the last grain. Not just Marwari, but even Brahmin money-lenders were facing the same fate.

The rebellion kept spreading. Money-lenders were trying their best to pacify the raving mobs, but generations of torment were not so easy to forget for those distressed people. They kept up their vicious attacks till finally, the police had to intervene. As a last resort, the police started indiscriminately imprisoning the rebelling farmers. It was only after hundreds of such farmers were locked up that the revolt started calming down. Honya Koli, one of the leaders of the revolt, was arrested. But, it was not until the government intervened, held peace talks with the farmers, and agreed to hear their complaints and pay them just compensation, that the rebellion truly stopped.

The government immediately instituted a committee to look into the problems of the farmers. The rebellion stopped but the dissent did not go away. It kept boiling within.

Jyotirao made a quick trip to Otur and Junnar along with Bhau Kondaji, Balaji Kusaji and Naro Babaji. He held several meetings with farmers at these places.

The government-appointed committee made an in-depth study of the problems that the farmers had been facing and suggested a few relief measures. Ceilings were put on the interest rate chargeable on loans. Confiscation of one's house and land against the non-repayment of loans, was banned. Lenders were asked to resolve disputes with mutual co-operation and understanding. In the later stages, the legal system was tweaked to encourage farmers to approach the courts for resolution of grievances. The number of courts was also increased. Even as the farmers got empowered to fight their battles systematically, the lenders became subdued – because, by now, they had realized what havoc tyrannized farmers could wreak on them.

Jyotirao returned to Pune with a lot of experiences and questions in mind. The farmers' agitation had given enterprising young leaders like Balaji Kusaji, Naro Babaji and Junnarkar Shete to the Satyashodhak Samaj. No one knew that time, but this agitation was to serve as the foundation stone of a much bigger revolution in the future.

The Samaj arranged for many lectures at various places, to educate the masses about what had brought about the farmers' revolution. That year's elocution competition also addressed the topic of what problems did consistent draught bring for farmers, and what measures could be undertaken to improve their lives. The student standing first in that competition, was to be awarded the prize instituted by the late Jaya Yalappa. At the same time, an essay competition was also organized. Students had to imagine that Queen Victoria was travelling around India and the Mahars and Maangs were telling her about their problems. They had to write essays imagining what problems would the Mahar-Maangs narrate to the Queen.

In the month of March, an annual report of the Satyashodhak Samaj was sent to be published to various newspapers and magazines. The members were waiting to see what reactions would the report elicit from the public at large.

58

Jyotirao had got a contract of mining boulders from the mine at Gorhaa. Gyaanoba had partnered with Jyotirao for this work, and would supervise the site everyday. One day, after a hurried visit to the site, Jyotirao had rushed to the shop and then come home for a quick lunch. He was waiting for Gyaanoba to come home for lunch; for, he had to return to the shop soon after.

Jyotirao had taken on this new contract after his work at the canal had ended. The commercial company, that had been started in partnership, was limping forward somehow. Internal disputes and disagreements were raising their head. Krishnarao had left the partnership. Ramchandrarao Shinde was in search of some other work.

From his perch in the living room, Jyotirao could see a group of beggars standing at the main door, waiting to get a piece of stale bhaakri from Savitribai. It had become a heart-wrenching sight; the draught, along with the accompanying inflation, had broken the back of many people. They had been reduced to begging along with their wife and children. It had become a common sight in Indapur, Miraj, and Tasgaon to see half-clothed women and children scrounging away for food. Starvation had reduced thousands of people into mere skeletons. Unable to feed their children, people had taken to leaving them alone in faraway wastelands. Those poor children would roam around the alleys, begging for a piece of bhaakri. People had gone to such deplorable levels that, there were some who would make small children go begging and then snatch away the money or food that they would get as alms. Humanity had become almost non-existent. No human being was ready to extend a hand of compassion to another. The biggest irony of it all was that, a farmer, who would feed thousands of people, had been reduced to begging for one piece of bhaakri for himself.

In order to get heavenly blessings for donating food, some rich people opened up shelters serving free food; but, these would be accessible only to the Brahmins. The donors held a misconception that serving free food to the poor Brahmins would expedite them straight to heaven after their death. Celestial maidens would be ready to welcome them with flowers and Lord Indra himself would come to lead them by the hand into that most coveted world. Even in abject poverty, the Brahmins had not lost their cunning. Promising the ignorant and illiterate rich donors that they would attain heaven after death, they would ask them to donate heartily to their Brahmin community. The most pitiable thing was that, most of these rich donors belonged to the Shoodra communities; yet, their compassion did not flow towards their own brethren! And of course, of that was the case with Shoodra donors, it would be foolish to expect a shred of humanity from the Brahmin donors.

While on one hand the draught had reduced many people to hellish depths of poverty, there were some who were getting richer or idling away on account of the freebies they were getting. The Brahmins who were getting free food, would spend all their time playing cards or gossiping, without a shred of compassion for the ravaged children and women roaming the streets in search of food. Their talks would revolve around how the loss of Peshwai had reduced their 'godly' selves to such disgraceful conditions.

Some Shastribuva would comment,

"Ohho.... If the Peshwas had been there today, we would never have been reduced to such a state!"

At this, caressing his belly extended shamefully in spite of the draught, another would reply,

"Curse these barbarians!! It is all the doing of these lowly heretics. The Peshwas had kept all these useless people below the thumb. But, these ignorant British....they allowed these lowly people to grow beyond their boots. No wonder, the heavens have cursed us all with draught. The Vedas have clearly stated that, a land that does not respect its Brahmins, will be cursed with famines and draught. Why so? Because, Brahmins are the embodiment of the supreme power Himself. A Brahmin can never go wrong. All the holy places reside in the toe of a

Brahmin. But alas, who will explain all this to these detestable people? This is nothing but Kaliyug! Everything is going to go up in smoke. Everything is going to be ruined, unless Brahmins are given their due respect and the low-lifes are flung back to the hellhole they came from. Do you know what the Manusmriti says? It says, even if the king of a land is going hungry, he should never dare to levy any tax or fine on a Brahmin. If a king, who is seen as an embodiment of Lord Vishnu, is prevented from committing such blasphemy, what chance do the others have?"

After gossiping about their importance and might for hours on end, the Brahmins would then go sniffing to see where they would get the tastiest food that day. Even those Brahmins who had jobs or had some business, would feel no shame in wolfing down free food given by donors. So many Shoodras would be dying every day due to lack of food, but no Brahmin would take pity on them. So many hungry children would keep encircling the food shelters to get a piece of bhaakri thrown to them, but they would never get a morsel. Jyotirao was tremendously uneasy on seeing the horrible conditions around. His heart would specially go out to the children. Adults could still do some work and earn their bread; but, what would the children do?! It was imperative that something be done immediately to resolve this problem. As it is, too many children had already succumbed to starvation…

Jyotirao knew that the only way to resolve this problem was to start another food shelter – but, it was not an easy task. He realized that it was imperative to tug the heart-strings of the rich Maratha donors and tell them that the roads to heaven did not open by only feeding Brahmins…!

Gyaanoba had still not arrived. Jyotirao picked up a copy of 'Vividh Dynaanvistaar', and started leafing through it. A journalist had written a cleverly laced sarcastic review about the Samaj's annual report. Coating a bitter pill in sugar, the journalist had opined that the Satyashodhak Samaj was taking 'more than necessary efforts to start a new sect' that was trying to unearth 'God knows what hitherto unknown truths'! Without trying to make an unbiased analysis of the principles that the Samaj functioned by, the journalist had alleged that the Samaj was trying to convert public opinion against the Brahmins and foster other lowly castes for its own gains.

Adding fuel to the fire, the journalist had further stated that 'the poor Brahmins had always been at the mercy of the rich Shoodras'. Reading that, Jyotirao called out to his wife and asked agitatedly,

"Savitribai, did you happen to read this nonsense?! What is this man saying?"

"Well, I did" Savitribai said with a wry smile.

"Now that we have started an organization to bring the Shoodras under one canopy, it seems this writer is feeling threatened on behalf of the Brahmin community! That is why all this nonsense has been written. And what kind of a mockery is this? Calling the Shoodras rich? When have the poor Shoodras ever been rich enough to patronize the Brahmins? Is this some kind of sick joke that this man is trying to make at the expense of Shoodras? That too, at a time when so many Shoodras are dying out of hunger?! How shameless can a person be?"

"It is nothing but a matter of convenience and hypocrisy, Shetji" replied Savitribai. "According to them, Brahmin is the only caste in society; there is no other caste worth mentioning. The very basics concepts regarding society that they hold and we hold, are diametrically different from each other. Plus, how did you ever think that they will not react acerbically, after what you have been writing about them?!"

Jyotirao banged the copy on the table in rage! He had no time or interest in reacting to this vitriol. He had too many things waiting to catch his attention.

After waiting for Gyaanoba till 1.30 pm, Jyotirao finally sat to have his lunch. But, the pitiful images of the half-naked, hungry children roaming the streets, refused to leave his mind, making it difficult for him to even swallow the morsels.

As Jyotirao was having his food, Gyaanoba came in.

"Come, Gyaanoba.... I was waiting for you, for long."

Sheepishly, Gyaanoba washed his hands and sat down to eat.

While eating, he kept stealing glances out of the door. At one point, he called out to someone saying,

"Take proper care of my blanket, alright?"

Jyotirao asked him,

"Who is it, Gyaanoba? Have you got someone outside?"

"Yes, Tatyasaheb. I have brought along one boy from our site. We have to carry back some material..."

"So then, why have you made him wait outside in the heat?" asked Jyotirao.

Seeing Gyaanoba silent, Jyotirao locked a steady gaze on him and asked,

"Has the boy eaten?"

Gyaanoba looked downwards in reply. In an instant, Jyotirao rose from his half-eaten meal, and went outside. He saw a young, emaciated boy waiting on the steps, looking after Gyaanoba's blanket and footwear.

"Son, have you eaten anything?" Jyotirao asked him gently, knowing that the answer would be in the negative.

Seeing the boy nod in a 'no', Jyotirao said,

"Come inside and have some food. Savitribai, please serve some food to this boy."

Then, he went inside and asked Gyaanoba in an infuriated tone,

"How could you even think of sitting for lunch by keeping this boy hungry?!

Gyaanoba was well aware of Tatyasaheb's rage. He found it prudent to keep mum, instead of giving any explanations. As it is, in hindsight, Gyaanoba was feeling ashamed of his behavior.

Jyotirao stopped his meal and waited for Savitribai to bring a plateful of food for the boy. Only after the boy started eating, did Jyotirao resume his lunch. However, his rage had still not abated. He continued berating Gyaanoba saying,

"Gyaanoba, I simply fail to understand how could you bring yourself to eat, knowing that there's a hungry boy sitting outside? It was your duty to first feed him and then yourself."

The rest of the meals were finished in an uncomfortable silence. Thereafter, Gyaanoba took all the material he needed for the site and left with the boy. Jyotirao too set off for his shop.

Lately, Jyotirao had been engrossed in writing an essay about how the building of canals had become beneficial for the Shoodras, and how a foreign government had thought more about this aspect, than an indigenous one.

There had been a lot of misunderstandings among the farmer community with regards to the canals. Many farmers would disallow the canals from going through their fields. They were afraid that if they allowed a canal to be built across their land, the government would claim ownership of the land. To begin with, they would scoff in disbelief that it was indeed possible to divert a river's water directly into their fields. In order to let the government continue its work unbridled, it was imperative to explain the workings of the canal to these farmers.

As soon as he reached the shop, Jyotirao sat to write the essay. While writing, a resolve shaped up in his mind. He decided to start a food shelter that would provide 2000 bhaakris every morning and evening. He started thinking about how to manage the logistics and who all to meet for this ambitious plan.

That evening, he went to meet Ramshet Uravane. After Shetji promised to help the cause, Jyotirao went to meet Hari Raoji.

Meeting Hari Raoji would always bring back old memories for Jyotirao. A young orphan who had come seeking Jyotirao's help all those years back, had carved a successful niche for himself as Hari Raoji Chiplunkar Shinde.

Hari Raoji had won over Bholageer Maharaj by toiling incessantly and sincerely at his shop. Maharaj had deployed Baba Gokhale as a tutor to coach Hari, and had then got his daughter married to Hari in later years. After marriage, Hari stayed at Bholageer Maharaj's house and after the latter's demise, Hari became heir to a vast fortune, comprising of many properties and the business.

Hari Raoji had not forgotten his humble beginnings. He would proactively participate in the Samaj's activities, physically as well as financially.

This time too, he assured Jyotirao of full support for the food shelter.

Jyotirao also had a meeting with the Municipal Health Officer, Dr. Shivappa Rajanna. At the following Sunday's meeting, Jyotirao read out his essay and put forth the proposal of the food shelter, which was tentatively called 'Balashram'. The proposal received unanimous response, and soon, Jyotirao started sending out letters of requests to the Samaj members in Mumbai, Pune etc.

"Dear members of the Satyashodhak Samaj, Pune, Mumbai etc.,

This letter is to apprise you all that, the Samaj has decided to start a food shelter called 'Victoria Balashram'. You all are aware of the draught situation in Pune. As a result of the draught, many people, who are unable to feed their young children, are leaving them on the streets. Similarly, except from the Brahmin caste, many other people from Indapur, Miraj and Tasgaon, are coming into Pune in search of food and basic clothing. However, food and clothing both are scarce in Pune right now. It has become a daily sight to see scraggly, half naked children, weakened by starvation, roaming the streets in search of scraps. The Samaj has decided to do something definitive to help these poor souls. We request you to kindly donate generously for this cause and lend your valuable support to the upkeep of humanity.

Date: 17 May 1877
Yours sincerely,
Jyotirao Phule,
Secretary,
Satyashodhak Samaj"

59

The Samaj members responded very generously to Jyotirao's appeal. The next four days saw cartloads of food and clothing come in. They also received liberal financial help. The 'Victoria Balashram' was started on an open land in Dhankawadi. 2000 bhaakris would be distributed every morning and evening. People would come in with children, all the way from Hadapsar and Bhamburde. The shelter had become a big respite for parents who had become frantic with worry about where would they get the next meal for their children from.

It was a rule of the Balashram that the children had to eat over there itself. They could not take the bhaakris outside. The rule was put across to ensure that the bhaakris would be eaten by the children only; not by anybody else.

Savitribai took on the responsibility of looking after the ashram. Bajubai Nimbankar, and Jyotirao's niece Thakubai Waghole, would come to make the bhaakris. Gyaanoba Sasane, Sahadu Waghole were also ever ready for any support required.

The draught had brought even the toughest of people down to their knees. The Phule household was also not an exception. Rajarambhau left for Mumbai with his wife and children. They were going to return only after the draught ceased.

News poring in from adjacent villages were heart-rendering to say the least. People were routinely dying out of hunger and thirst. The government had initiated some relief measures, but they were not proving enough. Inflation had skyrocketed. Cattle were dropping down dead without grass to eat. The government had opened up jungles for them, but it was almost of no use, because most of the foliage there had also dried up. The cattle would walk for miles on end in search of food and water, and would simply drop dead owing to exhaustion. People had become so desperately hungry, that they would scavenge for the flesh off those carcasses.

In this bleak scenario, 'Deenbandhu' was still pulling on valiantly, in spite of lack of subscribers and non co-operation by the Satyashodhaks. Nevertheless, Krishnarao did not lose hope. He kept pulling on by writing back-to-back articles about how the government needed to do more to tackle the draught . He also published many articles written by Jyotirao regarding the probable solutions to the situation. Apart from handling the work of 'Deenbandhu', Krishnarao was also writing a book called 'Baliba Patil and the draught of 1877'. The book was aimed to explain how every aggressor from Aryabhatt to the British, made themselves co-sharers of the farmers' earnings and completely subjugated them bit by bit. Krishnarao wanted the society to see that once again, the farmer was being made to live in utterly horrific conditions, even as the others scavenged on his toil.

One day, there came a huge storm. The sky lit up with lightning and a torrential rain ensued.

But then, once again, nothing! After that solo appearance, the rain did a disappearing act.

That intermittent rain wreaked a terrible epidemic of plague. The people, already at their wits' end with the draught, were now falling prey to the deadly disease. They started running away to the forests in a bid to escape the epidemic. However, there seemed no respite from the plague. People started dropping down dead like flies. Jyotirao's children - Lakshmi, Babu, Shivaji – also perished.

It was a mayhem ordained straight from hell!

60

The deaths of Babu, Shivaji and Lakshmi caused tremendous grief to the Phule couple. All of a sudden, they were bereaved of the children who had come to them as babies and grown on to become family.

Finally, at long last, the rain showered its grace on the city. People started returning from Mumbai; those who had left their villages and come to Pune also started returning to their villages. But, where were their houses? Everything had been wiped off, either by the draught or by errant thieves scrounging for any little thing they could sell. Jyotirao knew that he could not close down the Balashram yet. There were many who still required their help.

Jyotirao was trying to get his heart engaged in work, to push back the tormenting memories of his dead children. Shivaji, who would look ditto like Shantaram.... the playful Lakshmi and Babu.... their memories refused to cease. Nevertheless, he kept himself engaged in looking after Yeshwant, who had miraculously survived, and a few more new children who had enrolled in the orphanage.

That year brought in quite some negatives for the Phules. The hitherto unified Satyashodhak Samaj started rotting from within, owing to internal disputes. That year's elocution competition brought out the divide prominently. The Samaj Chairman Dr. Vishram Ramji Ghole presented vocal opposition to Jyotirao's views that the Brahmins were responsible for the suffering of the Shoodras. He had not liked the topic of that year's competition at all. During his thanksgiving speech on the eve of the competition, Dr. Ghole said that he found it whimsical when people claimed that 'not just Brahmins but even low caste people were equal contributors to the rise of the Hindu dharma'. He also stated that he found the comparison between slavery in America and untouchability in India, to be unfounded and incorrect.

Jyotirao was stunned by Dr. Ghole's volte face. He was saddened to see how Dr. Ghole took a convenient stand, in spite of seeing the suffering unleashed on the poor Shoodras during the draught. Dr. Ghole's speech put a curtain on the fact that this elocution competition had been organised to encourage the children of Shoodra, Ati Shoodra communities. Jyotirao simply did not fathom why Dr. Ghole had suddenly changed his views so drastically.

A few Brahmin journalists had come to cover the competition. They were bubbling with joy on seeing that the Samaj was facing opposition from its own Chairman. They had a field day with this unexpected turn of events. 'Dynaanprakash', which was a sworn enemy of the Samaj, published Dr. Ghole's speech word-to-word, and started lecturing the 'foolish', 'narrow-minded', and 'prejudiced' members of the Samaj to take the learned Dr. Ghole's advice seriously.

A few days later, the same journal carried a published version of Dr. Ghole's resignation from the Samaj. In reality, there was no need for Dr. Ghole to go public with his resignation. He could have resigned in private. But, things had reached to such a stage wherein Dr. Ghole felt like rubbing salt on the Samaj's wound by getting his resignation public. Jyotirao had realized that Dr. Ghole was shunning the Samaj, but he had never imagined that the Dr. would resort to such lowly means.

It was a very insulting occurrence, which further served to fan gossip in the city.

People started murmuring that Dr. Ghole was treating Prof. Krishnashastri Chiplunkar and it was Chiplunkar who had sown the seeds of rebellion in Ghole's mind. Some others said that a group of aggressive Brahmins had threatened Ghole with 'due treatment', if he did not quit the Samaj. Overall, the tone of the allegations was that the Brahmin group was responsible for weaning off Ghole from the Samaj.

Jyotirao was waiting for Rajarambhau to return. It was time

to start sowing seeds for this time's harvest. Every year, Rajarambhau would sow the seeds. Jyotirao would look into the farm, as and when time permitted. However, Rajarambhau did not return, and Jyotirao had to take up all the farm-related work in his own hand.

Jyotirao had written a letter asking Rajarambhau to return. He did not; instead, a letter written by Ganpati reached Jyotirao. It said that Rajarambhau had fallen ill.

On receiving the letter, Jyotirao had immediately rushed to Mumbai; but, it was too late. Rajarambhau had expired on the previous day itself!

Seeing her brother-in-law, Rajarambhau's wife had howled in distress; but, there was nothing anyone could do. Jyotirao had tried his best to prevent Rajarambhau from going to Mumbai, but the latter had not heeded any advice. He took his family and settled in a small hutment at Kamathipura. Father and son were doing odd jobs to keep the kitchen fires burning. They had decided to return to Pune after the draught ended.

But the climate of Mumbai did not agree with Rajarambhau. He soon fell ill. Ganpati took on the responsibility of running the house till Rajarambhau got well. But, instead of getting well, Rajarambhau's health kept deteriorating. The monsoons served to make him even more ill, and finally, death claimed him.

Jyotirao took Rajarambhau's bereaving family members and returned to Pune.

The labourers' colony on the fringes of Kamathipura was teeming with people who had left their draught-prone village and come to Mumbai in search of a half-decent life. However, the influx served to bring several epidemics along.

These people would stay in cubbyholes and keep roaming around looking for the day's work. They would take up any manual labor that came their way – be it in a mill, or in the market. However, money was tremendously scarce to come by. Starvation and the polluted air started making people fall violently ill. Many of them would soon fall prey to death. They were all caught between the devil and the deep sea. The city had epidemics, and their villages back home were reeling under famines. Add to that the merciless treatment by money-lenders. The poor farmers would find it better to die in the city with at least half their stomachs filled.

After Jyotirao returned to Pune, Chimna Aai came to meet her bereaved daughter-in-law. After Dada's demise, Chimna Aai had been staying alone in the house that Dada had willed to her. Jyotirao again requested his mother to come stay with them; but, she refused.

Cuddling her grandchildren for one last time, Chimna Aai left for her home.

61

"Tatyasaheb, how dare these people overstep their boundaries like this?! Does this critique make any sense? Does it serve any logic? What way is this to have a debate? How dare they drag our sisters into this matter?" Krishnarao was spewing venom, holding the latest copy of 'Nibandhamala' in his hand.

He started reading out flagrantly written passages from the journal, each more derogatory than the other for Jyotirao. After some time, Jyotirao took the copy from Krishnarao's hand and started reading it aloud himself.

Using the excuse of reviewing the Satyashodhak Samaj's report, Vishnushastri Chiplunkar had heavily criticized 'Gulamgiri' and 'Brahmananche Kasab' as well. Chiplunkar had lamented the fact that Brahmins were seen in such a contemptuous light due to Jyotirao's 'twisted' thoughts, and had even expressed unhappiness at being 'compelled to' write about the Satyashodhak Samaj in their journal, owing to the orders of the powers that be.

Pointing out that, in the four years of the Samaj's existence, it had not received societal sanction beyond its members,

Chiplunkar predicted that the Satyashodhak Samaj was soon going to go down the Arya Samaj way. He prophesised that, like the Arya Samaj founder, Jyotirao too would soon tire of finding the 'ultimate truth' (whatever that meant) and decamp to Jerusalem in search of his 'real God'.

Chiplunkar had also given a small yet interesting biography of Jyotirao's, mentioning him to be an 'all-rounder and multifaceted personality' who was a poet, writer, historian, linguist, orator and a social worker par excellence, 'who could not see any form of suffering and would take immediate steps to rectify it'.

Cracking down especially heavily on Jyotirao's linguistic skills, Chiplunkar wrote that "just as Jyotirao's ancestors – the demons named Shankasur and Hiranyaksha – had created a ruckus on earth with their antics, so also, Jyotirao is following in their steps to create a ruckus in the world of letters, with his 'flowery prose'. He has broken down all the rules of grammar laid down by the erstwhile scholars, to devise his own meanings of words like Brahmin, Vipra, Sanskrit, Martand and so on. Not being satisfied at just devising these meanings, this scholar has been taking all necessary steps to see that his alterations get percolated amid all the rungs of society. One does not expect much from this 'wise man' who has announced all literature written by Brhamins thus far as trash; but at least, he should have had better self-respect than taking his 'novels' for approval from those whose feet he licks and ducking behind whose backs, he scowls on the others."

Chiplunkar was understandably incensed about Jyotirao expressing gratitude towards the British, for opening up the doors of education for the Shoodras and Ati Shoodras. He further went onto 'laud' Jyotirao for writing a completely new history in his 'Gulamgiri', sans any reference points or proofs. Making sarcasm-laced commentary on Jyotirao's 'erudition', Chiplunkar said that hitherto, whatever they had gleaned about Jyotirao's intelligence from his consistently anti-Brahmin writings in journals like 'Dynaanoday' and 'Nanavidh Charchasangraha', was far less than what they experienced after reading 'Gulamgiri' and 'Kasab'.

"Ohoho! Such luminous thoughts... such fantastic logic... such a thirst to unearth the truth... such pride in being the one to unearth the truth... such loyalty towards the British... The ink of my pen will dry up, but not the paeans that I can sing in the praise of this erudite man in our midst. We fold our hands before the Guru of this scholar, who has blessed our great country with this diamond. Surely, this Guru must not be a Brahmin. Anyways, I would like to clarify one thing here: even though we Brahmins have to pay double the price to acquire a copy of 'Kasab' and 'Gulamgiri', I would recommend every Brahmin to please keep these two 'greatest literary works of this century' in their personal libraries, to pass on to their future generations as well."

Chiplunkar had not wasted a single line of his review while berating Jyotirao. Since he did not have any firm thoughts by which to challenge Jyotirao's claims with, he had resorted to saying that Shoodras were exaggerating and even downright lying about being harassed by generations of Brahmins.

In the conclusion, Chiplunkar wrote,

"We, as a society, really need to think about how much courage there really is when people like Jyotirao keep barking on Brahmins; how much loyalty and patriotism is displayed when people are willing to lick the ruler's feet for a few pieces of bread; and how wise is it to establish random groups to keep berating each other. Anyways, Jyotirao's Samaj is still too small. It hardly stretches from Hadapsar to Bhamburde. We Brahmins have no interest in expending our energies on such a tiny speck of nothingness. When (and if) it grows to the scale of the Arya Samaj, and when Jyotirao's marble statue gets erected in front of the Samaj's headquarters, that's when we may deem it necessary to take cognizance of the existence of that anti-Brahmin outfit."

It was a matter of sadness that the erudite writer Chiplunkar, who could write reams about patriotism and pride in one's religion, did not think about Shoodras as human beings who also deserved to be treated humanely. No wonder, he prickled due to the gratitude expressed by Jyotirao towards the British.

Chiplunkar had even expressed criticism towards this aspect by labeling Jyotirao as a 'poet of Shoodras', 'founder of the Shoodra religion', and so on.

Each word written by Chiplunkar, was pouring over with his ego and the rage he felt towards people other than Brahmins. Of course, there was also a pointed reason for his anger. In 'Gulamgiri', Jyotirao had written some text expressly criticizing Vishnushastri. Obviously, he was not going to keep quiet without giving any reaction.

Instead of feeling sad about the acerbic article, Jyotirao was happy that at least on that pretext, Krishnarao had come to him, forgetting all their differences. He said to Krishnarao,

"Let us not get agitated over this silly article. 'Nibandhamala' has become Vishnushastri's personal fiefdom; his watering hole to settle all his scores. We should not pay much attention to all this."

"No, Tatyasaheb! We will only encourage more such writing, if we decide to keep quiet. This criticism must be answered in equally strong words" argued an incensed Krishnarao.

"Not needed. Just because he has used big words to criticize us, does not mean our views are incorrect or untrue. We know the truth; our heart knows the truth; and that is enough. If the Satyashodhak Samaj had not been so threatening for Shastribuva, he would not have bothered spending so much time writing about it. Everyone is entitled to his/her opinion. Why should we waste time refuting these arguments? Time will tell, who is true, and who is not. We should concentrate on our work. If we are true to our thoughts and our work, no criticism should affect our resolve. If we engage in carrying this argument further, we shall only lose our time and focus, and nothing will be gained by the end of it all. Today our state is in the grips of such a terrible famine. Is this the time to be arguing about history and language skills? But, who will tell this to these high and mighty people? Where does their patriotism go at such times? Do they not see their Shoodra brethren dying out of hunger? Or, just because they are Shoodras, do they not qualify as humans?...."

Jyotirao continued,

"What is their concept of nation, pray tell me? A nation is a concept where everyone is equal and unified. But, a country like ours where so many people are bound by religious binds; where human beings are segregated like cattle owing to their caste; how can it ever qualify as a nation?! But, such things will never enter the brain of these prejudiced people. It is a waste of time trying to make them see sense. They can never understand the real pain of the Shoodras, sitting as they are on their high pedestals. Today, there is no Shoodra who is learned enough to pay these people back in their own coin; but, one day, such a Shoodra will definitely stand up."

Krishnarao said,

"Shastribuva has conveniently forgotten that, even though the doors of education may be open to all in theory, in reality, how many people really have the means to get that education? Such things take time to come by for the masses..."

Jyotirao replied,

"That is a true sign of being ignorant about social realities. Yet, he has no qualms commenting on our condition. And what about the hypocrisy? While commenting freely on the British, Shastribuva has conveniently forgotten about the torment wreaked by the Brahmins on the lower caste people, hasn't he? He finds no compunction in that slavery heaped upon us by his caste-brethren. Rather, he justifies the slavery by saying that such subjugation of the weak by the strong, is a universal phenomenon, and, the Satyashodhak Samaj is creating hullabaloo about a very common thing, just to gain mileage. What kind of a person is this, who expects tormented people to accept the misery as his fate and do nothing about it?! When we try to change these deplorable conditions by spreading education among the masses, that is also unacceptable to people like Shastribuva. Obviously, they do not want Shoodras and Ati Shoodras to become literate. How will they remain in slavery otherwise? Shastribuva and his ilk are incensed because we have taken up the cause of breaking their monopoly over education and making the entire society educated, so that they can see the reality with their own eyes. Don't give much thought to such write-ups. These writings do not care a penny about the suffering of our countrymen. They are under the fallacy that the Shoodra community will always remain illiterate. Instead of fighting to make them change their views, let us think about how we can work for the betterment of the subjugated class."

However, Krishnarao remained adamant that Jyotirao should give a befitting reply to Shastribuva. He was specially incensed by Shastribuva's claim that he did not know Jyotirao personally.

"What a liar this man is!" yelled Krishnarao. "Even his father knows you personally."

"It's okay, Krishnarao. Let it be" Jyotirao tried explaining calmly.

But, Krishnarao did not keep quiet. Seeing the Tatyasaheb was not going to react, he took the onus upon himself and wrote a big article in 'Deenbandhu', in response to Vishnushastri's write-up.

When Jyotirao picked up the next copy of 'Deenbandhu', this is what he saw written by Krishnarao:

"Malakar (i.e. Vishnushastri Chiplunkar) is a great scholar who has written many books so far. But his style seems to be quite odd. He takes pride in using the power of his pen as a sword to wound the sentiments and repute of others. If the writings of Jyotirao Phule had been in keeping with Shashtribuva's views, he would have been lavish with praise about Phule. But, since that is not the case, Chiplunkar has not wasted a single line in berating Phule. Thanks be to God that we now have a British regime. It has opened the doors of education for all those classes, that the Brahmins had selfishly kept away from getting learned and literate. Clearly, Malakar does not like the idea of an entire society progressing. He is as narrow-minded and selfish as his caste brethren. I do not know what to speak of the personality of a man who takes joy in wielding his power over the already subjugated, poor, and illiterate people, simply on the behest of his caste."

Krishnarao had written a very befitting and apt response; but, Jyotirao knew that it would not affect Vishnushastri in the least. Rather, by writing this article, Krishnarao had only invited further trouble in the form of additional quarrels.

62

Narayanrao Lokhande had come from Mumbai to meet Jyotirao. He had heard a lot about Jyotirao from Mama Parmanand and Ramji Santuji Aawate, as well as, members of the Samaj in Mumbai. Having worked in the Railways and the postal department for some time, Lokhande was now working as a storekeeper in the Mandavi mill.

Mills were flourishing in Mumbai, but the mill-workers were living in pitiful conditions. Unable to bear their plight any longer, Lokhande decided to meet Jyotirao to see if anything could be done to help the workers. During their meeting, a lot of discussion ensued about creating a workers' union to resolve their problems. Jyotirao had also invited Krishnarao to join the discussion. Being of the same age, Lokhande and Krishnarao struck up a good friendship. Currently, Krishnarao was using his 'Deenbandhu' as a platform to breathe fire on the Prarthana Samaj, who he had nicknamed 'Matlabsindhu Samaj' (an organisation that operates only on selfish motives). He had named it so, because I his opinion, the Prarthana Samaj thought nothing about the poor and downtrodden, especially the Shoodras. In that sense, Krishnarao and Jyotirao were on the same page; they both felt the need to have another organization that would purely look after the problems of the neglected classes. Another sector that would routinely face the barbs of 'Deenbandhu', were the Marathi princes, who were catering to the Brahmins. Krishnarao was firm in his view that, only technical education and abolition of caste differences would lad our country to progress.

It had been three days since Lokhande had come to Pune. On the day of his proposed departure, many people had come to meet him. Lokhande was supposed to leave after lunch.

Just then, Sitaram came announcing the arrival of a few young men. Jyotirao glanced outside and saw that three youngsters, presumably farmers, had come to meet them. Jyotirao welcomed them within. The more talkative of those three, said,

"Namaskar, Tatyasaheb. We are residents of Vetaal Peth. We heard your speech on Saturday, and thus came to invite you at our place."

"Thank you, but it won't be possible today. Our guest is due to leave for Mumbai today" said Jyotirao.

"Please, Tatyasaheb... Please don't refuse. In fact, do bring your esteemed guest too. When, otherwise, would we get the good fortune of hosting someone from Mumbai?"

The youngsters persisted so much, that finally, Jyotirao could not refuse. Even Shaahir said,

"Well, let's go, Tatyasaab."

Thus, Jyotirao, along with Narayanrao Lokhande, Shaahir Dhondiram, and Bhimajirao Birmal set off for Vetaal Peth. One amongst the three youngsters ran ahead to let his neighborhood know that Tatyasaheb was arriving.

Soon, the group was lead to a bungalow in Vetaal Peth.

The structure seemed incongruent for a farmer's family. Nevertheless, Jyotirao and his guests received a hearty welcome. Many people had congregated to hear Jyotirao speak. One of them asked,

"Tatyasaheb, I have been hearing your lectures about Satyadharma for a long time. I have also been ruminating about what you express. Who, according to you, qualifies as a Satyadharmi?"

"What is your name, gentleman?" asked Jyotirao.

"Balwant Hari Sakvalkar. I stay close by. I was very keen to meet you."

Jyotirao smiled and replied,

"Thank you. To answer your question, a person who does not lie; does not steal; does not do any morally wrong act; and also does not help anybody doing the same, can be called a Satyadharmi. A person who does not maintain segregations between human beings; who does not fleece innocent people in the name of religion or caste; and, who also does not support anyone doing so, can be called a Satyadharmi. A person who, instead of finding God in stone idols, finds Him in living beings; who believes that God is One; and who believes in according all living beings their due freedom to live, can be called a Satyadharmi."

Jyotirao spoke some more on the topic. Sakvalkar was listening intently. He was impressed by Jyotirao's thoughts, and said,

"Tatyasaheb, why don't you publish a book elucidating on the views that Satyadharma stands by?"

Shaahir had been requesting the same thing to Jyotirao for many months already. He was happy to find an ally in Sakvalkar.

Jyotirao smiled and said,

"I appreciate your thought, but I do not see any benefit in publishing a book just yet. The people for whom we would be publishing this book, are illiterate; and as for those who are literate...I doubt they would want to even touch such a book.

Nevertheless, whenever I get time, I will be penning down the tenets of Satyadharma. But, there's still time for that. Till then, speeches are the best way to get our views across to the masses."

The talks continued for a long time after that. Then, it was time for Jyotirao to leave.

"Well then, friends, thank you for having us over. We shall take your leave now" said Jyotirao, folding his hands to his hosts.

Just then, the talkative youngster from before, rushed inside and brought a garland for Jyotirao. He came forward, garlanded Jyotirao, and swiftly stepped behind. No one would have been aware of anything had it not been for Bhimaji Birmal who screamed,

"Tatyasaheb, there are scorpions in the garland!!!"

Hearing this, Jyotirao instantly tore the garland and flung it away. The audience was horrified to see four-five half-dead scorpions squirming from where they were strung to the garland!!

"See...see those scorpions!!" thundered Bhimaji.

Shaahir Dhondiram was infuriated! He had been suspicious of the youngsters' movements from a long time, but had not been able to place a finger on what was wrong.

"Is this why you wanted our Tatyasaab to come to your home? To insult and harm him like this?!" Shaahir bellowed.

Seeing his companions enraged, Jyotirao intervened and said,

"Brothers, calm down. See, these people gave us the opportunity to show that, with the right advice and counsel, even the most harmful animals can become sane. It does not suit us to be angry on them. Instead, we should be thankful to them for giving us this opportunity. And, we must not forget that, whatever their intentions were, it is because of their invitation that so many of these good people could hear something nice about our Satyadharma."

The three youngsters felt ashamed of their actions. They

stood with their heads bowed low. Unable to bear the weight of their heinous act, one of them dived at Jyotirao's feet to ask for his forgiveness.

But, Jyotirao stepped back and said,

"I'm too small a human being to forgive you. If you are really feeling repentant of your actions, ask forgiveness from the Almighty."

The youngsters became even more embarrassed on hearing this. Jyotirao realized that they had carried out this act at the behest of someone. He told them,

"I know that you have done this act, not on your own volition, but at the behest of someone else. But tell me, how long are you going to be puppets in the hands of others? Learn to think and act according to your intellect. Who have we started this Samaj for? For our Shoodra, Ati Shoodra brethren itself, right? We all need to join hands to take this work forward, instead of wasting time in such worthless pursuits."

"Sorry, Tatyasaheb, sorry...please forgive us. We were wrong!" the three youngsters pleaded.

Jyotirao pacified them and took everyone's leave.

The visit might have been marred by this unpleasant incident, but it certainly did not go waste. The Samaj got three young and able volunteers, apart from keen members like Sakvalkar.

63

The Khadakwasla lake was overflowing with water. After the kharif season, the canals would be flowing with water. The raabi crop was to grow on this water. Jyotirao's assurance was indeed going to come true.

But God knows who started a vile rumor that, the farmers who drew water from the canal, would find their lands confiscated! Rumors flew thick that it was the government's ploy to grab their lands, and Jyotirao was an agent of that government itself.

As these rumors started gaining strength, panic spread among the people. They conveniently forgot the speeches that Jyotirao had given over summer, about the benefits of the canals.

It took immense energy and time for Jyotirao to convince the people that these rumors were baseless, and that, it was not a sin to divert the holy water of river Ganges to their farms!

Dynaanoba Patil of Maanjri announced that he was selling his land holding of 60 acres. Jyotirao decided to purchase the land with his savings from the contracting business, and give a live example to the farmers about the benefits of canalling.

64

'Deenbandhu' had fallen behind the government like a battle-axe, to get them to pass laws that would benefit the farmers. Wielding to their persistence, the government had finally appointed a committee to look into the issues. In spite of stiff opposition, Krishnarao was somehow pulling on the paper with sheer grit and determination.

During this time, Vishnushastri Chiplunkar launched a scathing attack on 'Deenbandhu'. Shastribuva was worried that a 'Christianity oriented organisation' like Satyashodhak Samaj, and a paper like 'Deenbandhu', spelt nothing but trouble for the society's moral fabric. Shastribuva did not give a grain of importance or credence to Jyotirao. He would determinedly refute any and every theory that Jyotirao would propound in his speeches and writings. Referring to Jyotirao in deliberately derogatory terms like 'Shoodra dharma sansthapak' and 'Shoodra deshitecchuk', Shastribuva would advise Jyotirao to concentrate his efforts only on bringing up his downtrodden caste brethren, instead of trying to snub the elite Brahmins. In the latest issue, Shastribuva had also predicted an imminent doom for the Satyashodhak Samaj.

Some gems from Shastribuva's latest write-up, were as

follows:

"We do not claim that all Brahmins are God-gifted and faultless; just as, we do not claim that the laments that the Shoodras keep harping on every day, are entirely false. We are honest enough to admit that people of our caste also bear some minor faults within themselves. We have never tried to hide or discredit this fact. Just as, we also do not say that the troubles that our Shoodra brethren have borne till date due to casteism and other segregations, are false. Rather, we Brahmins are sensitive enough to want to help them get rid of their pain."

However, anyone with a bit of logical sense could see that, the intent of the write-up was diametrically opposite to its claims. Shastribuva felt no compunction in berating his own countrymen and then taking doubt about their loyalty to the country. He also felt no compunction in blatantly blowing the trumpet of his own coterie. He wrote,

"Our Shoodra brethren should always remember that we Chitpavans have been blessed with immense intellect and other wonderful qualities – the greatness of which has been displayed time & again, for generations on end. Irrespective of whether we have risen from the ashes, or, hailed from Iran; our greatness remains indisputable. No amount of scathing writing by some little writer, is going to erase generations of our greatness. We may be cunning…we may be cruel…but, no one can challenge the fact that we hold the keys to all intellectual greatness. And hence, unless we help them, no person from any other caste can ever rise high in life."

Shastribuva's words dripped with the venom of his punctured ego. He may be promising the Shoodras that Brahmins are there to help them, but it was unlikely that any Shoodra would trust these claims; especially not the Satyashodhaks.

Krishnarao came to meet Jyotirao with the latest issue of 'Nibandhamala' in hand, and remarked,

"Tatyasaheb, you were right. There is no point is stretching the argument with Shastribuva. The chaos is simply getting elevated instead of getting unraveled."

"That's what I have been trying to tell you, Krishnarao. These scholars will use the last drop of their intellect to sing praises of the caste system; because, that is beneficial to them. Casteism is deeply entrenched in their blood. They will do everything to see that these segregations do not go away; because, if that happens, it will uproot them from their self-proclaimed superiority. They are least interested in the plight of the lower castes. Instead, they will do everything possible to maintain their status quo in the society. Why waste our time and energy in trying to change their stance?" said Jyotirao.

"That means, you have read this issue..." remarked Krishnarao.

"Yes, I have read it and have also decided not to retaliate. I look at these things in a different way, Krishnarao. I welcome criticism – howsoever scathing it may be. For, it only helps me introspect and improve. For instance, look what is written here..."

"If Jyotirao truly wishes to uplift his community, he needs to do something more proactive than simply writing books like 'Gulamgiri'."

"Krishnarao, people like Vishnupant think that, just as they cannot see beyond their Brahmin caste, so also, I cannot see beyond the Mali community. What else can we expect from these people, who do not shed a single tear for the sufferings of their own widowed sisters? It would be futile to expect them to soften their hearts towards the condition of the Shoodras. They claim to be eager to help the Shoodras, but all that is humbug. In reality, they want the Shoodras to remain where they are. Such writing only serves to tell me that we need to expand the scope and speed of our work even more. Let these people keep forming vocal bubbles; we shall get on with our work and let it talk for itself."

Krishnarao conceded, and the topic ended there.

65

After the kharif season, water was let out into the canals. Jyotirao had decided to cultivate vegetables and sugarcane, apart from a few fruit. He had admired the fruit orchard near the bungalow of the Governor at Aundh and wanted to make something similar in his land too. The only problem was that of water supply – Jyotirao tried to resolve this problem by setting up a separate water connection for his land. The adjacent farms were also going to benefit due to this connection.

Jyotirao was worried about how was he going to look after the work of the farm by staying in Pune; but, Sahadu Waghole took the lead in this respect, and eased Tatyasaheb's worries.

The area of Maanjri and Hadapsar started getting soaked in water. The happy farmers began cultivating vegetables, fruit, and sugarcane. After finishing the work on his farm, Jyotirao went to Mumbai, to meet Mama Parmanand.

Mama Parmanand was an ideal of what a truly detached life is all about. Instead of being an eminent scholar and thinker, he would be rarely seen on any dais. He shunned publicity of any kind; preferring to do his work in isolation and away from public eye. He had played an important role during the movement to start widow remarriages.

During this meeting, Jyotirao and Mama spoke a lot about the former's work for the farmer community. Patil Ramappa had also accompanied Jyotirao during this trip. Jyotirao pledged to write articles highlighting the plight of farmers.

Swami Ramaiyya Ayyavaru, a very active member of the Samaj in Mumbai, had been doing yeoman service in the field of education in his locality of Kamathipura. Presently, he was working as a Chairman of the committee working to educate people about the ill-effects of alcoholism. Plus, he was also running a library. Himself a voracious reader and analyzer of various texts and scriptures, Swamiji held progressive and open-ended views about religion and related issues. Even though the atmosphere in his house was steeped in spirituality, Swamiji himself was a borderline atheist, so to say. In recent times, his views had shaped up to believe (and propagate) that, one should behave in keeping with truth, not because God is watching; but because, that is the correct way of life. That was what gave peace of mind and a fulfilling life to a person.

Swamiji and Jyotirao would have a lot of discussions, debates, and even disagreements. But, those disagreements never marred the wonderful friendship they shared.

After Jyotirao returned to Pune following his brief visit to Mumbai, a couple of pleasant and unpleasant events took place. Dr. Ghole received the honorable title of 'Raobahadur'. The senior Chiplunkar Shastribuva left for his heavenly abode. In spite of his differences with Vishnushastri, Jyotirao went for the funeral; because, he could never disregard all the help that the senior gentleman had given him.

Jyotirao was also equally engaged in his work as a member of the Municipal Corporation. His focus was on improving the conditions of the Shoodras through the empowerment that this post accorded him. With Hari Raoji's help, Jyotirao was looking into various issues plaguing the Shoodras; such as, sanitation, education, employment and so on. Of course, it was not at all an easy road for Jyotirao. Every step was a battle with the Brahmins clerks and officials. Anything proposed for the betterment of the Shoodras, was being stonewalled. However, this was just the beginning. The future would see a lot of Jyotirao's friendships, as well as, principles put to test.

Even as he was taking on newer tasks, Jyotirao's old tasks also continued demanding his attention. That year's elocution competition made quite a ripple with its controversial topic which asked the participants to examine as to, why was it that the Shoodra communities, that bore valiant men like Shivaji Maharaj, Shinde and Holkar, had now taken to pandering to the Brahmin men, and even women. Why couldn't they maintain their self respect like the Brahmins, who steadfastly refused to do anything below their level?

Jyotirao's intention was to make his community brethren see how they had become subtly enslaved; but, the intention got distorted because of a few ignorant and short-sighted Shoodras, who, fed on the Brahmins' jibes, felt that Jyotirao was mocking their work. It was ironical that, Jyotirao's efforts to free his brethren from generations of slavery, were being met with stiff opposition from those same people, just because they had become used to the phenomenon.

66

Prickly winter had set in. On one particularly cold morning, Jyotirao mounted his horse and set off for his farm. On the way, he saw many pieces of land still dry and unfertilized; because, many people still refused to use the canal water for farming.

However, some farms were laden with juicy sugarcanes standing majestically on the backdrop of the sky. Water was reaching them through the canals. Farm labourers had already started their work for the day. Jyotirao could not help but hope that such a sight would soon become common, all around.

Soon, Jyotirao reached his own farm. Sahadu was irrigating the sugarcane crop, while some more laborers were tending to the banana plantation.

Jyotirao tied his horse to a nearby tree and started walking around, inspecting the farm. He was happy to see a good crop of green, leafy vegetables; cauliflowers; deep purple brinjals; and , parrot-green chilies. Going ahead, he saw the mango saplings gaining good growth. He made a mental note to bring in more banana saplings, apart from papaya, sweet lemon and oranges.

Sahadu Waghole had indeed eased Jyotirao's worries about tending to the farm. In spite of being a son-in-law, Sahadu had never thrown any airs, and was more than happy to help Tatya.

Jyotirao cherished Sahadu for being the hard-working and co-operative individual that he was. Such people were rare to come by. Sahadu had also taken the lead in undertaking the responsibility of the 'Victoria Balashram'. His wife Thakubai was also a very good lady. She would help Savitribai roast bhaakris at the Balashram. After Rajarambhau's demise, Jyotirao had become the father-figure in Thakubai's life. He had seen Thakubai from her birth, and hence was naturally affectionate towards her. However, Jyotirao could never forget the pain of having to attend Thakubai's wedding like a distant relative, owing to petty family quarrels.

After some time, Sahadu came to the small hutment where Jyotirao was resting, and asked him,

"Tatya, the vegetables will be ready for sale in the next week. Have you made any arrangement for selling them?"

"We will sell it at Mumbai. Pune markets do not yield much profit" said Jyotirao.

Sahadu was astonished to hear this. He found the idea unfathomable. Seeing his surprised, Jyotirao explained,

"See, Sahadubuva... How is it justified that we toil so much in our farms, and the agents and middlemen decide the price of our crop?! These practices are detrimental to the farmers' progress. As it is, most farmers are carrying heavy debts on their heads. Getting lower rates for their crop will only subjugate them further. This cycle needs to stop somewhere. It is our crop; we should decide where do we want to sell it, and for what price. Who are the main customers of our crop in Pune markets? The miserly Brahmins, who will prefer to eat dried up vegetables for a smaller price, instead of eating fresh ones at their proper rate. How, then, will a farmer ever get due returns on his investment? The middlemen take undue advantage of the innocent, illiterate farmer's ignorance and fleece him out of his last penny. He does not get back even that money which he spends on transporting the vegetables; leave alone that which he invests in harvesting the crop."

Sahadu understood what Tatya was trying to say, but he still had his doubts about how were they going to manage the transportation to Mumbai, and keeping the accounts of such big transactions? He asked his query to Jyotirao, who said,

"Don't worry. We shall search for the right person to do this work."

"Yes, Tatya; but where shall we get him from?" asked Sahadu.

Jyotirao also started racking his brains. Gyaanoba would have been the correct person for this task, but he had taken up a government job. Ramchandra Hari had taken up the contract of Bhaatgar lake. The Poona Commercial and Contracting Company had all but closed down, after Krishnarao withdrew his partnership.

In spite of all these problems, Jyotirao could only think of one name: Gyaanoba Sasane. He told as much to Sahadu, who exclaimed,

"Yes, Tatya. He would be perfect! But...Isn't he in a job? How will he be able to help us then?"

"That's what even I am thinking" mused Jyotirao. "If we were to request him to leave his job, we should be able to pay him at least as much as he is getting in the job, if not more."

Knowing the misfortunes of Commercial Company, Sahadu kept silent. The company had seen more partners leave than it had got contracts. However, after some time, unable to contain himself, Sahadu ventured,

"But, Tatya... Now, this will be our own venture. Not a partnership with someone, isn't it?"

Jyotirao had been thinking on the same lines; he was happy to get Sahadu's explicit support. Buoyed by it, Jyotirao said,

"I shall write a letter to Gyaanoba, today itself."

Just then, Jyotirao saw Ganpatrao tilling his farm. Ganpatrao was a tailor by profession, but encouraged by Jyotirao's talks, he had also taken to farming. Today, he had again got his son, Govinda, along. Seeing that, Jyotirao called out to Ganpatrao and asked,

"Oh, has Govinda's school declared a holiday today also?"

Ganpatrao was not too keen about his son's education. He had enrolled Govinda into a school, but would take every opportunity to not send him there. Govinda was one of Ganpatrao's youngest sons. Thus, he looked at Govinda as his apprentice and support for old age. He was more keen on Govinda taking over the farm, than 'wasting time' in learning books. Ganpatrao was even planning to get Govinda married and settled into domesticity. Jyotirao would use every opportunity to make Ganpatrao see sense on both the aspects.

Hearing Jyotirao's question, Govinda lowered his head in shame. His father simply refused to budge. Jyotirao again prodded,

"Ganpatrao, it seems, today also you have made Govinda miss his school. If you stop his school, I shall be forced to cut off the water supply to your farm!"

Ganpatrao's farm was being tilled on the water supply fro Jyotirao's canals. Realizing the gravity of the situation, Ganpatrao made a sorry face and commented,

"Tatyasaheb, I have no hopes of Govinda getting educated. Education is for the rich; not for poor people like us."

"Ganpatrao, the poor are remaining poor because they do not get themselves educated. It is easy to curse one's fate, rather than attend school and become learned. Govinda, do you wish to attend school?" asked Jyotirao.

Surprised yet thrilled by the unexpected question thrown at him, Govinda nodded in the positive, his eyes sparkling. His father could see Govinda's enthusiasm, but he tried to deflect the topic saying,

"Tatyasaheb, thanks to you, he did learn so much. What is the use of further education for a farmer's son like Govinda? And, as it is, where do we send him for higher education? Out of this village?"

"Don't worry about that" said Jyotirao. "I shall take him

along with me to Pune. We can start an English medium school at Hadapsar; that won't be too difficult. Along side, you also teach him farming. So, he will not feel ashamed holding a plough after finishing his education."

"Thank you, Tatyasaheb! You echoed my sentiments indeed. I was afraid of that itself. Of what use will it be if my son gets educated and sits in an office wearing a trouser and shirt? Who will tend to the farm then?"

"I empathize with your sentiments, Ganpatrao. Our country does not accord due dignity to manual labor. Over here, the public sentiment is that, the one who sits in an office and pushes a pen is more important than the one who tills the land or does any kind of manual labor. That is why, our future generations must be taught from a young age that, no work is small or big. Having an agriculture-oriented school is a good way to ensure that. Apart from that, our children need to be given moral education too. Sadly, that does not happen. Christian schools teach their students about their religion. The Brahmin schools lecture their students about the importance of caste segregation. They are not interested in enrolling our children; rather, they are keen to see that our children do not get educated at all. That is why, we need to open more schools and encourage our children to study in them. Those children should be taken on as teachers when they grow up. Our schools will teach the students to wield a pen, but will also teach them to pull a plough. This cannot be achieved by Brahmin schools. We need more public schools for that. The government collects such huge taxes from our farmer brothers; why does it not use a portion of those collections to start schools for the farmers' children? But, they have conveniently shut their eyes to this possibility. Sadly, our farmer brethren are also not very keen on educating their children. As it is, many schools are shutting down owing to lack of students. If you continue to remain disinterested in the bright future of your sons and daughters, it won't be long before all the schools shut down, and your children lead the same ignorant, poverty-filled life that their forefathers lived."

Ganpatrao understood his folly; he promised to send his son to school regularly from tomorrow, and took Tatya's leave.

After some time, Jyotirao called Ganpatrao and Govinda to partake of a light breakfast with him and Sahadu. Govinda came running. He loved the breakfast of fresh produce that Tatya would offer. Soon, they all sat to eat fresh baby carrots, nuts, and roots along with bhaakri and tasty chutney. After breakfast, Jyotirao finished some pending work, and left for Pune.

On the way, as he crossed Hadapsar, Jyotirao came across the dry well in Krishnarao's farm. He had promised himself that he would fill this barren farm with nature's bounty again. He also thought about his idea of starting an English school at Hadapsar. Making a mental note of writing to Gyaanoba soon, Jyotirao went ahead.

After discussing with Savitribai, Jyotirao wrote a letter to Gyaanoba and promised to give him a 4 aana share in his business.

Gyaanoba came to Pune, as soon as he received the letter. The Poona Commercial and Contracting Company again came into business. Sacks of vegetables from Jyotirao's farm, started going to Mumbai's Byculla market. Subsequently, Jyotirao began purchasing the produce of other farmers at reasonable rates to supply it to Byculla market as well. The Poona Commercial company started doing well, but it served to antagonize the agents, who soon ganged up against Jyotirao. They started plotting conspiracies to put Jyotirao out of business.

As a result, Jyotirao was going to be compelled to take some important decisions very soon.

67

Yeshwant took the letter from the postman and ran to Tatya, who was busy writing a letter himself. Tatya took the letter from Yeshwant and started reading it.

The letter had brought some good news. Bapuji Hari, who was running a wing of Satyashodhak Samaj very successfully in Vidarbha, was coming to Pune. In spite of being in a government job, Bapuji had not used it as an excuse to shirk his responsibility towards the Samaj. Instead, he had duly taught a lesson to the Brahmin senior who was troubling him, and had surged ahead with the Samaj's work regardless. His sincerity was an ideal for other Samaj members.

The children were playing outside. Yeshwant had started going to school by now; he had also got a good friend in Lakshman Devrao Thosar. Tatya knew that this chatter would continue till the school time got near.

Jyotirao immediately started writing a letter to Bhaatgar. He would be happy if he got to meet some of his brothers on the occasion.

The next Sunday, Jyotirao and Moropant Walvekar were present at the railway station to welcome Bapuji personally. As Bapuji alighted, a young girl of about 26-27 years, also alighted with him. Dressed in a nauvari (nine-yard) sari with kumkum on her forehead and thick spectacles resting on the bridge of her nose, the short statured girl's fair-toned face was shining with intelligence and confidence. This was Bapuji's daughter, Tarabai.

Tarabai was very fond of education, but after her marriage, she had faced immense difficulties in continuing her studies. Unable to send Tarabai to school due to societal problems, Bapuji had taught her at home. As the sole sister to four brothers, her childhood had been a happy one. In order to let his only daughter stay close to him, Bapuji had got a son-in-law who would agree to stay in their house (instead of needing to send his daughter away, according to usual customs). He had felt that such an arrangement would make his daughter happy. But, the fates willed otherwise. Tarabai's marriage was an unhappy one. Not being able to conceive a child, only worsened the problems more. As time went by, Tarabai started finding solace in burying herself in books.

Her heart would go out to the women who suffered incessant atrocities at the hands of men, in our male-dominated society. Her own experiences were, of course, the foundation of her grief and empathy she felt towards the pain of her ilk. She found it specially shocking that men would conveniently blame a woman for everything that was wrong in their life, even though clearly, they were the ones responsible for the plight. As time went by, the flame of fighting for women's rights, started burning bright in Tarabai's heart. Bapuji had already told her about Jyotirao's work in the spheres of women's education and widow education & remarriage. After reading Jyotirao's books, Tarabai's feelings about doing something concrete for women's rights, intensified even more. She was extremely keen to meet the great man who spoke in favor of women's rights and had done so much to achieve the same.

Taking Bapuji's trunk in his hands, Jyotirao smiled and asked,

"Bapuji, is this Tarabai?"

"Indeed. This is my daughter, Tarabai. And daughter, this is the great man, Jyotirao Phule, who we fondly address as Tatyasaheb" replied Bapuji.

Tarabai was looking at the simply yet statuesque man in front of her, with tears in her eyes. She was surprised to see how humble and simple Tatyasaheb was. Dressed in a simple jacket, dhoti and turban, the middle-aged Tatyasaheb had a determined face illumined by grace and simplicity. She could not believe that such a big man could be so humble. With a lot of sincerity, Tarabai prostrated at Jyotirao's feet.

"Live a long, happy life" Jyotirao blessed her, adding,

"Bapuji, I am happy you got Tarabai along.

"Tara insisted that she had to come to meet you and Savitribai. She was wanting to meet you for a long time" said Bapuji.

"Is it? Well, that's very good! Come along, let us go home."

Soon, they all sat in a horse carriage and started for Ganj Peth.

Tarabai was even more overwhelmed on seeing Savitribai – a rural woman with a genteel face, etched with determination and intelligence. She could immediately see that Savitribai was the wind beneath Tatyasaheb's wings. Tarabai knew that Savitribai had also faced a lot of storms in her journey with Tatyasaheb. But, she bore those scars with grace, with her face shining like a gentle lamp – content and happy. She had also kept her home spick and span.

Tarabai prostrated before Savitribai with the same reverence with which she had done before Tatyasaheb.

Tarabai's stay at the Phule bungalow proved to be a very memorable one. In a mere few days, she became like a family member to the Phule couple. Jyotirao was very proud to see that a girl from a Maratha family, had ingrained so much of knowledge. Tarabai was adept in Marathi, Sanskrit and English. Her knowledge of Marathi literature was astonishing to say the least. Her thoughts about women's equality, the British regime, ill effects of the Peshwai regime, and the havoc wreaked by Brahmins, aligned very well with those held by Jyotirao. Tarabai would become specially aggressive while talking about women's equality and the treatment being meted out to women. Her oratory was as astounding as her study. She spoke animatedly against the male-dominated view of blaming women for everything, and against, male authors who unrepentantly accorded all rights to men, leaving the women as putty in their hands. She agreed with Jyotirao that books advocating the slavery of women, were written by cunning, biased male authors.

Among the feverish discussions that would ensue between Jyotirao and his guests, there would also be a sprinkling of humor due to the presence of Moropant, who had come from Mumbai and was staying with the Phules. Moropant was a humorous man, who took joy in teasing Jyotirao. Jyotirao's latest tryst as a vegetable seller had become the topic for poking fun. Moropant and Jyotirao would keep pulling each other's legs, till the audience would erupt in waves of laughter.

At that time, Jyotirao's student Gopalbaba Walangkar was enrolled in the army. He had also come to meet Jyotirao at the same time.

Jyotirao had a habit – anybody who would come to meet him, would be included in at least one meal of the day. He/she would not be allowed to leave without partaking at least one meal with the Phules. Even if the servant would be absent, Savitribai would herself cook for all the people who would be present for the meals. As it is, the Phules were well-known for their generosity when it came to food. Apart from running the food shelter, they would also keep feeding poor children from neighboring households, beggars, and people tormented by the draught. Some times, Jyotirao would pull his wife's leg saying,

"Savitribai, you are over-extending our household budget..."

On this, Savitribai would reply with a smile,

"Shetji, are we going to take anything of this with us to heaven?!"

Even after the Dhanakwadi ashram shut down, the Phules kept helping draught-ridden people from their own pockets. So many people would come straight to the Phules house in Ganj Peth, in the assurance that Tatya and Kaku would not disappoint them.

With fond memories of her stay with the Phules stored in her heart, Tarabai left for Buldhana. She assured Tatya that she would indeed think seriously about writing extensively on the plight of women and the need for women's equality.

As for Jyotirao's vegetable business, he soon had to fold it up, owing to the conspiracies of the cunning middlemen. The simple-minded Gyaanoba could not keep up with those games, and soon, the business started making huge losses. After the business folded up, Gyaanoba became unemployed. He started searching for a job frantically. Jyotirao gave him a letter of reference, wherein he described Gyaanoba as a loyal and hard worker. His reference proved useful in securing Gyaanoba a job of a clerk, in the public works department. Jyotirao was relieved after Gyaanoba became gainfully employed once more.

68

The air was extremely humid; almost suffocating. A smattering of rain had brought in waves of heat in its wake.

After finishing his dinner at 8 p.m., Jyotirao sat reading a book. But today, his mind was constantly wavering from the book, towards the thoughts of the elocution competition he had attended that afternoon. Justice Raosaheb Ranade and Sadashivrao Govande had organized the first-ever elocution competition for women. Jyotirao had been invited for the same. People had thronged to see how the women of Pune speak on a public dais. Just as the first participant began to speak, it started raining cats & dogs. The rain lasted for the entire duration of the competition, but it did not deter the participants in the least.

Jyotirao narrated the happenings of the entire event to Savitribai, and went to sleep with dreams of a bright future for women, wherein they would soon start speaking up more, followed by writing more. He realized that this competition was the harbinger of brilliant avenues opening up for women in Maharashtra; but all the same, he knew that it would take much more time for the waves of change to reach Shoodra community women. The women in Ganj Peth and Vetaal Peth had no idea of the forward step taken by the women in Sadashiv Peth that day. He was waiting for that day when, Shoodra women too would stand on a dais and talk fearlessly….!

Jyotirao was tossing and turning in his bed. The heat was unbearably stifling.

Just them, he heard some commotion from outside. Someone was yelling,

"Fire! Fire! The Budhwar mansion is on fire!"

"The rebels have come…they have come…!"

Jyotirao woke up with a start and rushed outside. He could see smoke billowing from a distance. The yellow and red flames were rising high to lick the sky. Someone was screaming,

"Run, save your lives…the rebels are here!"

Standing in his courtyard, Jyotirao could hear the sound of people running….horses galloping away…doors and windows being banged shut…. People were hiding inside to save their lives.

Just then, another huge ball of fire rose in the sky. Looked like, another house was torched. The atmosphere became even more stifling.

Lately, Pune had been reeling under the attack of the rebels.

….An aggressive youngster by the name of Vasudeo Balwant Phadke, had lately been kicking up a storm in Maharashtra, by instigating impressionable youngsters against the ill-effects of a foreign regime. He was zapped with the goal of upturning the British government, which he saw as the main anathema for India's development. Phadke's idols were Chhatrapati Shivaji and Tatya Tope; he dreamt of establishing a Hindavi Rashtra like they had done. Phadke was determined to stop the outflow of Indian wealth to foreign nations. He was determined to stop the spread of Missionary values and toil towards re-establishing the greatness of Hinduism in the minds of youngsters.

Phadke had begun looting nearby villages and towns to extort money to raise an army to fight the oppressive powers.

Resultantly, the houses of landlords and money-lenders were being indiscriminately looted and razed. The government was trying its level best to stop this rebellion. It had announced a reward of Rs. 50,000 for anyone who would present Phadke before the government.

Jyotirao had seen Phadke in Lahujibuva's akhaada. He would speak very aggressively against the British regime. He was a very effective orator and poet. From his student days, Phadke had started working towards social benefit. He started a school; he even educated his own wife to set an example for other women to follow. He would travel far & wide to give speeches. Phadke's oratory was so captivating that, his speeches would always run a full house.

After completing his education, Phadke had enrolled himself in the army. But, his bitter experiences in the army, led him to becoming a rebel. As things came to a head one day, Phadke abruptly resigned from his job and from there on, he became a full-fledged rebel, who vowed to drive out the British.

The whirlwind named Phadke had now reached Pune. He had taken up the task of enlisting youngsters to his cause. Before the break of dawn every day, Phadke would give army training to a batch of young boys near the Khunyaa Maruti temple at Pune. He had also made his wife, Gopikabai, adept in rifle shooting. For a long time, Pune was abuzz with fear-filled murmurs about Vasudeo Balwant Phadke.

However, what began as a volcano, soon petered into a trickle due to the non co-operation of idle barons and scared 'patriots'. Their promises of help and co-operation remained mere bubbles of words. Still, Phadke did not lose heart. He teamed up with the brave and self-respecting Ramoshis and Bhil-Kolis who had been oppressed due to the draught, random police cases, and ban on carrying weapons. The Ramoshis were already tremendously irked with the government for having sent Raje Umaji Naik to the gallows. Soon, a mini-army of Ramoshis, Kolis, Bhils, Mahars, Maangs, and even Muslims, started congregating under Phadke's leadership. The farmers, who had suffered immensely during the famine due to the government's apathy, also poured their rage out by joining Phadke.

The government was afraid of a full-fledged rebellion, that seemed to be round the corner. Even though they had taken preventive steps by passing a law that banned people from carrying weapons, the newspapers were pouring oil on fire by writing instigating reports. The Governor, Sir Litton, was toying with the idea of passing a Press Act to contain the anti-government reportage. It was just then that, Phadke's rebellion rose its head!

However, in spite of all the preparations, lack of proper strategies and enough human strength, the rebellion was bound to lose its steam soon. It was clear that Phadke could be arrested at any moment.

Jyotirao had been thinking: 'Why don't these patriotic youth work for social upliftment, instead of instigating illiterate people to join a rebellion that worked like a headless chicken?! What kind of regime do they wish to establish after driving out the British? Is their any vision in front of them? Is it even right to call them patriots, when they do not think of according human rights to their oppressed brethren in a peaceful manner? Whose independence are they really fighting for? Are these illiterate and ignorant people really going to become independent? The British regime is bound to go some day. Once the Shoodra communities start realizing their political and social rights, they are definitely going to upturn the British regime. But, at this moment at least, the British regime is just what the doctor ordered! If nothing else, it is at least letting them lead a life of peace and dignity, isn't it? These people have undergone generations of oppression at the hands of home-grown rulers. Right now, they have no strength and resources to stand up against the British. If these so-called patriots really want our nation to progress, then they should first work towards breaking down the internal barriers of caste and religion. Social equality is the base to achieve social unity, and social unity is what will lead us to freedom. Indian people are too busy fighting for their daily needs to be even interested in the fight for independence. Farmers, their cattle, their children are all sleeping hungry. A laborer does not get enough pay to even suffice for his daily needs. All these aggrieved people are jumping into the rebellion thinking that the British government has wreaked this havoc onto them. But, have they thought about, what kind of ruler are they going to get after driving out the British?'

Jyotirao too dreamt of a free India; but, the fabric of his dreams was different from that of Phadke and his followers. He knew that until today's Shoodras became rich in terms of money and education, they would not be strong enough to drive out the British and elect a ruler whose regime did not recognize untouchability and casteism. In the free India of Jyotirao's dreams, all people were going to live in equality and fraternity. Everyone was going to get enough to live a basic decent life, at least. But Jyotirao knew that, in order to manifest this dream into reality, people needed pens, not swords, in their hands.

Sadly, the end of the tunnel was not yet in sight. People were still dreaming of either getting the Peshwai regime back, or then, were happy to live a complacent life under a foreign regime.

After some time, Jyotirao could hear the tapping of police boots on the road outside. It was followed by the sounds of windows and doors opening, and people rushing outside towards the Budhwar Peth. They saw that, the Vishrambaug wada had also been torched along with the Budhwar wada.

People rushed with canisters of water to extinguish the fire. Some brave ones went inside to save as many documents as they could. However, a lot of damage was done. Most of the documents and books had been burnt; almost half of those structures had been demolished in the raging fire.

No one knew who had started the fire. Murmurs and gossips started ganing strength, with most blame falling upon the rebels. Some people surmised that a bunch of clerks from the Budhwar wada started the fire to hide the hara-kiri they had done in the accounts; they had torched the Vishrambaug wada, just to mislead others.

Gyaanoba was in Hadapsar when the news of this terrible incident reached him. He ran to the Phule mansion, and was relieved to see that the Phules and their house was safe.

There were many who believed that Vasudeo Phadke had the covert support of Jyotirao; because, after all, they both were the disciples of the same guru. Add to that, Phadke and his gang had been supplied with bhaakris at their hiding place in Katraj. People were quick to put two and two together and start murmuring that indeed, Jyotirao was helping fuel the rebellion.

The fire at these two prominent buildings in Pune, led the government to take decisive action against the rebels. Four days after the incident, Vasudeo's main accomplice, Daulatrao Naik, was killed in an encounter between the police and the rebels. Another accomplice, Vishnupant Gadre, went into hiding. The rebels lost two strong supporters!

However, this did not serve to cool down the suspicions raised about Jyotirao and his ilk. Raosaheb Ranade started being followed to see where all he went. His mail would also be rifled through. Somebody had a brainwave that the fire was directly connected to the farmers' uprising; and since, Raosaheb had supported the uprising, he was also responsible for the fire! As a matter of precaution, Raosaheb was transferred to Dhule on an immediate basis.

However, there were certain people in Pune who were also on Raosaheb's side, and who were agonized to see an upright man like Raosaheb being penalized for no reason. They decided to find out the real culprit and prove Raosaheb's innocence. In a matter of few days, a clerk working in the government's book depot was found to be the main culprit behind the fires. Coincidentally, the clerks' name was also Ranade.

The government started legal action against clerk Ranade, and Raosaheb Ranade was given a clean chit.

In the interim period, Gyaanoba had left his job and was staying in his village. The Brahmin clerks in his office had made life a living hell for Gyaanoba. Tired of facing them day in and day out, Gyaanoba finally resigned from the job and re-started the school in his village, that had shut down some time back. The school had been started by the Wanowrie Mission, but had shut down owing to lack of enough students. People had stopped sending their children to school in the fear that they would be converted. But now, since Gyaanoba had taken over the school's responsibility, the parents were relieved that no such thing was going to happen. On his part, Gyaanoba had decided that he was not going to take up any job henceforth, and pledged to devote his life to the cause of education. Bernard madam of the Wanowrie Mission was happy to help Gyaanoba in every way.

News about the rebels continued to filter in and excite the city of Pune from time to time. Vasudeo Phadke was still absconding – he was rumored to be hiding in some forest. Major Daniel was on Phadke's heels. In search of Phadke, Major Daniel treaded onto the Nizam's territory. He had received information that Phadke was hiding in Gaangapur and was building up an army with the help of the Rohillas. An arrest warrant was issued for Phadke. He was finally arrested at Devarnagadi, in the Nizam's territory.

Phadke's arrest poured iced water on the flames of rebellion. Phadke was charged with traitorship and sentenced to the dreaded imprisonment in the black waters. The case went on for barely a fortnight; during which, no advocate from Pune. came forward to represent this brave freedom fighter. On his part, Sarvajanik Kaka tried his best to represent Phadke. The famous advocate from Mumbai, Adv. Mahadev Chimnaji Apte, also came to lend his intellectual help for the case. However, all their efforts went vain, and Phadke was immediately sent to the prison at Aden. The Aden jail was an embodiment of hell on earth. Prisoners would be subjected to atrocious torture at this jail. They would be made to press seeds to extract oil and make flour out of tonnes of grain. A prisoner would either end up becoming mentally unstable, or would die due to extreme fatigue or infection.

Vasudeo Balwant Phadke's story was indeed a very tragic one. A promising, intelligent young man had gotten his wings burnt in the flames of rebellion. The tragic end to what could have been a very different life, set Jyotirao thinking. While on one hand, youngsters like Phadke were walking down the dangerous path of rebellion, on the other hand, people like Jyotirao were thinking on the lines of a social revolution. They were closely observing what was happening in England. England was on the verge of passing a law that made basic education compulsory for all. Jyotirao started preparations to lobby for a similar law in India. He started by writing articles in 'Deenbandhu' on the need and necessity of such a law in India.

Jyotirao started off by demanding compulsory primary education for all Indians. He advocated that, primary education was the foundation of all knowledge; and, in order to enable the spread of education, it was pertinent that everyone first receive good primary education. This topic brought the question of education for the Shoodras and Ati Shoodras, on the anvil once again.

69

Along side the rebellion, the government was also compelled to look into the farmers' agitation. 'Deenbandhu' was making it impossible for the government to ignore the topic any more, due to its incessant barrage of provoking articles. As a result, the government had to pass the 'Deccan Agriculturist Relief Act', which, apart from other things, had provisions to arrest the indiscriminate behavior of money lenders. The act gave some relief to the farmers; now, they were at least assured that if they took loans from money lenders, their lands would not be gobbled up by those greedy, unscrupulous individuals.

The public meetings being held by Sarvajanik Kaka, were helping the farmers' complaints reach upto the government's ears. But, it was unclear as to how much did the government really care about the farmers, and how much did it care about the money-lenders. Jyotirao did not have much faith on that primarily Brahmin-oriented gathering, which held no representation for the Shoodras.

Once the Agriculturist Act was passed, the Brahmin-run newspapers began lamenting on the behalf of the money lenders. However, only 'Deenbandhu' kept pushing for strict legal action and enforcement of the act. It also wreaked unsparing criticism on organizations like the 'Prarthana Samaj', which did not utter a word against the government in favor of the downtrodden.

'Deenbandhu's lashings put Brahmin-run newspapers in a quandary; but 'Deenbandhu' refused to soften its stance. However, after a point, when 'Deenbandhu' started criticizing the Christian religion, Jyotirao was filled with angst. It did not fall within the parameters of the Satyashodhak Samaj to criticize a religion which was much more generous and lenient than Hindu religion. Also, what had begun as an opposition to the principles of Brahmin caste, started becoming personal and vicious attacks on Brahmin people. Obviously, the Brahmin-run newspapers were quick to retaliate on 'Deenbandhu' and the Satyashodhak Samaj.

When he next met Krishnaji, Jyotirao advised him,

"Krishnarao, please think coolly about who exactly is our

enemy; who are we fighting against? It is not a sign of a stable mind that you sometimes attack the Brahmins, sometimes attack Christianity. The Christian religion is much more lenient than Hinduism. There is no point in finding silly faults in it. If you really wish to criticize, then criticize the unfair principles of the Brahmin caste. But while doing that too, remember that our battle is against the caste, not against the people born as Brahmins. It is not necessary that every Brahmin behaves oppressively. There are many Shoodras who also behave cunningly and oppressively towards their own brethren. And remember, a newspaper is the society's mouthpiece. It is a very powerful tool, which must be used very responsibly. Something is going drastically wrong, Krishnarao. I could see this happening; which is why, I was hesitant to give the press in your hands."

In spite of Jyotirao's explanation, Krishnarao stuck to his guns. Again, a storm of disagreement started brewing between both of them.

Krishnarao was facing a severe lack of funds for keeping 'Deenbandhu' afloat. He was suffering lot of losses to keep his paper running. Krishnarao had hoped that funding would start coming in, after the famine; but that did not happen. He had mortgaged his house, farm, and his wife's jewelry for running the paper. The condition worsened to such an extent that, his house came up for liquidation. Adding to his problems, his disagreements with Jyotirao kept earning him the displeasure of other Satyashodhaks. Jyotirao was also not uttering a word about 'Deenbandhu's financial health.

Finally, in the winter of 1879, 'Deenbandhu' downed its shutters. The Satyashodhaks were upset that a prominent voice of the Samaj, got strangled for ever. Jyotirao was away at Phaltan when Krishnarao took this decision.

Even though upset at having to shut down his labour of love, Krishnarao did not sit still. He kept organizing programs like 'essay reading competitions for women'. On the side, he also kept making efforts to restart 'Deenbandhu'. One of his plans included asking Ramji Santuji Aawate and Narayanrao Lokhande to operate the paper from Mumbai. Narayanrao was happy with the proposal; he got a good platform to boost his workers' movement. Damodar Savlaram Yande also joined hands with Narayanrao, and in mere four months, the paper started running successfully from Mumbai.

The new owners changed the whole look of the paper. It started being published in Marathi and English, both.

Krishnarao's relationship with the paper ended forever. Burdened with debts, Krishnarao decided to take the land that baron Atmarambuva was offering him at Chincholi, and went to become a farmer there.

70

Jyotirao was carrying out his municipal responsibilities sincerely. He was doing a lot of work in relation to cleanliness, providing employment to people, and maintaining accounts. He had kept one firm principle behind each work – that, anything he did should be of benefit to the common man. It was out of that thought that he decided to raise a strong objection about the liquor-serving joints that had mushroomed all over Pune.

With liquor licenses being given out like toffees, it was a common sight to see drunk men lolling on the streets. This was another 'gift' from the Peshwai. The Brahmins would merrily consume alcohol, anointing it as 'Somras' . Now, the newly educated class was finding it fashionable to emulate the Westerners and consume alcohol. The parties in the houses if barons and the nouveau rich, would be overflowing with liquor. It had become 'forward' and 'progressive' to have parties serving alcohol. Add to that, the government was doling out licenses for liquor shops, resulting in hitherto marginalized liquor shops coming into the mainstay.

With alcohol being available so easily, it became a common sight to see drunk men raving on the roads. Laborers started going in to these shops for a quick drink before going home. But, what started as a small indulgence, soon morphed into a dangerous addiction. People started blowing away their entire earnings in this poison; thinking nothing about their starving wife and children back home.

Jyotirao could bear it no more. He wrote a letter to Sir Plunkett, the Chairman of the Managing Committee of Pune Municipality, and a good friend of Jyotirao's. In the letter, he wrote that by giving out liquor licenses indiscriminately, the Municipality – which is supposed to be the upholder of its citizens' health – is heavily compromising on the same.

Not stopping at just writing the letter, Jyotirao insisted the Municipality's executive committee to pass a resolution regarding this problem. The resolution, along with a copy of Jyotirao's letter, was sent to the Collector Riche.

Around the same time, a resolution was passed to erect a market at Vetaal Peth. Jyotirao showed strong opposition to this resolution because, a plush market was bound to render many poor vegetable vendors out of business. When the topic of renovating the old market came up, Jyotirao insisted that the poor vendors should not be charged a rent of more than 4 aanas per month.

With regards to the problem of curbing the spread of alcoholism, the government was imply pushing papers around. It was in no mood to lose a huge chunk of its revenue. Another senior official, Dickson, and the police superintendent of Pune, were called upon to give their opinions on the matter. While Riche and Dickson were in favor of Jyotirao's views, the police superintendent put forth a number of silly arguments, all pointed at not curbing the licenses.

Finally, after many twists and turns, the resolution came back to the Municipal Corporation with a surprise comment from Riche: 'It cannot be said that the increase in licenses is responsible for increase in alcohol consumption in Pune'.

However, Jyotirao's efforts did not go entirely waste. From the next time, the government had to consider the Municipality's resolution while issuing licenses to any new liquor shop.

71

Jyotirao was sitting in his living room, reading the latest issue of 'Subodh Patrika'. Suddenly, he frowned and called out to Savitribai.

Savitribai was having her lunch. Hearing her husband's distinctively sharp call, she hurried outside. Seeing her, Jyotirao remarked,

"I'm sorry, I forgot that you were eating."

"It's okay. What happened?" asked Savitribai.

"This issue of 'Subodh Patrika' has expressed some really weird ideas about tonsuring of widows. It says, a widow should be tonsured by some woman from her own household, or then by some female barber. The article has also mentioned the name of one such barber in Nasik, and has exhorted people to support her for the higher social good. My friend has mouthed some really surprising gems here!" remarked Jyotirao, referencing to Moropant, who was the editor of the journal.

"I don't think he has written this article" Savitribai said.

"He may have not, but he is the editor, isn't it? Not a single word in the journal can be published without his express consent. I don't understand why these Brahmins are so afraid to tackle the issue of tonsuring directly, for the social evil it is? Tonsuring, whether done by a family member or a female barber, is an evil and heinous practice. It should be stopped altogether" said Jyotirao.

Jyotirao had been requesting Savitribai for many years to visit barbers and make them understand what trauma a woman undergoes when she is tonsured. He was sure that the barbers would understand a woman's plight better, when it was explained by a woman. However, shouldering so many responsibilities already had left Savitribai with no time to devote to this work.

Such a convenient, soft stance being taken by Brahmin-led journals, was not a new thing. In the fear of antagonizing their community, they would be afraid to rock the boat too much. A Parsi gentleman called Behramji Malbari had started another journal called 'Indian Spectator', which was quite open and brazen in expressing its views. However, people found it 'over-smart' for a Parsi man to comment on the happenings within the Hindu realm. Vishnushastri Chiplunkar was also planning to start another newspaper, but based on the past experience of 'Nibandhamala', Jyotirao was not very hopeful about what the content of the new paper would be.

Today, Jyotirao was strongly feeling the void left by the demise of 'Deenbandhu'. Had its editorial policy been well etched out, and had Krishnarao been a bit more flexible in his views, the paper would have done very well. But alas, Krishnarao had never left smarting about Jyotirao's refusal to give him the press, and had always operated with a tainted viewpoint.

Even after 'Deenbandhu' started again, it soon came into trouble with the new partners Aawate and Lokhande constantly bickering with each other.

Savitribai was emotional about the closure of 'Deenbandhu' and felt very sad about Krishnarao's condition after the closure. He had not been able to do farming at Chincholi, and had then shifted to Beervadi where he had taken up a job as a Sub Overseer at a canal.

"You should not have been so stern with Krishnarao" Savitribai reprimanded Jyotirao for the umpteenth time.

Jyotirao agreed that things could have been different, but somehow, the situations did not allow events to shape up in a more amiable way; and now, it was too late to cry over spilt milk. In a bid to pacify his wife, Jyotirao said,

"How long can one compromise and keep agreeing to things that one does not inherently agree with, Savitribai?"

"But, I don't understand... Why did you get so incensed just because Krishnarao criticized Christianity? Everyone is entitled to their options, and every religion has its pros and cons...." argued Savitribai.

"Even then, Savitribai, no one can deny that Christianity is much lenient and generous as compared to Hindu religion. Earlier, even Christianity was plagued by torment from Popeism; but, religious reformers like Thomas Penn and Martin Luther King have long since replaced that era with progressive views and principles. And, I personally feel that, the behavior of Brahmins is much more evil, as compared to, that of the religious heads in the darkest times of Christianity. At least those people accepted that there is a God, a higher power sitting up in the heaven. But Brahmins? They have embodied themselves as God and have been shamelessly looting the ignorant masses on that pretext...."

Realising that her husband was not going to change his mind, Savitribai stopped the discussion there. She knew that Jyotirao was not going to listen to anybody when it came to his views about the Brahmins.

In the afternoon, Jyotirao left for the Municipal Corporation's office. He had to speak on an important topic today. The Viceroy of India, Lord Litton, was due to visit Pune next month. The Corporation wanted the city to be beautified in lieu of his visit. The proposed expenses for this beautification drive had been pegged at Rs. 1000. Fearing that a formal proposal would probably face dissent, the Chairman had written to each member of committee separately, requesting their approval for the plan. 31 out of the 32 members had given their consent; just one consent remained, and that was on Jyotirao Phule.

Jyotirao was absolutely against this criminal waste of money, and that too for someone who had exerted the Press Act and heartlessly strangled the freedom of press. However, this time, Jyotirao was alone in his struggle. Not even Hari Raoji, his usual supporter, was with him in this matter. That did not deter Jyotirao, though. He expressed his dissent to the Chairman frankly, and asked him to instead use the amount for the education of poor children.

Sir Plunkett was unhappy with Jyotirao's stance and disregarded the suggestion. However, the incident was one more proof of the fact that Jyotirao would keep fighting for the upliftment of the marginalized sections of society, even if that meant taking on the displeasure of others.

72

One evening, Jyotirao took out all the children for a stroll. Devrao Thosar's son, Lakshman, was of Yeshwant's age. Ganpatrao Kale's son, Govind, was staying at the Phule residence to partake of education in English. Jyotirao would keep a stringent watch on the children's schooling, physical activities, and reading routine.

After coming back from the stroll, Jyotirao asked the children to sit for their studies, and himself started writing a letter to Tarabai. In her last letter to Tatyasaheb, Tarabai had written that she could no longer bear to sit quiet on seeing how the society was pushing women to the brink of 'unacceptable behavior ', and was then conveniently pointing fingers at them for conducting themselves inappropriately. Thus, Jyotirao was writing back to her that indeed, she should start writing about these things, especially on the backdrop of certain incidents that had happened recently. In a village called Udpaad, in Gujarat, a young widow called Vijayalakshmi had been sentenced to be hung till death for committing the 'crime' of feticide. Some people were fighting to reduce her punishment, but orthodox newspapers such as 'Pune Vaibhav' were adding fuel to the fire, without caring a bit about the pitiable state of widows and instead labeling them as morally corrupt. They had even started advising the government to not interfere in their religious matters by issuing laws in favor of widows. The hypocrisy and hard-heartedness was infuriating Jyotirao to no end, and he knew that a woman's writings would have more effect than any else.

That night, Devrao Thosar came to chat with Jyotirao. After having retired from his job in the police department, Thosar was now working as an honorary magistrate. There were many topics to talk about. Shastribuva's 'Nibandhamala', its constant and vicious attacks on Jyotirao, Lokahitawadi and Raobahadur.... all these were usual topics of discussion at the Phule house. At night, a group of Satyashodhaks would gather at Jyotirao's house and feverish discussions would continue till past midnight.

Sometimes the talks would go to Vishnushastri's affinity to European writers like Max Muller for having lent credence to the greatness of Brahmin-written scriptures like the Vedas. Jyotirao would pooh-pooh away Vishnushastri's loving words towards such writers saying, "Let them come to India and experience the torment in the name of religious segregations. I shall then ask them, how great do they still think Brahmin scriptures are?"

Influenced by Brahmin teachings, when some youngster would start cursing the Christian religion, Jyotirao would explain to him,

"My son, why are you expending your energy in getting angry on Christianity when our own country has the Brahmin way of life, which has reduced generations of Shoodras to ashes? Recognize a religion for what it really is. Do not base your views on biased propagandas. Shoodras have never been allowed to learn about what their real religion is; hence, they find it easiest to follow the Brahmins and become their slaves. However, these Brahmins who have reduced a whole mass of people to slavery, put a blot on the name of the same God who they claim to follow religiously. These people are very clever, son. Realizing that their fraudulent claims are being exposed, they are now trying to portray themselves as religious reformers via the Prarthana Samaj and Arya Samaj. But remember, we do not need their shams for reforming ourselves. We have chosen our path – the path of truth – already."

"Tatyasaheb, the Brahmins say that there are only two castes remaining in Kaliyug – Brahmin and Shoodra. Is that correct?" asked one Satyashodhak, who had been mulling over the question for many days now.

Jyotirao replied,

"Well, in a way, it is true. After the Aryans invaded Hindustan in the yore, there remained only two castes. The Aryan Brahmins, Kshatriyas and Vaishyas defeated and enslaved the original Kshatriyas on our land. Then, the three Aryan sub-groups began referring to themselves collectively as Brahmins. One among those Brahmins – Parshuram – thought nothing of bringing about a massacre of thousands of people, including women and children. So to cut a long story short, today there remain only two main castes – them, Brahmins; and the rest of us, Shoodra and Ati Shoodras who were the original Kshatriyas of this land."

Someone else asked,

"Tatyasaheb, is there any evidence to prove that indeed the Brahmins have made the caste system?"

This question had been posed to Jyotirao many a times. In fact, he and Dr. Ghole had several intense discussions and disagreements regarding this topic. Nevertheless, Jyotirao stuck to his stance and was presently engaged in researching Sanskrit texts to gather constructive evidence. He said to the querent,

"At the moment, I have no solid evidence to corroborate or refute this question. But, I can only say, these are the people who have written scriptures that praise casteism. Presently, I'm reading a lot of these scriptures and I have realized that casteism being of benefit to them, the Brahmins have always spoken in its favor. It has always been of benefit to Brahmins to keep the other caste people subjugated on the pretext that they have been born with inferior qualities. However, a person's qualities are determined by his education and upbringing; not by which family he is born into."

Many such discussions would ensue on various topics. Lately, Pune was in the grips of another controversy. Madhavrao Barve, a prominent minister from the princely state of Kolhapur, had filed a legal case on Tilak and Agarkar, alleging that their newspapers 'Kesari' and 'Maratha', were spreading social and political discontent through their flagrant reportage. Jyotirao felt satisfied that he had stood by Chhatrapati Shivaji Maharaj in the matters going on in the Kolhapur princely state regarding the ascension of the throne. For the last four years, Kolhapur was running rife with rumors and plots. It was being said that Shivaji Maharaj was mentally unstable. But this was not true. It was yet another ploy to remove the young king from the throne. The king was an orphan who had been adopted by the erstwhile ruler of Kolhapur. After finishing his education, the young king had started looking after the affairs of the kingdom. This caused immense heartburn to Madhavrao Barve and rumoredly, even the queen. It was feared that the king was going to be poisoned and eliminated.

The legal case made the entire Maharashtra turn its wrath onto Barve. Except for one-two papers like 'Belgaum Samachar', every other paper from 'Deenbandhu', to 'Native Opinion', to 'Dynanprakash', all wreaked havoc on Barve. Nana Bhide, a member of the Kolhapur court, responded to an invitation to speak at a public meeting in Pune and described what was transpiring at Kolhapur. He revealed that there was a big conspiracy brewing to prove the the king was mentally unstable, and many eminent people from the Kolhapur court were part of this conspiracy.

The government jumped into the fray and imprisoned Shivaji Maharaj in the Ahmadnagar fort. The government was hand-in-glove with Barve and they tortured the king very badly while he was in captivity. He would be beaten, kicked and abused badly.

On his way to Ahmadnagar, Shivaji Maharaj halted for a few days at Pune. He had been given a tiny bungalow at the riverside. He was staying in pitiable conditions along with his mother Radhabai. People would throng to see the king but would be saddened to see his plight. When the king was shifted to Ahmadnagar, many people had come to Daund railway station to see him off. They were deeply shaken to see a ruler, a king, picking up remnants of *shev* from a small paper ball that he held in his fist! Who was responsible for reducing a ruler of one of the richest states of Maharashtra to such pitiful conditions?!

Tilak and Agarkar did a lot of research and started expressing the truth in their papers. They decided to stand by Shivaji Maharaj and appeal to popular support in this regard. Jyotirao felt very proud of this stance taken by the two young editors.

When Shivaji Maharaj was suffering from inhuman torture in the prison, arrest warrants were also issued for Tilak and Agarkar. The people who had egged them to write against the government, conveniently backstabbed them at the last minute. A bail of Rs. 10,000 was demanded to release both of them from custody. Letters of request were circulated to gather the amount. When Jyotirao received the letter, he immediately went to Uravane shetji. The latter had also got the same letter. He agreed to donate as much amount as he could. Tilak and Agarkar were relieved when the bail amount was paid.

73

The Kolhapur case reached a crescendo, all over Maharashtra. The gossip mills began churning overtime. Madhavrao Barve was trying every trick in the book to bring Tilak and Agarkar to their knees. But, even though the legal system was on Barve's side, justice was on the side of Tilak and Agarkar. They had the goodwill of entire Maharashtra. The eminent advocate Firozshah Mehta was representing them in court.

Shivaji Maharaj was still being inhumanly tortured at the Ahmadnagar fort. The people's blood was boiling to hear newer episodes of torture ever day. Newspapers were describing the happenings in gory detail. Readers were reacting strongly to the injustice being meted out to the king. The legal eagles from both sides were burning the midnight oil in preparation for the case. Tilak and Agarkar became busy with their work. In spite of his delicate health, Vishnushastri Chiplunkar was doing everything possible to help them.

While all this was going on, one day, Shaahir Dhondiram came rushing to Jyotirao's house.

"Tatyasaab... please come outside fast, Tatyasaab..." he called out.

Jyotirao came outside. Seeing Shaahir's worried face, he asked,

"What happened, Shaahir?"

"Tatyasaab, Vishnushastri is no more!"

Jyotirao was taken aback to hear the news!

"What?? How is that possible? At such a young age?" he exclaimed.

"Yes, Tatyasaab. It is true. He developed stomach ulcers. Even while running a high fever, he kept muttering about Kolhapur Maharaj's case."

Vishnushastri had been taking immense efforts to bring justice for Shivaji Maharaj. But now, he was no more.

In spite of their ideological differences, Jyotirao could not help reminisce about all the work that Vishnushastri had done in a small span of time. He had left a well-paying government job to start a school. He started a newspaper too. At a young age of 24, he had launched 'Nibandhamala', which he ran successfully for eight years.

"It's a very sad news, Shaahir... Just when an intellectual revolution was beginning in Maharashtra, we have lost a very capable and promising young man. We need to carry forward the work of education that Vishnushastri had started" said Jyotirao.

"Tatyasaab, people are saying that Vishnushastri committed suicide by consuming poison" the Shaahir informed.

Jyotirao rebuked him saying,

"We should not speak like this about the dead, Shaahir..."

"I know, Tatyasaab. But, I am only telling you what the people are saying. Things have gone quite ahead. The police are refusing to release his mortal remains. They was a doctor's certificate to prove that it was not a suicide. Unless a post-mortem is done, they are not allowing for the funeral rites to take place."

"Why have such rumors started spreading?" Jyotirao asked.

"People are saying, Vishnushastri got afraid of an unsuccessful outcome of the Kolhapur case, and hence consumed poison."

Jyotirao was saddened to hear this. He said to Dhondiram,

"We have to go there. Right now. Come on."

Shastribuva had been ill for the last two months. Dr. Garde and Vishram Ramji, both had been tending to him. It was true that Vishnushastri was also quite worried about the Kolhapur case. But, the reason for his death turned out to be something different itself – in fact, he died out of something quite trivial.

Vishnushastri had planned to have a group photo of all his family members. A Portuguese photographer from the military, had been deployed for the task. The first day, the photographer came to Shastribuva's house and clicked separate photographs of the men and women. The next day, the whole family trooped to the photographer's house to have photos clicked together. Towards the end of the session, someone requested Shastribuva to get his solo photo clicked. Heeding the request, Shastribuva stood outside (for the photographer to get proper sunlight). Suddenly, he swooned and fell down. His face and teeth got hurt in this episode. From thereon, somehow he always ran a fever. As days went by, Shastribuva stopped responding to medicines. The temperature kept increasing, and finally, it lead to his demise.

On the night prior to Buva's demise, his fever had become very strong. The family had stopped allopathic medicines and had started the treatment of Vaidya Ganeshbuva Sakurdikar. He prescribed medicines and diet that would act as coolants. However, after taking that afternoon's medicine and eating some watermelon, Buva's fever escalated even more; to the extent that, it started affecting his brain. He started mumbling incoherently. At around 10 pm, Sitarampant called Dr. Vishram Ramji to check on Buva. Seeing him, Buva screamed out,

"Kaka, save me!! I'm dying, Kaka! Give me a sip of water…water Kaka…water…"

Vishram Ramji started preparing a medicine to give to Buva. In that condition too, Buva told him,

"I will not take this medicine. Be warned! I will not be poisoned like this. You will be held to task. This is the Kolhapur case…very big case…"

Seeing Vishnushastri's condition, Dr. Vishram Ramji found it prudent to not force him to take the medicine.

Sitarampant apologised for Buva's behavior and requested the doctor to compel him to take the medicine. But, Dr. Vishram Ramji refused and said,

"That won't be right. I think, please call Vaidyabuva in the morning and give his medicine to Shastribuva."

Saying thus, Dr. Vishram Ramji went home. However, late that night, Buva's health worsened. It became impossible to wait till morning. So, Vaidya Sakurdikar was called for urgently. It was almost 1 am when Vaidyabuva gave medicine to Shasitrbuva. All the family members were awake that night, hoping for a miracle which never came. Shastribuva left for his heavenly abode at 5.30 am.

The news of Shastribuva's demise spread like wildfire. People started gathering at his house in Dolkar alley. The atmosphere was tense. Prof. Keronana Chhatre, Baba Gokhale, and Rambhau Sane were huddled up in a corner, deep in discussion.

Seeing Jyotirao approach, Keronana remarked,

"Tatyasaheb, good you came. We were coming to you itself. The doctor's certificate is getting difficult to come by. We need to meet Dr. Vishram Ramji."

"Come on, let's go" said Jyotirao.

Accompanied by Keronana, Jyotirao went to meet Dr. Vishram Ramji, who could not refuse Jyotirao's request and thus came along with them, back to Shastribuva's home. As soon as the police got the death report that they wanted, they ordered for the police-watch to be lifted and gave permission to start carrying out the last rites. However, all this led to a delay of almost six hours since Buva's demise. It was 11 am by the time they got permission for the last rites. The mortal remains were taken to Omkareshwar, where the last rites were conducted with due rituals. Before leaving for Omkareshwar, there was a prayer meeting held for the departed soul. This was a newly started concept in Pune in those times.

Vishnushastri's disciple Rambhau Sane began speaking. Few more people wanted to speak but Keronana was getting antsy; he still feared a police backlash. He knew that the police had not been totally convinced with the death certificate issued. Not wanting anything unpleasant to mar the funeral proceedings, before anyone else could stand up to speak, Keronana intervened and said,

"Please do not waste any more time in speaking. We do not want further interference from the police. Let us get going and finish the funeral rites first. That is more important."

Everyone agreed. It was indeed dangerous to court more trouble from the police. Soon, they all reached Omkareshwar.

Shastribuva's cousin brother, Vinayakrao, conducted the last rites.

After the funeral pyre was lit, everyone started returning home. Jyotirao kept thinking about his bitter-sweet relations with the Chiplunkar family. Vishnushastri's father, Prof. Krishnashastri Chiplunkar, had been an avid supporter of Jyotirao's work. He would give a monthly donation of 4 aanas for the school that Jyotirao ran for Mahar-Maang children. He would also be present for many meetings and discussions, and would be ready to extend any form of help, as the need arose. Thereafter, Jyotirao's relations with Vishnushastri were not that happy. However, he could never forget everything that the Chiplunkar family had done for him.

The older generation was approaching its dusk. Times were changing and accordingly, people and situations were bound to change. Yet, in spite of the strained relations between him and Vishnushastri, Jyotirao could not accept that such an illustrious, capable and intelligent man should be dead at a young age of 32! On the basis of his intelligence, perseverance, hard work, and determination, Vishnushastri had achieved a lot in a short span of time. It was rare to find such perseverance and readiness for toil in the youngsters of the present. Keeping aside the criticism and arguments between the two, today Jyotirao could only see the good things that Vishnushastri had achieved. He found it more important to acknowledge the yeoman service that Vishnushastri had done in the field of education. Maharashtra had lost a great educationist and patron of the arts.

Wiping his tear-filled eyes with his scarf, Jyotirao returned home with a heavy heart.

74

"When a woman's husband dies, you force her to tonsure her head, become unattractive, and spend a lonely life sequestered in her house. Then, why don't you men shave off your moustaches and beards, and lead a similarly isolated life after your wives die? Men can have as many wives as they like; then, why can't a woman have as many husbands as she likes? Unscrupulous people who turn mendicants to loot women, are also men, isn't it? Even a prostitute is a woman who falls prey to the devious minds of men."

Tarabai's words were scathing, piercing a reader's heart straight through. All her inner rage was seen poured out in those words. As promised to Jyotirao, Tarabai had started writing her thoughts down. Jyotirao was also taken aback at the force of her words!

Tarabai had fearlessly questioned the men for applying separate laws for themselves and women; as also for, even writing mythological tales that upheld men as superior and believed that a woman's life was best spent in mindless sacrifice.

She had also come down heavily on the mythological character of Mandodari, who had convinced Sita to listen to her husband, Ravan.

"I don't understand why women feel that the only true way to happiness is to do what their husbands tell them to do? Why do husbands also feel happy and powerful when the wives do their bidding? Did Mandodari never feel like thinking what an unfortunate position she was bringing Sita into, by asking her to listen to Ravan? Wow! What a wonderful way to show loyalty to one's husband!"

Tarabai had also criticized writers like Ramji Ganoji who wrote lascivious books that portrayed women to be evil and morally corrupt temptresses. She also let her anger let loose on so-called educated men who gave zero value to a woman's intellect and abilities. However, Tarabai had not forgotten to thank the government for thinking compassionately about women's problems and making due laws for their upliftment.

Jyotirao had tears of joy in his eyes on reading Tarabai's powerful and emphatic writing. It was a matter of pride that a young girl from the conservative Maratha community had broken off her shackles and voiced her opinions so fearlessly.

After Savitribai finished reading Tarabai's draft, Jyotirao sent it off to the printing press.

Meanwhile, the social conditions in Pune were showing no signs of progress. Narrow-minded 'scholars' continued to uphold the greatness of Hindu religion for all the dogmatic principles it prescribed. Lately, another such scholar – incidentally, a woman – had appeared on the scene and was propounding the greatness of Hindu religion anew.

The scholar, Pandita Ramabai, was staying at Abhyankar's house. She knew heavy scriptures like the Bhagwad Geeta and Upanishads by heart. She had been able to defeat the great scholars of Kashi and Calcutta in religious debates, and had thus earned the title of 'Pandita' aka lady scholar.

Pandita Ramabai was holding weekly discourses at Pune. People were attending her lectures out of sheer curiosity to see what a lady scholar would talk like. They would go away impressed by her knowledge, charismatic personality, and sweet way of talking. Regular attendees to Ramabai's lectures included eminent people like Raosaheb Ranade and Keronana Chhatre. The orthodox group was thrilled to see the winds of change blowing in their favour once again.

Ramabai had another intention of coming to Pune. She had started the Arya Mahila Samaj in Mumbai, and now wanted to open another chapter of the same at Pune. However, had she heard the opinions of Pune's women regarding herself, Ramabai would not have waited in the city for a minute longer. The women of Pune detested Ramabai for having married a Shoodra. They opined that she had blackened the face of all Brahmins by marrying a low caste person, and was now trying to corrupt the minds of innocent women by telling them nonsense about men.

Ramabai came to meet Savitribai once or twice. Her affinity towards the cause of women empowerment was real; but, it was odd that she would take recourse to the Puranas, all the same. It was a contradictory behavior; one that did not impress the Phules.

Shaahir Dhondiram would regularly go to Ramabai's discourses. Often, he and Jyotirao would discuss upon the views expressed by Ramabai in her speeches. One day, Jyotirao remarked,

"I find it to be the height of ignorance that a scholar – and a lady scholar at that – should sings paeans to the religion that has continuously advocated and practiced subjugation of women. It goes to prove that the Pandita has not done in-depth study of the very ancient Hindu scriptures. She will be appalled to read what those texts say about the treatment that should be given to women and Shoodras."

Shaahir did not answer, but he was prompted to think about what Jyotirao had said.

75

Today, Tatya had taken the children for an excursion to see the newly arrived steam engine. They also went for a quick trip to the David Sassoon Hospital while returning from the train station.

After making a debut in Mumbai, the steam engine had recently started running in Pune. People were extremely curious to see the iron monstrosity hissing steam and running on impossibly small tracks. Few of them felt that it was indeed some demon who had come down from the skies, in the form of a train! They prayed to it, offering coconuts and cow urine, requesting it to not wreak its wrath on them.

However, the train kept functioning as it was bound to. After quite a few weeks of prayers and offerings, people started believing that it was a machine, and not a demon. Nevertheless, they could not fathom as to how it could keep moving relentlessly without consuming any food or water. They also could not understand that how exactly was it being pulled at such a speed. Many logical-illogical explanations later, they decided to let the issue be, and concentrated on daring to step onto the train!

Then, it became a common pastime to sit on the station to see the train approaching or leaving. Some brave-hearts even ventured to climb aboard and travel to a distance, returning with excitement-laced narratives about how fast the train moves and how comfortable it feels.

After months of fear and speculation, the people of Pune then started getting cocky about the train, claiming that the British must have read about the 'agnirath ' in their Puranas, and simply copied their idea to make a train.

However, the children's excursion turned out to be quite a joyful one, especially due to Tatya's informative narration about the workings of the engine and so on.

After they came home, Tatya sent the children to study and caught a small nap beneath the banyan tree in the courtyard. The children finished their studies and came back to Tatya, clamouring for a story.

"But Tatya, we want some other story, apart from the ones in Aesop's Fables. We do like Aesop's Fables, but why don't you tell us something from the Puranas?" requested Yeshwant.

Hearing this unusual request, Jyotirao replied,

"My son, the stories written in the Puranas are full of lies and immorality. Those stories will not have a desirable effect on your tender minds. Rather, they will only corrupt and confuse you. You will become idol-worshippers and shall start searching for God in mute stone idols. Instead, listen to stories from Aesop's Fables. They will have good effect on your mind and intellect. The history described in Ramayana and such other Purana-related scriptures, is false and illogical. For instance, the Ramayana says that during Sita's *swayamvar*, Ravana fell down while trying to string the bow that Sita used to play with during her childhood. Then, if Sita was so strong, how come Ravana could lift her up and flee into the jungles? Does it make any sense to you? Plus, if he was a demon (and not a human like Sita), then how did he even enter into the contest to win Sita as his wife? And what about Ram? A man who can leave his wife in the jungles and can hurt another woman by mutilating her, how can he even be called God?!"

Just then, Sitaram came and said to Jyotirao,

"Tatyasaheb, Uravane Shetji's family has called you urgently."

Jyotirao was anticipating this message to come at any moment. He got up in an instant and told Savitribai about the message. Leaving the children in Sitaram's care, they both started hurrying towards Uravane Shetji's house in Bhavani Peth.

Ramji Uravane had been ill for the last few days. His health had kept deteriorating. As Jyotirao and Savitribai neared the Uravane house, they saw a big group of people standing outside, and understood what had happened. Jyotirao's heart was filled with immense sadness. His eyes filled with tears.

Bapushetji's son, Ram, was a childhood friend of Jyotirao's. A pampered boy from a rich family, Ram had sobered down quite a lot after getting Jyoti Phule's company. Thus, Bapushet was very affectionate towards Jyotirao. Jyotirao reminisced about their days together in Father Mitchell's school. After Father Mitchell, Jyotirao was Ram's second teacher. Time went by; they both grew up. Ram became Ramshet and Jyoti became Jyotirao. Yet, the teaching continued. Ramshet used to like reading about social reformers. Jyotirao would keep sourcing such books for him. Jyotirao remembered reading reams of Thomas Penn's books in the company of Ramshet and Vasudeo Navrange.

Jyotirao's teachings to Ramshet helped make him a good human being. He became a stanch supporter of all the activities that Jyotirao took up – be it, starting a school at Bhide mansion, or, opening up the Victoria Balashram food shelter. Ramshet had also taken on the responsibility as a Treasurer of the Samaj. During the Kolhapur case, when a bail of Rs. 10,000 had been demanded to release Tilak and Agarkar, Ramshet had pushed aside all his health problems to come to his office at night and made arrangements to reach the bail money to Mumbai immediately. Jyotirao had lost a wonderful friend and a very generous and good human being.

Ramshet house was reverberating with loud cries. Satyashodhaks were thronging to his house to see him for the last time. Keronana Chhatre, Bholageer Maharaj, Hari Raoji, Dynaangiri Maharaj, Adv. Lingu, Dr. Vishram Ramji, Tilak, Agarkar and many other eminent people of Pune came to see off their dear friend.

The funeral took place the following morning. Jyotirao returned home with a heavy heart. In the privacy of his house, he let his emotions run amok...!

76

A meeting was in full force at Jyotirao's house. Jyotirao was saying,

"We do not need an educational system that will churn out good clerks for the government. We need an educational system that will help build a moral foundation for our children, while also equipping them with future-oriented practical knowledge. Children should get an education that will make them compassionate about the society's problems. Today, the farmers are toiling and their money is being blown up on idle Brahmins. The effects of this are going to be horrible. It is futile to hope that the society's upper layer will some day start teaching the lower classes. Nowhere has this ever happened. No country ever has such a benevolent government."

Recently, the government had instituted the William Hunter Commission to examine the lacunae and suggest due improvements in the Indian education system. The committee members were speaking with eminent and educated people in major cities and towns, to get their opinions on the subject.

However, Jyotirao strongly felt that this modus operandi would not yield any valid results for the government. He felt that the commission members had to visit the poorest of people living in urban and rural pockets and ask them what difficulties they faced while trying to educate their children.

Jyotirao had decided to write a letter to the government, expressing his thoughts on the topic and bringing to their notice what was wrong in the way they were gathering information.

The Hunter Commission also made a visit to Pune. They had held a big meeting at Town Hall, which incidentally saw a lot of women in attendance. The commission members inspected many schools in Pune, and also asked for data from the Municipal Corporation about how many schools they ran for boys, and how many for girls. The Corporation could give them no data for girls' schools; simply because, they did not run any! The schools for girls and Mahar-Maangs that Jyotirao Phule and Sadashivrao Govande had handed over to the Corporation to run, had long been shut down by narrow-minded Brahmin officials. In his speech, William Hunter made a pointed mention about this unfortunate fact and expressed deep regret about this apathy.

Following Hunter's speech, Raosaheb Ranade and Pandita Ramabai also gave long speeches about the need for women's education.

However, the government conveniently side-lined what Jyotirao had been saying about this issue over the last two years, via 'Deenbandhu'. Thus, he decided to take matter sin his hands and wrote a letter to the government directly.

In his letter, Jyotirao held the government responsible for spending indiscriminate amounts of money on the current educational system, which benefitted no one but only the upper castes, while shoving the lower castes further down the alley of ignorance. He further said that, if the government thought that the people who got education in this system, would do something for their less fortunate brethren, then that was a very rosy and idealistic view it held. He wrote:

"Please give us some examples of where you have seen it happening that, the educated class is doing something concrete for their uneducated counterparts? What steps have they taken to achieve such lofty aims? Have they started any classes for the uneducated section of the population? No. Instead, they have always kept their knowledge to themselves; probably thinking that by proliferating it to the ignorant masses, their education will get maligned!"

Jyotirao requested the government to look at the issue in a macroscopic and open way and then aid the spread of education to the lower classes, to help free themselves from the shackles of slavery that they have been bound in for generations on end. He demanded that primary education be made compulsory and freely available for all. He further said that the government should stop spending on the education of those who are financially well off and capable of paying for their own education. Instead, it should open the doors of education for those people from whom it gets tax, and who is the true pillar of society – the lower and working class.

Jyotirao had also identified the loopholes in the primary education being offered at present, and had outlined some suggestions to rectify those problems. Some of these included making primary education compulsory till the age of 12; simplifying the syllabus of schools in rural areas; employing trained teachers in rural schools; try employing teachers from farmer backgrounds in rural schools; according these teachers enough payment so that they would not feel the need to leave their profession; inspecting the schools from time to time; and making the education department keep a check on expenses from time to time.

He had not asked the government to stop paying attention to higher education; for, he understood that higher education was the foundation of a better tomorrow. But, he had suggested that the government divert more funds towards primary education instead of higher education; avoid the privatization of higher education; offer scholarships to students from marginalized sections; and, work towards including more women in the higher education bracket. Speaking to Gyaanoba about the issue, Jyotirao said,

"Just as England has made education compulsory for all in its own country, so also it should happen in India too. Sir Macaulay's old rules are not working in the new order of things.

Jyotirao held a meeting of all his friends and Satyashodhaks and read out the draft of his letter to them. As the meeting was in progress, Shaahir Dhondiram barged in huffing and announced,

"Tatyasaab, I am going to go to Kashi!"

Everyone was stunned with this announcement. No one understood what had prompted this outburst!

"What happened, Shaahir? Why this sudden decision to go to Kashi?" asked Jyotirao.

"I'm going to go there to study the Vedas!" the Shaahir replied.

"And what has prompted this sudden decision?" Jyotirao persisted.

"Tatyasaab, the Brahmins of Bhamburde have insulted us Satyashodhaks."

"What happened?" Jyotirao asked calmly.

"At yesterday's program, when I said the Veda-granthas were actually Bheda-granthas (scriptures promoting divisiveness), they started cursing me in public. They said I had no brain of my own, and I only parroted what you taught me."

Hearing this, Jyotirao said,

"Shaahir, first of all, remove the thought of having being insulted, from your mind. What's so new in what those Brahmins said? They have been saying all this for years. One day, everyone will realize what is the truth and what is not. Till then, we should continue doing our work. That's it. Anyways, why did you come so late? I was expecting you earlier..."

Shaahir did not respond. He was still agitated. Seeing that, Jyotirao again pacified him saying,

"Shaahir, if someone presses our weak nerve, don't we react in anger? It is the same thing with the Brahmins. And, why are you getting so agitated at being called brainless by those people who themselves have been behaving brainlessly for years on end? Do they themselves know their scriptures properly? They have only been learning the words by rote and parroting them before the ignorant audience who looks at them as God. Do not react in haste. Do learn the Vedas by all means, but why do you need to go to Kashi for that? You will find hundreds of Brahmin teachers in Pune if you wish to learn the Vedas."

"No, Tatyasaab. Those hypocrites will prefer teaching a British man, but will not teach their own countryman from a lower class."

Jyotirao tried a lot to dissuade Shaahir, but he had come decided that he would go to Kashi. Finally, Jyotirao said to him,

"Well, if you are so sure about going to Kashi, then please go. But then, study the Vedas in such a way that you will be able to identify the seeds of divisiveness cleverly hidden in them. Unless someone like you comes back armed with solid proof, we will not be able to issue a formidable challenge to the Brahmins. The Vedas hold proof to how the Aryans invaded our land and enslaved the original inhabitants. Go and search for those proofs that will enlighten our ignorant masses and empower them for a better tomorrow. I wish you all the luck."

Soon after, Shaahir Dhondiram indeed left for Kashi. A group of Satyashodhaks had gone to see him off at the railway station.

In due course, the vacuum left by Shaahir Dhondiram was filled by a young shaahir named Bhimrao Mahamuni.

The labor movement had started gaining momentum in

Mumbai. They were wanting Jyotirao to come to Mumbai and give a few speeches. However, after submitting his report to the Hunter Commission, Jyotirao had become busy with yet another important task.

It was being proposed to pass a resolution for sanctioning Rs. 3.25 lakhs for building the new vegetable market. However, that was going to escalate the costs of the individual lots in the markets, beyond the reach of the poor vendors. Jyotirao decided to strongly protest this resolution – not just for the benefit of the vendors, but also to exhort the Corporation to spend a chunk of that money on education of the masses.

Of course, as always, there were many opponents to this view too. In fact, there were many vocal opponents of Jyotirao's work, who showed their narrow-mindedness in myriad ways on various occasions. For instance, when Tukaram Nathuji Naik retired from his job in the Corporation, it was decided to honor him with a farewell gift of a nice clock. However, the proposal was shot down out of casteist views, just because Naik was a Christian. But, the same people thought nothing of giving a great farewell to a corrupt official like Narso Ramchandra, just because he was of their caste.

When Jyotirao had tried to expose the corrupt actions of Narso Ramchandra in the purchase of asbestos sheets and tried to move a no-confidence vote against him, the latter received unanimous support from his clique who claimed that there were not enough proofs against Narso Ramchandra to prove that he was corrupt!

Jyotirao voiced strong opposition to the proposal of the vegetable market, as soon as it was tabled. However, the cunning Brahmin lobby managed to cow down this opposition very soon.

Nevertheless, Jyotirao was not disheartened. He decided to take up another important matter with the Corporation. The heat had become unrelenting, and Jyotirao could see many thirsty Mahars and Maangs roaming around the streets, begging for a sip of water. He decided to table a proposal, demanding that all public drinking water facilities should be made open for even the Ati Shoodras.

77

One afternoon, a horse carriage was running on the streets of Mumbai. It was taking Jyotirao Phule, Narayanrao Lokhande, Yeshwantrao Manerikar, and Anandrao Talcherikar to the Mumbai market.

This time, Jyotirao had stayed in Mumbai for quite a long duration. His speeches regarding the conditions and problems of the farmers, were becoming hugely appealing for the laborers who were thronging for Jyotirao's meetings. Many of these laborers had originally been farmers. The famine, and continuous torment by money-lenders, had forced them to give up farming and move to the city to become laborers. Thus, Jyotirao's speeches held a lot of importance for them.

Many eminent people of Mumbi would also attend Jyotirao's speeches. They would be impressed by his thorough study and passionate oratory. The speech that he gave at the Phoolmali Hall, proved specially popular. From then on, Jyotirao began getting requests to write a book on the problems being faced by farmers.

This Mumbai visit accorded many good friends for Jyotirao. These included, Anandrao Talcherikar, Nagu Sayaji from Tardeo, and Madhavrao Rokade from Mandvi.

Madhavrao Rokade's dedication and hard work proved to be an inspiration for Jyotirao himself. Madhavrao was a paraplegic. Yet, he ran a school that was so renowned for its excellent education, that students would come from far off areas to seek admission in the same.

Madhavrao did not have enough funds to run the school, but he never spread his hands before anybody to help him with money. Whatever money would be collected via fees, would go in disbursing salaries to the teachers. Madhavrao would not take a penny out of those earnings, for himself. His son would also work in the school as a teacher. His wife and daughter would sell vegetables to run the household expenses.

Madhavrao was renowned for being a just and generous teacher. Born in a small hamlet called Nirgudi in Junnar, Madhavrao's childhood was filled with immense toil. He grew up in abject poverty, and in his teenage years, he came to Bhiwandi to work at his aunt's hotel. During this time, Madhavrao lost both his legs and thus it became difficult for him to continue working in the hotel. He then started a school to earn a living, but that earned him the wrath of his own mother, who turned Madhavrao and his teenage wife out of their house. Ridden with poverty with no roof over their heads, the couple took shelter in an empty, crumbling house that was left alone by others for apparently being haunted. Nevertheless, Madhavrao started living there and also started his school in the same house. In a small time, that school became so famous that even the Brahmins and Prabhus started sending their children to study there alongside children of the lower castes! After a while, Madhavrao left Bhiwandi and came to Mumbai, where he started a school at Chinchbunder. When that space started falling short, he shifted the school to Mandvi. Jyotirao held a very high opinion about Madhavrao, who had committed himself dedicatedly to the cause of education, in spite of all the challenges that came in his way.

In spite of it being winter, Mumbai was humid and hot. Jyotirao was walking down a street, when he was a marriage procession at a distance. It was a grand procession. The bride was decked up in jewelry and made to sit in an equally bedecked horse carriage.

As the procession came closer, Jyotirao noticed that the accompanying bridesmaids all wore a tell-tale bright red vermillion mark on their forehead and had left their hair loose. With a start, Jyotirao realized that this was not an ordinary marriage procession, but in fact that of a Devdasi's wedding to God! The procession was moving ahead slowly to the beat of cymbals and praises being sung to the Goddess Yalamma.

At that moment, Anandrao, who was accompanying Jyotirao, said,

"Tatyasaheb, you are doing so much work to reform our society. Please also do think about doing something to stop this heinous practice. It may not have proliferated that much in Pune yet, but in Mumbai, and especially among the lower classes, this practice has taken a strong root. Falling prey to superstitious beliefs, many ignorant and illiterate people are getting their young, pre-teen daughters 'married' to the Gods. In reality, this is just a sweet way of pushing those tender girls into prostitution! These people are as much responsible as the Brahmins who allow this ritual under the name of religion, and the rich strata who does not oppose it for obvious reasons, for spoiling the lives of hundreds of girls under the pretext of religious beliefs. Men from rich households pay enormous amounts of money to take the virginity of such tender girls. The girls are wedded to a sword and then sent to bed with God. Now since God Himself cannot come down for the 'ritual', it is the temple priest who gets the honor of deflowering the girl. After that, the girl is supposed to serve any man who comes to her, thinking of him as an embodiment of God! How horrific is all this?! Something needs to be done immediately to stop girls from being made into nothing but playthings and prostitutes like this, Tatyasaheb!"

Jyotirao could feel the fervency of Anandrao's words as he now saw the face of the innocent young girl as the procession moved in front of him. Her large eyes gazed around in curiosity; she was oblivious to the horrors that awaited her. The people, including women, dancing around her did not care a bit for the torment that lay in front of the poor girl. They were dancing as if it was some merry occasion. The enormity of it all caused Jyotirao to reel back in horror.

He looked at Anandrao with determination on his face and remarked,

"We need to stop this marriage! At any cost! Immediately!"

Anandrao was taken aback at Jyotirao's stance. He stammered,

"But.... Tatyasaheb...."

"No, Anandrao. There is no time to counsel these people. They are beyond counseling. We need to file a police complaint immediately."

Anandrao could see the repercussions of that act. The mother of this girl, who was being made a Devdasi, was a renowned and powerful rich woman. She ad the support of many big people behind her. He explained to Jyotirao,

"Tatyasaheb, the mother of this girl is a rich woman. However, she has fallen prey to superstition to fulfil her greed. Probably, this is her only daughter. Yet, she has become ready to sacrifice the child's life."

Jyotirao replied,

"The superstition is bad enough, but what is worse is the naked greed that is pushing this innocent girl into hell. I'm sure that the woman will not listen to any counsel. We need to take legal action."

Yeshwantrao, who was also accompanying them, remarked,

"In that case, Tatyasaheb, we should go to the Police Superintendent of Girgaon Police Station. He must be at home right now. Let us go and meet him."

Yeshwantrao shared a good rapport with the Superintendent, as he have lessons in Marathi to the latter. The trio went to the Superintendent's house. After hearing out Jyotirao's complaint, the officer said,

"I agree with you. But, this subject involves religious sentiments. We have strict orders from above to not interfere in subjects involving the religious sentiments of the natives."

After the bad experience of 1857, the Queen had issued orders that no British officer would henceforth intervene in any religious matter pertaining to the natives.

Jyotirao tried explaining in various ways that this issue was not religious in nature; but, the officer refused to budge from his stance. Finally, Jyotirao requested him,

"Okay. If you cannot stop this ceremony from happening, then please come along with us to the Police Commissioner's house. We will try speaking to him."

The Superintendent agreed. He was ready to look into the matter if the Commissioner permitted him to do so. They all went to meet Commissioner Sauter at his sprawling bungalow. The Superintendent sounded the Commissioner out about Jyotirao's complaint. Jyotirao also explained that it was necessary to stop such degrading rituals and hand out strict punishments to those parents who thought nothing about spoiling their girls' lives like this.

Commissioner Sauter patiently heard them all out, and ordered the Superintendent to take due steps to stop the ceremony on an urgent basis.

Jyotirao, Anandrao and Yeshwantra were immensely relieved! They profusely thanked the Commissioner and came out of his bungalow to see the Superintendent rushing out to issue due orders.

Soon enough, a never-before incident happened. A Devdasi's marriage ceremony was halted! All the people who were responsible for bringing about this 'marriage', were arrested. Mumbai was shaken to the core. The rich and powerful people started bubbling in anger, even as the religious men started trembling in rage at this unwanted interference in their domain! Thankfully, they never got to know who was behind starting this revolt against their traditions; and it was just as well, because had they got to know the name of the person, a terrible revolt would have ensued in Mumbai!

Tilak and Agarkar were due to finish their sentences in a few days. Narayanrao had planned for a grand program to welcome them both; but, it was not possible for Jyotirao to wait any longer. The seeds of a new book had been sown in his mind. He was getting reminded of the promise he had made to Mama Parmanand, five years ago. Jyotirao could no longer put off writing about the problems and conditions of farmers.

Promising Narayanrao that the Satyashodhak Samaj would soon host another welcome for the brave and forthright editors in Pune soon, Jyotirao left Mumbai.

However, even after returning from Mumbai, Jyotirao kept a keen eye on what was happening over there. After the episode of a Devdasi' marriage ceremony being halted, the Brahmins had started yelling aloud about the government interfering in their 'personal and religious' matters. Many of Mumbai's rich and powerful men were also displeased with the government. Everyone knew that their real grouse was that, after this, they were not going to be able to exploit innocent young girls for free!

However, after a few weeks, Anandrao wrote to Jyotirao, informing him that the marriage ceremony that he had so successfully halted, finally did take place. Jyotirao was immensely sad to read that news.

A few days later, Tilak and Agarkar came back to Pune after receiving a warm welcome in Mumbai. Pushing away his despondency over the Devdasi episode, Jyotirao started making preparations to welcome the young men with pomp. Nevertheless, he did not forget about the subject of the Devdasis. He wrote a big article in 'Deenbandhu', highlighting the evils of the Devdasi practice and exhorting the government to ban the practice with immediate effect. Jyotirao also appealed to people to support the ban...but in spite of many such articles, popular response to stopping the practice, was lukewarm. Albeit, that did not dishearten Jyotirao; he kept on writing in the hope that some day, people would realize the injustice being meted out to innocent girls and would stand unified against the same....

78

Jyotirao was immersed in writing his latest book, 'Aasud'. He had already finished two chapters and was working on the third one. In order to be able to concentrate on his writing, Jyotirao had come to the farm early in morning, savoring the peace and quietude he got there. After finishing the first two chapters, Jyotirao had read them out to a bunch of farmers from Wangani and Kurul. After they affirmed that the writing indeed touched their hearts, Jyotirao moved onto the third chapter.

His head was buzzing with myriad thoughts. After having written fearlessly about the Shoodra princes who revered Brahmins as God, and about the Brahmins who felt no compunction in looting the poor Shoodras by making them undergo empty rituals for every occasion, Jyotirao moved onto the new chapter. In this chapter, he was writing about how the British government was hand-in-glove with the Brahmins in subjugating the already tormented lower castes. The chapter was going include information about how the Aryan Brahmins came from Iran, how the Shoodra farmers are the original inhabitants of Hindustan, and how attributes like courage and good sense are not transferred by heredity but by education. Once again, Jyotirao had cracked his whip on the clerical and administrative class that was shamelessly enjoying on the money that they would gather from poor farmers by the way of enormous taxes. The rich were getting richer, and the poor were getting poorer. Farmers continued to be oppressed by indeterminate monsoons and indiscriminate taxation. The tax-free British merchandise had caused many indigenous merchants to go to the lowest depths of poverty. Not knowing what else to do, the thus tormented people were drowning their sorrows in cheap liquor. Jyotirao wrote:

"…. See how the native worker is taking bribes from our own farmers and dancing like a rabbit in front of the European workers. This extravagance has to be curtailed with immediate effect. Instead of paying unjustly high salaries to its officers and clerks, it will do well for the government to think about educating the lower class masses, and also freeing them of the burden of indiscriminate taxes and tolls. If this change does not happen soon, it won't be long before the tormented people surge up in a revolt that will have catastrophic effects for their tormentors."

After finishing the third chapter, Jyotirao started feeling a bit lighter – as if, some burden had been lifted off his chest. However, far from becoming complacent, he immediately started thinking about the fourth chapter, which would include topics like the present condition of agriculture, ways to bring improvements in this situation, and how to build a spirit of entrepreneurship in the farmers.

Soon, it was lunchtime. Jyotirao came out of the thatched hut that he had built in the farm and was working out of, to see farmers coming back from the farms to eat their meals in the shade.

One day, Gyaanoba had suggested to Jyotirao that he build a small bungalow in place of this thatched hut. That time, Jyotirao had said to him,

"What is the need for that, my son? For us farmers, a thatched hut is a true mansion. My hut provides ample ventilation, and also gives enough shelter from rain and sunlight. Why do I need anything more?"

But now, his mind was toying with the idea that Gyaanoba had proposed. Jyotirao had built the thatched hut with Sahadubuva's help. It was a nicely built structure with a small staircase that led to an attic upstairs. The surrounding banana plantation made the atmosphere cool and pleasant, according a peaceful sleep to the person staying inside.

Add to that, the neighboring farms of Maanjri had also become beautiful; what with the farmers emulating Jyotirao and turning their once-arid lands into paradise.

Jyotirao's farm remained the biggest attraction for his neighbors at Maanjri. Every Sunday, Jyotirao would organize a farm-party for which his family members and neighbors would be invited. He would himself take a horse carriage to Hadapsar, bring along his friends to the farm, and then, the whole day would be spent in fun-filled chatter, singing, and lending a helping hand in the farm. In the afternoon, Jyotirao would excuse himself to go to the attic of his thatched hut and would get immersed in reading and writing. Teatime would be another fun time, with fresh produce from the farm being laid out for the attendees. By evening, someone would inevitably come with a message that some person is waiting to see Jyotirao. He would then set off on horseback to Pune, to meet his guest and start a new week the next day.

However, this particular Sunday was different from the rest. It had been ten days since Ganpatrao Kale had expired, and Jyotirao was going to go to Hadapsar for the tenth-day ritual.

Jyotirao fed some grass to his horse and started inspecting the rows of flowery shrubs. Earlier, there were many fruit trees in the farm, but after they suffered a loss in the sale of fruit, now they only grew flowery shrubs, sugarcane, and bananas.

He drew Sahadubuva's attention to some shrubs that were drying out owing to lack of water. Sahadubuva assured him that he would look into it after breakfast and asked Jyotirao to join in with the neighboring farmers to eat.

"No, thank you, Sahadubuva. I have eaten an early breakfast today, and I need to leave for Hadapsar soon" replied Jyotirao, adding, "In fact, you go ahead and eat your breakfast. I shall water the plants. Get me the can here."

Seeing Jyotirao manning the canister of water, the other farmers started laughing in disbelief. Jyotirao said to them with a smile,

"Why are you laughing? Is it so unbelievable that I'm tending to the plants? I have been farming since my childhood. In fact, watering the plants is one of my favorite tasks."

Usually, while working in the farm, Jyotirao would sing some a rural melody at the top of his voice. His singing would cause bouts of laughter, prompting Jyotirao to remark,

"My friends, I cannot help it! We farmers toil in the burning sun with no entertainment to keep us engaged. Thus, we are compelled to turn or own entertainers; and, nothing better than singing to entertain us while we work."

However, today there was no song of Jyotirao's lips. He kept watering the plants wordlessly.

Some time later, Sahadubuva's son Mahadu came and hid behind his father. Mahadu was very afraid of Tatya. He had not gotten into a habit of attending school regularly, but there was a time when Mahadu would like to bunk school and while away his time in the farms. Nothing angered Jyotirao more than seeing the children of poor people, wasting their time doing nothing. He had thus scolded Mahadu a couple of times; even spanked him a bit. From there on, Mahadu would be afraid to go into front of Tatya.

When Jyotirao realized that young Mahadu had started feeling afraid of him, he felt very sad, and decided that henceforth he would not spank any child, whatsoever the reason may be.

In the afternoon, Jyotirao fed grass to the bullocks, gathered his writing supplies, and climbed his horse. Another topic was swirling in his head for the last few days. The Municipal elections were round the corner. From this time onwards, a people-chosen candidate would be becoming Sheriff, instead of a government-chosen one.

Jyotirao came towards Gyaanoba's house. Gyaanoba was sitting with his students. Seeing Jyotirao, he got up and welcomed him warmly, saying,

"Welcome, Tatyasaheb, welcome."

The students also bowed reverentially before Jyotirao.

Gyaanoba kept some notebooks in Jyotirao's hands, for him to inspect how the studies were going on. One particularly elder student had already caught Jyotirao's eye. His name was Sitaram Tarkunde. He would be present for every speech that Jyotirao would give in the village. Sitaram was an intelligent boy with a very good handwriting. He had written the final drafts of the first two chapters of 'Aasud'. Generally, Jyotirao would find it difficult to rewrite the final drafts, but had never hired a writer for the same. However, for 'Aasud', Jyotirao was looking out for a writer, when he came across Sitaram in Gyaanoba's school. On his part, Sitaram had been happy to help Tatyasaheb.

Sitaram's father, Ragunathrao Tarkunde, had a farm where he grew betel leaves. In spite of being born in a Brahmin household, Sitaram did not have parents who valued education. The family also did not have much value in the Brahmin community. In such a scenario, when Sitaram enrolled himself in Gyaanoba's school, he found more than a teacher in Gyaanoba – he found a parent and a mentor – and soon became a part of Gyaanoba's family.

When Jyotirao handed the draft of the third chapter of 'Aasud' to Gyaanoba, he was very happy to hand them over to Sitaram, with due instructions to make the changes.

That afternoon, Jyotirao and Gyaanoba went to Ganpatrao Kale's house. Many people had congregated there. Jyotirao offered his condolences to the family members and consoled Govinda. Soon, lunch was served. Jyotirao had his lunch with the others, and took their leave after agreeing to have a public reading of the first chapters of 'Aasud' in the meeting on Saturday.

79

Many Satyashodhaks, including Ramji Santuji Aawate and Damodar Savlaram, had gathered at the Tardeo bungalow of contractor Nagu Sayaji. Narayanrao Lokhande of 'Deenbandhu' was presiding over the meeting. Jyotirao had come down from

Pune to read out the three chapters of 'Aasud'.

After a brief welcome speech, Jyotirao stood up to read the extracts:

"Dear audience, I'm writing this book to highlight and analyze the over-worsening plight of our Shoodra farmer brethren. There are many political and religious reasons for this degradation. The hypocritical and cruel Brahmins are tormenting our farmers in the religious realm, as well as by the virtue of the fact that they are getting an upper hand in the government machinery because the government's European workers are lazy and useless. This book, which I have decided to title as 'Shetkaryache Aasud' , is being written to make our farmer brethren aware of their rights and how they can exercise them in order to have a better and free life."

Jyotirao's profound oratory was at its best as he spoke emphatically about the social conditions of farmers, the torment and problems they undergo, and the role of the British, the money lenders, and the Brahmins in all this. He spoke fearlessly about how this trio of tormentors is stripping a farmer off the cloth of this back. The farmer's whip was crackling boldly on the issues and problem-creators. Speaking about the princes of the princely states, Jyotirao bellowed:

"The Brahmin clerks and officials working for the princely states are so sly and selfish, that they do not let the princes develop a fondness for education and morality. While these princes can do so much for the upliftment of their Shoodra brethren, they are blindly wasting their time in nodding to whatever their Brahmin officials are asking them to do."

"What more do I say about the Machiavellian antics of the Brahmins? Their intelligence is 'best spent' is opposing us. But the fault lies with our community members too. They do not bother to even think of a Brahmin is incompetent or a dumb fool. As long as he can parrot the verses from some scripture, they are happy to prostrate at his feet and pay him ridiculous amounts of money, food, clothing and what not. It is because of our ignorant behavior that these Brahmins get easy opportunities to make every small festivity an occasion for extorting money and favors from us."

"The Brahmins have etched clever segregations between work of intelligence and work of physical labor. The root cause of all our problems is the proliferation of a big class of Brahmin priests who earn pots of money by sitting idle. Since the doors of knowledge have been closed for Shoodras, they have not been able to contribute to the productivity of the nation. Even the religious reformers do not feel like doing anything to uplift the lower classes, especially the farmers. The farmer class is badly caught between the Brahmins and the British."

Further, Jyotirao exhorted the government to do something proactive to save the farmers from this vicious cycle of ignorance, poverty, torment by the Brahmins, and the clerical class.

He was speaking for almost three hours straight. After he finished reading all the three chapters, Jyotirao drank a whole tumbler of water. There was pin-drop silence among the audience. They were stunned by the intensity of Jyotirao's writings, and wondered that if three chapters could have such a profound effect on their minds, what would the rest of the book shape up to be like?!

After a while, Nagu Sayaji broke the silence and said to Jyotirao,

"Tatyasaheb, please finish this book and get it published. It needs to reach to the government. Until then, they are not going to be roused from their convenient sleep. We all are ready to chip in with the expenses that will be incurred for the publishing process."

Everybody agreed with Nagu Sayaji. After that, Jyotirao gave an idea of what the rest of the chapters would entail, and then the meeting was called to an end. Narayanrao Lokhande gave a vote of thanks, in which he requested Jyotirao to allow 'Deenbandhu' to publish the first three chapters of 'Aasud'.

During this trip to Mumbai, Jyotirao was staying at Swami Aiyyavaru's house. A lot of credit for this trip of Jyotirao's, went to Swamiji. The work of the Neetiprasarak Sabha that Swamiji had established, was spreading fast all across Mumbai region. The Sabha had already established branches at Mandvi, Paydhonie, Dongari etc., from where, it was working incessantly towards promoting social causes like women empowerment, alcohol de-addiction, spread of education and so on. His work for women empowerment was receiving a specially good response. He got immense help from people like Simian Benjamin and his wife Rebecca for this work. Swamiji had arranged for a lecture of Jyotirao's during the upcoming Sunday's meeting of the Sabha.

One day, Swamiji and Jyotirao were going to Kamathipura for a meeting. While returning home, Swamiji said to Jyotirao,

"Tatyasaheb, you say that God is the ultimate justice and most loving of all. But then, does He not see the pitiable conditions of the farmers? Does He not see the little girls who are being offered as Devdasis? Does He not take cognizance of the injustice going on in His name?"

In recent times, Swamiji's thoughts were leaning towards atheism. Even though he was a Satyashodhak, he did not blindly follow everything propounded in that sect; instead preferring to weigh every principle against his rational mind and only then accepting it. For instance, he opined that it is good to speak the truth, not because God is watching, but because truth is what prevails and gives you peace of mind. He also did not agree with the mixture of religion and morality that, thinkers like Agarkar had started doing in their writings and speeches. Swamiji's views would confound many people. Even Jyotirao did not agree with a Satyshodhak leaning towards atheism. He said,

"Swamiji, it won't be right to hold God responsible for these happenings. I would rather hold the Brahmins – who see themselves as embodiment of God – to be responsible for all these social and economic evils. On this earth, a man has become man's worst enemy. Man has stopped fearing God. What can we expect from such people, who have stopped fearing the omnipresent and all-pervading higher power? They are going to fall to the lowest depths of being that can ever be. The time is not too far when the children of Shoodras and Ati Shoodras will be educated and empowered enough to fight off the injustice meted out to them."

Swamiji knew that he and Jyotirao would never concur on their views on this subject. The horse carriage reached Swamiji's house and the discussion ended there itself.

Swamiji invited Jyotirao for lunch and soon, a group of small children congregated around him, clamoring for stories and treats that their favorite Tatya was famous for.

That evening, as Jaya Karadi, Raju Babaji, Bhagoji Dulaji etc., sat chatting with Jyotirao, word came in that Ramchandrarao Dhamanaskar had arrived from Baroda. This gentleman had kept the Satyashodhak Samaj's flag flying high in Baroda. Jyotirao was very pleased to see him.

"Tatyasaheb, I'm very sorry to have missed today morning's meeting. I was not aware that you were in Mumbai" said Ramchandrarao.

"No problem. I would be happy to read out 'Aasud' to government officials like you, again. If the message reaches via you to the Maharaj of Baroda, and something good comes out of it for the farmers, I would be the happiest person around" replied Jyotirao.

"Tatyasaheb, then please come to Baroda. I shall arrange a reading of 'Aasud' over there."

Ramchandrarao had been insisting Jyotirao to visit Baroda since many years. Jyotirao remembered meeting the Maharaj of Baroda as a young man who had recently taken over the reins of the kingdom. An intelligent, sensitive and educated man, this king was very different from other rulers who did not think about their subjects. The Maharaj of Baroda was well-known for initiating many projects for his subjects' benefit.

Thumbing through the draft of 'Aasud', Ramchandrarao again said,

"Tatyasaheb, I'm telling you, Maharaj will be very pleased to host you in Baroda for a reading."

"But...the book is not yet complete. How can I read an incomplete draft before such a big man?" Jyotirao wondered.

"Oh, not to worry. Whatever you have written, is enough to give an idea to Maharaj. The rest of the book is bound to follow. I would say, please come along with me to Baroda from here itself" Ramchandrarao insisted.

"From here? Directly?"

"Yes, Tatyasaheb. Then again, monsoons will begin and you will get busy in farming. I shall write a letter to Kaku myself. She can berate me all she wants; I shall even come to Pune to take her scolding. But for now, please come with me."

Jyotirao could not refuse anymore. Seeing this, Ramchandrarao added,

"Maharaj would also like to meet Mama Parmanand. He really admired Mama's article in 'Indian Spectator'".

Jyotirao was pleased to know that the Maharaj of Baroda, Sayajirao Gaekwad, had liked the article written by Mama, in spite of its scathing language. Before this also, Mama had written a series of strongly-worded articles regarding the brash and thoughtless ways in which several Hindi princes operated their kingdoms. The articles had started after a particular incident with the prince of Jamnagar, and were supposed to serve as advice for the newly-minted Maharaj of Baroda, who had ascended the throne just then. His subjects were looking at the young king with lot of hopes.

Jyotirao was happy that the Maharaj of Baroda was hoping to meet Mama Parmanand; it signified that he was not displeased with Jyotirao, who had also written scathingly about Hindi princes who were operating blindly on the advice of their Brahmin clerks.

However, Mama Parmanand was not keeping too well, and

it would not be possible for him to make the long journey to Baroda. Ramchandrarao said to Jyotirao,

"I did give him Maharaj's message, but seeing his delicate health, I could not insist too much. But, Tatyasaheb, you must come. Please do not refuse."

Ramchandrarao's requests also received support from Swamiji. Jyotirao simply could not refuse.

"Tatyasaheb, I'm also going to meet Ramji Santuji and Yande Shetji. Maharaj has really liked their newsletter, 'Shetkaryancha Kaivari'. He feels that such a newsletter should be published from Baroda as well. Dr. Shivappa has already recommended them to Maharaj. If you also tell them, it will be really nice..." insisted Ramchandrarao.

However, Jyotirao refused the request saying,

"Ramchandrarao, our movement has also started getting eclipsed by petty disagreements and arguments. Thus, it will be better if you speak to them yourself, please."

Both these people had extracted their capital invested in 'Deenbandhu', and started their own newsletter. Jyotirao had faced immense distress in this matter, even though he was not directly related to it in any way.

Ramchandrarao understood Jyotirao's predicament; the topic ended there itself.

Then, Ramchandrarao broached the topic of the new palace that Maharaj was intending to build at Baroda. While on a lookout for a good contractor for this work, Ramchandrarao had suggested Swami Aiyyavaru's name. Ramchandrarao had already met Swamiji two-three times in this regard. This time, the talks went to the next level.

The next morning, Ramchandrarao sent a message for Aawate and Yande to come and meet him. After they came, he told them about Sayajirao Gaekwad's wish to meet both of them for the proposed newsletter. He also promised them that they would receive all possible help for this work.

The next day was a Sunday. After finishing the lecture in

front of the Neetiprasarak Sabha's members, Jyotirao started off for Baroda along with Ramchandrarao Dhamanaskar. A huge crowd had come to the railway station to see them off. The Satyashodhaks were thrilled that the problems of farmers were going to get an audience with the renowned king of Baroda.

This was the first time that Jyotirao was going to Baroda. He had heard a lot about Sayajirao's goodness, but still he wondered if the busy king would have time to listen to the plight of poor farmers.

Jyotirao's doubts were unfounded. He received such a warm welcome from Sayajirao Gaekwad, that he was overwhelmed beyond measure. Sayajirao well remembered his first introduction with Jyotirao at Pune.

Over the next few days of Jyotirao's stay, Sayajirao would cull out time from his busy schedule to listen to the reading of 'Aasud' and hold fervent discussions with Jyotirao about the problems of farmer men and women. Sayajirao was impressed with Jyotirao for his dedication and perseverance towards achieving the betterment of farmers and women. Sayajirao himself was a welcome change in the array of Hindi princes who, otherwise, would blindly follow the advice of their administrative officers. Sayajirao would listen to everyone and then take decisions as per how they appealed to his intellect and heart, both.

Jyotirao was stunned to see the various projects that Sayajirao had initiated for the social and economic betterment of his subjects.

During his Baroda visit, Jyotirao also met a lot of Satyashodhaks. Devrao Thosar's son-in-law Vasudeorao Lingoji Birje, was serving in the palace. Dr. Shivappa Rajanna, who had helped Jyotirao in many projects while in Pune, was serving as Sayajirao's personal physician. Dr. Shivappa had offered stellar help while starting the 'Victoria Balashram'.

What started as a two-day stay, went on for several days.

Finally, Jyotirao took everyone's leave and set off for Pune. He was requested to complete the book at the earliest and send a copy to the Baroda palace.

From Baroda, Jyotirao returned to Mumbai. He handed over the three chapters of 'Aasud' to Narayanrao, and met with Moropant, Mama Parmanand, Madhavrao Rokade and Behramji Malbari, the editor of 'Indian Spectator'. Then, he returned to Pune.

During his return journey, the fourth chapter of the book started shaping up in Jyotirao's mind. He was going to elucidate about the pitiful conditions of farmers and farming, topping it up with solutions to improve these conditions, in the fifth chapter.

On returning home, Jyotirao started penning down the fourth and fifth chapters without wasting any time. Monsoons were due any moment, and he wanted to finish off these chapters before getting busy with sowing new crops.

Jyotirao started writing the rough drafts; Govinda Ganpat Kale got busy in making final copies of the same.

In the meantime, the first two chapters of 'Aasud' got published in 'Deenbandhu'. As expected, they kicked up a storm in the government's face!

Jyotirao got emboldened; he remembered the encouragement given by Maharaj Sayajirao Gaekwad, and Nagu Sayaji. He was soon going to start the publishing process for 'Aasud'. But just then, an unpleasant event occurred that put brakes on Jyotirao's plans. The third chapter of 'Aasud' came back unpublished from 'Deenbandhu'. The editors thought that the writing in the third chapter had become overtly fiery and would cause more harm than good. They feared facing lawsuits if they published this chapter. Whether Narayanrao Lokhande's fear was real or unfounded, was a question in itself. But all said and done, he had retreated after giving massive promises of support.

Jyotirao's dream of seeing 'Aasud' published, thus got

canned. No other publisher was ready to take on this challenge. 'Deenbandhu' press was the only one that had shown readiness for publishing this 'scandalous' book, and now, even that dream had been crushed to bits. Jyotirao did not wish to mull over why this happened. He did not want to even discuss the topic anymore; nor did he hope that Narayanrao would change his mind. If he got so afraid of publishing three chapters, there was no hope that he would dare to publish the whole book.

Nevertheless, Jyotirao did not stop writing. There were many events happening around him – some pleasant, some unpleasant – but Jyotirao steadfastly concentrated on his writing.

Krishnarao had resigned from his job and returned to Pune. With the support of Lokahitawadi, Raosaheb Ranade, Dr. Vishram Ramji, and Adv. Gangarambhau Mhaske, Krishnarao had started the 'Su-Shikshan Gruha' in Somwar Peth. It was a hostel that provided lodging and food at subsidized rates, for students whose parents did not have the time or means to pay attention to their wards' studies. Even though Krishnarao's work was in keeping with the Satyashodhak principles, he did not receive any substantial support from the Samaj members. He also did not approach the Samaj for help; preferring to ask outsiders for support instead. Jyotirao was systematically eliminated from this whole process.

Monsoons arrived; Jyotirao finished his work at the farm and again sat to write 'Aasud'. He made three copies of the book and sent one copy to Maharaj Sayajirao Gaekwad. Tiding over many roadblocks, the second copy was sent to Governor General of India, Lord Dufferin at Calcutta. Many of Jyotirao's friends and well-wishers, including Devrao Thosar and Vinayak Bapuji Bhandarkar, opined that Jyotirao was making a big mistake by sending 'Aasud' to the government. They feared that this act would earn displeasure of the government for Jyotirao. However, Jyotirao was firm about doing what he had decided – repercussions unheeded. Explaining his stance to his friends, Jyotirao said,

"If 'Aasud' manages to open the eyes of this sleepy government, ultimately it will be to their benefit itself. If they read unbiased-ly about the problems faced by farmers and heed the solutions suggested to improve their conditions, ultimately it will lead to an increase in revenue for the government coffers itself. As of now, they have been mislead by the selfish Brahmin officials. Someone needs to rouse them from that slumber. Why should that person not be me? I do not care about the repercussions. This message needs to reach the government on an imminent basis."

Around 2 months after a copy of 'Aasud' was dispatched to Lord Dufferin, the 'Deenbandhu' carried a very confusing editorial in which, the editor thanked God for giving him the good sense to not publish the third chapter of the book, and strangely, even alleging that Jyotirao was not a friend but actually a foe of 'Deenbandhu' and had conspired to bury 'Deenbandhu' under a sea of defamatory lawsuits by asking them to publish excerpts from his controversial book.

Even though Jyotirao had faced many such false accusations till date, this one hurt him immensely, because it was made by a fellow Satyashodhak. He did not react, but in his heart, Jyotirao was very sad that the editor of 'Deenbandhu' felt that Jyotirao was out to harm him, and that he felt that publishing the excerpts would cause them loss instead of benefit.

It was clear that the once unified Satyashodhak Samaj was now being hollowed by the termites of divisive politics for selfish gains.

80

Jyotirao went to the farm in the morning, and soon, that message reached the Phule house. Sadashivrao's health had deteriorated badly since the previous night. Savitribai asked Govinda to take the second horse and go to Maanjri, and herself went to the Govande's house.

Sadashivrao had been ill for many months. Before that, he had resigned from social work and devoted himself wholeheartedly to spirituality. Saraswatibai had also resigned completely from her social work.

It was very strange that Sadashivrao, who had once done so much work for the education of Shoodras and Ati Shoodras; who had taken the oath of Swadeshi, along with Sarvajanik Kaka; should change to this extent. Jyotirao was painfully surprised to see such a sea-change in his friend who, in the past, had been attracted to Christianity because he had got disillusioned with the Hindu religion for its web of rituals and mindless laws that he blamed for making his widowed sister go Sati.

In the last few years, most of Sadashivrao's time would go sitting near his father's memorial. He would spend hours on end, chanting mantras and meditating. He was obsessed with the idea of travelling on the Bhaktimarga , to reach moksha . He was frantically searching for a Guru who would lead him on this path. Apparently, one day he saw a dream wherein a Guru Maharaj told him that he was waiting for Sadashivrao at the mental hospital at Yerawada! Without further thought, Sadashivrao went to Yerwada and got back an old man along, claiming that this was his Guru Kaalbuva. No one ever understood what the real name of this man was. The man would keep cursing the people who came to meet him, and at times, would just yell, "Kaal aala", "Kaal aala " . That is how he came to be addressed as Kaalbuva.

Sadashivrao would devotedly look after Kaalbuva. Many people would throng to take his blessings. However, Kaalbuva did not live for too long. After his demise, Sadashivrao again set out in search of another Guru. He brought back another mendicant by the name of Kashinathbuva. Nevertheless, Sadashivrao and Kashinathbuva's paths separated sooner than expected. It so happened that, Sadashivrao took Kashinathbuva along with his family members, to Pandharpur for the annual pilgrimage. Over there, he had the misfortune of seeing his Guru engaged in some immoral act. The vision disillusioned Sadashivrao immensely, and he immediately left Kashinathbuva's company.

After this incident, he fell immensely ill. Many incidents and disillusionments had added up to making him a very broken man. Add to that, when his friend Prof. Keronana Chhatre died a sudden death, it turned out to be the last straw of Sadashivrao's tolerance. He kept chanting that, he would go behind his friend. Sadly, that is precisely what happened. Sadashivrao never got well, and soon left for his heavenly abode.

As she stepped into the Govande's house, the entire shared past flashed before Savitribai's eyes. Her husband had run his school from the Govande house. Savitribai would teach at that school. Sadashivrao would give stationery to the children. Saraswatibai would give them fresh food. In this period, Savitribai had bonded closely with Saraswatibai. The bond had later developed into pooling their resources for bringing about women empowerment.

In due course, even though ideological differences had risen among Jyotirao and Sadashivrao, the bond between the two families had remained intact as ever. Savitribai and Saraswatibai had also remained good friends through it all.

When Savitribai went to the Govande's house, she saw a visibly tired and pale-faced Saraswatibai sitting near her husband. She burst into tears on seeing Savitribai.

People were coming in and sitting wherever they could manage to get place. Sadashivrao was living his final few moments. Everyone was nervous.

Jyotirao came as soon as the message reached him at Maanjri. He sat besides his oldest friend, and held his hand in his own. Sadashivrao opened his eyes and smiled weakly at his friend. It was as if he was waiting for Jyotirao to come. Jyotirao felt a stab of sadness in his heart. Sadashivrao was trying to say something by moving his eyes and fluttering his lashes. But sadly, he never managed to convey what he wanted to. Death claimed him in the next few minutes!

Saraswatibai started howling in grief. Savitribai held her close and began comforting her.

As the news spread, people started coming in to see Sadashivrao for the last time. The Satyashodhaks began preparing for the last rites.

Raosaheb Ranade, Lokahitawadi, Sitarampant Chiplunkar, Krishnajipant Nulkar and many more people participated in the funeral. It was late evening by the time the funeral procession reached Omkareshwar. The flames of the funeral fire rose to lick the dark sky, even as Sadashivrao bid his adieu to the world.

That night, Jyotirao could not eat or sleep properly. The flames of his friend's pyre were still dancing in front of Jyotirao's eyes. He kept thinking about their days together at the Mission school.

'We were such idealistic youngsters that time! Every day would bring some or the other idea into our over enthusiastic brains. From thinking of converting to Christianity after being disillusioned by Hinduism, to thinking of becoming armed rebels to upturn the British government... we had seen so many dreams together. And now, my dear friend is gone...'

Jyotirao kept thinking that, had they not read books by authors like Thomas Penn, or not met people like Baba Sane at an impressionable age, probably they all would have shaped up differently. But life had definite plans etched out for them. Which is why, they kept meeting people like Baig chacha, Dr. Mitchell, Rev. Mitchell, Erskin Perry, Major Candy, Ram Jaykar, Dadoba Pandurang and so on. They were also supported by people like Keshavrao Bhavalkar, Annasaheb Chiplunkar, and Jagannathrao Sadashivji. Sadashivrao and Jyotirao had a lot of disagreements, arguments, and even fallouts in this entire journey; but never did it all affect their friendship adversely.

Their affection for each other and their familial ties, remained untouched. Their ideological differences never marred their personal relationship.

While working for the Sarvajanik Sabha, Sadashivrao would often come for the meetings of Satyashodhak Samaj. He never became a member of Satyashodhak Samaj, but he still respected the work they were doing. After Jyotirao excused himself from the work of running schools for the Mahars and Maangs, Sadashivrao took over that responsibility on Jyotirao's behalf. After he joined the Sarvajanik Sabha, he passed over the responsibility of those schools to the government's education department. His professional graph had also been one of sincerity and honor. After working as a teacher and clerk, he worked in the Imaan Commission department for 23 years. Having honourably retired from that job, Sadashivrao devoted all his time to the Sarvajanik Sabha. But, in the last few years of his life, he had withdrawn from all social work and concentrated his energies on spirituality.

Once enchanted with the idea of becoming Christian, in the final years of his life, Sadashivrao had given himself up to the mystical spiritual world of Hinduism.

A free-willed life had met an untimely end.

Jyotirao could not shake himself out of the waves of memories that kept crashing on his heart.

The last six months had brought a run of bad luck for Jyotirao. He had lost in the Municipal elections, even after running for candidature from two places. A few days later, Chimna Aai left for her heavenly abode. Till the end of her life, Chimna Aai earned her own living and lived alone in the house at Kasba Peth. In spite of Jyotirao's repeated requests, she refused to become a burden on him; preferring to be self-sufficient till the end. Jyotirao knew that it would never have been possible for his mother to walk on the path he had etched for himself; but, the difference of opinions should lead to such a wide chasm between mother and son, was something that he could never reconcile with.

His mother's death left a tremendous vacuum in Jyotirao's heart. He cried so much that no one dared to even pacify him. Jyotirao had not cried this much even after Saguna Aau's demise.

However, he did not get much time to mull over his grief. Pune was in the eye of yet another storm. Pandita Ramabai had got herself baptized during her stay in London. The fundamentalists of Pune were shell-shocked! They started screaming aloud that Ramabai had become corrupted. Newspapers started overflowing with heavy criticism regarding this 'morally corrupt' act of who the orthodox group had made their poster-girl. Jyotirao's prophecy had come true. Albeit late, but Ramabai had become disillusioned with the hypocrisy of Hinduism, and thus had opted to convert her religion.

On the other side, plans were afoot to start the 'Deenbandhu Sarvajanik Sabha' under the leadership of Krishnarao. The main aim of this Sabha was to reach the troubles of the farmers, to the government. In Baroda, the administration had started taking the suggestions of 'Aasud' seriously. Accordingly, officers were appointed to hear the farmers' problems and take due steps to rectify the same.

A meal of khichadi used to be served to Hindu and Muslim priests near the temple of Kedareshwar. That custom was stopped and the Rs. 30 lakh that used to be spent in this exercise, were diverted towards educating children and youngsters. The princely state of Baroda also gave impetus to women's education. Separate schools were opened up for girls and women. A newsletter by the name of 'Baroda Vatsal' was launched. Aawate and Yande shut down 'Shetkaryancha Kaivari' and shifted lock, stock & barrel to Baroda.

One day, Jyotirao received a letter containing some good news from Baroda. At the recommendation of Diwan Bahadur Shahabuddin Qazi (who took counsel from Mama Parmanand), Dhamanaskar was promoted to the post of Naib Subhedar . The Satyashodhak Samaj received formal recognition from the princely state of Baroda.

On the other hand, the Junnar and Otur provinces again rose in agitation against money lenders. Bhau Patil was leading the agitation started by a group of farmers. Just when it seemed like the agitation was becoming successful, the Brahmin newspapers started writing reams about how the money lenders were actually helping the farmers. Jyotirao could not bear this hypocrisy. He felt the need to speak up. Coincidentally, just then, Bhau Patil proclaimed his intention of holding a huge public meeting of farmers. He sent an invitation to Jyotirao, who decided to participate in the meeting and immediately, left for Otur.

81

News of Jyotirao's arrival in Otur spread like wildfire. People started rushing to meet him and tell him of their problems. Bhau Patil said,

"Your message in 'Aasud' has proven right. The farmers are incensed. We are planning to hold a big revolt."

Jyotirao replied,

"A revolt is definitely necessary; but, it should have a proper direction. Without a properly etched path, the revolt will get scattered on the wind, and hot-headed, aimless 'patriots' will take undue advantage of the situation. Farmers need to recognize that their main enemy is the bracket of money lenders. If everybody's financial position has to be brought at par, then first, it is necessary to smash the money lenders."

A spate of public meetings began in villages, near and far. Messages were spread all across to declare that a large public meeting was planned to be held at Junnar. In response, thousands of farmers began making plans to head for the meeting, without worrying about the consequences and the rage it would elicit from money lenders.

On the day of the meeting, a huge crowd of almost 16,000

farmers had congregated in the open ground just before the village of Junnar. A dais had been created for the speakers, and rugs had been placed all around for the audience to sit on. People were waiting to hear what Jyotirao Phule was going to tell them. Incidentally, many amongst those people were so naïve, that they did not even know what a meeting was! They only went by what their friends told them – that, a meeting was a place where a few educated, learned and experienced men would tell them how to behave in current circumstances, and that they would do well to listen to their advice.

Apart from large numbers of Kunbi farmers, the meeting was also attended by Muslims, Christians, and even a few government officials.

After all preparations were in place, Junnarkar Shete escorted Jyotirao Phule, Bhau Kondaji, and Balaji Kusaji onto the dais. Pin-drop silence ensued. The rustle of leaves overhead was the only sound to be heard.

Bhau Kondaji got up to speak first. He said,

"My farmer brethren, this country has been built by the toil of farmers and such other working class people. But today's unfortunate condition is that, the farmers have become slaves to the money lenders, Brahmins, and rich merchants. He is deliberately kept away from education and religious knowledge. Recognizing that a religion that keeps away a major chunk of society away from its fold, can be nothing but selfish in its aims, we all have embraced the Satyadharma. When the great revolutionary Martin Luther King rose in revolt against the tormentors in the West, it was the farmer class that supported him the most. When all we farmers come under the canopy of Satyadharma to get educated and enlightened, it will spell a death-knell for the corrupt and selfish purveyors of that religion which segregates rather than unifying all."

After Kondaji, Jyotirao stood up to speak. He was happy to see such a large crowd in front of him.

"My dear farmer brethren... Today, our real enemy is not

the foreigner British regime, but sadly, the internal Brahmin regime that has spawned evil practices like money lending to subjugate the lesser people. Those who we today know as Aryas or Brahmins, were originally inhabitants of Iran. They came here, defeated Baliraja, the grandson of Prahlad, and enslaved his subjects. To subjugate them further, they drafted the Manusanhita and gave it religious color so that no one would dare to oppose its principles. The people who these Aryas have tormented for generations on end, are us, Shoodras and Ati Shoodras. It is due to their continual scheming and plotting that we are still living a deplorable life of poverty, ignorance, and torment. What was happening till the reign of the last Bajirao Peshwa? When a farmer would fail to pay taxes owing to abject poverty, he would be made to stand bending for hours in the sun, with a heavy stone kept on his back. Sometimes, they would make him bend, place his wife on his back, and burn red chilies below them both! I'm sure that no other regime in the world must have tormented and terrorized their subjects in this inhuman manner. For the Peshwas, ruling was equated with looting, torturing, and snuffing out their subjects while they themselves lolled in idly acquired riches….."

"Thankfully, today even though we are under a foreign regime, it is a much lenient and merciful one than our home-grown Peshwai. At least this government has a legal structure in place. Anyone can approach them for justice, unlike the Peshwai wherein all decisions would be taken by the Brahmins, for the Brahmins…"

Jyotirao halted for a moment to gauge the audience reaction. Seeing them listening in rapt attention, he continued,

"Brothers, the Company Sarkar regime is our sole opportunity for progress. Think of the British regime as one sent by God for our upliftment. The British have brought so many progressive things and concepts to our country. They have introduced concepts like artificial ponds and canals to help us farmers grow our crop properly. We may well wish that this government stays on for ever; but realistically speaking, that is not to be. One day, this government is bound to return to its own country. Ironically, we will be the ones to drive them out. Right now, we are ignorant and poor and thus dependent on the British government. But, the day we become educated and well-off, our people will like to take the affairs of our country into their own hands. The government knows this very well; thus, even though they are undertaking so many good projects, they are doing nothing to educate the farmers' children. Thus, it is us who need to take matters into our own hands. We need to shrug off the yoke of Brahmin slavery. For that, we first need to stop following mindless rituals that are nothing but the Brahmins' ploy to get money and food from us all. Have you ever seen one Brahmin donating food and money to another Brahmin? Never! They place these burdens on us, because they know we are ignorant and will do anything they tell us to do. But, wasting one's hard-earned money on aimless pursuits in the name of religion, is the most unreligious act ever. These Brahmins use every occasion as an excuse to cement their riches. They advice ignorant people to conduct elaborate rituals to ward off their misfortunes and collect enormous amounts of money and food in the name of dakshina for the same. These people are so lowly that, they take home the suparis and coconuts offered before God and use them for their own food or recreation. Else, they sell these goods, make money, and then lend the same money to enslave the farmers even further. It is a vicious cycle indeed."

"Not satisfied by simply monopolizing the religious realms, these Brahmins have now penetrated into government offices, using their education to their advantage and taking up high posts in legal, postal and police departments to name a few....No wonder, we get no response in these places. The British government, who has become complacent by handing over matters to these duplicitous people, is least bothered about what happens at the grassroots."

People were listening in rapt attention. It was a very new phenomenon for many of them to see one man speaking, and the rest of the crowd listening without interruption.

Just then, some activity at the end of the crowd caught everyone's attention. Three-four men got up and started huffing away. Such an experience was not new for Jyotirao. He had faced even more rude and weird audience members, who would keep asking stupid questions or would keep arguing just for the sake of it. This time at least, the interrupters had just walked away. From their costume, it was evident who those people were.

Jyotirao continued calmly,

"But brothers, tell me one thing....Is it right for anyone to forget those very people on whose toil all the salaries, pensions and other benefits of the upper class are going on so seamlessly? It is such an ironical tragedy that the people on whose shoulders these upper class people are standing and enjoying life in all ways...those people are starving and living half-naked! Not just that, they are constantly living under the threat of governmental action on them. It is tragic that not even the otherwise generous British government feels like addressing the plight of farmers. We have been kept away from education for centuries on end. The British are visitors, but the Brahmins who are responsible for our plight, will certainly have to face the music for their sins, every soon!"

"The ancestors of all us Shoodra and Ati Shoodra people viz. Mali, Kunbi, Maratha, Dhangar, Mahar, Maang, Chaambhar, Bhilla, and Koli, are one. They all used to live in harmony and unity, in the kingdom of Bali. Then, the Brahmins came in and put the yoke of slavery on our necks. Now, it is up to us to throw off this yoke and stand unified once again. For that, let us begin with treating our Shoodra and Ati Shoodra brethren with love and compassion."

"Brothers, now my work is done. Now, Bhau Kondaji and Balaji Kusaji are going to take my work ahead. They have taken on a lion's share of this work, thus relieving me of the same. I wish them all the luck to take forward the work of Satyashodhak Samaj in the same spirit that we have been upholding so far. Let us unite and fight the evil money lenders. Let us put a social ban on the Brahmins who make our lives miserable. The Brahmins have the audacity to consider you inferior and untouchable enough to not let you drink from their wells, and not let you participate in their events. But, those hypocrites have no qualms coming to your homes on the pretext of conducting poojas and getting money from you. Stop inviting Brahmins to conduct poojas at your home. Stop providing any services to the homes of money lenders. Let them stay bereft of barbers, cobblers, vegetable vendors, launderers etc. Then only, they will realize your worth...."

Jyotirao kept repeating his thoughts about the government's policies, the false alarms raised by newspapers, the cunningness of Brahmins, and the evil attitude of money lenders. It was having the desired effect. People were getting ready to fight the oppression in their own villages. After the meeting ended that evening, when they set off for their villages, the people were determined to ban the money lenders and Brahmins with all their might.

Jyotirao, Balaji, and Kondaji returned to Otur. Thereafter, they kept having small meetings wherein Jyotirao would also talk frankly about where the farmers were going wrong, as well.

One day, Bhau Patil said,

"Tatyasaheb, our farmers are also equally responsible for their plight. You keep advising them to live a frugal life, but these people go and marry four women at a time! What can we expect out of them, tell me?"

Jyotirao laughed and replied,

"I would suggest, these people should go and marry one more woman. So then, when one wife dies, the other four can carry her corpse at the funeral!"

Thereafter when Jyotirao would make this 'suggestion' in his meetings, the guilty farmers would hid their faces in shame.

While these meetings were going on, on the other hand there was also a spate of weddings happening. Jyotirao conducted the marriage ceremonies of many Satyashodhak youngsters. Balaji Patil also arranged for the marriage of two of his daughters. Finishing all that work, Jyotirao returned to Pune.

82

Otur and Junnar saw a rebellious upsurge like never before! Farmers refused to go work in the farms of lenders and landlords. Brahmins were banned from conducting any ritual at the house of lower castes. They tried threatening and sweet-talking the masses. The landlords agreed to give them lands for cultivation by only levying taxes on whatever produce they would have. But, nothing worked. People were simply not ready to relent till their loans were called off.

As is the law of nature, the actions started getting reactions. Farmers started getting tormented even more. Farmers in debt got legal cases thrown in their faces. Brahmin teachers refused to teach the children of rebellious farmers. As a solution for the last problem, Jyotirao and Bhau Kondaji met the Director of the education department and requested him to appoint non-Brahmin teachers at such schools. Bhau Patil started a separate school for the farmers' wards, at Otur.

The revolt was spreading like wildfire. Now, it reached Konkan and Thane districts. In Thane, people from the Mahadev Koli sub-caste started conducting marriage ceremonies without any Brahmins. When they could not find any person in their clique who knew the mantras for conducting marriage ceremonies, they simply started chanting 'Har Har Mahadev' to pronounce a marriage ceremony to have finished successfully.

While all this was happening, the Brahmins of Otur and Junnar filed a police case on Balaji Kusaji Patil. Their allegation was that the Satyashodhak Samaj had committed grave injustice by countering their birth-rights!

Balaji came to Pune to take Jyotirao's advice on the matter. Jyotirao asked Gangarambhau for legal help, but he refused to proffer any. Then, Jyotirao went and met Adv. Lingu.

This case was an important milestone for the Brahmins and non-Brahmins, especially Satyashodhak Samaj. If the Brahmins lost, they would lose all rights to conduct rituals and demand money and food from other castes as dakshina for the same. However, it was not going to be an easy battle, considering the legal heads were all Brahmins. In recent times, Sadashiv Hari Madhave had conducted some rituals without inviting the Brahmin head-priest. The head-priest, Dinanath Abaji, had filed a case asking for indemnity from Madhave. Raosaheb Ranade was the judge at the proceedings of this hearing, and he had weighted in favour of Abaji, citing,

"Whether a host wants it or not, it is a Brahmin priest right to conduct holy rituals and ask for compensation in terms of dakshina for the same."

Gangarambhau was close to Raosaheb Ranade. Jyotirao knew that it would be futile to expect help from him, but he had nevertheless tried. Jyotirao knew that this was an uphill battle, considering the open stance of Brahmin judges like Ranade, and even non-Brahmin legal eagles like Gangarambhau. But, he was not a man to give up. He would fight till the end.

The battle raged on.

In Junnar, the revolt became even more aggressive. Bhau Kondaji Patil wrote to the government, requesting it to provide protection to the farmers against the money lenders and landlords. Complaints and cases against Brahman clerks and officers in the government department, began increasing.

A year went by. Finally, the money lenders held their noses in their fists and came to talk out mutually beneficial agreements with the government officials and the leaders of the revolt. After that, the farmers lifted their ban on the lenders, landlords, and the Brahmins.

The Deccan Agriculturist Relief Act clearly proved insufficient to address the problems of the farmers. After thinking about the problem from many angles, the government passed the insolvency regulation act. This was going to prove a big lifeline for the farmers, but yet again, the Brahmin-run newspapers began to rant in favor of the money lenders. Instead of looking at the money lenders' attitudes in an unbiased manner, they started blaming the poverty of the farmers, and the taxation system of the government, for all the problems in the interim. A so-called progressive journal like 'Induprakash', wrote:

"It is not just the greed and craftiness of the lenders that is responsible for the plight of the farmers. There are many other factors on the farmers' side that also contributed equally to their misery. But, it has become a fashion of sorts to make a scapegoat out of money lenders for every problem. It is to extricate the 'innocent' farmers from the 'wolf-like jaws' of the money lenders that officer Hoppel has got the 'Relief Act' sanctioned. The resolution for insolvency regulation brought forth by Hart-Davies is going to raze the money lenders to the ground, while allowing farmers to conveniently escape from the promises they had given. One can see what results has the insolvency regulation act has yielded in Mumbai. People have been swindling money and conducting the most corrupt acts. Truth remains that farmers and money lenders are two sides of the same coin. They both need each other. Bringing in the insolvency regulation act will wash off all the unity that had been brought about by the Deccan Agriculturist Relief Act, and will make the society limp and unstable."

'Induprakash' had further noted that, bringing about the insolvency regulation act would be akin to interfering in the personal give n' take between farmers and lenders. Releasing them easily from their promises would only lead to more poverty for the farmers in the long run. They needed to be taught the importance of honesty, sincerity and hard work, instead of giving them a convenient escape route. Further, the journal also suggested other means of achieving compromise, such as, increasing the tenure of loan repayment, lowering the rate of interest, and so on.

Actually, this was an old sore point. The upper castes never wanted any kind of relief act for the farmers. Earlier too, they had to keep quiet because of the revolt. Now, they started ranting that the insolvency regulation act would completely finish off the money lenders.

But by then, the farmers had become clever enough to not get affected by these crocodile tears.

Even though the revolt against money lenders came under control somewhat, the revolt against Brahmins continued blazing as ever. In that regard, Jyotirao decided to travel to Baroda. Before that, he had to sort through many urgent matters; a very important among them being, responding to a letter received from the government. Behramji Malbari, the editor of 'Indian Spectator', had written to the government requesting stringent laws to be passed against child marriage and forced widowhood. In that regard, the government had requested several eminent members of the society, including Jyotirao, to convey their thoughts. The orthodox groups and newspapers had already started ranting that the government had no business interfering in their private religious matters. But, ignoring them all, Behramji had kept his efforts going. It angered the orthodox group even more that a Parsi man was putting his head into their matters! They started openly berating Behramji at any given occasion.

Actually, there should have been no argument about whether these inhumane practices needed to be stopped. But the textbook-ish priests had closed their eyes to the plight of little girls and young women. They would come on track only with the cane of legality whooped on their backs.

Jyotirao wrote two separate letters. Thanking Behramji for his efforts, Jyotirao went onto describe the horrific life that the girls and women are forced to lead owing to getting married off at a tender age and becoming widows in their youth. Describing their plight as being similar to the slaves in America, Jyotirao suggested that the government make it illegal for any boy below 19 years and any girl below 11 years to be married off. He further suggested levying strict fines on people who dared to break these laws, and use those fines for the education of young children so that they could grow up more aware. He also said that the government should ensure that this education should be given by someone apart from the fundamentalist Brahmins, who are bound to fill nothing but more illogical nonsense in their impressionable minds.

Jyotirao's mind was filled with sad memories while writing about the plight of child brides and widows. He remembered the widow Kashibai who worked in Sadashivrao's house; the way she had been compelled to kill her own child; and how that led to the formation of a shelter for children of widows.

Jyotirao mused that, 'even now, the situation of widows was not as pleasant as it should have been. Even though fewer children are dying at the hands of their hapless mothers, the widows are still not getting a dignified treatment at their homes. So many widows from good, wealthy, and known families are still being forced into prostitution owing to the lack of family support and the societal biases against them. Terrified at the fate of living the life of a tonsured widow, so many women have run off to become dancers at brothels. The vile practice of forced widowhood is responsible for all their ill-effects. It is necessary to describe all this to the government, so as to help them make the right decision and create proper laws to protect women in the future.'

The volcano of thoughts and memories that lay dormant in Jyotirao's mind for all these years, came to the fore. He started writing in impeccable English. 'Forced widowhood is a terrible practice that leads to a woman to the path of moral corruptibility, without her choice. Many young, Brahmin widows are also burning in the flames of this evil practice. So many Brahmin men regularly visit prostitutes in brothels and come home with sexually transmitted diseases, that render them sterile. They then force their wives to have physical relations with them and also torture them otherwise. They start doubting their wives of having affairs, while themselves wearing a mask of being God-fearing and true to religious principles. Even after such vile husbands die, the suffering of the women does not end. They are forced to tonsure their heads, forsake all the pleasures of life, and live life like some lowly animal. The Brahmin men have no compunction in marrying several women, but their 'morality' comes to the fore while allowing their widowed and sad young sisters to remarry. It is because of these biased and unjust societal attitudes that the widowed women get compelled to commit heinous crimes.'

Jyotirao further went onto describe the story of Kashibai and how it led to him and Savitribai to start a shelter for the children of widowed women. Further, he suggested that the government should take measures to educate the barbers engaged in tonsuring of widows about why this act is such a heinous one and how it adversely affects the psyche of the widows. He finished his letter by emphasizing that 'the Hindu scriptures are written by selfish and evil men who have conveniently made different laws for themselves and their women. They have allowed themselves multiple marriages, but have noted widow remarriages to be immorality of the highest order. They have deliberately made these segregations, so as to keep the women subjugated and make them dance to their tunes, all their life.'

While the government was trying to abolish evil practices like child marriage and forced widowhood, journals like 'Pune Vaibhav' were having as field day in tarnishing the image of scholars like Pandita Ramabai.

Jyotirao sent the final drafts of both letters via post, and taking Sahadubuva along, he started off his journey to Baroda.

PART 3

83

The city of Pune was in the grip of nationalistic sentiments. Hoards of people would be seen visiting the homes of Sitarampant Chiplunkar, Krishnajipant Nulkar, and Raosaheb Ranade. Plans were afoot to set up a national congress under the leadership of Sir Allan Hume and Sir William Wedderburn. Leaders like Pherozeshah Mehta, Dadabhai Naoraji, and Umeshchandra Banerjee had come together. The Governor General of India, Lord Dufferin had also empathized with the need for a national congress. The Bombay Association, East India Association of Calcutta, and Sarvajanik Sabha of Pune were going to be incorporated in the congress on a national scale. Umeshchandra Banerjee was going to preside over the first meeting that was going to be held at Pune.

Sitarampant Chiplunkar became

the leader of the host committee that was established to organize the meeting. A huge canopy was to be built in the garden of Peshwas, located at the foothills of Parvati.

At that time, the main aim of the national congress was to push for more official posts for Indians, in the predominantly British administrative system. They were talking about doing something for the farmers, but for now at least, farmers had not been invited for the meeting.

Jyotirao had been constantly falling ill after returning from Baroda. His growing age was not permitting his body to take on the strain of so much work and travel. Nevertheless, even in his illness, he kept on writing about how the country was conveniently forgetting the farmers, who were the backbone of India's economy. The book was nearing completion. He had not yet decided on the name, but the book was going to be an eye-opener for the leaders and the government that was conveniently ignoring the agricultural class at their own peril.

Jyotirao knew that he should have rested; but, he had no time to rest. He was set upon starting his own newsletter very soon. It came as no surprise that publications like 'Pune Vaibhav' and 'Dynaanchakshu' should make fun of Pandita Ramabai's religious conversion; but when a self-proclaimed Satyashodhak newsletter like 'Deenbandhu' also did the same, Jyotirao was incensed to the core. He was utterly displeased that 'Deenbandhu' should go to such lowly depths and make fun of a woman.

Jyotirao had become disillusioned with 'Deenbandhu' ever since they sent back the third chapter of 'Aasud'; but, the episode with Ramabai became the last straw of his tolerance. That was when Jyotirao decided to start his own newsletter.

During this time, Pune was suddenly gripped in the epidemic of cholera. The host committee of the national congress meeting, were sent into a tizzy. The meeting was shifted from Pune to Mumbai. Eminent people like V.S. Apte, Krishnajipant Nulkar, Gopalrao Agarkar of 'Sudharak', and

Gangarambhau Mhaske went to the meeting in Mumbai, as representatives from Pune.

Around this time itself, a big episode happened in Pune with regards to the female high school. Sir Wedderburn, who had come to Pune as a Commissioner, had decided to start in girls' school in memory of his late brother. He himself contributed a generous donation for erecting the school, even as people like Raosaheb Ranade also raised funds for this project on their own steam. Reformists like Gopal Ganesh Agarkar welcomed this step, but there were many people in Pune who felt that while education in English medium was important, it was not a right thing for girls to study English! Many protests were staged to not let the school open. Nevertheless, tiding over all the opposition, the Female High School did start off. Every morning, the principal, Madam Hartford, would take a sepoy along and go around the alleys of Pune, requesting parents to let their girls attend the school. Once again, women's education received a boost in Pune, but the orthodox group got yet another issue to barrel the government about.

Jyotirao had yet not recovered fully from the bout of cholera. However, one day, he was compelled to leave his bed to protect the vegetable vendors who had been mercilessly beaten up for refusing to shift to the newly constructed market. The market had been built with a huge budget of Rs. 3.5 lakhs. Naturally, the costs and rents of the individual lots in that market were too high to be affordable to the poor vendors. They would have to pay almost Re. 1 per day as rent, apart from monthly taxes. It was clear that yet again, they would get engulfed in a vicious cycle of debt. Jyotirao met the Municipality officers and tried to explain them the problems that the vendors would face. But, it was all in vain. The officers refused to listen to a word. The market was named after Governor Lord Ray.

Jyotirao did not understand why the Pune Municipality felt like competing with the Mumbai Municipality. After the

Crawford market was erected in Mumbai, the Pune Municipality started hankering to build a similar market in Pune. For that, they purchased the Khasgiwale's garden in Shukrawar Peth for Rs. 40,000. Rs. 3 lakhs were sanctioned for building the market. Jyotirao and Hari Raoji staged a lot of protests to not let the market be erected, and instead spend that money for the education of poor children. But, the requests went unheeded and the market was built at an extended budget of Rs. 3.5 lakhs. Obviously, the brunt of this exorbitant cost was gong to fall on the heads of the vendors.

Nevertheless, Jyotirao did not stop his agitation. He stood firmly in support of the vendors who kept selling vegetables from the old market opposite Shaniwarwada. They all were prepared for whatever calamity would befall them.

On the eve of Padwa, a procession of the Satyashodhak Samaj's flag was taken out all over Pune. This was the first time that the Samaj had arranged such a procession. The young members of the Samaj, such as Krishnarao Bhalekar and Shaiwale Ghorpade, had taken the lead in this endeavor. Hundreds of Satyashodhaks from the neighboring villages came to Pune to lend a helping hand. The procession began from the temple of Lord Vitthal, in Bhavani Peth. Enthusiasm was in the air as young Satyashodhaks carried the flag reverentially ahead, to the accompaniment of drums and cymbals.

Jyotirao was accompanied by Raosaheb Ranade, Gangarambhau Mhaske, Swami Aiyyavaru, Devrao Thosar, Dr. Santuji Lad, Dr. Sadoba Gawde etc. The procession began at 4 pm and went through areas like Saat Toti, Ravivar Peth, Phadke gate, Budhwar chowk, Kotwal chaavdi, Vetaal Peth, Bhavani Peth etc, to return to Dr. Gawde's house by 9 pm. The procession was followed by an impromptu meeting that saw Jyotirao, Raosaheb and Swami Aiyyavaru making speeches.

Jyotirao had come across many problems that the Satyashodhaks would face in routine life. For instance, they did not know what mantras to chant while conducting marriage proceedings without Brahmins. Thus, Jyotirao had written a different set of chants (known as 'mangalashtaks') for Satyashodhaks to chant during their marriage ceremonies. During this meeting, he read out those chants and specified that they did not require any Brahmin to say these. The chants were vows regarding duties and responsibilities that a bride and groom were supposed to say to one another, during the ceremony.

After the winds of the national congress meeting died down, Pune got gripped by the upcoming literary conference of Marathi litterateurs. Raosaheb Ranade had organized this conference, which was now in its second year. Krishnashastri Rajwade was chosen to preside over the conference. The first conference had been abruptly cancelled; thus, Raosaheb had taken all efforts to see that this year's conference would be a very successful one.

However, Jyotirao was not in favor of such an event that he opined was nothing more than a gimmick. According to Jyotirao, just as the Sarvajanik sabha and national congress did little to alleviate the real problems of the country's people, so also, the literary conference was going to be nothing but a battle of wits and empty words. Thus, in reply to the invitation sent to him by Raosaheb, Jyotirao said:

"Thank you for your kind invitation. However, I do not find it prudent to be present at a conference of people who do not care a drop for the real sufferings of people around them. These people write books with a safety valve intact. They are afraid to touch the topics of equal rights for all, and have conveniently 'forgotten' to write about how the upper castes have been subjugating the lower castes for generations on end. Neither do they know, and nor are they bothered about the torment that so many social classes have been going through. How, then, can their writing be lauded as a mirror for social conditions? My participation in this half-baked conference is not going to yield anything good for the people I toil for. Hence, it is better I stay away. Rather, I would suggest that, if this letter of mine serves to create some change in the mind-set of authors and they get brave enough to talk about the sufferings and torment of Shoodras and Ati Shoodras in their upcoming books, I shall be happy to attend the next literary conference."

Savitribai was upset with Jyotirao for having written such a strong-worded letter. She said,

"Shetji, I can understand if you do not wish to attend the conference. But, why write such a strong letter to Raosaheb, when you know he is a very peaceful and calm man? He will be so hurt by these harsh words of yours!"

Jyotirao replied,

"I agree, but Raosaheb is also known to respect and accept contradictory opinions, without being biased against them. We have known to have differing opinions since long. He participated in the Satyasamaj procession; I had also participated in the procession for Swami Dayanand. But, that did not translate into him becoming a member of Satyashodhak Samaj, or me becoming a member of Prarthana Samaj. He is simply not ready to talk anything against the Brahmins, who are clearly at the root of all the problems faced by the Shoodra and Ati Shoodras. On whose behest did Dr. Ghole resign from Satyasamaj? At whose behest did Gangarambhau Mhaske refused to give legal advice during the Otur revolt? Now, Raosaheb has started the Deccan Maratha Association, in which our Bhalekar has also joined in. But tell me, will this organisation benefit the lower classes in any way?"

Savitribai as listening intently. Jyotirao continued,

"We are not against Raosaheb in any way. We are against these writers who write fiction under the name of facts. What do these people know about the utter poverty-ridden life that the lower classes lead? What do they know or even care about what these people suffer? Have they ever tried to do anything to lessen their sufferings? No! Rather, these people, who have been fortunate to get good education by going to college…they simply use their linguistic skills to make jokes about whatever work the reformists are doing. Instead of using the power of their pens to make a difference in someone's life, they are happy making little fictional books to please a section of people. Of course, what can one expect from these writers who cannot even see the suffering of their own sisters?! Tell me Savitribai, why should I waste my time going to conferences that will fête these insensitive and hypocritical writers who think nothing of writing farces on the reformists' work, and then shamelessly proclaiming themselves to be progressive as well? I know that I have written the letter in harsh words, but sometimes, only the sharpest spear can make a thick-skinned bullock move….

….Tell me, who opposed the founding of female high school? These so-called educated progressives itself, isn't it? How double-standard can they be? They got themselves educated in view of the changing times, but when it came to the education of their sisters and daughters, they chose to keep them away from it all. These people are only fit for talking about the need for education from glorified daises. When it comes to implementing their thoughts practically, they run away faster than a horse! Taking education to keep up with changing times, and taking education because it is a basic human right, are two different things, Savitribai."

Savitribai knew that what Shetji was saying, was right. Raosaheb had supported the female high school in myriad ways. In fact, his own wife, Ramabai, was a student in that school. But, that did not do anything to curb the opposition that so many educated people of Pune had staged during setting up the female high school.

When Jyotirao's letter reached the literary conference committee, it created a huge furor! The letter was read out at the beginning of the conference. The Brahmin authors began spitting fire over the contents of the letter. Brahmin journalists scrambled to publish the most scandalous excerpts from the letter in their newspapers, the next day This was followed by several critical writings about how and why did Phule say what he said. Owing to all this, the literary conference became famous, not for its programs but for the controversy that was stoked due to Jyotirao Phule's letter.

84

One morning, a Muslim betelnut seller left to come to Jyotirao's house in Ganj Peth. He had a complaint to lodge with Jyotirao. Even though Jyotirao was no longer the Sheriff then, the man was sure that he would certainly do something to redress his grievance.

The man's problem was that, a whole community of ironsmiths used to keep working day & night near his house. The incessant hammering had become too much to bear. Thus, he was coming to Jyotirao's house to request him that the Municipal Corporation give some place at the Ray market to the ironsmiths.

As he entered the alley of Jyotirao's house in Ganj Peth, the man saw a row of scavengers walking in front of him, carrying buckets of human waste on their heads. The scavengers kept walking till Jyotirao's house, whereupon they disappeared towards the backside of the house.

The man called out to Jyotirao saying,

"Tatyasaheb, may I come in?"

Jyotirao got up to answer the door, asking,

"Who is it? Please come in."

"Aadab , Tatyasaheb…" the man said as he greeted Jyotirao.

"Aadab… Tell me, what may I do for you?"

The man described his ordeal to Jyotirao and put forth his request of asking the corporation to give the ironsmiths a place at the Ray market.

The problems of Ray market were yet unresolved. The vegetable vendors were not ready to shift there, owing to high rents and no guarantee of being able to get that much business, even if they opted to take lots in the market. The Municipality officers were just not ready to compromise in any way. Instead, they had started troubling Jyotirao and other Satyashodhaks who were working in favor of the vendors. One of the ways to trouble Jyotirao was to ask the scavengers to deposit the human waste collected from all over the city, in the depot behind Phule's house! There were several depots in the city, but the municipal officers instructed the scavengers to only use the depot behind Phule's house. The alleys of Ganj Peth were deliberately kept unclean without sweeping. All this was done to only trouble Phule.

Even though Jyotirao was incensed by this torment, he did not speak up a word against the same. He felt bad for his neighbors who had to undergo a lot of trouble just because they were his neighbors. Instead of ranting against the officials, Jyotirao chose to befriend the scavengers and would spend time with them to understand their problems.

Listening to the man's suggestion, Jyotirao told him,

"What you are proposing is nice, but the poor workers and vendors cannot afford the high rents and rates that the corporation has levied on the shops. I don't know how or why the corporation has turned a blind eye to the fact that the people for whom they have started this market, are so poor that they cannot afford a daily rent of Re. 1 also! Even if they take loans for paying rents, they are not assured of getting good business to pay off the loans, because their main customers will be Brahmin people who are extremely stingy with their money. They will prefer taking stale vegetables but will never think of paying due money for fresh goods. That is why they are sticking on to the old market itself. The Governor General Lord Rippon is one over-smart fellow. I don't know how he ever thought that the British and Brahmin officials would ever think of collective societal benefit.?!"

"Then, what can be done, Tatyasaheb?" the man asked.

"That is what even I am thinking about. Instead of helping the poor, they are being tortured for no reason. I have also not been spared from their evil tactics. For the last ten-twelve days, the entire human waste of Pune city is being dumped only in the depot of my Ganj Peth, instead of distributing it in depots available at Vetaal Peth, Meethganj Peth etc. It becomes impossible to set out of the house before 12 noon. There are rows and rows of scavengers who keep bringing in human waste from all around. I'm done with this Municipal Corporation and their evil Brahmin officials!"

Suddenly, Jyotirao realized that he had been speaking in a very harsh tone. He apologized to the man, realizing that he too was looking very incensed. The man said,

"I'm sorry, Tatyasaheb. I was not aware of all this. I'm an educated person. I shall write about all this in newspapers."

"Not needed, sir. I prefer looking at the good in every situation. Due to this decision of the Municipality, I could understand the terrible problems faced by these poor scavengers. They clean up the whole city with their bare hands, but they receive the lowest wages of all. One day, we are going to have to fight for their rights too."

"Alright, Tatyasaheb. I shall take your leave now" the man said.

"Alright, Sir. It was nice meeting you" said Jyotirao, as he came to leave the man till the door.

The meeting left Jyotirao very dejected. This was the first time that he had not been able to help someone who had come asking for his assistance. He felt very helpless in front of the corrupt and vile officials sitting in the municipality, who thought nothing about alleviating the real problems of people, and who instead kept supporting corrupt and criminal people. It was due to these tainted people that a project for supplying fresh water to Pune city, had collapsed even before it started. An artificial lake was being built near Zagdewadi, for supplying fresh water to Pune city. The limestone being used for the construction was of a very inferior quality. Jyotirao tried many times to bring this to the notice of the concerned officials; but, he was conveniently ignored. Instead, officials who knew nothing about construction, were employed to give a project report about the construction. They gave a glowing report! When the monsoons came, the lake filled up, only to get drained off the very next day! Such was the case when Jyotirao was the Sheriff. Hence, he knew that it was futile to even think that he would receive any support now.

The next day, Ramchandrarao Dhamanaskar made a flying visit to Pune. After being promoted to Naib Subhedar, Ramchandrarao would often come for work to Mumbai. Very often, he would also make a quick visit to Pune. This time however, he had a definite purpose for visiting Pune. Maharaj Sayajirao Gaekwad had sent a portrait of himself for Jyotirao.

After greetings were exchanged between them both, Ramchandrarao said,

"Today, there's a special reason behind my visit."

"Is that so? What is it?" asked Jyotirao.

"Do you remember, you had requested Maharaj for his portrait?"

"Yes, absolutely."

"Well, please see what I have got here for you..."

Saying thus, Ramchandrarao beckoned to the clerk who had accompanied him. The clerk came forward with a huge portrait of Maharaj Sayajirao.

Jyotirao was extremely overwhelmed to note that such a busy and great king had actually remembered his request and honoured it in such a wonderful way.

The clerk set down the heavy trunk that he was carrying, and removed a big frame from it. The frame was covered in plush red satin. He handed it over to Dhamanaskar, who then reverentially placed it in Jyotirao's hands.

Jyotirao gratefully accepted the gift, and slowly removed the satin covers.

Maharaj's portrait was indeed a beautifully painted one. He had worn the ceremonial garb. A big pugree sat on his head. His neck was adorned with strings of shiny pearls. A sword hung from his waist, sitting tucked in its sheath. A dagger was tucked into the pleats of the cummerbund that Maharaj wore on his waist. Overall, he looked regal and elegant; just as a king of a rich province should. The attire and accessories were complemented by the confident smile on his beatific face.

However, unexpectedly so, Jyotirao frowned on looking at that beautiful portrait. The Maharaj that he remembered having met in person, was very different from what this painting portrayed him to be. That Maharaj was a people's person – one who took time out of his busy schedule to mull over the problems of poor farmers; one who stopped all the wasteful practices in the palace of Baroda; one who would eat a simple fare of millet bhaakri and vegetables, when he could have afforded any gourmet delight in the world. That Maharaj did not wear pearls or silken tunics. He did not stand in front of people in his royal regalia. Jyotirao was desirous of having 'that real portrait' of Sayajirao Gaekwad; not this unrecognizable and unreal one.

Jyotirao asked Kaku,

"Savitribai, did you like the portrait?"

"Yes, I did" Savitribai answered innocently, not understanding the reason behind her husband's question.

However, Ramchandrarao sensed something amiss, as Jyotirao was not saying anything about the painting. He prodded,

"Tatyasaheb, you did not tell us whether you liked the painting or not..."

Jyotirao ventured,

"Well....the painting is nicely done...but, I don't want it. This is not the Maharaj I met...the Maharaj I know. When I requested for a portrait of Maharaj, it was to commemorate the good human being I saw in him; not the king that he obviously is. Please take this back with you."

Ramchandrarao was stunned at Jyotirao's answer. The unexpected reaction put Ramchandrarao in a quandary. He did not understand, how was he to take the painting back? He tried requesting Jyotirao,

"Well, Tatyasaheb... now that I have got the painting for you, please do accept it. What will I explain to Maharaj if you refuse it?"

Jyotirao replied,

"No. Please take it back. Tell Maharaj exactly what I told you. He will understand. If possible, please send me the portrait that I have requested for."

Ramchandrarao could not argue any further. He kept the painting back in the trunk and promised Jyotirao that he would get the desired portrait soon.

Then, talks moved onto the formation of the national congress. Ramchandrarao said,

"Tatyasaheb, the Satyshodhak Samaj needs to make its stance clear about the national congress."

Jyotirao replied,

"Ramchandrarao, first we need to examine whether this congress, that calls itself 'national', is it really national in the first place?! The concept of nation that they are trying to apply to our country made up of innumerable castes, sub-castes and myriad segregations among those all, can never be applicable to India. That concept of a 'nation' has stemmed from the thoughts of European thinkers. It may fit their countries well, but can never be applicable to a country as diverse as India. Till the time all our countrymen come under a canopy of true equality, we cannot become 'national' in the real sense."

He continued,

"Tell me, Ramchandrarao; does this so-called national congress have at least one Shoodra or Ati Shoodra representative on its panel? While demanding more places for themselves in the civil services cadre, are they asking for commensurate places for the lower castes, in keeping with their percentage in the total population? Even though they are saying Hindu, the reforms that are proposing are going to only benefit the Brahmins."

"They do not consider Shoodras and Ati Shoodras to be at par with themselves. They only want benefits for themselves. We are not going to gain anything by supporting them. Rather, we will face a loss on two accounts: people who are thinking of our good, will stop doing so; and the government too will go against us. The government has recently freed us from centuries of slavery. Imagine, in spite of the British ruling us today, we are still facing so much trouble. What will happen when they go? It is true that some day the British are bound to go. Ironically, it is our people who will drive them away. But that is still some time away..."

"Even though the government departments have been Indianized, who really rules them in practical life? The Brahmins, isn't it? Even though the chiefs night be British, but the main officers beneath them are Brahmins. They are clever enough to work in a way that they reap maximum benefits. Sometimes, even the topmost British officers become nonplussed before the cunning of their Brahmin officers. Once the British go home, it is these over-clever officers who are going to benefit the most. That is why, it is pertinent that we first work to weed out the corruption, bribery and nepotism that runs rampant in the system. Why doesn't the national congress do anything about this? They won't! They have never cared for the entire population of the country, which incorporates a large chunk of Shoodras and Ati Shoodras. All their talk about national integration, is just that – talk! Just as they have never tried to bring about religious equality, so also, they will never strive for national integration in the truest sense. We lower class people know that it is a lonely battle for us, but we are ready to fight it. We do not need false promises or crocodile tears."

Jyotirao continued,

"Till this congress has at least representative from the agricultural class, and till it really works towards alleviating the problems of the agricultural class which is the backbone of our country, whatsoever meetings they hold are going to prove futile for us, because our problems are never going to reach to the ears of the higher powers. If they really want a true 'national congress', then they should get representatives from each and every caste and sub-caste on board. But, that will never be done. They want these segregations for their own benefit; they will never do anything to erase them."

Ramchandrarao was stunned to hear Jyotirao's lucid views. He had never thought about all this in such depth. He began introspecting whether indeed the national congress was as national as it claimed to be?

However, seeing Jyotirao enraged, Ramchandrarao thought it best to change the topic at that moment, rather than take it further. He asked Jyotirao,

"By the way, Tatyasaheb, when do you plan to publish 'Shetkaryache Aasud'?"

Hearing this question, Jyotirao gave a wry smile and said,

"Ramchandrarao, till the time we have cowardly Shoodra and Ati Shoodra printers in our midst, that work looks difficult... So, for now, I have put the publishing on a backburner and am working on a newsletter called 'Satsaar'. The aim of 'Satsaar' will be to highlight, or rather remind (people), of the principles of the Satyashodhak Samaj. Some so-called Satyashodhaks seem to have lost their way. They are finding pride in making fun of women..."

Being aware of how 'Deenbandhu' had stepped back from publishing the third chapter of 'Aasud', and how it was publishing articles that heckled good women like Ramabai and Tarabai, Ramchandrarao could see a point in Jyotirao's decision to start 'Satsaar'.

He said,

"Tatyasaheb, I agree with you....'Deenbandhu' had no business writing those derogatory articles about the ladies."

"What can I say, Ramchandrarao? On one hand, the Samaj works incessantly for the empowerment of women; and then, we have people affiliated with the Samaj, doing monkey tricks like these! They fear being slapped with defamation suits if they publish 'Aasud', but then, how come they have no compunction in writing nonsense about the women? What right do these journalists have, criticizing Tarabai in the vile way they have? Is there anything false in what she has written? If her truth hurts so badly, then people should not behave that ways, in the first place. Satyashodhak Samaj does not stand by such behavior wherein a woman, who gives birth to a man, is criticized and insulted so badly. We specially discredit such behavior when men behave hypocritical enough to first mistreat a woman and then criticize her for speaking about the mistreatment meted out to her. Actually, Tarabai should be praised for writing so fearlessly; but, these cowards are afraid that their wrong behavior will get exposed if they do so. Thus, they found the safe way out and criticized her. After this incident, I have severed all ties with Krishnarao. Presently he is finding it rewarding to run the work of Deenbandhu Sarvajanik Sabha and Sushikshan Gruha according to the advice of Brahmin intellectuals. He does not need me now. In fact, I seem to have become an enemy of sorts for him."

Jyotirao's speech was laced with as much anguish, as it was with anger. Savitribai gently broke him midway, asking,

"Shetji, are you now going to keep fighting with your own Satyashodhaks?"

Jyotirao replied,

"Do you mean to say that we keep mum and not retaliate to even the most unfair things happening in front of our eyes?! Till recently, we were criticizing Vishnushastri Chiplunkar, but now, I'm afraid to see what pops up in the upcoming issues of 'Deenbandhu'! Isn't it 'Deenbandhu' that wrote that I made people wash my feet and drink that water, during my stay at Wangani? How absurd is that? Can I ever think of behaving like this? I know why they are writing all this against me. It is so that their faults can get hidden under the blanket of criticism against me. It is bad enough that my own friends and co-members are behaving like this; but even sadder is that, I have to contest my own people."

Seeing her husband getting more agitated, Savitribai said,

"Shetji, do criticize them, but for now, stop this discussion and come have dinner."

Jyotirao understood what his wife was trying to say. He invited Ramchandrarao and the clerk to join in for dinner. It was a simple fare of millet bhaakri, curd, and a vegetable salad, but they enjoyed it heartily.

The guests stayed over at Jyotirao's place for the night. Talks went on till the wee hours. The next day, Ramchandrarao and the clerk left for Baroda.

85

Jyotirao was talking to Bhau Patil. The furious Brahmins had plunged to lower depths in tormenting Patil. An officer from Junnar had filed a police case on Patil. It was beyond doubt that Patil would come out unscathed from those trumped-up charges.

Bhau Patil and Jyotirao's association went back almost ten years by then. Jyotirao would often tell him,

"Address me as Tatya. Why this formality of calling me Tatyasaheb? I hardly have anyone left in my life who can call me endearingly. At least you spare me that ceremony."

But Patil had too much respect for Jyotirao to call him anything other than Tatyasaheb.

That day, Jyotirao insisted that Bhau stay over at his place for the night. Maharaj Sayajirao Gaekwad had come to town. Many programs had been planned in his honor, all over Pune.

He had been visiting many schools and extending help from the Baroda treasury. Krishnarao's Sushikshan Gruha was one such school to receive Maharaj's benevolence.

The Satyashodhak Samaj had also planned a big program in Maharaj's honor.

Jyotirao was busy putting together the first issue of 'Satsaar', even as he was attending many programs that were being held in honor of Sayajirao Gaekwad. The newsletter was almost ready. He had planned to print 2000 issues to begin with. One of the highlights of the first issue of 'Satsaar' was going to be Jyotirao's counter-article to all the critics who had panned Pandita Ramabai. Other articles included a critique on Brahmins who misled people in the name of religion, and, an article highlighting the inherent differences between theory and practical with regards to what the Prarthana Samaj and Brahmo Samaj preached and followed, respectively.

Jyotirao had decided that if the first two issues received a good response, then he would publish 'Satsaar' on a weekly basis. He had even prepared a rough draft of the second issue. In that, he was going to drive some sense into the minds of people who thought nothing about berating women.

Jyotirao had recovered from the bout of cholera, but the weakness was still lingering. Nevertheless, he had planned a trip to Thane and Mumbai after publishing the first two issues of 'Satsaar'. After giving a speech at the laborer settlement in Mumbai, he was going to attend the annual celebration of Satyashodhak Samaj that was planned to be held at Thane that year. Dr. Santuji Lad had spent weeks in preparation of this event.

That day, Raosaheb Ranade was going to give a speech on behalf of the Pune Vaktrutva Sabha . Maharaj Sayajirao Gaekwad was going to be the chief guest for the event. The topic of Raosaheb's speech was going to be, 'prevalent condition of agriculture in the country'.

When Jyotirao came back along with Bhau Patil after

attending the speech, his face had turned red with rage! The reason for his anger was the views that Raosaheb had expressed in his speech. He had said:

"Even though there was rigid caste segregation in the earlier times, it did not really hamper the country's progress in any way. Today, the condition of agriculture and agriculturists is quite good. Farmers are getting a good price for their crop in the market. Many reforms have been brought about in the agricultural sector. The situation had become bad after the famine that hit us a decade back, but we have come a long way since then…."

Jyotirao had spoken after Raosaheb and had countered him on many points, but he was still enraged that an educated and informed man like Raosaheb should speak so casually.

"Did you see, Bhausaheb?! Did you see how that so-called intellectual man was painting a false picture before Maharaj? What can I say about statements like 'casteism has not hindered the progress of the nation'?! Just because he feels ashamed to admit that the Brahmins had indeed razed the agriculturist class to the ground with their torment, and that the Christians have brought in at least some relief since then, he conveniently claims that all is well?! How is that possible? Can we just forget about the decades of pain that our farmer brethren went through?"

Bhau Patil had also been enraged with what Raosaheb had spoken. He remarked,

"All this is nothing but blanketing their own faults, Tatyasaheb. People like Raosaheb do not have the courage to admit that their ilk has indeed committed thousands of sins; nor do they have the face to admit that we required foreigners to come and improve the social conditions of our land."

Jyotirao added,

"Do they even realize what misery our forefathers have been through due to their casteist attitudes? How can they even dare to talk about such a prominent issue in such a light vein? Does even one woman or child from the Brahmin household know the anguish of toiling for hours and days on end without one meal a day? Has even one Brahmin man ever lifted human excreta with his bare hands and carried it on his head for dumping? Why do people like Raosaheb never dare to utter a word about men of his ilk who loot our ignorant brethren in the name of mindless rituals and blow off that money on dancing girls?!"

Two days later, 'Dýnaanprakash' published . They also gave glowing reviews to Raosaheb's speech while berating Jyotirao for being narrow-minded and stubborn in his views.

Jyotirao decided to crack a whip in retaliation to Raosaheb and Dynaanprakash by printing the first issue of 'Satsaar'. The highlight of that issue was an article written with the title of 'Ishaara ', in which he berated Raosaheb for making casual statements about casteism not having affected the country's progress adversely, and for making false claims that the condition of Shoodras and Ati Shoodras is better today than what it was in the past. He cautioned that, making such false claims would serve to paint the Brahmins in a good light for the short term, but in the long term, it would only backfire on them. He further said that, using religion to mislead the ignorant Shoodras and Ati Shoodras has been a ploy long employed by the Brahmins; but now, the British government has been taking steps to educate the lower classes, so it would be better if Brahmins like Raosaheb think twice before making false statements casually.

After sending the first issue of 'Satsaar' to print, Jyotirao went off to Mumbai. After spending four days in Mumbai, he to Thane went along with Narayanrao Lokhande. The Satyashodhak Samaj's annual event proved to be a good event, which also resulted in bridges getting rebuilt between Jyotirao and Lokhande. Narayanrao agreed to start featuring a periodical column in 'Deenbandhu', reflecting the Satyashodhak ideologies. It was also decided to send Satyashodhak messengers all over Maharashtra, to help spread the ideology of the Samaj. They planned to have a meeting about the same in December. Soon after, Jyotirao returned to Pune.

The first issue of 'Satsaar' received tremendous response. Buoyed with that success, Jyotirao immediately sent the next issue for printing. That issue comprised of a scathing article on Narayanrao Lokhande; but Jyotirao did not remove that article out just because they had renewed their relations in the interim.

86

Everyone was waiting for Gopalbuva to arrive at Dhondiba Rode's house. Apart from Jyotirao, there were Marutrao Navle, Bhimajirao Birmal, Raynaak Ghadge and a few more people.

Raynaak Ghadge was the latest addition to the anti-untouchability movement initiated by Jyotirao. After joining the army, he had been introduced to Subhedar Major Daryajirao Thorat and Gopalbuva Walangkar. He had gone along with them to hear a couple of Jyotirao's speeches, and had returned with an all-new vision about how an ideal society should be. Then one day, he went along with Gopalbuva to meet Jyotirao and while speaking with the latter, Raynaak Ghadge felt like he was meeting a human embodiment of God Himself. It was a unique experience for him to meet a man who did not believe in untouchability, and who instead vouched for treating every human being at par.

Every Sunday, Jyotirao would visit the army cantonment and deliver lectures to the sepoys. He would also give them books to read. Jyotirao was of the opinion that the government should join hands with the army to build dams, lakes, roads and such other public utility services. The British officers did not heed Jyotirao's opinion, but nevertheless, he kept on pushing his demand ahead. It was during one such lecture that Ghadge had first seen Jyotirao, and had been stirred by Jyotirao's views as he said:

"The minds of Kshatriya warriors have been enslaved by the Brahmins. The reins of our country should come into the hands of us Kshatriyas who have always given our lives in the service of the nation. The more the reins remain in the hands of Brahmins, the further we will be from progress."

Addressing the Marathi sepoys in particular, Jyotirao had said:

"Mahars and Maangs are the original Kshatriyas of this land, but the Brahmins have consistently chipped away at their self-respect by subjugating them in more ways than one. What is even more disturbing is that, centuries of conditioning have led the Mahars and Maangs to believe that what the Brahmins a redoing is right. Worse still, even we have been treating the Mahars and Maangs in an inferior manner. We all need to think if what we are doing, is justified? We need to help our Mahar Maang brethren, not torture them more. We need to teach self-respect to the children of all non-Brahmin children, so that they can lead a life of dignity."

Jamadar Lakshmanrao Desai, Havaldar Shivajirao Desai and many more people from the army had become Jyotirao's disciples. Together, they had embarked on the anti-untouchability movement.

Dhondirao Rode was an able lietenant of the Satyashodhak Samaj, who was carrying forward Jyotirao's work in an able manner. Gopalbuva was Jyotirao's student; he was naturally involved in Jyotirao's work.

Ghadge could see the many obstacles that lay in Jyotirao's way as he kept working for social equality, and he was also duly impressed by the manner in which Jyotirao continued working in spite of all those problems and obstacles.

After having waited for Gopalbuva for a long time, Jyotirao decided to go to his house to ask his whereabouts. The group set off from Bhavani Peth to go towards Gopalbuva's house. Just as they were crossing the locality of Mahars, they saw a small boy crying loudly. No adult was along with him. Jyotirao's heart melted on seeing the small child. He lifted him up, wiped his tears, and asked him why he was crying. The boy could not answer. Just then someone said,

"This is our Kisan's son. Both husband and wife must have gone to work. They work at the Municipality..."

Jyotirao asked the others to hold the boy while he got some snacks for him from an adjacent store.

A so-called progressive man was seeing all this from the sidewalk. Unable to control himself, the man grimaced and asked Jyotirao,

"Tatyasaheb, how could you feel like picking up that dirty child? That too, a child of a Mahar?"

"Why? What's wrong with that?" Jyotirao asked the man. "His being a Mahar is not by choice. No one decides where they want to be born. And, as for him being dirty...he is dirty because people like you and me do not allow his parents to get sufficient water for their daily needs."

"But, do you not feel unclean when that dirt gets rubbed onto your clothes and body?" the man persisted.

"Not at all. This dirt can be easily washed off. What I am worried about is the dirt of casteist segregation that has stuck onto minds of people like you. How can that be washed away, is the real question!"

"What do you mean?"

"I think, you very well know what I mean. It is easy to stand on a dais and give speeches."

Jyotirao's caustic comment hit bull's eye. The man turned pink in embarrassment. Not knowing how else to counter Jyotirao's comment, he huffed,

"Only a fool can go to spar with you...!

Saying thus, the man walked away.

Dhondiram Rode was looking at the man's retreating figure, with an enraged face. Jyotirao noticed Dhondiram fuming and pacified him saying,

"Don't be angry. Our entire Shoodra and Ati Shoodra

community is facing the same prejudicial attitudes. But some day, these people are going to repent their sins. Some day, the human being in them shall come alive. That day is not too far..."

By then, the small child had stopped crying. Jyotirao kept him down and soon, he toddled off to his house. Then, they went off to Gopalbuva's house.

When Jyotirao returned home after meeting Gopalbuva, he was surprised to see two clerks from the Baroda palace waiting for him. They had brought along a new portrait of Maharaj Sayajirao Gaekwad for him.

Jyotirao was very happy to see the new portrait, in which, Maharaj Sayajirao was wearing simple clothes without any accessories, and riding on horseback.

One of the clerks, Vamanrao, said,

"Tatyasaheb, Maharaj had this portrait made specially for you."

Jyotirao replied,

"Please tell Maharaj that I'm very happy to have received the real depiction of Maharaj Sayajirao!"

Then, he called out to Sitaram and asked him to hang the portrait above the main door, facing inside. Sitaram was confused. He asked,

"Tatyasaheb, if we hang the portrait here, it will not be visible to anyone coming inside."

Jyotirao smiled and replied,

"It is okay if the portrait is not visible to anyone coming inside; it should be visible to everyone going outside from here!"

That afternoon, Jyotirao received a letter from Mama Parmanand, requesting Jyotirao to send some powadas written on historically eminent men. The over-Secretary of the department that Mama Parmanand worked in, was making a compilation of such powadas. He was being assisted by Mama and Shankarrao Shaligram in this work. Mama had written to Jyotirao, requesting him to send powadas on Chhatrapati

Shivaji Maharaj, if he had any.

But, Jyotirao had not come across any such powada on Maharaj that he could confidently say, was based on real events. He had long removed from his personal collection the powadas that sung excessive paeans to Dadoji Konddev, Samarth Ramdas, or to Shivaji Maharaj as a patron of cows. He had always criticized the European authors who would write about the life and times of Shivaji Maharaj on the basis of these powadas, without ascertaining their factuality.

Jyotirao was convinced that Shivaji Maharaj's valor was not a gift of someone's blessings or simply Dadoji Konddev's teachings. It was a ploy of Brahmin authors to exaggerate the role of men of their ilk and take away from the single-handed heroism of Shivaji Maharaj.

Jyotirao immediately started penning a reply to Mama Parmanand, in which he wrote,

"I have been consistently coming across powadas written on the Chhatrapati's life and times by young Brahmin writers. However, I do not collect such powadas that do not go by fact, by instead by fiction."

Jyotirao felt sad that he could be of no help to Mama, but he also felt good that he could clarify the truth instead of mutely contributing to the false writing about Maharaj that was already floating around.

The next day, the clerks from Baroda took Jyotirao's leave.

"Please convey my heartfelt thanks and greetings to Maharaj Sayajirao" said Jyotirao, as he bade them goodbye.

87

The Otur case came for hearing, two whole years after languishing in the court of Junnar. After going through all the evidences and listening to all the witnesses, Justice Mahadev Shridhar Ranade gave the verdict that Balaji Patil should give a compensation of 8 aanas to the head priest of the village, for conducting the marriage ceremonies without the latter in attendance. The verdict served to embolden Brahmins even more. They started dancing in joy!

The Satyashodhak Samaj immediately took their case to the District court. They also spread the message to neighboring villages that, people should conduct marriage and other ceremonies without calling Brahmins, and just send 4 aanas as dakshina to their homes.

The Samaj had won half the battle by keeping Brahmins out of religious ceremonies. Now, the next step was to eliminate their self-imposed financial 'rights'. However, the Brahmins were not giving up without a fight. They kept spreading rumors and false news about the Samaj's intentions.

On 5th December 1886, a letter sent by a man named Tamboli, was published in 'Deenbandhu'. It gave a detailed description of how the upper class was making life hell for a man who was doing yeoman service for the lower classes. The letter served to stop human waste being dumped in the depot behind Jyotirao's house, apart from also elevating Jyotirao's value in the eyes of his followers.

The Satyashodhak movement was getting stronger by the day. Many ceremonies were being conducted without Brahmins. The Brahmin priests continued to spread rumors that the Satyashodhaks had lost the case, and, the Satyashodhaks had surrendered before the Brahmins etc. But in reality, it was the Brahmins who were facing a tough time. Bhau Patil had made it impossible for Brahmins to conduct any ceremony in his region. If need be felt, they would take police protection but would not yield to the Brahmins.

A big issue happened at Talegaon-Damdhere. A young barber was to be wed in keeping with the Satyashodhak rituals. A few more such weddings were to take place in Kasari as well. All the balutedars came together to ban Brahmin priests from conducting these weddings.

Narayan Kashirao Karhekar from Talegaon came to Pune

to invite Jyotirao for the weddings. He was accompanied by the lady Satyashodhak Shivubai Bhujbal. Jyotirao would be specially proud of Shivubai for defying Vithoba Bhujbal who followed all scripture-instructed rituals, and following the Satyashodhak path in spite of many obstacles. Vithoba was also responsible for the problems that arose in Talegaon. He would promote superstitious beliefs and would then turn leader to instigate people to follow his instructions. It was high time that Vithoba received a dose of his own medicine.

When Narayanrao and Shivubai came to meet Jyotirao, he was busy in writing a small booklet about what rituals could be followed in marriage ceremonies such that they would be in keeping with the Satyashodhak principles. His health was not that good yet. When Savitribai requested him to rest a bit and then continue his work, Jyotirao said to her,

"I do not have the time and liberty to rest, Savitribai. Mere mangalashtaks are not proving enough for people to get convinced that they are conducting an important ritual like marriage. They are asking for rituals. So, I'm writing down rituals which will make sense in giving credibility to a marriage ceremony. A marriage is a lifetime contract between a man and a woman. It should be done taking into consideration their ages, thoughts, and mutual affection. It should also be done with the man and woman's complete consent and prudence. A marriage should receive heartfelt blessings from the elders. Ceremonies conducted by priests who are essentially strangers for the couple, and who mutter indecipherable chants, really have no significance."

Jyotirao sent Gyaanoba and a few other men ahead to Talegaon. By the time he handed over the booklet to Narayanrao for printing and himself reached Talegaon, a lot of things had happened in the interim.

The balutedars managed to hold a successful marriage ceremony of the barber, without letting the Brahmins interfere. The Brahmins tried their best to ruin the plan, but they were shaken to the core after the Satyashodhaks came in from Pune. Still, they tried to break the Satyashodhaks apart by plying some of them with liquor, and sweet-talking some others by apologizing to them. But, none of their tricks worked.

Irked with the non-responsive attitude of the balutedars, the Brahmins started spreading rumors that they have only ostracized the balutedars and that, it was a part of that ban that they had started shaving each others heads without going to a barber for the same. But, the barbers and the other balutedars did not care two pennies about these stories. Their leader, Jyotirao Phule, had himself arrived at Talegaon-Dhamdhere; hence, the Satyashodhaks had become even more emboldened.

People started making fun of these Brahmin barbers. This was not the first time that they had taken the razor in their own hands, literally and figuratively. Before this too, whenever barbers would raise their prices, the Brahmins would take each others heads and razors in their own hands! The matter had become a point of joke for everyone. People started wondering aloud that if the Brahmins were thus themselves converting into barbers, then why should they object to a barber's marriage ceremony being conducted by a barber?!

That night, a meeting was arranged at Narayanrao Karhekar's house. Many balutedars were in attendance. They all wanted the weddings at Kasari to be conducted by Jyotirao. It was decided that till the time Brahmins toiled to earn their bread, no villager would let them earn idly by simply chanting some indecipherable mantras.

Just as this meeting was happening, they could hear Narayanrao's father Kashiba singing a devotional hymn from inside the house. Hearing that, Jyotirao realized that while the younger generation was changing its views, it was going to be a tough job to convert the elders.

Some time later, Kashiba came outside and sat in the meeting. Jyotirao said to him,

"Kaka, do you not agree with our thoughts?"

"Of course I agree with your thoughts. But, at the age that I am in, it is difficult – nay, impossible – to change age old habits. Tomorrow, Narayan's son will not follow our path."

Hearing that answer, Jyotirao was reminded of his own father, Dada. He would also agree with Jyoti's views but would also find it difficult to follow on his path. Jyotirao realized that there was little he could do to bridge this generational difference. The silver lining to this was that, the upcoming generations would not follow the beaten path.

Still, Jyotirao said to Kashiba,

"Kashiba, just as you sign hymns in praise of Saint Dynaneshwar, so also we sing hymns that praise the truth in all its forms. That's the only difference – rest, the aim is the same."

Narayanrao then requested Jyotirao to sing the Adisatya hymn that he had himself written.

Talks went on till midnight, after which everyone left for their own homes.

The atmosphere in the village was a tense one. Everyone was looking at each other with suspicion. Finally, four days later, the Brahmins had to come nose-in-fist. They had realized that no one was falling for their ploys. They had to finally come and apologize at a meeting of all the balutedars. The head priest, Sitaram Yeshwant Bhawalkar apologized with tears in his eyes, saying, they had started shaving each other's heads to strip the barbers of their livelihood.

The balutedars forgave the Brahmins, but as the meeting came to an end, one of the young Brahmins, Lakhoba Gopal, started screaming:

"You foolish, lowly balutedars! You made us Brahmins beg for forgiveness from you? Who do you think you are?! I'm a Kulkarni; so many of my friends and relatives are on high positions in the government. I shall personally see to it that you shall suffer for this insult heaped upon us."

Lakhoba had been tremendously incensed by the fact that

the Brahmins had been made to lower their heads in front of the balutedars. His proclamation poured oil on the fire that was dying out! Dulerao Sakhaji Pingle and Narayanrao Karhekar reiterated their resolve to conduct all the weddings in Kasari in the Satyashodhak way. Once again, the Brahmins were banned!

The Kasari weddings were to take place that day itself. Late that afternoon, Jyotirao and the others set out for Kasari. But by then, the Brahmins had already laid their trap. Taking the traitor Vithoba Bhujbal into confidence, they threatened the hapless villagers with the fear of conducting black magic and got one young man married with Brahmin rituals. As that wedding ceremony was coming to a close, the Satyashodhaks reached the venue. Seeing them in front of him, the back-stabbing Bhujbal got scared and hid in a stack of hay! The Brahmins too gathered their dhotis and started running away, leaving the ceremony incomplete.

However, when Jyotirao and the Satyashodhaks came forward to complete the ceremony, the bride and groom's parents objected to letting them do so. They were insistent that their ceremony should be done by Brahmins only, because, even though they were Shoodras, they belonged to the higher rung of Malis in the Shoodra community, and thus would not allow some barber to conduct their ceremony. Jyotirao tried driving sense into their head by telling them that the Brahmins had brainwashed them into going against their own people. He also spoke to them extensively about the Otur case. But none of this yielded any result.

One of their relatives spoke up,

"Tatyasaheb, we understand what you are saying. But we are caught in a Catch 22 situation. Today these Brahmins may behave contrite, but later, they are bound to sharpen their claws and come back at us. They have an upper hand in every walk of life. The regime of our country might be British, but the real rulers are the Brahmin clerks and officials who are present everywhere. How and till where do we escape them, tell us?"

Jyotirao and the Satyashodhaks had to concede defeat. The Brahmins aside; a fight ensued between the balutedars and Vithoba Bhujbal. He became more responsible than the Brahmins for puncturing the confidence of the Shoodra community in Kasari.

Jyotirao was incensed. On returning to Pune, he started writing a caustic article about a traitor who has no compunction in wagging his tail before the Brahmins and causing harm to his own people for short-term selfish gains. In the article, Jyotirao interspersed couplets that sought to explain to Bhujbal that he was the biggest loser in this game that he was playing. For, the Brahmins were sure to kick him away once their aim was fulfilled; and, by then, he would have lost favor with his own people too.

88

One morning when Savitribai woke up, she felt something amiss. It seemed that her husband had not yet woken up – a possibility that was enough to startle Savitribai out of her sleep, because howsoever late it might have been the previous night, Jyotirao would always be up by 4 am. By the time Savitribai would wake up, Jyotirao would have long finished his ablutions and gone for his morning walk. During the monsoons, he would start reading instead of going for a walk.

Savitribai got up and went near her husband's bedside. Seeing him in deep sleep, she felt a twang of worry. She quickly went inside to start the cooking stove and returned to Jyotirao's bedside.

As she scanned his face, Savitribai noticed that her husband was looking much tired and older than she remembered him. The years of toil were making their presence more prominent by the day. His beard and hair had started greying; his face looked weary.

Savitribai gently woke up Jyotirao. He opened his eyes but did not say anything in response.

"Are you not feeling well, Shetji?" she asked with concern.

Jyotirao nodded in the negative and tried to get up by propping himself on his right hand; but suddenly, the hand fell limp, as if all its strength had been sapped away!

"What is happening, Shetji?" Savitribai asked, more worried now.

"Nothing…just a lot of weakness…" he replied feebly.

"This does not seem a sign of simple weakness…." Savitribai urged.

Jyotirao had never been the one to complain about his health. He neither had the time nor the inclination to keep pampering his health. But seeing his condition now, Savitribai realized with a start, that her husband had been bearing out a lot till now. It pained her even more that her husband, who would not do a single thing without taking her into consideration, had not felt the need to confide in her about his health problems. Her eyes filled with tears. Seeing that, Jyotirao strained his voice and said,

"Savitribai… why do I see tears in your eyes? Don't worry. I'm okay. Sometimes these things happen. It is a human body after all. Sometimes it does seem to lose all its strength. I don't know why this happens…but I'm sure, there's no cause for real worry…"

Savitribai did not respond. Jyotirao held her hand tenderly, and called out,

"Savitri…."

It was after many years later that Jyotirao had called her by that endearment. Savitribai looked at him with surprise. Jyotirao continued,

"Do you think I do not understand your worry, your care? But see, the troubles of the society are much more than our personal ones. They require immediate care than my health does. But I do know that this attitude of mine causes a lot of trouble for you..."

"What is this now? Is this what you want to say to me at this time?" Savitribai rebuked him gently.

"No, Savitri...Please hear me out. You have spent so many years of your life doing so much for me. You have been my pillar of support, my silent shadow...Always helping me wordlessly. But....but...I have not been able to do anything for you..."

Savitribai started feeling a pang of worry again. This was not the Shetji she knew. She couldn't understand why he was talking like this today. Jyotirao continued,

"Don't be upset, Savitri. I never cared for anyone in my life, but my heart begins melting when I think about you. Nowadays, I don't feel that carefree about my health. Add to it, our own relatives have been behaving like enemies. I'm worried, if something were to happen to me, they will not have any compunction in troubling you for getting a share of the pie. That is why I feel, I must make legal provisions for you and Yeshwant while I'm alive...."

"Means?" Savitribai asked confusedly.

"Means...I feel like I should make a will."

Hearing her husband talk in such a way, Savitribai started crying. Jyotirao had anticipated this reaction, but he felt it necessary to think practically and also exhort his wife to do the same. He kept explaining to her,

"See Savitri...our Satyashodhaks will always be with you. But, it is pertinent to think practically and make due provisions while one is still active. Think about Yeshwant... He is our responsibility. We cannot leave him high & dry."

After long last, Savitribai said to Jyotirao,

"Please do one thing..."

"Yes, Savitri?..."

"Stop talking about all these things for now. You require to rest. You have many things to accomplish before that stage of life comes by; so, don't think about those extremities just now.

What made you think about all this today in the first place?"

Jyotirao laughed and replied,

"You are right, Savitribai. There is so much more work to do. We need to win the Otur case. I'm yet to write a book on Sarvajanik Satyadharma. It will not be enough to just tell what we do not want. We need to be clear about what we do want. Else, I shall be maligned for starting a community whose sole purpose was to spread malice about the Brahmins and not do anything more. Also, I need to pay more attention to our family life. I go around telling people how to have a happy personal life...and look at me here! I hardly ever stay at home. That won't do. I shall now pay equal attention to domestic matters. What have you decided about Yeshwant's marriage?"

Savitribai was happy to hear Jyotirao echo her thoughts. Yeshwant had become 14 years old. Most of his friends had been married by then. Knowing Jyotirao's views about the ideal ages for a girl and boy's marriage, Savitribai had not broached the topic before Jyotirao. But, now that he himself had broached the topic, Savitribai replied,

"What are your views on this, Shetji?"

"Well, I think that he is to young to be married off right now; but, we can start thinking about it. If possible, we can get him betrothed to some good girl and then conduct the ceremony when he comes of proper age. Who knows what the future might bring? Whether or not people will be ready to give him their daughter in the future?...."

Savitribai was surprised to see Jyotirao thinking about Yeshwant's marriage. He surprised her even further by saying,

"Savitribai, what do you think of our Gyaanoba's daughter, Radha? For Yeshwant?"

Savitribai was elated on hearing Radha's name. They had known the girl since she was a baby, and the Phule couple was very fond of her.

"Radha would be the apt girl for our Yeshwant" she exulted, adding, "But, will Gyaanoba agree?"

"Why not, Savitribai? And, we are not going to be compelling Gyaanoba in any way. We shall reach out to him with a formal proposal. He has every right to accept or decline, as he deems fit. Having said that, I do not think he shall refuse. You do remember the chaos that had ensued during Gyaanoba's own wedding, don't you? The Brahmins had speculated that the marriage would be proven illegal…children born out of that wedlock would be proved illegitimate…That time, I had promised Gyaanoba that the marriages of his children will be my responsibility. So, in a way, today I am looking at fulfilling my responsibility…."

Savitribai suggested,

"Then, let us do one thing. Let us bring Radha to live with us. Let her and Yeshwant study together, play together. Let them come closer by heart…Then we shall think of getting them married."

"Very good idea, Savitribai. Radha is an intelligent girl. Let us educate her well. She has the potential to become a doctor like Anandibai Joshi. We have already suffered the loss of Dr. Joshi. Who knows, maybe Radha can take her work ahead and serve her sisters in this land? There are so many epidemics happening…so many people dying an untimely death in those epidemics… We need more and more doctors to stop this unfortunate cycle. There is no more altruistic profession than medicine. Our Yeshwant will also become a doctor. Both of them can then serve the country together…" mused Jyotirao.

Anandibai Joshi's name caused Savitribai to wince in pain. It had barely been five months since this intelligent and courageous young lady who got a degree in medicine from America, had been snatched away at the cruel hands of death at a tender age of 21.

Gopalrao Joshi had saddled the then-17 year old Anandibai with a huge responsibility. But, the determined young girl had seen it through, only to be taken away by fate before she could start using her knowledge for the betterment of people.

Kaku remembered the day when news filtered in that Anandibai had left for America. Pune was in the spasms of disbelief, shock, and rage after hearing that a young Brahmin girl had been sent across seven seas, and that too for higher education. The orthodox people of Pune, who had once made eminent men like Raobahadur Gopal Hari and Raosaheb Ranade to conduct atonement for their sins', were frothing at their mouths in fury about this blasphemy. However, Gopalrao Joshi proved stronger tan hundreds of orthodox Brahmins put together. He bravely declared that he was also going to join Anandibai abroad, and if need be felt, they were both going to convert to Christianity!

Gopalrao Joshi's courage was indeed commendable, to say the least. Without caring about the social repercussions, he enrolled Anandibai into a Mission school. When his child died in sickness after a Brahmin doctor refused to treat him for being a reformer's child, Gopalrao Joshi took the most courageous oath ever. He decided to send Anandibai to America to gain the best medical knowledge possible.

Joshi knew that it was difficult to gather the funds required for this endeavor, on his mere job as a clerk. Yet, he doggedly started saving money. At one point he realized that he had enough money to sponsor Anandibai's trip, but he could not join her – he did not have the additional funds. Joshi then became ready to convert his religion if that was going to simplify matters, but Anandibai strongly refused to allow him to do so.

Then, Joshi started writing to several people in America, requesting them for help. After many tries, he met with success. A lady named Mrs. Carpenter agreed to help him, and thus, Anandibai left for foreign shores.

She got admission with scholarship at the Pennsylvania Women's Medical College. Anandibai would study day and night. Her health had started weakening in the strong cold of America, but without paying much attention to that, she kept studying with determination. Having lost a child before coming to America, Anandibai would find her heart getting gainfully distracted while studying.

The young girl kept her efforts on for three years in the face of bone-chilling cold, deteriorating health, and Gopalrao's eccentric behavior.

Gopalrao was a good man. He held Anandibai's best interests at heart. But if only his perseverance had been supported with some patience, then probably Anandibai would have not suffered so much. But that was not to be...Gopalrao could not wait for the day his wife became a doctor.

As a result, when Anandibai returned as a qualified doctor to India, she came with Tuberculosis embedded in her bones. Shahu Maharaj of Kolhapur had already kept her a job reserved as royal physician in his durbar, but that was not meant to be. Anandibai could not fulfill her dream of serving her sisters. The tuberculosis had turned so potent by then that she could barely get up from her bed.

Gopalrao requested Vaidyashastri Mehendale to treat her, but he strongly refused to even see the face of a woman who had conducted a blasphemy of going across the seven seas! The mother died on account of the same illness as her child.

Barely four months after returning from America, Anandibai left for her heavenly abode. All her efforts went waste.

Savitribai could still remember the Anandibai who had come to visit them at their house...

The horse was neighing in the courtyard. Savitribai got up to tell Sitaram to feed him. On her way out, she told Jyotirao,

"I'm calling a doctor home. It is better that someone checks you now..."

Hearing this, Jyotirao said,

"Then please send for Dr. Vishram Ramji."

Savitribai was very happy to hear this request from Jyotirao himself. Jyotirao had met Dr. Vishram Ramji after he received the title of Raobahadur, but the relations between both the friends had not come to a very comfortable plain yet. Hence, she asked,

"Really? Do you mean it?"

In response, Jyotirao sighed and replied,

"Nowadays, I don't feel like staying angry with anyone for long. Life is too short for holding grudges. And as it is, he had heeded my request during Shastribuva's funeral, hadn't he?..."

Dr. Vishram Ramji was more than happy to come see his old friend. The visit served to remove the cobwebs that had accumulated over a good friendship during the years in the interim.

The next day, Jyotirao sat down to pen his will. After penning a brief history about Yeshwant's birth and life with them, Jyotirao willed their entire estate and property to him. Yeshwant was to get this right only after he legally became an adult or after the demise of both Jyotirao and Savitribai; whichever came first. He further obliterated all his brothers and nephew Ganpatrao Rajaram Phule from claiming any part of his property and earnings. Jyotirao further specified that at the time of writing this will, Yeshwant was not an adult, and he and Savitribai were taking due care of him as foster parents in the hope that one day, he would use his education to serve the needy and ignorant Shoodra, Ati Shoodra people. They wished that Yeshwant would use his life to educate his ignorant brethren by making them aware of their human rights and thus saving their future generations from a life of slavery to the evil, cunning, and selfish Brahmins. Jyotirao also specified that when he and his wife Savitribai die, all the post-demise rituals should be conducted by Yeshwant (irrespective of whether he is married by then or not), in keeping with the Satyashodhak Samaj rituals. If for any reason, Yeshwant is not present during their demise, Jyotirao asked one of the Satyashodhak Samaj members to conduct their rites. He also specified that instead of burning their corpses on a funeral pyre, they should be embalmed in salt and cremated in the earth. He mentioned that he had opted for this method, so as to be of use to nature even after his death, and also to ensure that post death, no Brahmin would need to even cast a shadow on his or his wife's dead body.

Even though Jyotirao had made the will in a way such that it would completely benefit Yeshwant, he had not become blind with love while doing so. In the same will, Jyotirao had mentioned that after the demise of their both, if Yeshwant is seen squandering away his time, energy, and the bequeathed money in futile pursuits, then he should immediately be removed from the said estates; a small sum be paid to him every month from Jyotirao's Pune or Khanwadi estate's revenue; and the rest of money be given to some intelligent, capable, and promising youngster from the Satyashodhak Samaj. He would be made responsible for conducting all affairs of Jyotirao's estate. The rights to determine such a person would remain with Savitribai and the Samaj members.

After writing out the will, Jyotirao explained it to Savitribai and Yeshwant too. He elucidated to Yeshwant, the reasons behind why he had written all this.

After they all were duly convinced with the contents of the will, Jyotirao went along with Dr. Vishram Ramji to the sub-registrar's office; took Dr. Vishram Ramji's signature certifying his mental health to be sane while writing the will; took the signatures of two more witnesses; and thus sealed the will.

One day, in order to depict the condition of farmers in the progressive British regime, Jyotirao painted the picture of a tree. The tree had Parsis sitting on the top. Brahmin s occupied by the branches immediately below the Parsis. The third rung of branches had Marwaris, the fourth rung held Bengalis, while the fifth rung held MUslims. Below all of them, holding the huge tree on his head and bent at the spine owing to the load, was the humble farmer.

He got several prints made of that picture and pasted it on the walls all around the city. He also sent a few copies to nearby villages.

Bhau Patil found the picture so apt in its description that, he decided to put it up in front of the national congress' conference.

Even though Jyotirao had decided not to get angry with anyone, certain things would so happen that he could not help but react in an enraged manner. The latest person to irk Jyotirao was his close friend Swami Ramaiyya Venkaiah Aiyyavaru.

Swami had written a small booklet titled 'A Request To All My Christian Friends'. The booklet showed the discrepancies between the teachings of Bible and the tenets of Christianity. It also had mild criticism of the faults of Christianity. He opined that Christianity also held several parables that were illogical and false. Also, he wrote that, while criticizing other religions for its tenets, Christianity should first introspect about what is good and bad in their own religion.

The newspapers got an idle topic to chew upon. A spate of reviews started appearing in newspapers, most of which served to fling mud upon Christianity. Sadly, 'Deenbandhu' also participated in these attacks.

Jyotirao was very incensed with the going-ons. He started writing articles and parables asking why are people finding joy in denouncing Christianity without knowing facts, and, elucidating on the good teachings that Christianity proffers if one is willing to take it in an unbiased way.

He sent all these writings under the pen-name of Swamibandhu for publication in 'Dynaanoday'.

There was another reason for Jyotirao's rage to rise up in such a manner. In the Neetiprasarak Sabha started by Swami Aiyyavaru, baseless debates would ensue regarding the existence of God. They would also debate about the connection between religion and morality. Jyotirao, who firmly believed in the existence of a higher power, could not reconcile with questions being raised about the very existence of God.

The Sushikshan Gruha also served to add to the confusion in the biases and prejudices. The children of Raju Babaji, Jaya Karadi etc. had started attending the Sushikshan Gruha at the behest of Swamiji. Now, they began complaining to Jyotirao through a spate of letters. One such letter was published in Jyotirao's 'Satsaar'; that served to worsen the relations between Jyotirao and Krishnarao even more. Krishnarao felt that Jyotirao had deliberately published that letter, in order to malign the image of Sushikshan Gruha.

'Swamibandhu's' articles began appearing in 'Dynaanoday'. It did not take much time for people to realize that this was Jyotirao writing under a pen-name. Many of them were displeased that Jyotirao should criticize in such a harsh manner. Swami Aiyyavaru also became quite unhappy with Jyotirao.

Soon after, people started demanding that Jyotirao should apologize to Swami Aiyyavaru. But, it did not align with the former's principles to apologize to someone who had baselessly criticized the Christian religion. Around that time, even Ramji Santuji Aawate, the editor of 'Baroda Vatsal' criticized Jyotirao for the mess that had been created.

Finally, Jyotirao had to yield to the increasing pressure. He wrote an apology-cum-explanatory letter to Dynaanoday, in which he wrote:

"In my critique published in your newsletter on 8 September 2018, I expressed my views regarding the biased treatment being given to Christian religion by my friend, Swami Aiyyavaru. Many of the readers felt that some part of my criticism was directed towards Swamiji himself. However, I'd like to clarify that, that is not the case. My critique was only against the writing; not against any person. I have never wished to defame any person through any of my writings and other expressions so far. Nevertheless, if my views have hurt anybody's sentiments, I wish to apologize for the same."

The letter was published in the 27th October issue of 'Dynaanoday', finally drawing a curtain on the vexing issue.

89

The District court took cognizance of the Satyashodhak Samaj's views. Justice Nanavati ruled that, 'a Brahmin priest has the right to demand dakshina only if a marriage ceremony is conducted in keeping with rituals mentioned in Hindu scriptures. But, any such ceremony that does not follow the Hindu rituals, automatically obliterates the Brahmins' rights to ask for dakshina. Thus, Joshi has no right to ask for dakshina'.

The judgment created havoc among Brahmin circles! The Brahmins of Otur called for urgent meetings, as did the Brahmins in Pune. The enraged Brahmin class decided to approach the High court to safeguard their rights. They were furious that the Satyashodhak Samaj was casting blows on what they considered their 'birth rights'.

In order to meet the escalating legal expenses, Jyotirao sold off his farm at Maanjri. It was a sad decision but he put a stone on his heart and took the step because it would not do to look at expenses if they had to defeat the strong Brahmin class.

More such legal cases ensued in Varhaad region.

Jyotirao started making the rounds of Mumbai to fight the case on behalf of the Samaj. After much trouble, he could get the eminent lawyer Ghanashyam Neelkant Nadkarni to represent their side. The opposing side was being represented by Mahadev Chimnaji Apte.

The constant travel and the tension of the case started taking a toll on Jyotirao's already weak health. As his travels to Mumbai increased, so did the duration of his stay in every visit. During those stays, more and more people began coming to meet and talk to him.

Once, Jyotirao gave a speech at Madhavrao Rokade's school. Bhau Kondaji, Narayanrao Lokhande and many more rich and scholarly people from Mumbai were in attendance at this program. Jyotirao spoke extensively about the battle waging on at Pune and Varhaad. A lively discussion began after the speech. The attendees started asking various questions. Madhavrao was compliant with Jyotirao's views, but he did not agree that Brahmin priests be substituted by Satyashodhak priests. He believed that by doing so, they would give birth to another bracket of priests, who, after some time, were bound to become aggressive and uncontrollable as well.

Jyotirao thought about this for a while and replied,

"Yes, your fear is true. Religious reformers soon tend to become drunk on power and turn into religious lords. But, if we take due care to see that such a tendency does not arise among the Satyashodhaks, then we can avert such a disaster in our clique. Else, another suggestion is that, we do away with the need for priests altogether. Why do we need priests? Be it a marriage ceremony, house-warming ceremony or whatever else... if one person from every family can learn to conduct those rituals, there won't be any need to call upon a priest. That will stop the loot happening in the name of dakshina from all kinds of priests, be it Brahmins or probably the others in later times."

A young student, sitting in the crowd, seemed eager to speak something. Narayanrao Lokhande, who was presiding over the meeting, encouraged him to speak up saying,

"Do you wish to talk? Please stand up."

The student got up and said,

"Tatyasaheb, I feel that religious reform should begin from the root. If you think that Brahmin priests should not interfere during religious proceedings, then the religious scriptures that have accorded them the right to preside over such proceedings, should be proven incorrect and baseless. Unless such an extreme step is taken, the priests are bound to keep raising their heads on some occasion or other."

Jyotirao was pleased to see the young boy's courage and

also his suggestion. He remarked,

"What this boy is saying is very correct. But, in order to manifest this idea into reality, we need to write equally heavy scriptures that will counter the earlier written ones. For that, we need religious scholars who will be able to write such books/ scriptures. That is a time-consuming affair and can be looked into in the long term. But for now, we all should keep up the work of debilitating these greedy Brahmin priests whenever they try to con us in the name of religion. People in Otur and Junnar have been doing a lot of work in this direction. If we keep taking due efforts, it won't be long before people in other villages will follow suit. For now, even this much is enough."

The student did not say anything further.

After the meeting, Jyotirao beckoned to him and asked him his name.

"I'm Krishnaji Arjun Keluskar" the young boy replied.

During his stay in Mumbai, Jyotirao also met up with Swami Aiyyavaru and clarified his stance. The strain that had befallen their relationship in the interim, got wiped away with this meeting.

Sheth Raju Babaji had enrolled his son Nana and nephew Shamba at Krishnarao Bhalekar's Sushikshan Gruha. Jaya Karadi's children were also enrolled there. But, they were getting increasingly displeased with the situation in that place. Once, Raju Babaji's sister, Rajubai went to Pune to oversee the place personally. She came back with disheartening reports, after which Babaji and Jaya Karadi, both pulled their wards out of the Sushikshan Gruha.

Till then, many news had started floating about the Sushikshan Gruha. It was said that, in spite of enforcing strict discipline, the children would behave in an undisciplined manner. Since Jyotirao and Krishnarao's relation was at a low ebb, the former did not take part in the Sushikshan Gruha's work in any way.

However, Raju Babaji and Jaya Karadi started insisting to Jyotirao that they were willing to re-enroll their wards in the Sushikdhan Gruha, provided Jyotirao would allow them to stay with himself at his home. After many weeks of insistence, finally Jyotirao yielded. Then one day, Jyotirao returned from Pune with the resolve to open a students' hostel.

He pondered that if he started a students' hostel, he could make arrangements for ten-twelve poor children, along with the rich children who would come to stay there. He would take fees from the rich parents and would admit poor children free of charge.

In the meantime, Bhalekar's Sushikshan Gruha downed its shutters. He got a sub-contract for the Tansa lake being built inMumbai, and shifted to Mumbai for that work.

Starting a new hostel under those circumstances was going to invite more controversies for Jyotirao, but he was oblivious of that possibility. He was just caught up with the thought of how and when he could start the hostel...

One evening when Jyotirao returned home, he saw Pandit Dhondiram and a few other people waiting for him in the living room. Everyone was looking immensely happy to see Shaahir Dhondiram having returned from Kashi as a scholarly Pandit. It was nothing short of a miracle that a simple man from the Kumbhar community went to Kashi on the basis of sheer determination, learnt Sanskrit, and then conducted a deep study of the Vedas.

Pandit Dhondiram was eagerly waiting for Jyotirao. When he entered the room, Dhondiram rushed ahead and lay his head of Jyotirao's feet!

Jyotirao was taken aback with this sudden gesture. He asked,

"What are you doing, Pandit? Please get up. When did you come?"

"This morning itself" replied Dhondiram, still kneeling at Jyotirao's feet. "Tatyasaheb, please accept my gratitude... it was only due to you that this simple man could achieve something worthwhile in his life."

"No, Pandit. Whatever you have achieved is due to your hard work and perseverance. That credit is only yours" Jyotirao replied in an overwhelmed voice.

Jyotirao then asked Dhondiram about his experiences at Kashi. It was truly an inspiring story of grit and determination as to how Dhondiram had battled several obstacles and biases to fulfil his aim. It had taken him immense perseverance to learn Sanskrit and then master the Vedas.

Hearing his narration, Jyotirao said to Dhondiram,

"Pandit, many congratulations to you. I do not have words to express what I am feeling right now. I had always wanted to do something on these lines, but it never got possible for me. But you have seen your aim through. Now, it is your duty to prove to the world, with due evidences, that the Vedas and other ancient scriptures have been written by selfish and cunning people who wanted to subjugate others through those confounding verses."

Pandit Dhondiram replied,

"After all the studies that I did, I have come to realize that indeed the Hindu scriptures and religious rules have been written by a handful selfish people. In order to bring this truth out in the open, I'm going to write a book called Vedachaar'. But Tatyasaheb.... I have one request..."

"Yes, Pandit...What is it?"

"Please continue to address me as Shaahir, as you would do earlier."

Hearing this, Jyotirao smiled and replied,

"No, Pandit. You have earned the title of Pandit with immense efforts. Our address is a salutation to those efforts that you have taken. In fact, henceforth, all Satyashodhaks shall address you as Pandit."

90

Hari Raoji Chiplunkar's mansion was lit up in the glow of lampshades and chandeliers. Candelabras holding lit up candles were placed in almost every corner of the house. The courtyard was decorated with festoons and flowers.

A dais was created at one end of the living room. Chairs were arranged for the audience members. A retinue of sepoys was stationed outside the mansion.

It was the day of a special feast at Chiplunkar's home today. The Duke of Connaught was invited to be the chief guest at the feast which was arranged in his honor.

The Chiplunkar mansion was famed for the many feasts that would be arranged for the government officials who would be retiring and soon be leaving for their motherland. At times, dignitaries visiting Pune city would also be invited over for such feasts. Today's celebration had a special reason. Hari Raoji had been felicitated with the title of Honorary Magistrate. Given his fond friendship with the Duke, it was going to be double the celebration that day. Add to that, the Duke was going to come along with his wife; so, that served to increase the happiness of all attendees even more.

That evening, the mansion started seeing a whirlwind of activity. Palanquins and horse carriages started depositing eminent guests at the mansion, who were welcomed at the entrance in the glow of flambeaus and torches. The guests came wearing rich attires coupled with ornate accessories. The ladies especially were looking regal in their bedecked avatars. Strings of pearls, gold necklaces, gold bangles, and such other jewelry looked beautiful on their gorgeous, embroidered saris. The ladies were accompanied by their personal maidservants.

All the guests had received personalized invitation cards. Even though most of the guests were family friends of the Chiplunkars, the sentries and specially-appointed clerks were checking all invitation cards thoroughly so as to ensure no lapse in security. Hari Raoji was standing at the door of the living room, welcoming each guest as they entered, and showing them to their designated seats.

Just then, clerk Shivram came and whispered something in Hari Raoji's ears. Apparently, there had been some problem at the main entrance. A rural and unkempt looking man was insisting that he had been invited for the soirée; he even had an invitation card on him. But, seeing his appearance, the sentries were refusing to let him inside.

Hari Raoji was confounded. He did not remember sending an invitation to any such man. But, considering that he did hold an invitation, it became necessary to see who the person was.

He squinted from afar and saw that a middle-aged man, wearing a collarless tunic, a dhoti up to the knees and a turban on the head, was standing at the main entrance with a stick in his hands. Suspecting that this was who he thought he was, Hari Raoji went ahead... and sure enough, his suspicions were confirmed. In an instant, Hari Raoji folded his hands and said in an apologetic voice,

"I'm extremely sorry, Tatyasaheb... Please do come inside...Shivram did not recognize you. I'm very sorry for the lapse. Please come in."

Saying thus, he reverentially got Jyotirao inside and made him sit on the dais in a chair placed right next to the Duke's.

Seeing the unkempt man sitting near the regal prince, a ripple of murmurs started among the crowd. Many of them did not understand who was this man who was being given so much importance...

Just then, an announcement was made that the Duke and the Duchess' horse carriage had come near the mansion. Hari Raoji went to welcome them. The royal guests were ushered inside with due pomp and pageantry.

A few speeches were to be done in the Dukes honor, before dinner was commenced. The Duke himself was also slated to speak. Hari Raoji started by introducing all the guests sitting on the dais. However, everyone's attention was pulled by the rural-looking man sitting among the well-dress, sophisticated guests. Recognizing the curiosity sparked by Jyotirao, Hari Raoji introduced him saying,

"Your Highness, this is Jyotirao Govindrao Phule. Our social reformer. Leader of our peasants and workers."

The Duke extended his hand towards Jyotirao and asked Hari Raoji,

"Oh, so is he a peasant himself?"

"Yes, he is a peasant and also our social reformer" replied Hari Raoji.

"Oh...glad to meet you, Mr. Jyotirao Phule" said the Duke.

"Thank you. I have great pleasure to see you, Your Highness" Jyotirao replied.

Hearing this, the Duke realized that this rural-looking man was different than what he seemed on first glance. His curiosity was replaced by respect.

A spate of speeches ensued in the Duke's honor. Then, Hari Raoji requested Jyotirao to speak.

"Alright" said Jyotirao. "But, I shall require half an hour. Can Your Highness spare that much time?"

Hari Raoji realized that Jyotirao wanted to talk about something specific. He whispered,

"Please go on. The Duke is eager to hear you."

However, many of the attendees were displeased that this unkempt, rustic man was being given so much importance in a feast fit for kings. They did not like the idea of having to listen to him talk on such a joyous occasion. They figured that his speech was bound to be nothing more than a litany of complaints and barbs; but, they were helpless. They had to bear it out and listen to him.

However, some people in the audience, and especially the Duke, were quite eager to hear what Jyotirao was going to say.

Jyotirao had come with his speech prepared. He had

anticipated that he would be requested to talk, and had thus prepared a speech of request on behalf of the country's agriculturist population, to present in front of the Duke.

Jyotirao hung his walking stick to the chair, kept his shawl on the table, and began to speak in confident English. Cordially greeting the Duke and then the rest of the eminent people on the dais, he began:

"Brothers and sisters, you must be confounded to see me in this attire. But, what is there to be confounded by this? 90% of our country's people are dressed in a similar attire all their life. I myself am a farmer; so, I have dressed like one. Also, there is a particular reason for me to have come here in this attire..."

Hearing this, the Duke looked at Jyotirao expectantly. Jyotirao continued,

"Your Highness, seeing all these esteemed guests present here in rich, elegant dresses and ornate jewelry, you might come under the misconception that India is a very well-to-do country. But, that will be your fallacy; because, the reality is far removed and grim from what you see here. The real India is the one run by hard-working farmers, who never even see – let alone wear – even one such dress in their lives. Our real India is made up of those laborious farmers who toil incessantly, night & day, and yet remain barefooted, half-naked, and starving for all their lives. What I am wearing today is a much decent and clean version of what those farmers wear. If the Duke wishes to get a snapshot of the real India, I request him to please visit some villages and see the abject poverty over there. He may also kindly visit the localities earmarked for Mahars and Maangs, the lowest of our caste-hierarchy, and see the extremely unhygienic conditions that they are forced to live in..."

"Sir...that is the real India. The real Hindustan. Sadly, our farmers do not understand your language and you do not understand theirs. Hence, the cunning and corrupt Brahmin clerks and officers have got a big loophole to keep spinning their web of exploitation. I beseech you, kindly do not think that the esteemed people sitting in front of you are the real India. Please convey to Her Highness the Queen of England that a very huge chunk of our population is languishing in abject poverty for generations on end due to lack of education. We desperately require many more avenues of education to be made open for our people. That is what I came here to request you about."

The Duke was enchanted with Jyotirao. He had never come across such a man in India, who spoke so fearlessly, confidently, and yet humbly. The Duke had heard about a lot of so-called freedom fighters who would show that they were fighting for the people of India but would only end up creating more chaos; but, this was the first time that he was seeing a man who thought deeply and sanely about the long-term benefits of his countrymen.

The Duke had never seen such an intricately woven and complex society like India. In his speech, he thanked Jyotirao for opening his eyes to the realities of India and promised him that his message would surely reach to Her Highness, the Queen.

Then, the dinner gala started. Frankincense started wafting around the huge dining hall. Servers began running around obsequiously, carrying platters of delicious delicacies to serve to the guests. The food and the informal atmosphere caused several tongues to start wagging. Displeasure started getting expressed for inviting a rustic man like Jyotirao to pour water over the happy occasion. Nevertheless, those who agreed with Jyotirao's views, were happy that he had been given a chance to express his thoughts before the Duke.

The Duke invited Jyotirao to sit beside him during the feast. They both enjoyed the sumptuous dinner over more talks and discussion.

The regal feast and Tatyasaheb Phule's fearless speech on the occasion, served to keep the gristmills of Pune running for several weeks after that.

91

'Satsaar' shut down barely after two issues; but thankfully, by then, the relations between 'Deenbandhu' and Jyotirao had again become pleasant. So much so that, Jyotirao contributed the entire profits from the sale of the mangalashtak booklet, to 'Deenbandhu'.

After finishing the Tansa lake contract, Krishnrao returned to Pune and launched a new monthly newsletter called 'Deenmitra' with the help of his nephew Ganpat Sakharam Patil. His relations were Jyotirao were still bad. There seemed to be no possibility of a compromise now, because Krishnarao was convinced that Jyotirao was responsible for the closure of his Sushikshan Gruha. In order to compensate for the closure of Sushikshan Gruha, Krishnarao began efforts to launch the Deenbandhu Free School for poor students.

Picking on the chaos that was ensuing in religious occasions and festive celebrations due to the oddities that had crept up in the Satyashodhak-prescribed rituals, 'Deenmitra' started writing critical articles regarding the leaders of the Satyashodhak Samaj. The main attack would always be on Jyotirao Phule. Actually, Jyotirao was taking a lot of efforts to bridge the discrepancies in the various interpretations and practices of the Satyashodhak-prescribed rituals. He had even published small booklets to this end. But, it was getting challenging to proliferate these messages across all demographics. He had finished writing a couple of booklets more. The writing of 'Sarvajanik Satyadharma' had also finished by then. But, finances were falling short to begin the publishing process of these books.

But, 'Deenmitra' was not concerned about all these problems. Its sole aim, obviously interspersed with personal prejudices, was to keep cutting down Jyotirao to size.

From Jyotirao's side, irrespective of their strained personal relations, he still keep admiring Krishnarao for his industrious spirit. There had been many occasions when Krishnarao had gone against everyone's wishes – including Tatyasaheb – and done something unique. Whether or not he got success in every venture, was debatable; but, the courage and forward-thinking attitude he showed, had always made Jyotirao appreciative of Krishnarao.

During the inauguration of the Tansa lake, the Governor had been called as the Chief Guest. A decorative installation had been erected for the Governor's welcome. At the last minute, Krishnarao placed a board near the main entrance. The board read:

'This lake is sure to quench the thirst of many thirsty souls; but, how do you plan to quench the thirst for knowledge that millions of Indians are still thirsting for?'

Such fearlessness and quick-wit were what made Krishnarao the person he was. It was due to this attitude of his that Jyotirao took all his criticism in a composed manner. In fact, he asked Yeshwant to send a small monetary contribution to 'Deenmitra'. When Yeshwant protested, Jyotirao explained to him,

"My son, look at the bigger picture here. So what is 'Deenmitra' had been criticizing us and exposing our faults? That is only helping us get better. And, it is this fearless criticism that will one day help the whole society change for the better, because I'm sure, 'Deenmitra' is not going to stop at only criticizing me or our Samaj."

Yeshwant abided by Tatya's wishes and sent the contribution across.

At this time, something different was going on in Mumbai. People had started talking in reverential tones about the constant efforts that Jyotirao Phule had been taking for the betterment of society in myriad ways. His tremendous social work, the sacrifice that he did for the Otur case, the years of torment that he had wordlessly suffered from various sections of society, his indefatigable work even when his health

was deteriorating.... everything was being talked about with awe.

Jyotirao was going to complete 60 years of age in the upcoming month of May. The Satyashodhaks came together and decided to organize a big felicitation of their dear Tatyasaheb on this occasion. An important and unanimous decision was taken to honour Tatyasaheb with the title of 'Mahatma' on the eve of his 60th birthday.

The labor class of Mumbai was thrilled to hear this decision taken by its leaders. They also held immense respect for Jyotirao, who had constantly toiled to resolve the problems of the labor class and accord them a better quality of life. The birthday celebration was going to give each and every person an occasion to express his/her heartfelt gratitude towards their beloved Tatyasaheb.

Narayanrao Lokhande, Swami Aiyyavaru, Sheth Raju Babaji, Dr. Santuji Lad and hundreds of Satyashodhaks began toiling to put up a fantastic celebration for their beloved leader. Mama Parmanand, Behramji Malbari, Raobahadur Vitthalrao Vandekar, and Madhavrao Rokade pledged their unstinting support.

Lokhande, Swami Aiyyavaru, and a few other people went to Pune to request Jyotirao to kindly be present at the event and accept the honor. His affirmation lent even more excitement to the proceedings.

The date and time of the celebration was decided. The venue zeroed in upon was the community hall of the Mandvi koliwada . Accordingly, invitations started getting sent out to Satyashodhaks in even the remotest of villages. Many eminent people received the invite, prominent amongst them being the Maharaja of Baroda, Sayajirao Gaekwad.

On the 11th of May, the Mandvi koliwada community hall wore a lovely festive look. It was decorated with festoons and flowers. People started thronging in from morning for the program that was scheduled to begin in the afternoon. They couldn't wait to see the felicitation of the great man who had toiled for decades to arouse the self-respect in even the most downtrodden person's heart; to bring the invaluable gift of education to the most marginalized sections of society; to ingrain the importance of truth, morality, education, and de-addiction in all the strata of society. It was impossible

for a simple human being to achieve all this in one birth. Hence, no wonder, Jyotirao was being felicitated with the title of a 'Mahatma' – a great soul. For indeed, he was a great man. A great soul, who had touched their lives with a magic wand.

By 12 noon, the community hall was packed to the fringes with Satyashodhaks who had come down from the remotest corners of Maharashtra. Hundreds of people were standing in the compound and even on the road beyond the same.

Around noon, Bhau Kondaji Patil and a few other dignitaries from Pune, arrived at the hall. Soon after, Jyotirao Phule himself arrived at the venue, causing ripples of excitement to start flowing all around!

There was a visible difference between the 25-year old Jyotirao Phule who had received his first award from Major Candy for his work in the field of women's education, and the 60-year old senior man who was today going to be accorded the title of a Mahatma. His face had wrinkled, the red turban had given way to a white one…

Vandekar, Jaya Karadi, Swami Aiyyavaru etc got ready to welcome Jyotirao and Bala Kusaji Patil. Yande Shetji had come with a message from the Maharaj of Baroda. The latter had requested that Jyotirao Phule be also honored with the title of 'India's Booker T. Washington ', on the happy occasion.

As Jyotirao entered the hall, a sea of applause erupted from all around! He was overwhelmed to see the hall packed to the seams with happy faces beaming with joy and gratitude towards him.

A lot of speeches followed wherein each orator spoke about

Jyotirao and Savitribai's immense contribution to the society. He was constantly addressed as Mahatma, in all the speeches. Raobahadur Vitthalrao Vandekar and Swami Aiyyavaru's speeches took a lot of emotional turns.

Finally, the Justice of Peace Narayanrao Lokhande announced that Jyotirao Phule was being honorably accorded the title of 'Mahatma'. He also read out the message sent by Sayajirao Gaekwad and conferred the title of 'India's Booker T. Washington' on Jyotirao. Then, he was felicitated with a shawl, and gifts meant for Savitribai were also handed over to him.

The hall started reverberating with joyous proclamations of "Mahatma Jyotirao Phule ki jai!!!"

Balaji Patil, who had fought along side Jyotirao to eradicate the dominance of Brahmins, was also honored on the occasion.

Soon, the attendees began rushing to meet Tatyasaheb personally. The table and the dais was filled with garlands and flowers brought along by people. Jyotirao was immensely overwhelmed by all the praise, honor, and the love of people being showered upon him. In that emotional state, he got up with tears in his eyes and folded his hands to the audience, saying,

"Brothers and sisters, I have no words for the immense honor and love that you all have bestowed upon me today. But, I really do not know if I am indeed worthy of so much importance and affection? Have I indeed done so much work to deserve all this? Brothers and sisters, whatever little work I have done so far, has been in keeping with what appealed to my conscience and intellect. It was in response to what I thought was injustice to my Shoodra, Ati Shoodra brethren...."

"...A lot of my dear colleagues here spoke about the trouble I had to go through while doing all this work. But honestly, I'm not alone in this. All my colleagues have suffered similar torment. But, I hold no malice towards my tormentors. They did their work, I did mine... And I shall keep doing it till the end of my life..."

"Who are we Satyashodhaks? When the truth is deliberately hidden from the society to keep them in ignorance, we Satyashodhaks toil to unearth that truth. The truth about religious rules has been hidden by a handful of people to accord themselves dominance over the masses. But, Satyashodhaks are on a mission to uncover those truths and give a happy, dignified life to all."

"We have done what we could. We will still keep doing it for as long as we are alive. But, we also require the help of our young members to take this work ahead. I hope that you all with keep the flame of truth burning and keep showing our ignorant and illiterate brethren, the road to truth and light."

Saying thus, Jyotirao finished his speech. People kept coming up on the dais to meet him. It was late evening by the time Jyotirao could make his way out along with Narayanrao Lokhande. Even then, people kept coming to Lokhande's house to meet Tatyasaheb till late in the night.

A few more such felicitation programs were held for Jyotirao in the coming days. However, by then, his mind started getting diverted towards Pune. A few more evidences had to be submitted to the court soon.

Jyotirao met Adv. Nadkarni and then returned to Pune. A sea of mixed emotions filled Jyotirao's heart. While on one hand he was floating on a cloud of happiness and contentment, on the other hand he could see a mountain of problems awaiting him as he returned to Pune.

It was in this state of mixed emotions that Jyotirao returned to Pune where hundreds of Satyashodhaks had arrived at the railway station to greet him.

92

Finally Jyotirao fulfilled his dream of starting a student hostel. He took Alhaat's house on rent and started the hostel there. Whatever funds he had got on selling the farm at Maanjri, were deployed for the initial expenses of running the hostel, which could accommodate 25-30 students to begin with. Jaya Karadi's sons Venkaiah, Yalappa and Bapu; his nephew Linganna; Shet Raju Babaji's son Nana; Dr. Santuji Lad's son and few more children from Kalyan were the first few inmates of this hostel. These were parents who paid fees for their wards; these fees were going to be used to accommodate more students from poor households. The parents were happy that their wards were now directly in Tatyasaheb's hands.

Jyotirao became completely immersed in running the hostel with the help of Yeshwant, Sitaram, and Govinda. Jyotirao would personally take the children's studies and look after their physical fitness, diet, sleep schedules etc. Savitribai and a helper widow, Rangubai would cook for all the children. A strict discipline was maintained in the calendar of activities.

Jyotirao would wake up the children early in the morning. They would receive a wholesome, nutritious diet twice a day. They were disallowed from going outside after 9 pm. Every Saturday, post-dinner, Jyotirao would regale the children with stories having a moral base. Sometimes the children would sing songs and play games.

Jyotirao and Savitribai treated the children in the hostel with the same love and affection with which they treated Yeshwant and Gajanan. Raju Shetji's son Nana, was a bit less interested in studies. His attention would be more on games than books. But with Tatya and Kaku's affectionate guidance, he also started changing.

Barely a month after the hostel started, a very strange rumor erupted all around Pune. Some self-proclaimed astrological expert had declared that if some brother and sister want to meet each other, they will have to do so in the last five-six days of the Jyeshtha month, or else, they will not be able to meet each other for the next three years. If they meet each other in the next three years, one of them is bond to meet an untimely death! It did not take much time for this weird rumor to spread to the neighboring villages. Parents started panicking and arrived at the hostel to take there children back home to meet their siblings. Obviously, the carefully set routine of the hostel got immensely disturbed.

A spate of puja rituals and sacrifices started all around Pune and the neighboring villages. Yet again, Brahmins came in demand! It was crystal clear that this was a ploy by the Brahmins to regain their lost ground. Jyotirao tried his level best to make the harrowed parents understand that all this was nothing but a devious game being played for selfish games, and that, astrology and the position of stars did not determine a person's life or death.

But, mostly no one was in the mood to listen.

So it happened that, a lot of brothers went to meet their sisters in the designated dates; a lot of married sisters made hurried trips to see their brothers.

Jyotirao was tremendously pained to see the society collectively behaving so ignorantly. It distressed him that the Brahmins could so easily sway such a large mass – a huge chunk of them being Shoodras and Ati Shoodras – by issuing silly and baseless threats.

Nevertheless, the students who had been taken away by their parents, returned to the hostel and in the next few days, things returned to normalcy.

Just when everything was settling down again, a terrible incident occurred. One day, Jyotirao woke up as usual before dawn, and before he could realize what was happening, he crashed to the ground. Hearing the noise, Savitribai rushed to see what had happened and was aghast to see her husband sprawled on the floor.

Savitribai's heart came in her mouth as she lit a wicker lamp to see properly in the dark. She was flabbergasted to see a deep bloodied gnash on Jyotirao's head. Blood was also streaming down his nostrils. He was trying to say something but was not being able to. His legs and hands had turned numb.

All of a sudden, a wave of tremendous pain ran like lightning from the right side of his body to his brain, and Jyotirao fell unconscious!

"Yeshwant...Govinda...come fast children..." Savitribai ran sobbing, calling out to the youngsters for help.

Sitaram, Yeshwant, Govinda all came rushing. They laid the unconscious Jyotirao on a bed and went to fetch Dr. Vishram Ramji.

Dr. Vishram Ramji came rushing. He bandaged the wound. Some time later, Jyotirao regained consciousness but was still unable to talk. His tongue felt heavy and his limbs seemed to have all their strength. He had suffered a serious blow to the head while crashing down onto the leg of the bed.

The symptoms pointed towards a paralysis attack. Indeed, Jyotirao had suffered from a sudden paralytic stroke, which rendered the right side of his body weak and limp.

Savitribai was aghast! All the people in Phule house became equally dumbstruck by the sudden and unexpected turn of events. As news started spreading, people began thronging to the Phule house to see Jyotirao.

No one could believe what they were seeing. It was beyond comprehension to fathom that a human whirlwind had suddenly been arrested and pinned to his bed.

With Jyotirao's health problem, the household expenses ballooned beyond proportion. Apart from the regular domestic expenses and that required for the hostel, Savitribai now had to arrange money for his medicines too. However, kind-hearted people like Maharaja Sayajirao Gaekwad of Baroda and Nageshwargeer Maharaj sent some funds to lend a helping hand.

After a long time, Jyotirao started responding to Dr. Vishram Ramji's treatment. He began sitting up in bed and speaking a few words haltingly. However, the right side of his body was still limp, and he was advised complete rest. Thus, the entire responsibility of handling the household and the hostel fell on Savitribai. She handled all the work without a word of complaint.

The entire household was running around to assist Jyotirao, but it was not in his nature to sit still and get his work done from others. He was raring to get up from the bed and restart all his pending work, but his body refused to co-operate. It was extremely frustrating for him to not be able to talk or write anything. But then, he decided to engage his restless mind in reading.

Among the many journals and newsletters that he would keep reading, was 'Deenmitra', who had sent back the donation sent by Jyotirao and kept writing heavily critical articles on him and the Satyashodhak Samaj. In one of the issues of 'Deenmitra', a 'dire warning' had been issued to self-proclaimed 'new age religious gurus'. The article warned the founder of Satyashodhak Samaj about how his so-called followers were going behind his back and following the age-old Hindu rituals again. Cautioning that such hidden activities were bound to spell an imminent death for the Satyashodhak Samaj, the article also highlighted the chaos that had set in between the theoretical rules of the Samaj and their practical application during religious ceremonies. The writer of the article advised the leaders of Satyashodhak Samaj to introspect where they were going wrong and take immediate steps to rectify their mistakes, else the future looked bleak for the Samaj and its leaders.

Jyotirao never took any criticism to heart. He would take whatever was good in the criticism and rectify his behavior for better results. However, this particular article had hurt him very badly. He felt like doing many thing to retaliate but was tied down due to his paralysis.

After a long time of thinking, Jyotirao called out to Yeshwant.

Yeshwant came running and asked,

"Yes, Tatyasaheb... Do you need anything?"

"Yesh...Yesh...want... Gi...Give me...me...a

pen..pencil…and…a…a sl…slate" Jyotirao said haltingly.

Yeshwant could not understand what was in Tatya's mind. He looked at him in confusion, but by then, Jyotirao was already trying to get up on his own. Yeshwant came ahead and propped him up. Jyotirao looked at his limp right hand in frustration but kept thinking something.

Yeshwant got him a pencil and slate and stood by the side to see what was on Tatya's mind.

Jyotirao slowly picked up the pencil in his left hand and started writing on the slate! Initially, the words were turning out illegible, but still, he persisted! Yeshwant was stunned to see Jyotirao's tremendous determination even in this stage of health.

Just then, Savitribai came outside and she was equally flabbergasted to see what her husband was trying to do.

"What are you doing, Shetji?" she asked him in an alarmed voice.

Jyotirao looked at her calmly and replied,

"I'm practicing…"

"Practicing what…?" Savitribai asked in a confused voice.

"To write with my left hand…" Tatya replied, not taking his hand away from the slate.

"Ohho….why all this effort now? Dr. Ramji has asked you to rest!" Savitribai rebuked him.

In response, Jyotirao held up the issue of 'Deenmitra' in front of her. Savitribai quickly scanned through the write-up. Looking at the changing expressions on her face, Jyotirao said,

"It is a very hurtful and condescending allegation to be subjected to after all these years of work! But what face do I have to fight this allegation that the members of Satyashodhak Samaj are straying from the path, when it is a true fact? That is why, I need to finish 'Sarvajanik Satyadharma' at the earliest now. We cannot afford a delay of even a day now. I should not have let my other duties get in the way of writing 'Sarvajanik Satyadharma'. I should have realized that our Satyashodhak brethren are illiterate and thus ignorant. They can get easily swayed by contradictory claims. I should thank 'Deenmitra' for making me aware of what my imminent responsibilities are. I should be able to start writing with my left hand in the next 4-8 days. After that, I shall immediately start writing 'Sarvajanik Satyadharma'" said Jyotirao.

Savitribai said to him,

"Shetji, you dictate the content. Govinda will write it down."

But Jyotirao refused, saying,

"No...No... He has his studies, plus he also has to look at the hostel. I shall be ready to write with my left hand in the next few days. As it is, Govinda will have to help me later to prepare the final draft of my writing."

In spite of knowing that her husband will not listen, Savitribai again tried pleading with him to write after he felt a bit better. However, as expected, Jyotirao refused her suggestion saying,

"My medicines are going on. I should feel better any day now. But what do I do till then? I get very bored sitting at one place. This writing will keep me gainfully engaged."

Seeing his wife silent in reaction, Jyotirao said to her,

"Please don't be angry with me, Savitribai. I have never refused you in any important thing, but today, please allow me to follow my heart. This work needs to be finished before I breathe my last. There are many other things that are demanding my attention, but there are other people to take care of those. For instance, I am worried about the Otur case, but I know, there are other capable people to look after it. Yeshwant's marriage too will be done very well by you, in my absence...I'm sure of it. But, the responsibility of writing 'Sarvajanik Satyadharma' rests solely on me, and I need to see it through at any cost. I cannot entrust anyone else to pen down my thoughts because, if they are compromised or vilified in any way, it will wreak havoc in an already chaotic situation.

This book will aim to explain to the members of the Satyashodhak Samaj, those principles on which they should base their personal and social lives. If the book is not written in a proper way, then those principles will soon get lost in the mêlée, or probably, people will again get up to say that Phule's thoughts were divisive at the core. No, that will not do. I need to spell out very clearly as to what kind of a society is envisioned by the Satyashodhak Samaj. I cannot falter in this task."

Savitribai understood that Jyotirao was not going to alter his stance. She kept quiet and started going into the kitchen. Jyotirao stopped her saying,

"I had one more request, Savitribai…"

Savitribai looked at him wordlessly. Seeing her that ways, Jyotirao asked,

"Are you angry with me?"

"No…. I'm not. I do understand the importance of everything that you are saying. But, I also am worried about your health."

"I realize your concern. I shall also do this work taking due care of my health."

"Alright… by the way, what was that request you had for me?" asked Savitribai.

"Oh yes… Please do not tell Dr. Vishram Ramji anything about this…" requested Jyotirao.

93

Jyotirao was writing incessantly. The topics pertaining to how life could be bettered for men and women, both, were coming in front of his mind's eye, and he was writing… It had taken Jyotirao one and a half months before he could write properly with the left hand. He had tried taking Savitribai's suggestion to narrate the content to Govinda, but still, his words were slurred and speech was slow. Hence, irritated with the effort, Jyotirao took to penning down the content on his own.

The book was shaping up in a Q&A format, wherein a curious Satyashodhak was shown to ask questions and Jyotirao would explain his thoughts in the form of answers. He would rehash the excerpts of the many conversations he had had with Pandit Dhondiram, Subhedar Major Ganpatrao Thorat, Balwantrao Sakvalkar, Yeshwant, Govinda etc.

Every night, Govinda would collect the day's writing from Jyotirao and by the next morning, he would present it to him in a beautiful, legible handwriting.

How can a human being become truly happy? What are religious scriptures? Who has created this world? How do we pay obeisance to that creator? What offerings do we make to him? The differences and similarities between men and women… what is sin, what is goodness…these and many such topics were being handled by Jyotirao in his book.

While rewriting Jyotirao's work, Govind would start mulling on the advice therein. He realized that what Tatyasaheb was putting across, was a very new religious thought in a very simplified way. In this path, there was no scope for mysticism or blind dependence of any religious rules. Govinda was very impressed with the easy-to-follow thoughts which said, truth was the only way to make a human being truly happy; going against one's moral meter was sin; and, not troubling anyone for one's own happiness was true goodness of heart.

Jyotirao had also written that the creator of this world is too huge an entity to be seen and fathomed by our miniscule human brain. Hence, one should not spend precious time in trying to achieve this impossible task. He also denounced mystical concepts such as, seers could see God in his real form on the basis of tremendous mediation.

Balwant Hari Sakvalkar would come to Jyotirao with several questions in mind. Once he asked Jyotirao,

"What can we give as offerings to God?"

Jyotirao replied,

"God created the beautiful flowers and other natural things

for us humans to enjoy. Then, how does it make sense to offer Him the same things that He has made for us? Hence, I strongly denounce the selfish, manipulative people who thug the hard-working but ignorant brethren of ours. If at all flowers are to be offered, then they should be offered to those people who are working to extricate the ignorant ones from the web of deceit that is spun around them. For, in those saviors, God does rest."

He also opined,

"Instead of wearing saffron robes and going into hypnotic trances while chanting God's name, it is better to behave in a morally upright way; that would be the biggest service to God."

Yeshwant asked him,

"Do we not offer food to the Brahmin priests, as a service to God?"

Jyotirao answered,

"What is important here, is the donation of food. So why does one need to maintain segregations about who to donate food to? As long as one is giving food to any person – be it a Brahmin, or an American native, or even a Mahar-Maang - the fulfillment in their bellies reaches God's ears and makes the donation worthwhile."

One day as Govinda went to submit his rewritten stack of papers to Jyotirao, he found Balwant Hari and Yeshwant deep in conversation with Jyotirao, who was explaining how and why the Vedas are the root cause of all social evils.

"Vedas have been written by cunning, selfish and thieving individuals. However, their future generations are going to have to bear the ill-effects of their forefathers' karmas. If they feel they are so clever that they can even escape the court of God, they are very mistaken."

"But Tatyasaheb, is there no way in which they can atone their sins?" asked Govinda.

"Of course, there is. The Brahmins should leave their ego aside, ask for forgiveness for their generations of misdeeds, and should follow the path of truth. If they do so, the Shoodras, Ati Shoodras, Bhils, Kolis, Gonds....everyone will forgive them. They can also prevent their further social degradation by atoning their sins in this manner."

Then, Balwant Hari asked Jyotirao,

"Tatyasaheb, has the creator made any difference while creating human beings and other creatures?"

Jyotirao replied,

"Yes. He has elevated human beings over other living beings by giving them a rational brain. That has been the main tool of humankind's progress. Animals and birds have been living the same way as they did for last so many centuries. But, humankind has progressed from living in jungles and caves to now leading such a prosperous and well-endowed life – all due to the power of its rational and intelligent brain."

"Then does that mean that other living beings have no special attribute in them?" Balwant Hari asked.

Hearing that, Jyotirao smiled and replied,

"Not at all. How can that be? Birds and animals may only work to fill their stomachs, but they never leave the path of truth, which is the path that nature ordained for them. They do not cheat or hurt their own brethren. They do not conduct immoral or wring deeds like Nana Peshwa did. The creator bestowed human beings with a rational, thinking brain; but sadly, we have put that brain to more of a corrupt and wrong use tan for any good. In that comparison, I would say, birds and animals stand on a higher ground than us."

Everyone laughed. Jyotirao further said,

"Now think about this... These Brahmins keep looting the Shoodras on the pretext that the more they give to the Brahmins, the faster they will see heaven. But tell me, if these Brahmins are so virtuous that they can fast-track somebody to heaven, has even one of them himself seen what heaven looks like?! They just cannot – because, there is nothing like heaven. All these concepts of soul, salvation, heaven, hell are nothing but a figment of an over-wired brain that saw a good opportunity to brandish these words and thug ignorant people. By giving undue importance to the scriptures that promote these ideas, we are only further pushing an already-ignorant society into the realms of superstitious beliefs.

Govinda said,

"Then, Tatyasaheb, please expose these fraudulent practices of the Brahmins who are suing the name of God to thug innocent people. In this British regime, we have no need to fear these Brahmins."

Jyotirao replied,

"My son, I have been writing about them a lot thus far. Even that writing proved too heavy for them to digest. They have started influencing our Shoodra brethren against me now..."

All this talking exerted Jyotirao a lot. He started huffing. Govinda said,

"Tatyasaheb, the Shoodras are ignorant; thus they are getting easily influenced. Instead of thinking about them and getting distressed, I think we should focus on publishing the 'Sarvajanik Satyadharma' soon, so that they themselves can decided what is true and what is not."

The discussion stopped there. After a brief rest, Jyotirao again sat down to write. Govinda realized that if Tatyasaheb continued to write at this speed, the book should be ready in the next two months.

In the meantime, Gyaanoba agreed to the alliance between his daughter and Yeshwant. He knew that he was going to suffer societal antagonism for this decision, but that did not sway him.

It was decided to get them married in the coming February month. By then, Jyotirao's book as also going to get finished. Money was scant, so Jyotirao and Savitribai had been keeping a strict check on the expenses. While the funds sent by Sayajirao had been exhausted, those given by Nageshwargeerbuva were still remaining.

Many people came to meet Jyotirao during his illness. Quite a few of them - like Gangarambhau Mhaske - were those who had serious difference of opinions with Jyotirao. But they all kept aside their internal differences and came to meet him. Jyotirao was overwhelmed to see that people like Hari Raoji and Raosaheb Ranade took time out to meet and speak to him. Their discussions would invigorate Jyotirao like none other.

Jyotirao was in a quandary about how to repay Dr. Vishram Ramji; he had not taken a penny for his treatment so far. Yet, he would come rushing, every time Savitribai requested his presence. It was another overwhelming thing for Jyotirao that his illness had bridged the gap between him and Dr. Vishram Ramji. Jyotirao expressed his gratitude for well-wishers like Sayajirao and Dr. Vishram Ramji through a poem that said,

"A true brave-heart is one who goes to check on his enemy when the enemy falls ill;

He is truly large-hearted for not getting petty differences in between at such times;

He may again stand up in opposition after the enemy gets well;

But, that behavior is in keeping with what implies truth in its real form"

Seeing Savitribai's increasingly busy schedule, Gyaanoba sent Radha to stay at the Phule house and assist Kaku, even before the marriage ceremony.

Radha would remind Kaku of Lakshmi. Hence one day, she proclaimed that henceforth, Radha would be called Lakshmi.

Radha i.e. Lakshmi became an integral part of the Phule household. Jyotirao enrolled her in the Hujurpaga school. She was now in the 4th grade.

Lakshmi was diligent in her studies, and would also take part in the household work with interest. She would assist

Savitribai in the kitchen and would also help Jyotirao. The Phule couple would see to it that Lakshmi got ample time for her studies, play, and rest as well. They were happy to get a very good daughter-in-law.

Soon, the festival of Diwali arrived. Jyotirao and Savitribai decided to send Lakshmi back to her parents house at Hadapsar.

"She will miss school for a week, two weeks; but Savitribai, let her go. Her parents will feel very lonely if Lakshmi does not go there during the festival" opined Jyotirao.

Soon, Diwali got over. A few Satyashodhaks conducted the Tulshi Lagna . Jyotirao expressed displeasure over this saying,

"This ritual is not ours. The Brahmins have perpetrated it. I'm strongly against conducting a ritual wherein the Tulshi plant is married off to Lord Vishnu, who branded her as morally corrupt."

When one man tried arguing that they had been conducting the Tulshi Lagna without Brahmins for many years by then, Jyotirao rebuked him saying,

"It is never too soon to stop a wrong ritual. We had been going wrong, but now that we have realized our mistake, let us stop committing it. Else, our future generations will also fall prey to incorrect rituals and ideas."

The people agreed. Soon enough, messages to the effect reached the Satyashodhaks in various villages, and it was decided to stop Tulshi lagna ritual from the next year.

94

Winter was setting in. One morning, Jyotirao sat basking in the soft wintry sun, writing the final pages of 'Sarvajanik Satyadharma'. He had written extensively about religion, morality, logic, fate, astrology etc. Now, the final pages were going to focus on topics like marriage, death, rituals after death and so on.

However, that day, Jyotirao's mind was getting diverted

towards Mumbai. Today , the Otur case was going to be heard by Justice Sergeant and Kashinath Telang. The jury had shown a sympathetic inclination towards the Samaj. Jyotirao was hopeful that justice would prevail on their side.

He was feeling happy about reaching the final stages of 'Sarvajanik Satyadharma'.

Jyotirao kept writing... His left arm started paining. His back started getting rigid due to sitting for long stretches. But, he kept writing... the topic was 'birth'.

He wrote about how once they become parents, people should cast aside their vices and behave in a way that their son/daughter gets morally upright values. Further, he wrote about how Satyashodhaks should conduct the child's naming rituals, how can they start feeding the child solid foods, how and when they should start thinking of its education and so on.

Finally, as his body could take the strain no more, Jyotirao lay down in the courtyard itself. The air was still chilly. His blanket moved away as he tried to sleep. He could not pull the blanket closer with one hand.

Thus Jyotirao called for help, saying,

"Lakshmibai?"

"Yes, Tatyasaheb?" Lakshmi answered prancing out in a moment.

"My child, you should always answer elders saying 'Jee', alright? Do not forget..." Jyotirao once again reminded Lakshmi. He had been trying to inculcate this habit in the young girl for many days now, but she would inevitably forget. Yet, Jyotirao kept reminding her patiently.

"Jee..." she said, adding, "What may I do for you, Tatyasaheb? May I pull the blanket over you?"

"Yes my child...That is what I called you for," replied Jyotirao.

Lakshmi pulled the blanket over Jyotirao, arranged his papers properly, and went inside. The next 7-8 days went in the same way. Jyotirao kept writing, not paying attention to his aching body. Lakshmi had taken over the responsibility of looking after his medicines, fomentation etc.

Finally, after a lot of efforts, 'Sarvajanik Satyadharma' was finished! Jyotirao was immensely happy to have been able to achieve this seemingly impossible task, surmounting all odds. He decided to immediately write a letter to Gyaanoba.

Ever since Lakshmi had arrived, Jyotirao had written many letters to Gyaanoba, but all those had been penned by Govinda. Now, he himself sat to write to Gyaanoba.

II Satyameva Jayate II

21 December, 1888

To,

Shri. Gyaanoba Krishnaji Sasane,

Hadapsar.

Many blessings to you.

I was extremely caught up in finishing the book 'Sarvajanik Satyadharma' and thus found no time to write to you in the interim. Today, however, I had to write to specially tell you that our dear daughter-in-law Lakshmi is an intelligent and diligent young girl. She is also very affectionate and hard-working. It is our responsibility as her elders, to develop her inborn attributes in the proper way. To this end, I have a small suggestion: She needs to learn to answer an ender saying 'jee'; we have been taking due efforts for the same, but they have not yielded results thus far. Please do try from your side too. Apart from that, everything is fine. I would also request you to examine her on her studies, but also give her enough time to play.

P.S.: Last night, my health had deteriorated again, but Lakshmibai nursed me back to health in a wonderful way. She is indeed a very well brought up girl.

Yours truly,

Jyotirao Phule

That night, Jyotirao could hear the students in the hostel, chatting and laughing with each other. Suddenly, he felt like joining them. Slowly, he got up and walked to where they were sitting. The children were happy to see Tatyasaheb come there unexpectedly. They would enjoy his company – embellished as it would be with stories, humor, and laughter.

That day, one student asked him,

"Tatyasaheb, we are very curious to know about your childhood and what inspired you to take up all the work that you have been doing? Will you please tell us about it?"

Hearing the question, Jyotirao's mind instantly got transported to the past. It was as if a cave full of memories lay open in front of him. He smiled and said,

"It is a very big story, but I shall tell you all today... We originally hailed from a small village called Katgun, in the province of Satara. Our ancestors worked as Chougulas in the village. One of our ancestors, Ranoji, who was the son of Mudhoji Gore, worked as a chevalier in Chhatrapati Shivaji Maharaj's cavalry. He was martyred in the battle of Bijapur. My great grandfather, Kondaji Gore, belonged to the lineage of this Ranoji Gore. Kondaji was an upright man who could not tolerate any form of lies and injustice. He would thus get into constant skirmishes with the Kulkarni of the village, Vishnupant Kulkarni. Once, when the annual village fair was happening in Katgun, Vishnupant Klkarni was found brutally murdered. Knowing the constant tussles he and Kondaji would have, people were quick to point at Kondaji as the murderer. Whether or not there was any truth in this allegation, always remained a secret. But Kondaji decided to leave Katgun. One night, taking his entire family along, he fled from Katgun and settled in Khanwadi near Purandar."

"But Tatyasaheb, how did the Gores become Phules?" one student piped in.

"I'm coming to that... Kondaji started his life anew at Khanwadi. He started farming for a livelihood. They all soon forgot their old life at Katgun. Kondaji's son was Shetiba – who was my grandfather. Kondaji and his wife fell prey to an epidemic soon after Shetiba's marriage. The twists of fate rendered Shetiba poor in the later years of his life. His wife, that is my grandmother Lakshmibai, was from Pune. She and my grandfather came to Pune to get some help from Lakshmibai's father, Chafaji. Chafaji used to work for the Peshwas. He gave some farmland to Shetiba; they started their life anew. During this time, Narayanrao Peshwa was murdered. Chafaji was killed in the effort to save Narayanrao. Soon after that, Shetiba started a flower shop. He did well in that business. His flowers, garlands, and floral decorations would be in demand at the Peshwas mansions. Sawai Madhavrao was specially impressed with Shetiba. From then on, Shetiba Gore came to be known as Shetiba Phule. That is how the story goes.... We still have our ancestral house at Khanwadi..."

The children were listening intently, even as Jyotirao moved onto telling them about Saguna Aau, Murray Mitchell and so on. They were fascinated with the many twists and turns of Tatyasaheb's life.

The talks went on for a long time. Then, Jyotirao got tired, and asked the children to play something amongst themselves and sleep soon, lest their minds and bodies get too tired.

Jyotirao went off to sleep, but the memories of yore kept him awake for long. At long last, sleep showered her blessings on him. When he woke up, Savitribai was singing a poem praising her husband. Jyotirao's eyes filled with tears on hearing his wife's verses.

A glow of contentment on his face, Jyotirao got up and went to wake up the students of the hostel.

95

One night, the students of the hostel congregated around Jyotirao, and soon, the hostel came alive with chatter and laughter. That day, Sheth Raju Babaji and Jaya Karadi had also joined them from Mumbai. They were thrilled to see the students' progress, and gave them prize-money to get some sweets.

After the children went off to sleep, Jyotirao, Babaji, and Karadi sat down to talk. Apart from the Otur case, the other topic of discussion was Krishnaro's 'Deenbandhu Free School' that he had started at Shukrawar Peth. Krishnarao had been successful in getting the support of many people for this school, right from the middlemen in the vegetable market, to eminent ones like Raosaheb Ranade. In fact, Dharmaji Baburao Dhayarkar. the main middleman of the market, had kept a piggy bank in the market. The collections of that piggy bank would go for Krishnarao's school.

However, that did not mean that Krishnaro did not face any obstacles while running the school. He certainly did.

For instance, when Maharaj Sayajirao Gaekwad had come to Pune, he had promised a monthly donation of Rs. 100 for the school. However, there was no sign of the money for the next six months. Finally when the first donation came, it was only Rs. 50 and that minus the 50 paise it took to do the money order! It was a long time later that Krishnarao could understand why this had happened. Apparently, even before Sayajirao could reach Baroda from Pune, a committee of Brahmins led by Raoji Punekar, decided to meet Sayajirao with special recommendation from Matoshri Jamnabai. As expected, due to Matoshri Jamnabai's insistence, Punekar got an audience with Sayajirao, in which he gave gory descriptions about the 'real' work of Satyashodhak Samaj, and what havoc would ensue if Sayajirao gave such a big amount to Krishnarao's school.

"Maharaj, if you give such a large amount of Rs. 100 every month to the Satyashodhaks, the Brahmins of Pune will rise up in utter discontent. These Satyashodhaks have made life impossible for Brahmins. They keep speaking derogatorily against us. They desecrate God and religious rituals. Now they have started schools, undoubtedly to train children to hate their Brahmin counterparts. If they receive such huge financial help, they will get empowered enough to burn our houses and abduct our good wives. And if this happens, the sin will fall on your head, Maharaj. Thus, I'm earnestly requesting you to not do anything that will make you a sinner!"

After hearing all this, Maharaj was in two minds. Thus, he found a midway and sent Rs. 50 instead of the promised Rs. 100.

The Brahmins were overjoyed that their ploy had worked; but even then, they were not fully satisfied. The donation coming in from the vegetable market was still hurting in their eyes. They couldn't sit still before stopping those funds. To that end, they caught hold of Narayanrao Joglekar, a like-minded municipal officer. He gave so much trouble to Dhayarkar and other merchants, that finally they just stopped the fund!

The running of the school came in trouble. Krishnarao was left with no other option but to ask for fees from the students. He ended up displeasing a lot of parents with that decision. The future of the free school came in jeopardy.

However, Jyotirao knew that the perseverant Krishnarao will not give up so easily. They kept discussing about what would Krishnarao's next move possibly be.

The next morning when Jyotirao went to wake up the students, they started complaining about being woken up so early. The last night had been full of fun for them, and they were feeling very lazy to wake up so soon. But Jyotirao knew how to bring errant children in line with gentleness. He said to them,

"Children, I know how much you like to eat the sweets we serve once a week. But, if you wish to be able to keep eating such nice delicacies all your life, you need to wake up early and study. There is no point in being lazy or being displeased with me. If you do not study and become big, the educated people will sell you off in open markets just as the Americans did with the blacks."

This ploy worked wonders! The children were up in a minute!

Jyotirao had again started looking into the work of the hostel. He would make the rounds of the hostel to wake the children up, look after the general upkeep and basically do everything to ensure that the children were living in comfortable conditions so that they could pay complete attention to their studies. Jyotirao wanted to spare no effort in making educated adults out of these children; for, he knew that only that would ensure a bright future and good quality of life for them.

To that end, Jyotirao himself would brush up on his Sanskrit, English, Marathi and Hindi lessons, so as to be able to teach the children properly. He would personally take their Marathi grammar lessons and was insistent that the children be fluent in all three languages, apart from also understanding Sanskrit. To that end, he had hired a Sanskrit tutor called Pathak Sir, who would come at 7 am to teach Sanskrit to the children. That time, Jyotirao too would join in the class to brush up on his own skills. He would also discuss certain words from some book or scriptures with Pathak Sir, so as to understand and explain the concepts to the children better.

In recent times, Jyotirao had become fond of combing through the scriptures to find good and bad references about Shoodras, Ati Shoodras and analyzing the real meaning of those words or phrases in the context that they were written in. He would keep hashing-rehashing through the meanings, taking Pathak sir's help wherever necessary.

However, even though Jyotirao's mind had become fit & fine, his body had not yet become that capable to catch up with the flights of his mind. Hence, he would keep falling ill and become bed-ridden for a few days now & then. The frustration would get to him and he would crave to become well again.

During such times, people would come to meet Jyotirao and give him company. One day, Krishnarao Babar, the principal of the Training College, came to meet Jyotirao, bringing a student along. The student was in dire need of funds to continue his education.

Jyotirao fell in a quandary. Had it been the question of accommodating this student into his hostel, it would have been no trouble. But with his medical expenses mounting, Jyotirao did not have ready cash to offer to the boy. Till then, no student had gone back empty-handed from Phule's house. The helplessness that Jyotirao felt on this occasion was very big for him. He said to Krishnarao,

"I'm extremely sorry, Guruji; but presently, I'm not in a position of offer anything as financial help. I would suggest, please go to Gangarambhau Mhaske; he should be able to help you. Tell him that I have requested his help for this boy."

"Alright, Tatyasaheb. Your reference is also a big help. Please don't feel bad the fact that you could not help us directly" Krishnarao said solemnly, as he left to meet Gangarambhau.

A week later, a similar incident repeated itself. A few farmers from Fursungi came to meet Jyotirao to get justice for a fellow farmer whose house had been snatched away by an unscrupulous money lender. That time, while again directing them to Gangarambhau for legal advice, Jyotirao said to them,

"Brothers, please learn to see the winds of changing coming your way. Become wise. Get educated. I'm not going to be around for too long...."

Jyotirao was getting increasingly frustrated that after spending his whole life in helping people, fate had now rendered him helpless to offer even the smallest of assistance. It was in this phase of time that the excess efforts that he had taken in the post-recuperative stage led Jyotirao to get another paralytic stroke, rendering him completely bed-ridden once more!

PART 4

96

It was quite late at night by the time Jyotirao returned from the meeting of barbers, accompanied by Gyaanoba Sasane and Pandit Dhondiram. That day was special because, it was almost after a year that Jyotirao had stepped out of his house. Of course, the reason for him to take this step was also compelling.

Papers like 'Deenbandhu' and 'Indian Spectator' were writing reams & reams on the topic of tonsuring of widows. In opposition to the same, many groups were deciding to bring about a strike of the barbers. The Satyashodhak Samaj was at the forefront of this idea. The meeting at Bhavani Peth was held to discuss that itself.

While coming back, Jyotirao's ears were ringing with the terrible tales that the barbers had told them.

"What do we tell you,

Tatyasaheb… Our hands tremble while running our blades on the soft heads of those little girls. Their pleas keep ringing in our ears, but we cannot do anything. They cry….they fall at our feet…but no one's heart melts for them. They tie them up, stuff a piece of cloth in their mouths to shut them up, and place them in front of us to shorn their off all their hair. They curse her saying, "You have eaten up your husband…you are a sinner…you must be punished." Those little lamb-like girls keep looking at us with tear-filled eyes, but this wretched stomach of ours compels us to ignore them! Her relatives keep saying utmost ugly things about her hair. They say, the more hair you have, the more your husband will rot in hell. He will stay there for as many drops of water that will fall from your wet hair when you wash them. So, in order to liberate him from hell, you must give the sacrifice of your hair."

Everyone was listening with a stunned expression on their faces. Jyotirao had said to them,

"My brothers, why are you doing the sin of making an already tormented widow, even more sad? Why are you becoming the tools to rob them of the gift of hair that Mother Nature has given them? Just for those 2-4 aanas that you get? Are those 2-4 aanas going to give you a lifetime of luxury? No, the won't. Instead, they will burden you with the heart-rendering curses of those innocent lives, whose beauty, self-respect, and confidence you take away by tonsuring them. Please do not fall prey to this sin for a few pennies. Please do not fall prey to the web of deceit spun for decades on end by these crafty Brahmins."

One of the barbers got up and said,

"Tatyasaheb is telling the truth. These people take huge amounts of money to 'purify the widow' – whatever that means – and pay us mere pennies for tonsuring them. If we try to protest against this injustice, they threaten us with dire consequences."

"Brothers, this behavior in itself shall give you a glimpse of how deceitful and selfish these Brahmins can be. They have no qualms in pushing a helpless woman into the depths of misery simply to keep their own kitchen fires burning."

When the topic came up about those few barbers who had joined hands with Brahmins, Jyotirao said,

"Let them be. One day, they will themselves see the truth and come on our side. Till then, let us start waging our war against this inhuman practice."

"Hear, hear!!" the crowd shouted.

The meeting was proclaimed a success but still Jyotirao was doubtful as to how much this resolution would keep up in the face of life's practicalities.

That night, Jyotirao kept thinking about all the events that he had not been able to go to, in the last one year of being bedridden. The scavengers' strike at Mumbai, the sweepers' strike at Alibaug, the protest led by Krishnarao Bhalekar on the eve of Prince Albert's arrival in India, the erection of a farmer's statue done by the Satyashodhak Samaj members at the conference of Indian National Congress in Mumbai, and many more. He knew that henceforth, he would have to be satisfied by only hearing about such events; attending them was becoming a remote possibility with every passing day.

The work of Deenbandhu Sarvajanik Sabha was going on in full force, as was the scathing criticism of Jyotirao being continually done by 'Deenmitra'. Jyotirao's ill health had not served to soften 'Deenmitra's stance towards him.

In his free time, Jyotirao would reminisce about everything that had happened in his life. The lessons he learnt from Thomas Penn, Brihaspati, as well as his teachers like Dr. Mitchell; the continuous war that he waged against the Brahmins; the schools he had opened across Pune and so many neighboring villages; the orphanage that he and Savitribai had started at their home to give shelter to the innocent children of widows; Kashibai's death; Yeshwant's marriage; starting the Satyashodhak Samaj.... memories would doting the landscape of his mind, even as he would think about our society, still taking baby steps onto the turf of human rights.

He reminisced about the immense courage shown by Rakhmabai. In fact, so big was her courageous act that Raosaheb had given a special lecture about it in Pune. Rakhmabai was the daughter of Dr. Sakharam Arjun of Mumbai. She staunchly refused to continue her marriage with her illiterate and tuberculosis-ridden husband. The matter went to court. The court decreed that it was a Hindu woman's duty to live with and serve her husband – howsoever she may not approve of him; else, she could be imprisoned for her defiance. Rakhmabai replied that she would happily go to jail, but would not return to her husband, at any cost. Rakhmabai's frank decision served to open the judge's eyes. He decided to think over the issue once again. Everybody had thought that Rakhmabai would have no choice but to accept what the judge decided; but, she stood her ground firmly, thus changing the judgment in her favour. The effects of this unique case were felt across seven seas.

But, there were very few girls who had the courage and resources to take such a defiant stand.

Jyotirao would feel frustrated that the aims that he had held close to heart all these years and worked for, had not yielded much result. A major chunk of society was still lagging behind, embracing ancient, regressive ideas. Even though the doors of education had creaked open for women, it was just the beginning. There were a lot of people who were still against the very idea of basic education for women. The question of child widows was still on anvil. Laws were being made to protect them, but the social attitudes were not changing in tune with those norms. A rare person like Behramji Malbari was fighting dedicatedly to bring in a minimum legal age for girls to get married. Gopalbuva was fighting to abolish the social evil of untouchability.

Thankfully, the Shoodra and Ati Shoodra communities

were waking up to the reforms being cultivated by the Satyashodhak Samaj. They were changing their attitudes and outlook in order to better their own lives.

Yeshwant's marriage was done with, but the tension of Otur case still remained on Jyotirao's head. Nevertheless, when some Satyashodhak youngster would come bearing some good news, Jyotirao's would again start feeling rejuvenated.

The regions of Otur and Junnar were seeing a spate of Satyashodhak revelries, thanks to Bhimrao Mahamuni. The revelries would see people from many neighboring villages come to participate. Bhimrao would give effective speeches on the evils perpetrated by Brahmins, the importance of education, the need to remain without addictions and so on. His powerful oratory would result in hundreds of young people becoming members of the Samaj.

Satyashodhaks like Bhimrao were indeed doing a great service in spreading the work of the Samaj; for, it was not that easy to host these revelries. The fear of savage attacks from rivals was always a reality. Hence, the Satyashodhaks would always deploy armed guards, wherever they were travelling for the revelries.

Many youngsters would come to Pine to describe these 'adventures' to their Tatyasaheb and also take advice from him. Seeing their courage and excitement, Jyotirao would say,

"Now, my worries are over. The work which I started, is being carried ahead on able shoulders. Whenever death comes to claim me, I can go in peace with the knowledge that a great social reform is on the anvil for our society. Even if I may not be able to see it, the world will!"

In this same duration, Gopalbuva wrote a public appeal to all Hindu brethren. in the form of a booklet called 'Vitaal Vidhvansan'. In that booklet, he appealed the Hindu brethren to stop the casteist segregations and allied social evils like untouchability on their own accord; failing which, he and his accomplices would be forced to wage a legal battle on this account.

Then one day, finally, that golden day arrived when the Satyashodhak Samaj and its Satyadharma won the landmark Otur case!! Adv. Nadkarni had represented the Samaj's views in the most apt way. Arguing that since there had been no ritual conducted in those weddings, apart from the bride and groom exchanging floral garlands, there was no question of any Brahmin having the right to ask for dakshina. The opposition was completely taken aback by this argument, and the court gave the ruling in favor of the Samaj.

When Jyotirao received a copy of that historical ruling which snubbed the Brahmins in their face, he felt like a wave of excitement coursed through his weak body anew!

In the same phase, 'Deenbandhu' started a strong critical campaign against the inhuman practice of tonsuring of widows. They appealed to the human being in the barbers and asked them to stand up against the social evil on their own accord. Mama Parmanand also upheld these views and wrote critical articles against the widows' relatives and barbers for allowing such savage rituals to still continue. In his letter to 'Deenbandhu', Mama Parmanand praised their sincere efforts while also denouncing the paper tigers who did little but roar in solitude against such evils. He also said that 'Deenbandhu' was doing a courageous job in the crowd of mostly orthodox papers who would never dare to touch this issue. Agarkar's 'Sudharak' also expressed gratitude towards 'Deenbandhu' for taking up this sensitive but burning question.

However, Tilak's 'Kesari' expressed negative opinions about 'Deenbandhu's act.

It was impossible that Jyotirao Phule would sit still with all this activity going on. In spite of his failing health, Jyotirao decided to lead the barber's strike to the finish. He was intent on eradicating this social evil.

After the strike, not a single barber got ready to tonsure a single widow. The orthodox Brahmin group was hopping mad at this daredevilry shown by the barbers, but they would have to lock horns with Jyotirao Phule in order to express their rage – and they were definitely not ready to do that! On one hand, while they tried threatening barbers with ostracism, on the other hand, there also began a spate of Brahmins rubbing their noses on the floor, begging the barbers to tonsure their widowed girls. They were trying every trick in the book to break the spine of this strike; but, to no avail.

The movement spread from Pune to Mumbai. Narayanrao Lokhande of 'Deenbandhu', and, Sadoba Krishnaji held a massive meeting, which saw more than a thousand barbers in attendance. Many of them expressed their views about the inhumane practice. At the end of the meeting, the barbers took an oath to no longer be party to tonsuring of widows. Three more such meetings followed in Mumbai itself. The meeting in Mandvi saw almost 500 barbers from as far as Wai, Junnar, and Pune in attendance. It was decided that any barber who henceforth tonsured a widow, would be ostracized from the barber community! The news of this unique social movement reached all the way from Europe. Many congratulatory letters started pouring in from there, praising the barbers for taking the courageous and much-needed step.

However, the Brahmins were not going to give up so easily. Taking the few barbers on their side at hand, they kept waging tricks to break the strike.

Ill health, penury, and social torment notwithstanding, Jyotirao kept working incessantly. He kept meeting barbers, kept talking to them to help change their minds... The barbers' strike received backing from the reformists too.

Seeing all opposition stacked against them, the Brahmins finally removed their last weapon. They started shaving each other's heads. Using that as an opportunity, the traitor barbers started talking their counterparts into compromise.

Slowly, the barbers' resolution started falling weak in the face of hunger, financial worries, and the evil promises of moral turpitude. Jyotirao's hands fell short of rescuing his widowed sisters from a bleak fate! He kept hearing the pitiable cries of the young widows, but was helpless to do anything to help them!

97

Days and months were flying by. Jyotirao was almost permanently bed-ridden. His body would ache continuously.

Moropant took the draft of 'Sarvajanik Satyadharma' with him to Mumbai. He had decided to get the book published as soon as possible. Moropant also had his own financial worries, but he as determined to see his dear friend's last wish through, come what may.

On his part, Jyotirao was relieved that the book was getting published. Months and years of effort were finally reaching fruition. He felt immensely grateful to Moropant for his help.

The hostel was still running, in face of constant problems and continuous criticism by 'Deenmitra'. It was getting increasingly difficult to feed the students properly. Finances were very short; but Jyotirao and Savitribai would themselves sleep half-stomached at the cost of feeding the children.

Mama Parmanand was seeing Jyotirao's immense efforts even in the face of old age, ill health, and penury. He started feeling worried about the future of the Phule family. Yeshwant's education was still going on. Till he became a qualified doctor, the Phule family required money to carry on their daily expenses. Jyotirao would spend almost all his income on social work. It was impossible that he would ask for financial help from anybody; he was too self-respecting for that.

Mama Parmanand realized that he would need to appeal to a large-hearted patron, on behalf of Jyotirao. On the lookout for such a patron who realized the enormity of Jyotirao's contribution to society, Mama decided to contact Maharaj Sayajirao Gaekwad of Baroda.

Mama Parmanand was the epitome of grace and sacrifice. Actually, Maharaj Sayajirao had himself proffered financial help for Mama after getting to know of his delicate health. In response to that letter, Mama wrote to him:

"...Maharaj, my health is delicate but thankfully it is not as bad as that of the immensely dedicated social reformer Jyotirao Phule. Phule has been very ill due to two paralytic strokes; his financial situation is also not that comfortable. We have had our ideological differences in the past, but that does not take away from the fact that Phule is extremely large-hearted and principled gentleman. I would request the Maharaj to kindly take cognizance of his problems and extend some financial help to him...."

Before this, Dr. Vishram Ramji had also sent a letter of request to Maharaj Sayajirao, requesting financial help for Jyotirao Phule. Considering that Maharaj Sayajirao held Phule in great esteem, and Diwanbahadur Ramchandrarao Dhamanaskar was a good friend of Phule's, there did not seem to be a problem in getting this help.

Mama Parmanand decided to write a big letter to Ramchandrarao, reminding him of Dr. Vishram Ramji's letter, as well as, describing in great detail about the work done by the Phule couple till date. He wrote:

"Dear Ramchandrarao,

....I'm herewith attaching a formal letter of request for financial help towards Jyotirao Phule. If you wish to make any changes in the same, or if you have any suggestions for me to repair the appeal in any way, please do advise me so; I shall be glad to make the due changes and re-send the letter.

It is my earnest request to you to please present this letter of request before Maharaj Sayajirao Gaekwad. I'm sure, he shall take due note of the immense work that Jyotirao has done for the society so far, and shall accordingly extend a hand of help towards him in these difficult times. It was indeed a very tough task for a Maratha man to educate his wife, and then educate scores of Brahmins girls through her; and that to, in an orthodox city like Pune, which is but a haven of Brahmins. Instead of resting on those laurels, Jyotirao then went onto opening schools for the Mahars and Maangs, and appealed to the society to treat them as equal human beings. This task was no less onerous than walking into a lion's cave and plucking at its mane! He had the help of two Brahmin friends for this task. One of them parted ways with Jyotirao after they developed ideological differences, and has long expired. The other friend is still loyally with him, and in spite of not being of very sound financial health, has been toiling to get Jyotirao's book published on his own funds.

Jyotirao did a lot of work, but never thought about his own financial comforts or security. If he had, he would have probably been living a very comfortable life today. But, Jyotirao's mind-set was never inclined towards accumulating personal wealth. He chose to walk on a different path and spend maximum of his earnings for the same. Another lesser-known attribute of his is that, in his young age, since he was blessed with a handsome face and good health, Jyotirao had been the target of a couple of immoral ladies. But, never did he fall prey to those temptations; he kept walking on the path of morality and values all through, thus practicing what he preached. His selfless, humane nature can be seen from the immense work that he did for rehabilitation of widows, who would have otherwise been caught in a web of moral turpitude, or would have inevitably committed the sin of infanticide. Jyotirao looked after all those young women with the affection of a father. His biggest and most consistent contribution to the upliftment of society has been, his speeches, writings, and overall advice to the lower caste people to help them unshackle themselves of generations of mental slavery and learning to live a life of dignity. He has been working towards this cause for the last 25 years at least. He has faced immense obstacles on the way; so far as to, falling out of favor of many upper caste people, some of them his dear friends too. I do admit that Jyotirao's blunt manner and harsh language has also served to irk many people; but, that does not take away from his dedication towards the cause of bringing all people on a similar human plane, irrespective of their castes and sub-castes. Unfortunately, quite a few of his followers, who did not have the capabilities of their leader, went to emulate him and fell flat on their faces. That led to Jyotirao's work getting tainted, purely due to the reason of association, and nothing more.

In no way am I trying to say that Jyotirao has never made any mistakes, or that his mistakes should simply be forgiven and forgotten. However, in my humble opinion, his work far more exceeds his follies; and in view of the yeoman service that he has rendered to the society, we must take due cognizance of the penury that has befallen him in his ill health, coupled with old age. He does not have any affluent friends who can help him with large amounts. He is also too self-respecting to ask anybody for help on his own accord.

Hence, it is my humble request to Maharaj Sayajirao Gaekwad that, in view of the work that he knows has been done by Jyotirao, we will be extremely grateful if he can extend some financial help towards the Phules."

Stating that ideally, the government should have offered this help, but it is futile to expect that generosity from them, Mama further said,

"It is a humble proposal from my side that Jyotirao and Savitribai be given Rs. 30 per month for their expenses. After the demise of either one of them, the amount should be reduced as deemed fit, and should be entirely stopped after the education of their son Yeshwant, gets completed. It will be helpful to act on this proposal without much delay. Looking at Jyotirao's health, I daresay, the help will not be required to be given for too long, and, the amount is also not too much."

At the end of the letter, Mama also reminded Ramchandrarao of a similar letter sent earlier by Dr. Vishram

Ghole, saying,

"Dr. Vishram Ghole is a family friend and physician of the Phules. He has been treating Jyotirao free-of-cost. I understand that Dr. Ghole had also sent a letter of request to Maharaj Sayajirao, via Mr. Pestonji. I do not know the details of the request sent by him, but I understand that the reply that he received was as follows: 'We are in receipt of many such letters of request from different people. We cannot promise anything imminently. But, Maharaj has promised to look into the matter in the next few weeks.' In pursuance to that letter and the reply it received, this letter is to urge you to please treat Jyotirao Phule's requirement as urgent. I surmise that while there must be a lot of applicants for help at Maharaj's durbar, there will not be many like Jyotirao. Considering the magnanimity of his work, coupled with the seriousness of his health issues, any further delay in extending help will undermine the empathy and generosity that Maharaj Gaekwad is so famous for.

Yours truly,
N.M. Parmanand"

Mama's son, Babu, was a doctor at the Baroda princely state. Mama sent the letter to Dr. Babu, to personally hand over to Ramchandrarao Dhamanaskar. But, there was no reply forthcoming to both letters – the earlier one sent by Dr. Ghole, as well as, the one sent by Mama Parmanand. Mama could not understand why the princely state and its king who was so famous for his immense compassion and judiciousness, was dithering in responding to an appeal for Jyotirao.

Three weeks passed by without any reply. Unable to wait any more, Mama wrote another letter to Dhamanaskar. In this letter he wrote,

"... *If any part of my previous letter has served to displease you, kindly treat it as my personal opinion and not let it stand in the way of offering much-needed help to this selfless gentleman. I took the liberty of explaining so much about Jyotirao's work and condition, only so that the entire background for asking for help be lucid, so as to enable an expedited decision, considering Phule's dire circumstances. If my mentioning Phule's Maratha background has been a bone of contention, please be rest assured that there was absolutely no intention to signify that Maharaj Gaekwad maintains casteism and favoritism while proffering help. Maharaj has always supported people of all castes and sub castes, including the Brahmins. So, I'm sure that he can certainly find it in his heart to support a selfless man who is struggling with ill health, old age, and penury at the same time.*

I have been advocating Jyotirao's side because I feel that, irrespective of all his follies and faults, the enormity of the work that he has done should certainly be given due respect. Under normal circumstances, I myself would have given him some funds every month; but presently, my own health has become a cause for added expenditure, thus preventing me from doing much for him. Jyotirao's close friends will also chip in as and when they can; but, what he really requires is a consistent income every month. I sincerely wish that Maharaj finds it in his heart to extend this help.

On another note, I was sorry to hear that Maharaj Fattesingh's health has not been too well. I hope that the atmosphere of Mumbai helps him recuperate.

Yours truly,
N.M.Parmanand."

98

The festival of Diwali went by; winters set in. Jyotirao's health deteriorated even more. Many friends and well-wishers kept coming in to meet their dear Tatyasaheb, but Raobahadur Gopal Hari Deshmukh's visit proved specially distressful.

Raobahadur had suffered immense pain and grief in the last decade. His wife, elder brother, three young sons, one son-in-law, and two daughters had left for their heavenly abodes back-to-back. The sudden blows had reduced the once charming and smart Raobahadur to a shrunken old man. Nevertheless, keeping his personal grief aside, Raobahadur had come to see Jyotirao.

After serving as a judge at Mumbai, Nagar, Nasik, and Ahmadabad, Raobahadur had finally settled at Pune. Locking away his despondency in his heart, Raobahadur kept toiling away for social upliftment. Unaffected by his grief, the orthodox group still kept chipping away at his self-respect through intense criticism. In particular, Vishnushastri Chiplunkar's death anniversary would be the biggest day for denouncing Lokahitawadi, because he had dared to go against his own Brahmin caste. All through his working life, Lokahitawadi had suffered so many instances of public humiliation and ostracism.

But, Jyotirao knew the greatness of his work. He knew that while Lokahitawadi bowed down to the orthodox group at times, he never betrayed his ideals. The Raobahadur who invited people for a widow's remarriage and himself went off to Ahmadabad, or, the Raobahadur who sent his son abroad for higher studies were not separate people. He was the epitome of how desperate can an intelligent, thoughtful man become in the face of intense social pressure. Raobahadur had forever walked on a tight-rope – keeping one eye on the future, while fighting with the restrictions imposed by his caste. His life had been one long battle with people, as well as, his heart.

Raobahadur crossed swords with his caste brethren to send his son abroad for higher studies. He faced ostracism for the same, and even had to do atonement for his 'sin'. After all this, when his son returned as a barrister, his demeanor had changed so much that it brought in tremendous grief and heartache for Raobahadur. So much so that, the same man who used to advocate sending children abroad for a bright future, was reduced to exhorting people to never do that mistake.

However, Raobahadur remained the first Brahmin to fearlessly take on his own caste brethren. He exposed the evil ploys played by Brahmins to maintain their social superiority. Owing to his education in the English medium, he was very progressive in his views; but sadly, his own people never saw the good in what Raobahadur would propose.

Jyotirao had first met Gopal Hari Deshmukh at Lahujibuva's akhaada. The dandpatta-wielding youngster was a student of the English school at Budhwar Peth. The friendship grew from strength to strength thereafter. In due course, Gopal Hari took on the name of Lokahitawadi and published those famous hundred letters by that name. Jyotirao would eagerly wait for those letters that would come published in 'Prabhakar'.

Seeing the once lively Gopal Hari reduced to a tired, old man sitting in front of him, made Jyotirao's heart wrench. How he wished he could have taken some of Gopal Hari's troubles on his own self! Raosaheb and Jyotirao had always stood by each other's side during any form of trouble. Jyotirao was among the first one to stand up for Raobahadur after he was first ostracized, whereas, Raobahadur had been a great help when Jyotirao and Savitribai started the orphanage at their home.

It pained Jyotirao to see that this great social reformer who spent his entire life in the service of humankind; who ran a dispensary at home and would himself tend to the ailing poor patients, had turned so helpless in the dusk of his life. Nevertheless, without displaying his inner grief at any point, Raobahadur said,

"Jyotirao, whatever we did, it was for the betterment of our countrymen. It was to make them realize their standing in society. I know that whatever scriptures and literature we have criticized and faced so much flak for, are going to be collectively rejected by the people tomorrow, because they themselves will realize what was wrong in those. The orthodox group is not going to accept our views today; but soon, a day will come when the masses will go against them. Let us hope that at least that time, they shall keep their vacuous egos aside and heed the popular opinions."

The progressive thinker's message of hope was laced with fervor and worry, both. t was this attitude of his tat had always endeared Jyotirao to Raobahadur.

One day, a message came in from the Mission that Baba Padmanji was coming to meet Jyotirao.

After Madam Sera's demise, Baba Padmanji had left for Mumbai and was now working as an editor in the Bible & Tract Society. His third wife had recently left for her heavenly abode. Jyotirao was feeling sad that he could not go for her prayer meeting.

Baba Padmanji had converted to Christianity and was staying in Pune for many years now. His first Christian wedding had happened in Pune itself. He was a dedicated teacher, preacher and caretaker of the Free Church Mission. Constantly engaged in reading, writing and thinking, Baba was a fountain of knowledge to say the least. Jyotirao and Baba Padmanji had become friends when Baba was a member of the Paramhans Sabha. They both agreed that religious reforms could not be brought about by behaving safely. The bond of friendship became stronger after Baba came to stay at Pune.

Now, a sea of myriad memories rose in Jyotirao's heart, as he welcomed this old friend. A courageous man who converted to Christianity because its principles appealed to him; a religious-minded but stubborn Baba who refused to accept his first Hindu wife after getting married to Madam Sera; an avid writer and thinker who would talk for hours on end about religion; a learned man who would rectify the mistakes in powadas about the Chhatrapati and publish them in 'Satyadeepika'...

So many memories came rising to the surface... But nowadays, Jyotirao would tire of those memories too. Rehashing them would make him exhausted.

When Baba Padmanji came, Jyotirao could not even get up from his bed to greet him. Baba was looking tired and weak; his wife's demise had cast a shadow on his shingin face. Folding his hands, Jyotirao greeted him saying,

"Welcome Baba. I'm extremely sorry, I could not come for the prayer meeting...."

"Jyotirao, please do not apologize. Don't I know that you would have definitely come if you could? How are you feeling now?" replied Baba.

"I'm okay, Baba. How is your daughter, Esther doing?"

"She is well. She is the one who takes care of me now. Rest, all is in Lord Christ's hand."

"Father, I really liked the tract that you had written. Plus, my teacher, Father Mitchell has written to me from Scotland. He still remembers me. I know that he would have been really glad if I had converted to Christianity as well. I did agree with Lord Christ's teachings, but the mythological stories described in the Christian religion, did not agree with me. I would always say to Father Mitchell, 'Why do I need to convert to Christianity in order to follow Lord. Christ's teachings? I can always walk on his path without changing my religion.' We would have a lot of affectionate debates on this topic, but never did they cause any rift in our relationship. I'm so happy to see that he still remembers me and cares for me. He must have grown very old by now; how sad that I'm not in a state to travel and meet him now."

Govinda brought Father Mitchell's letter and handed it over to Baba to read. After reading the letter, Baba said,

"Dr. Mitchell is indeed a rare gentleman. He still holds you in great esteem and is genuinely concerned about your spiritual wellness." Halting for a moment, Baba asked, "Jyotirao, at the end of your life, would you say that you are spiritually content?"

"Yes" Jyotirao replied emphatically. "I can say so with full conviction. I have not harmed anybody. Whatever I have done, has been in keeping with my moral compass. I do not have any regrets."

"Well, Jyotirao, when the Lord asks us thousand questions on Judgment Day, we shall not be able to answer even a single one of those. May the Lord forgive us" said Baba.

"Amen."

Soon, news spread that Jyotirao was speaking as if he knew his end was near. This put his friends and well-wishers in worry. There was yet no reply from Baroda. Once again, Mama Parmanand wrote to Diwanbahadur Dhamanaskar, saying,

"If not for the selfless and great man that Jyotirao is, I beseech you to please do something for his equally great wife and adopted son. If nothing else, please at least show both my letters to Maharaj directly. If possible, please show my smaller letter to him in complete secrecy. If you can think of any other way to help Jyotirao, kindly advise."

Mama was repeatedly requesting the Baroda state for help, but none of his letters received any response whatsoever. Neither did any financial help come in.

One day, Jyotirao said to Dr. Ghole,

"Doctor, please tell my Satyashodhak friends that I wish to see them all for the last time."

99

One evening, Savitribai finished her evening's cooking with the help of Rangutai, and went to sit besides Jyotirao's bed. Generally, Jyotirao's evenings would be spent talking to the children, but today, he kept sleeping. In fact, he had not been moving from his bed since last morning. Kaku was extremely worried; she was working on autopilot, but her heart was engaged with Jyotirao's health.

Dr. Vishram Ramji would make a daily visit to check on Jyotirao, but even he had given up on hopes of recovery by now. Jyotirao's meals had become very small. Till two days before he would at least have one chapatti and some rice in a day, but lately, he had only been subsisting only on sago gruel and milk.

Mama Parmanand, Narayanrao Lokhande and Swami Aiyyavaru came from Mumbai to meet Jyotirao. Pandita Ramabai made a visit to see him too. Justice Raosaheb Ranade,

Ramkrishna Bhandarkar, Nageshwargeerbuva, Hari Raoji, Bhau Kondaji, Balaji Kusaji, Shastri Naro Babaji, Gangarambhau Mhaske...so many people kept coming to meet their dear Tatyasaheb, who was getting weaker by each passing day.

Soon, Satyashodhaks started pouring in from Baroda, Nagpur, Dhule, Jalgaon, Satara and Kolhapur. Jyotirao would ignore his frail health and keep talking to them. He would tell everybody,

"Brothers, this is the last time that we are meeting. I'm sure that what we could not achieve in the last 2000 years, we are bound to achieve in the next 50 years. Your ancestors were reduced to cowering lambs during Peshwai; but, you should now become tigers. The British are not going to be here forever. But, till they are here, use whatever resources they are offering you and make your life better. Educate your children. There is no better gift that you can give them. Always walk on the path of Satyadharma; this is the only path that shall ultimately bring the entirety humankind on one equal plane."

He would also constantly acknowledge Savitribai's support saying,

"It was only due to Kaku's unstinting support that I could do so much work in one lifetime. She has been my true partner for the last five decades..."

People would go back with tears in their eyes.

One day, Dr. Santuji Lad and a few more Satyashodhaks were expected to arrive from Thane. The Phule couple was awaiting them. Jyotirao was lying down with his eyes closed. At one point, Savitribai called out to him saying,

"Shetji..."

Jyotirao opened his eyes weakly.

"Are you feeling okay?" she asked.

In response, Jyotirao gave a weak smile and gestured Savitribai to sit next to him. Even as she did so, he again shut his eyes and remained so for a long time. Then, Savitribai said,

"Wait, let me get some food for you..."

"No, Kaku" Jyotirao responded in a tired voice. "Just get me some milk. Nothing more."

Savitribai said in a worried voice,

"...But, you have not eaten anything in the last two days, Shetji..."

"No, Savitribai. I really do not feel like eating anything." Waiting for a moment, he continued, "Please continue our work. Our Satyashodhak brothers and sisters like Savitribai Rode and Shivubai are there to help you. Do not let the hostel shut down. I feel very worried for you, but our Yeshwant is there to take care of you. He will soon begin earning. Take care of Lakshmi. It would have been nice if I could have met Ganpati..."

"Shall I send a message to Adgaon?" Savitribai asked.

"No, it's okay. Take care of Sitaram and Govinda too...." Jyotirao again kept quiet for some time and then said, "And please ensure one thing. Do not allow any of our brethren who feel happy being enslaved by Brahmins, to touch my corpse after I'm gone. Be sure to help the poor and students on the eve of my funeral rituals..."

Jyotirao was speaking haltingly. His tongue was getting heavier; words were getting unclear. Savitribai was listening to him with a heavy heart. She had resolved to see each of Jyotirao's wishes through till the end.

Jyotirao had one more wish. He wanted his body to be embalmed in salt and cremated in an already earmarked place, at the foot of a banyan tree in the Phule's compound. He did not want his corpse to be placed on a funeral pyre. Also, he had saved some money to spend for poor students; he told Savitribai to do the needful after his demise.

"I'm worried about one more thing, Savitribai" said Jyotirao. "After I'm gone, probably you will face a lot of societal torment. But please, do not give up. Remain courageous, as you always have. One day, we shall certainly see the fruition of our efforts, and that day is not too far off."

Hearing this, Savitribai's gentle eyes shone with the light of determination, as she replied,

"Don't worry, Shetji. Your teaching shall not go waste. We have not stepped ahead to go back. I shall continue your work with the same zeal as you have done so far."

Savitribai's answer brought tears to Jyotirao's eyes. He felt content and emotional at the same time. Trying to wipe the tears with his left hand, Jyotirao looked at Savitribai with tenderness and said,

"Indeed, I would not have been able to do anything at all, if you had not stood by me, Savitri! People can see me at the forefront, but the real strength behind all my endeavours has been you! Your unstinting support and efforts will not go waste. I will not be around to see it, but soon, our efforts will be seen bearing ripe fruit."

"Enough now, Shetji.... Shall I get you some milk and sago gruel? You need to eat something. Dr. Lad is going to come, isn't it?"

"If you say so..."

Savitribai got some milk and gruel for Jyotirao. He had a few sips of both and again laid down. Savitribai could see the writing on the wall clearly – Shetji had never forsaken food to this extent, in all these months of his illness.

That night, Jyotirao was awake long after midnight. Sometime late after midnight, his health started deteriorating rapidly. Things were not looking good even in the morning. He called Savitribai and said to her,

"My days are numbered, Savitri. But, do not lose courage after I'm gone. Be strong. You need to stand up strongly for our Yeshwant and Gajanan. I'm confident, you will manage everything well. Send a telegram to Mumbai and Otur. I want to meet my dear ones for one last time. Sitaram...."

"Yes, Tatyasaheb?"

"Do not leave my Yeshwant alone, please..."

"No...never, Tatyasaheb!" Sitaram promised, stifling the

sobs that threatened to spill over any moment.

Telegrams were sent quickly. People from the neighboring houses started gathering. Dr. Vishram Ramji came to check on Jyotirao. He declared that there was no cause for worry. Dr. Santuji Lad also reached in some time. He had got delayed in his arrival. He also checked Jyotirao and gave the same opinion as Dr. Vishram Ramji. But, Savitribai's heart was not ready to believe that.

Jaya Karadi, Swami Aiyyavaru, Raju Babaji, Narayanrao Lokhande and Moropant Walvekar rushed to Pune that afternoon. They all spoke with Jyotirao. Moropant gave him an update about the publication process of 'Sarvajanik Satyadharma'. They all felt that his health seemed okay and thus, were confounded as to what was going on in Tatyasaheb's mind. Pandit Dhondiram, Marutrao Navle, Dr. Vishram Ramji, Gyaanoba Sasane and Krishnarao Bhalekar were asked to come urgently to the Phule house.

As they all gathered, Jyotirao said,

"Brothers, please forgive me for summoning all of you here so urgently. But, I have a big request for you all. I'm not going to live for too long now. Hence, I wish to give the responsibility of Savitribai and Yeshwant in your able hands."

"Tatyasaheb...please do not talk like this.." said Swami Aiyyavaru.

"Swamiji, it is the truth. It is time for me to bid goodbye to all of you. Hence, I called all of you here today. This is our last meeting."

Everyone was overwhelmed. There was pin-drop silence, as they all struggled to control their tears. Seeing that, Jyotirao said,

"Brothers, please do not be sad. We all would like to be with each other for ever; but, death is certain for us all. No one can escape it. A living being is bound to die some day. As human beings, our duty is to live a good and moral life till the last breath. I'm happy that I could see you all before closing my eyes for ever. It would have been a great joy t see our Shoodra and Ati Shoodra brethren scaling the peaks of progress during my lifetime, but I will not have the fortune to see that. For, a lot of work remains to be done for that to happen. And, who better than you all to take up this responsibility? Please keep working to uplift our ignorant brethren. Make them aware of their rights and self-respect. Teach the importance of getting educated.... "

"..... I have done the work that God sent me on earth for. You all gave me tremendous support in this journey. I'm very thankful to you for that. But today, I'm also entrusting you the baton of this incomplete work. I can go in peace, knowing that you all will carry ahead this work and uplift our Shoodra and Ati Shoodra brethren."

"Tatyasaheb..." Dr. Vishram Ramji tried intervening.

"No, Doctor. Please let me talk today. Brothers, even if I leave this mortal body, please consider that I shall always remain with you all in spirit. I shall be there in every success and challenge you encounter. But please, do not forsake this responsibility. Please serve the society. Behave in keeping with moral values and justice. Do not meander from the path of truth. You may face immense challenges while doing so, but please realize that, ultimately, that is the only road to success. Our efforts shall not go waste. Our Shoodra, Ati Shoodra brethren shall certainly lead a dignified life soon...."

Talking so much led Jyotirao to have a strong bout of cough. He shut his eyes and laid still. Everyone around him sat in silence; tears streaming down their cheeks.

Savitribai was also crying silently. The Phule house was filled with people who simply did not want to leave after hearing Tatyasaheb speak with this finality.

Unable to control himself, Moropant cried out,

"Tatya... are you going to leave us suddenly like this? Don't you want to see your book in print?"

Jyotirao opened his eyes and looked at this childhood friend of his, who was now sobbing like a child. Memories came cascading down as Jyotirao kept looking wordlessly at his dear friend. So many people had come and gone in his life. So many friends morphed into enemies. Moropant also had his differences with Jyotirao, but he never let their friendship get affected adversely by them. Sadashiv had long parted ways; Sakharam went off to Mumbai for livelihood and never returned. But Moropant never went away from Jyotirao.

With much effort, Jyotirao said to Moropant,

"My dear friend, how can I ever thank you for all the beautiful moments you have accorded me with in your friendship? I hold our bond very dear to heart. Please do one last thing for me. Please see to it that 'Sarvajanik Satyadharma' sees the light of the day. The society will forever be indebted to you for that."

Soon, the people from Thane and Mumbai left. Narayanrao did not leave with them. He had to go to his wife's maiden home from there. By evening, other people also went home. Jyotirao requested Krishnarao to stay on. He wanted to talk to him.

Krishnarao had come as soon as he got the message that Jyotirao wanted to see him. It was many years later that he was setting foot in Phule's house. In spite of all their differences, Jyotirao had always admired Krishnarao for his ingenuity, courage, and persistence.

After everyone had left, Jyotirao called Krishnarao close and said,

"Please do not keep any malice in mind...."

Krishnarao answered,

"Tatyasaheb, please do not think like this. I have pushed everything behind and come to meet you. I promise you that we shall take your work forward. Please be rest assured."

"I have no doubt that, Krishnarao. But remember one thing – people will try to use you. They will praise you to the skies to get their selfish aims fulfilled. But, the picture of the uplifted society that we see in our dreams, is not the same that they see in theirs. They cannot think beyond the Brahmin caste. Do not get fooled into believing that they will do anything for the Shoodras and Ati Shoodras. Please get aware in good time before the crafty Brahmins tighten their noose around your neck. It was for the same reason that I had criticized Gangarambhau. He did not mind it so much, but, you did. I hold no personal enmity with anyone. My enmity has always been with the Brahmin way of thinking...with casteist segregations and the resultant torment wreaked on the masses. If I was against Brahmins per se, I would not have done so much for their widows."

"That's what I'm saying, Tatyasaheb..." Krishnarao interjected.

"I know what you are trying to say, Krishnarao. The mountain of problems in front of our lower caste brethren, still remains very big. I did whatever I could. Now, I'm entrusting you all to carry this work forward. As times change, so will the types of these challenges. But remember, whatever the challenge, the only way to resolve it, is truth."

"But Tatyasaheb, it surprised me that Agarkar should also snub you, calling you a Reverend..." ventured Krishnarao.

"What is there to be surprised about that? It is clear that he does not accept my views. No problem. If he thinks that I have not been able to explain how this divisive caste system came about, then he should explain it. It is an old habit of our home-grown reformers to play the blame game to evade uncomfortable questions. If we speak frankly about the caste system, they are quick to label us as converted Christians. But, that only serves to mislead people all the more, instead of bringing about some good. They forget that if we really want to bring about social and societal progress, we all need to candidly accept what is wrong with our own religions/castes and make due changes. But these people prefer to play ostrich, simply to keep the image of their caste well-coiffed."

Jyotirao halted a bit and then said,

"But still, Agarkar's 'Sudharak' is doing a lot more service in cracking down upon social evils, than any of the other Brahmin-run newspapers. I hold Agarkar in high esteem for the courage that he shows in expressing his thoughts. If we have more such people who are not afraid to speak their, whatever the consequences, our society shall soon be on the road to a bright future. Agarkar's insistence of social reform over political reform, is a very correct one. There can be no political reform unless there is social reform."

Again halting for some time, Jyotirao said,

"Krishnrao, it is not an easy task to work for the upliftment of society in the kind of society that we are in. It requires tremendous perseverance and persistence to achieve results in such a social set-up. You are one of those rare individuals who have been gifted with both these qualities. Hence, please use these qualities for social betterment. The problems are going to get more complex. Our Shoodra, Ati Shoodra communities are slowly waking up to their rights; but, they require a proper direction to that awakening. I will not be present, but I sincerely hope that you shall be able to see a new dawn to this night of ignorance and subjugation."

Tears sprung to Krishnarao's eyes. Thereafter, they kept talking for a long time. The years of strain and dissent seemed to have melted away with that one meeting.

100

Dusk went by, holding the night by its hand to take its place. Jyotirao was lying on his bed, watching the moon cast its calm beams on the earth. He was feeling especially tired and weak tonight. His eyelids were drooping as if they had a life of their own.

Jyotirao did not understand when sleep claimed him, but when he woke up, he saw Savitribai sitting at his bedside with a wicker lamp by her side.

"Savitribai..."

"Yes, Shetji?"

"Please have your food..."

"So early? It is hardly 8 pm."

"Is it? Then, why do I feel that it is late night?" Jyotirao asked in a confused voice.

"It's okay, Shetji. Come on, you need to eat something" Savitribai urged.

"No, I don't feel like having anything" Jyotirao replied.

But, Savitribai was not going to take a no for an answer. She made him have some milk. Then, they all sat for dinner; but no one was in a mood to eat.

Just then, Bhau Patil came rushing in and went directly to Jyotirao's bedside, crying ou,

"Tatya!!!"

It was the first time that Bhau was calling him by that endearment. Jyotirao remembered the conversation they had had many years back, when he had insisted Bhau to call him as Tatya instead of the formal Tatyasaheb. But, today was different. Bhau could not stop his tears as he cried out,

"Tatya!! How can a younger brother go before an elder one? Is that right? You tell me!!"

Jyotirao looked a him weakly and said,

"Bhausaheb, please don't be so sad. I'm going as a content man. Just take care of my Yeshwant.... Now there is nothing more to wait for. I hope God takes me soon..."

Jyotirao wanted to say a lot more but the weakness would not allow him to exert any more.

Savitribai asked Bhau Patil to join them for dinner. Savitribai said to Jyotirao,

"Please sleep. Do not exert yourself so much."

But, in spite of the weakness, sleep eluded Jyotirao. He kept awake, looking at all the people having a few morsels over a quiet dinner. Savitribai closed the kitchen and came to sit besides her husband. The others were also awake.

Jyotirao was going in and out of sleep. It was past midnight. Savitribai kept looking at her husband as he now lay awake. Her eyes were streaming with tears. At one point, Jyotirao held his wife's hand tenderly, and asked,

"Savitribai, do you wish to say something?"

Seeing her husband's bright eyes giving away their light, Savitribai could no longer control her sobs. She cried out,

"Shetji, how am I to live without you? Who do I have except you?"

"Savitribai, why are you saying this? Our Yeshwant is there, isn't it? Do you not trust him?" Saying thus, Jyotirao beckoned Yeshwant closer and said,

"My son, you will take care of your mother, won't you?"

Breaking into tears, Yeshwant replied,

"Yes, Tatyasaheb; she is the only mother I have known. I shall never forsake her."

Jyotirao smiled with contentment on hearing this.

"Never forsake her, son…never…"

"I won't, Tatyasaheb!" Yeshwant promised.

"Lakshmi, Govinda, Gajanan...come to me, my children…" Tatyasaheb said. As they came closer, he ran an affectionate hand over their wan faces and then said to Gyaanoba,

"Gyaanoba, start saying your prayers."

The exertion again claimed Jyotirao. His eyelids became heavy. After some time, he opened his eyes weakly and could hear Gyaanoba singing a devotional hymn. This was not what Jyotirao wanted to hear, but he felt too weak to even register that much.

Soon, his vision became hazy. His eyelids seemed to refuse to stay open for any more time. From the closing brackets of his eyes, Jyotirao could see people crying. He wanted to tell them to not cry, but somehow he could not.

Soon, the voice of the singers ceased to be heard by

Jyotirao's ears. He whispered, "Ishwara...Ishwara..." A small sigh let out from his dry lips...and in the next instance, the life went out of Jyotirao's body!!!

"Shetji!!!" Savitribai cried out the moment she realized that her husband of five decades had left her for ever!

"Tatyasaheb!!" cried out Gyaanoba.

As realization dawned, people started wailing in grief. Just then, Bhau Patil and Dr. Vishram Ramji reached there. Realizing that they were too late, Bhau Patil howled in distress,

"Tatya...Oh Tatya...!!!"

Soon, messages started flying all around Pune and neighboring villages. Telegrams were sent out. People from Meethganj, Bhavani Peth and other parts of Pune started rushing to the Phule house.

By that night, there was not an inch of space remaining even in the courtyard. People kept streaming in from Hadapsar, Wanowrie, Zagdewadi, Maanjri, Ghorpadi, Bhamburde and Yerawada.

101

Dr. Vishram Ramji took charge of the situation. It was necessary to look at certain formalities even in the midst of all the grief. Jyotirao had asked to be embalmed and cremated. It was necessary to obtain the Collector's permission for that. Dr. Vishram Ramji himself went to meet the Collector for this purpose, but he returned with a negative response. Hearing this, Bhau Patil said,

"Alright. Then, let us have a funeral for him and bury his ashes in the spot that he wanted to be cremated at. No one can refuse us for doing that."

Everyone agreed to this suggestion and preparations for conducting the funeral began in earnest. Just then, news filtered in that, Jyotirao's kin were arriving there with the intention of creating a ruckus. The people decided to cross the bridge when they came to it, and went about the preparations for the funeral.

People were still coming in to take a last look at the great man. Wails and cries were permeating the air. Dalit brethren came in from afar to see their messiah. Many eminent people were coming in for the last rites.

Jyotirao's body was given a bath and adorned with new clothes. Flowers were arranged on his body, which was then kept on the bier. A few Satyashodhaks came ahead to lift the body. Just then, Babaji Phule came running from somewhere with his son Mahadba and a few more people in tow. Looking at Dr. Vishram Ramji with blazing eyes, he bellowed,

"Doctor, Tatya was our brother. Our blood. Who have you the right to conduct his funeral rituals? That is entirely our right! Just as, it is only our right to lift his corpse."

"Yes, yes. It is only our right" Mahadba asserted.

"True, true... Mahadba is the righteous heir who has the right to conduct these rituals. We will not accept that adopted boy as eligible for these important things" said a few others who had accompanied Babaji.

As the crowd started creating a commotion, Bhau Patil stepped ahead and bellowed,

"Keep quiet, everybody!"

Everyone fell silent. Then, Bhau Patil said,

"Babaji... It was Tatyasaheb's wish that, none of his relatives or friends who voluntarily got themselves enslaved by Brahmins, should be let to touch his dead body. That is why, none of you are eligible to conduct Tatyasaheb's last rites. And, you may not consider Yeshwant as your own, but for Tatyasaheb, he was the only son they had. Hence, he has every right to conduct the last rites. Rest of the things shall happen as written down by Tatyasaheb in his will. You need not worry about that."

Seeing that Babaji refused to budge, Dr. Vishram Ramji warned,

"If you do not leave in peace, we shall be compelled to call the police."

Babaji stepped back a few steps on hearing the word 'police', but still he refused to change his stance.

"I still insist that Mahadba be allowed to take part in the rituals. After all, he shares the bloodline with Tatya."

Hearing this, one of the people who had accompanied Babaji, spoke up,

"Then why just Mahdba? In that case, Ganpat's son should also be allowed to participate."

Soon, an infighting broke out among Babaji's group itself. It was a sorry sight to see that, while thousands of people were waiting for the funeral to begin, Jyotirao's own kin were fighting like cats & dogs over irrelevant issues.

Savitribai was listening to this chaos from inside the house. Unable to bear it any longer, she finally charged outside like a tigress; looked at Babaji in the eye; and said,

"No one will participate in these rituals except for me and our son, Yeshwant. I do not want even your shadow to fall on Shetji's dead body. I know very well, why all of you have come rushing here today. Get out, everybody. If nothing else, at least think about all the good that he did for you and let him go in peace!"

Babaji lowered his neck in shame. He did not dare to look at the usually calm Savitribai's enraged face, now flaming red with rage.

Just then, Dr. Vishram Ramji came with the police in tow. Seeing the police, Babaji decided that it was prudent to not extend this topic any more. Soon, he and his cronies slunk away.

Then, Savitribai, Yeshwant and Gajanan started leading the funeral procession with Pandit Dhondiram, Tatyasaheb Rode, Gyaanoba and Bhau Kondaji carrying the bier on their shoulders. A sea of people was following from behind. The air was thick with cries and the fragrance of flowers that were being constantly heaped on Jyotirao's dead body.

Everyone's hearts were filled with their own memories of

their dear Tatyasaheb. Bhau Kondaji was grieving the loss of his younger brother, whose friendship was a matter of immense pride for him. He kept thinking about Jyotirao's dedication, impressive oratory, and the incessant work that he did till the end of his life. Jyotirao's calm, intelligent face and towering body were still dancing in front of Bhau's eyes. It was a pity that such a towering personality had been reduced to a heap of helplessness due to the deadly paralytic attacks he bore. However, even though the illness had slowed down Jyotirao's body, it had not been able to take away his indomitable spirit and willpower.

'The lone warrior named Jyotirao Phule, had waged a tremendously brave battle against everything that he felt was not right. He kept fighting – many a times, alone – with immense willpower and perseverance. He wade his way through terrible times and a sea of enemies, even backstabbers; but, never did he give up. He kept falling down only to get up with more strength and resolve. Jyotirao was insistent that the new age required new humanitarian rules. The brave-heart fought without thinking about success or defeat; but, his lonely battle opened up the way for a huge crusade. This man, who always shied away from recognition, was indeed as big as the sky! He wanted nothing more than a society that would give equal treatment to everyone, irrespective of his birth and caste. He dreamt of a country where everyone had complete religious freedom, and, where everyone's human rights would be upheld.

Jyotirao's dreams were simply too big to be held in the eyes of common people. He kept fighting to manifest those dreams, without caring about defeat or criticism. He did not let friendship or relations to stand in the way of his dreams. He kept working towards what appealed to his inner conscience, irrespective of how his actions would be perceived by close ones.

Jyotirao was the first to rush for helping any poor person, irrespective of what caste or religion he belonged to. There was not a single form of social good that remained unaffected by his Midas touch. It was a joke of fate that such a progressive thinker and reformer should be born in the lap of so many challenges. But, that did not deter him in any way whatsoever. He kept burning the flame of his life to spread light in the life of others – thus living up to his name , Jyotiba, in every way!

Jyotirao's greatness and the extent of his dreams were too large to be understood by all. But, it is those dreams that will carry the society ahead into a beautiful future. But that, he won't be there to see it...'

Bhau Kondaji could not control his sobs any longer. He broke down like a child. He remembered that yesterday, Tatya wanted to say something, but he could not. What did he want to say?... Then, Bhau's vision rested on Savitribai who was walking in front of the procession. Looking at her, Bhau thought, Jyoti may have gone, but his luminescence still remains. Savitribai can never be looked upon as separate from Jyotirao. She stood by him in the darkest of times. She was his true support – a friend, philosopher, guide who would sometimes become Jyotirao's mother, and sometimes his daughter too! The memories of their happy married life brought a fresh slew of tears to Bhau's eyes.

The Satyashodhaks were moving ahead, singing songs written by Jyotirao. It was early evening by the time the procession reached the place of the funeral. People sat on steps and the open ground. Pandit Dhondiram, Vishram Ramji, Krishnarao Bhalekar, Narayanrao Lokhande, Swami Aiyyavaru, Shastri Naro Babaji, Yeshwant Phule.... all gave speeches describing Jyotirao as a great reformer, thinker, humanitarian, as well as, a father and friend. People were listening intently, tears streaming down their faces.

Lastly, Bhau Patil rose to speak. He said,

".... Jyotirao Phule was a great man, who spent his life to accord equal human rights and a life of dignity to our Shoodra and Ati Shoodra brethren who have been leading a life of torment and subjugation for centuries on end. While Jyotirao Phule's mortal body may have left us, he remains with us in spirit through his work, thoughts, and writings. Today, our society is not capable enough to bear the weight of Mahatma Jyotirao Phule's progressive thoughts; but one day, they shall understand its greatness for themselves. In fact, I pray to the Lord that he make the society thus capable very soon. There will be no better tribute to Jyotirao Phule's incessant and immense work, than this. I pray to all of you to keep his work and sacrifice in mind, for ever. May the great man's soul rest in peace."

The prayer meeting got over. Jyotirao's body was laid on the funeral pyre. Pandit Dhondiram began chanting prayers.

Yeshwant came ahead and lit the pyre.

In a moment, the yellow & crimson flames began rising to lick the sky.

The live flame of dedication, perseverance, and continuous efforts got consumed in that blaze!!!

◆